FROM OFF THE STREETS OF CLEVELAND COMES...

AMERICAN SPLENDOR

THE LIFE AND TIMES OF HARVEY PEKAR

STORIES BY HARVEY PEKAR

INTRODUCTION BY R. CRUMB

Art by

Kevin Brown • Gregory Budgett • R. Crumb

Gary Dumm • Gerry Shamray

AND

FROM OFF THE STREETS OF CLEVELAND COMES...

More AMERICAN SPLENDOR

THE LIFE AND TIMES OF HARVEY PEKAR

STORIES BY HARVEY PEKAR

Art by

Gregory Budgett • Sean Carroll • Sue Cavey

R. Crumb • Gary Dumm • Val Mayerik

Gerry Shamray

A Ballantine Book
Published by The Random House Publishing Group

American Splendor copyright © 1976, 1977, 1978, 1979, 1980, 1981, 1982, 1983, 1984 By Harvey Pekar
Introduction to *American Splendor* copyright © 1986 by R. Crumb
American Splendor was originally published by Doubleday & Company, Inc., in 1986.

More American Splendor copyright © 1976, 1977, 1978, 1979, 1980, 1981, 1982, 1983, 1984,
1985, 1986, 1987 by Harvey Pekar
More American Splendor was originally published by Doubleday & Company, Inc., in 1987.

Published in the United States by Ballantine Books, an imprint of The Random House Publishing Group,
a division of Random House, Inc., New York, and simultaneously in Canada by Random House
of Canada Limited, Toronto.

Ballantine and colophon are registered trademarks of Random House, Inc.

www.ballantinebooks.com

Library of Congress Control Number is available from the publisher upon request.

ISBN 0-345-46830-9

Cover design by Derek Walls
Manufactured in the United States of America

First Ballantine Books Edition: August 2003

6 8 9 7

THE LIFE AND TIMES OF HARVEY PEKAR

INTRODUCTION

YEAH, I'VE KNOWN HARVEY PEKAR A LONG TIME...A LONG TIME...SINCE THE FALL OF 1962, WHEN I FIRST LEFT HOME AND WENT TO CLEVELAND, AND SHARED A BASEMENT APARTMENT WITH MY FRIEND MARTY PAHLS. PEKAR LIVED AROUND THE CORNER ON DEERING STREET AT THAT TIME. (NONE OF THESE BUILDINGS ARE STILL STANDING...THE WHOLE NEIGHBORHOOD WAS BULLDOZED IN THE 'SEVENTIES.) HARVEY WAS THE FIRST PERSON I EVER MET WHO I THOT WAS A GENIUNE "HIPSTER." I WAS VERY IMPRESSED. HE WAS HEAVILY INTO MODERN JAZZ, HAD BIG CRAZY ABSTRACT PAINTINGS ON THE WALLS OF HIS PAD, TALKED BOP LINGO, HAD SHELVES AND SHELVES OF BOOKS AND RECORDS, AND NEVER CLEANED HIS APARTMENT...AND HE WAS SEETHING, INTENSE, BURNING UP, ALWAYS MOVING, PACING, JUMPING AROUND ...JUST LIKE A CHARACTER OUT OF KEROUAC.

TWENTY YEARS LATER, STILL COMING OUT OF HIS SKIN, PEKAR STILL LIVES ON CLEVELAND'S EAST SIDE... THOSE SAME ABSTRACT PAINTINGS ARE NOW COVERED WITH DUST AND GRIME. ACTUALLY, IT TURNS OUT HE'S ONE OF THE MOST STABLE GUYS I KNOW. EVERYONE ELSE FROM THOSE OLD DAYS HAS LONG SINCE FLED, SCATTERED TO OTHER PLACES AND TOWNS, EXCEPT DANNY THOMPSON, SID GOLD, AND HARVEY. CLEVELAND IS A HARD TOWN...I CAME NEAR COMMITTING SUICIDE WHEN I LIVED THERE. I KNEW SEVERAL YOUNG SENSITIVE TYPES WHO DID END IT ALL IN CLEVELAND, THE POET D.A. LEVY BEING THE MOST FAMOUS.

YEAH, HARVEY IS AN EGO-MANIAC; A CLASSIC CASE...A DRIVEN, COMPULSIVE, MAD JEW....WATCHING HIM EAT—HE EATS FASTER THAN ANYONE I'VE EVER SEEN, SHOVELLING IT IN AS IF SOMEBODY HAD A GUN AT HIS HEAD AND WAS THREATENING TO KILL HIM IF HE DIDN'T GET IT ALL DOWN IN TEN SECONDS. IT'S SOMETHING TO SEE. BUT HOW ELSE COULD HE HAVE GOTTEN ALL THOSE COMICS PUBLISHED, WITH ALMOST NO MONEY, IN TOTAL ISOLATION FROM ANY COMIC-PUBLISHING "SCENE" SUCH AS EXISTS OUT HERE IN CALIFORNIA, OR IN NEW YORK; CONSTANTLY BROW-BEATING ARTISTS TO ILLUSTRATE HIS STORIES; HANDLING THE DISTRIBUTION HIMSELF... ONLY AN EGO-MANIAC WOULD PERSIST IN THE FACE OF SUCH ODDS.

BELIEVE ME, I KNOW FROM WHENCE I SPEAK, HAVING BEEN NAGGED AND BULLIED PLENTY BY HIM TO GET THE WORK IN...THE PHONE RINGS... THE DESPERATE YELLING, THREATENING, CAJOLING...AND ILLUSTRATING HIS STORIES IS NOT EASY. THERE'S SO LITTLE REAL COMIC-BOOK-STYLE ACTION FOR AN ARTIST TO SINK HIS TEETH INTO. MOSTLY IT'S JUST PEOPLE STANDING AROUND TALKING, OR JUST HARVEY HIMSELF ADDRESSING THE READER FOR PAGE AFTER PAGE...YOU HAVE TO REALLY SHARE HIS VISION, OR NEED THE FEW BUCKS HE PAYS FOR THIS TEDIOUS LABOR. IF HARVEY WASN'T SO DRIVEN, THERE WOULD NEVER'VE BEEN ANY AMERICAN SPLENDOR COMICS. IT'S NOT AS IF HE'S MADE A LOUSY DIME OFF OF THEM. I'M FAIRLY CERTAIN THAT THE SALES OF HIS COMIC BOOKS HAVE NEVER COVERED THE PRINTING COSTS.

IT'S A SAD FACT THAT YOU CAN'T SELL "ADULT" COMIC BOOKS TO AMERICAN ADULTS. COMIC BOOKS ARE FOR KIDS. ADOLESCENT MALE POWER

FANTASIES, THAT'S WHAT MOST COMIC BOOKS CONTAIN; ESCAPE FANTASIES FOR PIMPLY-FACED YOUNG BOYS...YEP. MOST COMIC SPECIALTY SHOPS WON'T EVEN CARRY BOOKS LIKE AMERICAN SPLENDOR. WHY SHOULD THEY? "ADULTS" NEVER GO IN SUCH PLACES, AND SO THE "ADULT" COMICS JUST SIT THERE TAKING UP SPACE ON THE SHELF.

MAYBE A "REAL" BOOK OF PEKAR'S COMICS, LIKE THIS, WILL SELL BETTER THAN THE CHEAP NEWSPRINT COMIC BOOKS. I WONDER IF DOUBLEDAY & CO. KNOWS WHAT THEY'RE GETTING THEMSELVES INTO HERE, BECAUSE, WHILE PEKAR'S WORK IS HIGHLY RESPECTED IN CERTAIN INTELLECTUAL CIRCLES, IT'S DEFINITELY NOT VERY COMMERCIAL.... BUT, WHO KNOWS? WITH DISTRIBUTION IN BIG BOOKSTORE CHAINS...WELL, HE'LL NEVER BE THE NEXT GARFIELD, THAT'S CERTAIN. THE SUBJECT MATTER OF THESE STORIES IS SO STAGGERINGLY MUNDANE, IT VERGES ON THE EXOTIC! IT IS VERY DISORIENTING AT FIRST, BUT AFTER AWHILE YOU GET WITH IT. MYSELF, I LOVE IT...PEKAR HAS PROVEN ONCE AND FOR ALL THAT EVEN THE MOST SEEMINGLY DREARY AND MONOTONOUS OF LIVES IS FILLED WITH POIGNANCY AND HEROIC STRUGGLE. ALL IT TAKES IS SOMEONE WITH AN EYE TO SEE, AN EAR TO HEAR, AND A DEMENTED, DESPERATE JEWISH MIND TO GET IT DOWN ON PAPER... THERE IS DRAMA IN THE MOST ORDINARY AND ROUTINE OF DAYS, BUT IT'S A SUBTLE THING THAT GETS LOST IN THE SHUFFLE... OUR PERSONAL STRUGGLES SEEM DULL AND DRAB COMPARED WITH THE THRILLING, SUSPENSE-FILLED, ACTION-PACKED LIVES OF THE CHARACTERS WHO ARE PUSHED ON US ALL THE TIME IN MOVIES, TV SHOWS, ADVENTURE NOVELS AND...THOSE OTHER COMICBOOKS.

WHAT PEKAR DOES IS CERTAINLY NEW TO THE COMICBOOK MEDIUM. THERE'S NEVER BEEN ANYTHING EVEN APPROACHING THIS KIND OF STARK REALISM. IT'S HARD ENOUGH TO FIND IT IN LITERATURE, IMPOSSIBLE IN THE MOVIES AND TV. IT TAKES CHUTSPAH TO TELL IT EXACTLY THE WAY IT HAPPENED, WITH NO ADORNMENT, NO GREAT WRAP-UP, NO BIZARRE TWIST, NOTHING. PEKAR'S GENIUS IS THAT HE PULLS THIS OFF, AND DOES IT WITH HUMOR, PATHOS, ALL THE DRAMA YOU COULD EVER WANT...AND IN A COMIC BOOK YET!

USUALLY HE WRITES HIS STORY IDEAS SOON AFTER THE EVENT, WHILE THE NUANCES OF IT ARE STILL FRESH IN HIS MIND. HE ALWAYS HAS A LARGE BACKLOG OF THESE STORIES, WHICH HE CAN CHOOSE FROM TO COMPOSE EACH NEW ISSUE OF AMERICAN SPLENDOR. HE WRITES THE STORIES IN A CRUDELY LAID-OUT COMIC PAGE FORMAT USING STICK FIGURES, WITH THE DIALOGUE OVER THEIR HEADS, AND SOME DESCRIPTIVE DIRECTIONS FOR THE ARTIST TO WORK FROM. THE NEXT PHASE INVOLVES CALLING UP VARIOUS ARTISTS AND HARANGING THEM TO TAKE ON PARTICULAR STORIES.

HARVEY IS OFTEN FRUSTRATED BY THE ARTISTS' LACK OF ABILITY TO BREAK OUT OF THE STANDARD HEROIC COMIC BOOK STYLE OF PORTRAYING CHARACTERS. INDEED, IT IS A CHALLENGING TASK TO DRAW ORDINARY PEOPLE REALISTICALLY, TO GIVE THEM UNIQUE PERSONAL QUALITIES IN A SERIES OF PANELS. ONE ARTIST, GERRY SHAMRAY, WENT ALL THE WAY, TAKING HUNDREDS OF PHOTOS OF PEKAR, HIS WIFE, HIS APARTMENT, THE STREETS OF HIS NEIGHBORHOOD, AND SO ON, AND DREW FROM THE PHOTOS. ONE OR TWO OTHER ARTISTS HAVE USED THIS METHOD WITH PEKAR'S STORIES. THE RESULTS OF THIS APPROACH ARE VERY SUCCESSFUL. MANY OF THE ARTISTS WHO HAVE WORKED FOR PEKAR OVER THE YEARS (HARVEY HAS BEEN WRITING COMIC STORIES SINCE 1975.) HAVE PUSHED THEIR ABILITIES TO HIGHER LEVELS OF SUBTLETY AND REALISM IN THE STRUGGLE TO CONVEY PEKAR'S IDEAS, OR MAYBE JUST TO GET HARVEY OFF THEIR BACKS — ME INCLUDED!

— R. CRUMB
APRIL, 1985

THE HARVEY PEKAR NAME STORY

STORY BY HARVEY PEKAR   ART BY R. CRUMB

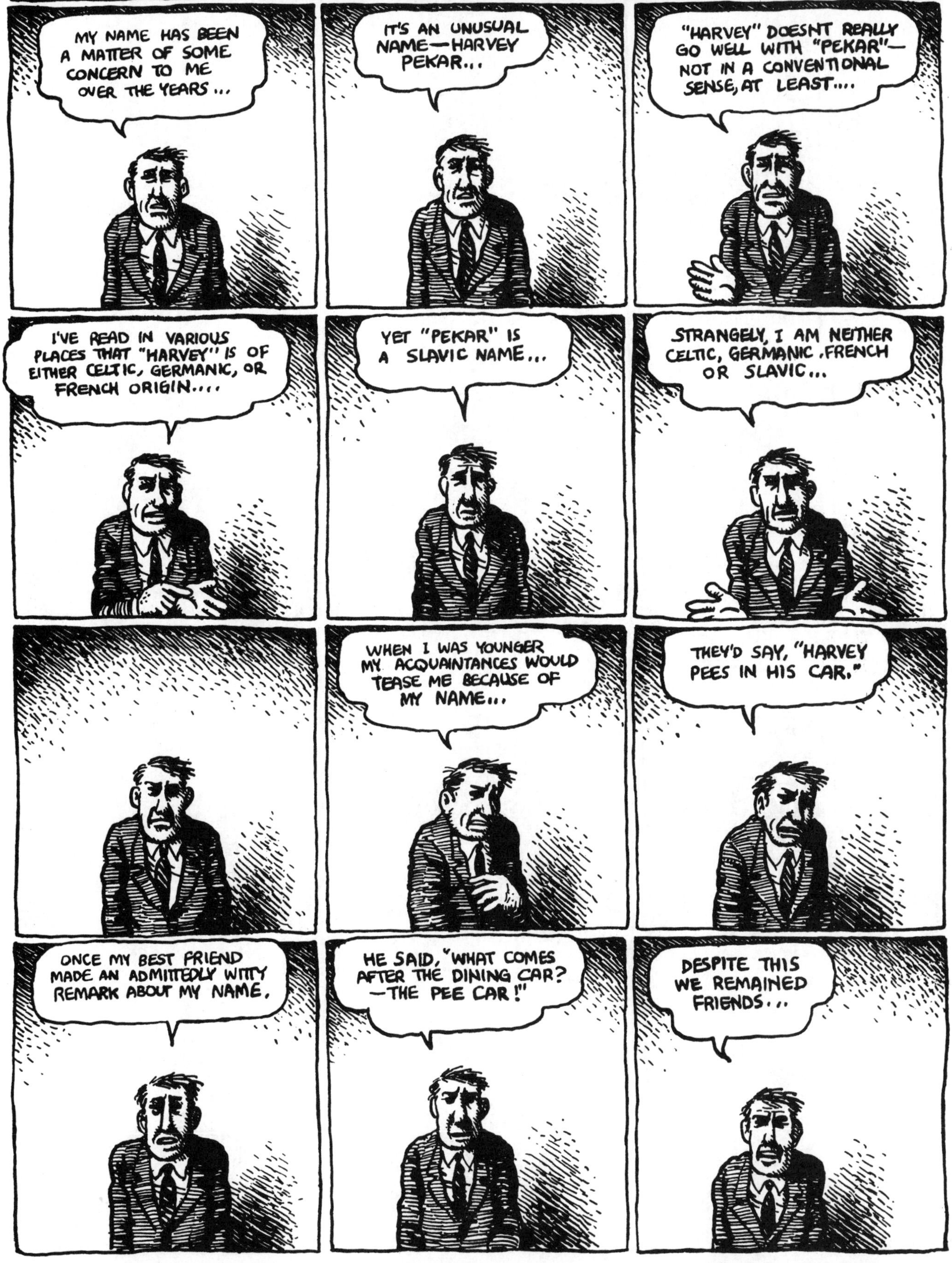

MY NAME HAS BEEN A MATTER OF SOME CONCERN TO ME OVER THE YEARS...
IT'S AN UNUSUAL NAME—HARVEY PEKAR...
"HARVEY" DOESN'T REALLY GO WELL WITH "PEKAR"— NOT IN A CONVENTIONAL SENSE, AT LEAST....
I'VE READ IN VARIOUS PLACES THAT "HARVEY" IS OF EITHER CELTIC, GERMANIC, OR FRENCH ORIGIN....
YET "PEKAR" IS A SLAVIC NAME...
STRANGELY, I AM NEITHER CELTIC, GERMANIC, FRENCH OR SLAVIC...
WHEN I WAS YOUNGER MY ACQUAINTANCES WOULD TEASE ME BECAUSE OF MY NAME...
THEY'D SAY, "HARVEY PEES IN HIS CAR."
ONCE MY BEST FRIEND MADE AN ADMITTEDLY WITTY REMARK ABOUT MY NAME.
HE SAID, "WHAT COMES AFTER THE DINING CAR? —THE PEE CAR!"
DESPITE THIS WE REMAINED FRIENDS...

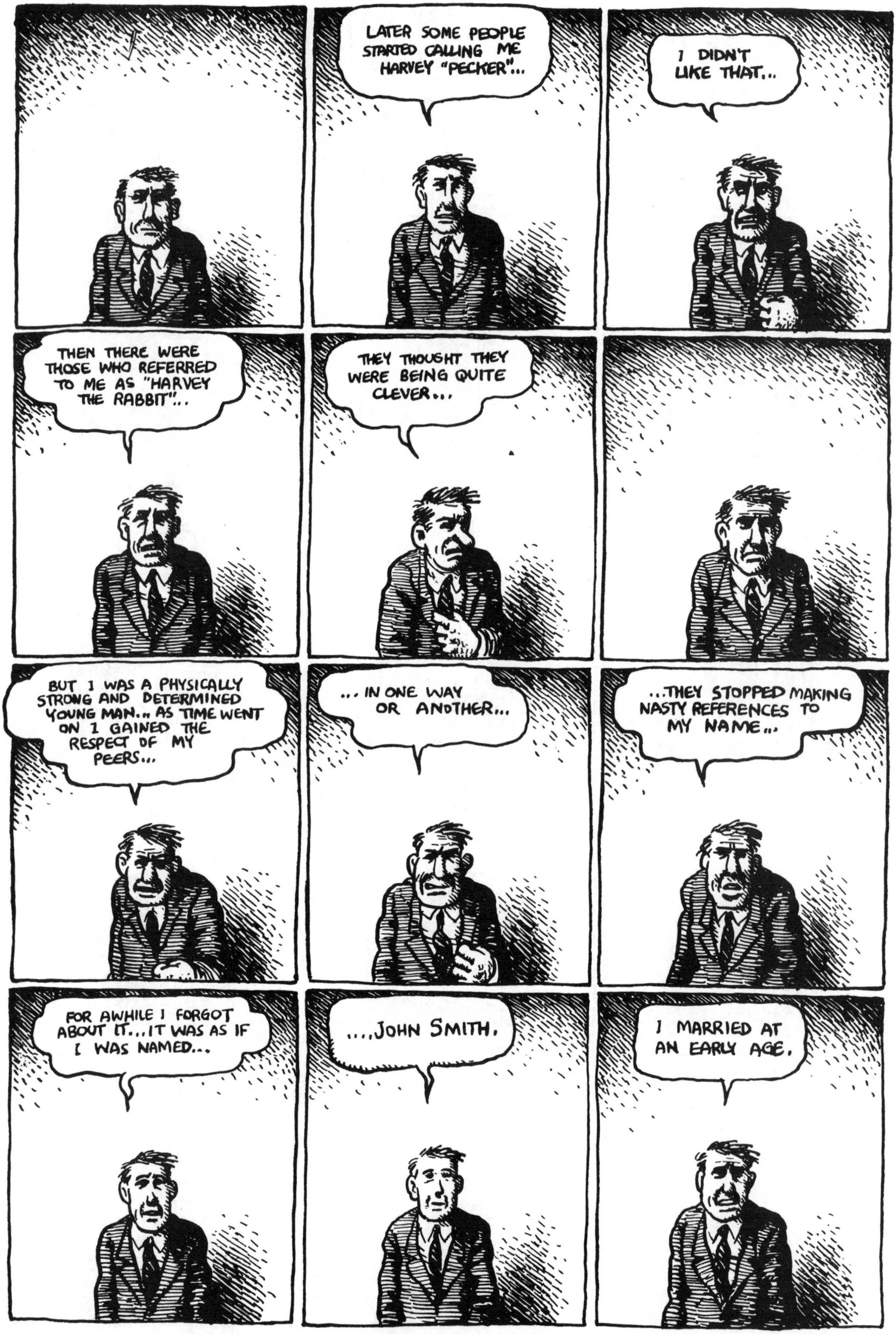
LATER SOME PEOPLE STARTED CALLING ME HARVEY "PECKER"...
I DIDN'T LIKE THAT...
THEN THERE WERE THOSE WHO REFERRED TO ME AS "HARVEY THE RABBIT"...
THEY THOUGHT THEY WERE BEING QUITE CLEVER...
BUT I WAS A PHYSICALLY STRONG AND DETERMINED YOUNG MAN.. AS TIME WENT ON I GAINED THE RESPECT OF MY PEERS...
... IN ONE WAY OR ANOTHER...
...THEY STOPPED MAKING NASTY REFERENCES TO MY NAME...
FOR AWHILE I FORGOT ABOUT IT... IT WAS AS IF I WAS NAMED...
....JOHN SMITH.
I MARRIED AT AN EARLY AGE.

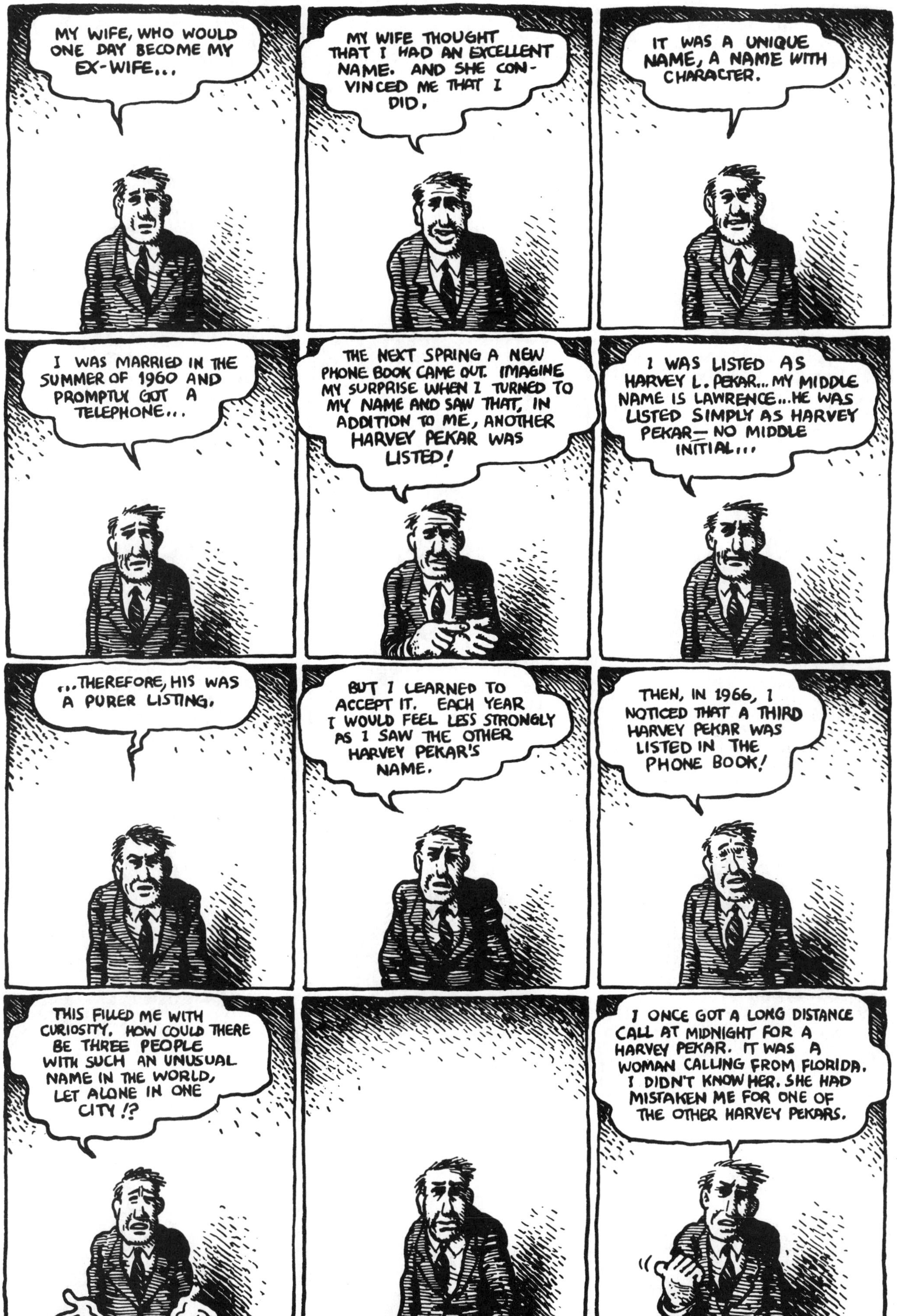
MY WIFE, WHO WOULD ONE DAY BECOME MY EX-WIFE...
MY WIFE THOUGHT THAT I HAD AN EXCELLENT NAME. AND SHE CONVINCED ME THAT I DID.
IT WAS A UNIQUE NAME, A NAME WITH CHARACTER.
I WAS MARRIED IN THE SUMMER OF 1960 AND PROMPTLY GOT A TELEPHONE...
THE NEXT SPRING A NEW PHONE BOOK CAME OUT. IMAGINE MY SURPRISE WHEN I TURNED TO MY NAME AND SAW THAT, IN ADDITION TO ME, ANOTHER HARVEY PEKAR WAS LISTED!
I WAS LISTED AS HARVEY L. PEKAR... MY MIDDLE NAME IS LAWRENCE... HE WAS LISTED SIMPLY AS HARVEY PEKAR— NO MIDDLE INITIAL...
...THEREFORE, HIS WAS A PURER LISTING.
BUT I LEARNED TO ACCEPT IT. EACH YEAR I WOULD FEEL LESS STRONGLY AS I SAW THE OTHER HARVEY PEKAR'S NAME.
THEN, IN 1966, I NOTICED THAT A THIRD HARVEY PEKAR WAS LISTED IN THE PHONE BOOK!
THIS FILLED ME WITH CURIOSITY. HOW COULD THERE BE THREE PEOPLE WITH SUCH AN UNUSUAL NAME IN THE WORLD, LET ALONE IN ONE CITY!?
I ONCE GOT A LONG DISTANCE CALL AT MIDNIGHT FOR A HARVEY PEKAR. IT WAS A WOMAN CALLING FROM FLORIDA. I DIDN'T KNOW HER. SHE HAD MISTAKEN ME FOR ONE OF THE OTHER HARVEY PEKARS.

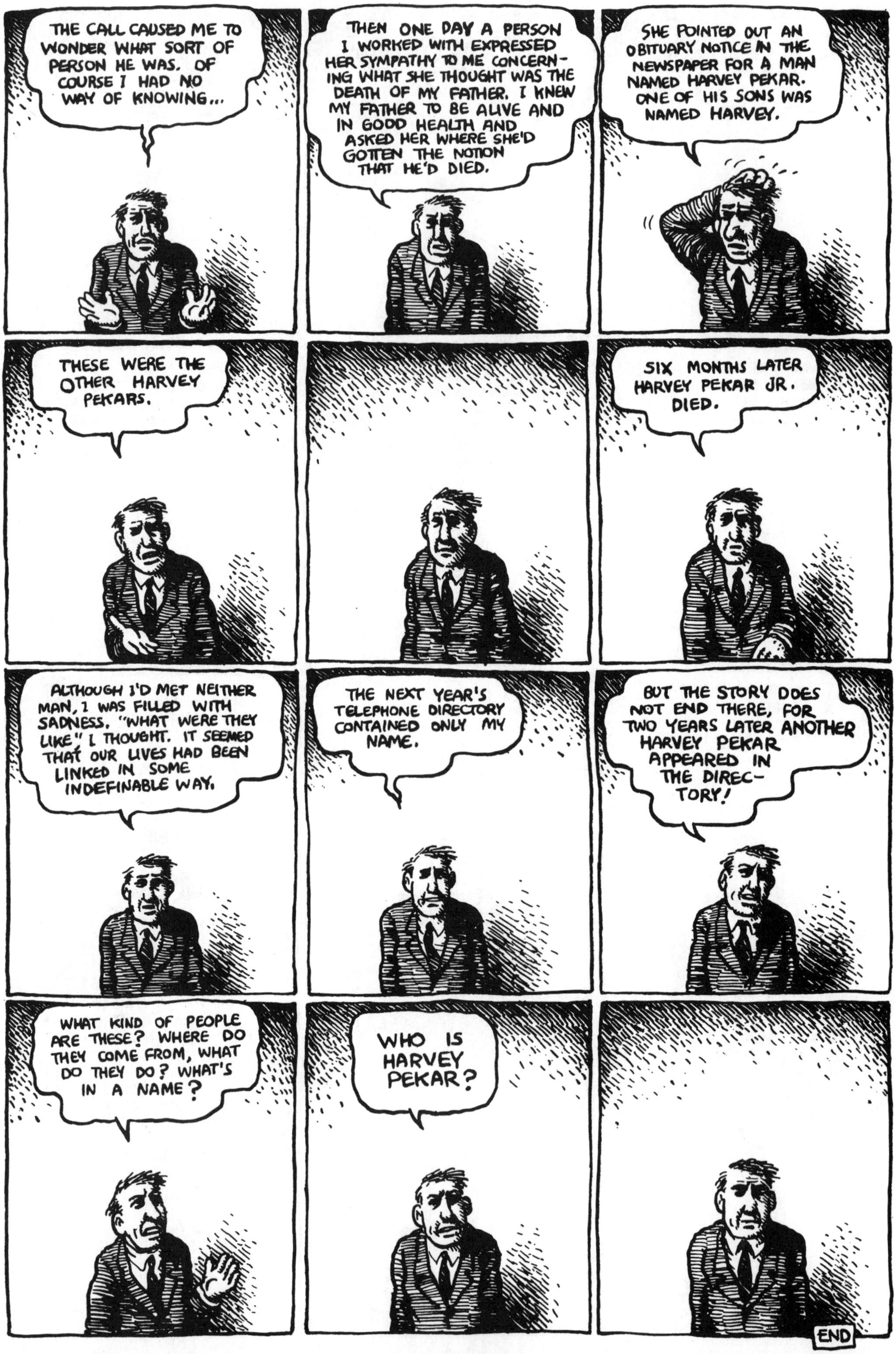
THE CALL CAUSED ME TO WONDER WHAT SORT OF PERSON HE WAS. OF COURSE I HAD NO WAY OF KNOWING...
THEN ONE DAY A PERSON I WORKED WITH EXPRESSED HER SYMPATHY TO ME CONCERNING WHAT SHE THOUGHT WAS THE DEATH OF MY FATHER. I KNEW MY FATHER TO BE ALIVE AND IN GOOD HEALTH AND ASKED HER WHERE SHE'D GOTTEN THE NOTION THAT HE'D DIED.
SHE POINTED OUT AN OBITUARY NOTICE IN THE NEWSPAPER FOR A MAN NAMED HARVEY PEKAR. ONE OF HIS SONS WAS NAMED HARVEY.
THESE WERE THE OTHER HARVEY PEKARS.
SIX MONTHS LATER HARVEY PEKAR JR. DIED.
ALTHOUGH I'D MET NEITHER MAN, I WAS FILLED WITH SADNESS. "WHAT WERE THEY LIKE" I THOUGHT. IT SEEMED THAT OUR LIVES HAD BEEN LINKED IN SOME INDEFINABLE WAY.
THE NEXT YEAR'S TELEPHONE DIRECTORY CONTAINED ONLY MY NAME.
BUT THE STORY DOES NOT END THERE, FOR TWO YEARS LATER ANOTHER HARVEY PEKAR APPEARED IN THE DIRECTORY!
WHAT KIND OF PEOPLE ARE THESE? WHERE DO THEY COME FROM, WHAT DO THEY DO? WHAT'S IN A NAME?
WHO IS HARVEY PEKAR?
END

The Young Crumb Story

Story by Harvey Pekar
Art by R. Crumb

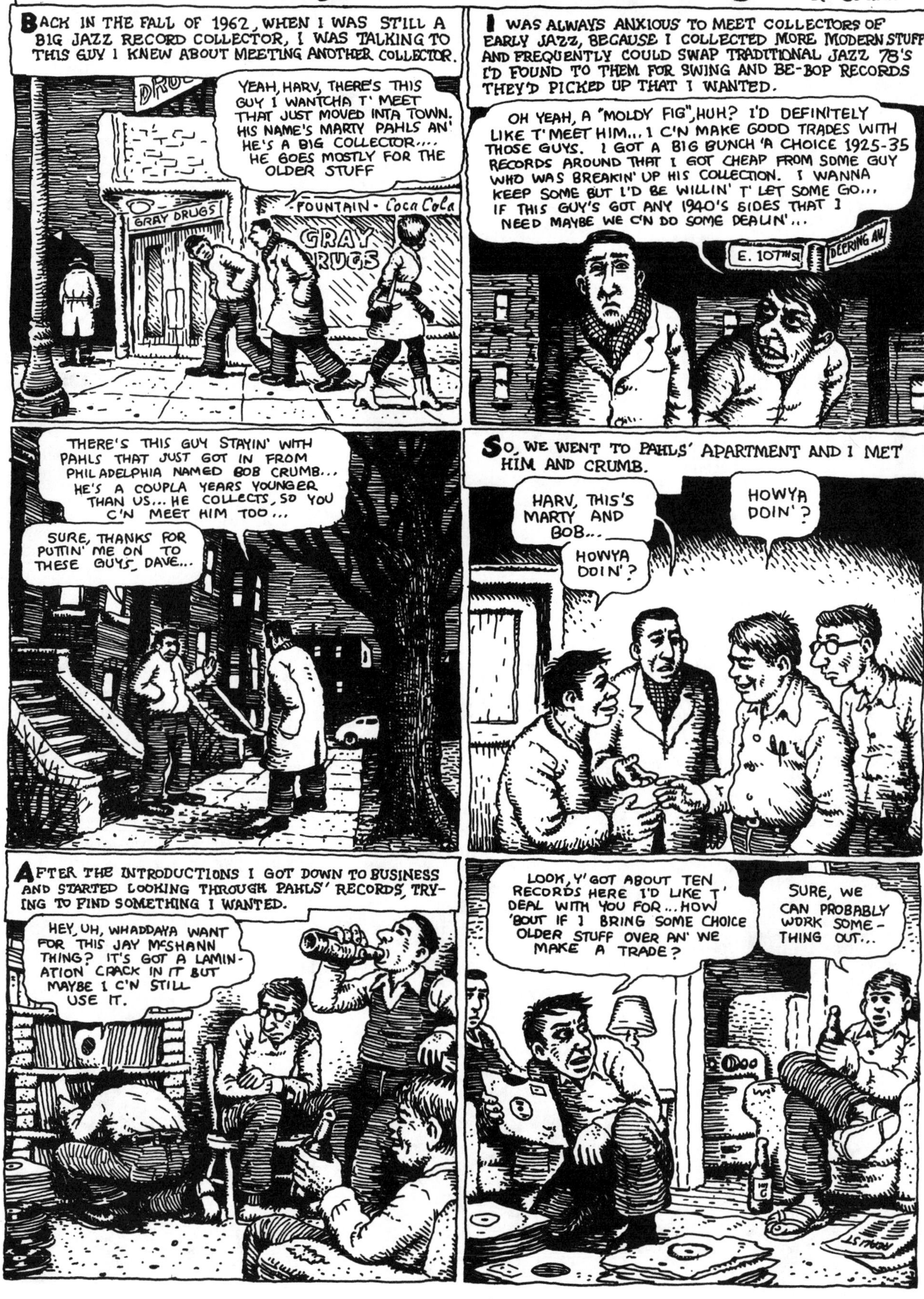

BACK IN THE FALL OF 1962, WHEN I WAS STILL A BIG JAZZ RECORD COLLECTOR, I WAS TALKING TO THIS GUY I KNEW ABOUT MEETING ANOTHER COLLECTOR.
YEAH, HARV, THERE'S THIS GUY I WANTCHA T' MEET THAT JUST MOVED INTA TOWN. HIS NAME'S MARTY PAHLS AN' HE'S A BIG COLLECTOR.... HE GOES MOSTLY FOR THE OLDER STUFF
GRAY DRUGS
FOUNTAIN - Coca Cola
GRAY DRUGS
I WAS ALWAYS ANXIOUS TO MEET COLLECTORS OF EARLY JAZZ, BECAUSE I COLLECTED MORE MODERN STUFF AND FREQUENTLY COULD SWAP TRADITIONAL JAZZ 78'S I'D FOUND TO THEM FOR SWING AND BE-BOP RECORDS THEY'D PICKED UP THAT I WANTED.
OH YEAH, A "MOLDY FIG", HUH? I'D DEFINITELY LIKE T' MEET HIM... I C'N MAKE GOOD TRADES WITH THOSE GUYS. I GOT A BIG BUNCH 'A CHOICE 1925-35 RECORDS AROUND THAT I GOT CHEAP FROM SOME GUY WHO WAS BREAKIN' UP HIS COLLECTION. I WANNA KEEP SOME BUT I'D BE WILLIN' T' LET SOME GO... IF THIS GUY'S GOT ANY 1940'S SIDES THAT I NEED MAYBE WE C'N DO SOME DEALIN'...
E. 107TH ST
DEERING AV
THERE'S THIS GUY STAYIN' WITH PAHLS THAT JUST GOT IN FROM PHILADELPHIA NAMED BOB CRUMB... HE'S A COUPLA YEARS YOUNGER THAN US... HE COLLECTS, SO YOU C'N MEET HIM TOO...
SURE, THANKS FOR PUTTIN' ME ON TO THESE GUYS, DAVE...
SO, WE WENT TO PAHLS' APARTMENT AND I MET HIM AND CRUMB.
HARV, THIS'S MARTY AND BOB...
HOWYA DOIN'?
HOWYA DOIN'?
AFTER THE INTRODUCTIONS I GOT DOWN TO BUSINESS AND STARTED LOOKING THROUGH PAHLS' RECORDS, TRYING TO FIND SOMETHING I WANTED.
HEY, UH, WHADDAYA WANT FOR THIS JAY McSHANN THING? IT'S GOT A LAMINATION CRACK IN IT BUT MAYBE I C'N STILL USE IT.
LOOK, Y' GOT ABOUT TEN RECORDS HERE I'D LIKE T' DEAL WITH YOU FOR... HOW 'BOUT IF I BRING SOME CHOICE OLDER STUFF OVER AN' WE MAKE A TRADE?
SURE, WE CAN PROBABLY WORK SOMETHING OUT...

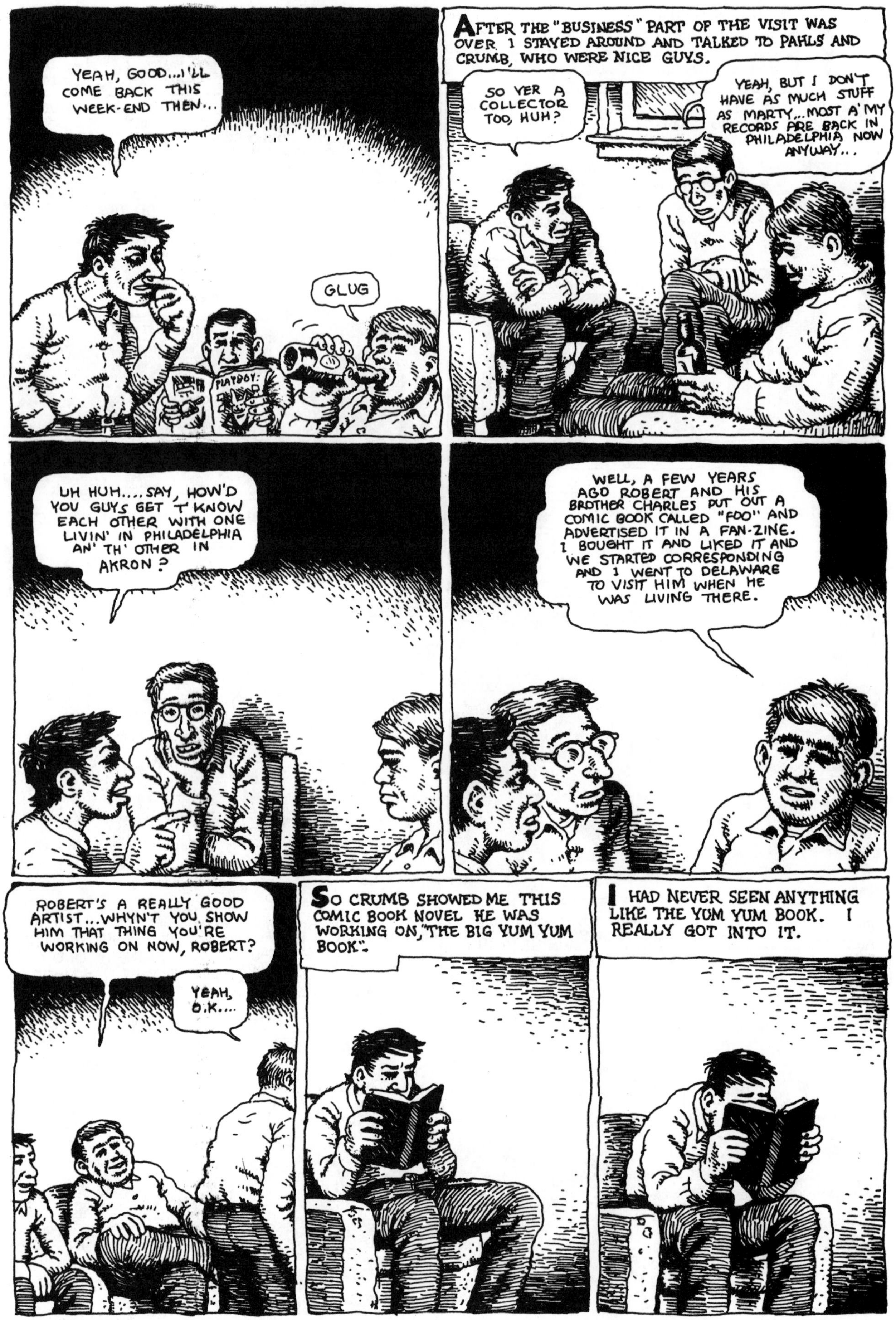
YEAH, GOOD...I'LL COME BACK THIS WEEK-END THEN...
GLUG
AFTER THE "BUSINESS" PART OF THE VISIT WAS OVER I STAYED AROUND AND TALKED TO PAHLS AND CRUMB, WHO WERE NICE GUYS.
SO YER A COLLECTOR TOO, HUH?
YEAH, BUT I DON'T HAVE AS MUCH STUFF AS MARTY... MOST A' MY RECORDS ARE BACK IN PHILADELPHIA NOW ANYWAY...
UH HUH.... SAY, HOW'D YOU GUYS GET T' KNOW EACH OTHER WITH ONE LIVIN' IN PHILADELPHIA AN' TH' OTHER IN AKRON?
WELL, A FEW YEARS AGO ROBERT AND HIS BROTHER CHARLES PUT OUT A COMIC BOOK CALLED "FOO" AND ADVERTISED IT IN A FAN-ZINE. I BOUGHT IT AND LIKED IT AND WE STARTED CORRESPONDING AND I WENT TO DELAWARE TO VISIT HIM WHEN HE WAS LIVING THERE.
ROBERT'S A REALLY GOOD ARTIST... WHYN'T YOU SHOW HIM THAT THING YOU'RE WORKING ON NOW, ROBERT?
YEAH, O.K....
SO CRUMB SHOWED ME THIS COMIC BOOK NOVEL HE WAS WORKING ON, "THE BIG YUM YUM BOOK".
I HAD NEVER SEEN ANYTHING LIKE THE YUM YUM BOOK. I REALLY GOT INTO IT.

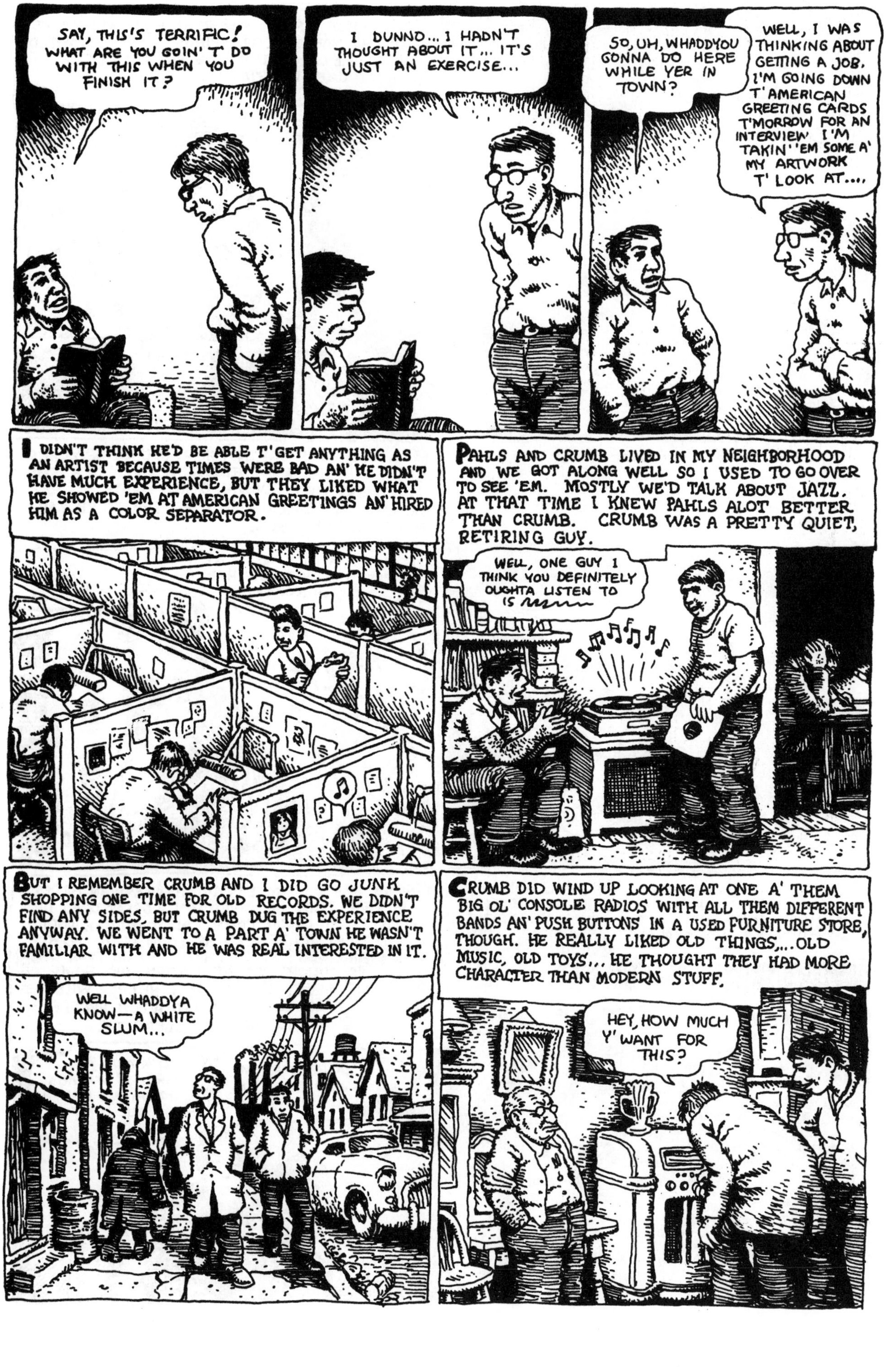

SAY, THIS'S TERRIFIC! WHAT ARE YOU GOIN' T' DO WITH THIS WHEN YOU FINISH IT?
I DUNNO... I HADN'T THOUGHT ABOUT IT... IT'S JUST AN EXERCISE...
SO, UH, WHADDYOU GONNA DO HERE WHILE YER IN TOWN?
WELL, I WAS THINKING ABOUT GETTING A JOB. I'M GOING DOWN T' AMERICAN GREETING CARDS T'MORROW FOR AN INTERVIEW I'M TAKIN' 'EM SOME A' MY ARTWORK T' LOOK AT....
I DIDN'T THINK HE'D BE ABLE T' GET ANYTHING AS AN ARTIST BECAUSE TIMES WERE BAD AN' HE DIDN'T HAVE MUCH EXPERIENCE, BUT THEY LIKED WHAT HE SHOWED 'EM AT AMERICAN GREETINGS AN' HIRED HIM AS A COLOR SEPARATOR.
PAHLS AND CRUMB LIVED IN MY NEIGHBORHOOD AND WE GOT ALONG WELL SO I USED TO GO OVER TO SEE 'EM. MOSTLY WE'D TALK ABOUT JAZZ. AT THAT TIME I KNEW PAHLS ALOT BETTER THAN CRUMB. CRUMB WAS A PRETTY QUIET, RETIRING GUY.
WELL, ONE GUY I THINK YOU DEFINITELY OUGHTA LISTEN TO IS
BUT I REMEMBER CRUMB AND I DID GO JUNK SHOPPING ONE TIME FOR OLD RECORDS. WE DIDN'T FIND ANY SIDES, BUT CRUMB DUG THE EXPERIENCE ANYWAY. WE WENT TO A PART A' TOWN HE WASN'T FAMILIAR WITH AND HE WAS REAL INTERESTED IN IT.
WELL WHADDYA KNOW—A WHITE SLUM...
CRUMB DID WIND UP LOOKING AT ONE A' THEM BIG OL' CONSOLE RADIOS WITH ALL THEM DIFFERENT BANDS AN' PUSH BUTTONS IN A USED FURNITURE STORE, THOUGH. HE REALLY LIKED OLD THINGS,...OLD MUSIC, OLD TOYS... HE THOUGHT THEY HAD MORE CHARACTER THAN MODERN STUFF.
HEY, HOW MUCH Y' WANT FOR THIS?

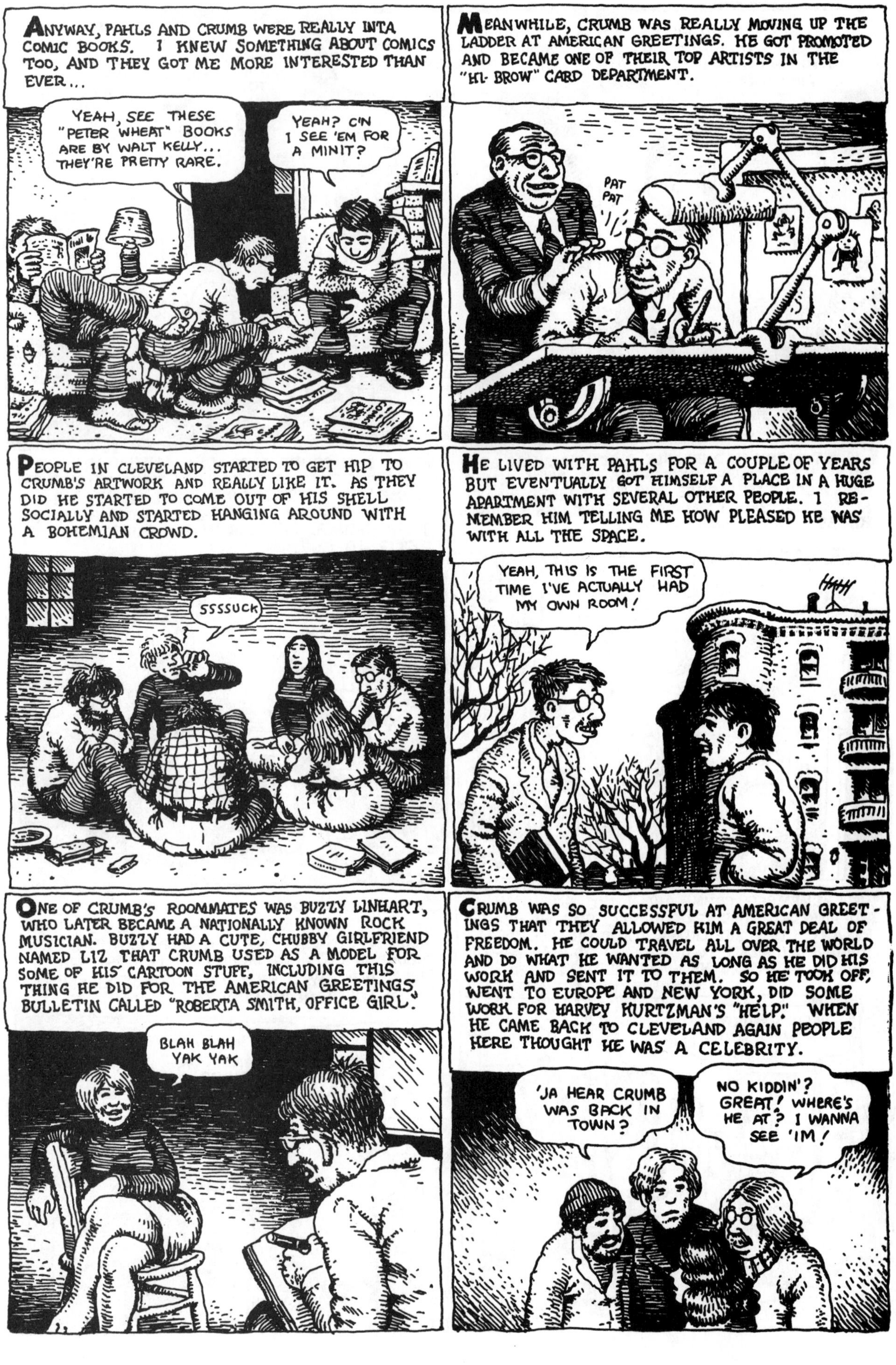
ANYWAY, PAHLS AND CRUMB WERE REALLY INTA COMIC BOOKS. I KNEW SOMETHING ABOUT COMICS TOO, AND THEY GOT ME MORE INTERESTED THAN EVER...
YEAH, SEE THESE "PETER WHEAT" BOOKS ARE BY WALT KELLY... THEY'RE PRETTY RARE.
YEAH? C'N I SEE 'EM FOR A MINIT?
MEANWHILE, CRUMB WAS REALLY MOVING UP THE LADDER AT AMERICAN GREETINGS. HE GOT PROMOTED AND BECAME ONE OF THEIR TOP ARTISTS IN THE "HI-BROW" CARD DEPARTMENT.
PAT PAT
PEOPLE IN CLEVELAND STARTED TO GET HIP TO CRUMB'S ARTWORK AND REALLY LIKE IT. AS THEY DID HE STARTED TO COME OUT OF HIS SHELL SOCIALLY AND STARTED HANGING AROUND WITH A BOHEMIAN CROWD.
SSSSUCK
HE LIVED WITH PAHLS FOR A COUPLE OF YEARS BUT EVENTUALLY GOT HIMSELF A PLACE IN A HUGE APARTMENT WITH SEVERAL OTHER PEOPLE. I REMEMBER HIM TELLING ME HOW PLEASED HE WAS WITH ALL THE SPACE.
YEAH, THIS IS THE FIRST TIME I'VE ACTUALLY HAD MY OWN ROOM!
ONE OF CRUMB'S ROOMMATES WAS BUZZY LINHART, WHO LATER BECAME A NATIONALLY KNOWN ROCK MUSICIAN. BUZZY HAD A CUTE, CHUBBY GIRLFRIEND NAMED LIZ THAT CRUMB USED AS A MODEL FOR SOME OF HIS CARTOON STUFF, INCLUDING THIS THING HE DID FOR THE AMERICAN GREETINGS BULLETIN CALLED "ROBERTA SMITH, OFFICE GIRL".
BLAH BLAH YAK YAK
CRUMB WAS SO SUCCESSFUL AT AMERICAN GREETINGS THAT THEY ALLOWED HIM A GREAT DEAL OF FREEDOM. HE COULD TRAVEL ALL OVER THE WORLD AND DO WHAT HE WANTED AS LONG AS HE DID HIS WORK AND SENT IT TO THEM. SO HE TOOK OFF, WENT TO EUROPE AND NEW YORK, DID SOME WORK FOR HARVEY KURTZMAN'S "HELP." WHEN HE CAME BACK TO CLEVELAND AGAIN PEOPLE HERE THOUGHT HE WAS A CELEBRITY.
'JA HEAR CRUMB WAS BACK IN TOWN?
NO KIDDIN'? GREAT! WHERE'S HE AT? I WANNA SEE 'IM!

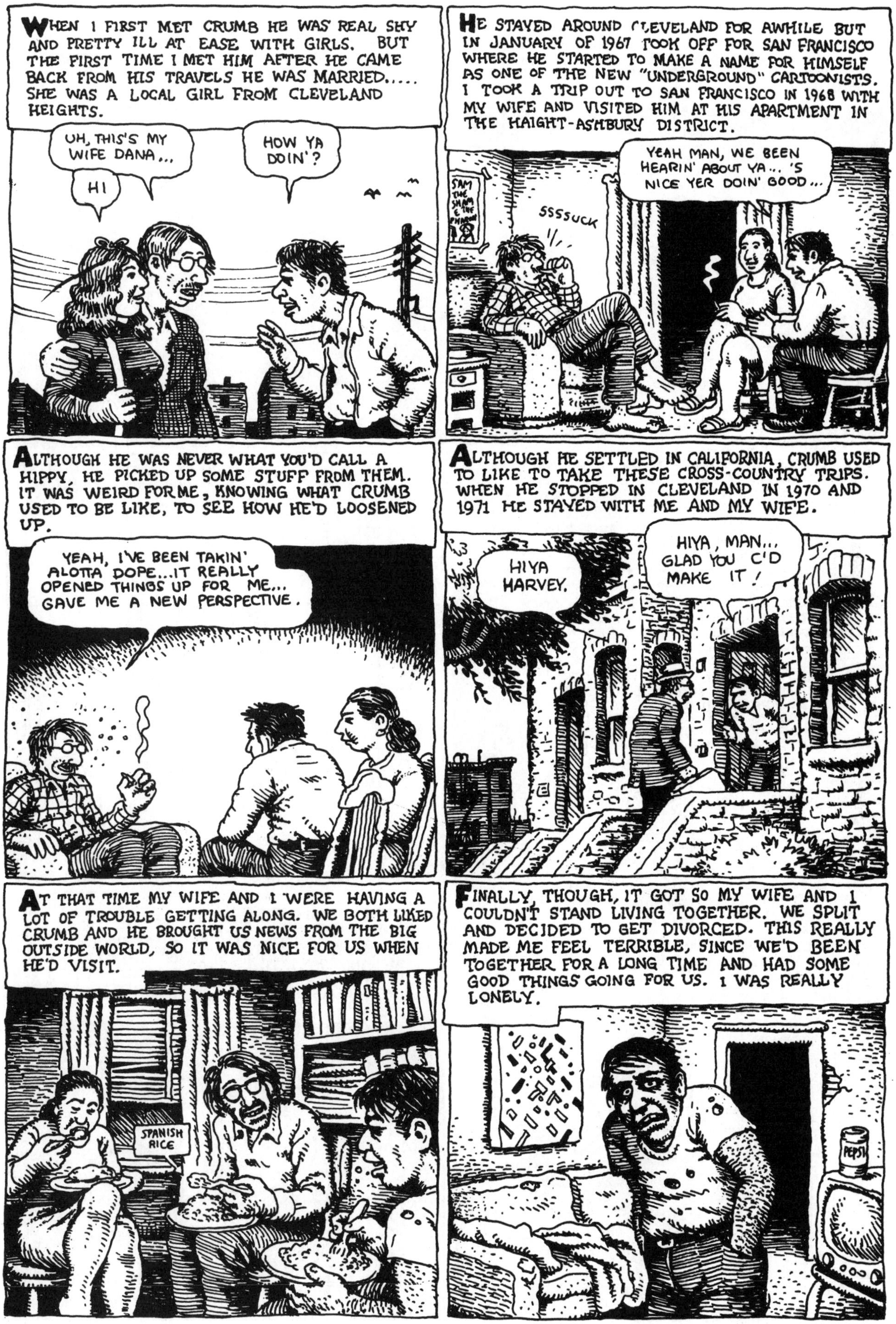

WHEN I FIRST MET CRUMB HE WAS REAL SHY AND PRETTY ILL AT EASE WITH GIRLS. BUT THE FIRST TIME I MET HIM AFTER HE CAME BACK FROM HIS TRAVELS HE WAS MARRIED..... SHE WAS A LOCAL GIRL FROM CLEVELAND HEIGHTS.
UH, THIS'S MY WIFE DANA...
HI
HOW YA DOIN'?
HE STAYED AROUND CLEVELAND FOR AWHILE BUT IN JANUARY OF 1967 TOOK OFF FOR SAN FRANCISCO WHERE HE STARTED TO MAKE A NAME FOR HIMSELF AS ONE OF THE NEW "UNDERGROUND" CARTOONISTS. I TOOK A TRIP OUT TO SAN FRANCISCO IN 1968 WITH MY WIFE AND VISITED HIM AT HIS APARTMENT IN THE HAIGHT-ASHBURY DISTRICT.
YEAH MAN, WE BEEN HEARIN' ABOUT YA... 'S NICE YER DOIN' GOOD...
SSSSUCK
ALTHOUGH HE WAS NEVER WHAT YOU'D CALL A HIPPY, HE PICKED UP SOME STUFF FROM THEM. IT WAS WEIRD FOR ME, KNOWING WHAT CRUMB USED TO BE LIKE, TO SEE HOW HE'D LOOSENED UP.
YEAH, I'VE BEEN TAKIN' ALOTTA DOPE...IT REALLY OPENED THINGS UP FOR ME... GAVE ME A NEW PERSPECTIVE.
ALTHOUGH HE SETTLED IN CALIFORNIA, CRUMB USED TO LIKE TO TAKE THESE CROSS-COUNTRY TRIPS. WHEN HE STOPPED IN CLEVELAND IN 1970 AND 1971 HE STAYED WITH ME AND MY WIFE.
HIYA HARVEY.
HIYA, MAN... GLAD YOU C'D MAKE IT!
AT THAT TIME MY WIFE AND I WERE HAVING A LOT OF TROUBLE GETTING ALONG. WE BOTH LIKED CRUMB AND HE BROUGHT US NEWS FROM THE BIG OUTSIDE WORLD, SO IT WAS NICE FOR US WHEN HE'D VISIT.
SPANISH RICE
FINALLY, THOUGH, IT GOT SO MY WIFE AND I COULDN'T STAND LIVING TOGETHER. WE SPLIT AND DECIDED TO GET DIVORCED. THIS REALLY MADE ME FEEL TERRIBLE, SINCE WE'D BEEN TOGETHER FOR A LONG TIME AND HAD SOME GOOD THINGS GOING FOR US. I WAS REALLY LONELY.
PEPSI

I WROTE TO CRUMB ABOUT IT. HE SENT ME BACK AN ENVELOPE CONTAINING A CAPTAIN MARVEL TIE CLIP, A 1941 "YOUR IDEAL LOVE MATE" CARD WITH A PICTURE OF A PLATINUM BLOND ON IT, AND A LETTER THAT BEGAN ——

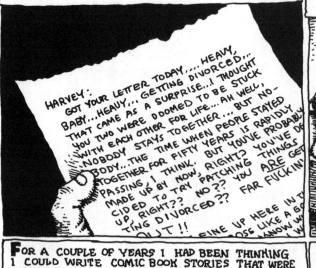

HARVEY:

GOT YOUR LETTER TODAY.... HEAVY, BABY...HEAVY... GETTING DIVORCED... THAT CAME AS A SURPRISE...I THOUGHT YOU TWO WERE DOOMED TO BE STUCK WITH EACH OTHER FOR LIFE.... AH WELL, NOBODY STAYS TOGETHER ... BUT NO-BODY...THE TIME WHEN PEOPLE STAYED TOGETHER FOR FIFTY YEARS IS RAPIDLY PASSING, I THINK. BUT YOU'VE PROBABLY MADE UP BY NOW, RIGHT? YOU'VE DE-CIDED TO TRY PATCHING THINGS UP, RIGHT?? NO?? YOU ARE GET-TING DIVORCED?? FAR FUCKIN' OUT!!

A FEW MONTHS AFTER MY DIVORCE CRUMB VISITED ME AGAIN FOR AWHILE. THIS TIME HE WAS WITH SOME OTHER PEOPLE, INCLUDING BOB ARMSTRONG, A MEMBER OF A STRING BAND CRUMB HAD FORMED, AND A FINE CARTOONIST HIMSELF. WE HAD A GOOD TIME LISTENING TO RECORDS AND TALKING.

FOR A COUPLE OF YEARS I HAD BEEN THINKING I COULD WRITE COMIC BOOK STORIES THAT WERE DIFFERENT FROM ANYTHING BEING DONE BY BOTH STRAIGHT CARTOONISTS AND UNDERGROUND CARTOONISTS LIKE CRUMB. NOW, WITH CRUMB AND ARMSTRONG THERE, I STARTED THINKING ABOUT IT AGAIN — IN MORE DETAIL THAN EVER.

THE GUYS WHO DO THAT ANIMAL COMIC AN' SUPER-HERO STUFF FOR STRAIGHT COMICS ARE REALLY LIMITED BECAUSE THEY GOTTA TRY T'APPEAL TO KIDS. TH' GUYS WHO DO UNDERGROUND COMICS HAVE REALLY OPENED THINGS UP, BUT THERE ARE STILL PLENTY MORE THINGS THAT CAN BE DONE WITH 'EM. THEY GOT GREAT POTENTIAL. YOU C'N DO AS MUCH WITH COMICS AS THE NOVEL OR MOVIES OR PLAYS OR ANYTHING. COMICS ARE WORDS AN' PICTURES; YOU C'N DO ANYTHING WITH WORDS AN' PICTURES!

ACTUALLY, THERE WERE SOME STORIES I WANTED TO WRITE THAT I HAD THOUGHT ABOUT SO MUCH THAT I HAD JUST ABOUT COMPLETED THEM IN MY MIND. ALL I HAD TO DO WAS WRITE 'EM DOWN ON PAPER. SO THAT DAY WHEN I GOT BACK FROM WORK, I SAT DOWN AN' WROTE ONE OF THE STORIES, USING PANELS, STICK FIGURES AN' WORD AN' THOUGHT BALLOONS.

I SHOWED THE STORY TO CRUMB AND ARMSTRONG AND THEY LIKED IT A LOT.

GREAT STUFF, HARVEY

THAT REALLY ENCOURAGED ME. I SAT AN' WROTE SOME MORE STORIES IN THE NEXT COUPLA DAYS. CRUMB AND ARMSTRONG TOOK A FEW WITH 'EM WHEN THEY LEFT AN' ILLUSTRATED 'EM. THE STORIES GOT PRINTED. THAT GOT ME STARTED.

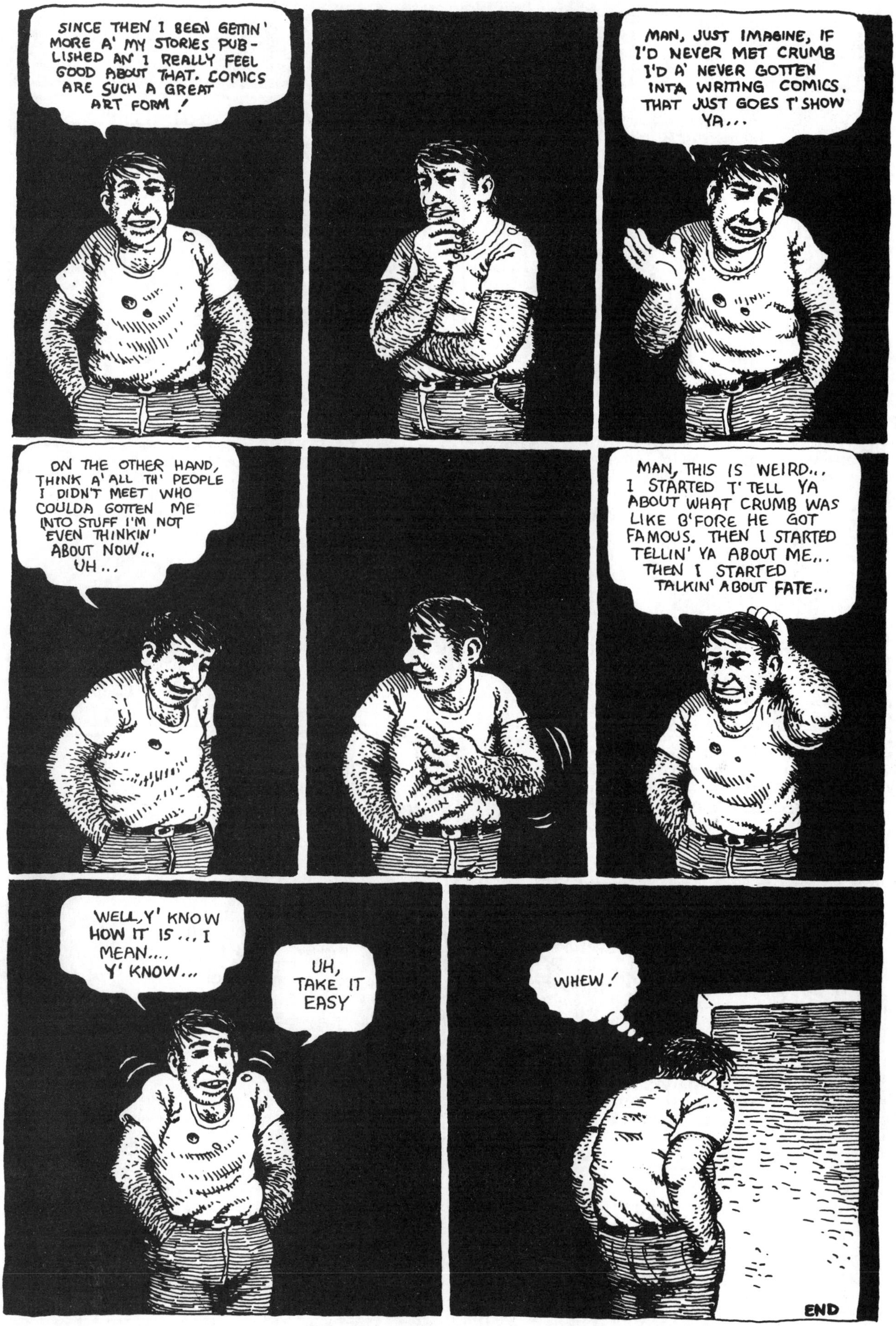
SINCE THEN I BEEN GETTIN' MORE A' MY STORIES PUB-LISHED AN' I REALLY FEEL GOOD ABOUT THAT. COMICS ARE SUCH A GREAT ART FORM!
MAN, JUST IMAGINE, IF I'D NEVER MET CRUMB I'D A' NEVER GOTTEN INTA WRITING COMICS. THAT JUST GOES T' SHOW YA...
ON THE OTHER HAND, THINK A' ALL TH' PEOPLE I DIDN'T MEET WHO COULDA GOTTEN ME INTO STUFF I'M NOT EVEN THINKIN' ABOUT NOW... UH...
MAN, THIS IS WEIRD... I STARTED T' TELL YA ABOUT WHAT CRUMB WAS LIKE B'FORE HE GOT FAMOUS. THEN I STARTED TELLIN' YA ABOUT ME... THEN I STARTED TALKIN' ABOUT FATE...
WELL, Y' KNOW HOW IT IS... I MEAN.... Y' KNOW...
UH, TAKE IT EASY
WHEW!
END

A Fantasy

Art by R. Crumb
Story by Harvey Pekar

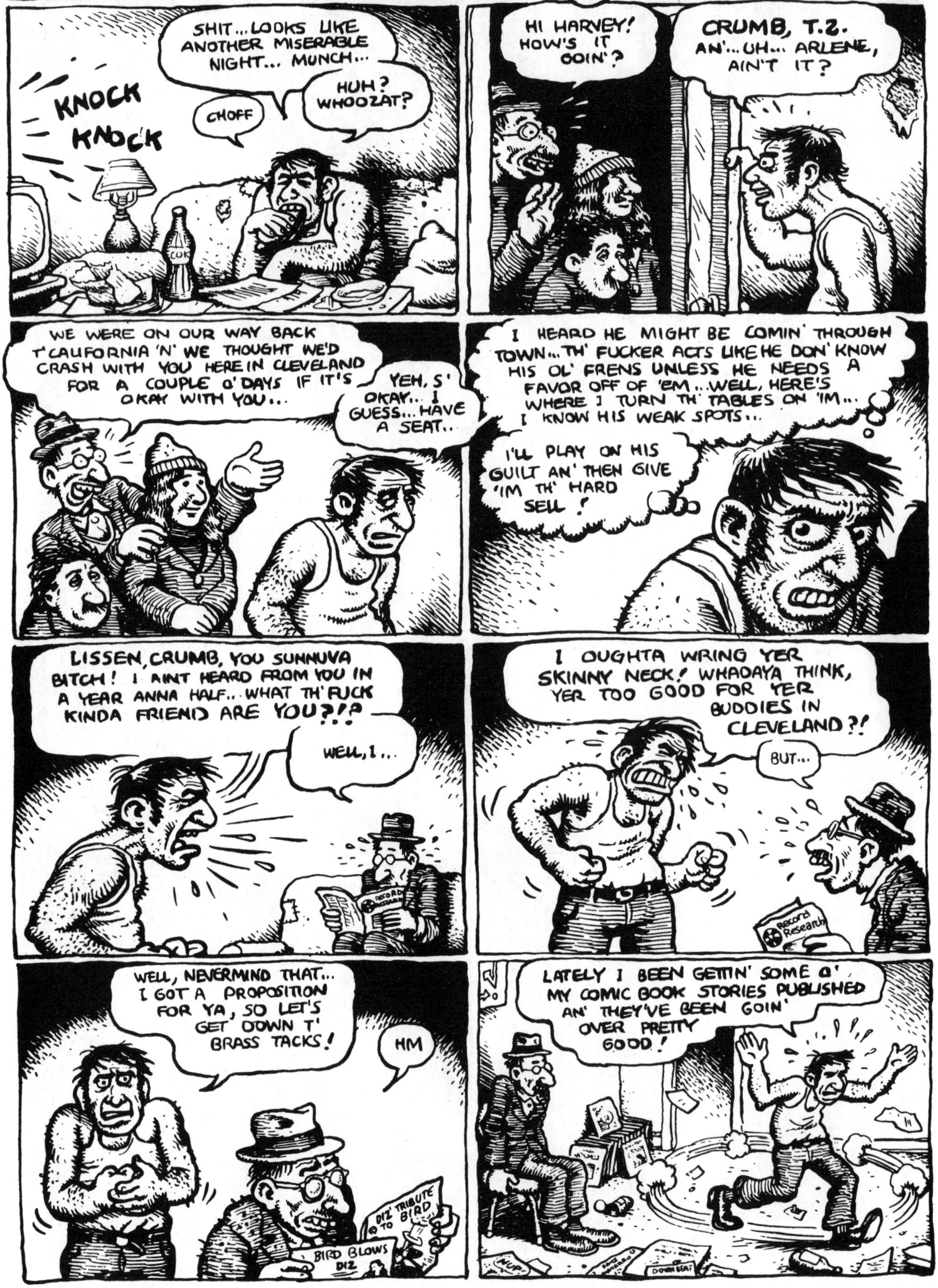

SHIT... LOOKS LIKE ANOTHER MISERABLE NIGHT... MUNCH...
CHOFF
KNOCK KNOCK
HUH? WHOOZAT?
HI HARVEY! HOW'S IT GOIN'?
CRUMB, T.Z. AN'... UH... ARLENE, AIN'T IT?
WE WERE ON OUR WAY BACK T'CALIFORNIA 'N' WE THOUGHT WE'D CRASH WITH YOU HERE IN CLEVELAND FOR A COUPLE O' DAYS IF IT'S OKAY WITH YOU...
YEH, S' OKAY... I GUESS... HAVE A SEAT...
I HEARD HE MIGHT BE COMIN' THROUGH TOWN... TH' FUCKER ACTS LIKE HE DON' KNOW HIS OL' FRENS UNLESS HE NEEDS A FAVOR OFF OF 'EM... WELL, HERE'S WHERE I TURN TH' TABLES ON 'IM... I KNOW HIS WEAK SPOTS...
I'LL PLAY ON HIS GUILT AN' THEN GIVE 'IM TH' HARD SELL!
LISSEN, CRUMB, YOU SUNNUVA BITCH! I AINT HEARD FROM YOU IN A YEAR ANNA HALF... WHAT TH' FUCK KINDA FRIEND ARE YOU?!?
WELL, I...
RECORD RESEARCH
I OUGHTA WRING YER SKINNY NECK! WHADAYA THINK, YER TOO GOOD FOR YER BUDDIES IN CLEVELAND?!
BUT...
Record Research
WELL, NEVERMIND THAT... I GOT A PROPOSITION FOR YA, SO LET'S GET DOWN T' BRASS TACKS!
HM
DIZ' TRIBUTE TO BIRD
BIRD BLOWS DIZ
LATELY I BEEN GETTIN' SOME O' MY COMIC BOOK STORIES PUBLISHED AN' THEY'VE BEEN GOIN' OVER PRETTY GOOD!
DOWN BEAT

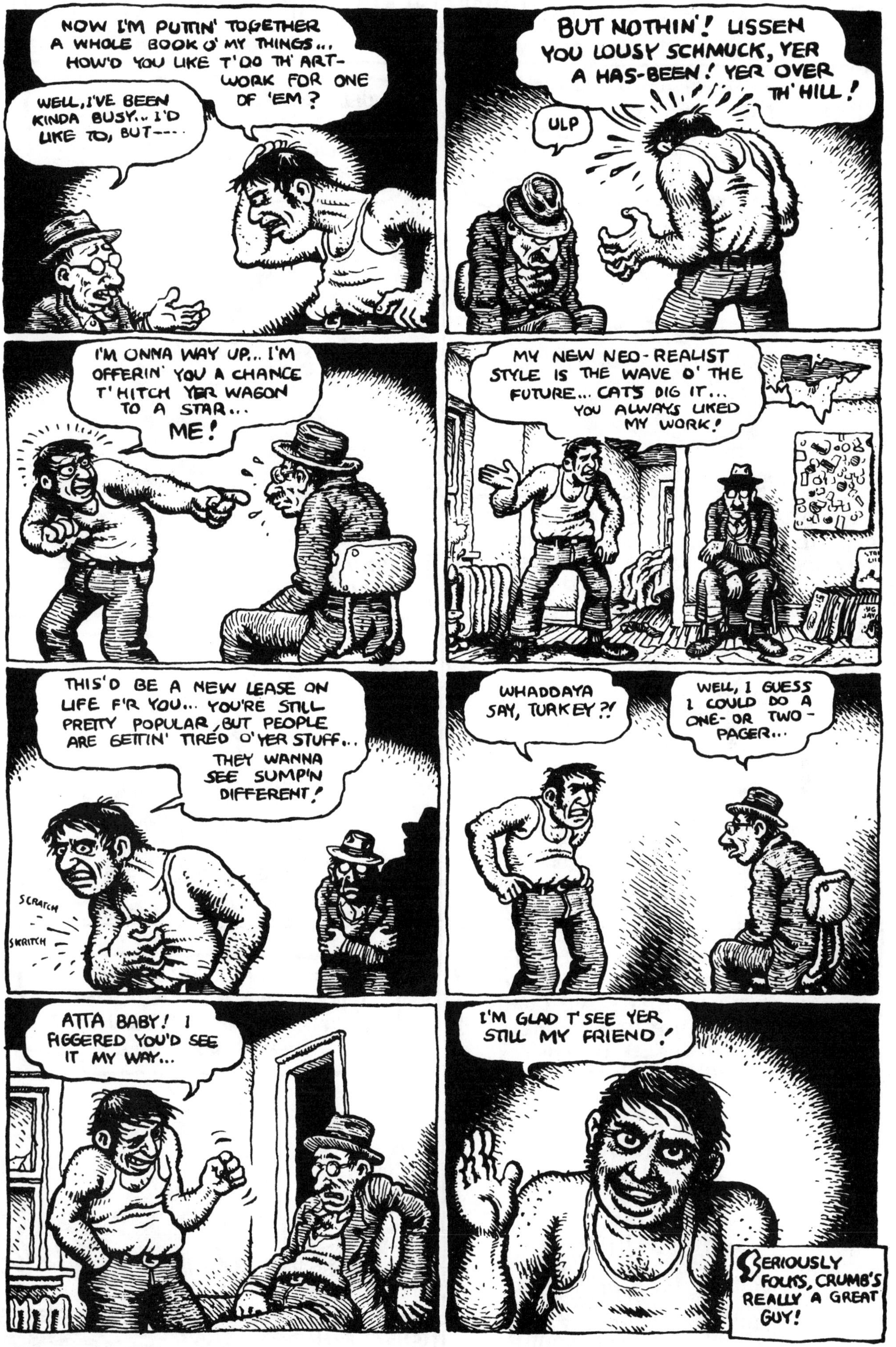
NOW I'M PUTTIN' TOGETHER A WHOLE BOOK O' MY THINGS... HOW'D YOU LIKE T'DO TH' ART-WORK FOR ONE OF 'EM?
WELL, I'VE BEEN KINDA BUSY.. I'D LIKE TO, BUT---
BUT NOTHIN'! LISSEN YOU LOUSY SCHMUCK, YER A HAS-BEEN! YER OVER TH' HILL!
ULP
I'M ONNA WAY UP... I'M OFFERIN' YOU A CHANCE T'HITCH YER WAGON TO A STAR... ME!
MY NEW NEO-REALIST STYLE IS THE WAVE O' THE FUTURE... CATS DIG IT... YOU ALWAYS LIKED MY WORK!
THIS'D BE A NEW LEASE ON LIFE F'R YOU... YOU'RE STILL PRETTY POPULAR, BUT PEOPLE ARE GETTIN' TIRED O'YER STUFF... THEY WANNA SEE SUMP'N DIFFERENT!
SCRATCH
SKRITCH
WHADDAYA SAY, TURKEY?!
WELL, I GUESS I COULD DO A ONE- OR TWO-PAGER...
ATTA BABY! I FIGGERED YOU'D SEE IT MY WAY...
I'M GLAD T'SEE YER STILL MY FRIEND!
SERIOUSLY FOLKS, CRUMB'S REALLY A GREAT GUY!

OZZIE NELSON'S OPEN LETTER TO CRUMB

STORY BY HARVEY PEKAR ART BY GARY DUMM (STORY WRITTEN IN 1972)

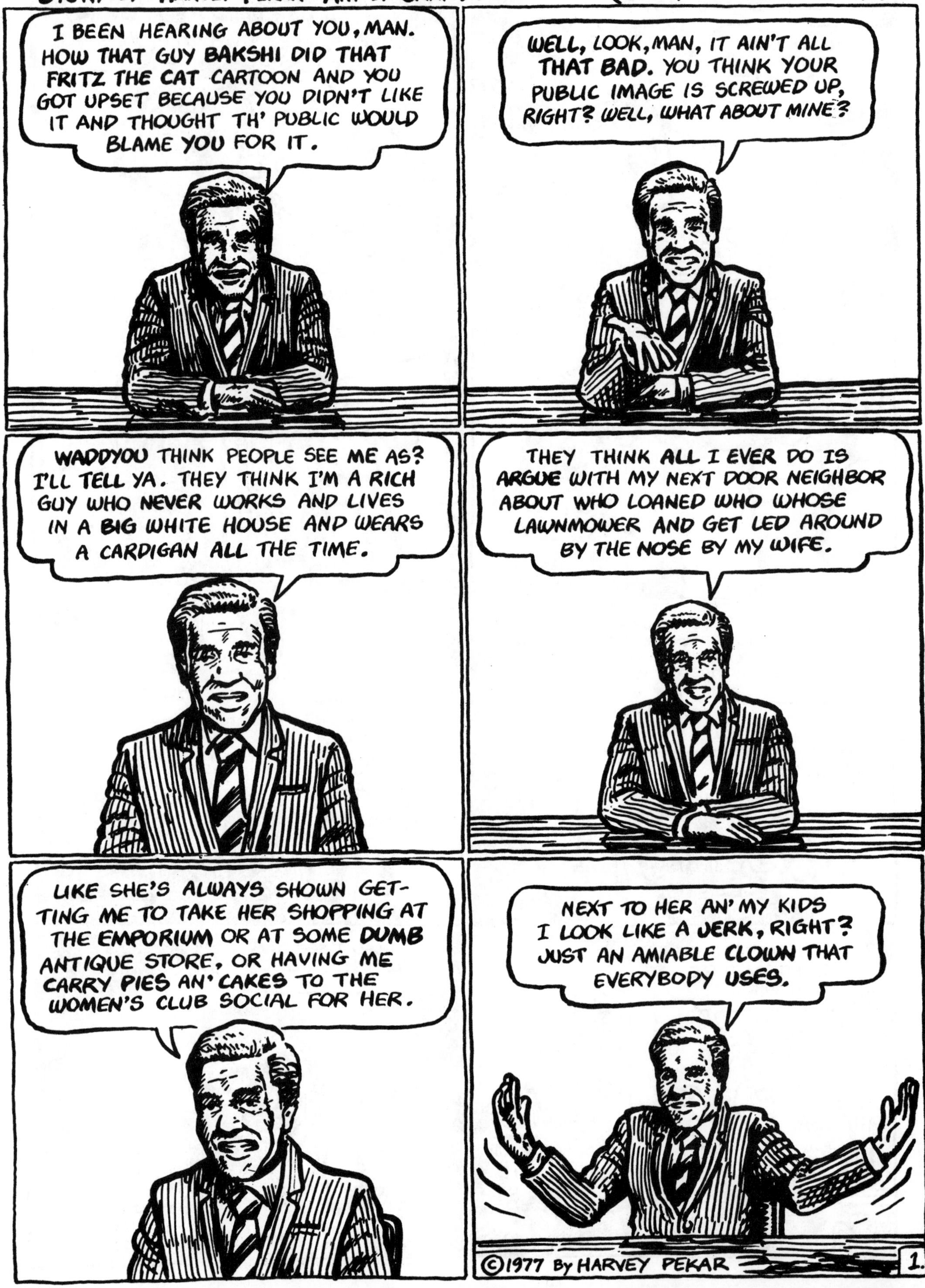

I BEEN HEARING ABOUT YOU, MAN. HOW THAT GUY BAKSHI DID THAT FRITZ THE CAT CARTOON AND YOU GOT UPSET BECAUSE YOU DIDN'T LIKE IT AND THOUGHT TH' PUBLIC WOULD BLAME YOU FOR IT.
WELL, LOOK, MAN, IT AIN'T ALL THAT BAD. YOU THINK YOUR PUBLIC IMAGE IS SCREWED UP, RIGHT? WELL, WHAT ABOUT MINE?
WADDYOU THINK PEOPLE SEE ME AS? I'LL TELL YA. THEY THINK I'M A RICH GUY WHO NEVER WORKS AND LIVES IN A BIG WHITE HOUSE AND WEARS A CARDIGAN ALL THE TIME.
THEY THINK ALL I EVER DO IS ARGUE WITH MY NEXT DOOR NEIGHBOR ABOUT WHO LOANED WHO WHOSE LAWNMOWER AND GET LED AROUND BY THE NOSE BY MY WIFE.
LIKE SHE'S ALWAYS SHOWN GETTING ME TO TAKE HER SHOPPING AT THE EMPORIUM OR AT SOME DUMB ANTIQUE STORE, OR HAVING ME CARRY PIES AN' CAKES TO THE WOMEN'S CLUB SOCIAL FOR HER.
NEXT TO HER AN' MY KIDS I LOOK LIKE A JERK, RIGHT? JUST AN AMIABLE CLOWN THAT EVERYBODY USES.
©1977 BY HARVEY PEKAR
1.

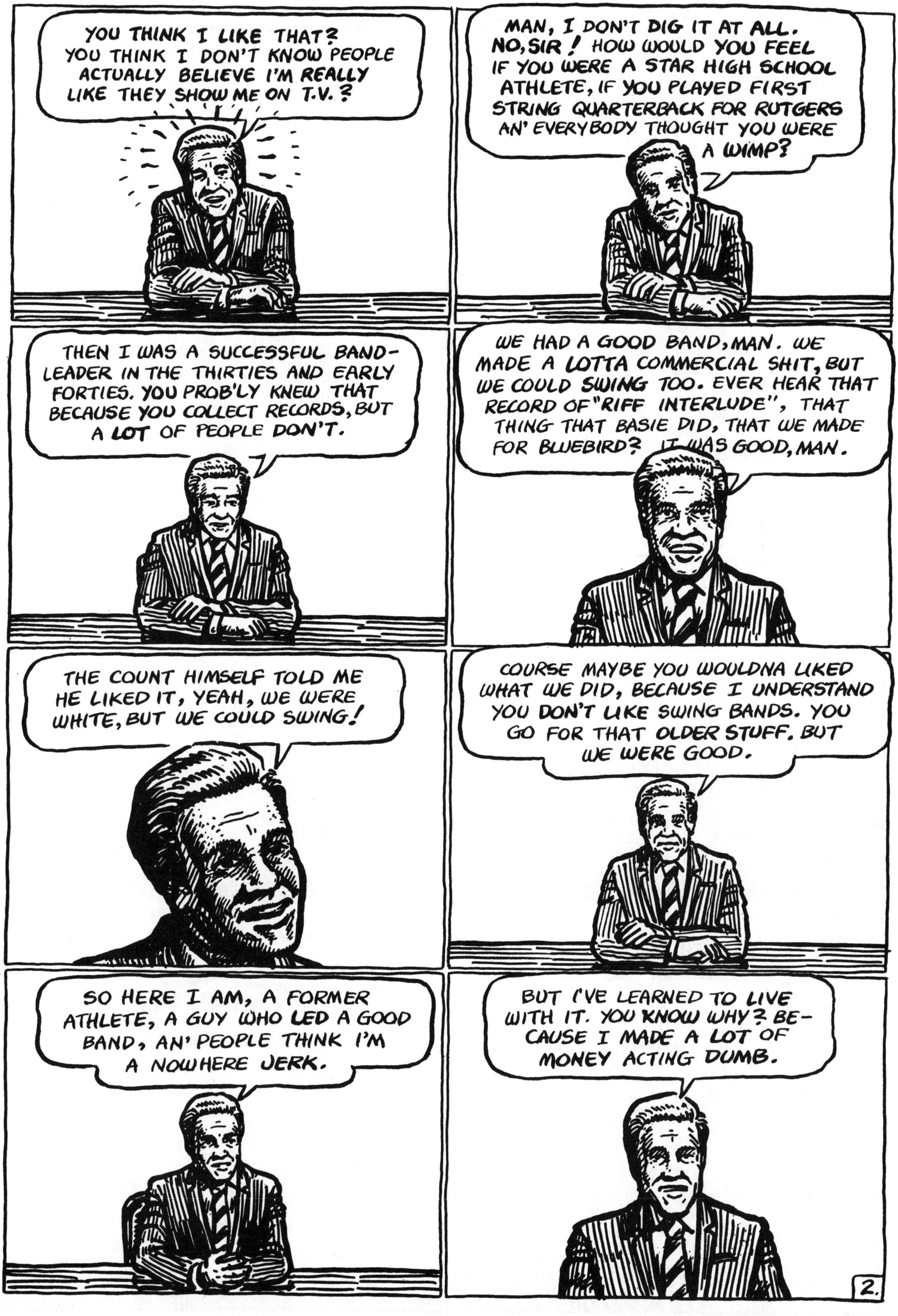
YOU THINK I LIKE THAT? YOU THINK I DON'T KNOW PEOPLE ACTUALLY BELIEVE I'M REALLY LIKE THEY SHOW ME ON T.V.?
MAN, I DON'T DIG IT AT ALL. NO, SIR! HOW WOULD YOU FEEL IF YOU WERE A STAR HIGH SCHOOL ATHLETE, IF YOU PLAYED FIRST STRING QUARTERBACK FOR RUTGERS AN' EVERYBODY THOUGHT YOU WERE A WIMP?
THEN I WAS A SUCCESSFUL BAND-LEADER IN THE THIRTIES AND EARLY FORTIES. YOU PROB'LY KNEW THAT BECAUSE YOU COLLECT RECORDS, BUT A LOT OF PEOPLE DON'T.
WE HAD A GOOD BAND, MAN. WE MADE A LOTTA COMMERCIAL SHIT, BUT WE COULD SWING TOO. EVER HEAR THAT RECORD OF "RIFF INTERLUDE", THAT THING THAT BASIE DID, THAT WE MADE FOR BLUEBIRD? IT WAS GOOD, MAN.
THE COUNT HIMSELF TOLD ME HE LIKED IT, YEAH, WE WERE WHITE, BUT WE COULD SWING!
COURSE MAYBE YOU WOULDNA LIKED WHAT WE DID, BECAUSE I UNDERSTAND YOU DON'T LIKE SWING BANDS. YOU GO FOR THAT OLDER STUFF. BUT WE WERE GOOD.
SO HERE I AM, A FORMER ATHLETE, A GUY WHO LED A GOOD BAND, AN' PEOPLE THINK I'M A NOWHERE JERK.
BUT I'VE LEARNED TO LIVE WITH IT. YOU KNOW WHY? BE-CAUSE I MADE A LOT OF MONEY ACTING DUMB.
2.

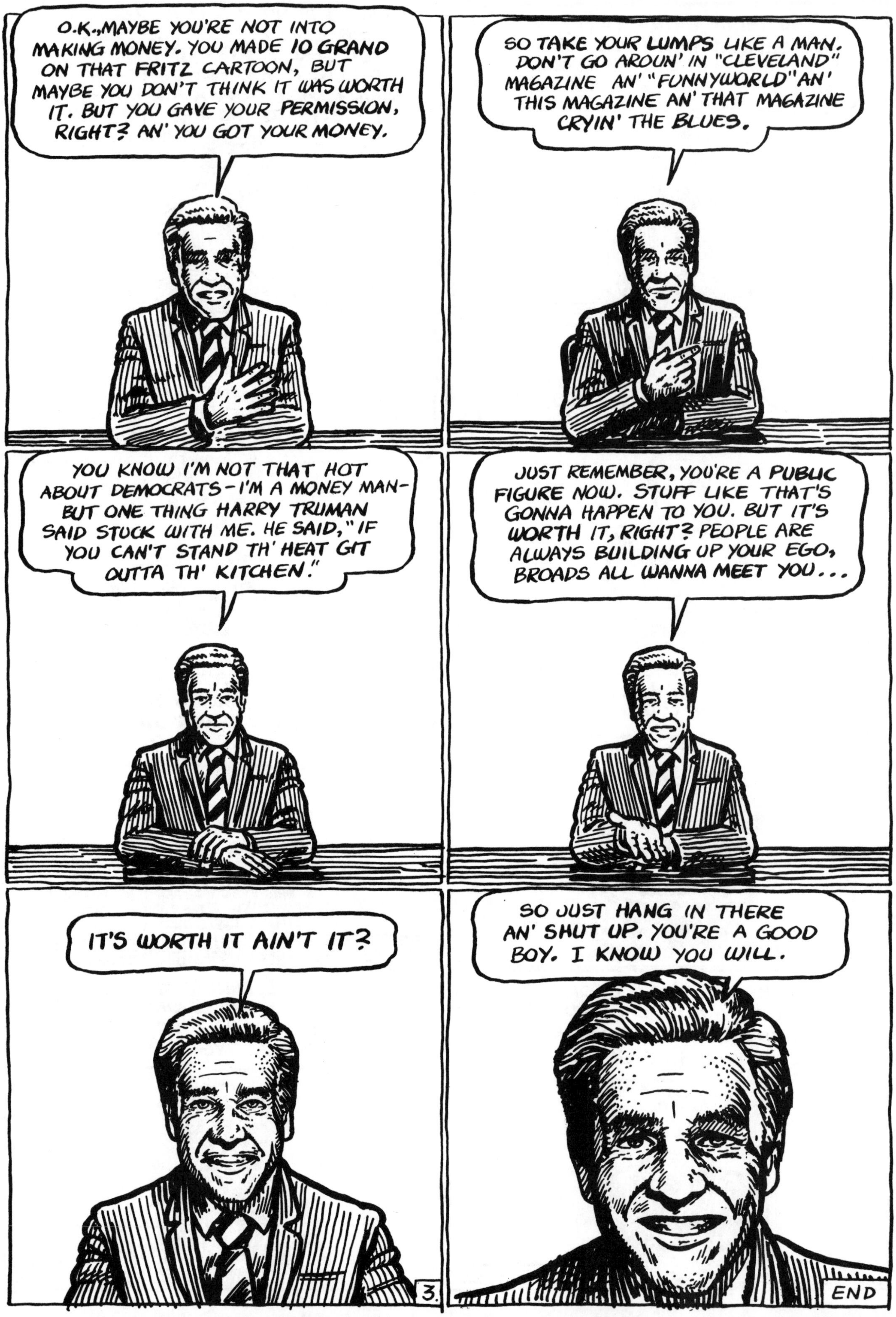
O.K., MAYBE YOU'RE NOT INTO MAKING MONEY. YOU MADE 10 GRAND ON THAT FRITZ CARTOON, BUT MAYBE YOU DON'T THINK IT WAS WORTH IT. BUT YOU GAVE YOUR PERMISSION, RIGHT? AN' YOU GOT YOUR MONEY.
SO TAKE YOUR LUMPS LIKE A MAN. DON'T GO AROUN' IN "CLEVELAND" MAGAZINE AN' "FUNNYWORLD" AN' THIS MAGAZINE AN' THAT MAGAZINE CRYIN' THE BLUES.
YOU KNOW I'M NOT THAT HOT ABOUT DEMOCRATS - I'M A MONEY MAN - BUT ONE THING HARRY TRUMAN SAID STUCK WITH ME. HE SAID, "IF YOU CAN'T STAND TH' HEAT GIT OUTTA TH' KITCHEN."
JUST REMEMBER, YOU'RE A PUBLIC FIGURE NOW. STUFF LIKE THAT'S GONNA HAPPEN TO YOU. BUT IT'S WORTH IT, RIGHT? PEOPLE ARE ALWAYS BUILDING UP YOUR EGO, BROADS ALL WANNA MEET YOU...
IT'S WORTH IT AIN'T IT?
3.
SO JUST HANG IN THERE AN' SHUT UP. YOU'RE A GOOD BOY. I KNOW YOU WILL.
END

HOW I QUIT COLLECTING RECORDS
AND PUT OUT A COMIC BOOK WITH THE MONEY I SAVED

Story by Harvey Pekar **Art by R. Crumb**

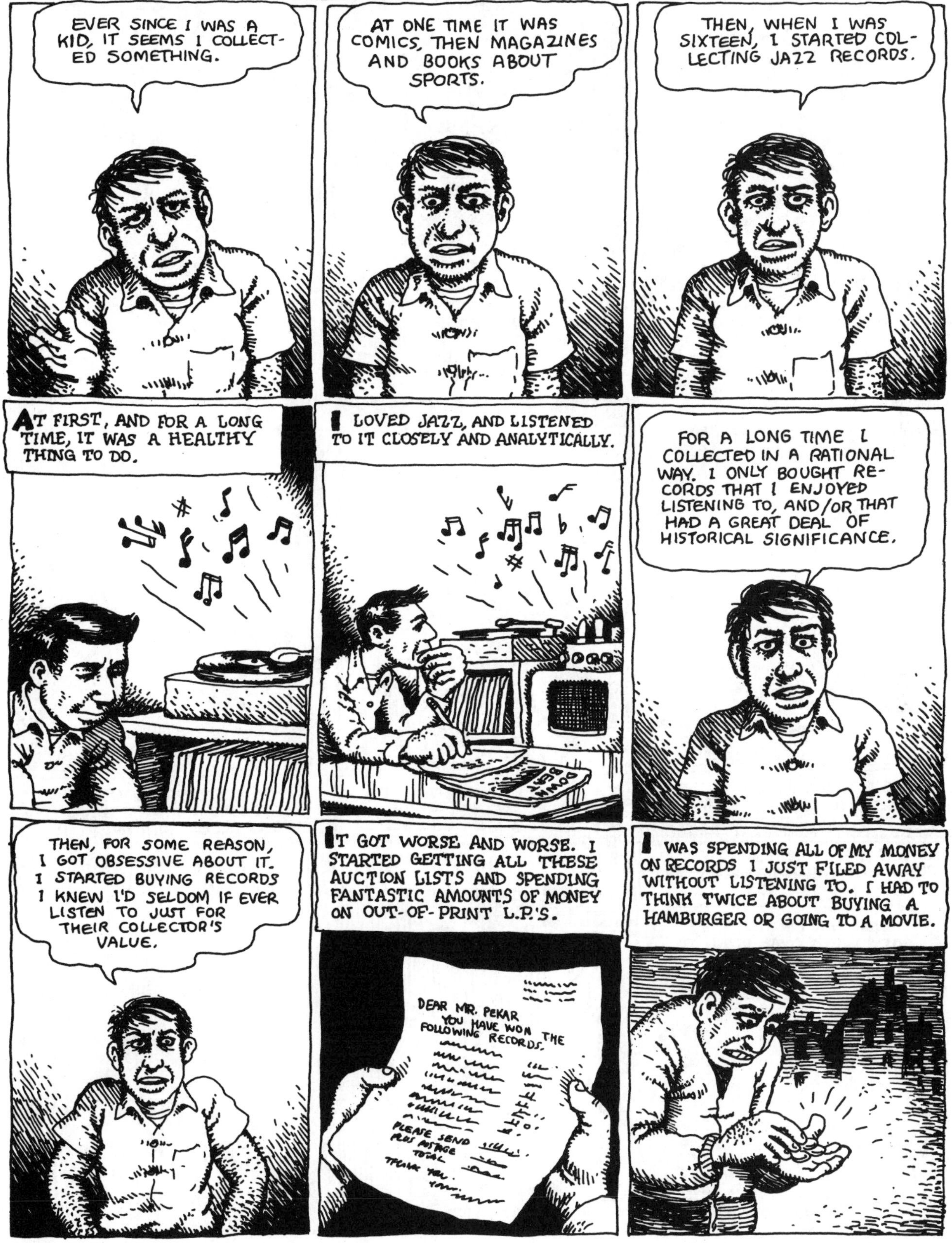
EVER SINCE I WAS A KID, IT SEEMS I COLLECTED SOMETHING.
AT ONE TIME IT WAS COMICS, THEN MAGAZINES AND BOOKS ABOUT SPORTS.
THEN, WHEN I WAS SIXTEEN, I STARTED COLLECTING JAZZ RECORDS.
AT FIRST, AND FOR A LONG TIME, IT WAS A HEALTHY THING TO DO.
I LOVED JAZZ, AND LISTENED TO IT CLOSELY AND ANALYTICALLY.
DOWN BEAT
FOR A LONG TIME I COLLECTED IN A RATIONAL WAY. I ONLY BOUGHT RECORDS THAT I ENJOYED LISTENING TO, AND/OR THAT HAD A GREAT DEAL OF HISTORICAL SIGNIFICANCE.
THEN, FOR SOME REASON, I GOT OBSESSIVE ABOUT IT. I STARTED BUYING RECORDS I KNEW I'D SELDOM IF EVER LISTEN TO JUST FOR THEIR COLLECTOR'S VALUE.
IT GOT WORSE AND WORSE. I STARTED GETTING ALL THESE AUCTION LISTS AND SPENDING FANTASTIC AMOUNTS OF MONEY ON OUT-OF-PRINT L.P.'S.
DEAR MR. PEKAR YOU HAVE WON THE FOLLOWING RECORDS.
PLEASE SEND
TOTAL
I WAS SPENDING ALL OF MY MONEY ON RECORDS I JUST FILED AWAY WITHOUT LISTENING TO. I HAD TO THINK TWICE ABOUT BUYING A HAMBURGER OR GOING TO A MOVIE.

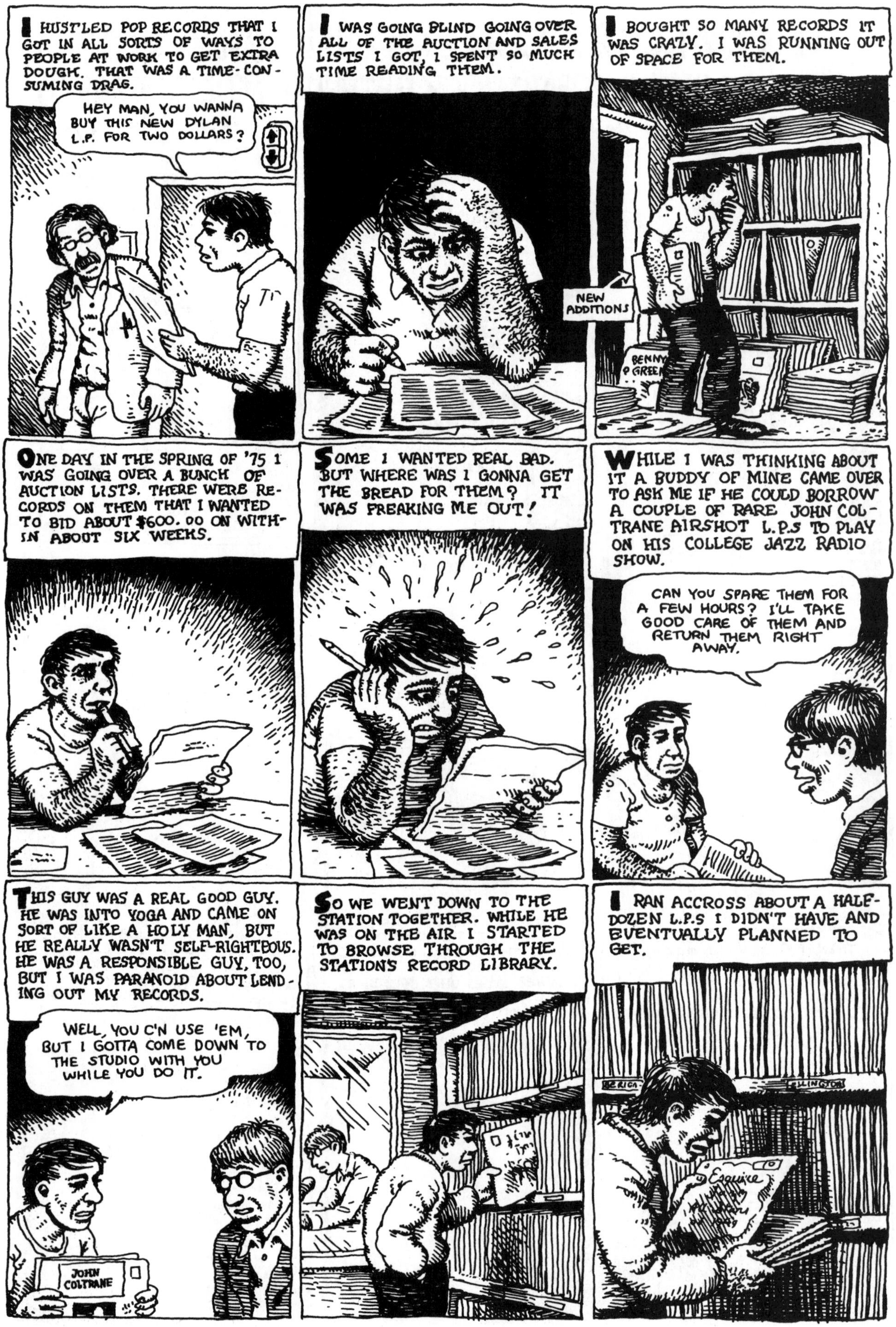
I HUSTLED POP RECORDS THAT I GOT IN ALL SORTS OF WAYS TO PEOPLE AT WORK TO GET EXTRA DOUGH. THAT WAS A TIME-CONSUMING DRAG.
HEY MAN, YOU WANNA BUY THIS NEW DYLAN L.P. FOR TWO DOLLARS?
I WAS GOING BLIND GOING OVER ALL OF THE AUCTION AND SALES LISTS I GOT, I SPENT SO MUCH TIME READING THEM.
I BOUGHT SO MANY RECORDS IT WAS CRAZY. I WAS RUNNING OUT OF SPACE FOR THEM.
NEW ADDITIONS
ONE DAY IN THE SPRING OF '75 I WAS GOING OVER A BUNCH OF AUCTION LISTS. THERE WERE RECORDS ON THEM THAT I WANTED TO BID ABOUT $600.00 ON WITHIN ABOUT SIX WEEKS.
SOME I WANTED REAL BAD. BUT WHERE WAS I GONNA GET THE BREAD FOR THEM? IT WAS FREAKING ME OUT!
WHILE I WAS THINKING ABOUT IT A BUDDY OF MINE CAME OVER TO ASK ME IF HE COULD BORROW A COUPLE OF RARE JOHN COLTRANE AIRSHOT L.P.S TO PLAY ON HIS COLLEGE JAZZ RADIO SHOW.
CAN YOU SPARE THEM FOR A FEW HOURS? I'LL TAKE GOOD CARE OF THEM AND RETURN THEM RIGHT AWAY.
THIS GUY WAS A REAL GOOD GUY. HE WAS INTO YOGA AND CAME ON SORT OF LIKE A HOLY MAN, BUT HE REALLY WASN'T SELF-RIGHTEOUS. HE WAS A RESPONSIBLE GUY, TOO, BUT I WAS PARANOID ABOUT LENDING OUT MY RECORDS.
WELL, YOU C'N USE 'EM, BUT I GOTTA COME DOWN TO THE STUDIO WITH YOU WHILE YOU DO IT.
JOHN COLTRANE
SO WE WENT DOWN TO THE STATION TOGETHER. WHILE HE WAS ON THE AIR I STARTED TO BROWSE THROUGH THE STATION'S RECORD LIBRARY.
I RAN ACCROSS ABOUT A HALF-DOZEN L.P.S I DIDN'T HAVE AND EVENTUALLY PLANNED TO GET.
Esquire

THEY WERE STILL IN PRINT BUT THEY WOULDA' COST ME AROUND THIRTY BUCKS TO BUY.

I KNEW THAT ALOT OF PEOPLE RIPPED OFF RECORDS FROM THAT STATION.

SO I FIGURED, " FUCK IT, WHAT'S THE DIFFERENCE" AND I DECIDED I WAS GONNA STEAL THE SIDES BUT I THOUGHT I'D BE SLICK ABOUT IT...

IT WAS SUNDAY, THE BUILDING WAS DESERTED. SO WHAT I DID, I SNEAKED THE SIDES OUT OF THE STUDIO AND STUCK 'EM IN A BATHROOM.

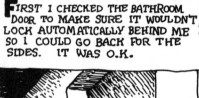

FIRST I CHECKED THE BATHROOM DOOR TO MAKE SURE IT WOULDN'T LOCK AUTOMATICALLY BEHIND ME SO I COULD GO BACK FOR THE SIDES. IT WAS O.K.

THEN I STUCK THE SIDES IN A BOX OF TOILET PAPER.

ACME TOILET TISSUE 100 ROLLS

THEN I WENT BACK TO THE STUDIO TO BULLSHIT WITH MY BUDDY. I FIGURED I'D TAKE THE COLTRANE RECORDS WHEN HE WAS THROUGH WITH THEM AND SPLIT WHILE HE WAS STILL ON THE AIR.

HE'D SEE ME WALKING OUT OF THE STUDIO WITH ONLY THE COLTRANE RECORDS IN MY HANDS, SO IF THE OTHER SIDES WERE MISSED HE WOULDN'T SUSPECT ME.

I MEAN, THE CAT TRUSTED ME AND I DIDN'T WANT HIM TO KNOW I WAS STEALING. LIKE HE WAS SUCH A MORAL DUDE, Y'KNOW. HE WAS EVEN AGAINST STEALING FROM STORES AND INSTITUTIONS.

SO HE FINISHES PLAYIN' THE COLTRANE SIDES, GIVES 'EM BACK TO ME AN' I SPLIT.

THANKS ALOT, MAN!

'S O.K....UH, LOOK, I GOTTA TAKE OFF NOW...

SO THEN I MAKE IT OVER TO THE BATHROOM TO GET TH' SIDES.

MEN

BUT THE DOOR IS LOCKED.

I COULDN'T BELIEVE IT. I HAD TESTED IT BEFORE TO MAKE SURE IT WOULDN'T LOCK ON ME. I YANKED ON IT AGAIN AND AGAIN. IT WAS LOCKED.

THAT BLEW MY MIND. I WAS ALREADY WONDERING ABOUT WHERE I WAS GONNA GET TH' $600.00 AND NOW I HAD THROWN AWAY ANOTHER $30.00 WORTH OF SIDES BECAUSE I'D DEVISED TOO ELABORATE A PLAN TO RIP THEM OFF.

IF I'D HAVE STUCK THEM IN THE HALL SOME PLACE THEY'D HAVE BEEN O.K. NO ONE WAS GONNA COME ALONG AND SEE THEM. BUT NO, I HADDA GET CUTE AN' STICK 'EM IN A TOILET PAPER BOX IN A BATHROOM.

I WALKED BACK HOME IN A DAZE.

HOW COULD I HAVE BEEN SO STUPID? IT WAS SO EASY TO STEAL THOSE SIDES! NOW I GOTTA COME UP WITH $30.00 MORE TO BUY THEM SOME DAY... WHAT IF THEY FIND THE SIDES IN THE TOILET PAPER BOX? WILL THEY SUSPECT ME??

MY HEAD WAS ALL FUCKED UP. I SAT DOWN TO RELAX AND THINK ABOUT MY SITUATION.

THIS RECORD COLLECTING IS DRIVING ME NUTS. IT'S TAKING ALL OF MY TIME AND MONEY.

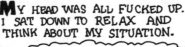
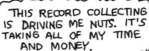

NO MATTER HOW MANY RECORDS I GET I'M NEVER SATISFIED; I GOTTA GET MORE. I'VE TRIED TO QUIT BUT I CAN'T. WHAT AM I GONNA DO? THIS IS LIKE BEING A JUNKY!!

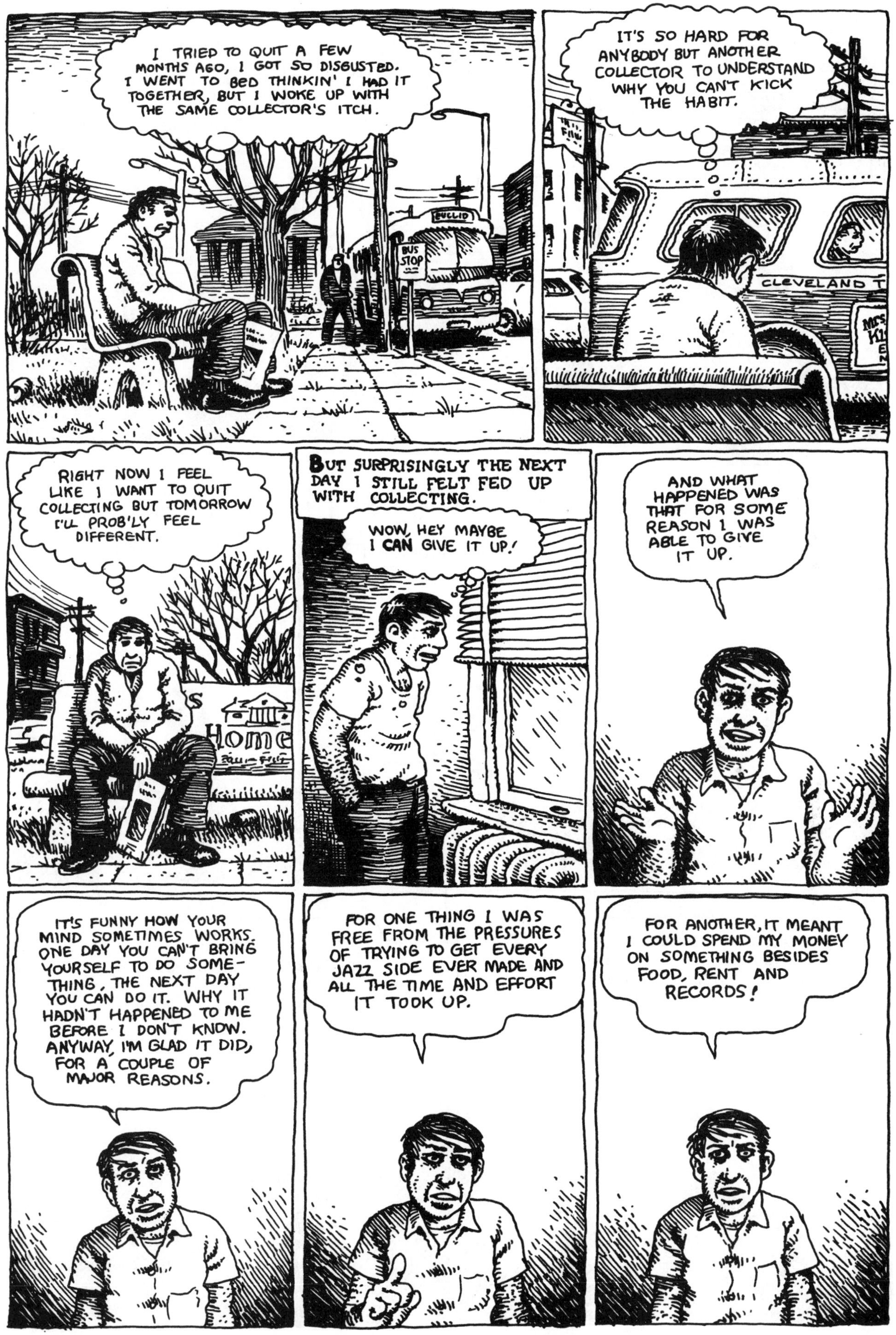
I TRIED TO QUIT A FEW MONTHS AGO, I GOT SO DISGUSTED. I WENT TO BED THINKIN' I HAD IT TOGETHER, BUT I WOKE UP WITH THE SAME COLLECTOR'S ITCH.
EUCLID
BUS STOP
IT'S SO HARD FOR ANYBODY BUT ANOTHER COLLECTOR TO UNDERSTAND WHY YOU CAN'T KICK THE HABIT.
CLEVELAND T
RIGHT NOW I FEEL LIKE I WANT TO QUIT COLLECTING BUT TOMORROW I'LL PROB'LY FEEL DIFFERENT.
Home
BUT SURPRISINGLY THE NEXT DAY I STILL FELT FED UP WITH COLLECTING.
WOW, HEY MAYBE I CAN GIVE IT UP!
AND WHAT HAPPENED WAS THAT FOR SOME REASON I WAS ABLE TO GIVE IT UP.
IT'S FUNNY HOW YOUR MIND SOMETIMES WORKS. ONE DAY YOU CAN'T BRING YOURSELF TO DO SOMETHING, THE NEXT DAY YOU CAN DO IT. WHY IT HADN'T HAPPENED TO ME BEFORE I DON'T KNOW. ANYWAY, I'M GLAD IT DID, FOR A COUPLE OF MAJOR REASONS.
FOR ONE THING I WAS FREE FROM THE PRESSURES OF TRYING TO GET EVERY JAZZ SIDE EVER MADE AND ALL THE TIME AND EFFORT IT TOOK UP.
FOR ANOTHER, IT MEANT I COULD SPEND MY MONEY ON SOMETHING BESIDES FOOD, RENT AND RECORDS!

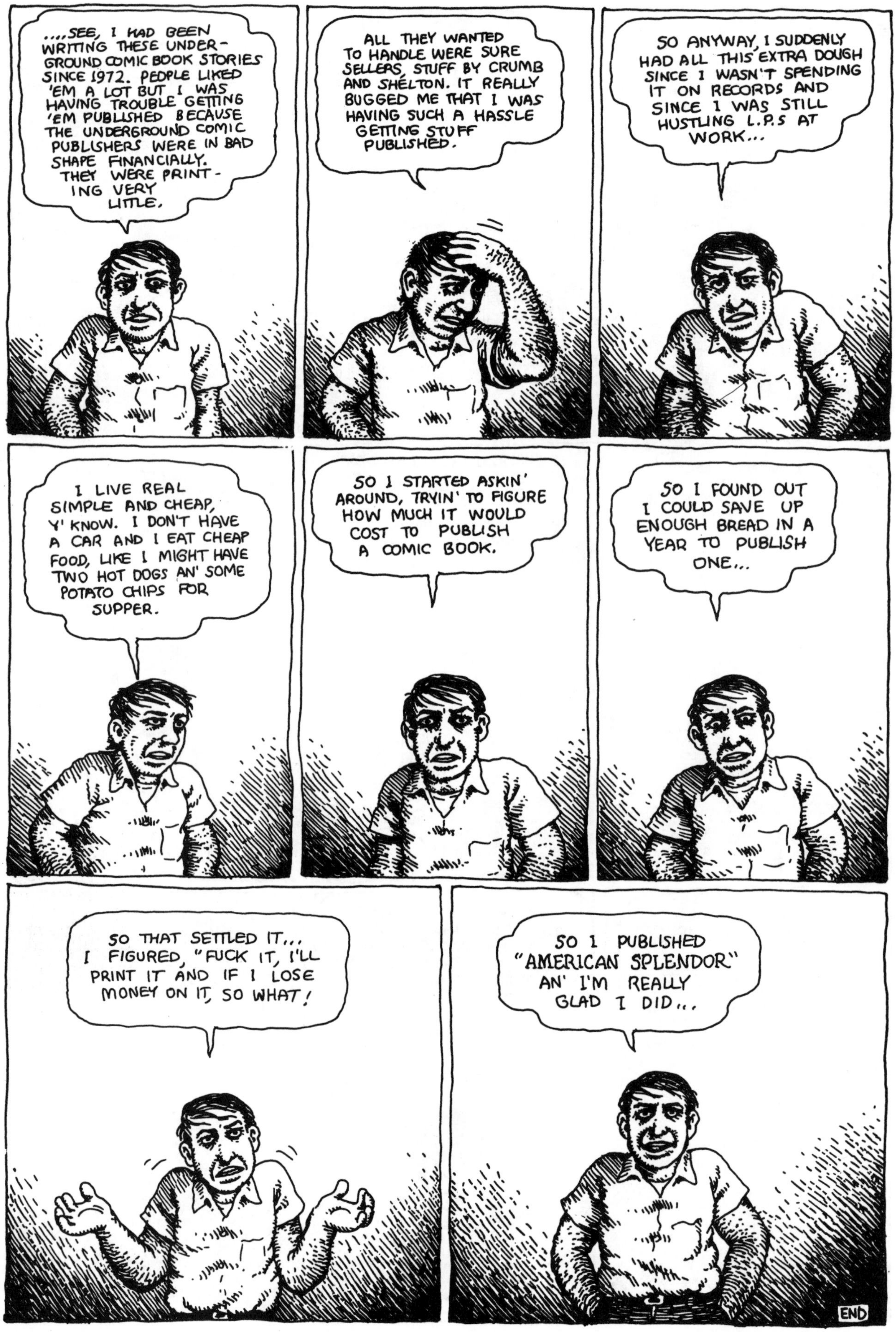
....SEE, I HAD BEEN WRITING THESE UNDERGROUND COMIC BOOK STORIES SINCE 1972. PEOPLE LIKED 'EM A LOT BUT I WAS HAVING TROUBLE GETTING 'EM PUBLISHED BECAUSE THE UNDERGROUND COMIC PUBLISHERS WERE IN BAD SHAPE FINANCIALLY. THEY WERE PRINTING VERY LITTLE.
ALL THEY WANTED TO HANDLE WERE SURE SELLERS, STUFF BY CRUMB AND SHELTON. IT REALLY BUGGED ME THAT I WAS HAVING SUCH A HASSLE GETTING STUFF PUBLISHED.
SO ANYWAY, I SUDDENLY HAD ALL THIS EXTRA DOUGH SINCE I WASN'T SPENDING IT ON RECORDS AND SINCE I WAS STILL HUSTLING L.P.S AT WORK...
I LIVE REAL SIMPLE AND CHEAP, Y' KNOW. I DON'T HAVE A CAR AND I EAT CHEAP FOOD, LIKE I MIGHT HAVE TWO HOT DOGS AN' SOME POTATO CHIPS FOR SUPPER.
SO I STARTED ASKIN' AROUND, TRYIN' TO FIGURE HOW MUCH IT WOULD COST TO PUBLISH A COMIC BOOK.
SO I FOUND OUT I COULD SAVE UP ENOUGH BREAD IN A YEAR TO PUBLISH ONE...
SO THAT SETTLED IT... I FIGURED, "FUCK IT, I'LL PRINT IT AND IF I LOSE MONEY ON IT, SO WHAT!
SO I PUBLISHED "AMERICAN SPLENDOR" AN' I'M REALLY GLAD I DID...
END

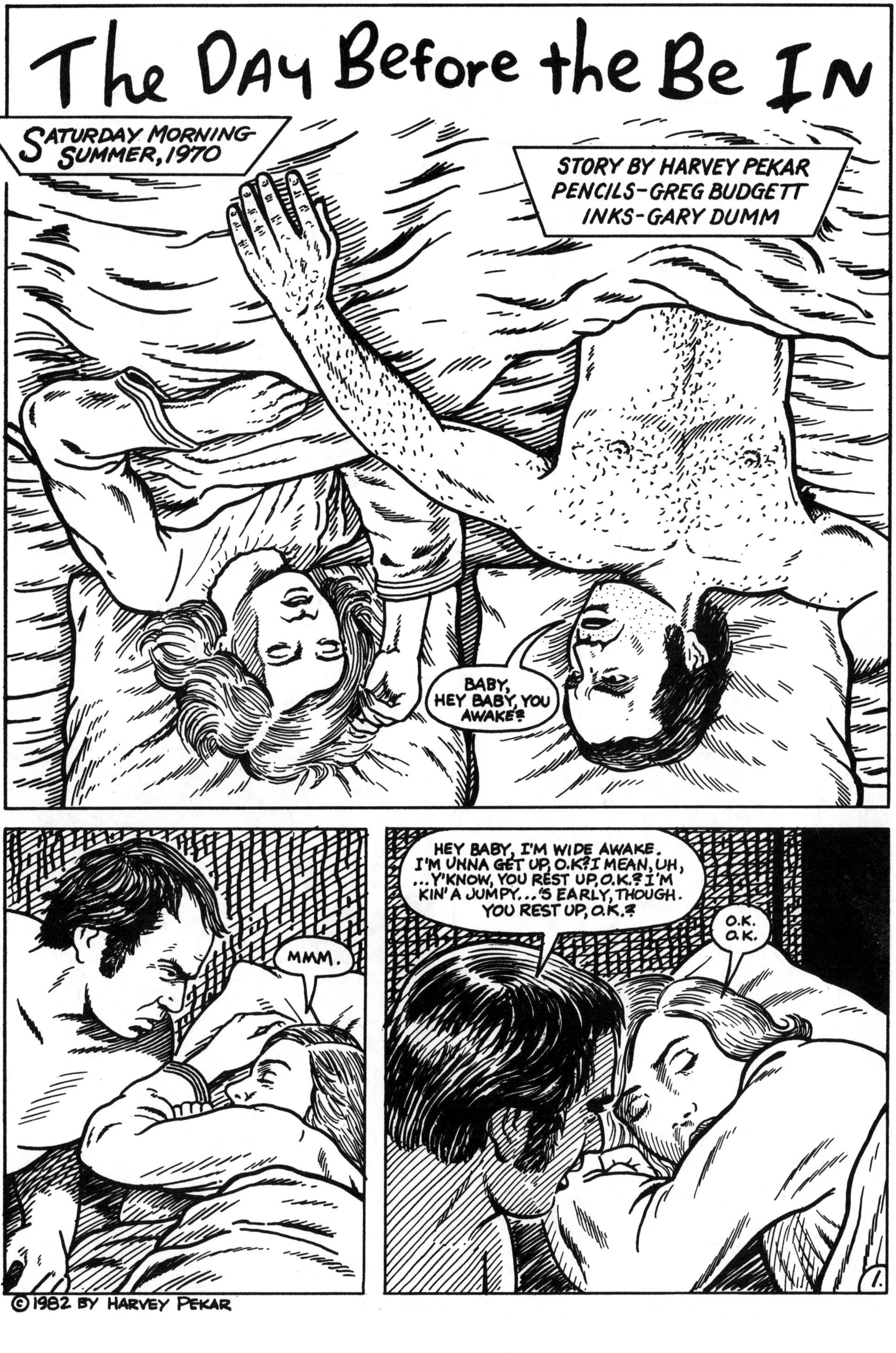
The Day Before the Be In
SATURDAY MORNING-SUMMER, 1970
STORY BY HARVEY PEKAR
PENCILS-GREG BUDGETT
INKS-GARY DUMM
BABY, HEY BABY, YOU AWAKE?
MMM.
HEY BABY, I'M WIDE AWAKE. I'M UNNA GET UP, O.K.? I MEAN, UH, ...Y'KNOW, YOU REST UP, O.K.? I'M KIN' A JUMPY... 'S EARLY, THOUGH. YOU REST UP, O.K.?
O.K. O.K.
1.

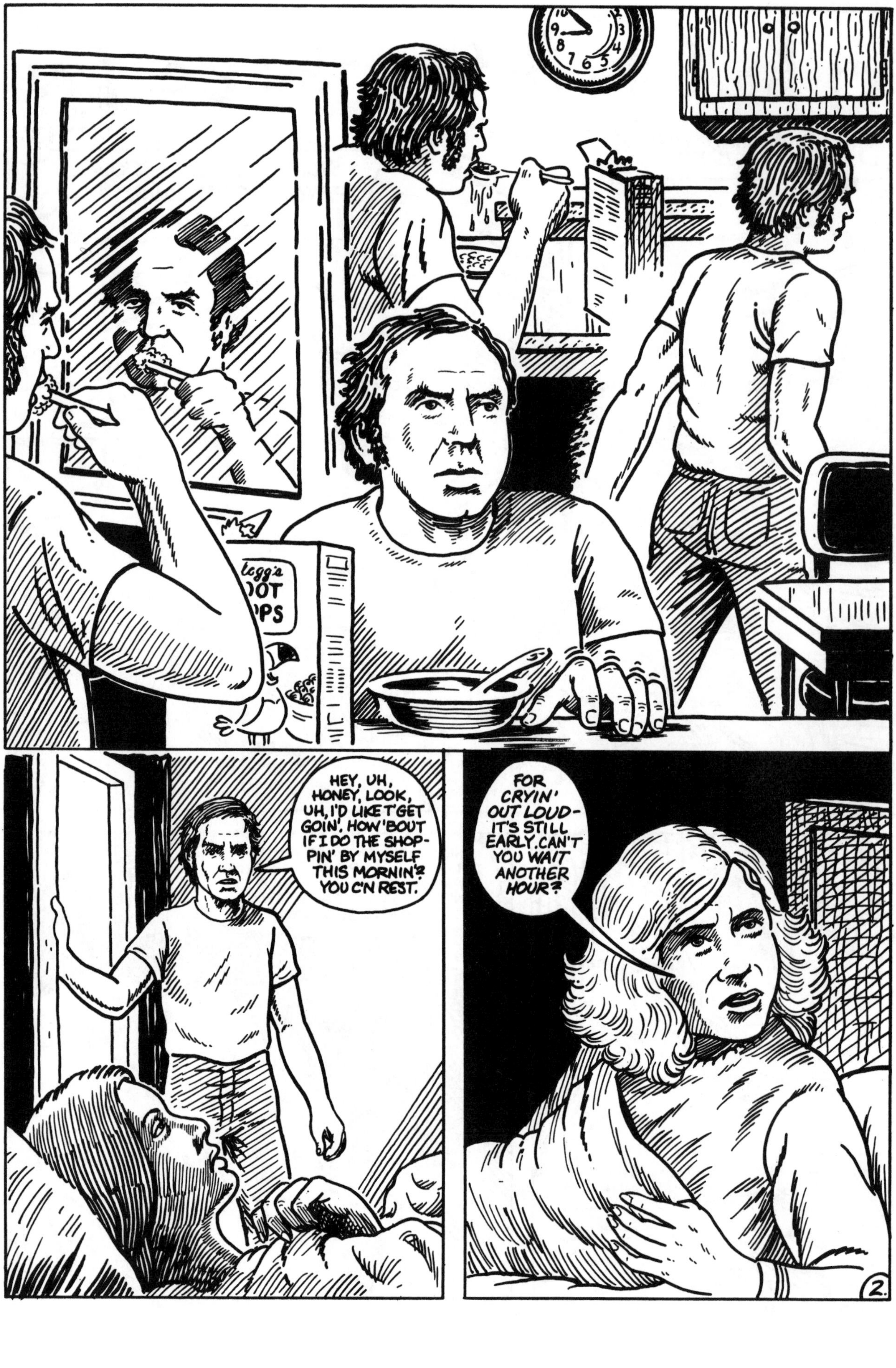
HEY, UH, HONEY, LOOK, UH, I'D LIKE T'GET GOIN'. HOW 'BOUT IF I DO THE SHOP-PIN' BY MYSELF THIS MORNIN'? YOU C'N REST.
FOR CRYIN' OUT LOUD- IT'S STILL EARLY. CAN'T YOU WAIT ANOTHER HOUR?

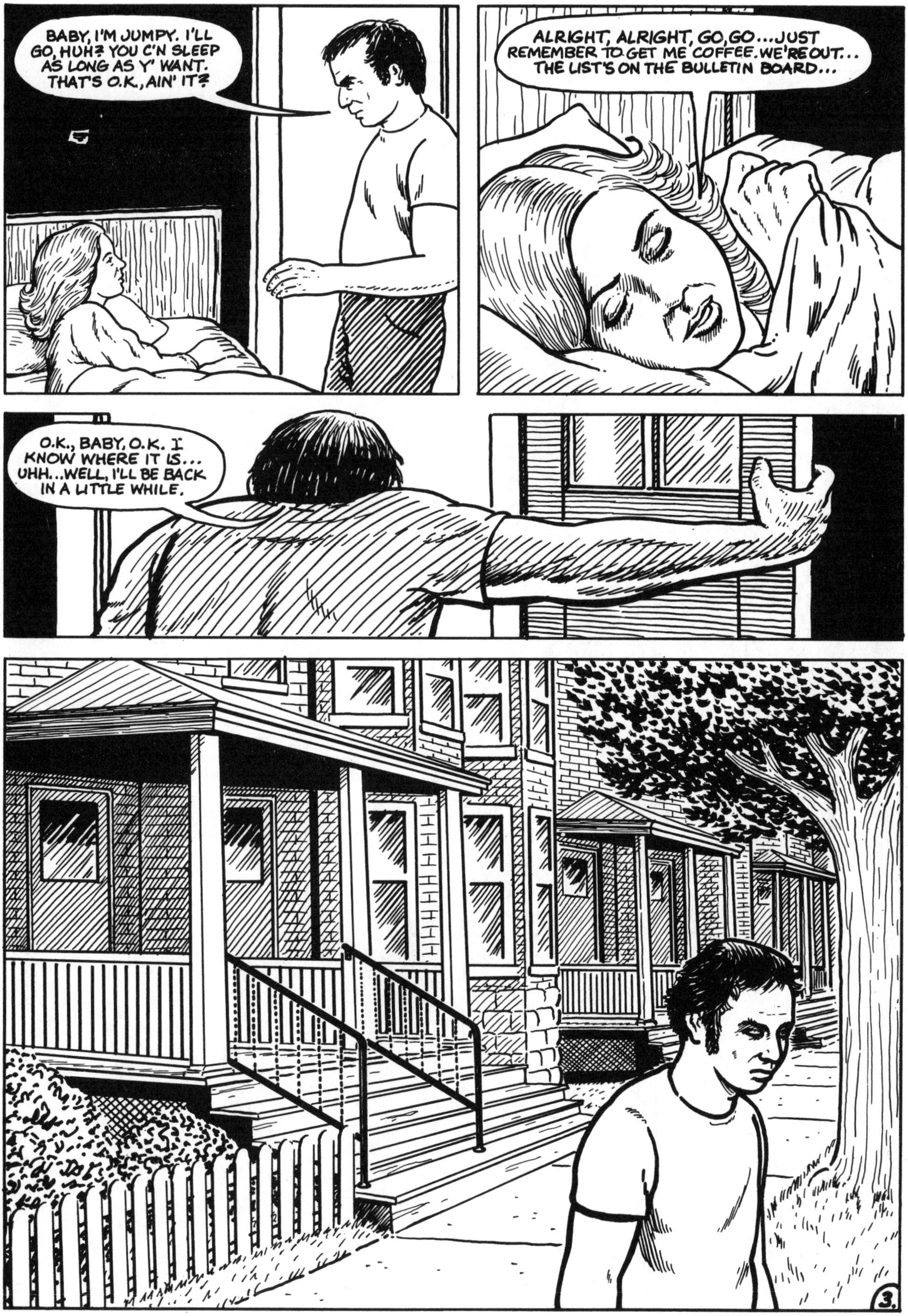
BABY, I'M JUMPY. I'LL GO, HUH? YOU C'N SLEEP AS LONG AS Y' WANT. THAT'S O.K., AIN' IT?
ALRIGHT, ALRIGHT, GO, GO... JUST REMEMBER TO GET ME COFFEE. WE'RE OUT... THE LIST'S ON THE BULLETIN BOARD...
O.K., BABY, O.K. I KNOW WHERE IT IS... UHH... WELL, I'LL BE BACK IN A LITTLE WHILE.
3.

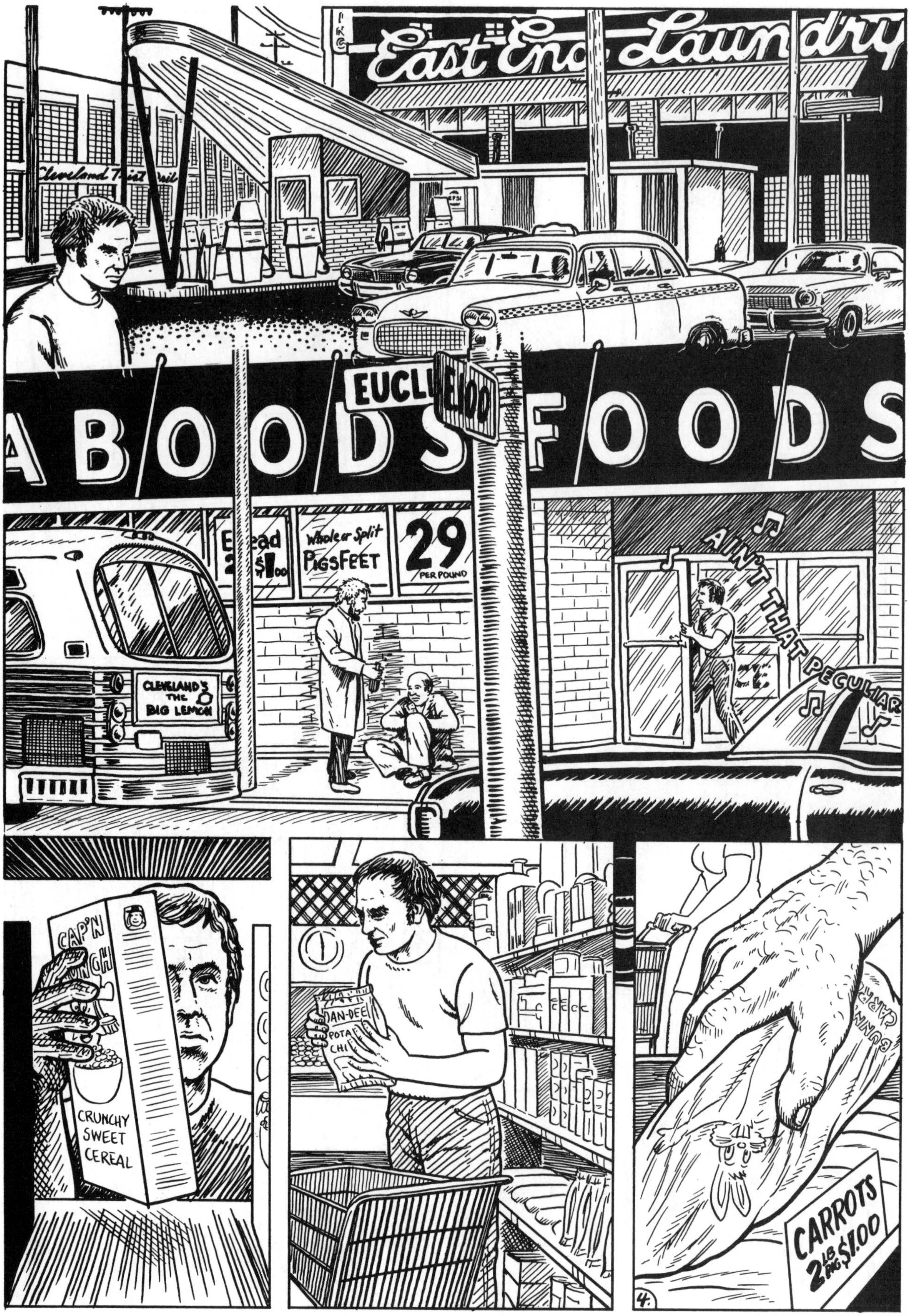
East End Laundry
EUCLI
ABOODS
FOODS
PIGSFEET
29
PER POUND
CLEVELAND'S THE BIG LEMON
AIN'T THAT PECULIAR
CRUNCHY SWEET CEREAL
DAN-DEE
CARROTS 2 LB BAG $1.00

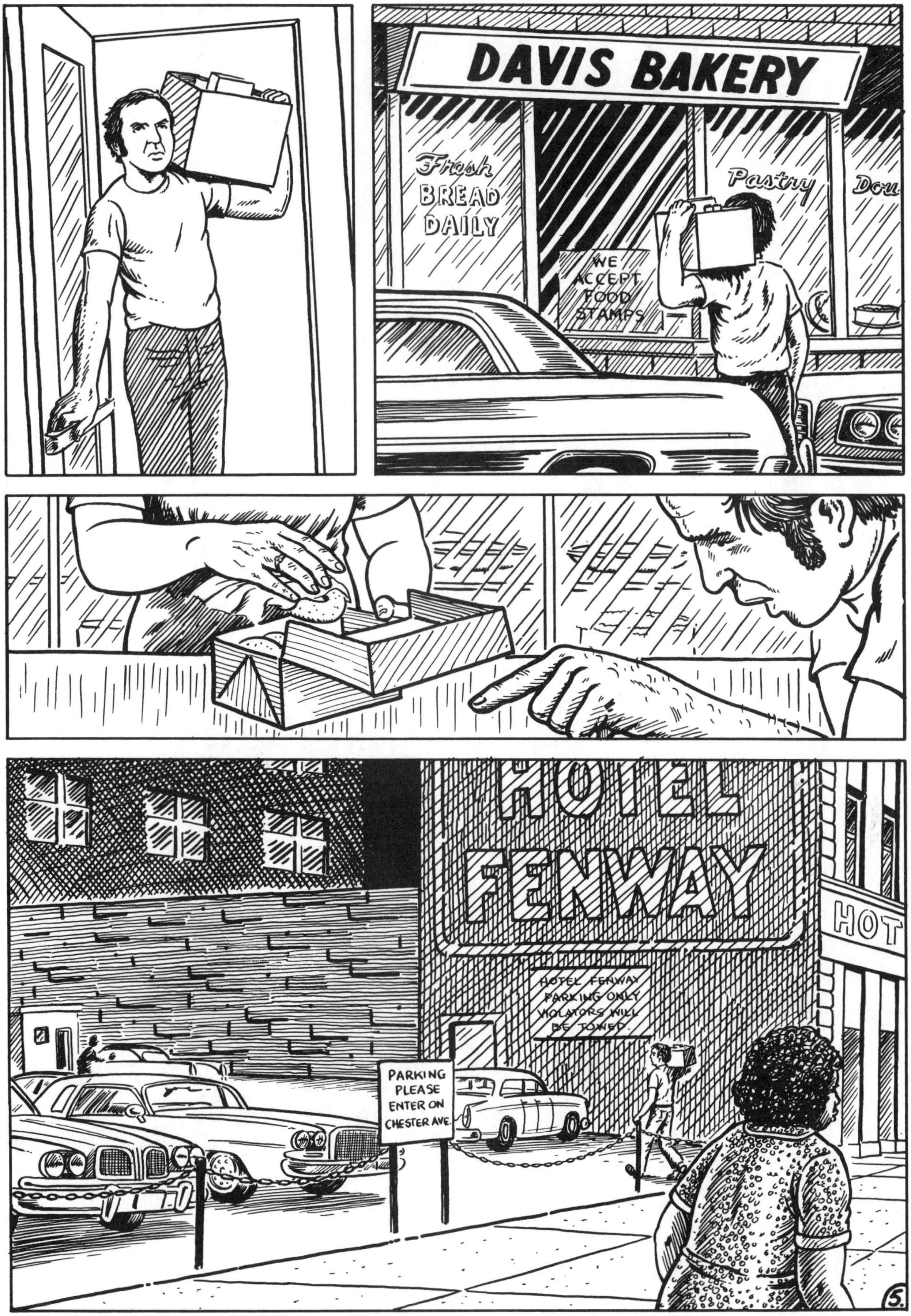
DAVIS BAKERY
Fresh
BREAD
DAILY
Pastry
Dou
WE
ACCEPT
FOOD
STAMPS
HOTEL
FENWAY
HOT
HOTEL FENWAY
PARKING ONLY
VIOLATORS WILL
BE TOWED
PARKING
PLEASE
ENTER ON
CHESTER AVE.

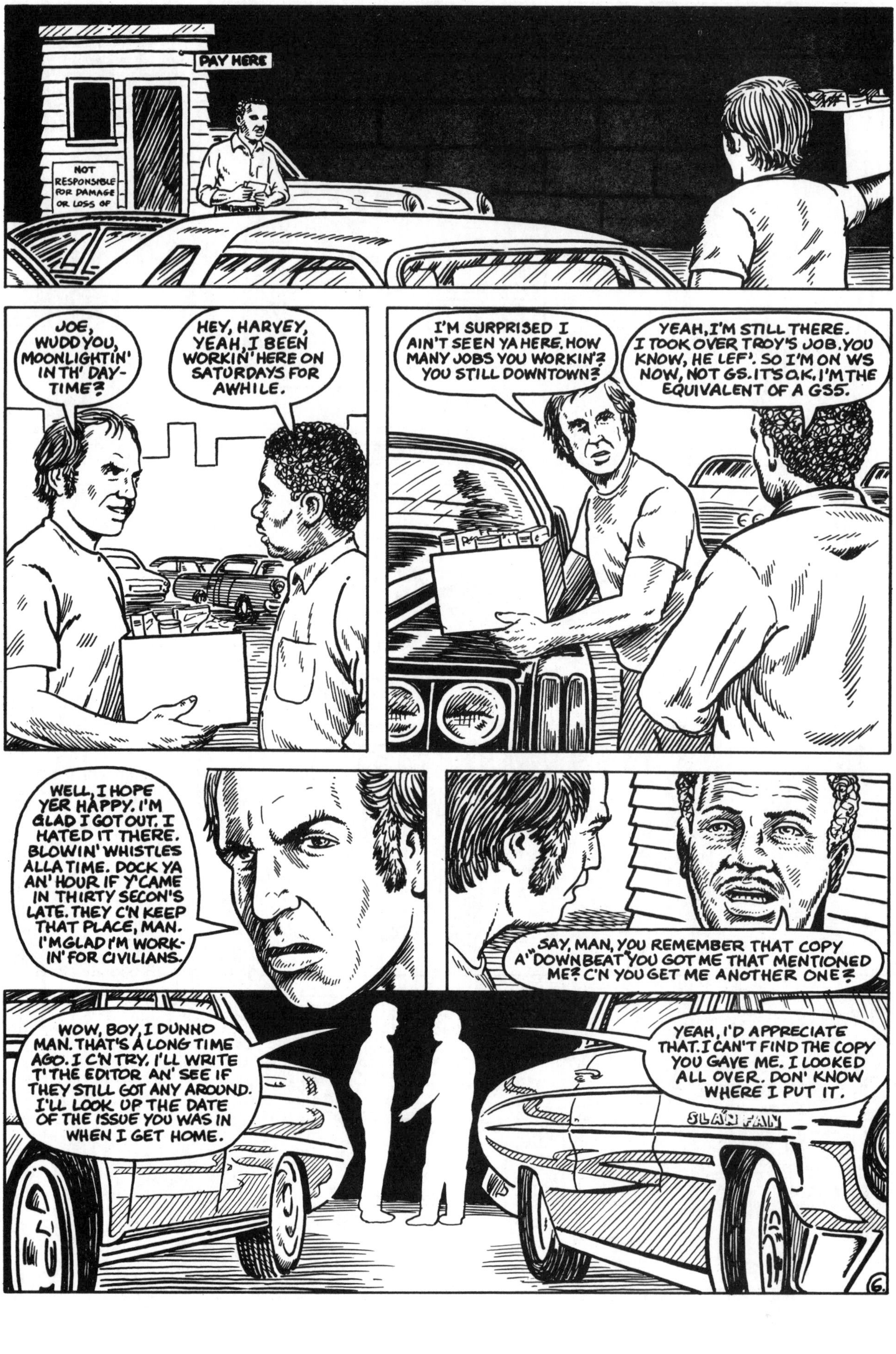
PAY HERE
NOT RESPONSIBLE FOR DAMAGE OR LOSS OF
JOE, WUDD YOU, MOONLIGHTIN' IN TH' DAY-TIME?
HEY, HARVEY, YEAH, I BEEN WORKIN' HERE ON SATURDAYS FOR AWHILE.
I'M SURPRISED I AIN'T SEEN YA HERE. HOW MANY JOBS YOU WORKIN'? YOU STILL DOWNTOWN?
YEAH, I'M STILL THERE. I TOOK OVER TROY'S JOB. YOU KNOW, HE LEF'. SO I'M ON WS NOW, NOT GS. IT'S O.K. I'M THE EQUIVALENT OF A GS5.
WELL, I HOPE YER HAPPY. I'M GLAD I GOT OUT. I HATED IT THERE. BLOWIN' WHISTLES ALLA TIME. DOCK YA AN' HOUR IF Y'CAME IN THIRTY SECON'S LATE. THEY C'N KEEP THAT PLACE, MAN. I'M GLAD I'M WORKIN' FOR CIVILIANS.
SAY, MAN, YOU REMEMBER THAT COPY A "DOWNBEAT" YOU GOT ME THAT MENTIONED ME? C'N YOU GET ME ANOTHER ONE?
WOW, BOY, I DUNNO MAN. THAT'S A LONG TIME AGO. I C'N TRY. I'LL WRITE T' THE EDITOR AN' SEE IF THEY STILL GOT ANY AROUND. I'LL LOOK UP THE DATE OF THE ISSUE YOU WAS IN WHEN I GET HOME.
YEAH, I'D APPRECIATE THAT. I CAN'T FIND THE COPY YOU GAVE ME. I LOOKED ALL OVER. DON' KNOW WHERE I PUT IT.
SLAN FAN

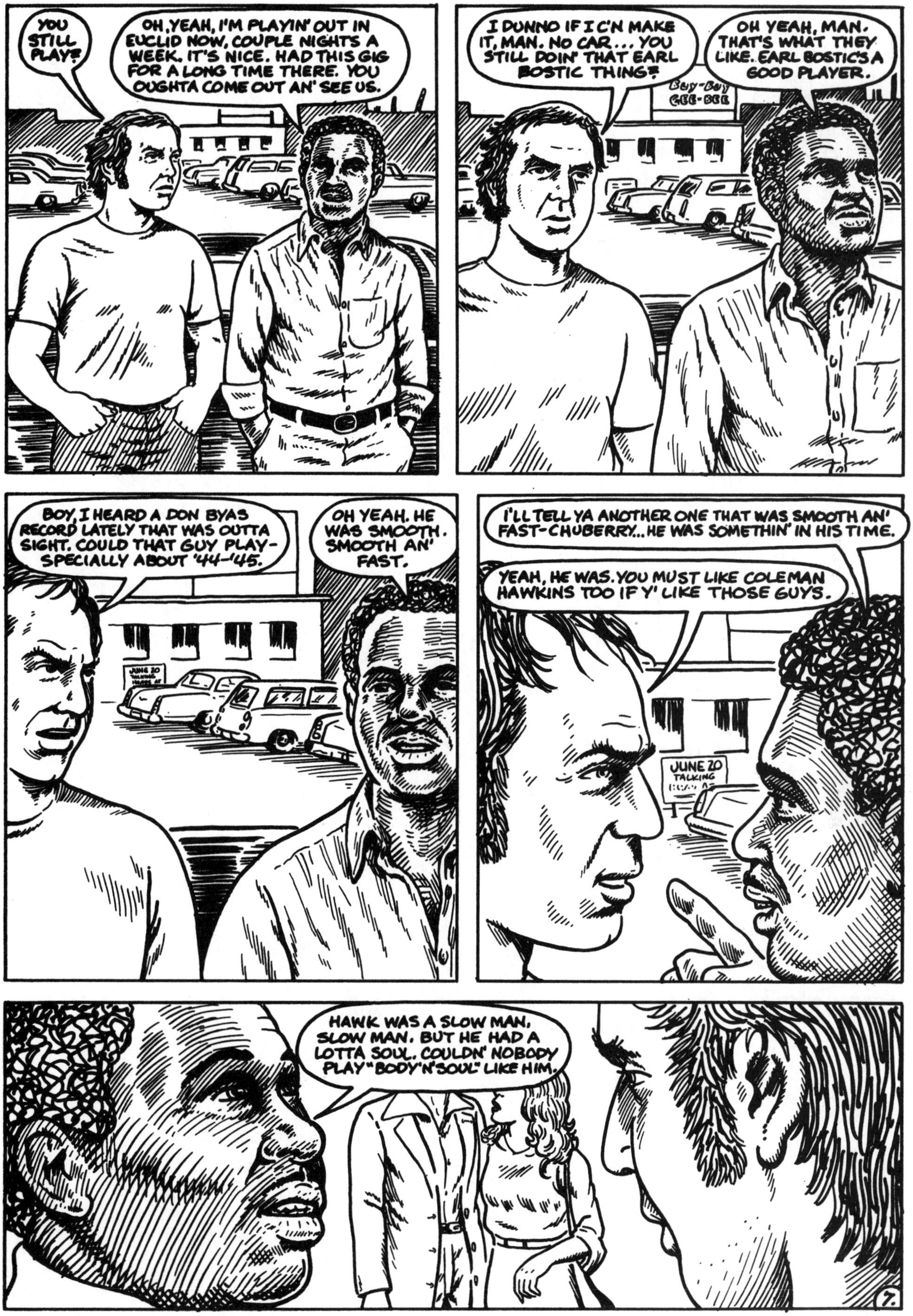
YOU STILL PLAY?
OH, YEAH, I'M PLAYIN' OUT IN EUCLID NOW, COUPLE NIGHTS A WEEK. IT'S NICE. HAD THIS GIG FOR A LONG TIME THERE. YOU OUGHTA COME OUT AN' SEE US.
I DUNNO IF I C'N MAKE IT, MAN. NO CAR... YOU STILL DOIN' THAT EARL BOSTIC THING?
OH YEAH, MAN. THAT'S WHAT THEY LIKE. EARL BOSTIC'S A GOOD PLAYER.
BOY, I HEARD A DON BYAS RECORD LATELY THAT WAS OUTTA SIGHT. COULD THAT GUY PLAY-SPECIALLY ABOUT '44-'45.
OH YEAH. HE WAS SMOOTH. SMOOTH AN' FAST.
I'LL TELL YA ANOTHER ONE THAT WAS SMOOTH AN' FAST-CHUBERRY... HE WAS SOMETHIN' IN HIS TIME.
YEAH, HE WAS. YOU MUST LIKE COLEMAN HAWKINS TOO IF Y' LIKE THOSE GUYS.
JUNE 20 TALKING
HAWK WAS A SLOW MAN, SLOW MAN. BUT HE HAD A LOTTA SOUL. COULDN' NOBODY PLAY "BODY 'N' SOUL" LIKE HIM.
7.

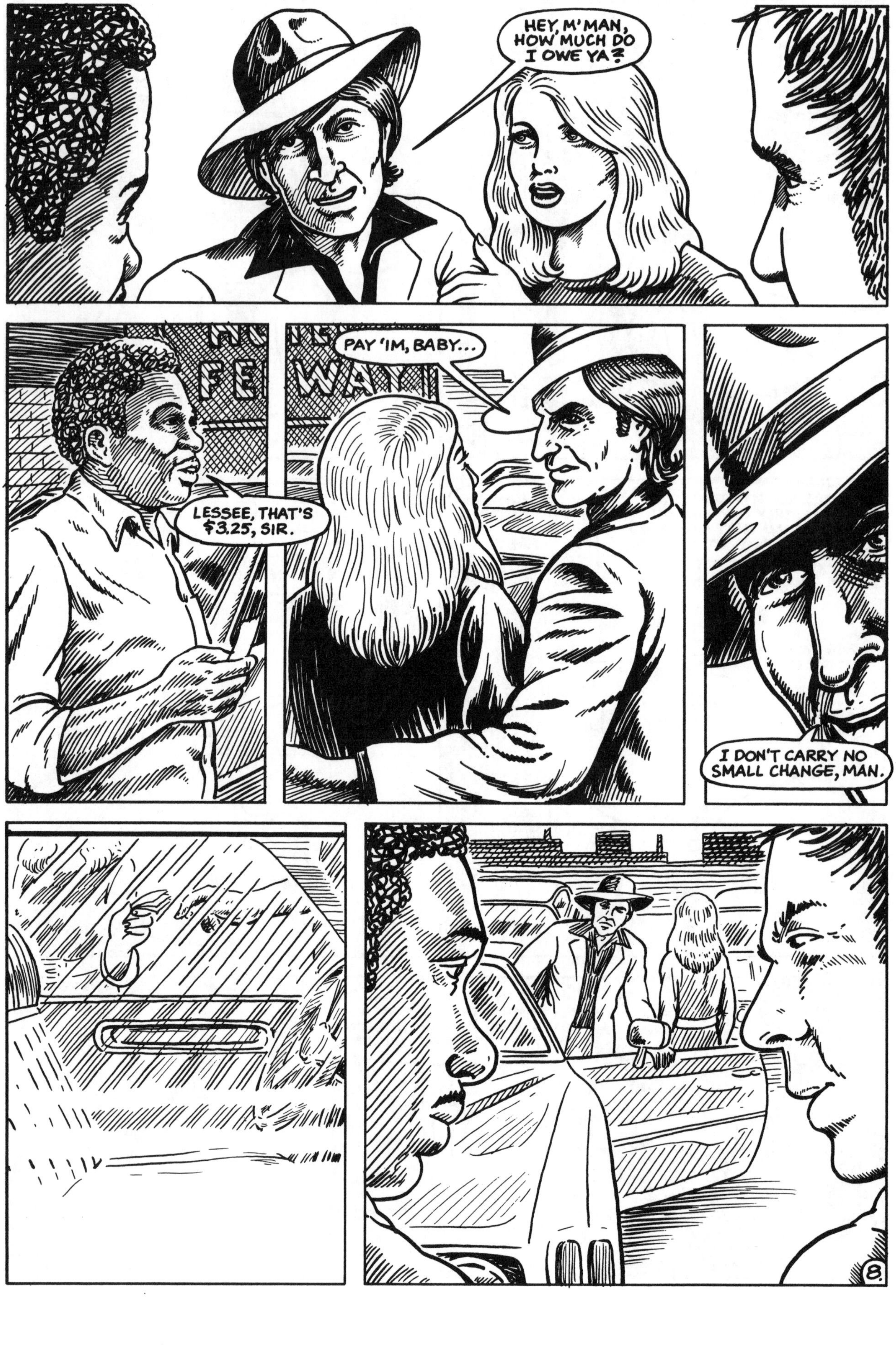
HEY, M'MAN, HOW MUCH DO I OWE YA?
LESSEE, THAT'S $3.25, SIR.
PAY 'IM, BABY...
I DON'T CARRY NO SMALL CHANGE, MAN.

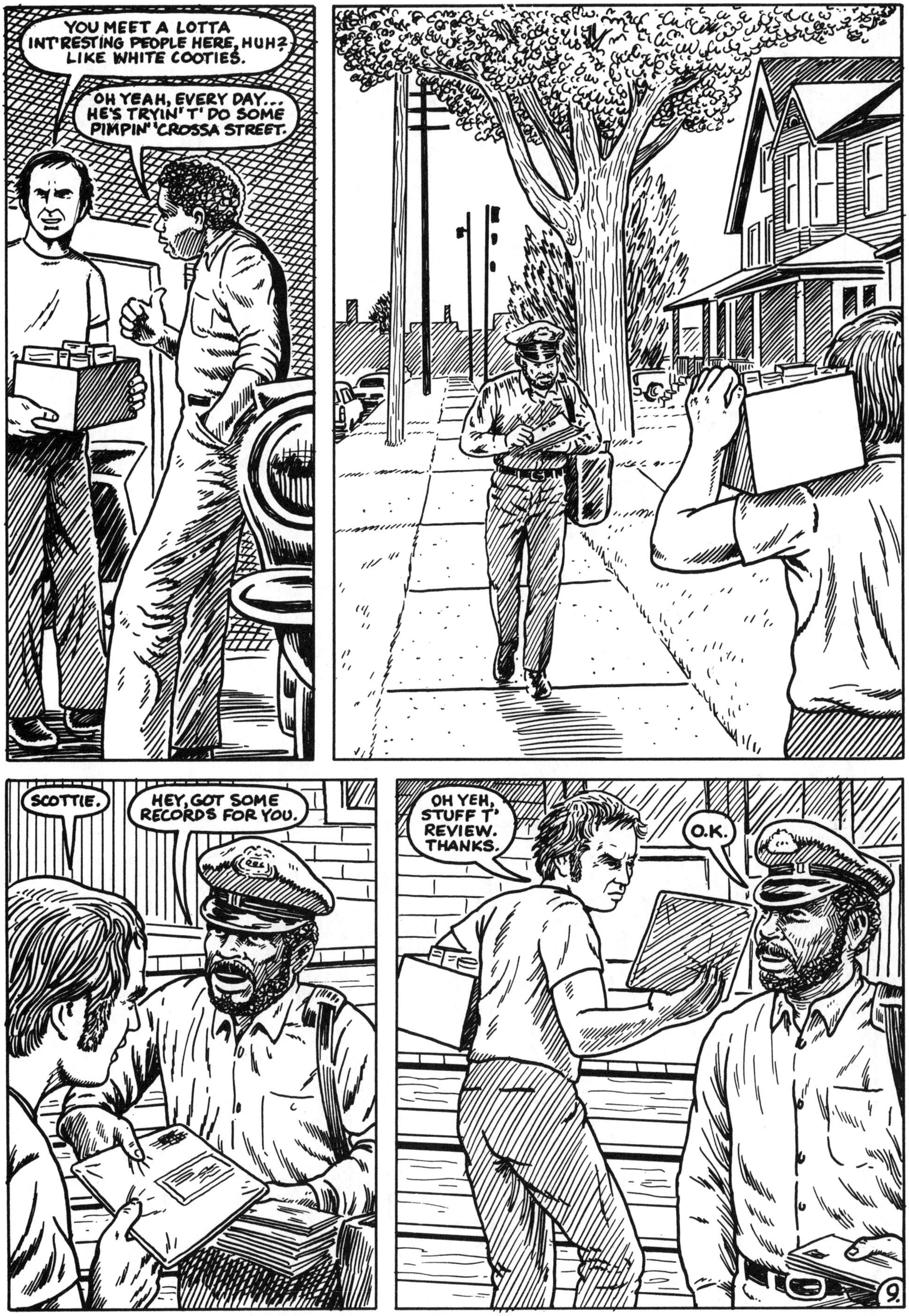
YOU MEET A LOTTA INT'RESTING PEOPLE HERE, HUH? LIKE WHITE COOTIES.
OH YEAH, EVERY DAY... HE'S TRYIN' T' DO SOME PIMPIN' 'CROSSA STREET.
SCOTTIE.
HEY, GOT SOME RECORDS FOR YOU.
OH YEH, STUFF T' REVIEW. THANKS.
O.K.

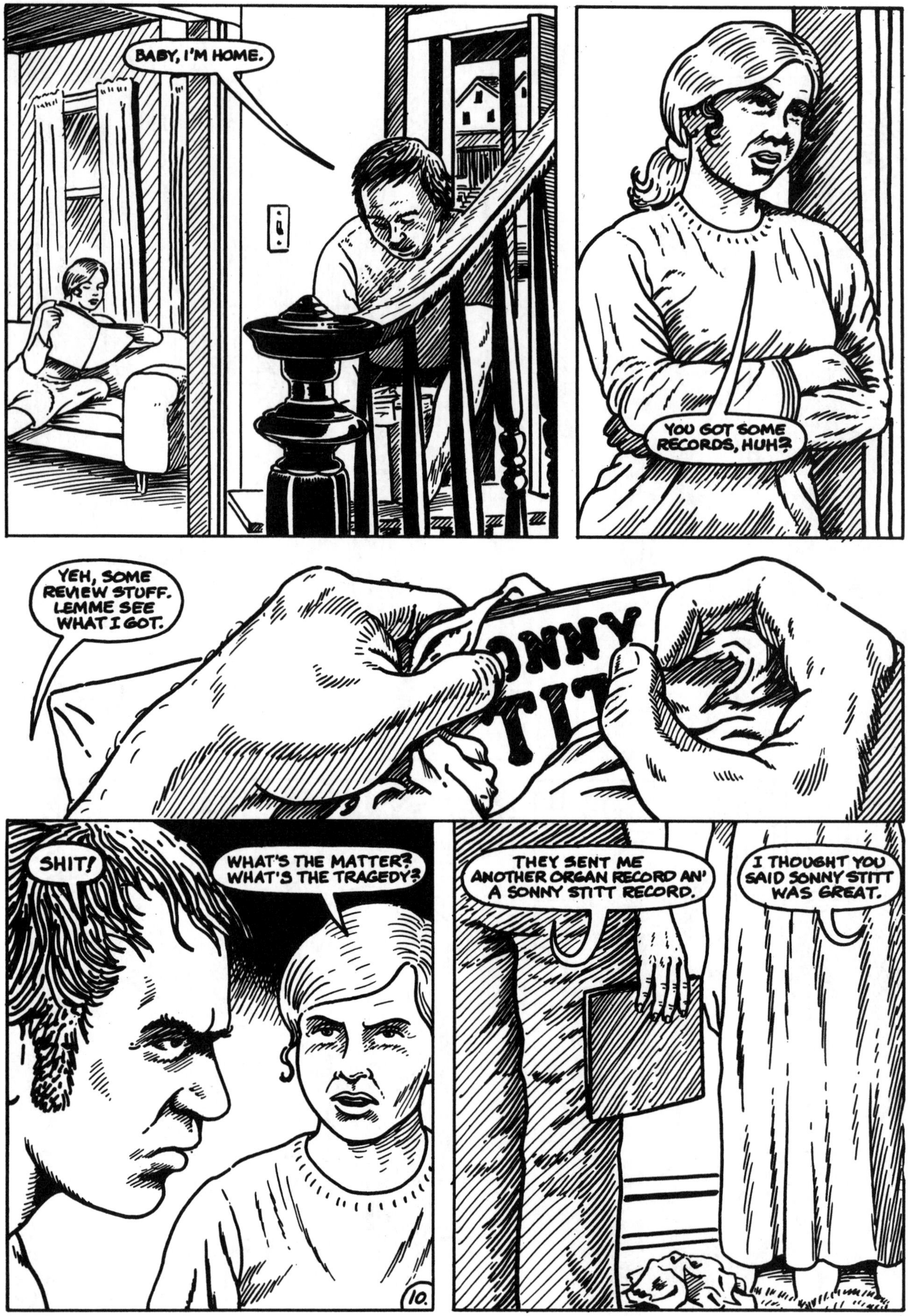
BABY, I'M HOME.
YOU GOT SOME RECORDS, HUH?
YEH, SOME REVIEW STUFF. LEMME SEE WHAT I GOT.
ONNY
TIT
SHIT!
WHAT'S THE MATTER? WHAT'S THE TRAGEDY?
THEY SENT ME ANOTHER ORGAN RECORD AN' A SONNY STITT RECORD.
I THOUGHT YOU SAID SONNY STITT WAS GREAT.
10.

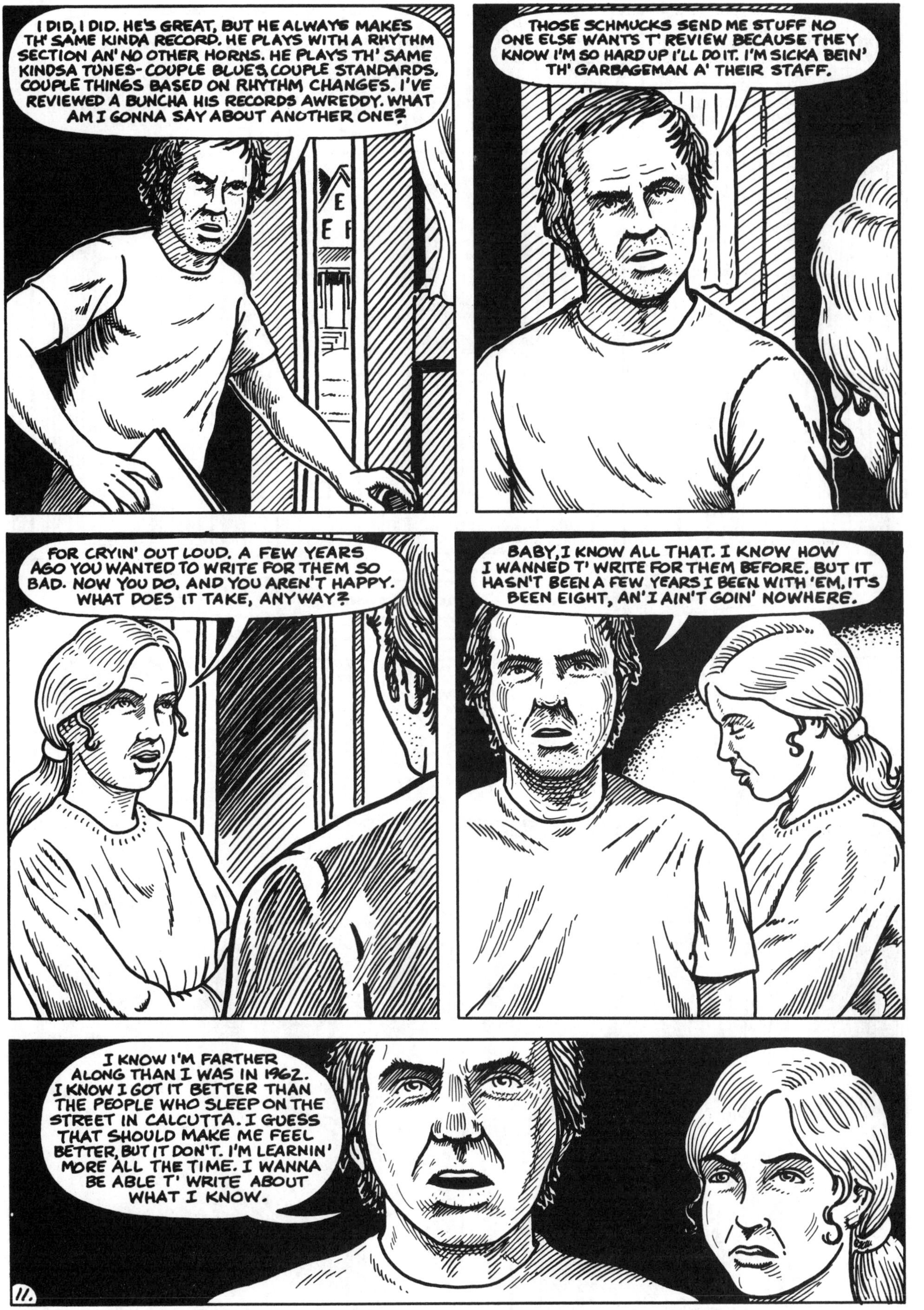
I DID, I DID. HE'S GREAT, BUT HE ALWAYS MAKES TH' SAME KINDA RECORD. HE PLAYS WITH A RHYTHM SECTION AN' NO OTHER HORNS. HE PLAYS TH' SAME KINDSA TUNES- COUPLE BLUES, COUPLE STANDARDS, COUPLE THINGS BASED ON RHYTHM CHANGES. I'VE REVIEWED A BUNCHA HIS RECORDS AWREDDY. WHAT AM I GONNA SAY ABOUT ANOTHER ONE?
THOSE SCHMUCKS SEND ME STUFF NO ONE ELSE WANTS T' REVIEW BECAUSE THEY KNOW I'M SO HARD UP I'LL DO IT. I'M SICKA BEIN' TH' GARBAGEMAN A' THEIR STAFF.
FOR CRYIN' OUT LOUD. A FEW YEARS AGO YOU WANTED TO WRITE FOR THEM SO BAD. NOW YOU DO, AND YOU AREN'T HAPPY. WHAT DOES IT TAKE, ANYWAY?
BABY, I KNOW ALL THAT. I KNOW HOW I WANNED T' WRITE FOR THEM BEFORE. BUT IT HASN'T BEEN A FEW YEARS I BEEN WITH 'EM, IT'S BEEN EIGHT, AN' I AIN'T GOIN' NOWHERE.
I KNOW I'M FARTHER ALONG THAN I WAS IN 1962. I KNOW I GOT IT BETTER THAN THE PEOPLE WHO SLEEP ON THE STREET IN CALCUTTA. I GUESS THAT SHOULD MAKE ME FEEL BETTER, BUT IT DON'T. I'M LEARNIN' MORE ALL THE TIME. I WANNA BE ABLE T' WRITE ABOUT WHAT I KNOW.
11.

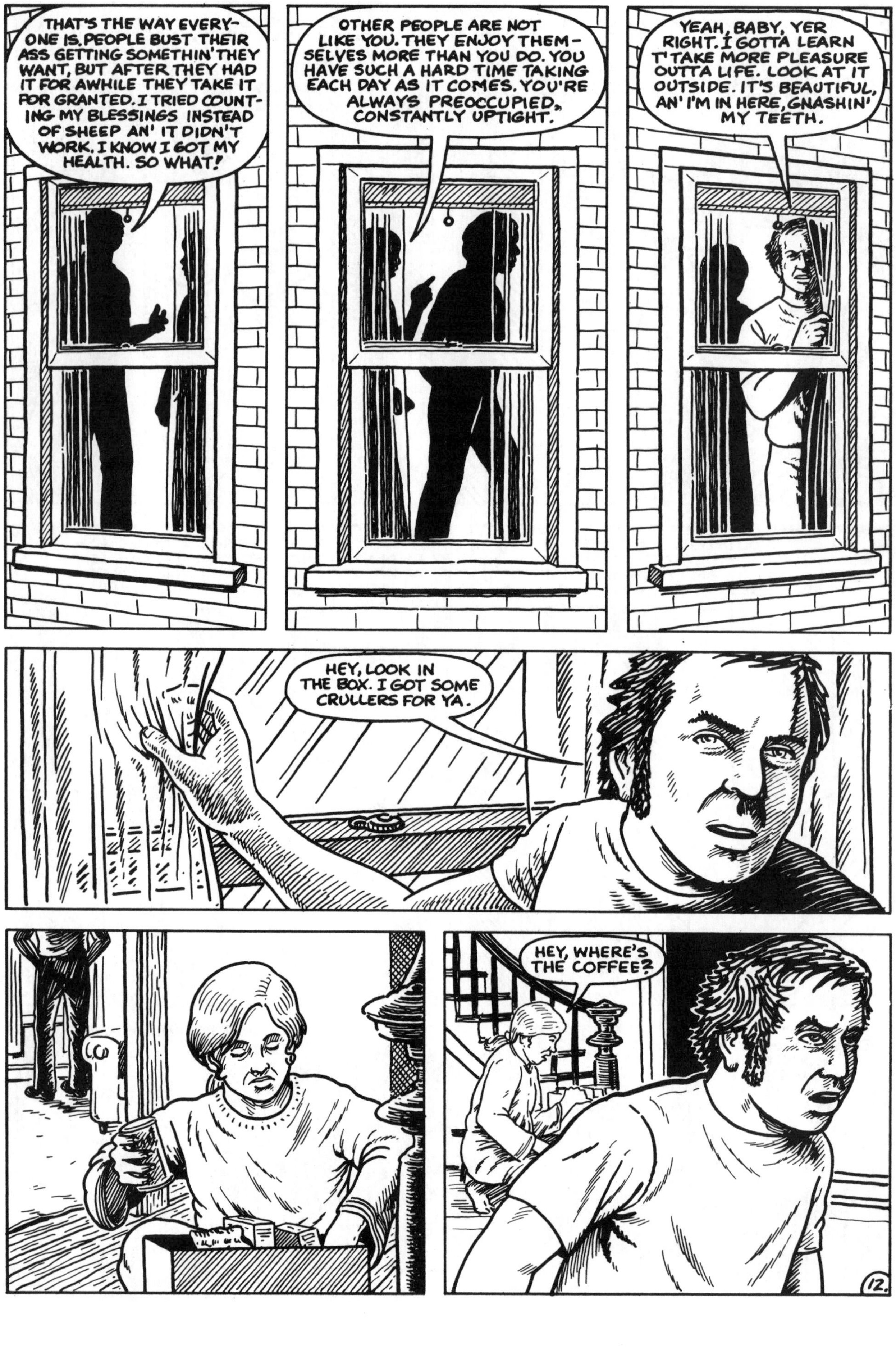
THAT'S THE WAY EVERYONE IS. PEOPLE BUST THEIR ASS GETTING SOMETHIN' THEY WANT, BUT AFTER THEY HAD IT FOR AWHILE THEY TAKE IT FOR GRANTED. I TRIED COUNTING MY BLESSINGS INSTEAD OF SHEEP AN' IT DIDN'T WORK. I KNOW I GOT MY HEALTH. SO WHAT!
OTHER PEOPLE ARE NOT LIKE YOU. THEY ENJOY THEMSELVES MORE THAN YOU DO. YOU HAVE SUCH A HARD TIME TAKING EACH DAY AS IT COMES. YOU'RE ALWAYS PREOCCUPIED, CONSTANTLY UPTIGHT.
YEAH, BABY, YER RIGHT. I GOTTA LEARN T' TAKE MORE PLEASURE OUTTA LIFE. LOOK AT IT OUTSIDE. IT'S BEAUTIFUL, AN' I'M IN HERE, GNASHIN' MY TEETH.
HEY, LOOK IN THE BOX. I GOT SOME CRULLERS FOR YA.
HEY, WHERE'S THE COFFEE?

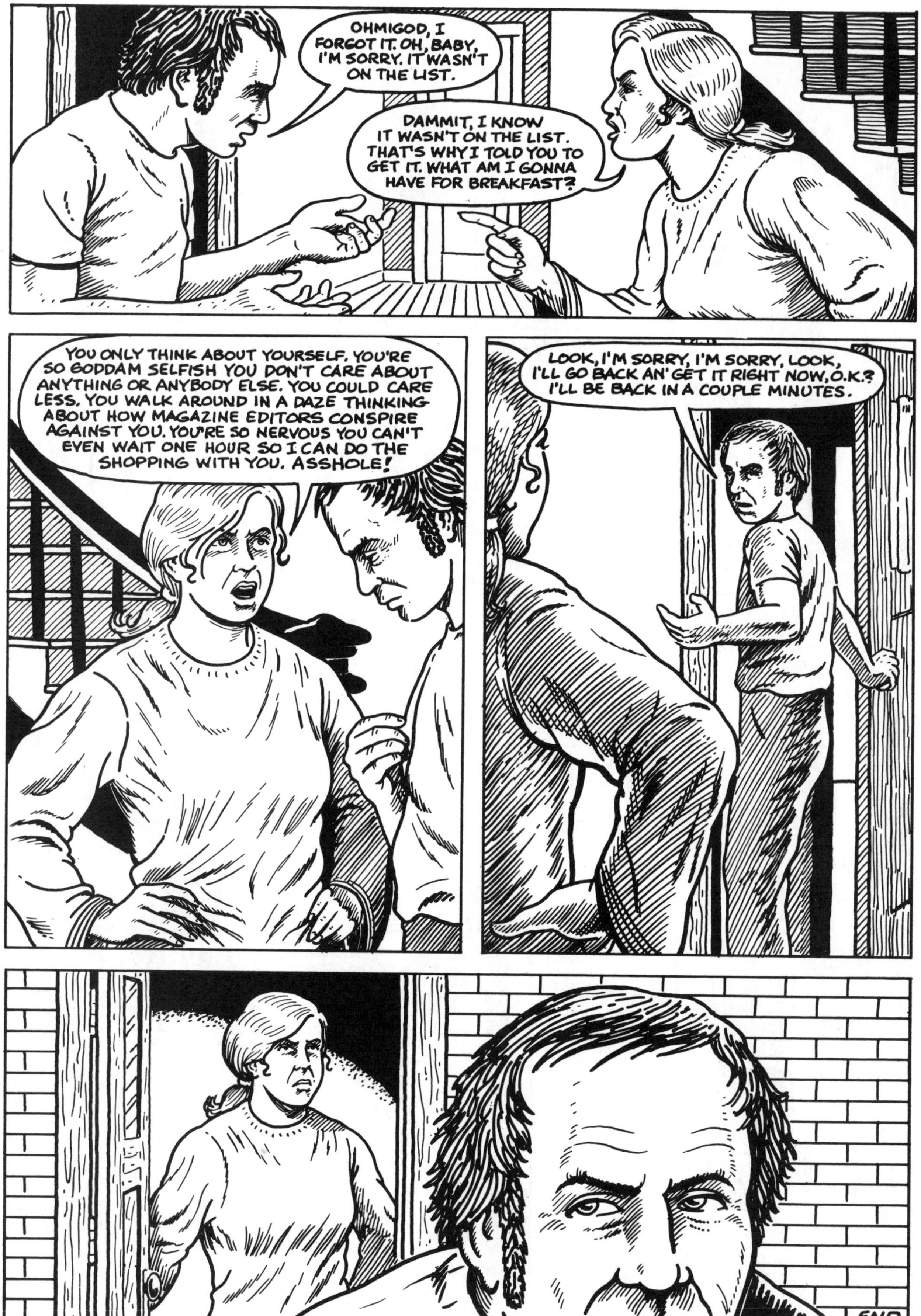
OHMIGOD, I FORGOT IT. OH, BABY, I'M SORRY. IT WASN'T ON THE LIST.
DAMMIT, I KNOW IT WASN'T ON THE LIST. THAT'S WHY I TOLD YOU TO GET IT. WHAT AM I GONNA HAVE FOR BREAKFAST?
YOU ONLY THINK ABOUT YOURSELF. YOU'RE SO GODDAM SELFISH YOU DON'T CARE ABOUT ANYTHING OR ANYBODY ELSE. YOU COULD CARE LESS. YOU WALK AROUND IN A DAZE THINKING ABOUT HOW MAGAZINE EDITORS CONSPIRE AGAINST YOU. YOU'RE SO NERVOUS YOU CAN'T EVEN WAIT ONE HOUR SO I CAN DO THE SHOPPING WITH YOU. ASSHOLE!
LOOK, I'M SORRY, I'M SORRY, LOOK, I'LL GO BACK AN' GET IT RIGHT NOW, O.K.? I'LL BE BACK IN A COUPLE MINUTES.
END.

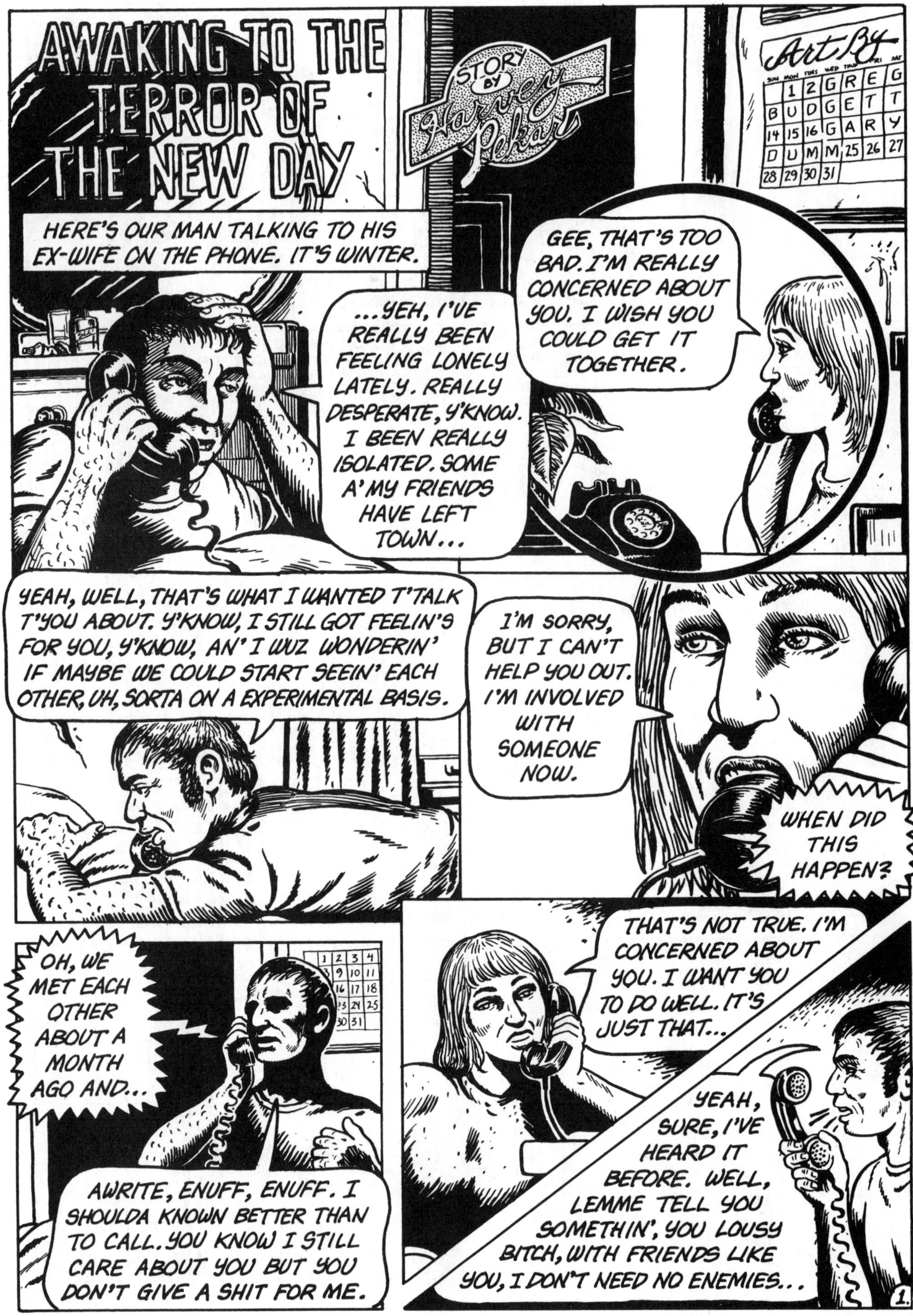
AWAKING TO THE TERROR OF THE NEW DAY
STORY BY Harvey Pekar
Art By GREG BUDGETT GARY DUMM
HERE'S OUR MAN TALKING TO HIS EX-WIFE ON THE PHONE. IT'S WINTER.
...YEH, I'VE REALLY BEEN FEELING LONELY LATELY. REALLY DESPERATE, Y'KNOW. I BEEN REALLY ISOLATED. SOME A' MY FRIENDS HAVE LEFT TOWN...
GEE, THAT'S TOO BAD. I'M REALLY CONCERNED ABOUT YOU. I WISH YOU COULD GET IT TOGETHER.
YEAH, WELL, THAT'S WHAT I WANTED T'TALK T'YOU ABOUT. Y'KNOW, I STILL GOT FEELIN'S FOR YOU, Y'KNOW, AN' I WUZ WONDERIN' IF MAYBE WE COULD START SEEIN' EACH OTHER, UH, SORTA ON A EXPERIMENTAL BASIS.
I'M SORRY, BUT I CAN'T HELP YOU OUT. I'M INVOLVED WITH SOMEONE NOW.
WHEN DID THIS HAPPEN?
OH, WE MET EACH OTHER ABOUT A MONTH AGO AND...
AWRITE, ENUFF, ENUFF. I SHOULDA KNOWN BETTER THAN TO CALL. YOU KNOW I STILL CARE ABOUT YOU BUT YOU DON'T GIVE A SHIT FOR ME.
THAT'S NOT TRUE. I'M CONCERNED ABOUT YOU. I WANT YOU TO DO WELL. IT'S JUST THAT...
YEAH, SURE, I'VE HEARD IT BEFORE. WELL, LEMME TELL YOU SOMETHIN', YOU LOUSY BITCH, WITH FRIENDS LIKE YOU, I DON'T NEED NO ENEMIES...
1.

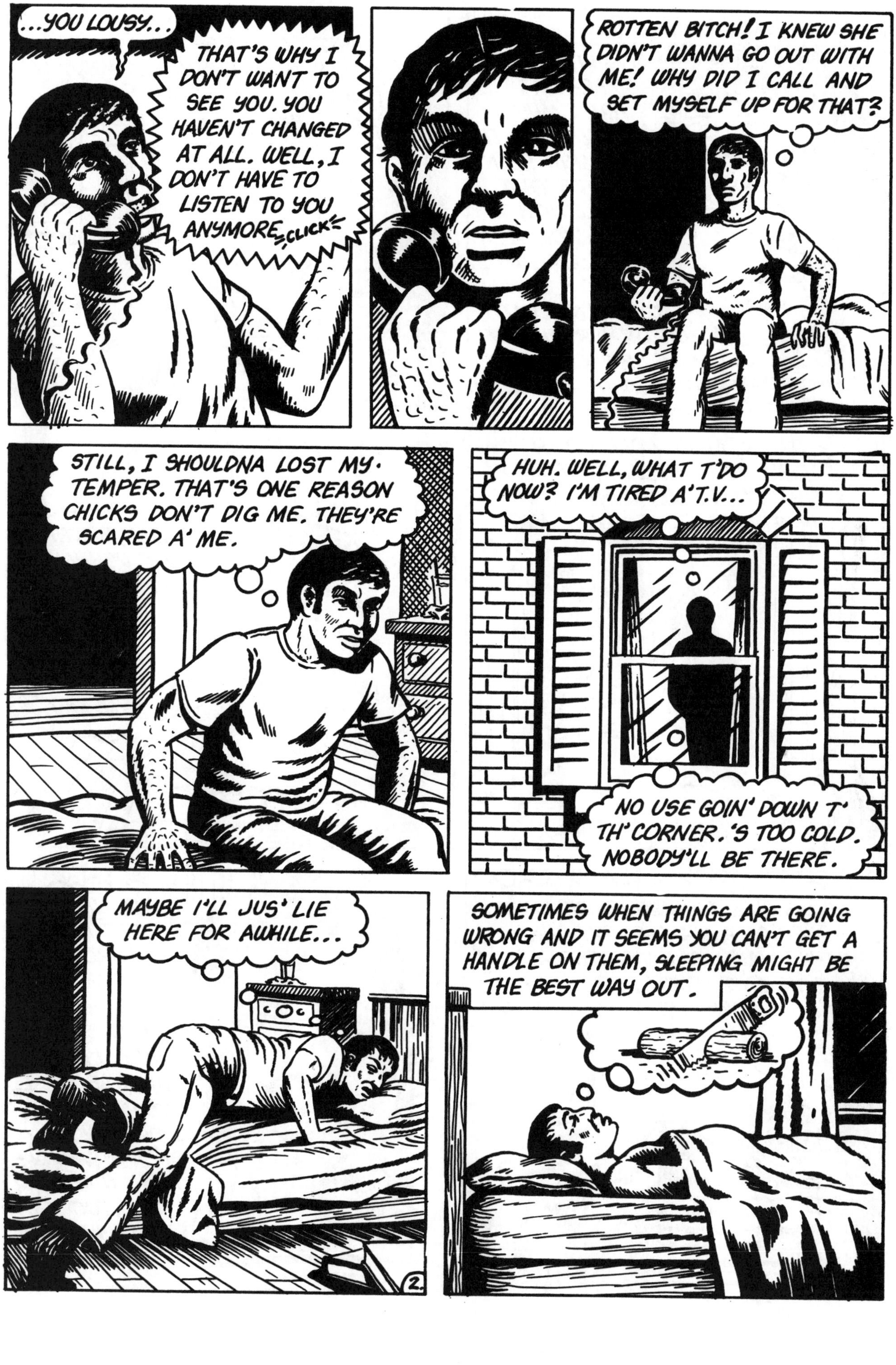
...YOU LOUSY...
THAT'S WHY I DON'T WANT TO SEE YOU. YOU HAVEN'T CHANGED AT ALL. WELL, I DON'T HAVE TO LISTEN TO YOU ANYMORE
CLICK
ROTTEN BITCH! I KNEW SHE DIDN'T WANNA GO OUT WITH ME! WHY DID I CALL AND SET MYSELF UP FOR THAT?
STILL, I SHOULDNA LOST MY TEMPER. THAT'S ONE REASON CHICKS DON'T DIG ME. THEY'RE SCARED A' ME.
HUH. WELL, WHAT T'DO NOW? I'M TIRED A' T.V...
NO USE GOIN' DOWN T' TH' CORNER. 'S TOO COLD. NOBODY'LL BE THERE.
MAYBE I'LL JUS' LIE HERE FOR AWHILE...
2.
SOMETIMES WHEN THINGS ARE GOING WRONG AND IT SEEMS YOU CAN'T GET A HANDLE ON THEM, SLEEPING MIGHT BE THE BEST WAY OUT.

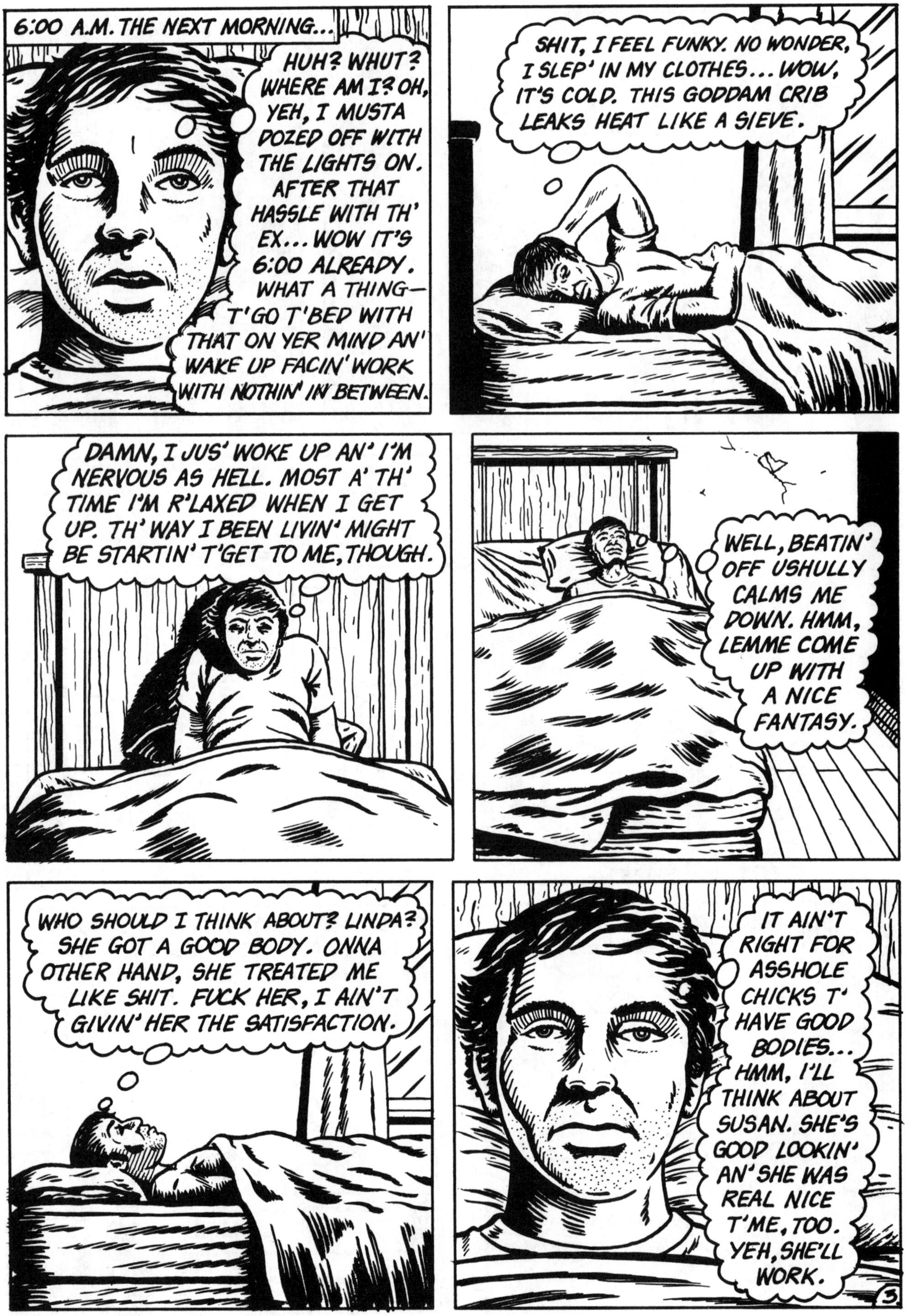
6:00 A.M. THE NEXT MORNING...
HUH? WHUT? WHERE AM I? OH, YEH, I MUSTA DOZED OFF WITH THE LIGHTS ON. AFTER THAT HASSLE WITH TH' EX... WOW IT'S 6:00 ALREADY. WHAT A THING— T'GO T'BED WITH THAT ON YER MIND AN' WAKE UP FACIN' WORK WITH NOTHIN' IN BETWEEN.
SHIT, I FEEL FUNKY. NO WONDER, I SLEP' IN MY CLOTHES... WOW, IT'S COLD. THIS GODDAM CRIB LEAKS HEAT LIKE A SIEVE.
DAMN, I JUS' WOKE UP AN' I'M NERVOUS AS HELL. MOST A' TH' TIME I'M R'LAXED WHEN I GET UP. TH' WAY I BEEN LIVIN' MIGHT BE STARTIN' T'GET TO ME, THOUGH.
WELL, BEATIN' OFF USHULLY CALMS ME DOWN. HMM, LEMME COME UP WITH A NICE FANTASY.
WHO SHOULD I THINK ABOUT? LINDA? SHE GOT A GOOD BODY. ONNA OTHER HAND, SHE TREATED ME LIKE SHIT. FUCK HER, I AIN'T GIVIN' HER THE SATISFACTION.
IT AIN'T RIGHT FOR ASSHOLE CHICKS T' HAVE GOOD BODIES... HMM, I'LL THINK ABOUT SUSAN. SHE'S GOOD LOOKIN' AN' SHE WAS REAL NICE T'ME, TOO. YEH, SHE'LL WORK.
3

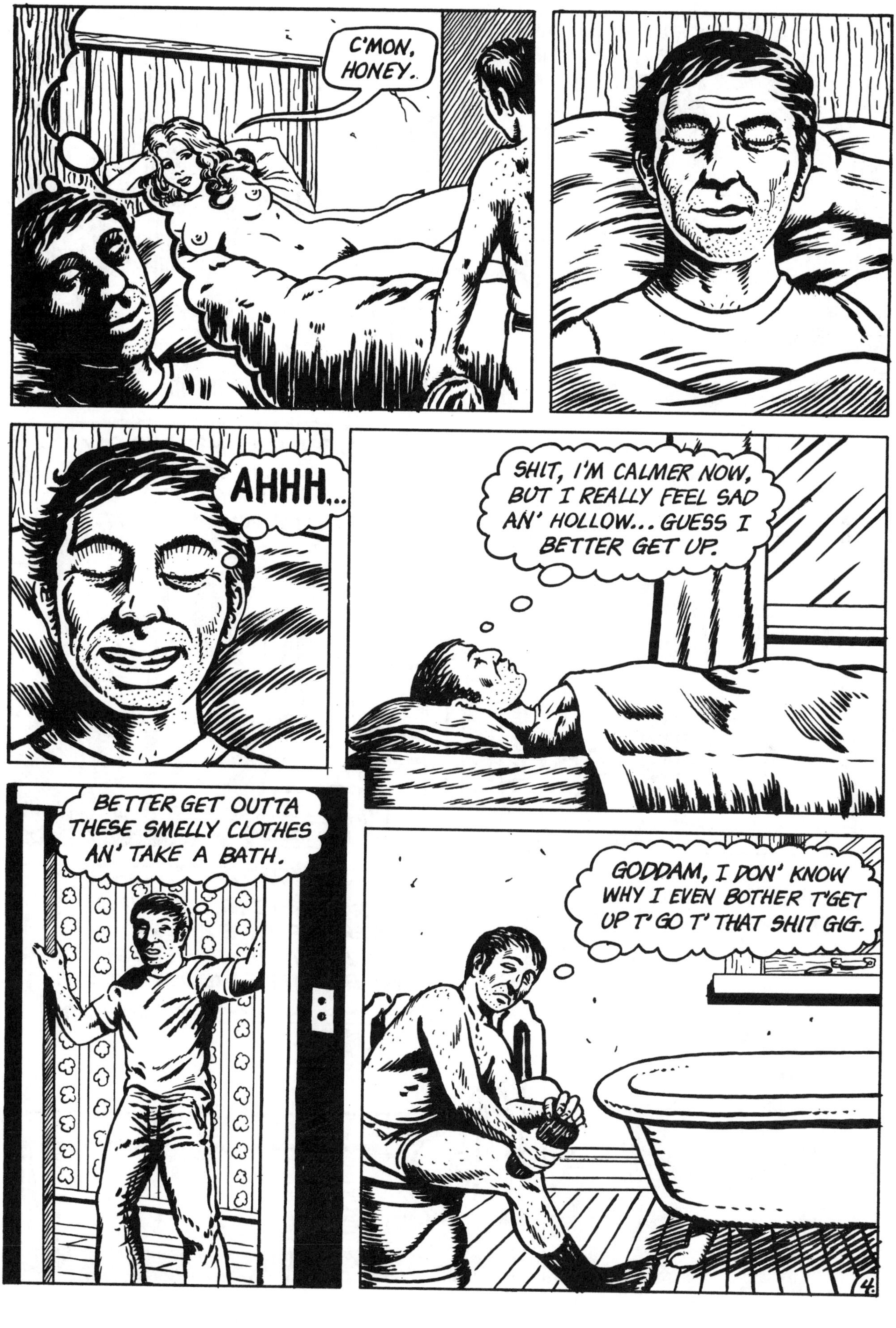
C'MON, HONEY.
AHHH...
SHIT, I'M CALMER NOW, BUT I REALLY FEEL SAD AN' HOLLOW... GUESS I BETTER GET UP.
BETTER GET OUTTA THESE SMELLY CLOTHES AN' TAKE A BATH.
GODDAM, I DON' KNOW WHY I EVEN BOTHER T'GET UP T' GO T' THAT SHIT GIG.
4.

WHAT'M I LIVIN' FOR ANYWAY? WHAT'VE I GOT T' SHOW FOR IT? SHIT GIG. NO OL' LADY FOR MONTHS. CRIB THAT'S FALLIN' APART...

...AN' NO RELIEF IN SIGHT.

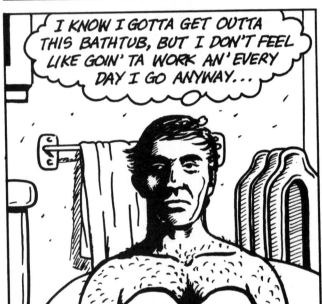

I KNOW I GOTTA GET OUTTA THIS BATHTUB, BUT I DON'T FEEL LIKE GOIN' TA WORK AN' EVERY DAY I GO ANYWAY...

'CEPT FOR THAT ONE DAY I QUIT THAT DOOR-TO-DOOR SALESMAN GIG. THAT JUS' WASN'T WORTH IT.

MMMM, IT'S SO NICE IN THIS WATER. I KNOW I'M GONNA GET OUT OF IT THOUGH.

SOMETIMES I WISH I COULD FREAK OUT, HAVE A NERVOUS BREAKDOWN, ANYTHING TO GET AWAY FROM THE SAME OLD ROUTINE.

5.

BUT I KNOW I WON'T. I GOT THIS FAR, I GUESS I'LL MAKE IT TH' REST OF TH' WAY.

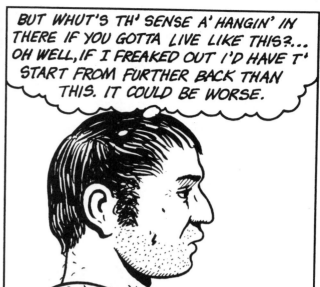

BUT WHUT'S TH' SENSE A' HANGIN' IN THERE IF YOU GOTTA LIVE LIKE THIS?... OH WELL, IF I FREAKED OUT I'D HAVE T' START FROM FURTHER BACK THAN THIS. IT COULD BE WORSE.

WELL, HERE GOES NUTHIN'.

BRRRR.

SHORTLY...

LE'S SEE—WHAT KINDA SPLENDID THREADS 'M I GONNA PUT ON T'DAY?

THESE THINGS 'R' FALLIN' APART. I GUESS I'LL HAVE T' GET SOME NEW CLOTHES PRETTY SOON. SHIT, I HATE T' SPEND MONEY ON CLOTHES. PEOPLE SPEND SO MUCH MONEY ON CLOTHES BUT THEY DON'T TAKE CARE A' THEMSELVES. THEY'RE NUTS. WHAT COULD BE MORE RIDICULOUS THAN FAT SLOBS SPENDIN' A LOT A' MONEY ON CLOTHES. THEY'RE GONNA LOOK LOUSY ANYWAY.

6.

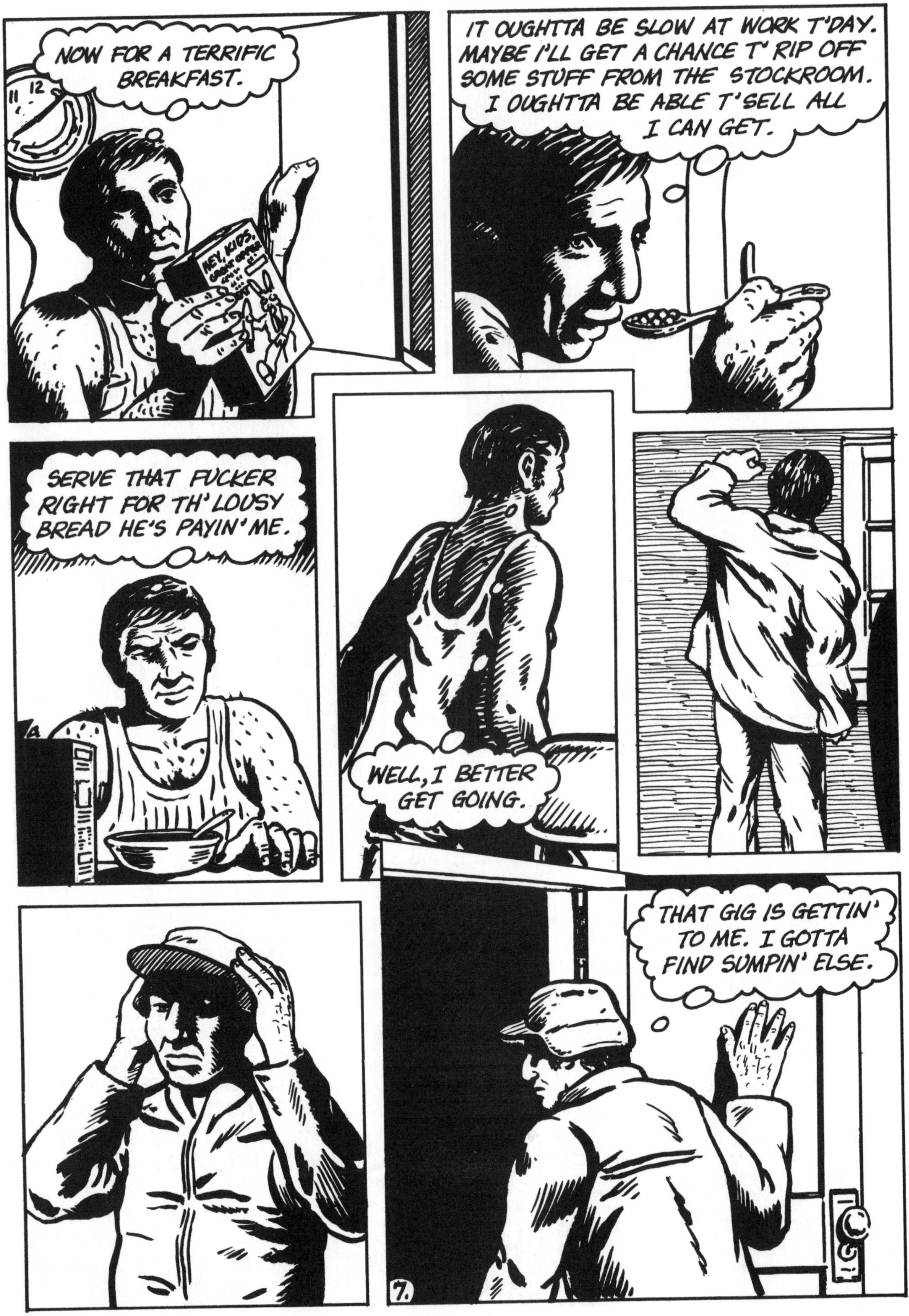
NOW FOR A TERRIFIC BREAKFAST.
HEY, KIDS, GREAT OFFER
IT OUGHTTA BE SLOW AT WORK T'DAY. MAYBE I'LL GET A CHANCE T' RIP OFF SOME STUFF FROM THE STOCKROOM. I OUGHTTA BE ABLE T'SELL ALL I CAN GET.
SERVE THAT FUCKER RIGHT FOR TH' LOUSY BREAD HE'S PAYIN' ME.
WELL, I BETTER GET GOING.
THAT GIG IS GETTIN' TO ME. I GOTTA FIND SUMPIN' ELSE.
7.

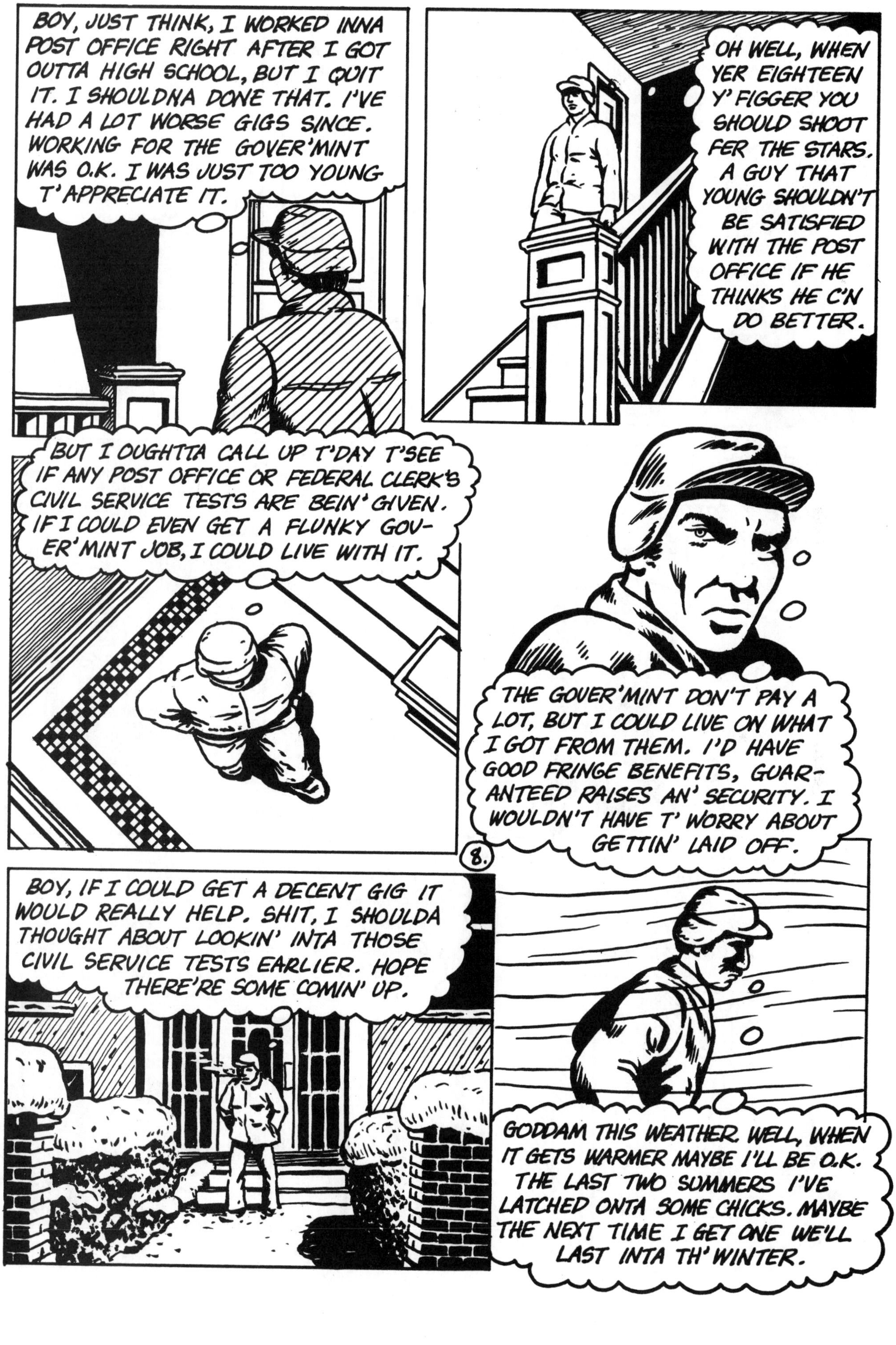
BOY, JUST THINK, I WORKED INNA POST OFFICE RIGHT AFTER I GOT OUTTA HIGH SCHOOL, BUT I QUIT IT. I SHOULDNA DONE THAT. I'VE HAD A LOT WORSE GIGS SINCE. WORKING FOR THE GOVER'MINT WAS O.K. I WAS JUST TOO YOUNG T'APPRECIATE IT.
OH WELL, WHEN YER EIGHTEEN Y'FIGGER YOU SHOULD SHOOT FER THE STARS. A GUY THAT YOUNG SHOULDN'T BE SATISFIED WITH THE POST OFFICE IF HE THINKS HE C'N DO BETTER.
BUT I OUGHTTA CALL UP T'DAY T'SEE IF ANY POST OFFICE OR FEDERAL CLERK'S CIVIL SERVICE TESTS ARE BEIN' GIVEN. IF I COULD EVEN GET A FLUNKY GOVER'MINT JOB, I COULD LIVE WITH IT.
THE GOVER'MINT DON'T PAY A LOT, BUT I COULD LIVE ON WHAT I GOT FROM THEM. I'D HAVE GOOD FRINGE BENEFITS, GUARANTEED RAISES AN' SECURITY. I WOULDN'T HAVE T' WORRY ABOUT GETTIN' LAID OFF.
BOY, IF I COULD GET A DECENT GIG IT WOULD REALLY HELP. SHIT, I SHOULDA THOUGHT ABOUT LOOKIN' INTA THOSE CIVIL SERVICE TESTS EARLIER. HOPE THERE'RE SOME COMIN' UP.
GODDAM THIS WEATHER. WELL, WHEN IT GETS WARMER MAYBE I'LL BE O.K. THE LAST TWO SUMMERS I'VE LATCHED ONTA SOME CHICKS. MAYBE THE NEXT TIME I GET ONE WE'LL LAST INTA TH' WINTER.

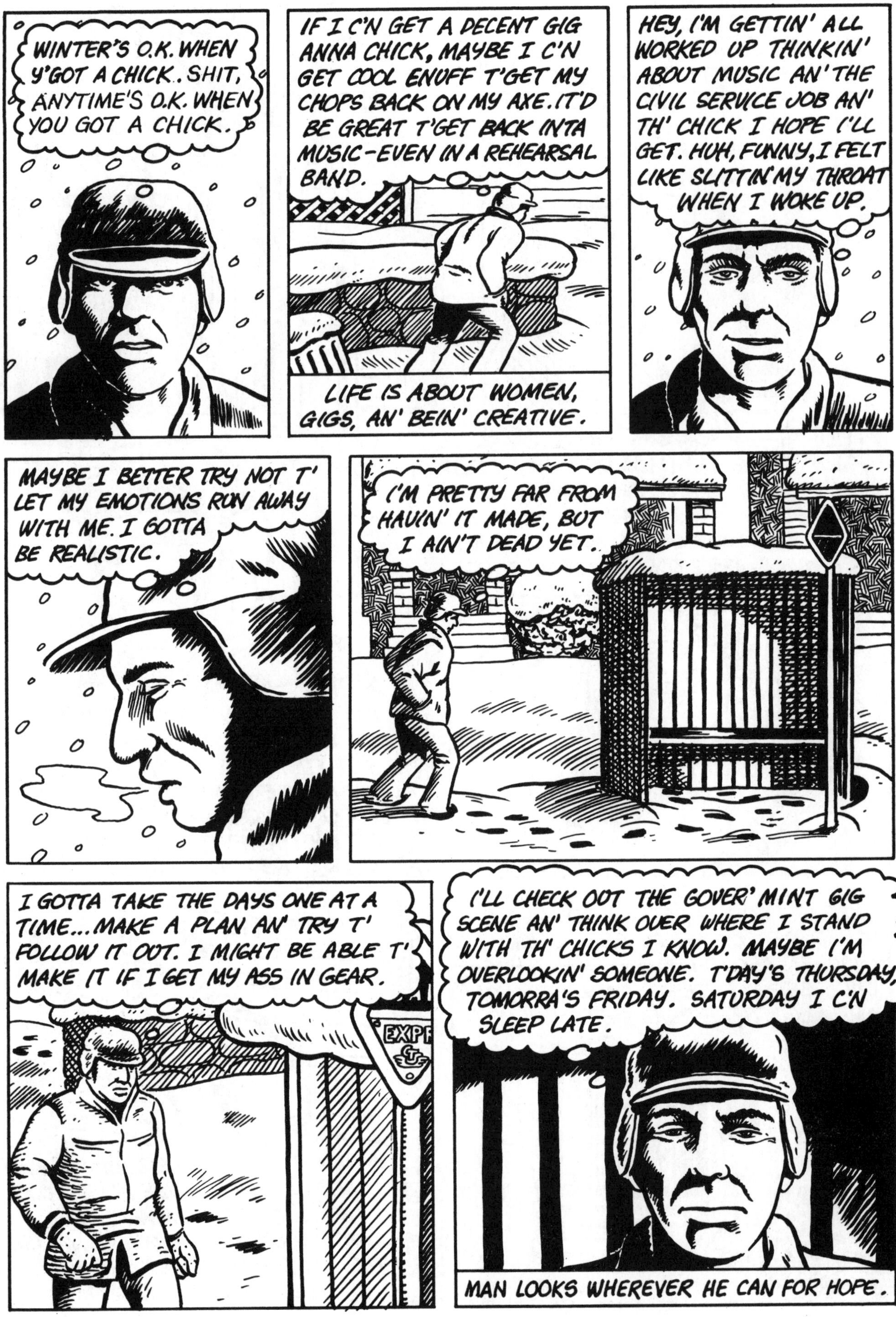
WINTER'S O.K. WHEN Y'GOT A CHICK.. SHIT, ANYTIME'S O.K. WHEN YOU GOT A CHICK.
IF I C'N GET A DECENT GIG ANNA CHICK, MAYBE I C'N GET COOL ENUFF T'GET MY CHOPS BACK ON MY AXE. IT'D BE GREAT T'GET BACK INTA MUSIC-EVEN IN A REHEARSAL BAND.
LIFE IS ABOUT WOMEN, GIGS, AN' BEIN' CREATIVE.
HEY, I'M GETTIN' ALL WORKED UP THINKIN' ABOUT MUSIC AN' THE CIVIL SERVICE JOB AN' TH' CHICK I HOPE I'LL GET. HUH, FUNNY, I FELT LIKE SLITTIN' MY THROAT WHEN I WOKE UP.
MAYBE I BETTER TRY NOT T' LET MY EMOTIONS RUN AWAY WITH ME. I GOTTA BE REALISTIC.
I'M PRETTY FAR FROM HAVIN' IT MADE, BUT I AIN'T DEAD YET.
I GOTTA TAKE THE DAYS ONE AT A TIME...MAKE A PLAN AN' TRY T' FOLLOW IT OUT. I MIGHT BE ABLE T' MAKE IT IF I GET MY ASS IN GEAR.
I'LL CHECK OUT THE GOVER' MINT GIG SCENE AN' THINK OVER WHERE I STAND WITH TH' CHICKS I KNOW. MAYBE I'M OVERLOOKIN' SOMEONE. T'DAY'S THURSDAY, TOMORRA'S FRIDAY. SATURDAY I C'N SLEEP LATE.
MAN LOOKS WHEREVER HE CAN FOR HOPE.

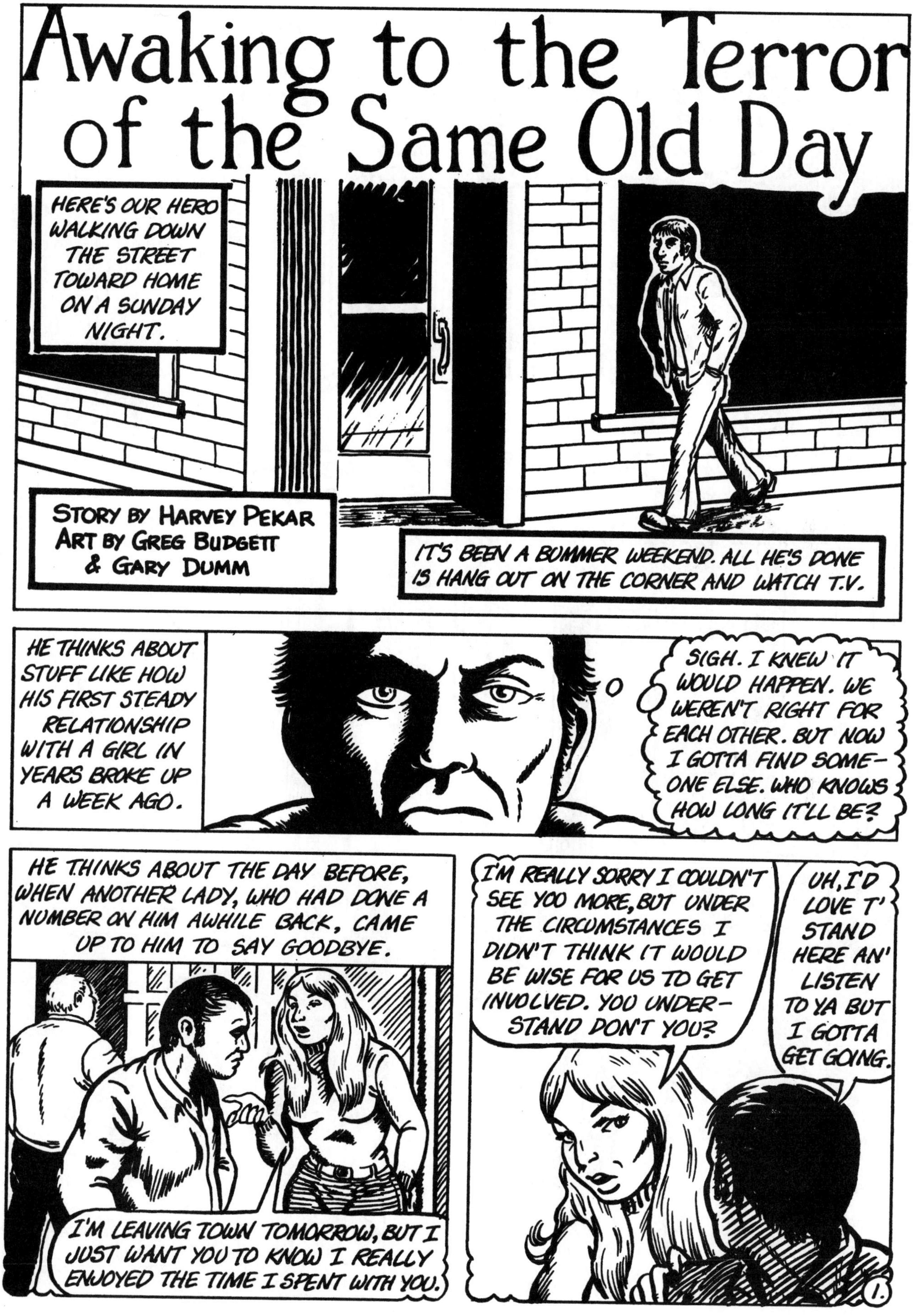

Awaking to the Terror of the Same Old Day
HERE'S OUR HERO WALKING DOWN THE STREET TOWARD HOME ON A SUNDAY NIGHT.
STORY BY HARVEY PEKAR
ART BY GREG BUDGETT & GARY DUMM
IT'S BEEN A BUMMER WEEKEND. ALL HE'S DONE IS HANG OUT ON THE CORNER AND WATCH T.V.
HE THINKS ABOUT STUFF LIKE HOW HIS FIRST STEADY RELATIONSHIP WITH A GIRL IN YEARS BROKE UP A WEEK AGO.
SIGH. I KNEW IT WOULD HAPPEN. WE WEREN'T RIGHT FOR EACH OTHER. BUT NOW I GOTTA FIND SOME-ONE ELSE. WHO KNOWS HOW LONG IT'LL BE?
HE THINKS ABOUT THE DAY BEFORE, WHEN ANOTHER LADY, WHO HAD DONE A NUMBER ON HIM AWHILE BACK, CAME UP TO HIM TO SAY GOODBYE.
I'M LEAVING TOWN TOMORROW, BUT I JUST WANT YOU TO KNOW I REALLY ENJOYED THE TIME I SPENT WITH YOU.
I'M REALLY SORRY I COULDN'T SEE YOO MORE, BUT UNDER THE CIRCUMSTANCES I DIDN'T THINK IT WOULD BE WISE FOR US TO GET INVOLVED. YOU UNDER-STAND DON'T YOU?
UH, I'D LOVE T' STAND HERE AN' LISTEN TO YA BUT I GOTTA GET GOING.
1.

ROTTEN BITCH. SHE WANTED ME TO FORGIVE HER AND TELL HER WHAT A NICE PERSON SHE IS. WHAT FUCKIN' NERVE SHE HAS.

SHE WAS DESPERATE FOR A GUY SO SHE CAME ON TO ME EVEN THOUGH SHE REALLY WANTED A DOCTOR OR SUMP'N. THEN SHE CHANGES HER MIND AND ACTS LIKE SHE DON'T KNOW ME. WHAT A ROTTEN LITTLE FLAKE SHE TURNED OUT TO BE.

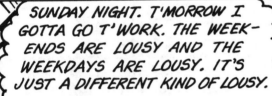

SUNDAY NIGHT. T'MORROW I GOTTA GO T'WORK. THE WEEK-ENDS ARE LOUSY AND THE WEEKDAYS ARE LOUSY. IT'S JUST A DIFFERENT KIND OF LOUSY.

SHOULD I WATCH T.V.? THERE'S A GOOD ABBOTT AN' COSTELLO MOVIE ON. NAH, FUCK IT. I'D RATHER SLEEP.

MAN, I DON'T FEEL LIKE DOIN' NOTHIN' THESE DAYS EXCEPT SLEEP.

2.

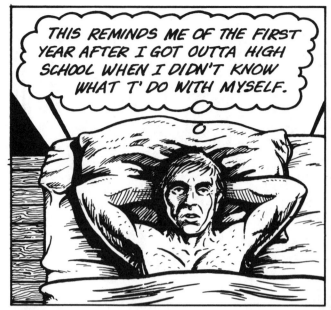

THIS REMINDS ME OF THE FIRST YEAR AFTER I GOT OUTTA HIGH SCHOOL WHEN I DIDN'T KNOW WHAT T' DO WITH MYSELF.

THAT'S ALL I DID WAS SLEEP THEN. JUST LIKE NOW. I DON'T FEEL LIKE DOING ANYTHING, NOTHING'S FUN THESE DAYS. I AIN'T ENTHUSIASTIC ABOUT ANYTHING.

ZZZZ

SOON...

RINNNG

HULLO... HUH?...IS IT IMPORTANT, MAN? WELL, LOOK, HOW 'BOUT IF I CALL YA BACK T'MORRA. I WAS SLEEPIN'.

THAT'S O.K., MAN. I CAN DIG YOUR CALLIN'. MOST GUYS WOULD BE AWAKE AT THIS HOUR. IT'S JUST THAT I BEEN GOIN' T' SLEEP REAL EARLY THESE DAYS. I'LL CALL YA T'MORRA, O.K.?

3.

SHIT, NOW I GOTTA FALL ASLEEP AGAIN... A' COURSE MAYBE THAT AIN'T SO BAD. I GUESS WHAT I REALLY LIKE IS GETTIN' SLEEPY AN' FALLIN' ASLEEP, NOT ACTUALLY SLEEPIN' ITSELF. WHEN YER SLEEPIN' NUTHING'S HAPPENING.

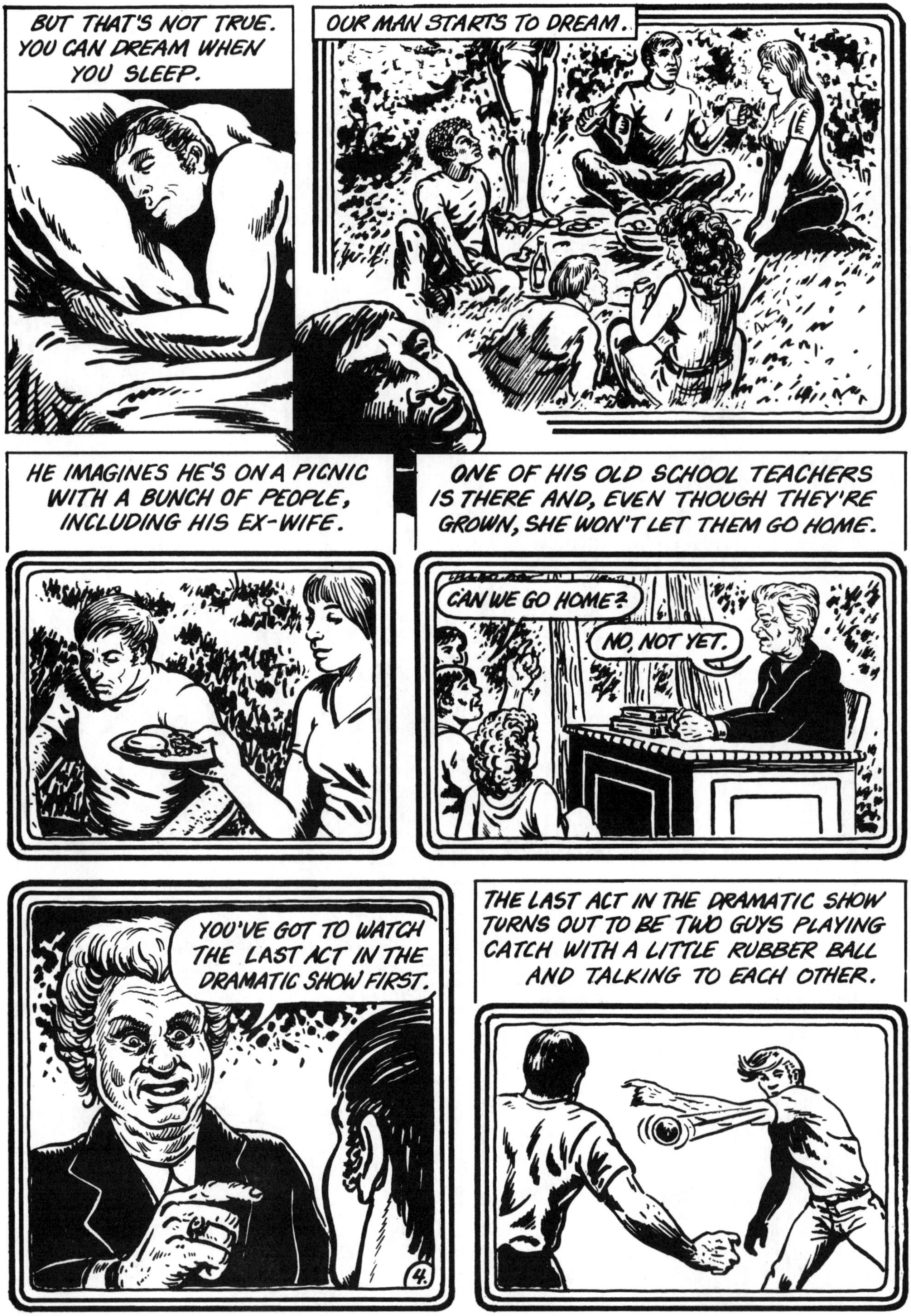
BUT THAT'S NOT TRUE. YOU CAN DREAM WHEN YOU SLEEP.
OUR MAN STARTS TO DREAM.
HE IMAGINES HE'S ON A PICNIC WITH A BUNCH OF PEOPLE, INCLUDING HIS EX-WIFE.
ONE OF HIS OLD SCHOOL TEACHERS IS THERE AND, EVEN THOUGH THEY'RE GROWN, SHE WON'T LET THEM GO HOME.
CAN WE GO HOME?
NO, NOT YET.
YOU'VE GOT TO WATCH THE LAST ACT IN THE DRAMATIC SHOW FIRST.
4.
THE LAST ACT IN THE DRAMATIC SHOW TURNS OUT TO BE TWO GUYS PLAYING CATCH WITH A LITTLE RUBBER BALL AND TALKING TO EACH OTHER.

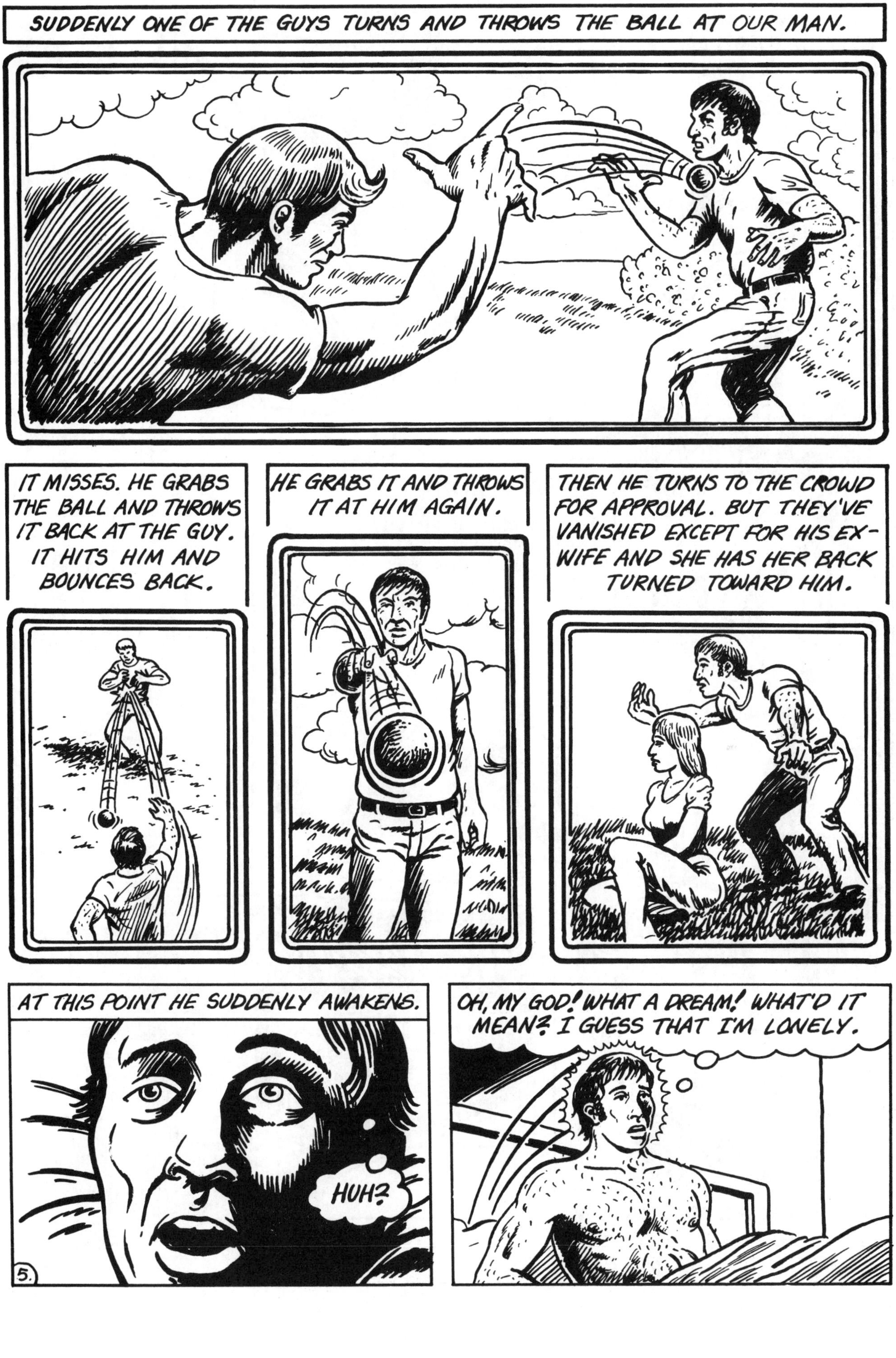
SUDDENLY ONE OF THE GUYS TURNS AND THROWS THE BALL AT OUR MAN.
IT MISSES. HE GRABS THE BALL AND THROWS IT BACK AT THE GUY. IT HITS HIM AND BOUNCES BACK.
HE GRABS IT AND THROWS IT AT HIM AGAIN.
THEN HE TURNS TO THE CROWD FOR APPROVAL. BUT THEY'VE VANISHED EXCEPT FOR HIS EX-WIFE AND SHE HAS HER BACK TURNED TOWARD HIM.
AT THIS POINT HE SUDDENLY AWAKENS.
HUH?
OH, MY GOD! WHAT A DREAM! WHAT'D IT MEAN? I GUESS THAT I'M LONELY.

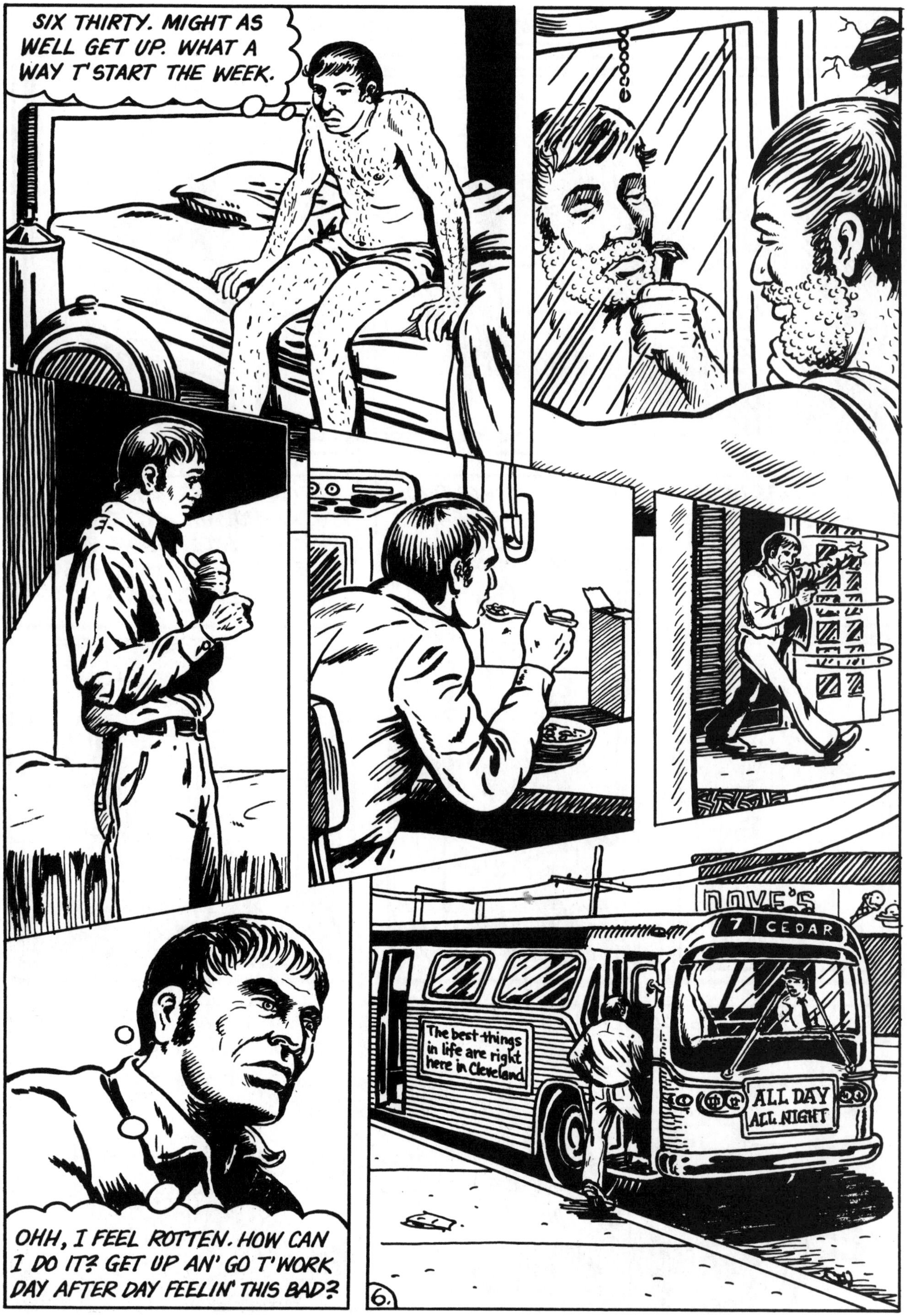
SIX THIRTY. MIGHT AS WELL GET UP. WHAT A WAY T'START THE WEEK.
DOVE'S
7 CEDAR
The best things in life are right here in Cleveland
ALL DAY ALL NIGHT
OHH, I FEEL ROTTEN. HOW CAN I DO IT? GET UP AN' GO T'WORK DAY AFTER DAY FEELIN' THIS BAD?
6.

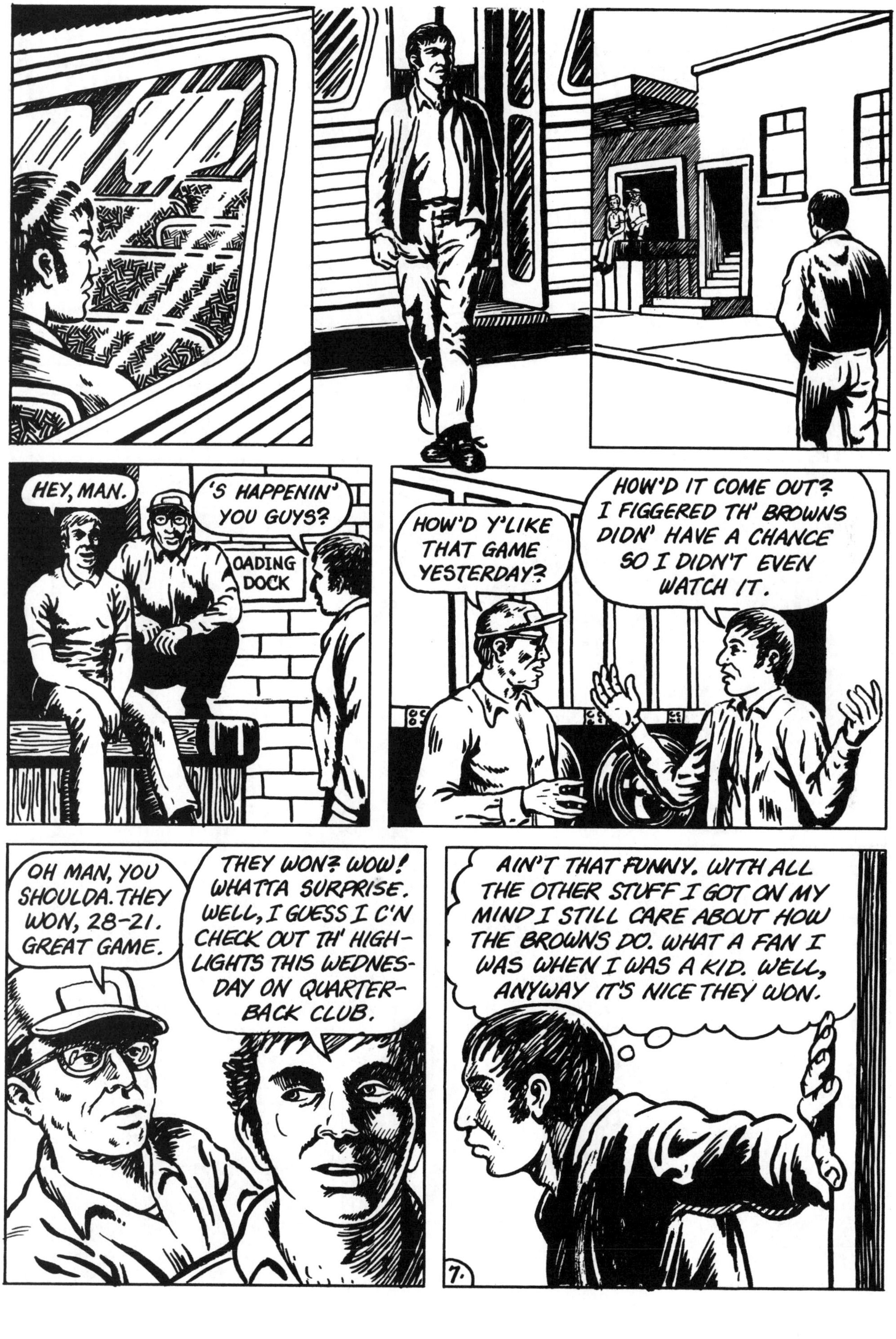
HEY, MAN.
'S HAPPENIN' YOU GUYS?
OADING DOCK
HOW'D Y'LIKE THAT GAME YESTERDAY?
HOW'D IT COME OUT? I FIGGERED TH' BROWNS DIDN' HAVE A CHANCE SO I DIDN'T EVEN WATCH IT.
OH MAN, YOU SHOULDA. THEY WON, 28-21. GREAT GAME.
THEY WON? WOW! WHATTA SURPRISE. WELL, I GUESS I C'N CHECK OUT TH' HIGH-LIGHTS THIS WEDNES-DAY ON QUARTER-BACK CLUB.
AIN'T THAT FUNNY. WITH ALL THE OTHER STUFF I GOT ON MY MIND I STILL CARE ABOUT HOW THE BROWNS DO. WHAT A FAN I WAS WHEN I WAS A KID. WELL, ANYWAY IT'S NICE THEY WON.
7.

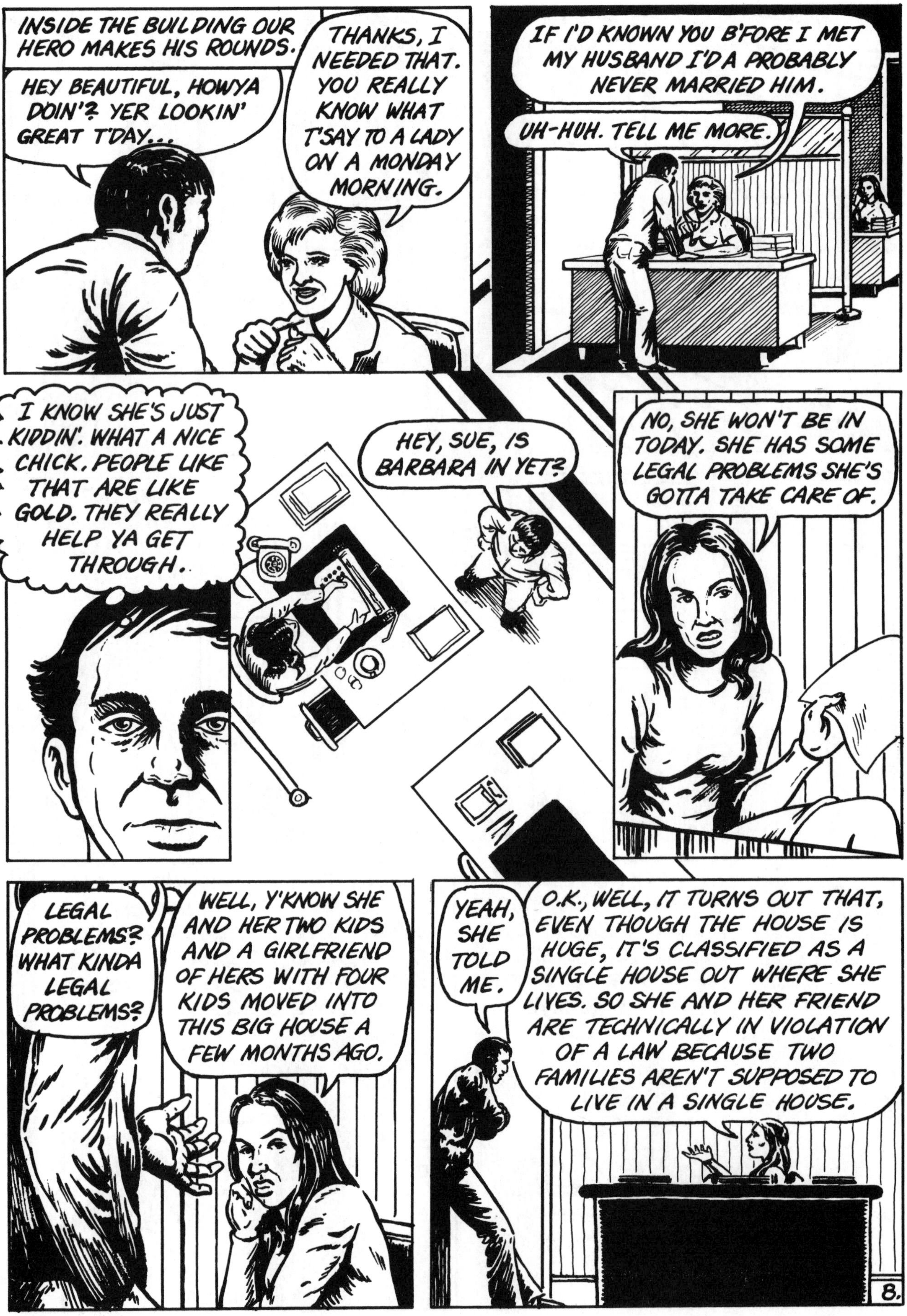
INSIDE THE BUILDING OUR HERO MAKES HIS ROUNDS.
HEY BEAUTIFUL, HOWYA DOIN'? YER LOOKIN' GREAT T'DAY...
THANKS, I NEEDED THAT. YOU REALLY KNOW WHAT T'SAY TO A LADY ON A MONDAY MORNING.
IF I'D KNOWN YOU B'FORE I MET MY HUSBAND I'DA PROBABLY NEVER MARRIED HIM.
UH-HUH. TELL ME MORE.
I KNOW SHE'S JUST KIDDIN'. WHAT A NICE CHICK. PEOPLE LIKE THAT ARE LIKE GOLD. THEY REALLY HELP YA GET THROUGH.
HEY, SUE, IS BARBARA IN YET?
NO, SHE WON'T BE IN TODAY. SHE HAS SOME LEGAL PROBLEMS SHE'S GOTTA TAKE CARE OF.
LEGAL PROBLEMS? WHAT KINDA LEGAL PROBLEMS?
WELL, Y'KNOW SHE AND HER TWO KIDS AND A GIRLFRIEND OF HERS WITH FOUR KIDS MOVED INTO THIS BIG HOUSE A FEW MONTHS AGO.
YEAH, SHE TOLD ME.
O.K., WELL, IT TURNS OUT THAT, EVEN THOUGH THE HOUSE IS HUGE, IT'S CLASSIFIED AS A SINGLE HOUSE OUT WHERE SHE LIVES. SO SHE AND HER FRIEND ARE TECHNICALLY IN VIOLATION OF A LAW BECAUSE TWO FAMILIES AREN'T SUPPOSED TO LIVE IN A SINGLE HOUSE.
8.

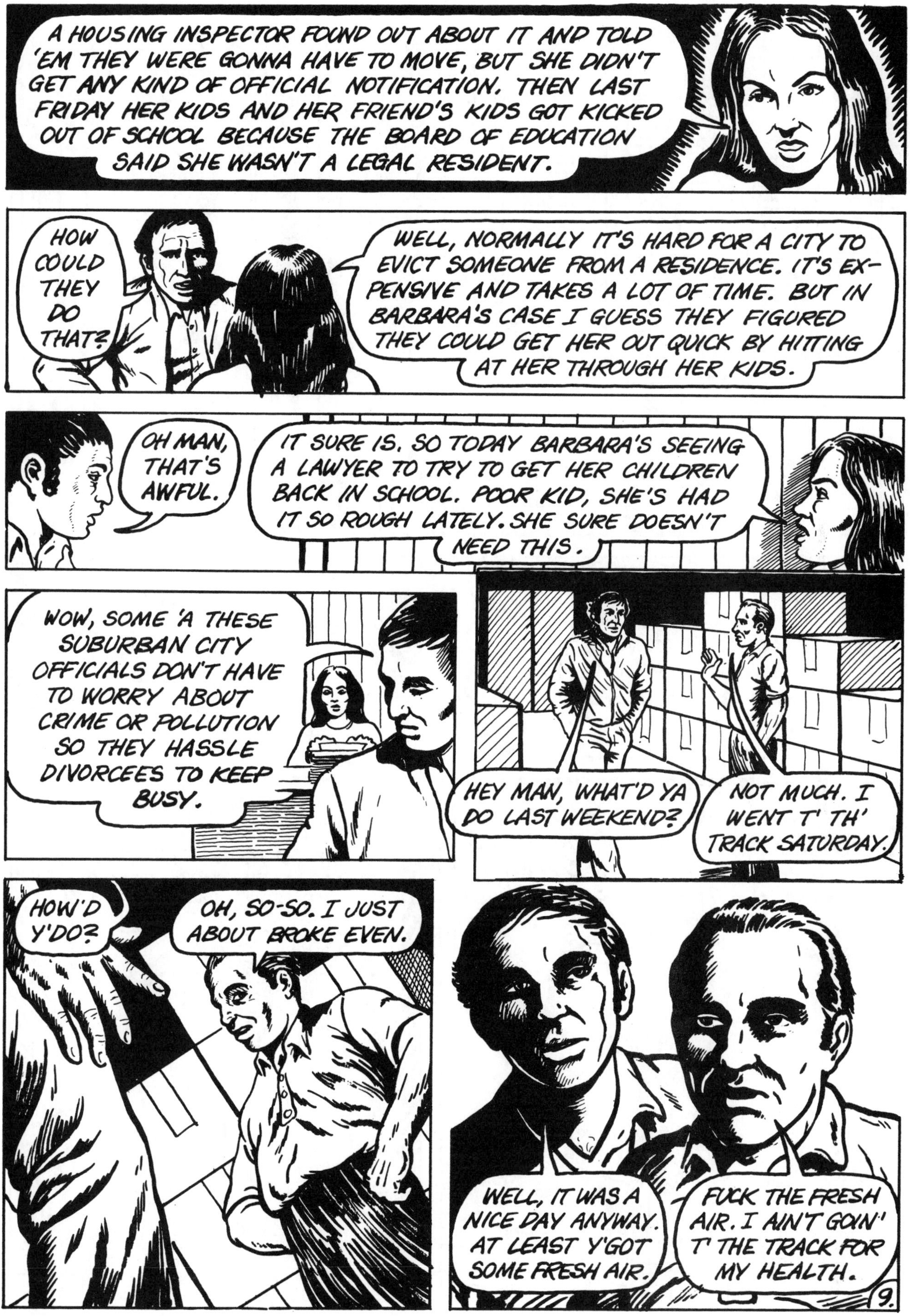
A HOUSING INSPECTOR FOUND OUT ABOUT IT AND TOLD 'EM THEY WERE GONNA HAVE TO MOVE, BUT SHE DIDN'T GET ANY KIND OF OFFICIAL NOTIFICATION. THEN LAST FRIDAY HER KIDS AND HER FRIEND'S KIDS GOT KICKED OUT OF SCHOOL BECAUSE THE BOARD OF EDUCATION SAID SHE WASN'T A LEGAL RESIDENT.
HOW COULD THEY DO THAT?
WELL, NORMALLY IT'S HARD FOR A CITY TO EVICT SOMEONE FROM A RESIDENCE. IT'S EXPENSIVE AND TAKES A LOT OF TIME. BUT IN BARBARA'S CASE I GUESS THEY FIGURED THEY COULD GET HER OUT QUICK BY HITTING AT HER THROUGH HER KIDS.
OH MAN, THAT'S AWFUL.
IT SURE IS. SO TODAY BARBARA'S SEEING A LAWYER TO TRY TO GET HER CHILDREN BACK IN SCHOOL. POOR KID, SHE'S HAD IT SO ROUGH LATELY. SHE SURE DOESN'T NEED THIS.
WOW, SOME 'A THESE SUBURBAN CITY OFFICIALS DON'T HAVE TO WORRY ABOUT CRIME OR POLLUTION SO THEY HASSLE DIVORCEES TO KEEP BUSY.
HEY MAN, WHAT'D YA DO LAST WEEKEND?
NOT MUCH. I WENT T' TH' TRACK SATURDAY.
HOW'D Y'DO?
OH, SO-SO. I JUST ABOUT BROKE EVEN.
WELL, IT WAS A NICE DAY ANYWAY. AT LEAST Y'GOT SOME FRESH AIR.
FUCK THE FRESH AIR. I AIN'T GOIN' T' THE TRACK FOR MY HEALTH.

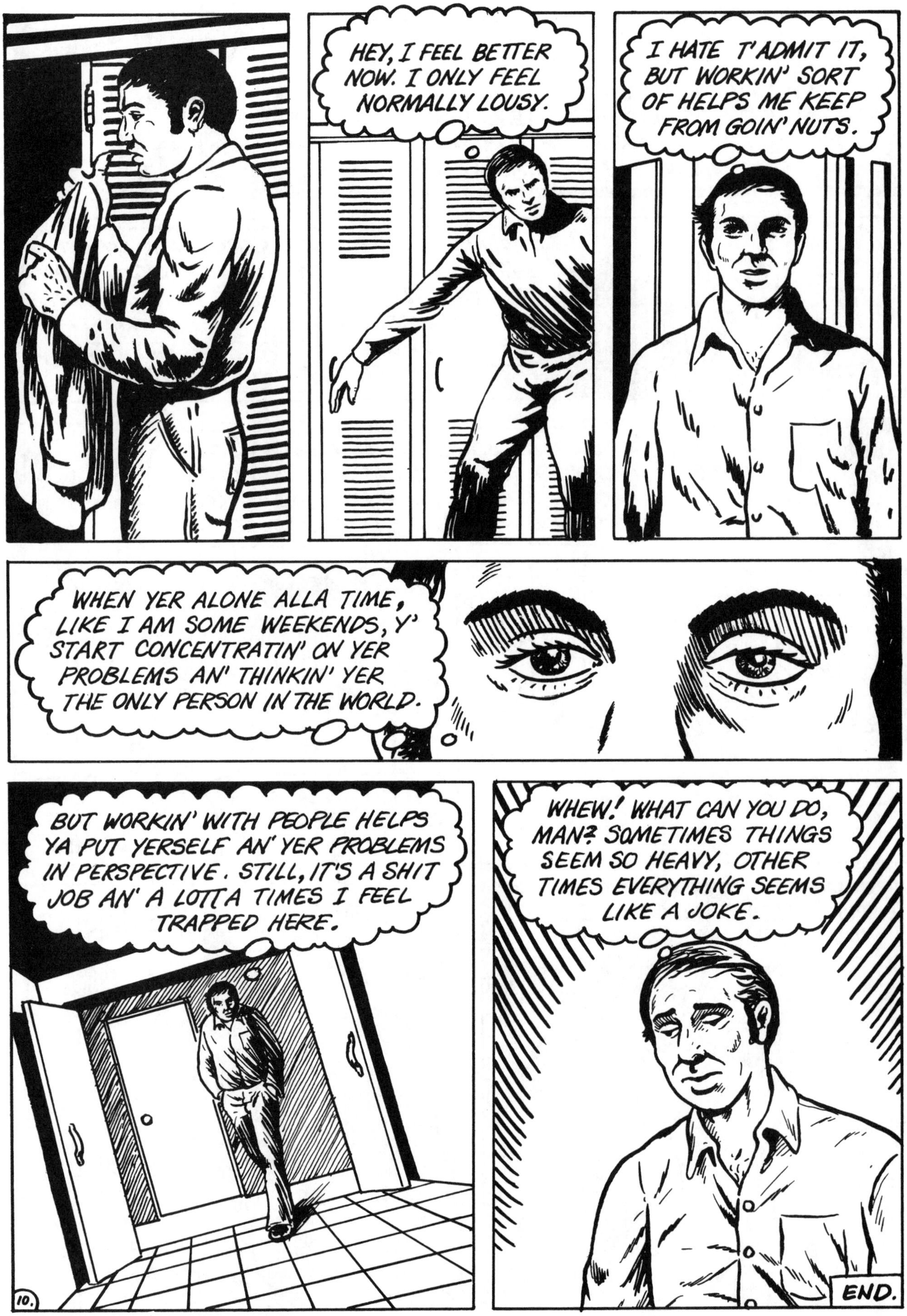
HEY, I FEEL BETTER NOW. I ONLY FEEL NORMALLY LOUSY.
I HATE T'ADMIT IT, BUT WORKIN' SORT OF HELPS ME KEEP FROM GOIN' NUTS.
WHEN YER ALONE ALLA TIME, LIKE I AM SOME WEEKENDS, Y' START CONCENTRATIN' ON YER PROBLEMS AN' THINKIN' YER THE ONLY PERSON IN THE WORLD.
BUT WORKIN' WITH PEOPLE HELPS YA PUT YERSELF AN' YER PROBLEMS IN PERSPECTIVE. STILL, IT'S A SHIT JOB AN' A LOTTA TIMES I FEEL TRAPPED HERE.
10.
WHEW! WHAT CAN YOU DO, MAN? SOMETIMES THINGS SEEM SO HEAVY, OTHER TIMES EVERYTHING SEEMS LIKE A JOKE.
END.

SHORT WEEKEND
A STORY ABOUT THE COSMIC AND THE ORDINARY

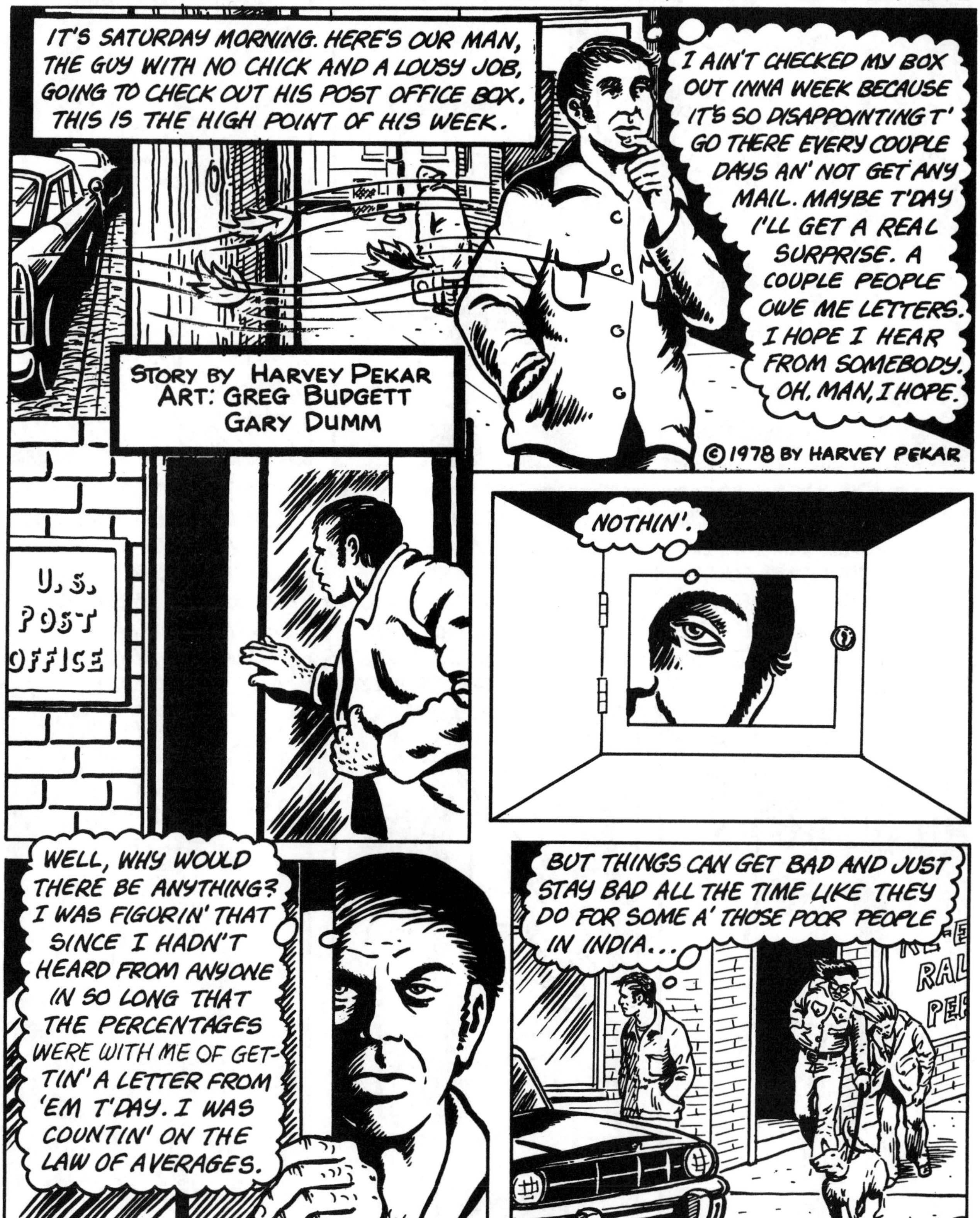
IT'S SATURDAY MORNING. HERE'S OUR MAN, THE GUY WITH NO CHICK AND A LOUSY JOB, GOING TO CHECK OUT HIS POST OFFICE BOX. THIS IS THE HIGH POINT OF HIS WEEK.
I AIN'T CHECKED MY BOX OUT INNA WEEK BECAUSE IT'S SO DISAPPOINTING T' GO THERE EVERY COUPLE DAYS AN' NOT GET ANY MAIL. MAYBE T'DAY I'LL GET A REAL SURPRISE. A COUPLE PEOPLE OWE ME LETTERS. I HOPE I HEAR FROM SOMEBODY. OH, MAN, I HOPE.
STORY BY HARVEY PEKAR
ART: GREG BUDGETT
GARY DUMM
© 1978 BY HARVEY PEKAR
U.S. POST OFFICE
NOTHIN'.
WELL, WHY WOULD THERE BE ANYTHING? I WAS FIGURIN' THAT SINCE I HADN'T HEARD FROM ANYONE IN SO LONG THAT THE PERCENTAGES WERE WITH ME OF GETTIN' A LETTER FROM 'EM T'DAY. I WAS COUNTIN' ON THE LAW OF AVERAGES.
BUT THINGS CAN GET BAD AND JUST STAY BAD ALL THE TIME LIKE THEY DO FOR SOME A' THOSE POOR PEOPLE IN INDIA...
1.

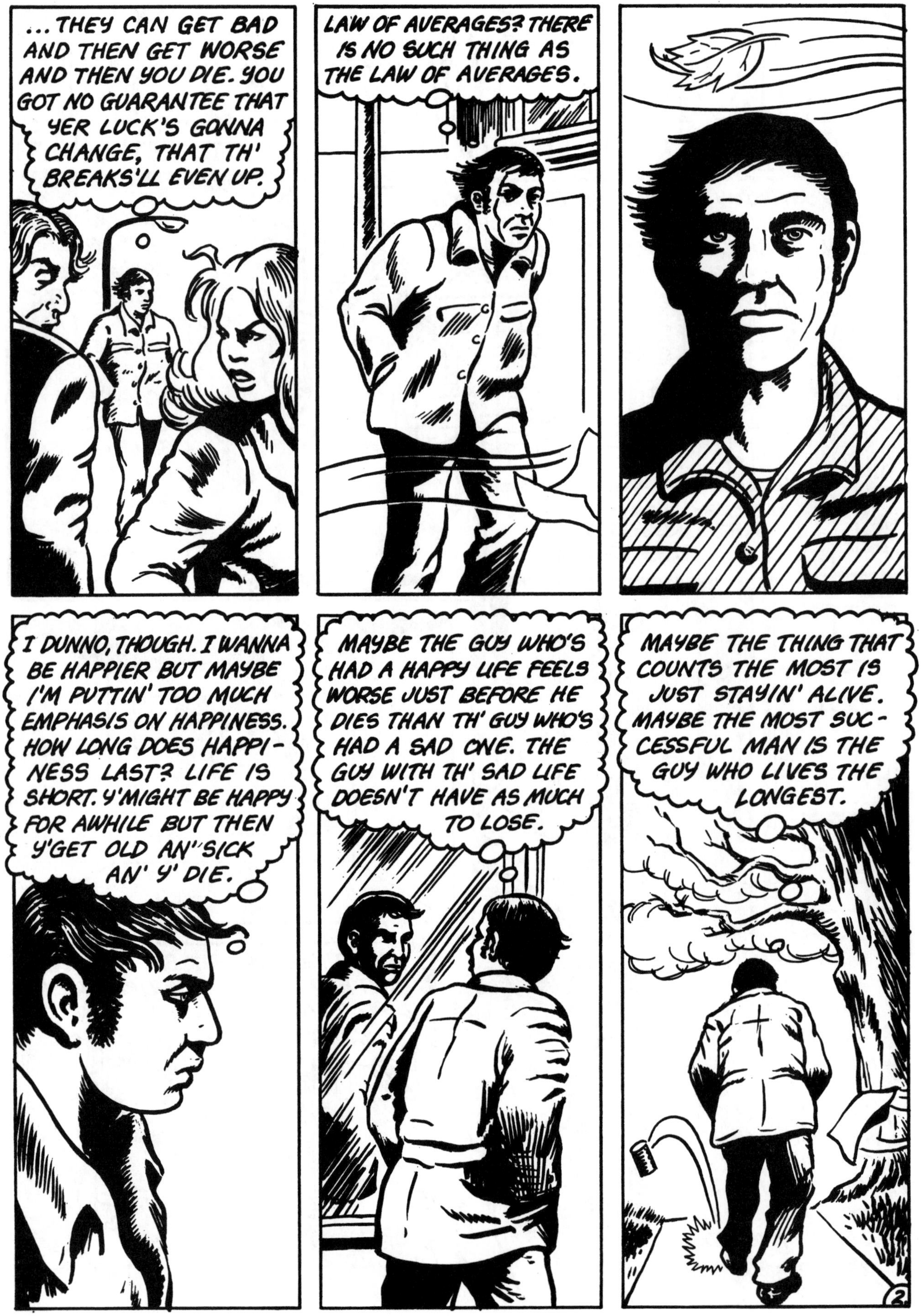
...THEY CAN GET BAD AND THEN GET WORSE AND THEN YOU DIE. YOU GOT NO GUARANTEE THAT YER LUCK'S GONNA CHANGE, THAT TH' BREAKS'LL EVEN UP.
LAW OF AVERAGES? THERE IS NO SUCH THING AS THE LAW OF AVERAGES.
I DUNNO, THOUGH. I WANNA BE HAPPIER BUT MAYBE I'M PUTTIN' TOO MUCH EMPHASIS ON HAPPINESS. HOW LONG DOES HAPPI-NESS LAST? LIFE IS SHORT. Y'MIGHT BE HAPPY FOR AWHILE BUT THEN Y'GET OLD AN' SICK AN' Y' DIE.
MAYBE THE GUY WHO'S HAD A HAPPY LIFE FEELS WORSE JUST BEFORE HE DIES THAN TH' GUY WHO'S HAD A SAD ONE. THE GUY WITH TH' SAD LIFE DOESN'T HAVE AS MUCH TO LOSE.
MAYBE THE THING THAT COUNTS THE MOST IS JUST STAYIN' ALIVE. MAYBE THE MOST SUC-CESSFUL MAN IS THE GUY WHO LIVES THE LONGEST.
2

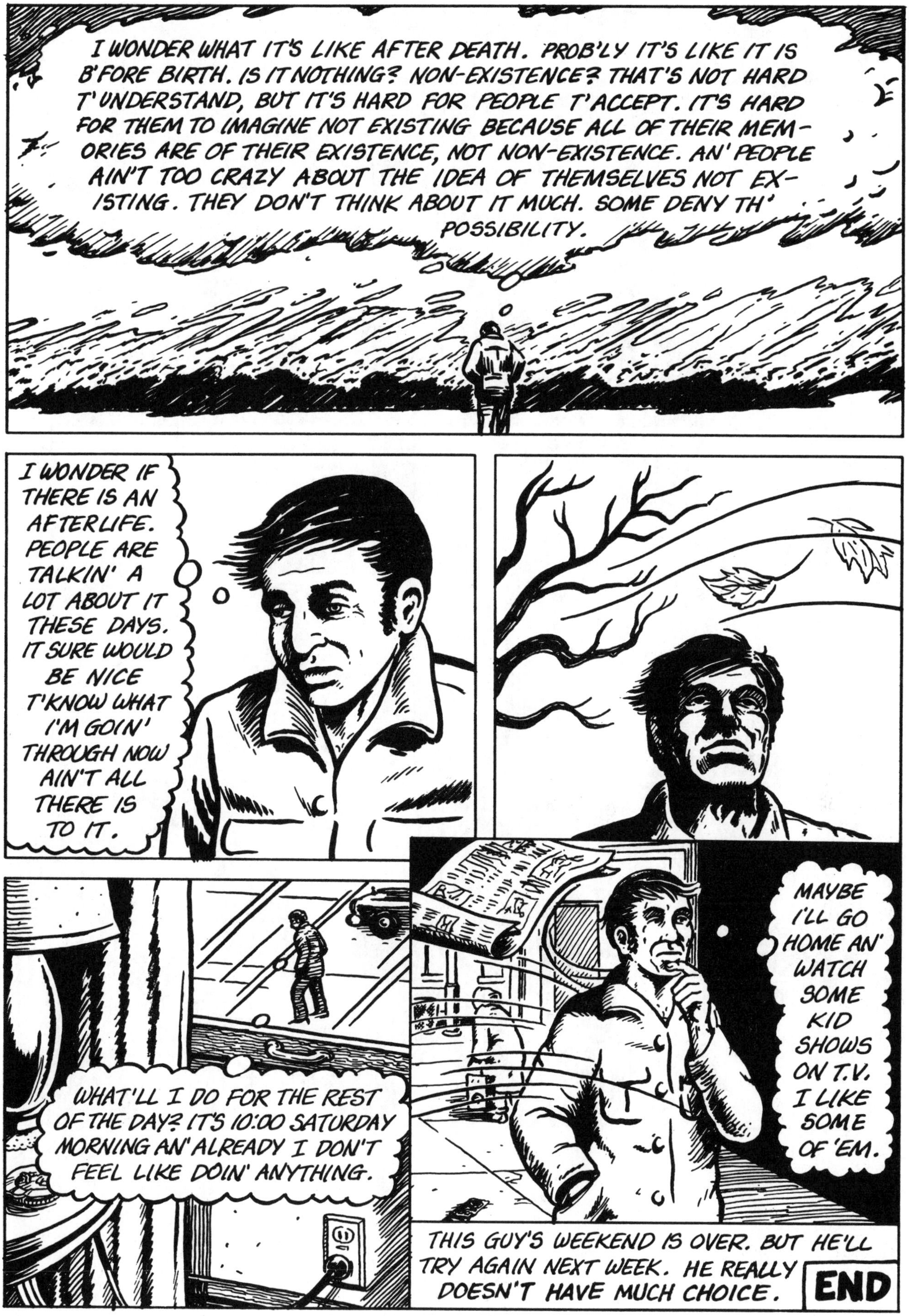
I WONDER WHAT IT'S LIKE AFTER DEATH. PROB'LY IT'S LIKE IT IS B'FORE BIRTH. IS IT NOTHING? NON-EXISTENCE? THAT'S NOT HARD T'UNDERSTAND, BUT IT'S HARD FOR PEOPLE T'ACCEPT. IT'S HARD FOR THEM TO IMAGINE NOT EXISTING BECAUSE ALL OF THEIR MEMORIES ARE OF THEIR EXISTENCE, NOT NON-EXISTENCE. AN' PEOPLE AIN'T TOO CRAZY ABOUT THE IDEA OF THEMSELVES NOT EXISTING. THEY DON'T THINK ABOUT IT MUCH. SOME DENY TH' POSSIBILITY.
I WONDER IF THERE IS AN AFTERLIFE. PEOPLE ARE TALKIN' A LOT ABOUT IT THESE DAYS. IT SURE WOULD BE NICE T'KNOW WHAT I'M GOIN' THROUGH NOW AIN'T ALL THERE IS TO IT.
WHAT'LL I DO FOR THE REST OF THE DAY? IT'S 10:00 SATURDAY MORNING AN' ALREADY I DON'T FEEL LIKE DOIN' ANYTHING.
MAYBE I'LL GO HOME AN' WATCH SOME KID SHOWS ON T.V. I LIKE SOME OF 'EM.
THIS GUY'S WEEKEND IS OVER. BUT HE'LL TRY AGAIN NEXT WEEK. HE REALLY DOESN'T HAVE MUCH CHOICE.
END

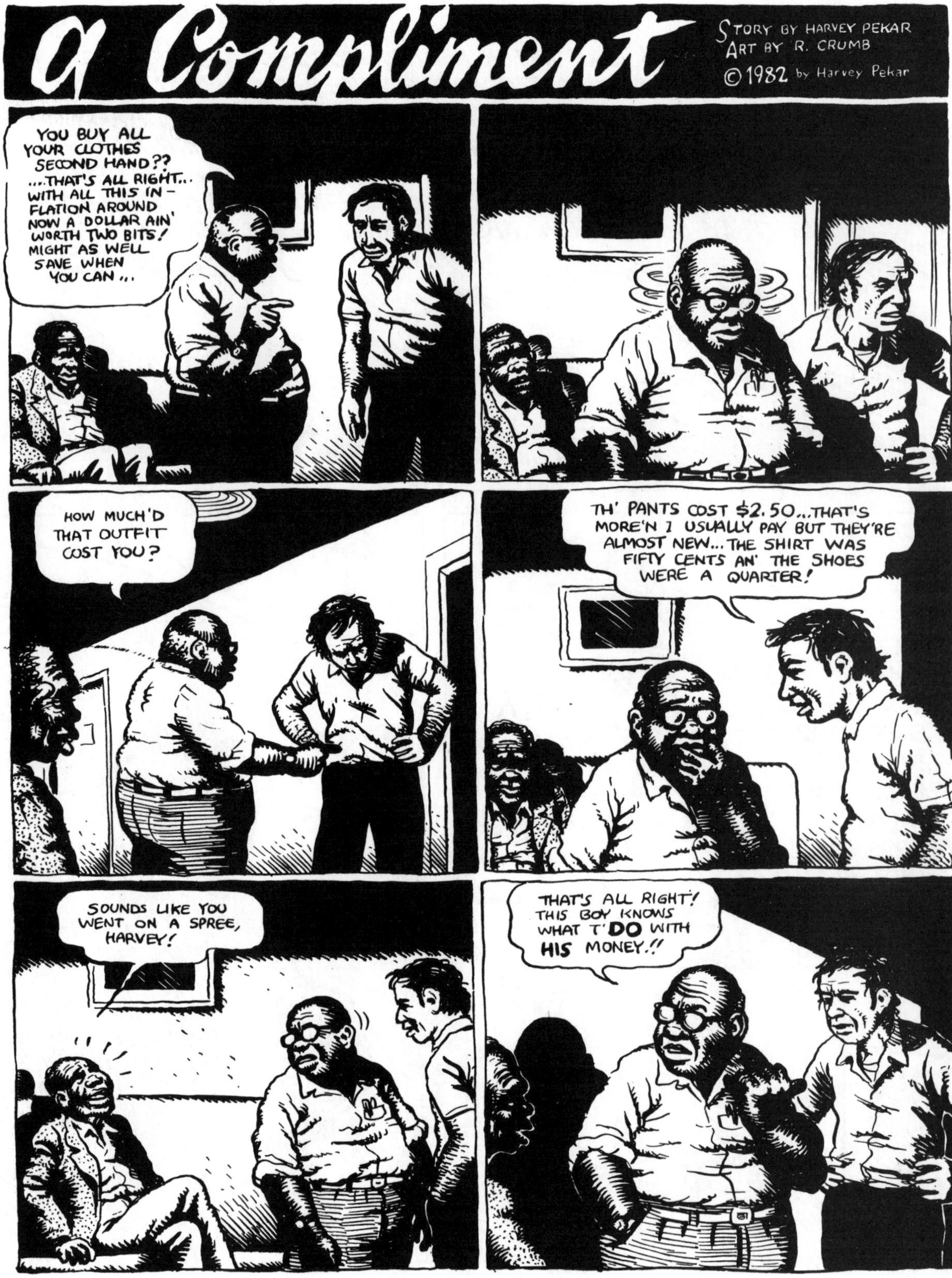
A Compliment
STORY BY HARVEY PEKAR
ART BY R. CRUMB
©1982 by Harvey Pekar
YOU BUY ALL YOUR CLOTHES SECOND HAND?? ...THAT'S ALL RIGHT... WITH ALL THIS IN-FLATION AROUND NOW A DOLLAR AIN' WORTH TWO BITS! MIGHT AS WELL SAVE WHEN YOU CAN...
HOW MUCH'D THAT OUTFIT COST YOU?
TH' PANTS COST $2.50...THAT'S MORE'N I USUALLY PAY BUT THEY'RE ALMOST NEW... THE SHIRT WAS FIFTY CENTS AN' THE SHOES WERE A QUARTER!
SOUNDS LIKE YOU WENT ON A SPREE, HARVEY!
THAT'S ALL RIGHT! THIS BOY KNOWS WHAT T' DO WITH HIS MONEY.!!

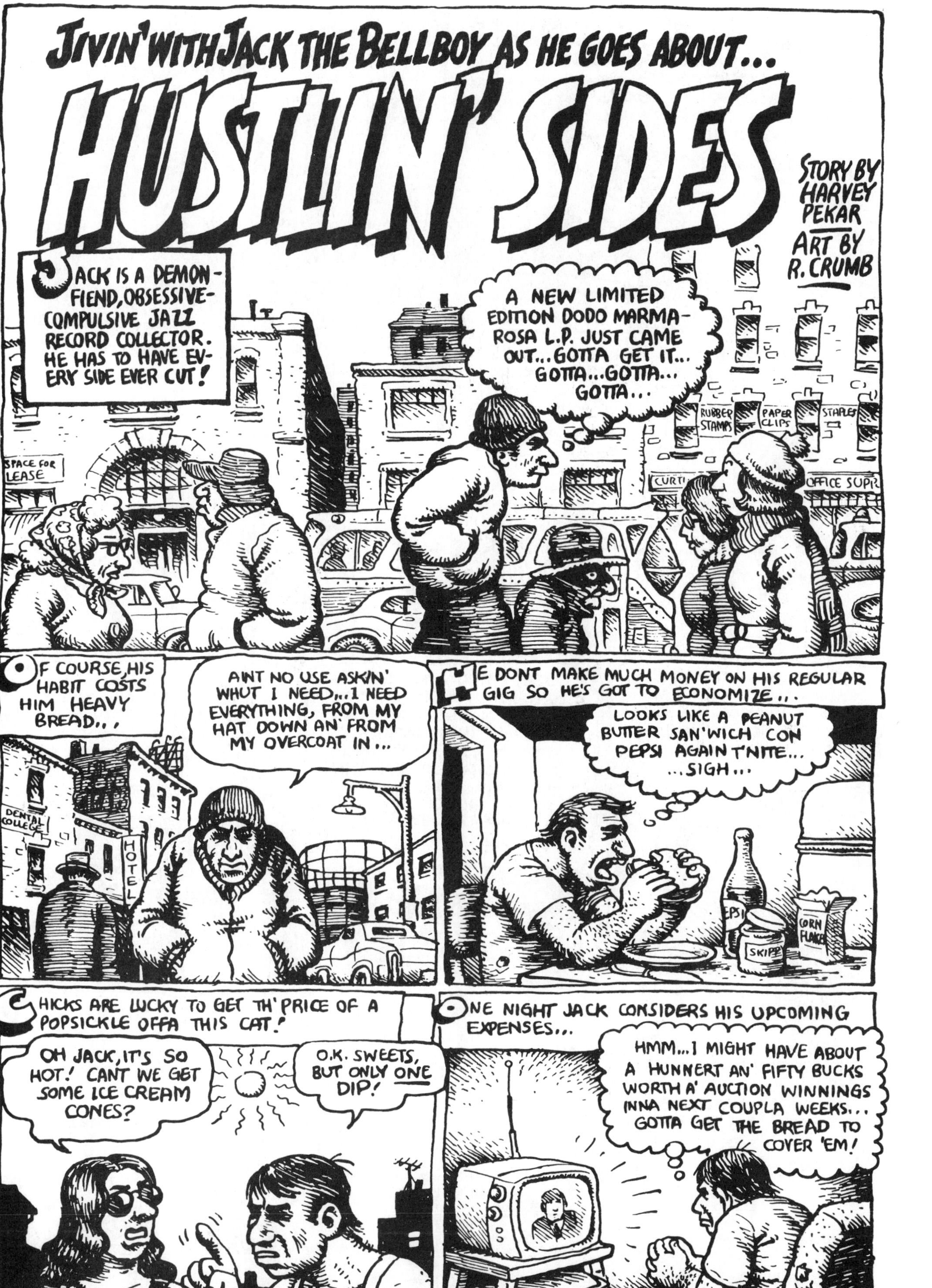
JIVIN' WITH JACK THE BELLBOY AS HE GOES ABOUT...
HUSTLIN' SIDES
STORY BY HARVEY PEKAR
ART BY R. CRUMB
JACK IS A DEMON-FIEND, OBSESSIVE-COMPULSIVE JAZZ RECORD COLLECTOR. HE HAS TO HAVE EVERY SIDE EVER CUT!
A NEW LIMITED EDITION DODO MARMAROSA L.P. JUST CAME OUT... GOTTA GET IT... GOTTA... GOTTA... GOTTA...
SPACE FOR LEASE
RUBBER STAMPS
PAPER CLIPS
STAPLES
OFFICE SUP
OF COURSE, HIS HABIT COSTS HIM HEAVY BREAD...
AINT NO USE ASKIN' WHUT I NEED... I NEED EVERYTHING, FROM MY HAT DOWN AN' FROM MY OVERCOAT IN...
DENTAL COLLEGE
HOTEL
HE DONT MAKE MUCH MONEY ON HIS REGULAR GIG SO HE'S GOT TO ECONOMIZE...
LOOKS LIKE A PEANUT BUTTER SAN'WICH CON PEPSI AGAIN T'NITE... ...SIGH...
PEPSI
SKIPPY
CORN FLAKES
CHICKS ARE LUCKY TO GET TH' PRICE OF A POPSICKLE OFFA THIS CAT!
OH JACK, IT'S SO HOT! CANT WE GET SOME ICE CREAM CONES?
O.K. SWEETS, BUT ONLY ONE DIP!
ONE NIGHT JACK CONSIDERS HIS UPCOMING EXPENSES...
HMM... I MIGHT HAVE ABOUT A HUNNERT AN' FIFTY BUCKS WORTH A' AUCTION WINNINGS INNA NEXT COUPLA WEEKS... GOTTA GET THE BREAD TO COVER 'EM!

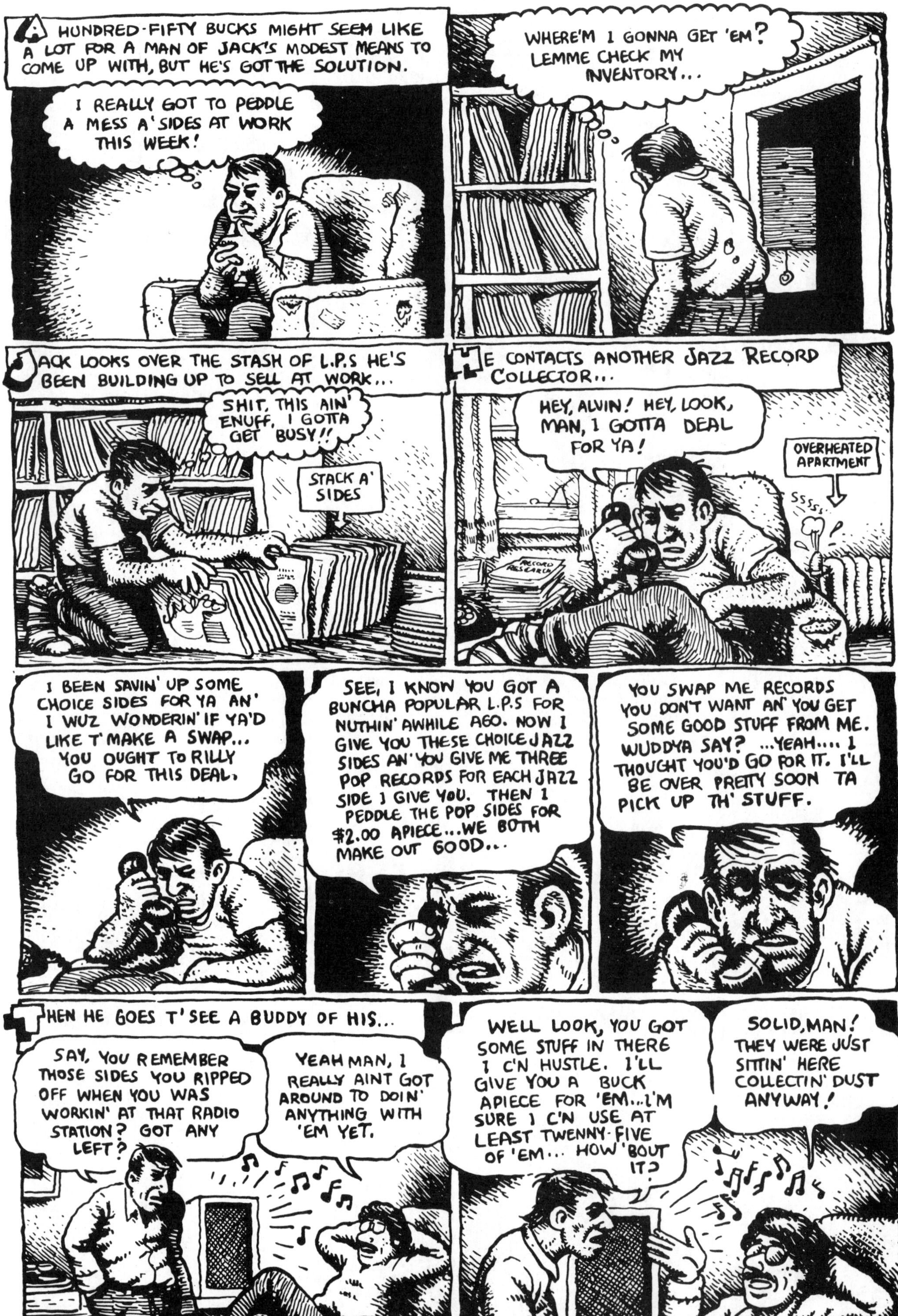
A HUNDRED-FIFTY BUCKS MIGHT SEEM LIKE A LOT FOR A MAN OF JACK'S MODEST MEANS TO COME UP WITH, BUT HE'S GOT THE SOLUTION.
I REALLY GOT TO PEDDLE A MESS A' SIDES AT WORK THIS WEEK!
WHERE'M I GONNA GET 'EM? LEMME CHECK MY INVENTORY...
JACK LOOKS OVER THE STASH OF L.P.S HE'S BEEN BUILDING UP TO SELL AT WORK...
SHIT, THIS AIN' ENUFF, I GOTTA GET BUSY!!
STACK A' SIDES
HE CONTACTS ANOTHER JAZZ RECORD COLLECTOR...
HEY, ALVIN! HEY, LOOK, MAN, I GOTTA DEAL FOR YA!
OVERHEATED APARTMENT
SSSSS
RECORD RESEARCH
I BEEN SAVIN' UP SOME CHOICE SIDES FOR YA AN' I WUZ WONDERIN' IF YA'D LIKE T'MAKE A SWAP... YOU OUGHT TO RILLY GO FOR THIS DEAL.
SEE, I KNOW YOU GOT A BUNCHA POPULAR L.P.S FOR NUTHIN' AWHILE AGO. NOW I GIVE YOU THESE CHOICE JAZZ SIDES AN' YOU GIVE ME THREE POP RECORDS FOR EACH JAZZ SIDE I GIVE YOU. THEN I PEDDLE THE POP SIDES FOR $2.00 APIECE...WE BOTH MAKE OUT GOOD...
YOU SWAP ME RECORDS YOU DON'T WANT AN' YOU GET SOME GOOD STUFF FROM ME. WUDDYA SAY? ...YEAH.... I THOUGHT YOU'D GO FOR IT. I'LL BE OVER PRETTY SOON TA PICK UP TH' STUFF.
THEN HE GOES T'SEE A BUDDY OF HIS...
SAY, YOU REMEMBER THOSE SIDES YOU RIPPED OFF WHEN YOU WAS WORKIN' AT THAT RADIO STATION? GOT ANY LEFT?
YEAH MAN, I REALLY AINT GOT AROUND TO DOIN' ANYTHING WITH 'EM YET.
WELL LOOK, YOU GOT SOME STUFF IN THERE I C'N HUSTLE. I'LL GIVE YOU A BUCK APIECE FOR 'EM...I'M SURE I C'N USE AT LEAST TWENNY-FIVE OF 'EM... HOW 'BOUT IT?
SOLID, MAN! THEY WERE JUST SITTIN' HERE COLLECTIN' DUST ANYWAY!

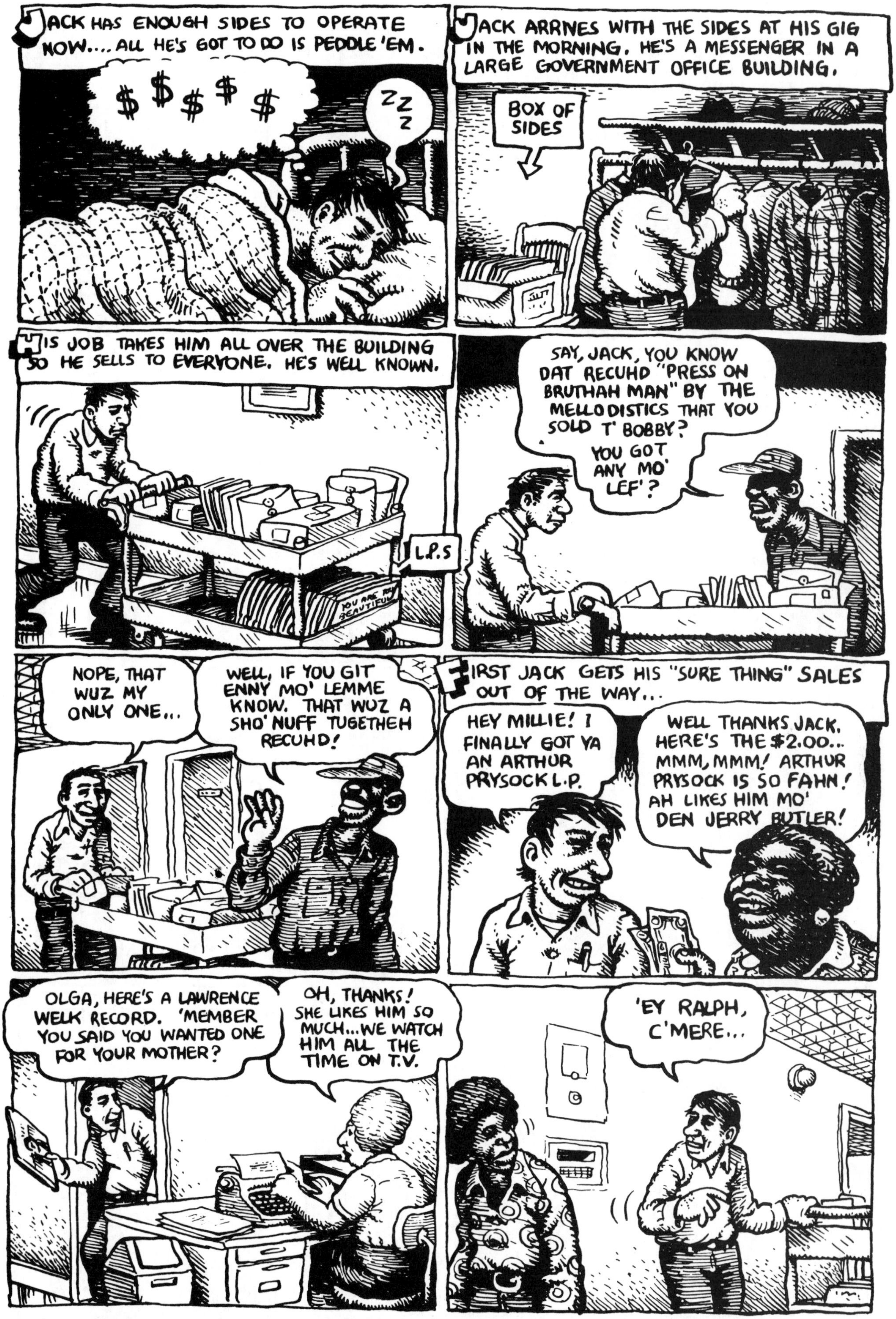
JACK HAS ENOUGH SIDES TO OPERATE NOW.... ALL HE'S GOT TO DO IS PEDDLE 'EM.
$ $ $ $ $
Z Z Z
JACK ARRIVES WITH THE SIDES AT HIS GIG IN THE MORNING. HE'S A MESSENGER IN A LARGE GOVERNMENT OFFICE BUILDING.
BOX OF SIDES
HIS JOB TAKES HIM ALL OVER THE BUILDING SO HE SELLS TO EVERYONE. HE'S WELL KNOWN.
L.P.S
SAY, JACK, YOU KNOW DAT RECUHD "PRESS ON BRUTHAH MAN" BY THE MELLODISTICS THAT YOU SOLD T' BOBBY?
YOU GOT ANY MO' LEF'?
NOPE, THAT WUZ MY ONLY ONE...
WELL, IF YOU GIT ENNY MO' LEMME KNOW. THAT WUZ A SHO' NUFF TUGETHEH RECUHD!
FIRST JACK GETS HIS "SURE THING" SALES OUT OF THE WAY...
HEY MILLIE! I FINALLY GOT YA AN ARTHUR PRYSOCK L.P.
WELL THANKS JACK. HERE'S THE $2.00... MMM, MMM! ARTHUR PRYSOCK IS SO FAHN! AH LIKES HIM MO' DEN JERRY BUTLER!
OLGA, HERE'S A LAWRENCE WELK RECORD. 'MEMBER YOU SAID YOU WANTED ONE FOR YOUR MOTHER?
OH, THANKS! SHE LIKES HIM SO MUCH... WE WATCH HIM ALL THE TIME ON T.V.
'EY RALPH, C'MERE...

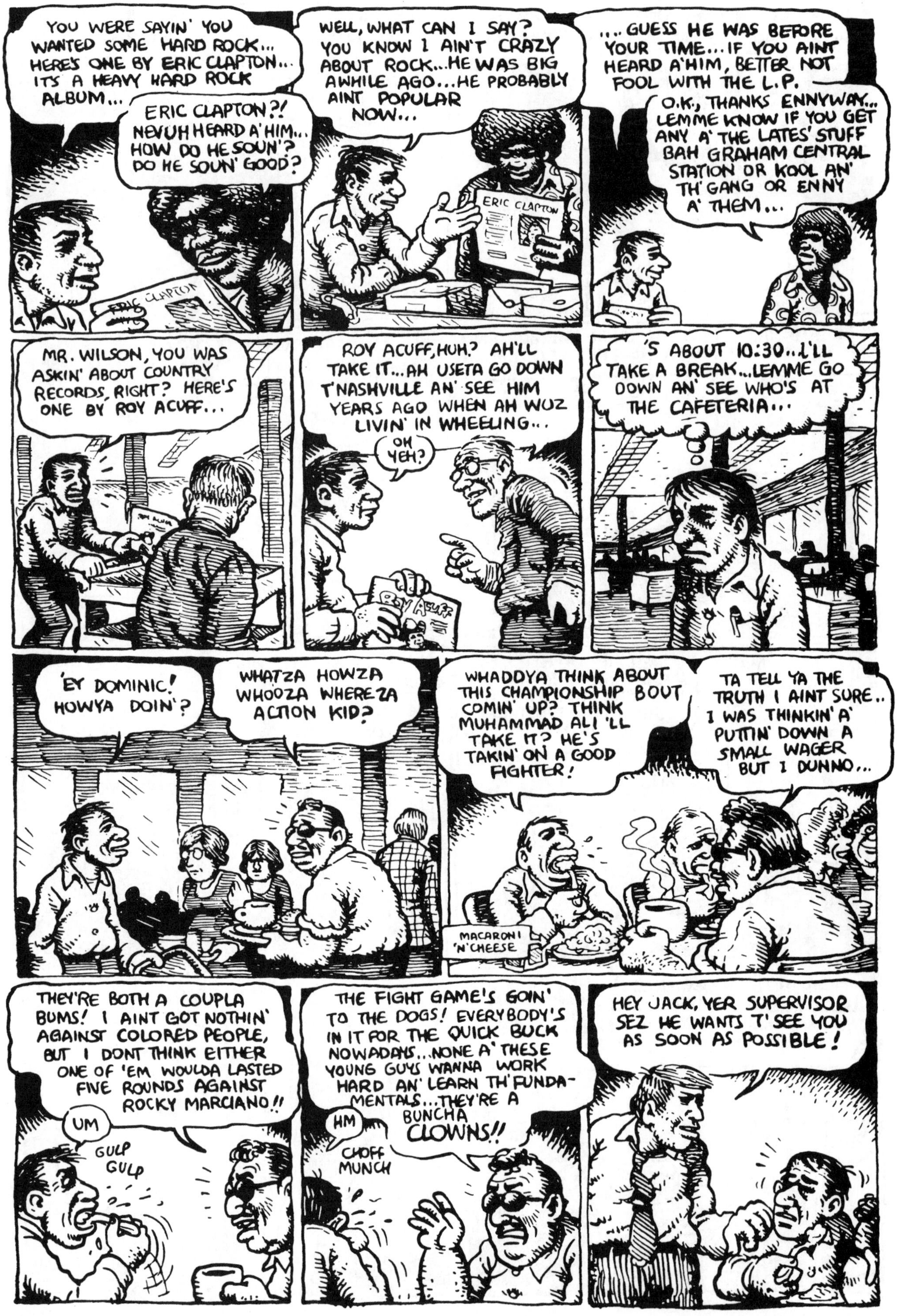
YOU WERE SAYIN' YOU WANTED SOME HARD ROCK... HERE'S ONE BY ERIC CLAPTON... ITS A HEAVY HARD ROCK ALBUM...
ERIC CLAPTON?! NEVUH HEARD A'HIM... HOW DO HE SOUN'? DO HE SOUN' GOOD?
ERIC CLAPTON
WELL, WHAT CAN I SAY? YOU KNOW I AIN'T CRAZY ABOUT ROCK...HE WAS BIG AWHILE AGO...HE PROBABLY AINT POPULAR NOW...
ERIC CLAPTON
...GUESS HE WAS BEFORE YOUR TIME...IF YOU AINT HEARD A'HIM, BETTER NOT FOOL WITH THE L.P.
O.K., THANKS ENNYWAY... LEMME KNOW IF YOU GET ANY A' THE LATES' STUFF BAH GRAHAM CENTRAL STATION OR KOOL AN' TH' GANG OR ENNY A' THEM...
MR. WILSON, YOU WAS ASKIN' ABOUT COUNTRY RECORDS, RIGHT? HERE'S ONE BY ROY ACUFF...
ROY ACUFF, HUH? AH'LL TAKE IT...AH USETA GO DOWN T'NASHVILLE AN' SEE HIM YEARS AGO WHEN AH WUZ LIVIN' IN WHEELING...
OH YEH?
ROY ACUFF
'S ABOUT 10:30..I'LL TAKE A BREAK...LEMME GO DOWN AN' SEE WHO'S AT THE CAFETERIA...
'EY DOMINIC! HOWYA DOIN'?
WHATZA HOWZA WHOOZA WHEREZA ACTION KID?
WHADDYA THINK ABOUT THIS CHAMPIONSHIP BOUT COMIN' UP? THINK MUHAMMAD ALI 'LL TAKE IT? HE'S TAKIN' ON A GOOD FIGHTER!
TA TELL YA THE TRUTH I AINT SURE.. I WAS THINKIN' A' PUTTIN' DOWN A SMALL WAGER BUT I DUNNO...
MACARONI 'N' CHEESE
THEY'RE BOTH A COUPLA BUMS! I AINT GOT NOTHIN' AGAINST COLORED PEOPLE, BUT I DONT THINK EITHER ONE OF 'EM WOULDA LASTED FIVE ROUNDS AGAINST ROCKY MARCIANO!!
UM
GULP GULP
THE FIGHT GAME'S GOIN' TO THE DOGS! EVERYBODY'S IN IT FOR THE QUICK BUCK NOWADAYS...NONE A' THESE YOUNG GUYS WANNA WORK HARD AN' LEARN TH' FUNDAMENTALS...THEY'RE A BUNCHA CLOWNS!!
HM
CHOFF MUNCH
HEY JACK, YER SUPERVISOR SEZ HE WANTS T' SEE YOU AS SOON AS POSSIBLE!

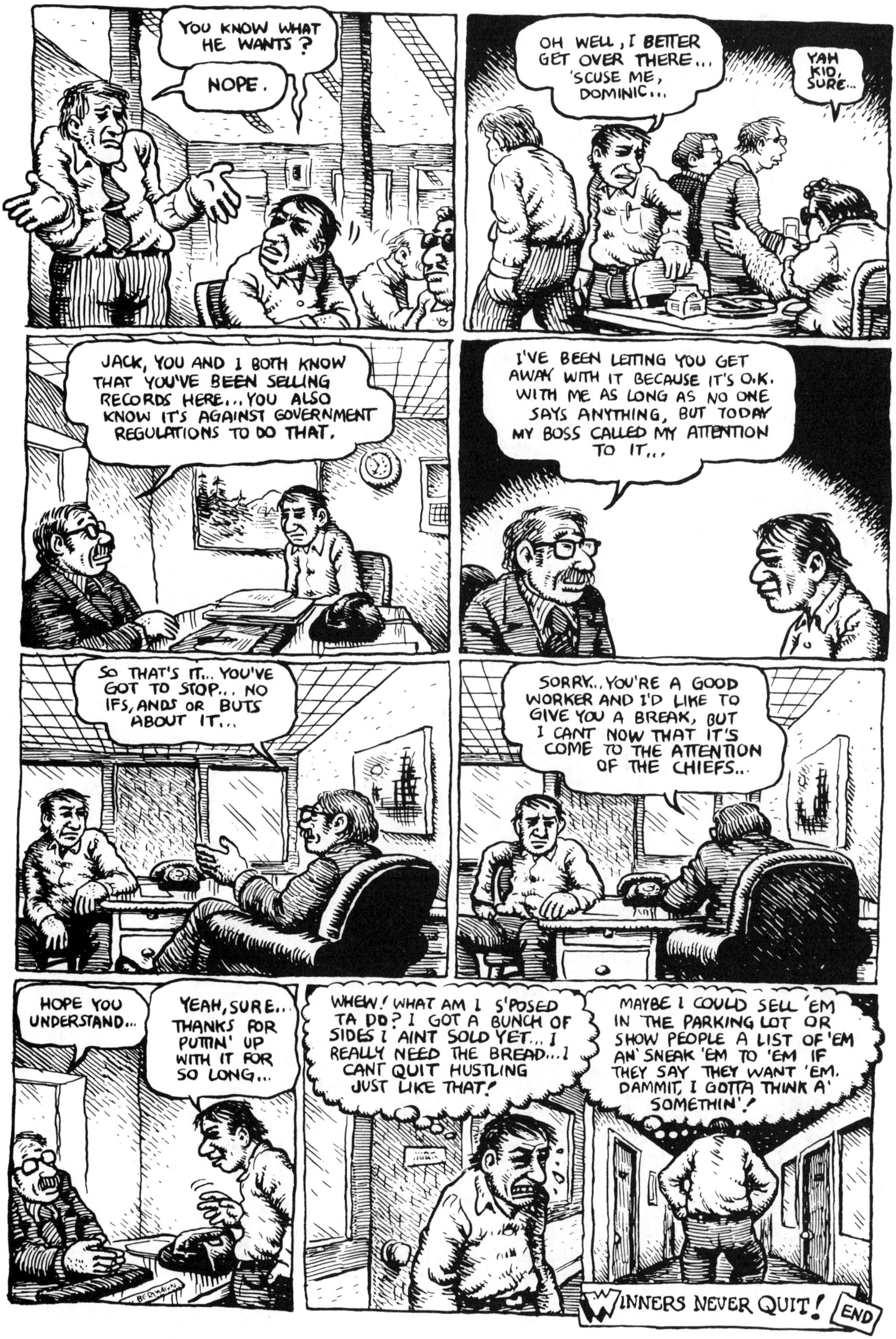
YOU KNOW WHAT HE WANTS?
NOPE.
OH WELL, I BETTER GET OVER THERE... 'SCUSE ME, DOMINIC...
YAH KID, SURE...
JACK, YOU AND I BOTH KNOW THAT YOU'VE BEEN SELLING RECORDS HERE... YOU ALSO KNOW IT'S AGAINST GOVERNMENT REGULATIONS TO DO THAT.
I'VE BEEN LETTING YOU GET AWAY WITH IT BECAUSE IT'S O.K. WITH ME AS LONG AS NO ONE SAYS ANYTHING, BUT TODAY MY BOSS CALLED MY ATTENTION TO IT...
SO THAT'S IT... YOU'VE GOT TO STOP... NO IFS, ANDS OR BUTS ABOUT IT...
SORRY... YOU'RE A GOOD WORKER AND I'D LIKE TO GIVE YOU A BREAK, BUT I CANT NOW THAT IT'S COME TO THE ATTENTION OF THE CHIEFS..
HOPE YOU UNDERSTAND...
YEAH, SURE.. THANKS FOR PUTTIN' UP WITH IT FOR SO LONG...
BERGMAN
WHEW! WHAT AM I S'POSED TA DO? I GOT A BUNCH OF SIDES I AINT SOLD YET... I REALLY NEED THE BREAD... I CANT QUIT HUSTLING JUST LIKE THAT!
MAYBE I COULD SELL 'EM IN THE PARKING LOT OR SHOW PEOPLE A LIST OF 'EM AN' SNEAK 'EM TO 'EM IF THEY SAY THEY WANT 'EM. DAMMIT, I GOTTA THINK A' SOMETHIN'!
WINNERS NEVER QUIT!
END

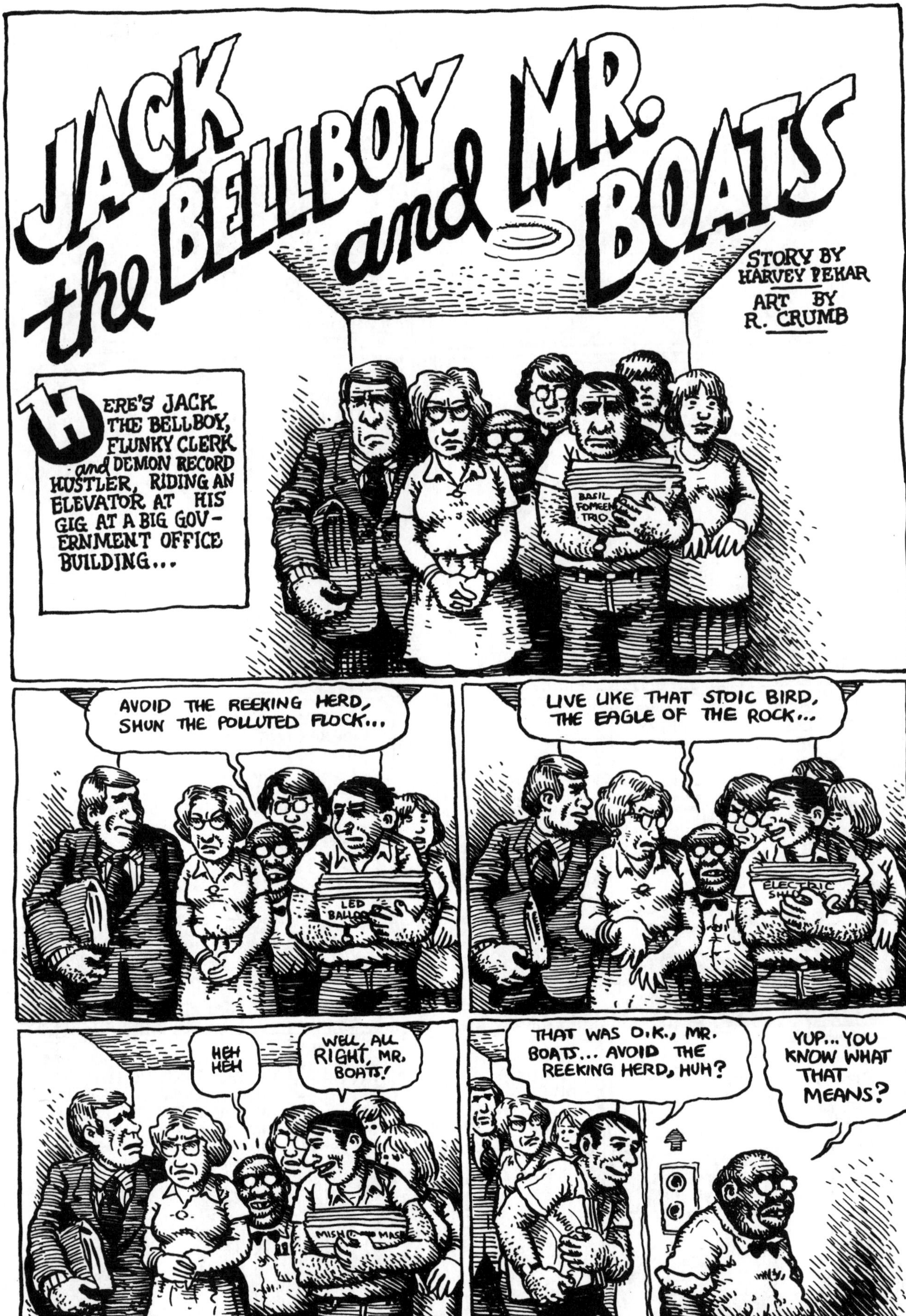
JACK the BELLBOY and MR. BOATS
STORY BY HARVEY PEKAR
ART BY R. CRUMB
HERE'S JACK THE BELLBOY, FLUNKY CLERK and DEMON RECORD HUSTLER, RIDING AN ELEVATOR AT HIS GIG AT A BIG GOVERNMENT OFFICE BUILDING...
BASIL FOMEEN TRIO
AVOID THE REEKING HERD, SHUN THE POLLUTED FLOCK...
LIVE LIKE THAT STOIC BIRD, THE EAGLE OF THE ROCK...
HEH HEH
WELL ALL RIGHT, MR. BOATS!
THAT WAS O.K., MR. BOATS... AVOID THE REEKING HERD, HUH?
YUP... YOU KNOW WHAT THAT MEANS?

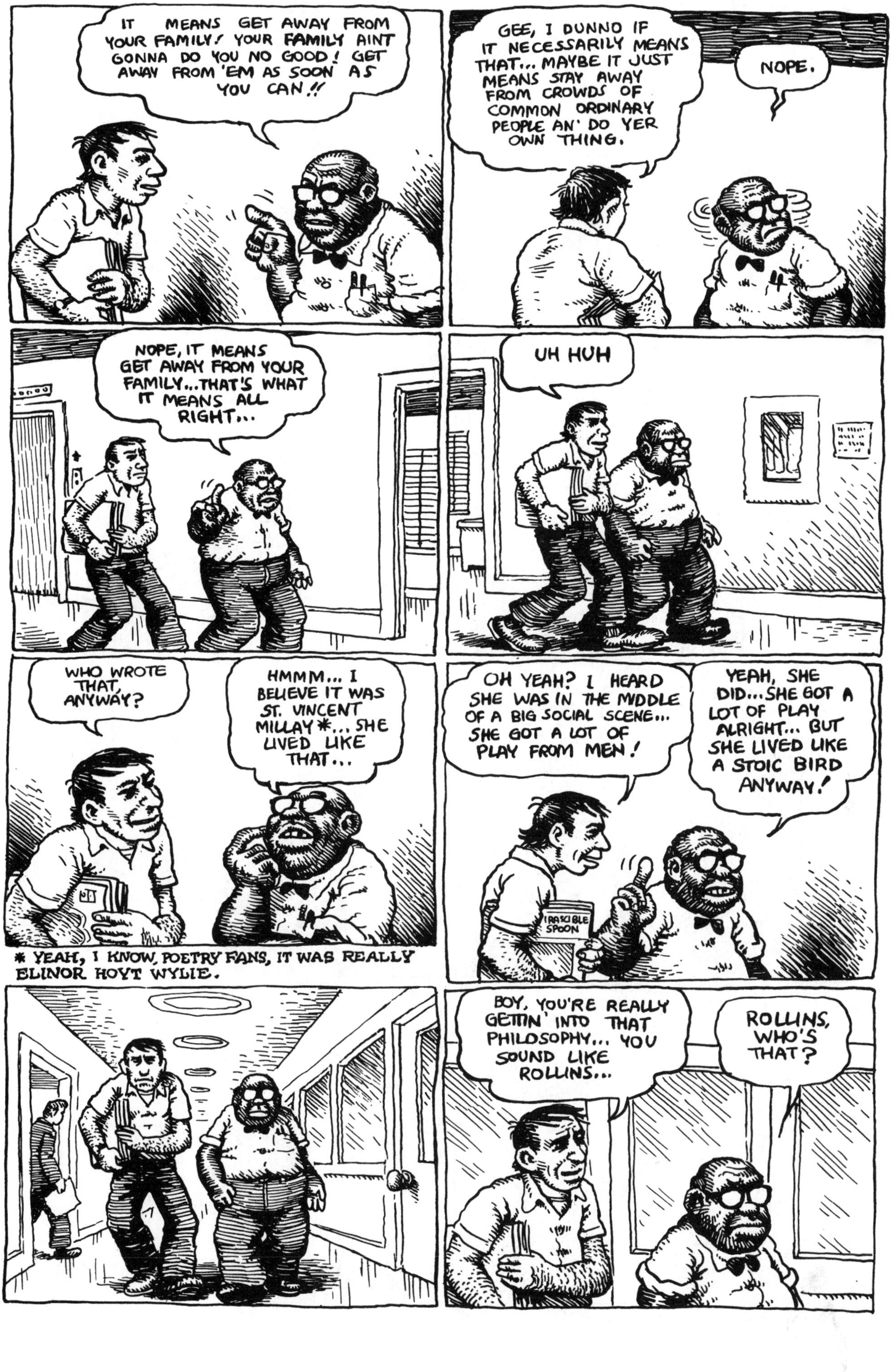
IT MEANS GET AWAY FROM YOUR FAMILY! YOUR FAMILY AINT GONNA DO YOU NO GOOD! GET AWAY FROM 'EM AS SOON AS YOU CAN!!
GEE, I DUNNO IF IT NECESSARILY MEANS THAT... MAYBE IT JUST MEANS STAY AWAY FROM CROWDS OF COMMON ORDINARY PEOPLE AN' DO YER OWN THING.
NOPE.
NOPE, IT MEANS GET AWAY FROM YOUR FAMILY... THAT'S WHAT IT MEANS ALL RIGHT...
UH HUH
WHO WROTE THAT, ANYWAY?
HMMM... I BELIEVE IT WAS ST. VINCENT MILLAY*... SHE LIVED LIKE THAT...
* YEAH, I KNOW, POETRY FANS, IT WAS REALLY ELINOR HOYT WYLIE.
OH YEAH? I HEARD SHE WAS IN THE MIDDLE OF A BIG SOCIAL SCENE... SHE GOT A LOT OF PLAY FROM MEN!
YEAH, SHE DID... SHE GOT A LOT OF PLAY ALRIGHT... BUT SHE LIVED LIKE A STOIC BIRD ANYWAY!
IRASCIBLE SPOON
BOY, YOU'RE REALLY GETTIN' INTO THAT PHILOSOPHY... YOU SOUND LIKE ROLLINS...
ROLLINS, WHO'S THAT?

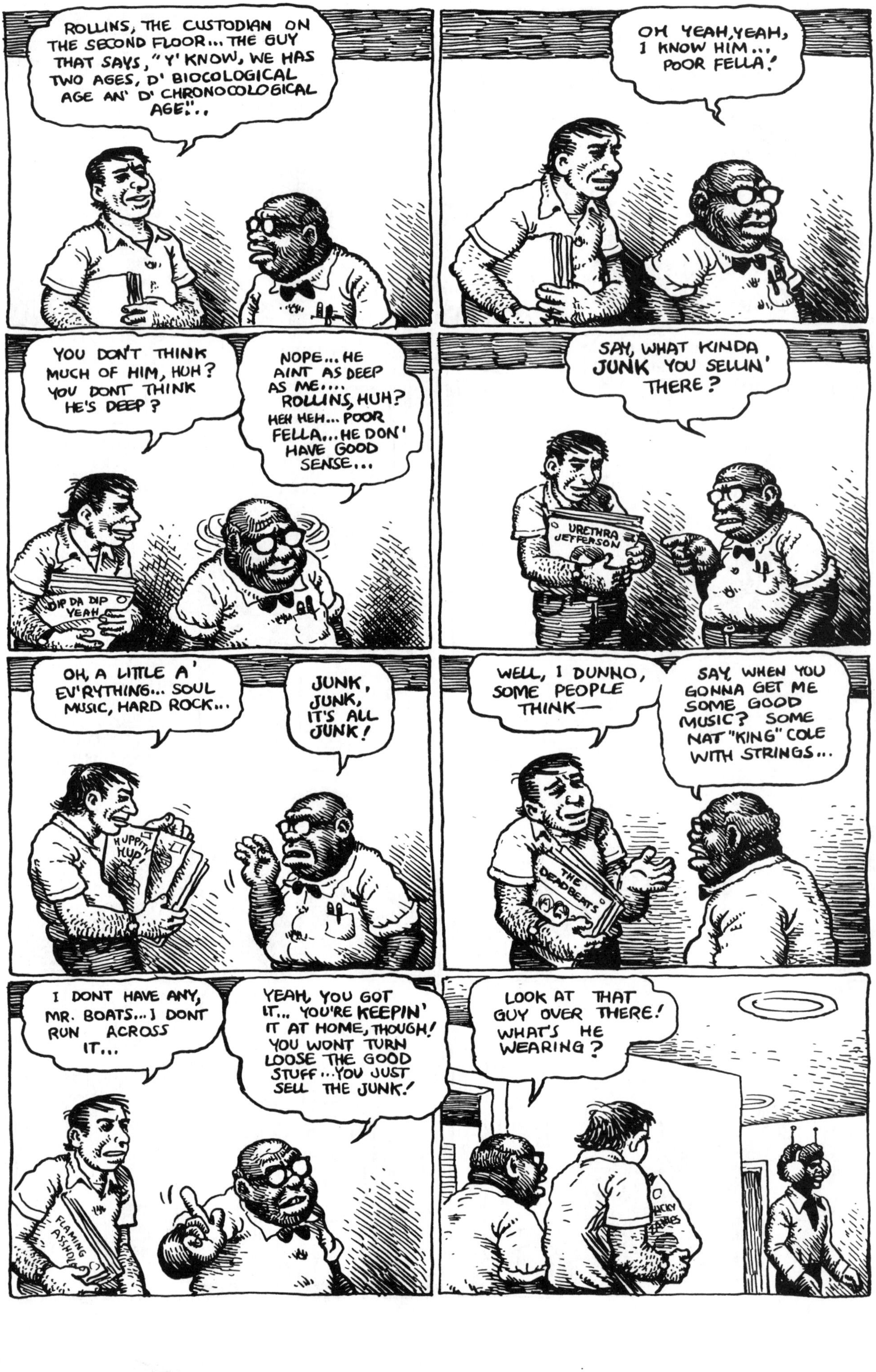
ROLLINS, THE CUSTODIAN ON THE SECOND FLOOR... THE GUY THAT SAYS, "Y' KNOW, WE HAS TWO AGES, D' BIOCOLOGICAL AGE AN' D' CHRONOCOLOGICAL AGE!"..
OH YEAH, YEAH, I KNOW HIM... POOR FELLA!
YOU DON'T THINK MUCH OF HIM, HUH? YOU DONT THINK HE'S DEEP?
NOPE... HE AINT AS DEEP AS ME.... ROLLINS, HUH? HEH HEH... POOR FELLA... HE DON' HAVE GOOD SENSE...
DIP DA DIP YEAH
SAY, WHAT KINDA JUNK YOU SELLIN' THERE?
URETHRA JEFFERSON
OH, A LITTLE A' EV'RYTHING... SOUL MUSIC, HARD ROCK...
JUNK, JUNK, IT'S ALL JUNK!
HUPPITY HUP!
WELL, I DUNNO, SOME PEOPLE THINK—
SAY, WHEN YOU GONNA GET ME SOME GOOD MUSIC? SOME NAT "KING" COLE WITH STRINGS...
THE DEADBEATS
I DONT HAVE ANY, MR. BOATS... I DONT RUN ACROSS IT...
YEAH, YOU GOT IT... YOU'RE KEEPIN' IT AT HOME, THOUGH! YOU WONT TURN LOOSE THE GOOD STUFF... YOU JUST SELL THE JUNK!
FLAMING
LOOK AT THAT GUY OVER THERE! WHAT'S HE WEARING?

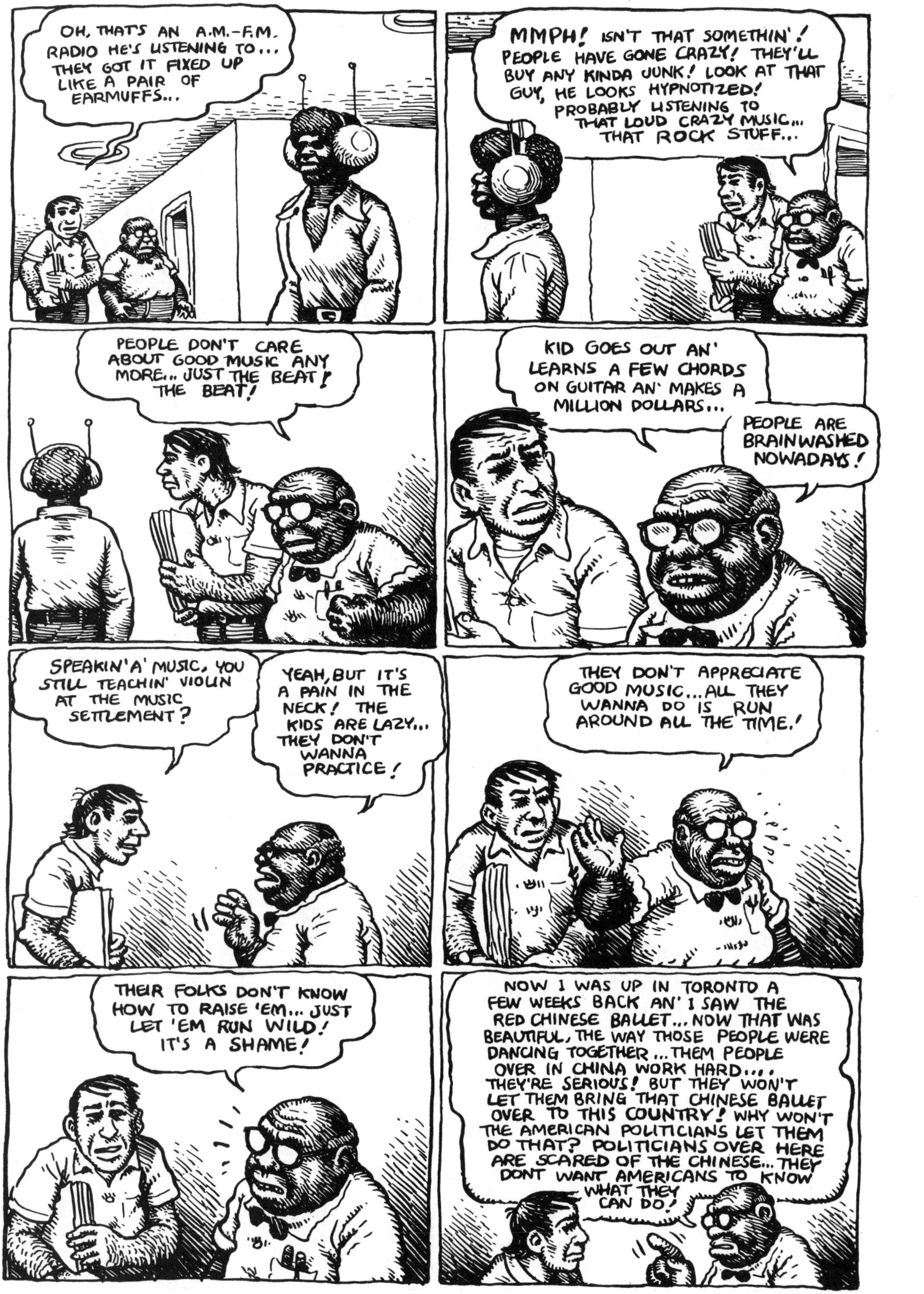
OH, THAT'S AN A.M.-F.M. RADIO HE'S LISTENING TO... THEY GOT IT FIXED UP LIKE A PAIR OF EARMUFFS...
MMPH! ISN'T THAT SOMETHIN'! PEOPLE HAVE GONE CRAZY! THEY'LL BUY ANY KINDA JUNK! LOOK AT THAT GUY, HE LOOKS HYPNOTIZED! PROBABLY LISTENING TO THAT LOUD CRAZY MUSIC... THAT ROCK STUFF...
PEOPLE DON'T CARE ABOUT GOOD MUSIC ANY MORE.. JUST THE BEAT! THE BEAT!
KID GOES OUT AN' LEARNS A FEW CHORDS ON GUITAR AN' MAKES A MILLION DOLLARS...
PEOPLE ARE BRAINWASHED NOWADAYS!
SPEAKIN' A' MUSIC, YOU STILL TEACHIN' VIOLIN AT THE MUSIC SETTLEMENT?
YEAH, BUT IT'S A PAIN IN THE NECK! THE KIDS ARE LAZY... THEY DON'T WANNA PRACTICE!
THEY DON'T APPRECIATE GOOD MUSIC... ALL THEY WANNA DO IS RUN AROUND ALL THE TIME.!
THEIR FOLKS DON'T KNOW HOW TO RAISE 'EM... JUST LET 'EM RUN WILD! IT'S A SHAME!
NOW I WAS UP IN TORONTO A FEW WEEKS BACK AN' I SAW THE RED CHINESE BALLET... NOW THAT WAS BEAUTIFUL, THE WAY THOSE PEOPLE WERE DANCING TOGETHER... THEM PEOPLE OVER IN CHINA WORK HARD.... THEY'RE SERIOUS! BUT THEY WON'T LET THEM BRING THAT CHINESE BALLET OVER TO THIS COUNTRY! WHY WON'T THE AMERICAN POLITICIANS LET THEM DO THAT? POLITICIANS OVER HERE ARE SCARED OF THE CHINESE... THEY DONT WANT AMERICANS TO KNOW WHAT THEY CAN DO!

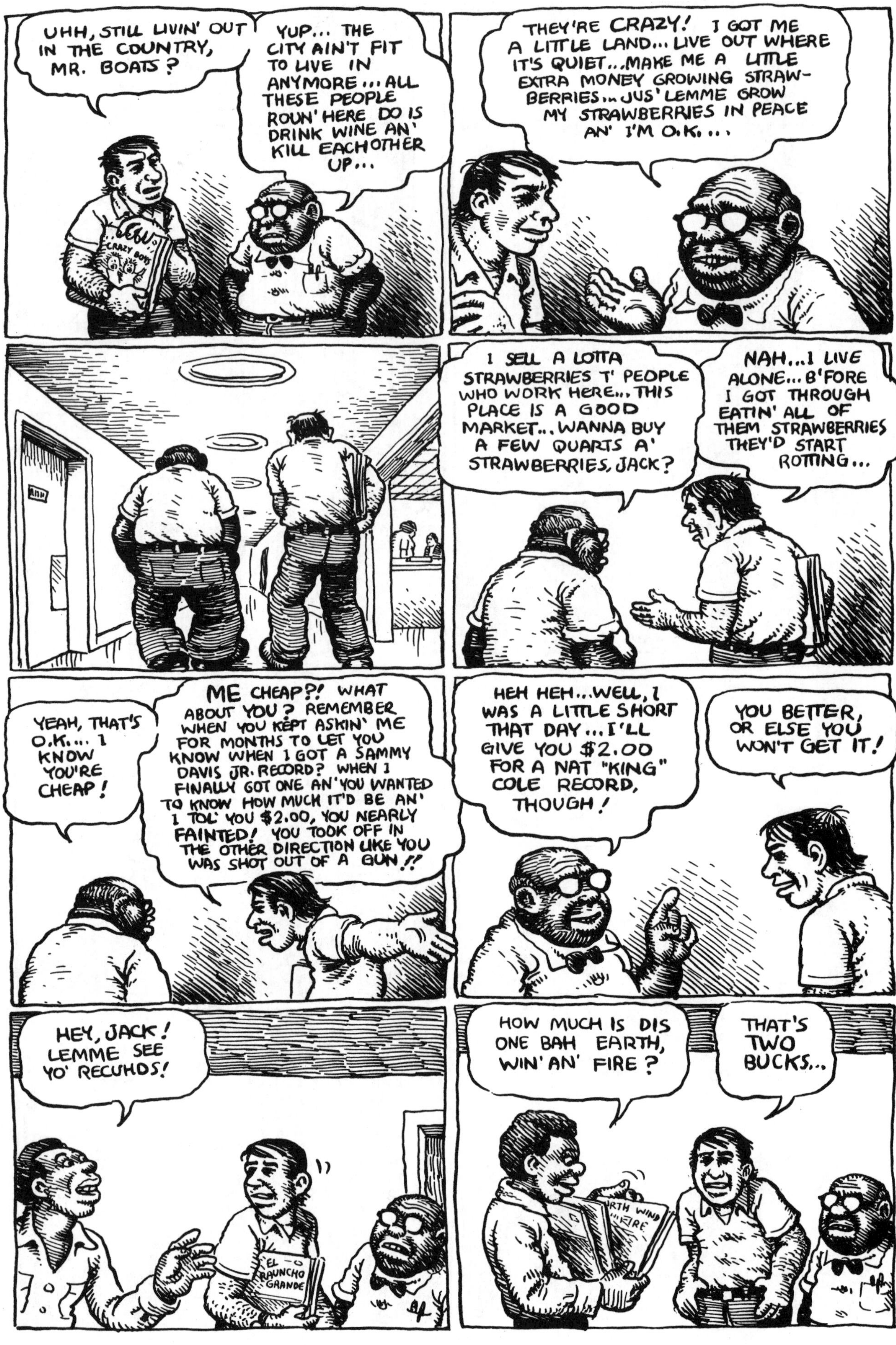
UHH, STILL LIVIN' OUT IN THE COUNTRY, MR. BOATS?
YUP... THE CITY AIN'T FIT TO LIVE IN ANYMORE... ALL THESE PEOPLE ROUN' HERE DO IS DRINK WINE AN' KILL EACHOTHER UP...
CRAZY BOYS
THEY'RE CRAZY! I GOT ME A LITTLE LAND... LIVE OUT WHERE IT'S QUIET... MAKE ME A LITTLE EXTRA MONEY GROWING STRAW-BERRIES... JUS' LEMME GROW MY STRAWBERRIES IN PEACE AN' I'M O.K....
I SELL A LOTTA STRAWBERRIES T' PEOPLE WHO WORK HERE... THIS PLACE IS A GOOD MARKET... WANNA BUY A FEW QUARTS A' STRAWBERRIES, JACK?
NAH... I LIVE ALONE... B'FORE I GOT THROUGH EATIN' ALL OF THEM STRAWBERRIES THEY'D START ROTTING...
YEAH, THAT'S O.K.... I KNOW YOU'RE CHEAP!
ME CHEAP?! WHAT ABOUT YOU? REMEMBER WHEN YOU KEPT ASKIN' ME FOR MONTHS TO LET YOU KNOW WHEN I GOT A SAMMY DAVIS JR. RECORD? WHEN I FINALLY GOT ONE AN' YOU WANTED TO KNOW HOW MUCH IT'D BE AN' I TOL' YOU $2.00, YOU NEARLY FAINTED! YOU TOOK OFF IN THE OTHER DIRECTION LIKE YOU WAS SHOT OUT OF A GUN!!
HEH HEH... WELL, I WAS A LITTLE SHORT THAT DAY... I'LL GIVE YOU $2.00 FOR A NAT "KING" COLE RECORD, THOUGH!
YOU BETTER, OR ELSE YOU WON'T GET IT!
HEY, JACK! LEMME SEE YO' RECUHDS!
EL RAUNCHO GRANDE
HOW MUCH IS DIS ONE BAH EARTH, WIN' AN' FIRE?
THAT'S TWO BUCKS...

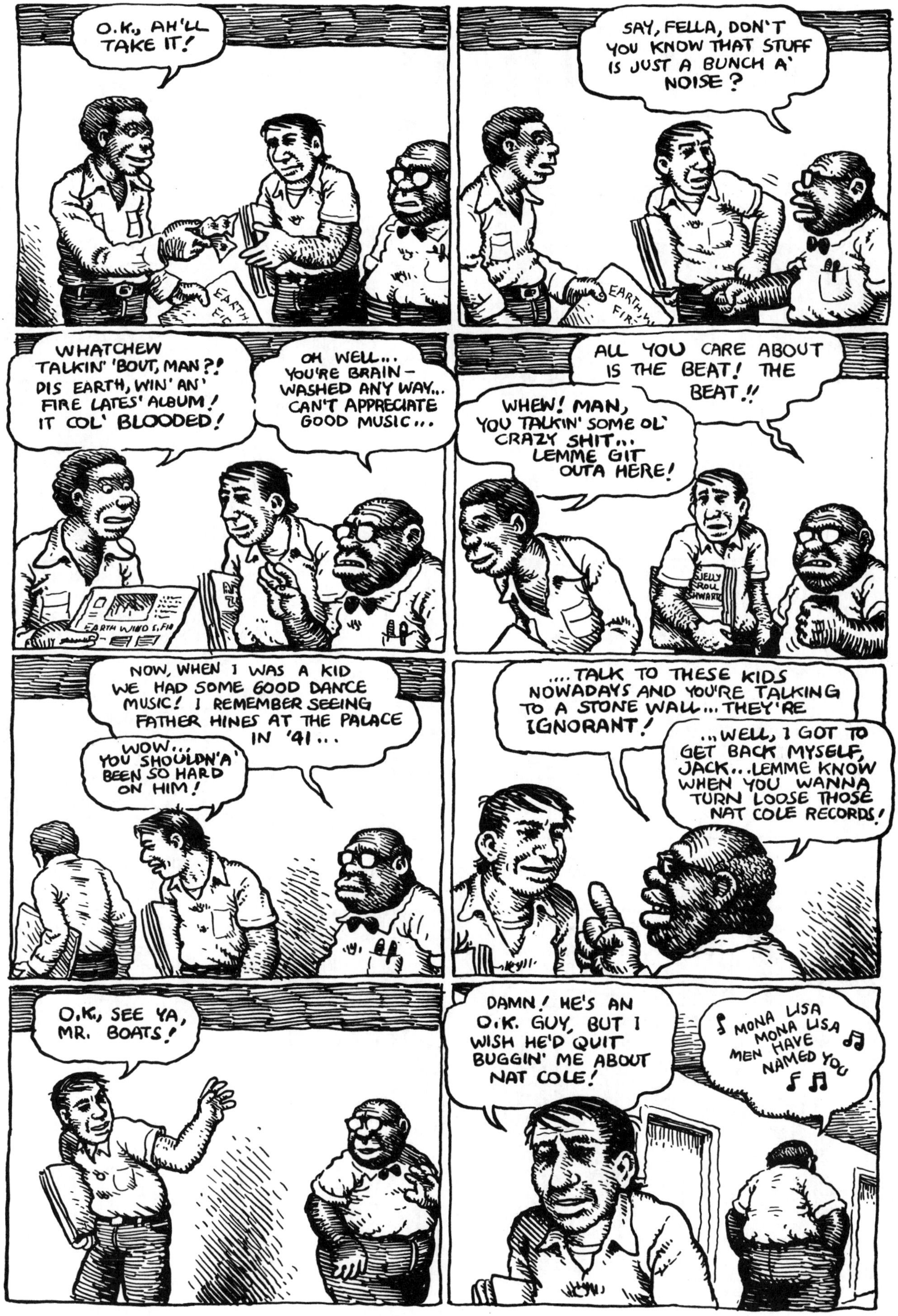
O.K., AH'LL TAKE IT!
EARTH FI
SAY, FELLA, DON'T YOU KNOW THAT STUFF IS JUST A BUNCH A' NOISE?
EARTH W FIR
WHATCHEW TALKIN' 'BOUT, MAN?! DIS EARTH, WIN' AN' FIRE LATES' ALBUM! IT COL' BLOODED!
OH WELL... YOU'RE BRAIN-WASHED ANY WAY... CAN'T APPRECIATE GOOD MUSIC...
EARTH WIND & FIR
ALL YOU CARE ABOUT IS THE BEAT! THE BEAT!!
WHEW! MAN, YOU TALKIN' SOME OL' CRAZY SHIT... LEMME GIT OUTA HERE!
JELLY ROLL SCHWARTZ
NOW, WHEN I WAS A KID WE HAD SOME GOOD DANCE MUSIC! I REMEMBER SEEING FATHER HINES AT THE PALACE IN '41...
WOW... YOU SHOULDN'A' BEEN SO HARD ON HIM!
....TALK TO THESE KIDS NOWADAYS AND YOU'RE TALKING TO A STONE WALL... THEY'RE IGNORANT!
...WELL, I GOT TO GET BACK MYSELF, JACK... LEMME KNOW WHEN YOU WANNA TURN LOOSE THOSE NAT COLE RECORDS!
O.K, SEE YA, MR. BOATS!
DAMN! HE'S AN O.K. GUY, BUT I WISH HE'D QUIT BUGGIN' ME ABOUT NAT COLE!
♪ MONA LISA MONA LISA ♫ MEN HAVE NAMED YOU ♪ ♫

READ THIS

STORY BY HARVEY PEKAR
ART BY GREG BUDGETT & GARY DUMM

BACK ABOUT FIFTEEN YEARS AGO WHEN I WAS REALLY INTA COLLECTIN' JAZZ RECORDS REAL HEAVY, THIS FRIEND A' MINE PUT ME ONTO A GUY I COULD BUY L.P.'S OFFA CHEAP.

HOW MUCH DO THEY COST?

HE CHARGES $2.00 APIECE.

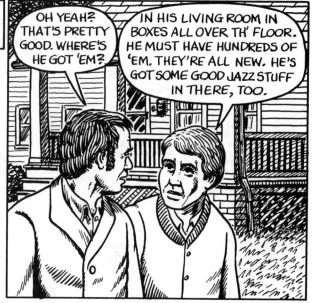

OH YEAH? THAT'S PRETTY GOOD. WHERE'S HE GOT 'EM?

IN HIS LIVING ROOM IN BOXES ALL OVER TH' FLOOR. HE MUST HAVE HUNDREDS OF 'EM. THEY'RE ALL NEW. HE'S GOT SOME GOOD JAZZ STUFF IN THERE, TOO.

WHATSA DEAL WITH THIS GUY, ANYWAY? HOW'S HE GET 'EM SO CHEAP? HOW DO YOU KNOW 'IM?

26

HE RUNS AN AFTER HOURS JOINT OUT OF HIS HOUSE. HE'S A COLLECTOR TOO. I DON'T ASK 'IM WHERE HE GETS HIS SIDES, THEY'RE PROB'LY HOT.

SO I CHECK TH' GUY OUT. HE DOES HAVE SOME GOOD STUFF, 'AN OVER THE NEXT FEW MONTHS I GET A LOTTA RECORDS OFFA HIM.

O.K. I GOT FOURTEEN SIDES HERE. THAT'S TWENNY-EIGHT BUCKS, RIGHT?

AFTER AWHILE I GET TO TRADIN' RECORDS WITH HIM AS WELL AS BUYIN' 'EM, AN' IN THE PROCESS I GOT TO KNOW 'IM

© 1981 BY HARVEY PEKAR

1.

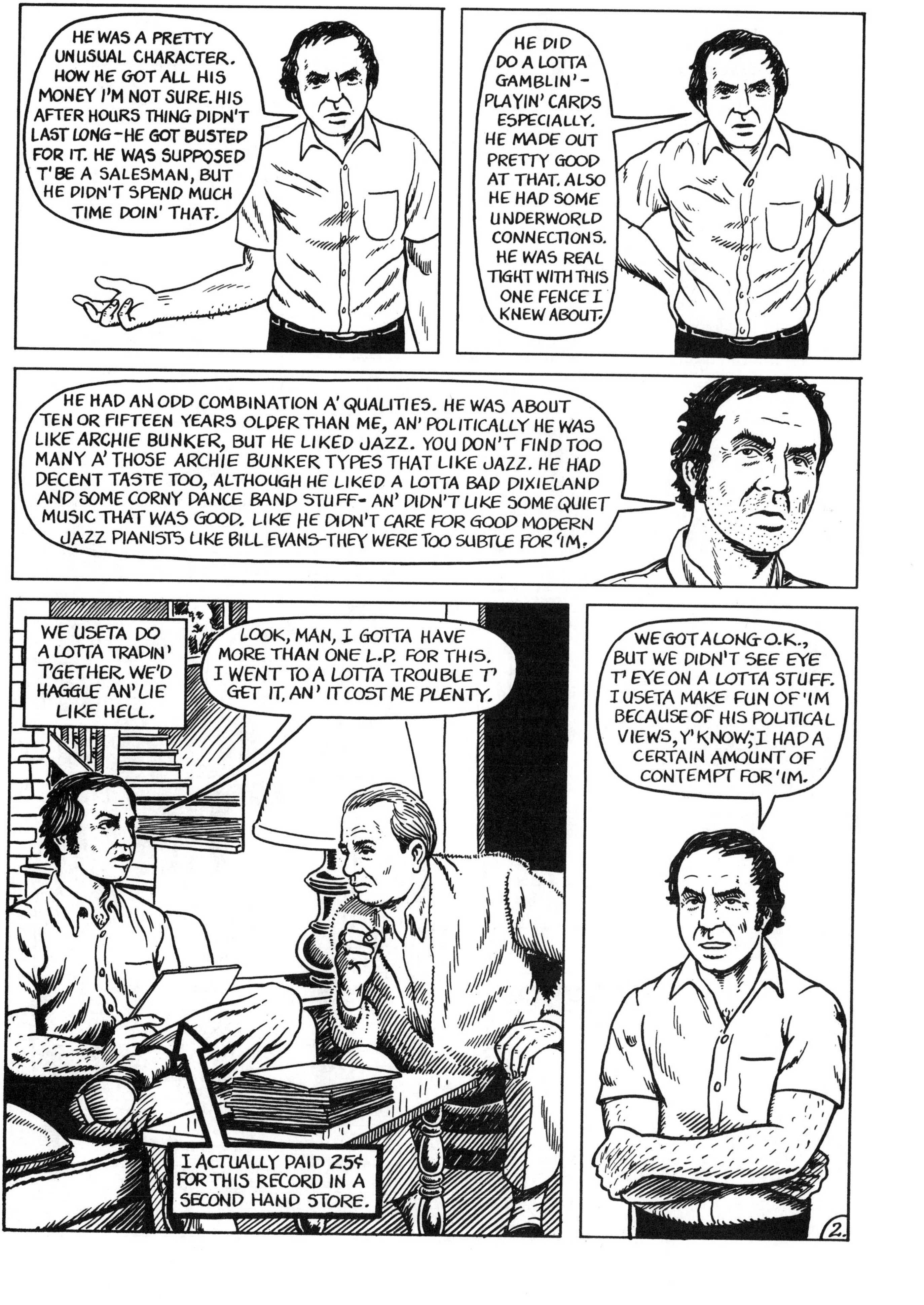

HE WAS A PRETTY UNUSUAL CHARACTER. HOW HE GOT ALL HIS MONEY I'M NOT SURE. HIS AFTER HOURS THING DIDN'T LAST LONG - HE GOT BUSTED FOR IT. HE WAS SUPPOSED T'BE A SALESMAN, BUT HE DIDN'T SPEND MUCH TIME DOIN' THAT.
HE DID DO A LOTTA GAMBLIN' - PLAYIN' CARDS ESPECIALLY. HE MADE OUT PRETTY GOOD AT THAT. ALSO HE HAD SOME UNDERWORLD CONNECTIONS. HE WAS REAL TIGHT WITH THIS ONE FENCE I KNEW ABOUT.
HE HAD AN ODD COMBINATION A' QUALITIES. HE WAS ABOUT TEN OR FIFTEEN YEARS OLDER THAN ME, AN' POLITICALLY HE WAS LIKE ARCHIE BUNKER, BUT HE LIKED JAZZ. YOU DON'T FIND TOO MANY A' THOSE ARCHIE BUNKER TYPES THAT LIKE JAZZ. HE HAD DECENT TASTE TOO, ALTHOUGH HE LIKED A LOTTA BAD DIXIELAND AND SOME CORNY DANCE BAND STUFF - AN' DIDN'T LIKE SOME QUIET MUSIC THAT WAS GOOD. LIKE HE DIDN'T CARE FOR GOOD MODERN JAZZ PIANISTS LIKE BILL EVANS - THEY WERE TOO SUBTLE FOR 'IM.
WE USETA DO A LOTTA TRADIN' T'GETHER. WE'D HAGGLE AN' LIE LIKE HELL.
LOOK, MAN, I GOTTA HAVE MORE THAN ONE L.P. FOR THIS. I WENT TO A LOTTA TROUBLE T' GET IT, AN' IT COST ME PLENTY.
I ACTUALLY PAID 25¢ FOR THIS RECORD IN A SECOND HAND STORE.
WE GOT ALONG O.K., BUT WE DIDN'T SEE EYE T' EYE ON A LOTTA STUFF. I USETA MAKE FUN OF 'IM BECAUSE OF HIS POLITICAL VIEWS, Y'KNOW; I HAD A CERTAIN AMOUNT OF CONTEMPT FOR 'IM.

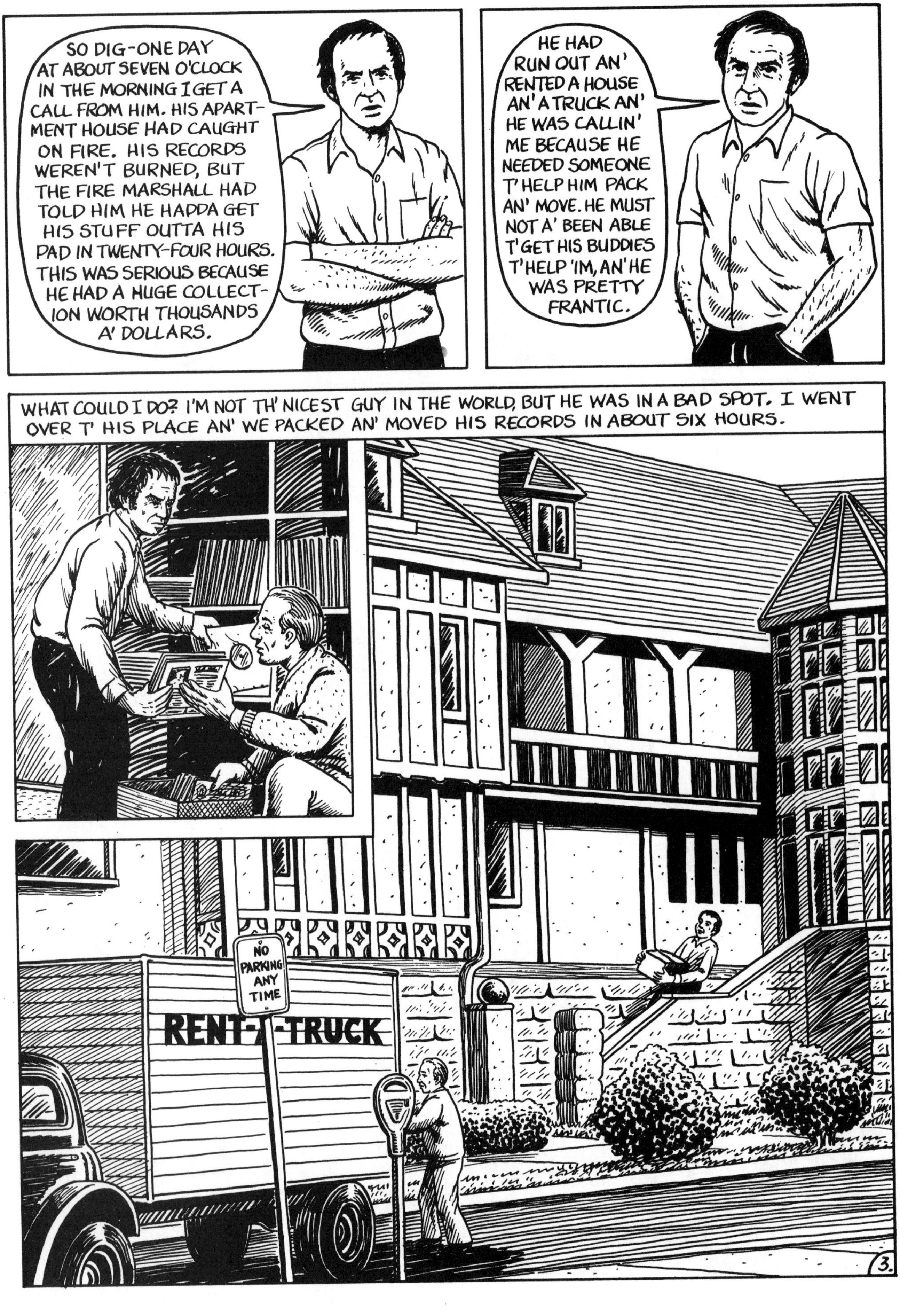
SO DIG-ONE DAY AT ABOUT SEVEN O'CLOCK IN THE MORNING I GET A CALL FROM HIM. HIS APARTMENT HOUSE HAD CAUGHT ON FIRE. HIS RECORDS WEREN'T BURNED, BUT THE FIRE MARSHALL HAD TOLD HIM HE HAPPA GET HIS STUFF OUTTA HIS PAD IN TWENTY-FOUR HOURS. THIS WAS SERIOUS BECAUSE HE HAD A HUGE COLLECTION WORTH THOUSANDS A' DOLLARS.
HE HAD RUN OUT AN' RENTED A HOUSE AN' A TRUCK AN' HE WAS CALLIN' ME BECAUSE HE NEEDED SOMEONE T' HELP HIM PACK AN' MOVE. HE MUST NOT A' BEEN ABLE T' GET HIS BUDDIES T' HELP 'IM, AN' HE WAS PRETTY FRANTIC.
WHAT COULD I DO? I'M NOT TH' NICEST GUY IN THE WORLD, BUT HE WAS IN A BAD SPOT. I WENT OVER T' HIS PLACE AN' WE PACKED AN' MOVED HIS RECORDS IN ABOUT SIX HOURS.
NO PARKING ANY TIME
RENT-A-TRUCK

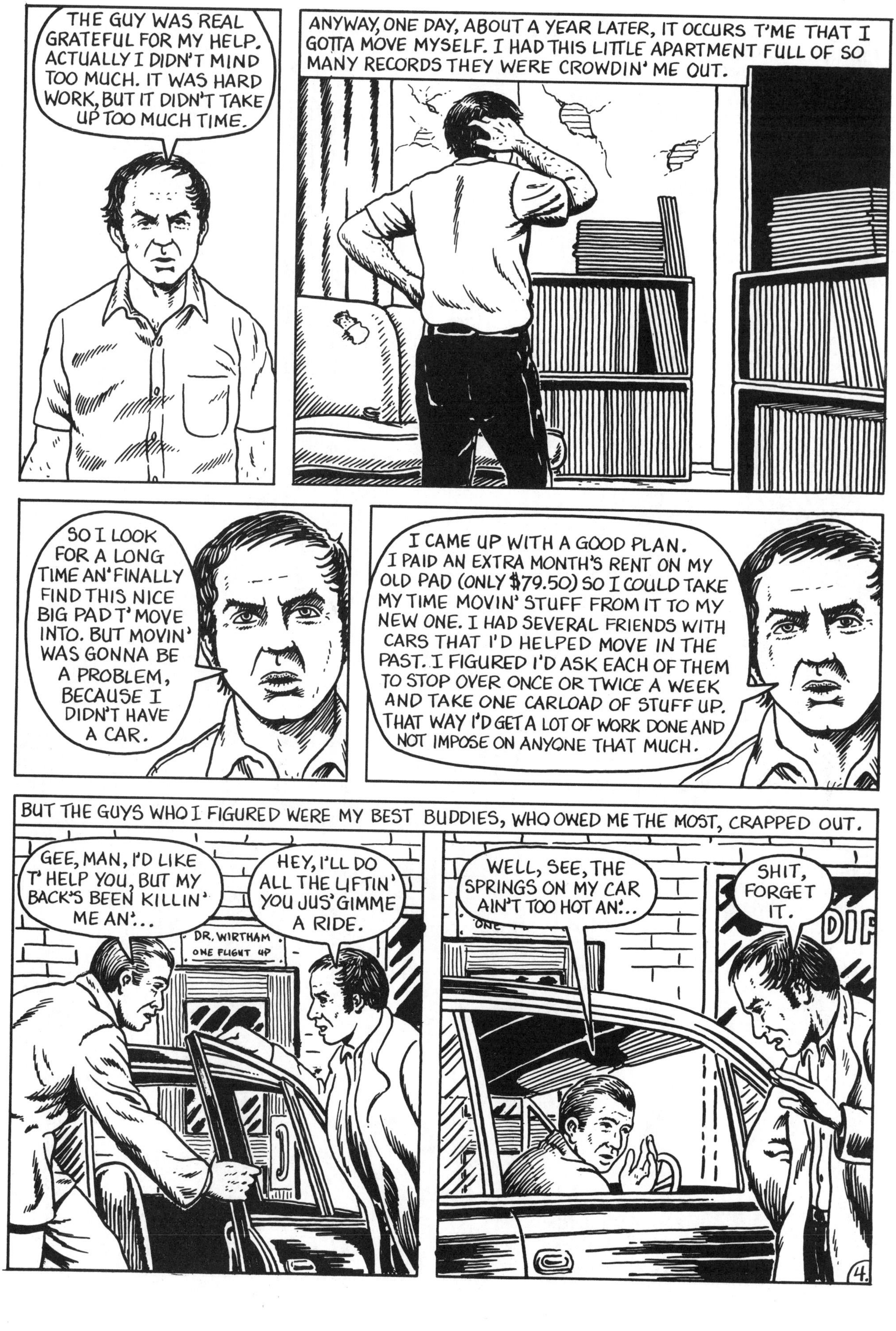
THE GUY WAS REAL GRATEFUL FOR MY HELP. ACTUALLY I DIDN'T MIND TOO MUCH. IT WAS HARD WORK, BUT IT DIDN'T TAKE UP TOO MUCH TIME.
ANYWAY, ONE DAY, ABOUT A YEAR LATER, IT OCCURS T'ME THAT I GOTTA MOVE MYSELF. I HAD THIS LITTLE APARTMENT FULL OF SO MANY RECORDS THEY WERE CROWDIN' ME OUT.
SO I LOOK FOR A LONG TIME AN' FINALLY FIND THIS NICE BIG PAD T' MOVE INTO. BUT MOVIN' WAS GONNA BE A PROBLEM, BECAUSE I DIDN'T HAVE A CAR.
I CAME UP WITH A GOOD PLAN. I PAID AN EXTRA MONTH'S RENT ON MY OLD PAD (ONLY $79.50) SO I COULD TAKE MY TIME MOVIN' STUFF FROM IT TO MY NEW ONE. I HAD SEVERAL FRIENDS WITH CARS THAT I'D HELPED MOVE IN THE PAST. I FIGURED I'D ASK EACH OF THEM TO STOP OVER ONCE OR TWICE A WEEK AND TAKE ONE CARLOAD OF STUFF UP. THAT WAY I'D GET A LOT OF WORK DONE AND NOT IMPOSE ON ANYONE THAT MUCH.
BUT THE GUYS WHO I FIGURED WERE MY BEST BUDDIES, WHO OWED ME THE MOST, CRAPPED OUT.
GEE, MAN, I'D LIKE T' HELP YOU, BUT MY BACK'S BEEN KILLIN' ME AN'...
HEY, I'LL DO ALL THE LIFTIN' YOU JUS' GIMME A RIDE.
DR. WIRTHAM
ONE FLIGHT UP
WELL, SEE, THE SPRINGS ON MY CAR AIN'T TOO HOT AN'...
SHIT, FORGET IT.

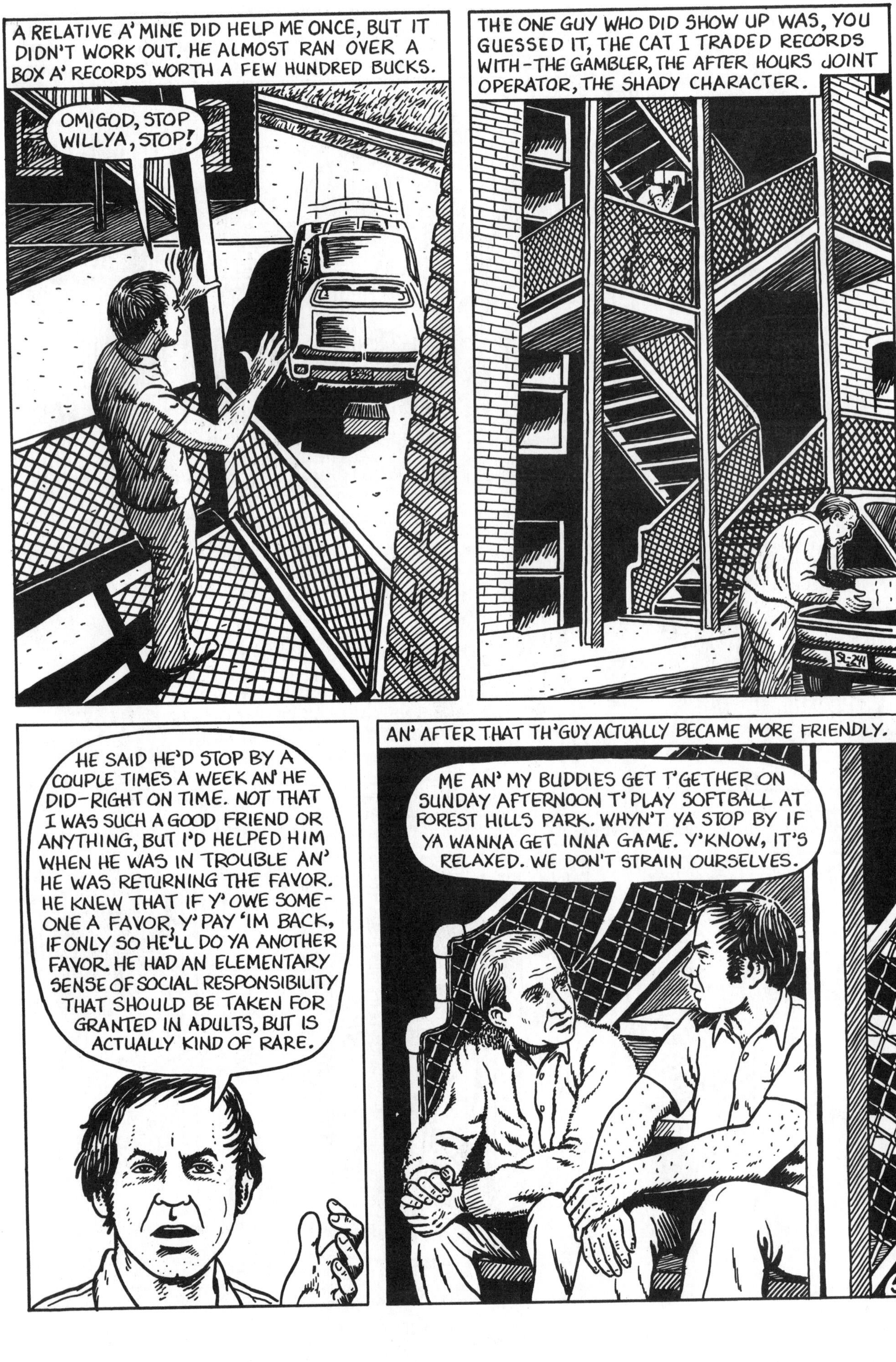

A RELATIVE A' MINE DID HELP ME ONCE, BUT IT DIDN'T WORK OUT. HE ALMOST RAN OVER A BOX A' RECORDS WORTH A FEW HUNDRED BUCKS.
OMIGOD, STOP WILLYA, STOP!
THE ONE GUY WHO DID SHOW UP WAS, YOU GUESSED IT, THE CAT I TRADED RECORDS WITH–THE GAMBLER, THE AFTER HOURS JOINT OPERATOR, THE SHADY CHARACTER.
HE SAID HE'D STOP BY A COUPLE TIMES A WEEK AN' HE DID–RIGHT ON TIME. NOT THAT I WAS SUCH A GOOD FRIEND OR ANYTHING, BUT I'D HELPED HIM WHEN HE WAS IN TROUBLE AN' HE WAS RETURNING THE FAVOR. HE KNEW THAT IF Y' OWE SOME-ONE A FAVOR, Y' PAY 'IM BACK, IF ONLY SO HE'LL DO YA ANOTHER FAVOR. HE HAD AN ELEMENTARY SENSE OF SOCIAL RESPONSIBILITY THAT SHOULD BE TAKEN FOR GRANTED IN ADULTS, BUT IS ACTUALLY KIND OF RARE.
AN' AFTER THAT TH' GUY ACTUALLY BECAME MORE FRIENDLY.
ME AN' MY BUDDIES GET T'GETHER ON SUNDAY AFTERNOON T' PLAY SOFTBALL AT FOREST HILLS PARK. WHYN'T YA STOP BY IF YA WANNA GET INNA GAME. Y'KNOW, IT'S RELAXED. WE DON'T STRAIN OURSELVES.

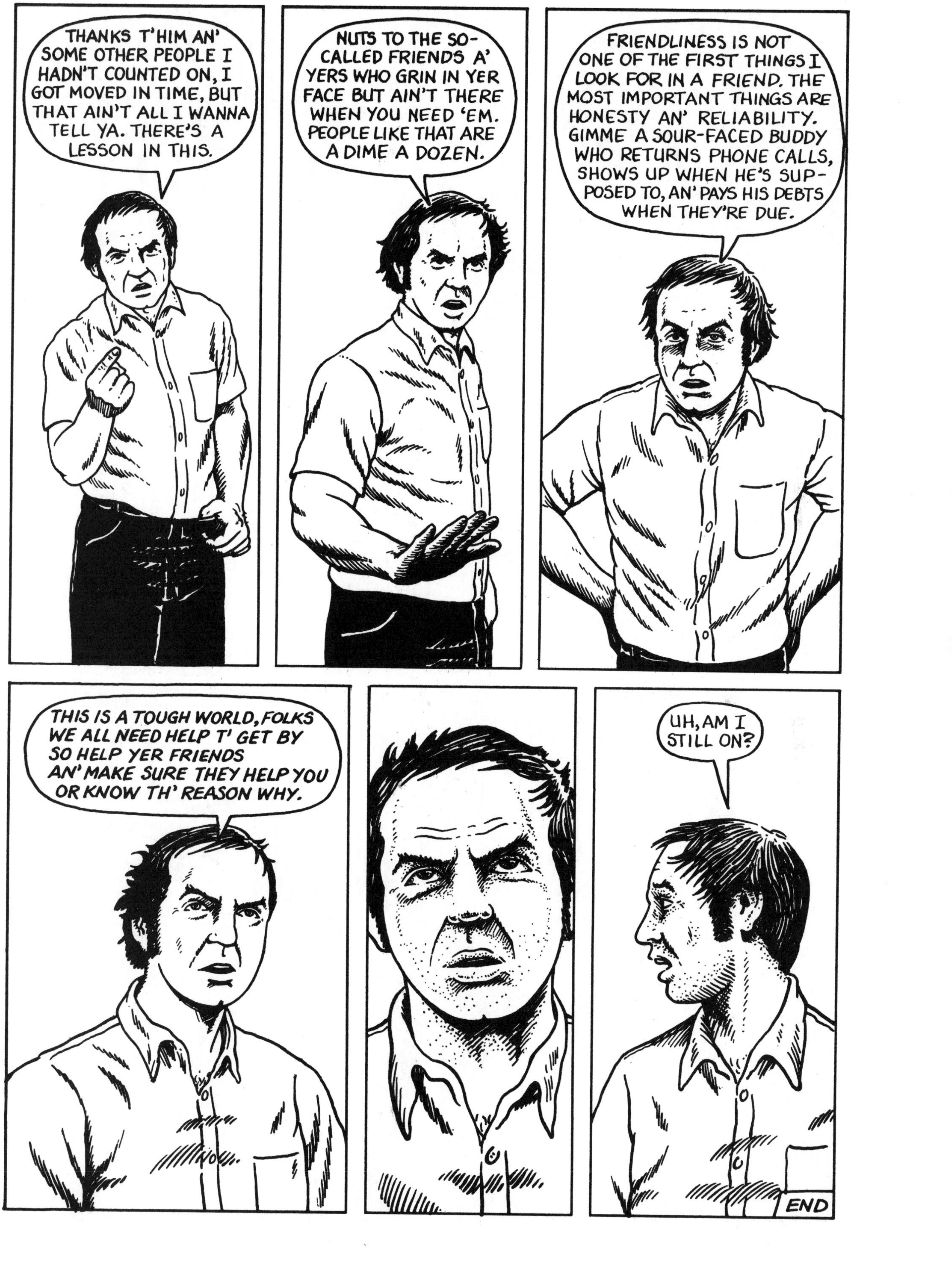
THANKS T'HIM AN' SOME OTHER PEOPLE I HADN'T COUNTED ON, I GOT MOVED IN TIME, BUT THAT AIN'T ALL I WANNA TELL YA. THERE'S A LESSON IN THIS.
NUTS TO THE SO-CALLED FRIENDS A' YERS WHO GRIN IN YER FACE BUT AIN'T THERE WHEN YOU NEED 'EM. PEOPLE LIKE THAT ARE A DIME A DOZEN.
FRIENDLINESS IS NOT ONE OF THE FIRST THINGS I LOOK FOR IN A FRIEND. THE MOST IMPORTANT THINGS ARE HONESTY AN' RELIABILITY. GIMME A SOUR-FACED BUDDY WHO RETURNS PHONE CALLS, SHOWS UP WHEN HE'S SUPPOSED TO, AN' PAYS HIS DEBTS WHEN THEY'RE DUE.
THIS IS A TOUGH WORLD, FOLKS WE ALL NEED HELP T' GET BY SO HELP YER FRIENDS AN' MAKE SURE THEY HELP YOU OR KNOW TH' REASON WHY.
UH, AM I STILL ON?
END

Standing Behind Old Jewish Ladies in Supermarket Lines

STORY BY HARVEY PEKAR   ART BY R. CRUMB

MAN, I REALLY HATE T'SHOP FOR GROCERIES... ESPECIALLY WHEN THE STORE IS CROWDED!

SOMETIMES Y' HAVE T' STAND IN THE CHECK-OUT LINE FOR SO LONG!

Y' HAVE T' WAIT AN ESPECIALLY LONG TIME IN MY NEIGHBORHOOD T' GET CHECKED OUT, BECAUSE SO MANY OLD JEWISH LADIES SHOP AT THE SUPERMARKET THERE...

MAN, THEY ARE REALLY PENNY-WISE! THEY WILL ARGUE FOREVER WITH A CASHIER ABOUT WHETHER SHE RUNG THE PRICES UP RIGHT, OR ABOUT COUPONS, OR ABOUT THE FOOD STAMP LAWS. GET BEHIND THEM IN A LINE AN' YER GONNA WAIT A LO-O-ONG TIME!

I'M A YID MYSELF, AN' THE WOMEN IN MY FAMILY ARE LIKE THAT... BUT I NEVER GOT USED TO IT... I MEAN, I'M KINDA CHEAP MYSELF, BUT I GOT LIMITS!

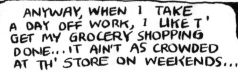

ANYWAY, WHEN I TAKE A DAY OFF WORK, I LIKE T' GET MY GROCERY SHOPPING DONE... IT AIN'T AS CROWDED AT TH' STORE ON WEEKENDS...

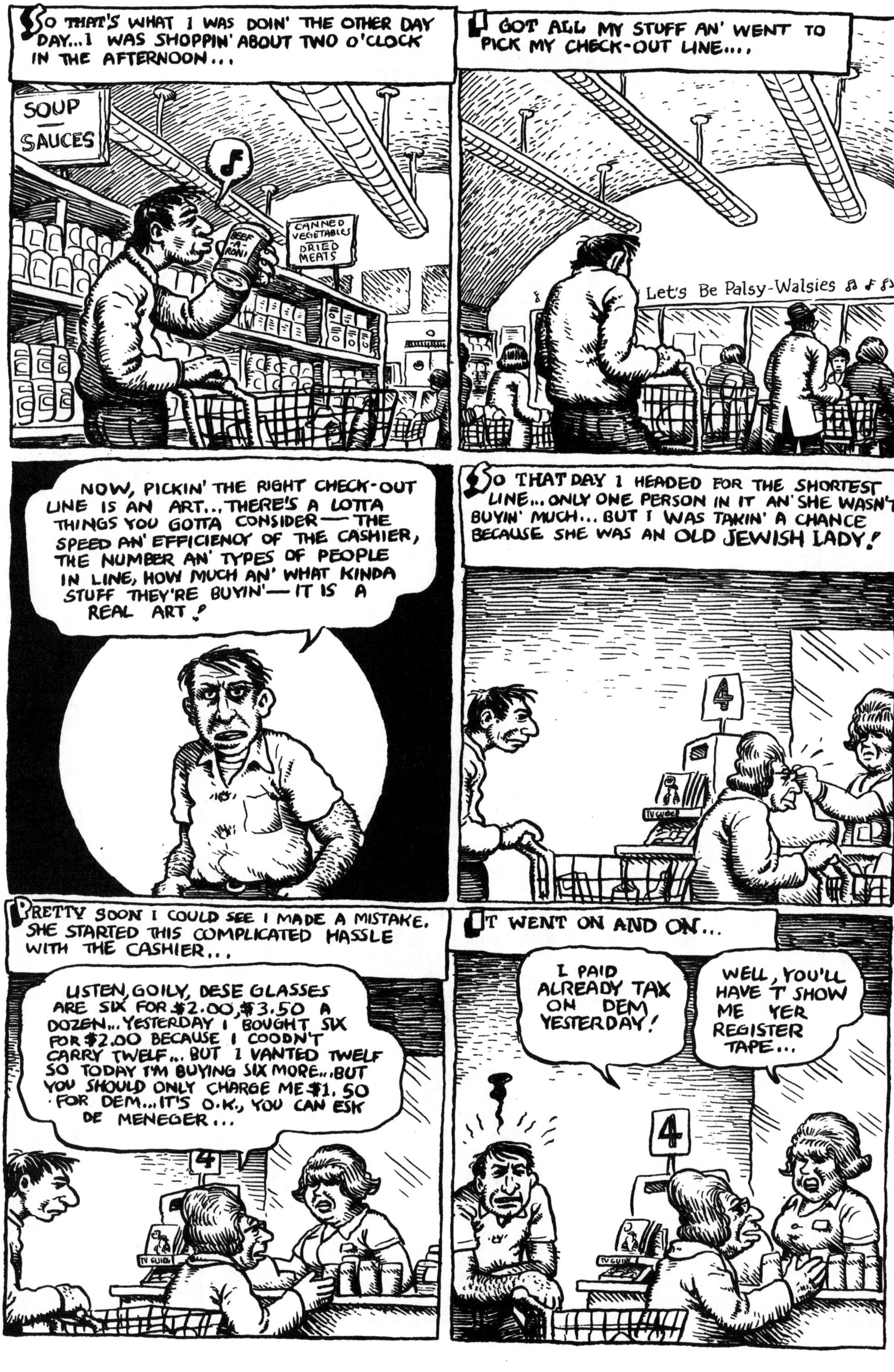
SO THAT'S WHAT I WAS DOIN' THE OTHER DAY DAY... I WAS SHOPPIN' ABOUT TWO O'CLOCK IN THE AFTERNOON...
SOUP — SAUCES
CANNED VEGETABLES DRIED MEATS
BEEF-A-RONI
I GOT ALL MY STUFF AN' WENT TO PICK MY CHECK-OUT LINE....
Let's Be Palsy-Walsies
NOW, PICKIN' THE RIGHT CHECK-OUT LINE IS AN ART... THERE'S A LOTTA THINGS YOU GOTTA CONSIDER — THE SPEED AN' EFFICIENCY OF THE CASHIER, THE NUMBER AN' TYPES OF PEOPLE IN LINE, HOW MUCH AN' WHAT KINDA STUFF THEY'RE BUYIN' — IT IS A REAL ART!
SO THAT DAY I HEADED FOR THE SHORTEST LINE... ONLY ONE PERSON IN IT AN' SHE WASN'T BUYIN' MUCH... BUT I WAS TAKIN' A CHANCE BECAUSE SHE WAS AN OLD JEWISH LADY!
4
TV GUIDE
PRETTY SOON I COULD SEE I MADE A MISTAKE. SHE STARTED THIS COMPLICATED HASSLE WITH THE CASHIER...
LISTEN, GOILY, DESE GLASSES ARE SIX FOR $2.00, $3.50 A DOZEN... YESTERDAY I BOUGHT SIX FOR $2.00 BECAUSE I COODN'T CARRY TWELF... BUT I VANTED TWELF SO TODAY I'M BUYING SIX MORE... BUT YOU SHOULD ONLY CHARGE ME $1.50 FOR DEM... IT'S O.K., YOU CAN ESK DE MENEGER...
4
IT WENT ON AND ON...
I PAID ALREADY TAX ON DEM YESTERDAY!
WELL, YOU'LL HAVE T' SHOW ME YER REGISTER TAPE...
4

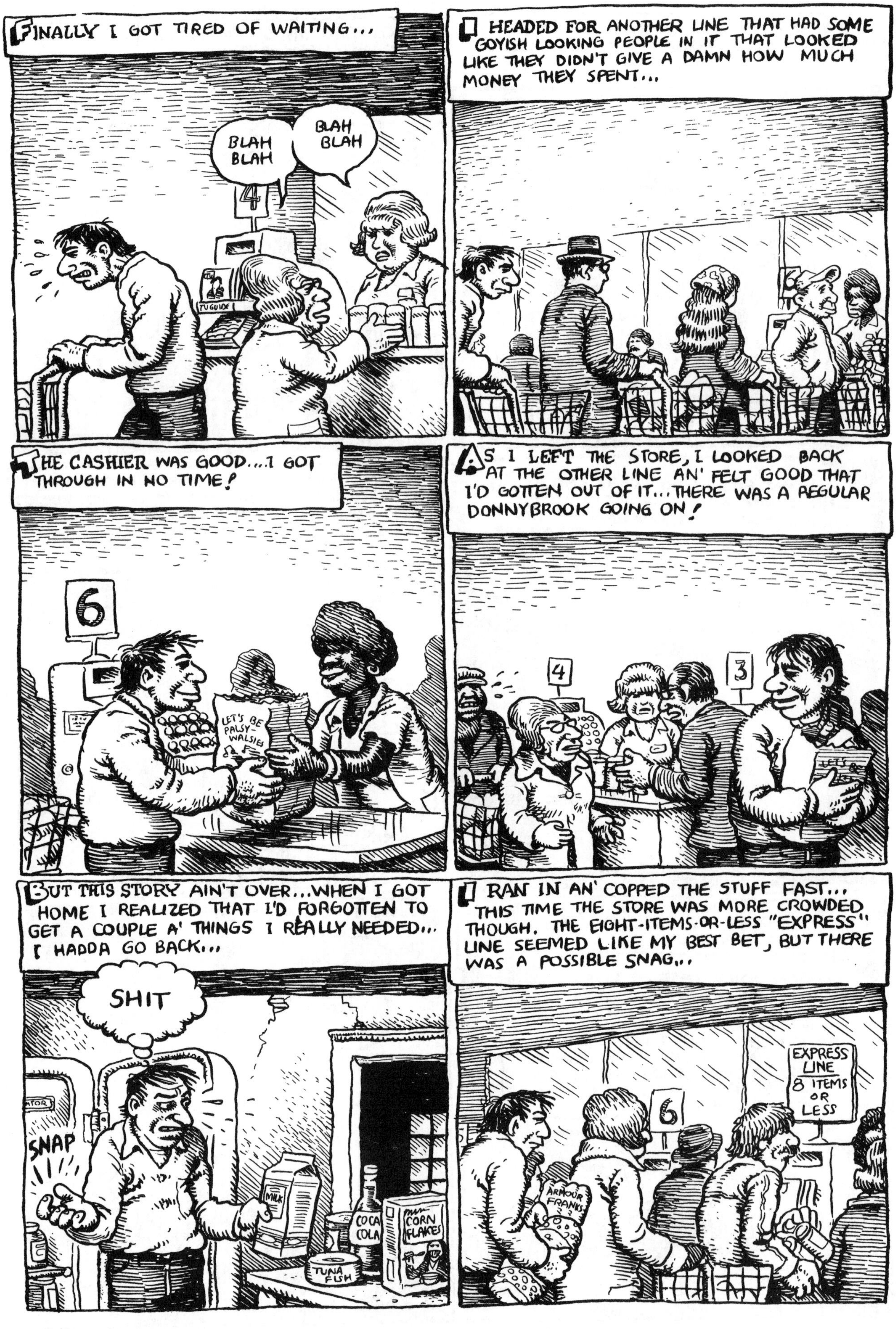
FINALLY I GOT TIRED OF WAITING...
BLAH BLAH
BLAH BLAH
4
TV GUIDE
I HEADED FOR ANOTHER LINE THAT HAD SOME GOYISH LOOKING PEOPLE IN IT THAT LOOKED LIKE THEY DIDN'T GIVE A DAMN HOW MUCH MONEY THEY SPENT...
THE CASHIER WAS GOOD...I GOT THROUGH IN NO TIME!
6
LET'S BE PALSY-WALSIES
AS I LEFT THE STORE, I LOOKED BACK AT THE OTHER LINE AN' FELT GOOD THAT I'D GOTTEN OUT OF IT...THERE WAS A REGULAR DONNYBROOK GOING ON!
4
3
BUT THIS STORY AIN'T OVER...WHEN I GOT HOME I REALIZED THAT I'D FORGOTTEN TO GET A COUPLE A' THINGS I REALLY NEEDED... I HADDA GO BACK...
SHIT
SNAP
MILK
COCA COLA
CORN FLAKES
TUNA FISH
I RAN IN AN' COPPED THE STUFF FAST... THIS TIME THE STORE WAS MORE CROWDED THOUGH. THE EIGHT-ITEMS-OR-LESS "EXPRESS" LINE SEEMED LIKE MY BEST BET, BUT THERE WAS A POSSIBLE SNAG...
EXPRESS LINE 8 ITEMS OR LESS
6
ARMOUR FRANKS

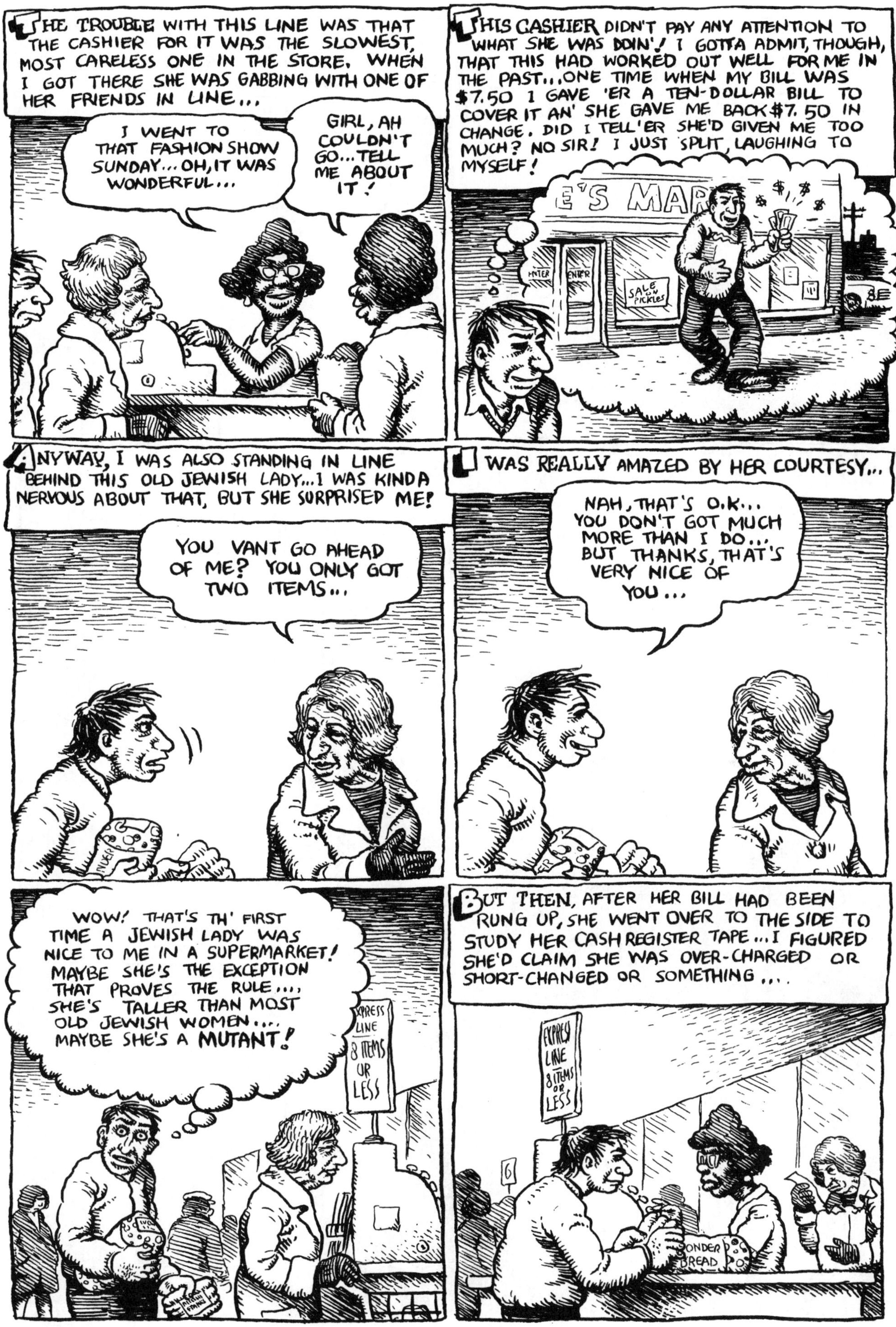
THE TROUBLE WITH THIS LINE WAS THAT THE CASHIER FOR IT WAS THE SLOWEST, MOST CARELESS ONE IN THE STORE. WHEN I GOT THERE SHE WAS GABBING WITH ONE OF HER FRIENDS IN LINE...
I WENT TO THAT FASHION SHOW SUNDAY... OH, IT WAS WONDERFUL...
GIRL, AH COULDN'T GO... TELL ME ABOUT IT!
THIS CASHIER DIDN'T PAY ANY ATTENTION TO WHAT SHE WAS DOIN'! I GOTTA ADMIT, THOUGH, THAT THIS HAD WORKED OUT WELL FOR ME IN THE PAST... ONE TIME WHEN MY BILL WAS $7.50 I GAVE 'ER A TEN-DOLLAR BILL TO COVER IT AN' SHE GAVE ME BACK $7.50 IN CHANGE. DID I TELL 'ER SHE'D GIVEN ME TOO MUCH? NO SIR! I JUST SPLIT, LAUGHING TO MYSELF!
E'S MAR
SALE ON PICKLES
ANYWAY, I WAS ALSO STANDING IN LINE BEHIND THIS OLD JEWISH LADY... I WAS KINDA NERVOUS ABOUT THAT, BUT SHE SURPRISED ME!
YOU VANT GO AHEAD OF ME? YOU ONLY GOT TWO ITEMS...
I WAS REALLY AMAZED BY HER COURTESY...
NAH, THAT'S O.K... YOU DON'T GOT MUCH MORE THAN I DO... BUT THANKS, THAT'S VERY NICE OF YOU...
WOW! THAT'S TH' FIRST TIME A JEWISH LADY WAS NICE TO ME IN A SUPERMARKET! MAYBE SHE'S THE EXCEPTION THAT PROVES THE RULE..., SHE'S TALLER THAN MOST OLD JEWISH WOMEN.... MAYBE SHE'S A MUTANT!
EXPRESS LINE 8 ITEMS OR LESS
BUT THEN, AFTER HER BILL HAD BEEN RUNG UP, SHE WENT OVER TO THE SIDE TO STUDY HER CASH REGISTER TAPE... I FIGURED SHE'D CLAIM SHE WAS OVER-CHARGED OR SHORT-CHANGED OR SOMETHING...
EXPRESS LINE 8 ITEMS OR LESS
6
WONDER BREAD

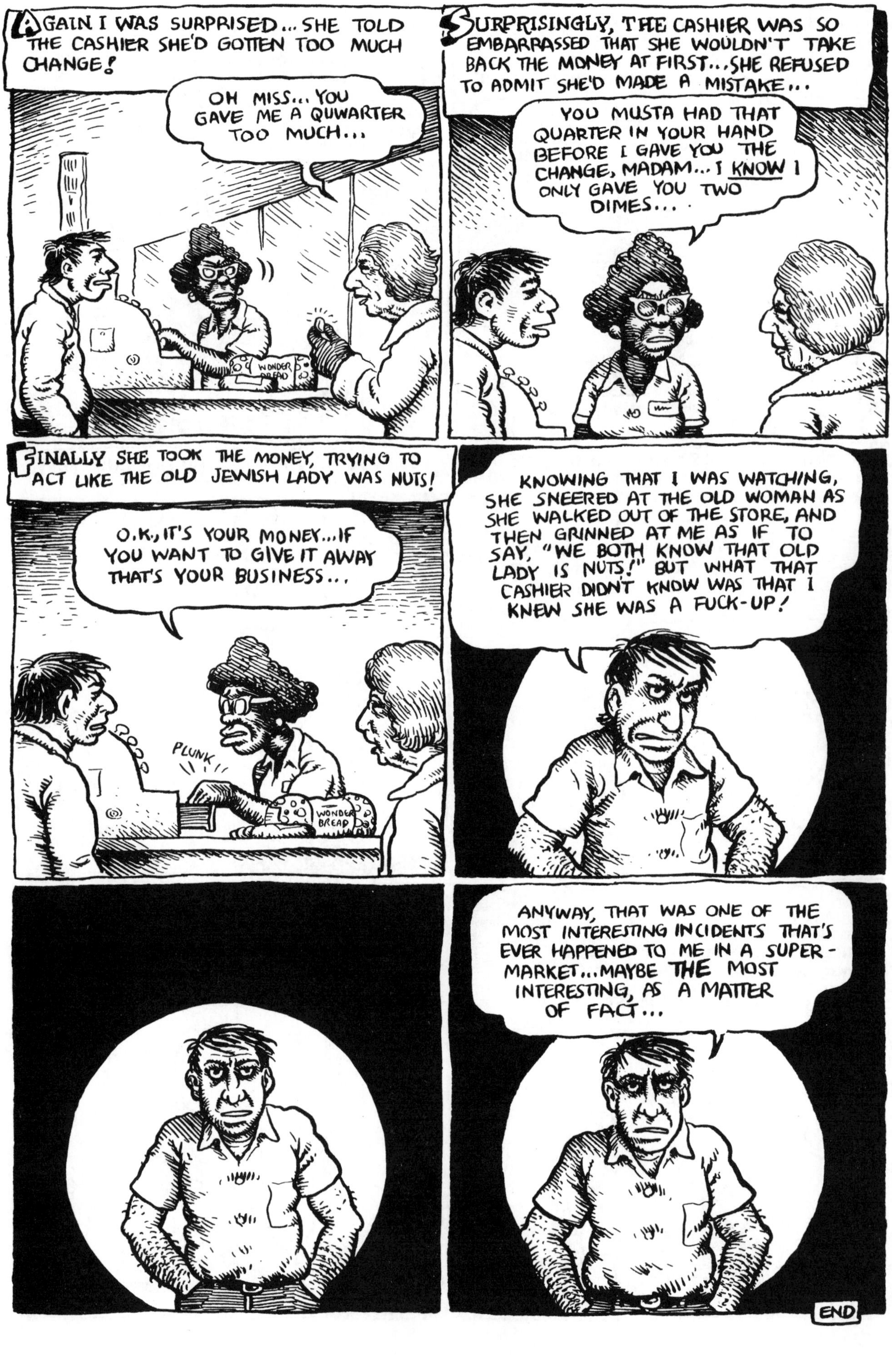
AGAIN I WAS SURPRISED... SHE TOLD THE CASHIER SHE'D GOTTEN TOO MUCH CHANGE!
OH MISS... YOU GAVE ME A QUWARTER TOO MUCH...
WONDER BREAD
SURPRISINGLY, THE CASHIER WAS SO EMBARRASSED THAT SHE WOULDN'T TAKE BACK THE MONEY AT FIRST... SHE REFUSED TO ADMIT SHE'D MADE A MISTAKE...
YOU MUSTA HAD THAT QUARTER IN YOUR HAND BEFORE I GAVE YOU THE CHANGE, MADAM... I KNOW I ONLY GAVE YOU TWO DIMES...
FINALLY SHE TOOK THE MONEY, TRYING TO ACT LIKE THE OLD JEWISH LADY WAS NUTS!
O.K., IT'S YOUR MONEY... IF YOU WANT TO GIVE IT AWAY THAT'S YOUR BUSINESS...
PLUNK
WONDER BREAD
KNOWING THAT I WAS WATCHING, SHE SNEERED AT THE OLD WOMAN AS SHE WALKED OUT OF THE STORE, AND THEN GRINNED AT ME AS IF TO SAY, "WE BOTH KNOW THAT OLD LADY IS NUTS!" BUT WHAT THAT CASHIER DIDN'T KNOW WAS THAT I KNEW SHE WAS A FUCK-UP!
ANYWAY, THAT WAS ONE OF THE MOST INTERESTING INCIDENTS THAT'S EVER HAPPENED TO ME IN A SUPER-MARKET... MAYBE THE MOST INTERESTING, AS A MATTER OF FACT...
END

Ridin' the Dog

STORY BY HARVEY PEKAR
ART BY R. CRUMB

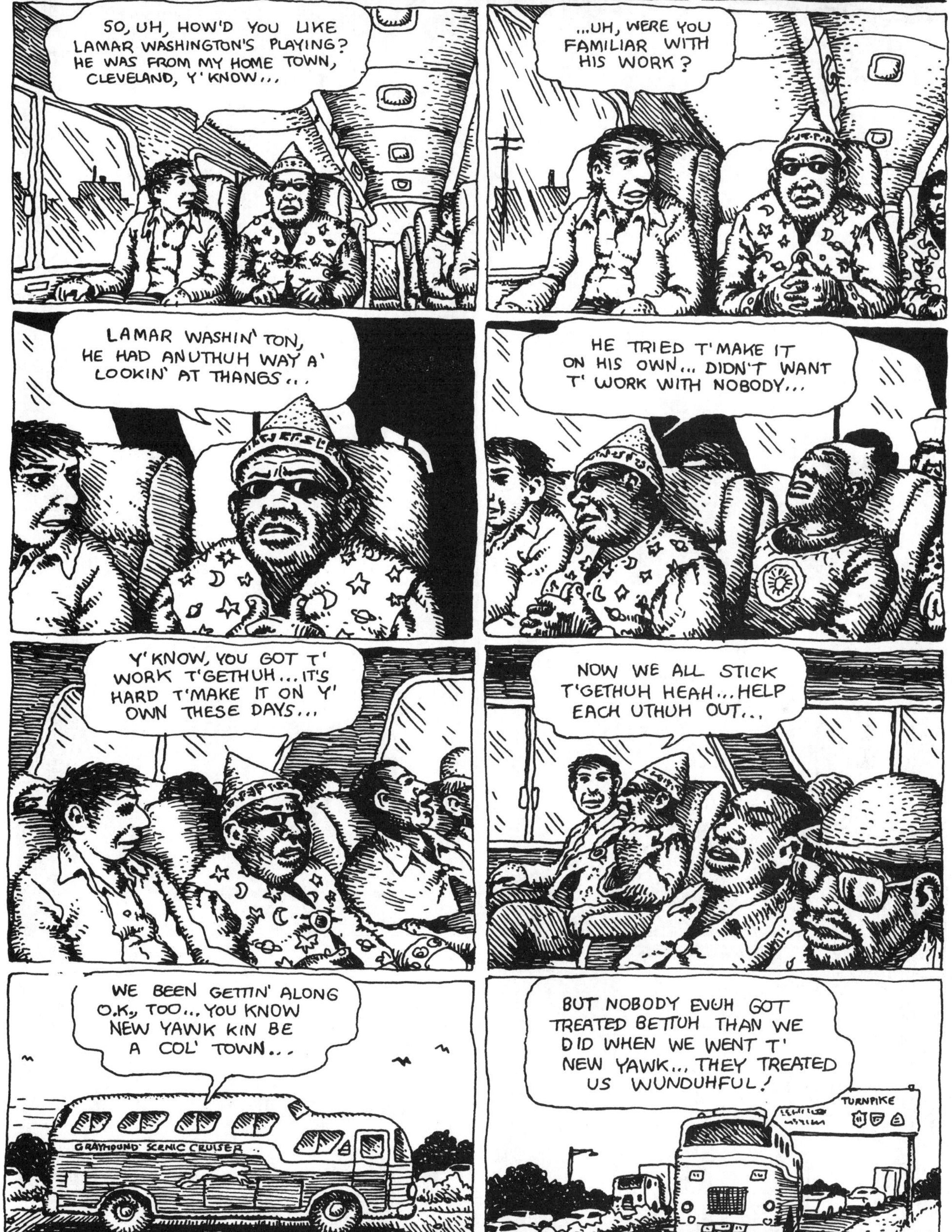
SO, UH, HOW'D YOU LIKE LAMAR WASHINGTON'S PLAYING? HE WAS FROM MY HOME TOWN, CLEVELAND, Y'KNOW...
...UH, WERE YOU FAMILIAR WITH HIS WORK?
LAMAR WASHIN' TON, HE HAD ANUTHUH WAY A' LOOKIN' AT THANGS...
HE TRIED T'MAKE IT ON HIS OWN... DIDN'T WANT T' WORK WITH NOBODY...
Y'KNOW, YOU GOT T' WORK T'GETHUH... IT'S HARD T'MAKE IT ON Y' OWN THESE DAYS...
NOW WE ALL STICK T'GETHUH HEAH... HELP EACH UTHUH OUT...
WE BEEN GETTIN' ALONG O.K., TOO... YOU KNOW NEW YAWK KIN BE A COL' TOWN...
GRAYHOUND SCENIC CRUISER
BUT NOBODY EVUH GOT TREATED BETTUH THAN WE DID WHEN WE WENT T' NEW YAWK... THEY TREATED US WUNDUHFUL!
TURNPIKE

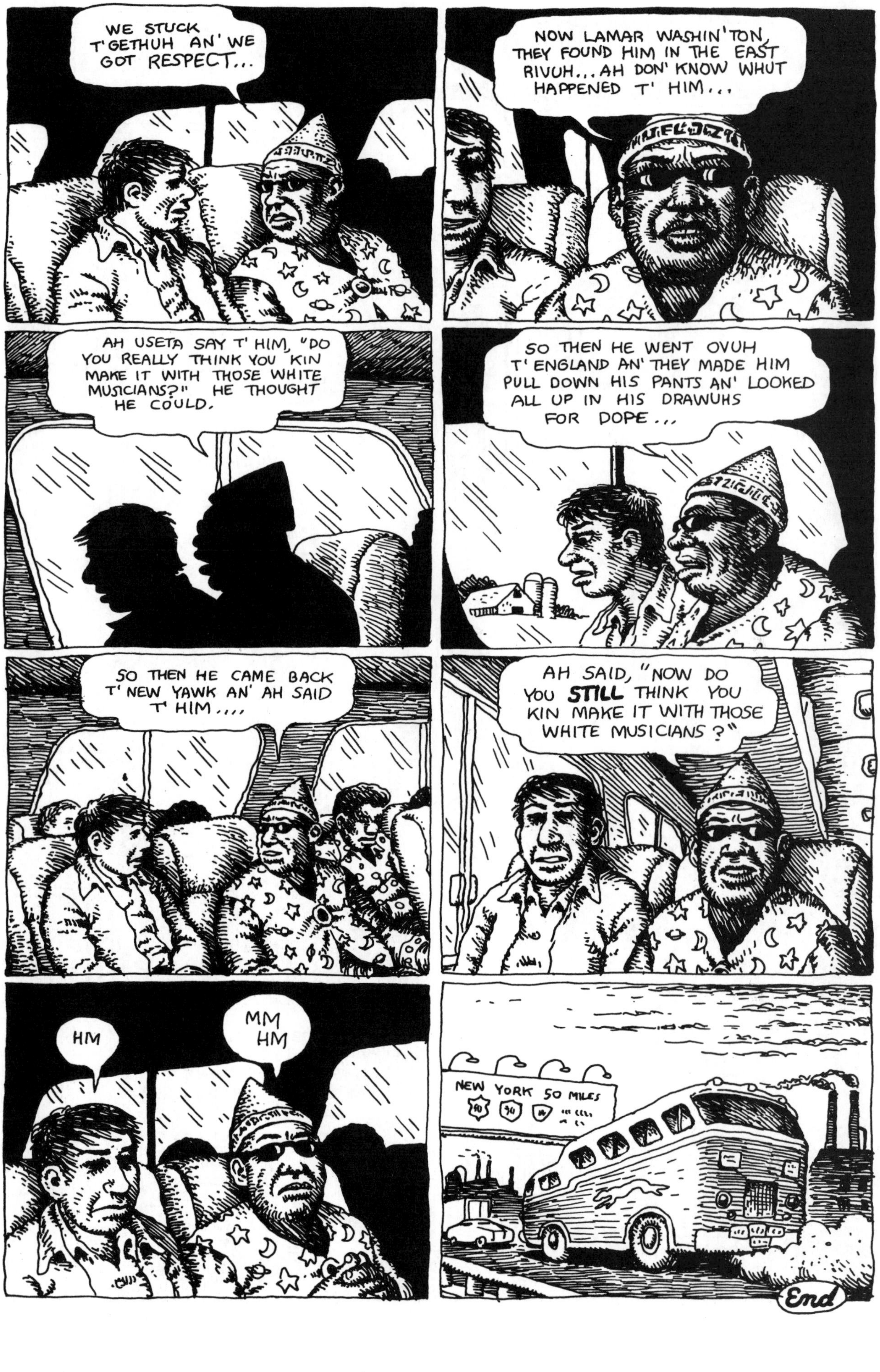

WE STUCK T'GETHUH AN' WE GOT RESPECT...
NOW LAMAR WASHIN'TON, THEY FOUND HIM IN THE EAST RIVUH... AH DON' KNOW WHUT HAPPENED T' HIM...
AH USETA SAY T' HIM, "DO YOU REALLY THINK YOU KIN MAKE IT WITH THOSE WHITE MUSICIANS?" HE THOUGHT HE COULD.
SO THEN HE WENT OVUH T' ENGLAND AN' THEY MADE HIM PULL DOWN HIS PANTS AN' LOOKED ALL UP IN HIS DRAWUHS FOR DOPE...
SO THEN HE CAME BACK T' NEW YAWK AN' AH SAID T' HIM....
AH SAID, "NOW DO YOU STILL THINK YOU KIN MAKE IT WITH THOSE WHITE MUSICIANS?"
HM
MM HM
NEW YORK 50 MILES
End

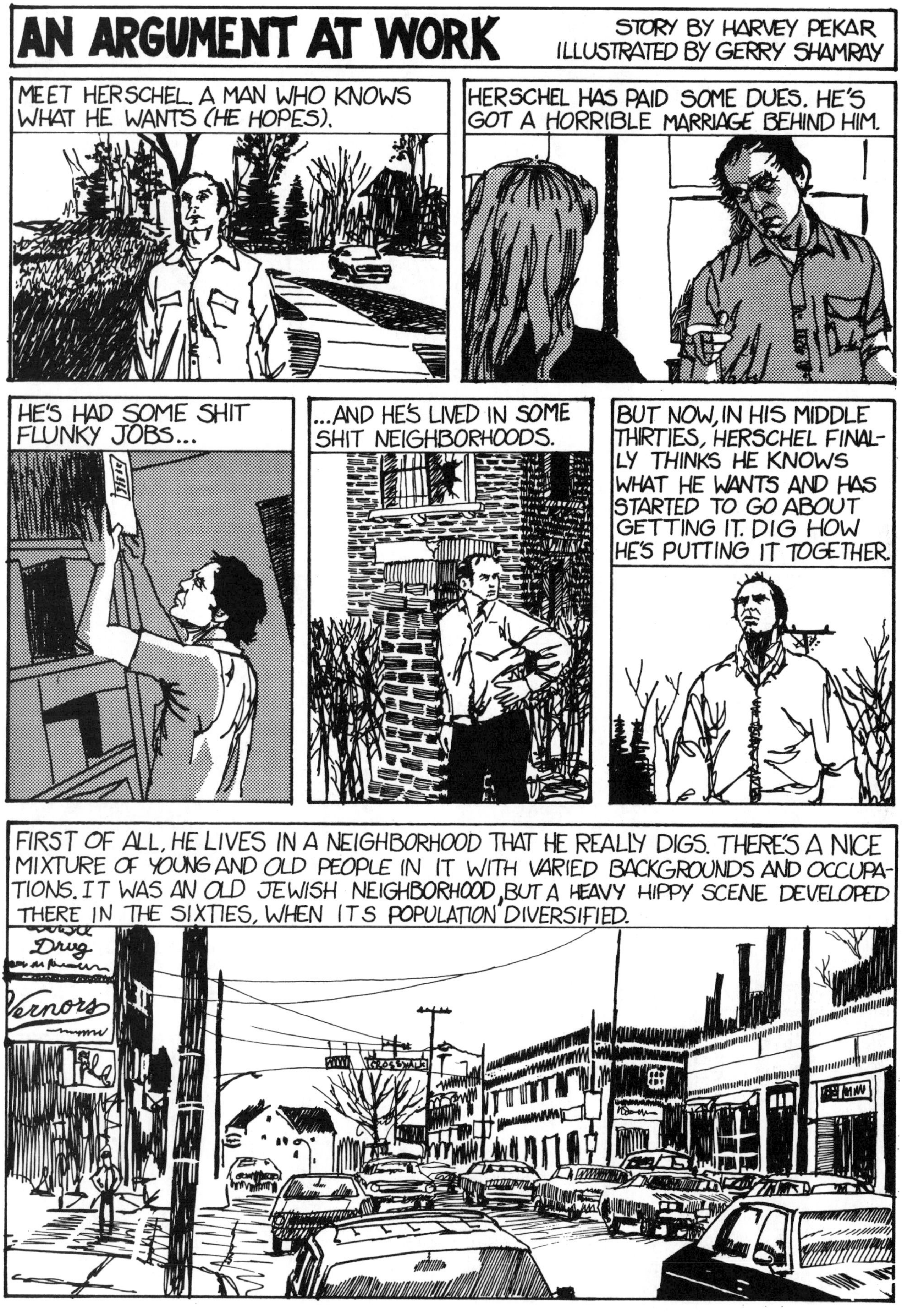
AN ARGUMENT AT WORK
STORY BY HARVEY PEKAR
ILLUSTRATED BY GERRY SHAMRAY
MEET HERSCHEL. A MAN WHO KNOWS WHAT HE WANTS (HE HOPES).
HERSCHEL HAS PAID SOME DUES. HE'S GOT A HORRIBLE MARRIAGE BEHIND HIM.
HE'S HAD SOME SHIT FLUNKY JOBS...
...AND HE'S LIVED IN SOME SHIT NEIGHBORHOODS.
BUT NOW, IN HIS MIDDLE THIRTIES, HERSCHEL FINALLY THINKS HE KNOWS WHAT HE WANTS AND HAS STARTED TO GO ABOUT GETTING IT. DIG HOW HE'S PUTTING IT TOGETHER.
FIRST OF ALL, HE LIVES IN A NEIGHBORHOOD THAT HE REALLY DIGS. THERE'S A NICE MIXTURE OF YOUNG AND OLD PEOPLE IN IT WITH VARIED BACKGROUNDS AND OCCUPATIONS. IT WAS AN OLD JEWISH NEIGHBORHOOD, BUT A HEAVY HIPPY SCENE DEVELOPED THERE IN THE SIXTIES, WHEN ITS POPULATION DIVERSIFIED.
Drug
Vernors
CROSSWALK

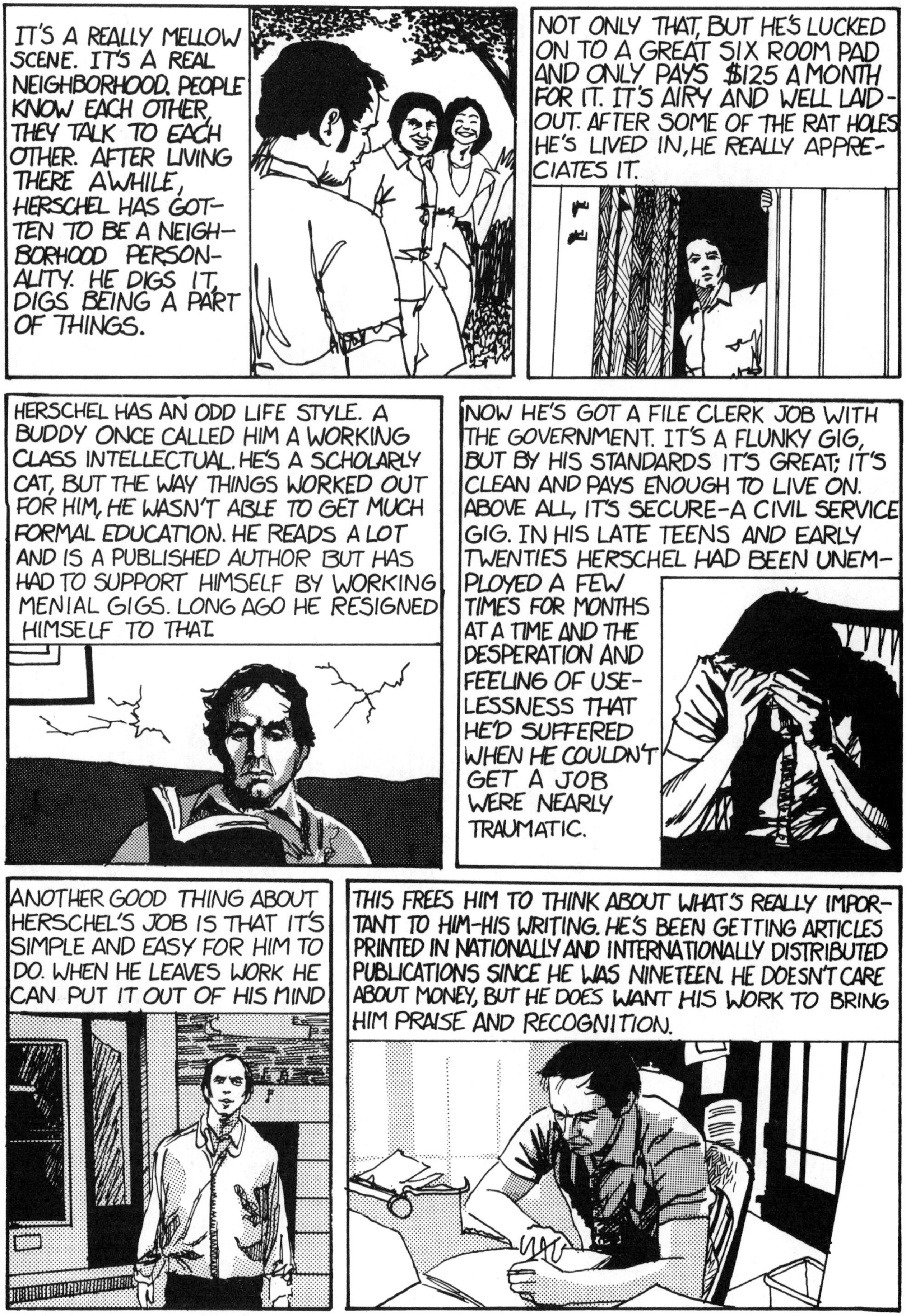
IT'S A REALLY MELLOW SCENE. IT'S A REAL NEIGHBORHOOD. PEOPLE KNOW EACH OTHER, THEY TALK TO EACH OTHER. AFTER LIVING THERE AWHILE, HERSCHEL HAS GOTTEN TO BE A NEIGHBORHOOD PERSONALITY. HE DIGS IT, DIGS BEING A PART OF THINGS.
NOT ONLY THAT, BUT HE'S LUCKED ON TO A GREAT SIX ROOM PAD AND ONLY PAYS $125 A MONTH FOR IT. IT'S AIRY AND WELL LAID-OUT. AFTER SOME OF THE RAT HOLES HE'S LIVED IN, HE REALLY APPRECIATES IT.
HERSCHEL HAS AN ODD LIFE STYLE. A BUDDY ONCE CALLED HIM A WORKING CLASS INTELLECTUAL. HE'S A SCHOLARLY CAT, BUT THE WAY THINGS WORKED OUT FOR HIM, HE WASN'T ABLE TO GET MUCH FORMAL EDUCATION. HE READS A LOT AND IS A PUBLISHED AUTHOR BUT HAS HAD TO SUPPORT HIMSELF BY WORKING MENIAL GIGS. LONG AGO HE RESIGNED HIMSELF TO THAT.
NOW HE'S GOT A FILE CLERK JOB WITH THE GOVERNMENT. IT'S A FLUNKY GIG, BUT BY HIS STANDARDS IT'S GREAT; IT'S CLEAN AND PAYS ENOUGH TO LIVE ON. ABOVE ALL, IT'S SECURE-A CIVIL SERVICE GIG. IN HIS LATE TEENS AND EARLY TWENTIES HERSCHEL HAD BEEN UNEMPLOYED A FEW TIMES FOR MONTHS AT A TIME AND THE DESPERATION AND FEELING OF USELESSNESS THAT HE'D SUFFERED WHEN HE COULDN'T GET A JOB WERE NEARLY TRAUMATIC.
ANOTHER GOOD THING ABOUT HERSCHEL'S JOB IS THAT IT'S SIMPLE AND EASY FOR HIM TO DO. WHEN HE LEAVES WORK HE CAN PUT IT OUT OF HIS MIND
THIS FREES HIM TO THINK ABOUT WHAT'S REALLY IMPORTANT TO HIM-HIS WRITING. HE'S BEEN GETTING ARTICLES PRINTED IN NATIONALLY AND INTERNATIONALLY DISTRIBUTED PUBLICATIONS SINCE HE WAS NINETEEN. HE DOESN'T CARE ABOUT MONEY, BUT HE DOES WANT HIS WORK TO BRING HIM PRAISE AND RECOGNITION.

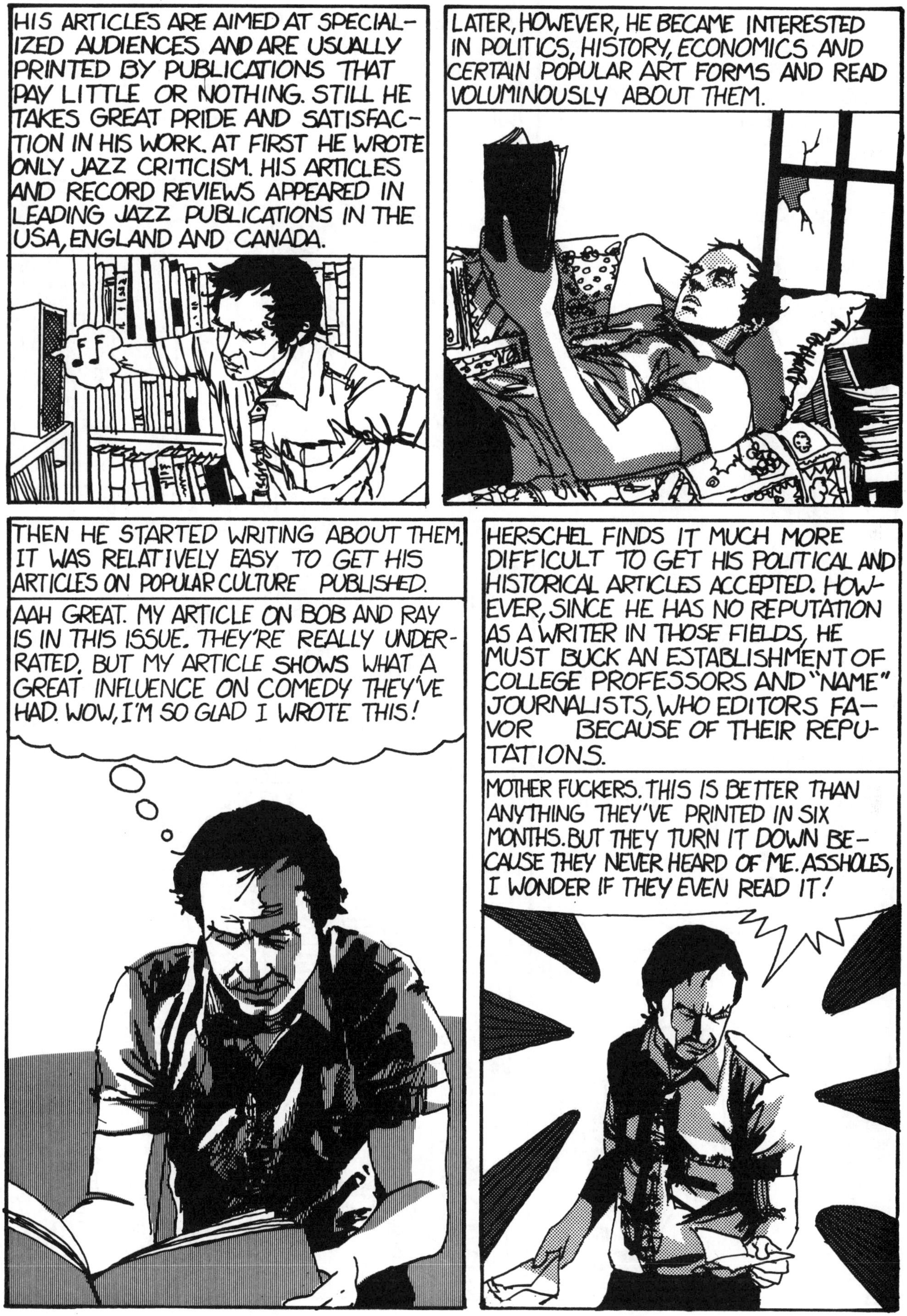
HIS ARTICLES ARE AIMED AT SPECIALIZED AUDIENCES AND ARE USUALLY PRINTED BY PUBLICATIONS THAT PAY LITTLE OR NOTHING. STILL HE TAKES GREAT PRIDE AND SATISFACTION IN HIS WORK. AT FIRST HE WROTE ONLY JAZZ CRITICISM. HIS ARTICLES AND RECORD REVIEWS APPEARED IN LEADING JAZZ PUBLICATIONS IN THE USA, ENGLAND AND CANADA.
LATER, HOWEVER, HE BECAME INTERESTED IN POLITICS, HISTORY, ECONOMICS AND CERTAIN POPULAR ART FORMS AND READ VOLUMINOUSLY ABOUT THEM.
THEN HE STARTED WRITING ABOUT THEM. IT WAS RELATIVELY EASY TO GET HIS ARTICLES ON POPULAR CULTURE PUBLISHED.
AAH GREAT. MY ARTICLE ON BOB AND RAY IS IN THIS ISSUE. THEY'RE REALLY UNDERRATED. BUT MY ARTICLE SHOWS WHAT A GREAT INFLUENCE ON COMEDY THEY'VE HAD. WOW, I'M SO GLAD I WROTE THIS!
HERSCHEL FINDS IT MUCH MORE DIFFICULT TO GET HIS POLITICAL AND HISTORICAL ARTICLES ACCEPTED. HOWEVER, SINCE HE HAS NO REPUTATION AS A WRITER IN THOSE FIELDS, HE MUST BUCK AN ESTABLISHMENT OF COLLEGE PROFESSORS AND "NAME" JOURNALISTS, WHO EDITORS FAVOR BECAUSE OF THEIR REPUTATIONS.
MOTHER FUCKERS. THIS IS BETTER THAN ANYTHING THEY'VE PRINTED IN SIX MONTHS. BUT THEY TURN IT DOWN BECAUSE THEY NEVER HEARD OF ME. ASSHOLES, I WONDER IF THEY EVEN READ IT!

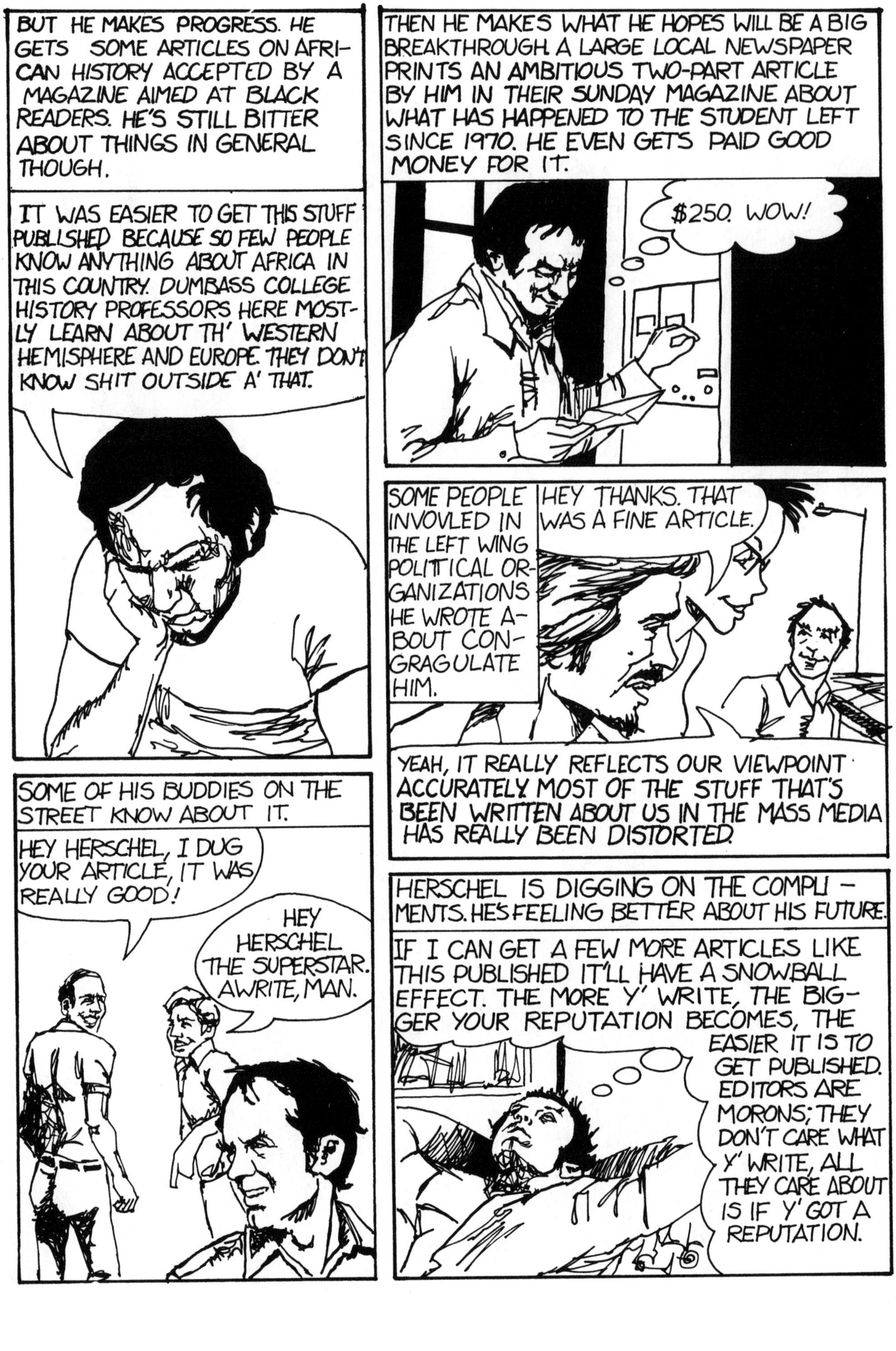
BUT HE MAKES PROGRESS. HE GETS SOME ARTICLES ON AFRICAN HISTORY ACCEPTED BY A MAGAZINE AIMED AT BLACK READERS. HE'S STILL BITTER ABOUT THINGS IN GENERAL THOUGH.
IT WAS EASIER TO GET THIS STUFF PUBLISHED BECAUSE SO FEW PEOPLE KNOW ANYTHING ABOUT AFRICA IN THIS COUNTRY. DUMBASS COLLEGE HISTORY PROFESSORS HERE MOSTLY LEARN ABOUT TH' WESTERN HEMISPHERE AND EUROPE. THEY DON'T KNOW SHIT OUTSIDE A' THAT.
SOME OF HIS BUDDIES ON THE STREET KNOW ABOUT IT.
HEY HERSCHEL, I DUG YOUR ARTICLE, IT WAS REALLY GOOD!
HEY HERSCHEL THE SUPERSTAR. AWRITE, MAN.
THEN HE MAKES WHAT HE HOPES WILL BE A BIG BREAKTHROUGH. A LARGE LOCAL NEWSPAPER PRINTS AN AMBITIOUS TWO-PART ARTICLE BY HIM IN THEIR SUNDAY MAGAZINE ABOUT WHAT HAS HAPPENED TO THE STUDENT LEFT SINCE 1970. HE EVEN GETS PAID GOOD MONEY FOR IT.
$250. WOW!
SOME PEOPLE INVOVLED IN THE LEFT WING POLITICAL ORGANIZATIONS HE WROTE ABOUT CONGRAGULATE HIM.
HEY THANKS. THAT WAS A FINE ARTICLE.
YEAH, IT REALLY REFLECTS OUR VIEWPOINT ACCURATELY. MOST OF THE STUFF THAT'S BEEN WRITTEN ABOUT US IN THE MASS MEDIA HAS REALLY BEEN DISTORTED.
HERSCHEL IS DIGGING ON THE COMPLIMENTS. HE'S FEELING BETTER ABOUT HIS FUTURE.
IF I CAN GET A FEW MORE ARTICLES LIKE THIS PUBLISHED IT'LL HAVE A SNOWBALL EFFECT. THE MORE Y' WRITE, THE BIGGER YOUR REPUTATION BECOMES, THE EASIER IT IS TO GET PUBLISHED. EDITORS ARE MORONS; THEY DON'T CARE WHAT Y' WRITE, ALL THEY CARE ABOUT IS IF Y' GOT A REPUTATION.

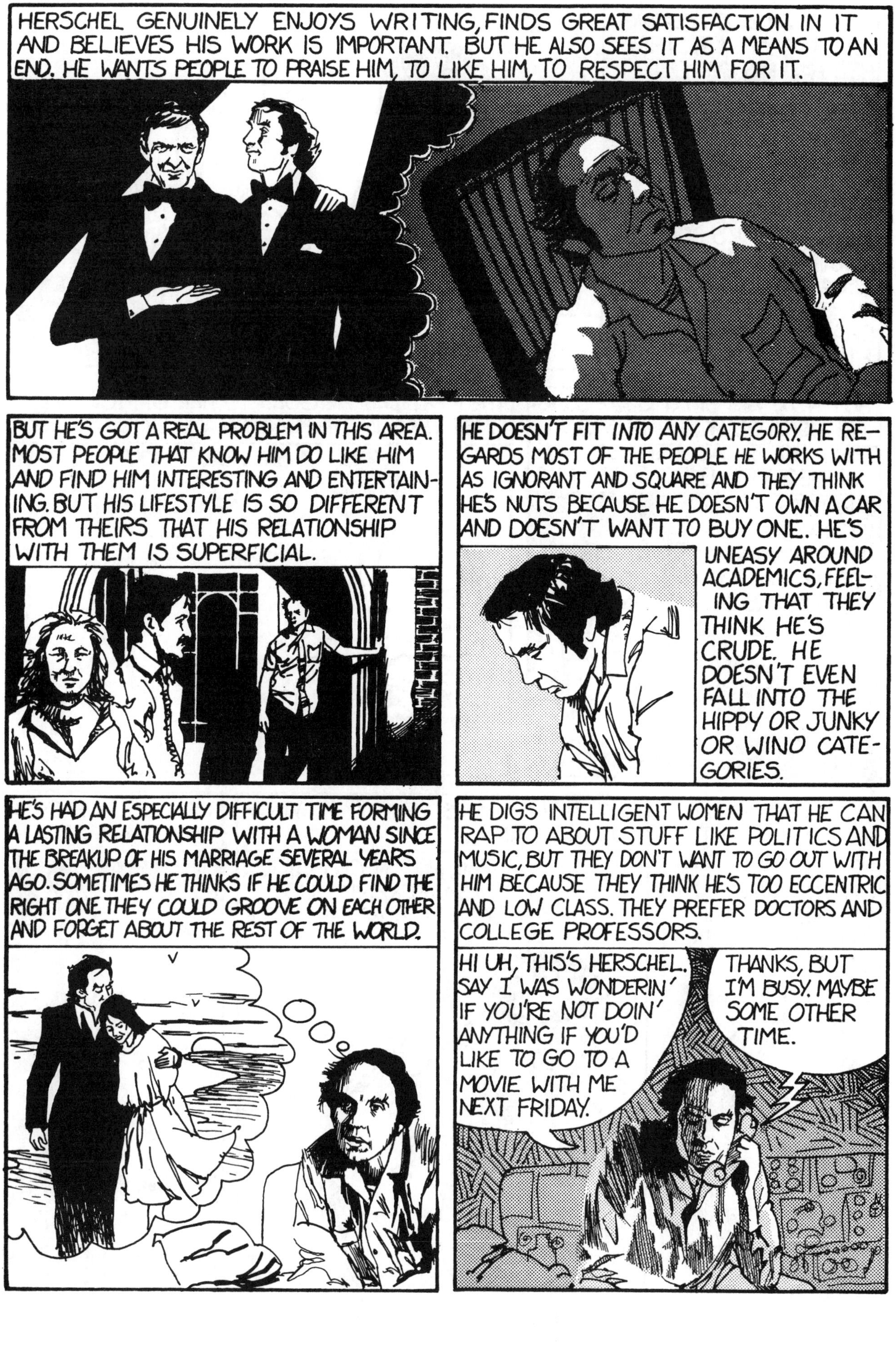
HERSCHEL GENUINELY ENJOYS WRITING, FINDS GREAT SATISFACTION IN IT AND BELIEVES HIS WORK IS IMPORTANT. BUT HE ALSO SEES IT AS A MEANS TO AN END. HE WANTS PEOPLE TO PRAISE HIM, TO LIKE HIM, TO RESPECT HIM FOR IT.
BUT HE'S GOT A REAL PROBLEM IN THIS AREA. MOST PEOPLE THAT KNOW HIM DO LIKE HIM AND FIND HIM INTERESTING AND ENTERTAINING. BUT HIS LIFESTYLE IS SO DIFFERENT FROM THEIRS THAT HIS RELATIONSHIP WITH THEM IS SUPERFICIAL.
HE DOESN'T FIT INTO ANY CATEGORY. HE REGARDS MOST OF THE PEOPLE HE WORKS WITH AS IGNORANT AND SQUARE AND THEY THINK HE'S NUTS BECAUSE HE DOESN'T OWN A CAR AND DOESN'T WANT TO BUY ONE. HE'S
UNEASY AROUND ACADEMICS, FEELING THAT THEY THINK HE'S CRUDE. HE DOESN'T EVEN FALL INTO THE HIPPY OR JUNKY OR WINO CATEGORIES.
HE'S HAD AN ESPECIALLY DIFFICULT TIME FORMING A LASTING RELATIONSHIP WITH A WOMAN SINCE THE BREAKUP OF HIS MARRIAGE SEVERAL YEARS AGO. SOMETIMES HE THINKS IF HE COULD FIND THE RIGHT ONE THEY COULD GROOVE ON EACH OTHER AND FORGET ABOUT THE REST OF THE WORLD.
HE DIGS INTELLIGENT WOMEN THAT HE CAN RAP TO ABOUT STUFF LIKE POLITICS AND MUSIC, BUT THEY DON'T WANT TO GO OUT WITH HIM BECAUSE THEY THINK HE'S TOO ECCENTRIC AND LOW CLASS. THEY PREFER DOCTORS AND COLLEGE PROFESSORS.
HI UH, THIS'S HERSCHEL. SAY I WAS WONDERIN' IF YOU'RE NOT DOIN' ANYTHING IF YOU'D LIKE TO GO TO A MOVIE WITH ME NEXT FRIDAY.
THANKS, BUT I'M BUSY. MAYBE SOME OTHER TIME.

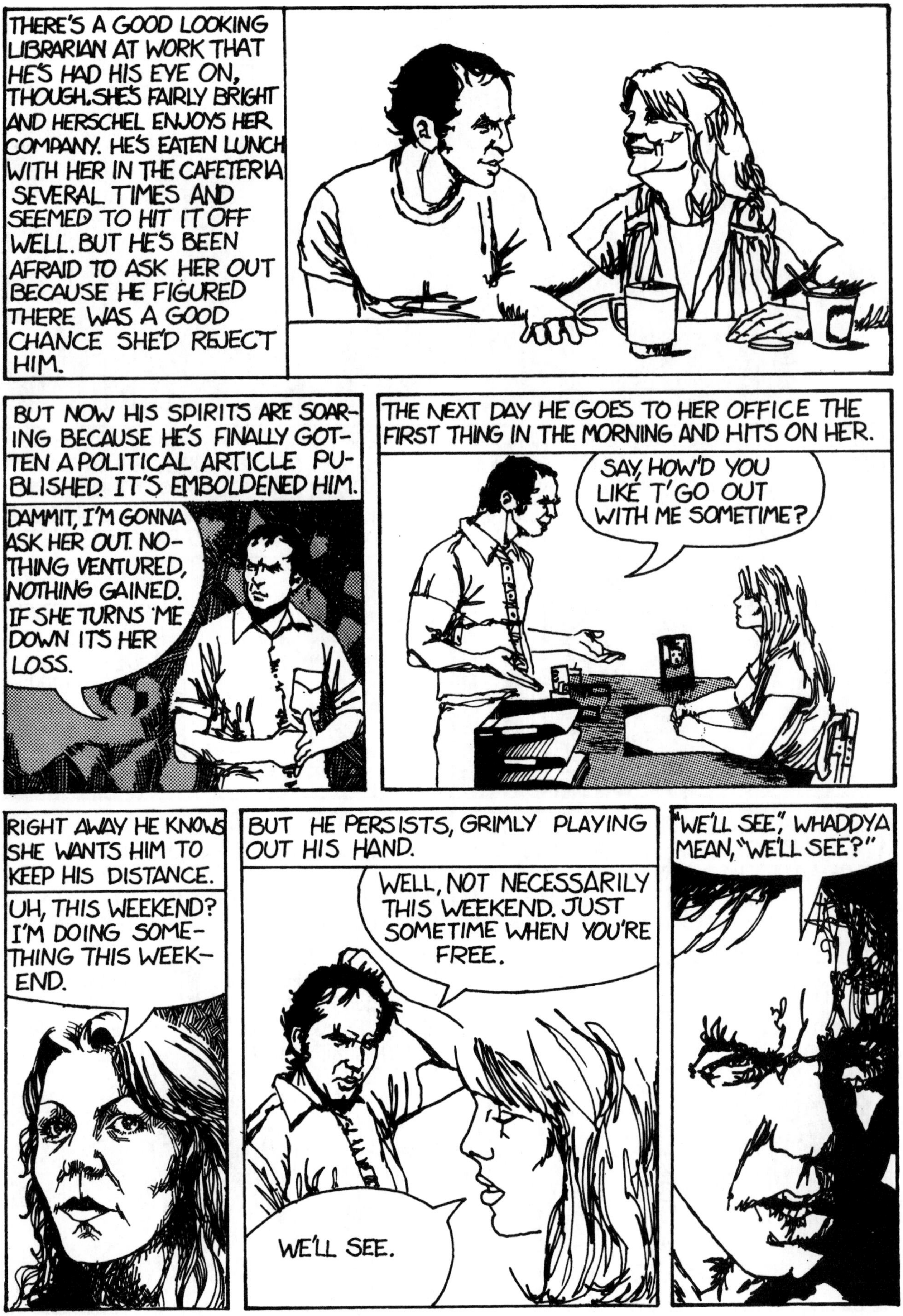

THERE'S A GOOD LOOKING LIBRARIAN AT WORK THAT HE'S HAD HIS EYE ON, THOUGH. SHE'S FAIRLY BRIGHT AND HERSCHEL ENJOYS HER COMPANY. HE'S EATEN LUNCH WITH HER IN THE CAFETERIA SEVERAL TIMES AND SEEMED TO HIT IT OFF WELL. BUT HE'S BEEN AFRAID TO ASK HER OUT BECAUSE HE FIGURED THERE WAS A GOOD CHANCE SHE'D REJECT HIM.
BUT NOW HIS SPIRITS ARE SOARING BECAUSE HE'S FINALLY GOTTEN A POLITICAL ARTICLE PUBLISHED. IT'S EMBOLDENED HIM.
DAMMIT, I'M GONNA ASK HER OUT. NOTHING VENTURED, NOTHING GAINED. IF SHE TURNS 'ME DOWN ITS HER LOSS.
THE NEXT DAY HE GOES TO HER OFFICE THE FIRST THING IN THE MORNING AND HITS ON HER.
SAY, HOW'D YOU LIKE T'GO OUT WITH ME SOMETIME?
RIGHT AWAY HE KNOWS SHE WANTS HIM TO KEEP HIS DISTANCE.
UH, THIS WEEKEND? I'M DOING SOMETHING THIS WEEKEND.
BUT HE PERSISTS, GRIMLY PLAYING OUT HIS HAND.
WELL, NOT NECESSARILY THIS WEEKEND. JUST SOMETIME WHEN YOU'RE FREE.
WE'LL SEE.
"WE'LL SEE," WHADDYA MEAN, "WE'LL SEE?"

HE WALKS AWAY FROM HER, KNOWING HE'S BEEN BRUSHED OFF.

OOOH, WHY'D I DO THAT? I KNEW SHE WOULDN'T GO OUT WITH ME.

GRADUALLY, THOUGH, HIS FEELINGS OF HURT ARE DRIVEN AWAY BY RAGE.

LOUSY CUNT. I'M TEN TIMES AS SMART, AND KNOWLEDGABLE AS HER OR ANY GUY SHE EVER WENT OUT WITH. SHE GOT A NERVE BRUSHIN' ME OFF.

SHE DIDN'T EVEN HAVE THE GUTS TO GIVE ME A FLAT-OUT NO. "WE'LL SEE," WHAT KINDA CHICKEN SHIT ANS-WER IZZAT?

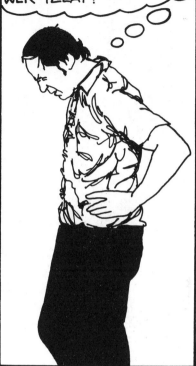

HE'S PREOCCUPIED AT WORK THAT DAY, PERFORMING HIS DUTIES IN A HAZE OF ANGER AND FRUSTRATION.

GODDAM WOMEN. IF THEY THINK A GUY'S BE-NEATH THEM SOCIALLY OR AIN'T RESPECTABLE, THEY DON'T CARE HOW MUCH HE'S GOT ON THE BALL OR HOW NICE HE IS. MOST WOMEN SUCK RE-SPECTABILITY FROM A MAN LIKE A VAMPIRE SUCKS BLOOD.

FORTUNATELY HE'S PRETTY MUCH HIS OWN BOSS AT WORK SO HE'S LEFT ALONE TO WORK HIS FEELINGS OUT. HE KNOWS HIS JOB, AND HIS SUPERVISORS REALIZE THIS AND PRETTY MUCH LET HIM DO IT HIS OWN WAY. HE'S REALLY TREATED LIKE A PRIVI-LEGED CHARACTER.

BUT IT'S A BUSY DAY AND HE HAS TO WORK AT A FRANTIC PACE TO KEEP UP WITH WHAT'S HAPPEN-ING. WHEN SOMETHING GOES WRONG IT REALLY BUGS HIM.

WHERE'S MR. SANTORELLI'S FILE? HE WAS IN HERE YES-TERDAY AN' I GOTTA GET IT FOR THE CODING SECTION!

I SENT IT BACK ALREADY.

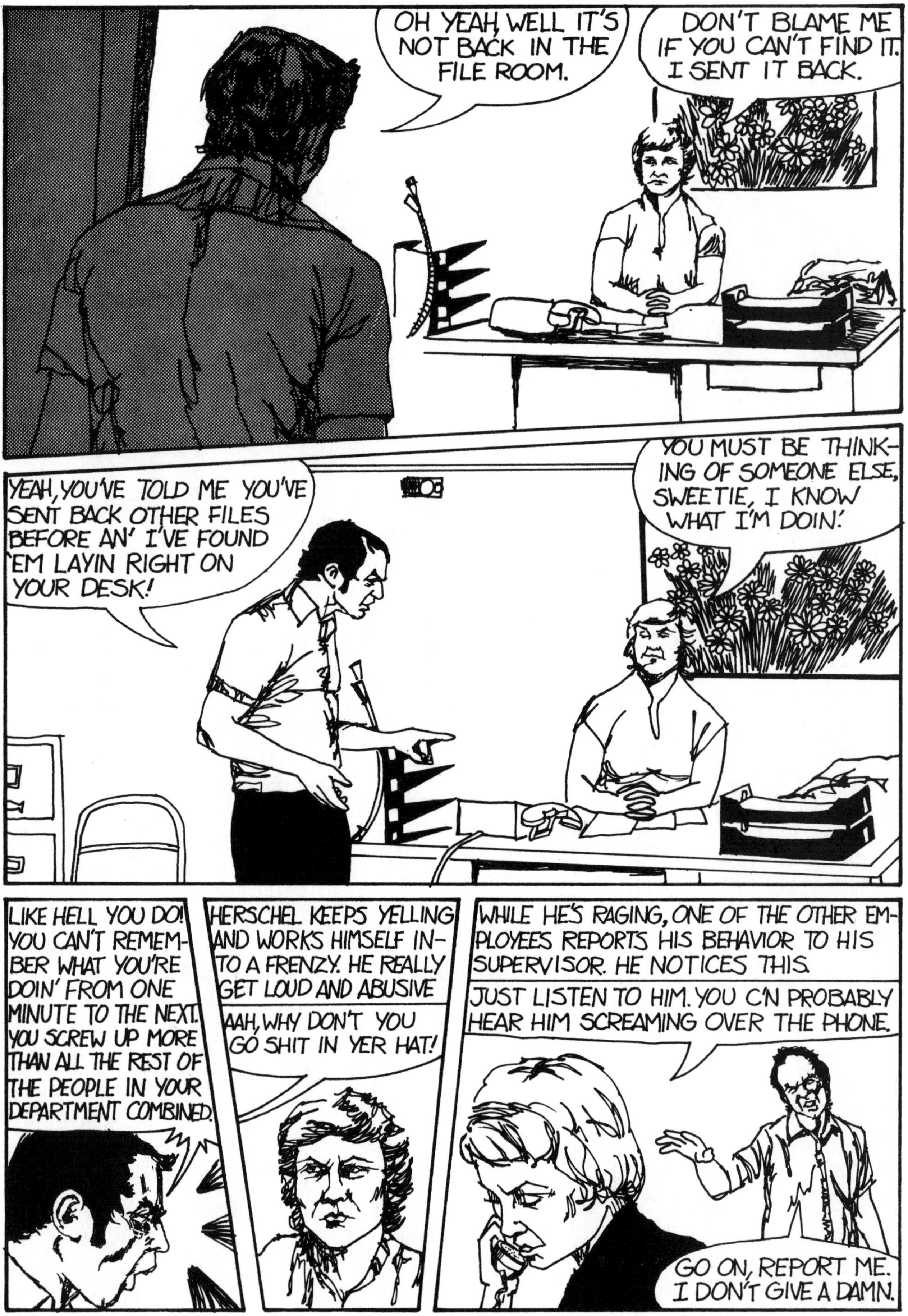
OH YEAH, WELL IT'S NOT BACK IN THE FILE ROOM.
DON'T BLAME ME IF YOU CAN'T FIND IT. I SENT IT BACK.
YEAH, YOU'VE TOLD ME YOU'VE SENT BACK OTHER FILES BEFORE AN' I'VE FOUND 'EM LAYIN RIGHT ON YOUR DESK!
YOU MUST BE THINKING OF SOMEONE ELSE, SWEETIE, I KNOW WHAT I'M DOIN'.
LIKE HELL YOU DO! YOU CAN'T REMEMBER WHAT YOU'RE DOIN' FROM ONE MINUTE TO THE NEXT. YOU SCREW UP MORE THAN ALL THE REST OF THE PEOPLE IN YOUR DEPARTMENT COMBINED.
HERSCHEL KEEPS YELLING AND WORKS HIMSELF INTO A FRENZY. HE REALLY GET LOUD AND ABUSIVE
AAH, WHY DON'T YOU GO SHIT IN YER HAT!
WHILE HE'S RAGING, ONE OF THE OTHER EMPLOYEES REPORTS HIS BEHAVIOR TO HIS SUPERVISOR. HE NOTICES THIS.
JUST LISTEN TO HIM. YOU C'N PROBABLY HEAR HIM SCREAMING OVER THE PHONE.
GO ON, REPORT ME. I DON'T GIVE A DAMN.

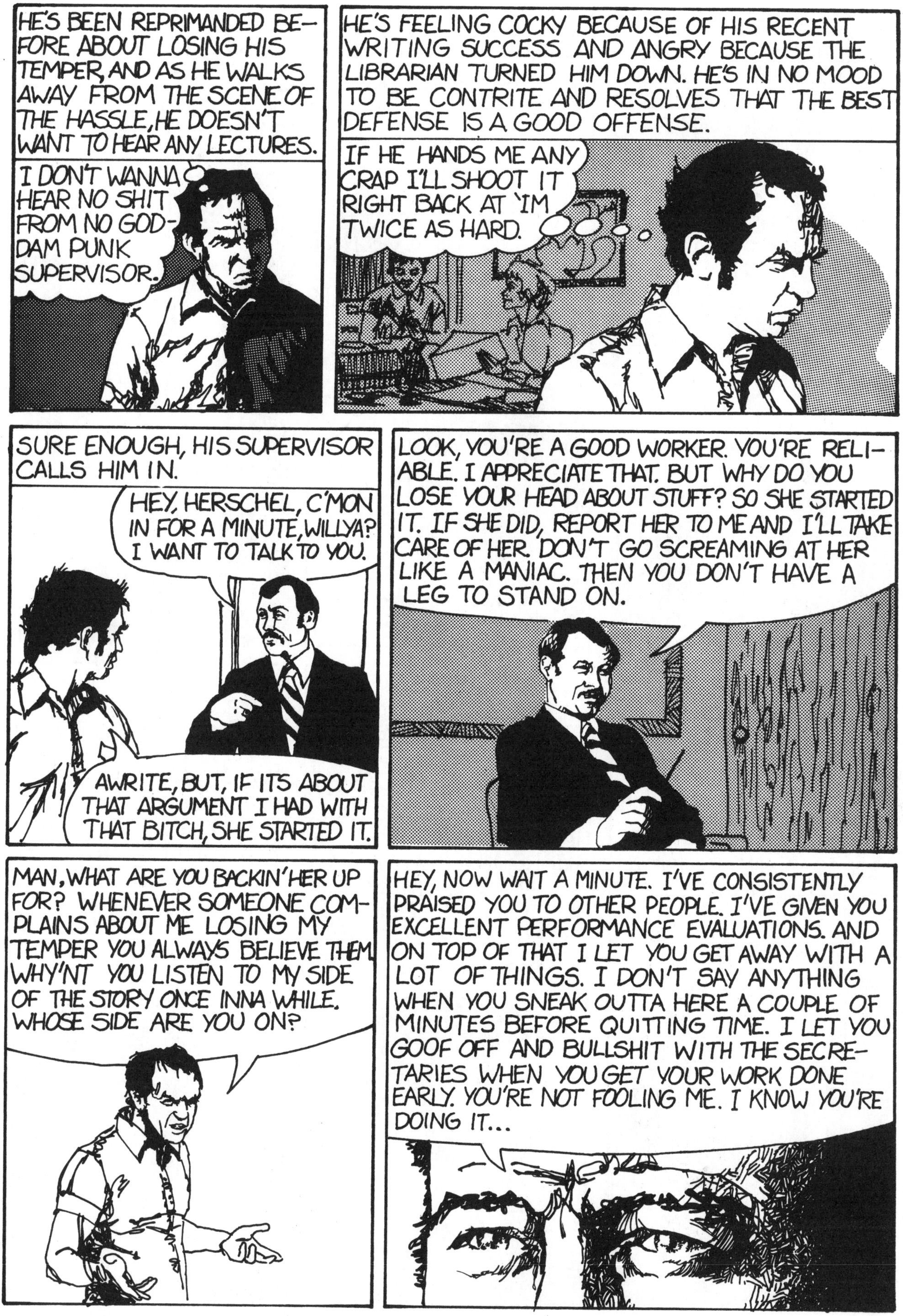
HE'S BEEN REPRIMANDED BEFORE ABOUT LOSING HIS TEMPER, AND AS HE WALKS AWAY FROM THE SCENE OF THE HASSLE, HE DOESN'T WANT TO HEAR ANY LECTURES.
I DON'T WANNA HEAR NO SHIT FROM NO GOD-DAM PUNK SUPERVISOR.
HE'S FEELING COCKY BECAUSE OF HIS RECENT WRITING SUCCESS AND ANGRY BECAUSE THE LIBRARIAN TURNED HIM DOWN. HE'S IN NO MOOD TO BE CONTRITE AND RESOLVES THAT THE BEST DEFENSE IS A GOOD OFFENSE.
IF HE HANDS ME ANY CRAP I'LL SHOOT IT RIGHT BACK AT 'IM TWICE AS HARD.
SURE ENOUGH, HIS SUPERVISOR CALLS HIM IN.
HEY, HERSCHEL, C'MON IN FOR A MINUTE, WILLYA? I WANT TO TALK TO YOU.
AWRITE, BUT, IF ITS ABOUT THAT ARGUMENT I HAD WITH THAT BITCH, SHE STARTED IT.
LOOK, YOU'RE A GOOD WORKER. YOU'RE RELIABLE. I APPRECIATE THAT. BUT WHY DO YOU LOSE YOUR HEAD ABOUT STUFF? SO SHE STARTED IT. IF SHE DID, REPORT HER TO ME AND I'LL TAKE CARE OF HER. DON'T GO SCREAMING AT HER LIKE A MANIAC. THEN YOU DON'T HAVE A LEG TO STAND ON.
MAN, WHAT ARE YOU BACKIN' HER UP FOR? WHENEVER SOMEONE COMPLAINS ABOUT ME LOSING MY TEMPER YOU ALWAYS BELIEVE THEM. WHY'NT YOU LISTEN TO MY SIDE OF THE STORY ONCE INNA WHILE. WHOSE SIDE ARE YOU ON?
HEY, NOW WAIT A MINUTE. I'VE CONSISTENTLY PRAISED YOU TO OTHER PEOPLE. I'VE GIVEN YOU EXCELLENT PERFORMANCE EVALUATIONS. AND ON TOP OF THAT I LET YOU GET AWAY WITH A LOT OF THINGS. I DON'T SAY ANYTHING WHEN YOU SNEAK OUTTA HERE A COUPLE OF MINUTES BEFORE QUITTING TIME. I LET YOU GOOF OFF AND BULLSHIT WITH THE SECRETARIES WHEN YOU GET YOUR WORK DONE EARLY. YOU'RE NOT FOOLING ME. I KNOW YOU'RE DOING IT...

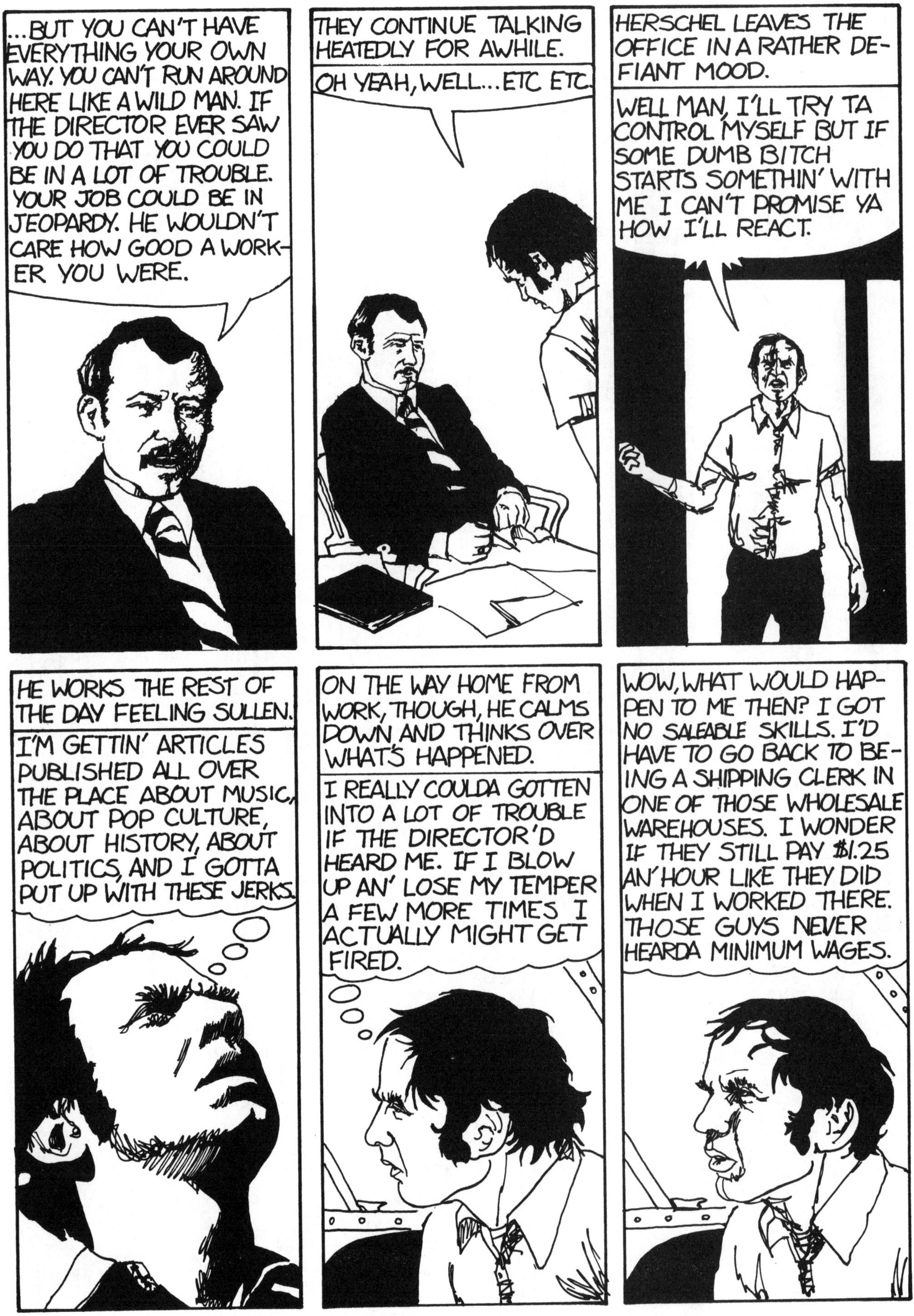
...BUT YOU CAN'T HAVE EVERYTHING YOUR OWN WAY. YOU CAN'T RUN AROUND HERE LIKE A WILD MAN. IF THE DIRECTOR EVER SAW YOU DO THAT YOU COULD BE IN A LOT OF TROUBLE. YOUR JOB COULD BE IN JEOPARDY. HE WOULDN'T CARE HOW GOOD A WORKER YOU WERE.
THEY CONTINUE TALKING HEATEDLY FOR AWHILE.
OH YEAH, WELL... ETC ETC.
HERSCHEL LEAVES THE OFFICE IN A RATHER DEFIANT MOOD.
WELL MAN, I'LL TRY TA CONTROL MYSELF BUT IF SOME DUMB BITCH STARTS SOMETHIN' WITH ME I CAN'T PROMISE YA HOW I'LL REACT.
HE WORKS THE REST OF THE DAY FEELING SULLEN.
I'M GETTIN' ARTICLES PUBLISHED ALL OVER THE PLACE ABOUT MUSIC, ABOUT POP CULTURE, ABOUT HISTORY, ABOUT POLITICS, AND I GOTTA PUT UP WITH THESE JERKS.
ON THE WAY HOME FROM WORK, THOUGH, HE CALMS DOWN AND THINKS OVER WHAT'S HAPPENED.
I REALLY COULDA GOTTEN INTO A LOT OF TROUBLE IF THE DIRECTOR'D HEARD ME. IF I BLOW UP AN' LOSE MY TEMPER A FEW MORE TIMES I ACTUALLY MIGHT GET FIRED.
WOW, WHAT WOULD HAPPEN TO ME THEN? I GOT NO SALEABLE SKILLS. I'D HAVE TO GO BACK TO BEING A SHIPPING CLERK IN ONE OF THOSE WHOLESALE WAREHOUSES. I WONDER IF THEY STILL PAY $1.25 AN' HOUR LIKE THEY DID WHEN I WORKED THERE. THOSE GUYS NEVER HEARDA MINIMUM WAGES.

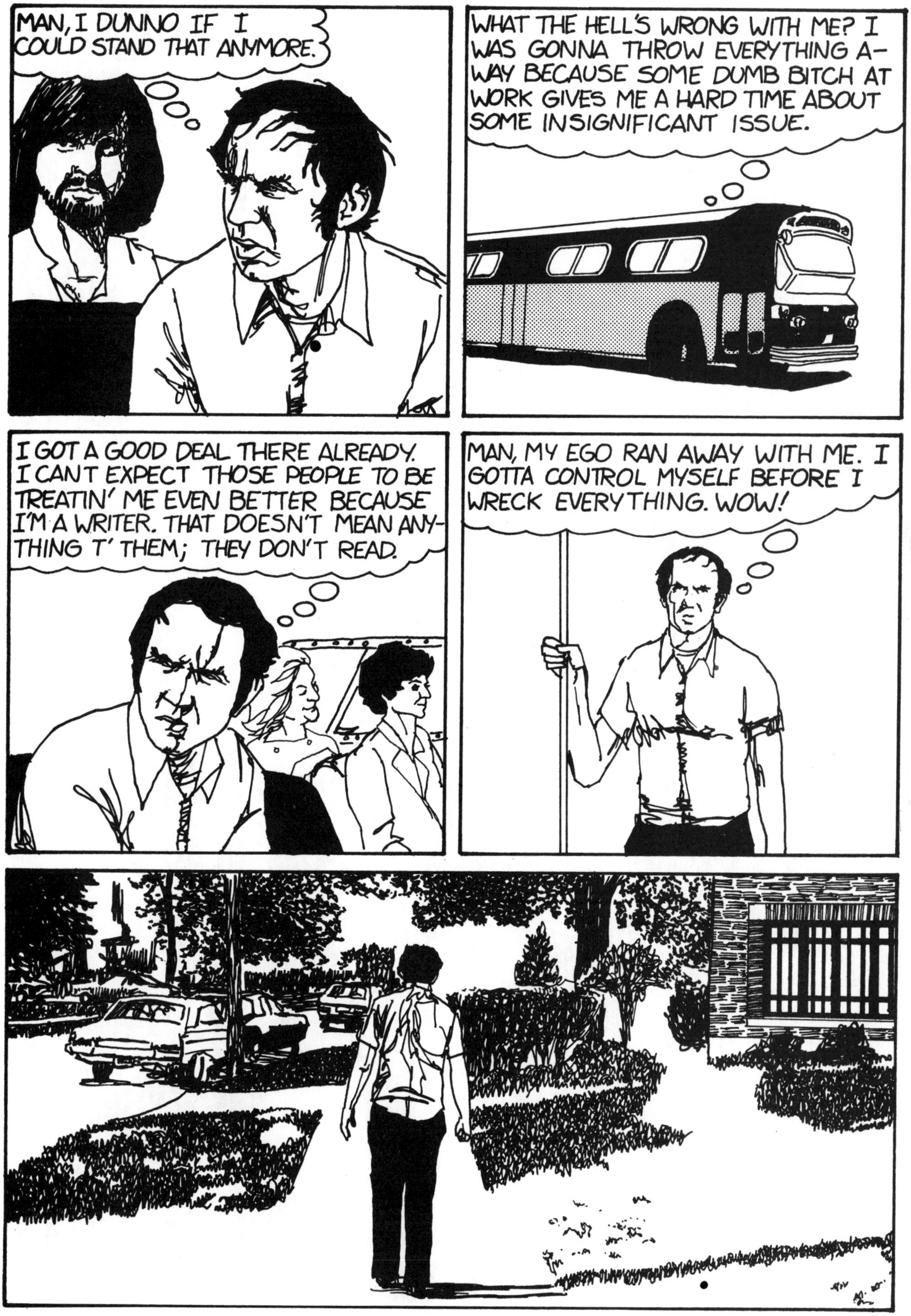
MAN, I DUNNO IF I COULD STAND THAT ANYMORE.
WHAT THE HELL'S WRONG WITH ME? I WAS GONNA THROW EVERYTHING A-WAY BECAUSE SOME DUMB BITCH AT WORK GIVES ME A HARD TIME ABOUT SOME INSIGNIFICANT ISSUE.
I GOT A GOOD DEAL THERE ALREADY. I CAN'T EXPECT THOSE PEOPLE TO BE TREATIN' ME EVEN BETTER BECAUSE I'M A WRITER. THAT DOESN'T MEAN ANY-THING T' THEM; THEY DON'T READ.
MAN, MY EGO RAN AWAY WITH ME. I GOTTA CONTROL MYSELF BEFORE I WRECK EVERYTHING. WOW!

working man's nightmare

STORY BY HARVEY PEKAR
ILLUSTRATED BY GERRY SHAMRAY

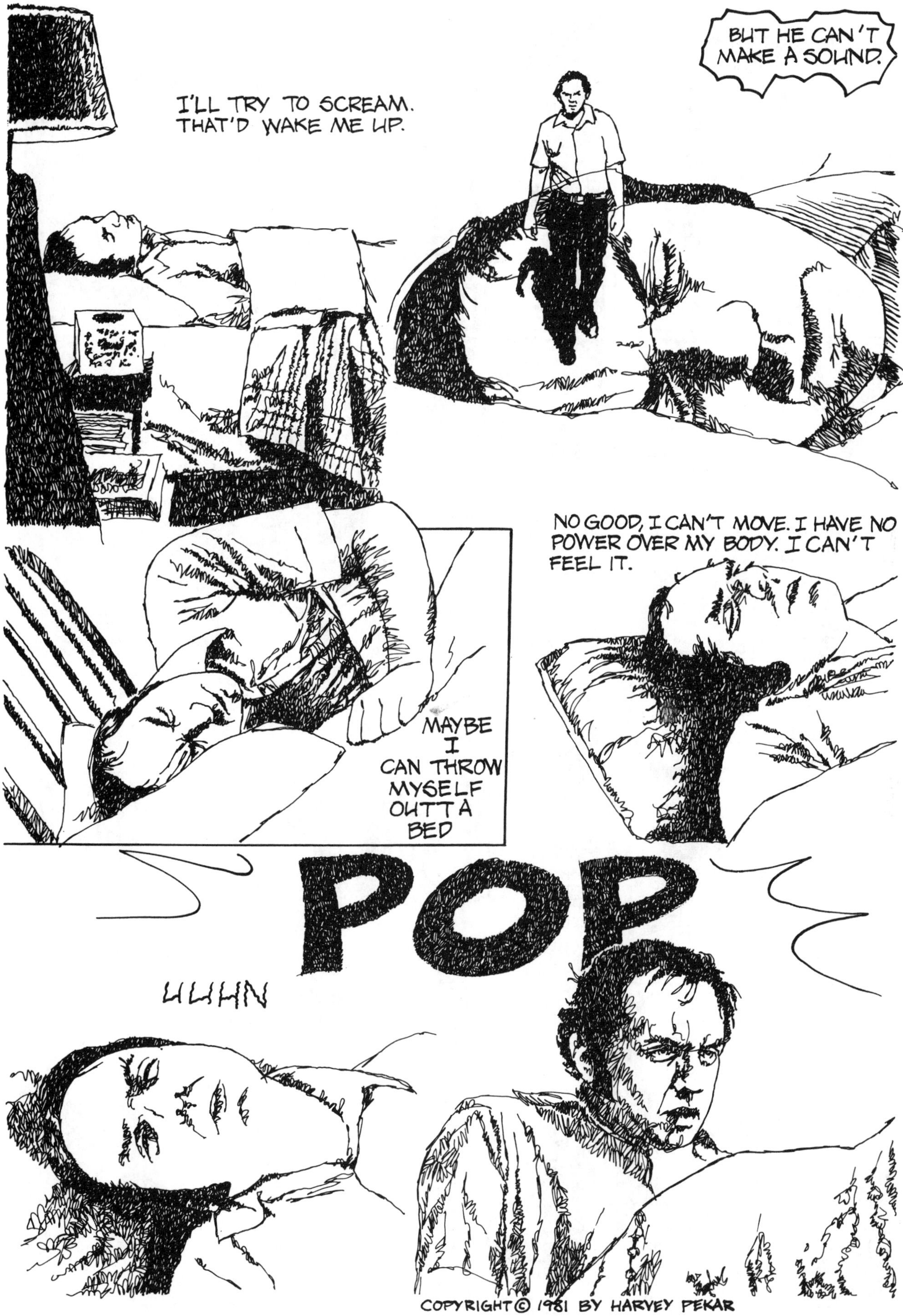
I'LL TRY TO SCREAM. THAT'D WAKE ME UP.
BUT HE CAN'T MAKE A SOUND.
MAYBE I CAN THROW MYSELF OUTTA BED
NO GOOD, I CAN'T MOVE. I HAVE NO POWER OVER MY BODY. I CAN'T FEEL IT.
POP
UUHN

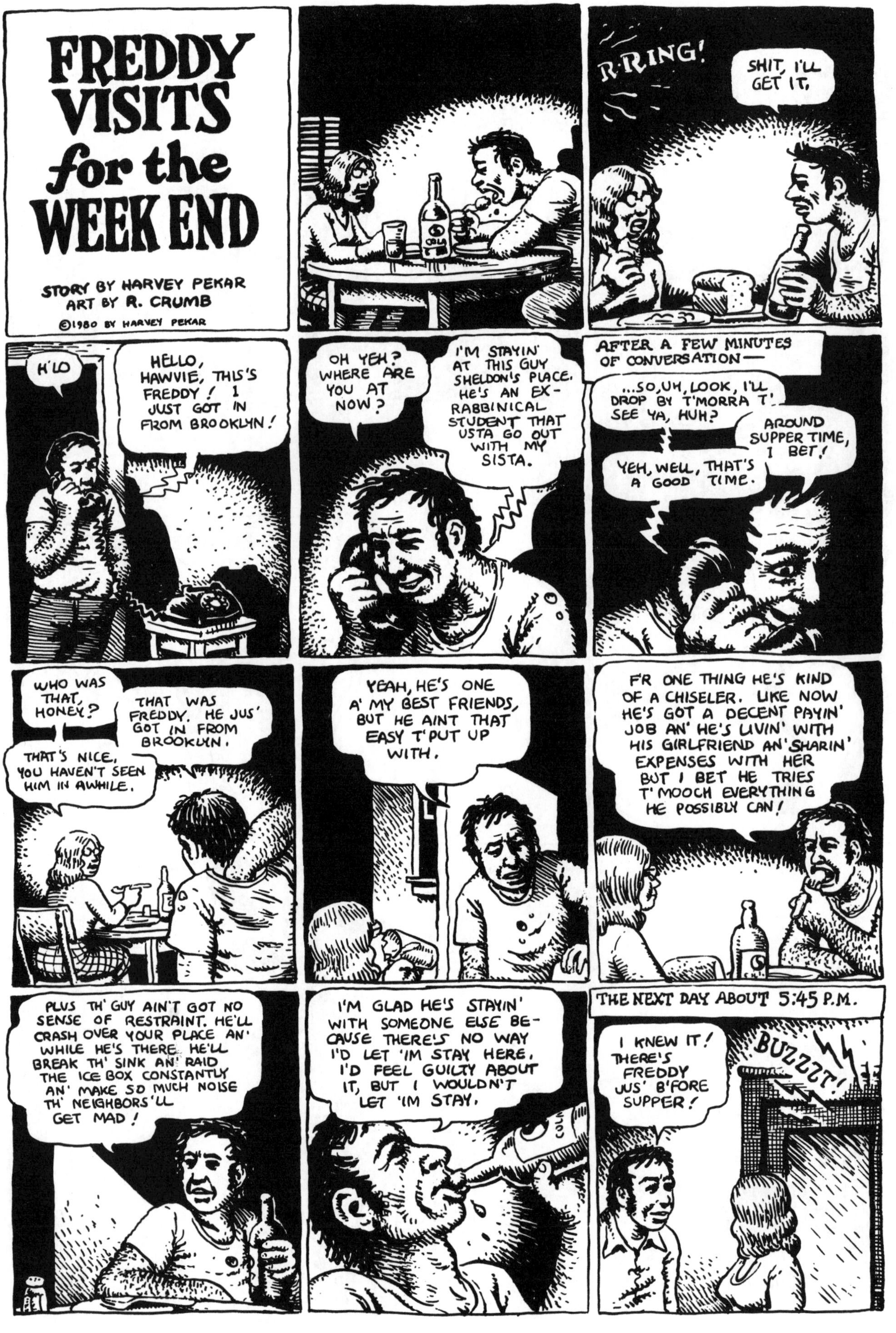
FREDDY VISITS for the WEEK END
STORY BY HARVEY PEKAR
ART BY R. CRUMB
©1980 BY HARVEY PEKAR
R-RING!
SHIT, I'LL GET IT,
H'LO
HELLO, HAWVIE, THIS'S FREDDY! I JUST GOT IN FROM BROOKLYN!
OH YEH? WHERE ARE YOU AT NOW?
I'M STAYIN' AT THIS GUY SHELDON'S PLACE. HE'S AN EX-RABBINICAL STUDENT THAT USTA GO OUT WITH MY SISTA.
AFTER A FEW MINUTES OF CONVERSATION—
...SO, UH, LOOK, I'LL DROP BY T'MORRA T' SEE YA, HUH?
AROUND SUPPER TIME, I BET!
YEH, WELL, THAT'S A GOOD TIME.
WHO WAS THAT, HONEY?
THAT WAS FREDDY. HE JUS' GOT IN FROM BROOKLYN.
THAT'S NICE, YOU HAVEN'T SEEN HIM IN AWHILE.
YEAH, HE'S ONE A' MY BEST FRIENDS, BUT HE AINT THAT EASY T'PUT UP WITH.
F'R ONE THING HE'S KIND OF A CHISELER. LIKE NOW HE'S GOT A DECENT PAYIN' JOB AN' HE'S LIVIN' WITH HIS GIRLFRIEND AN' SHARIN' EXPENSES WITH HER BUT I BET HE TRIES T'MOOCH EVERYTHING HE POSSIBLY CAN!
PLUS TH' GUY AIN'T GOT NO SENSE OF RESTRAINT. HE'LL CRASH OVER YOUR PLACE AN' WHILE HE'S THERE HE'LL BREAK TH' SINK AN' RAID THE ICE BOX CONSTANTLY AN' MAKE SO MUCH NOISE TH' NEIGHBORS'LL GET MAD!
I'M GLAD HE'S STAYIN' WITH SOMEONE ELSE BE-CAUSE THERE'S NO WAY I'D LET 'IM STAY HERE. I'D FEEL GUILTY ABOUT IT, BUT I WOULDN'T LET 'IM STAY.
THE NEXT DAY ABOUT 5:45 P.M.
BUZZZZT!
I KNEW IT! THERE'S FREDDY JUS' B'FORE SUPPER!

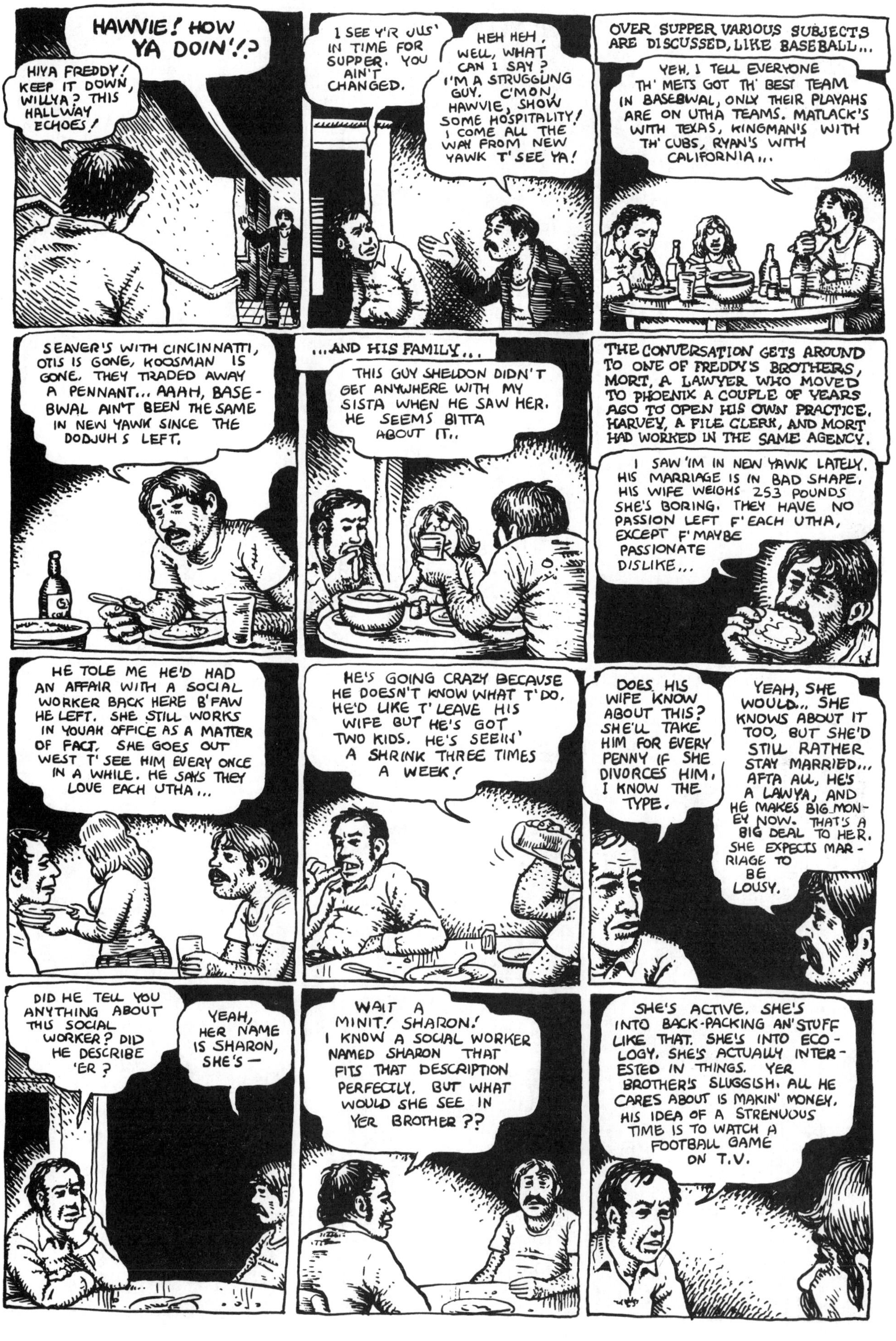
HAWVIE! HOW YA DOIN'!?
HIYA FREDDY! KEEP IT DOWN, WILLYA? THIS HALLWAY ECHOES!
I SEE Y'R JUS' IN TIME FOR SUPPER. YOU AIN'T CHANGED.
HEH HEH. WELL, WHAT CAN I SAY? I'M A STRUGGLING GUY. C'MON, HAWVIE, SHOW SOME HOSPITALITY! I COME ALL THE WAY FROM NEW YAWK T' SEE YA!
OVER SUPPER VARIOUS SUBJECTS ARE DISCUSSED, LIKE BASEBALL...
YEH, I TELL EVERYONE TH' METS GOT TH' BEST TEAM IN BASEBWAL, ONLY THEIR PLAYAHS ARE ON UTHA TEAMS. MATLACK'S WITH TEXAS, KINGMAN'S WITH TH' CUBS, RYAN'S WITH CALIFORNIA...
SEAVER'S WITH CINCINNATTI, OTIS IS GONE, KOOSMAN IS GONE. THEY TRADED AWAY A PENNANT... AAAH, BASE-BWAL AIN'T BEEN THE SAME IN NEW YAWK SINCE THE DODJUH'S LEFT.
...AND HIS FAMILY...
THIS GUY SHELDON DIDN'T GET ANYWHERE WITH MY SISTA WHEN HE SAW HER. HE SEEMS BITTA ABOUT IT..
THE CONVERSATION GETS AROUND TO ONE OF FREDDY'S BROTHERS, MORT, A LAWYER WHO MOVED TO PHOENIX A COUPLE OF YEARS AGO TO OPEN HIS OWN PRACTICE. HARVEY, A FILE CLERK, AND MORT HAD WORKED IN THE SAME AGENCY.
I SAW 'IM IN NEW YAWK LATELY. HIS MARRIAGE IS IN BAD SHAPE, HIS WIFE WEIGHS 253 POUNDS SHE'S BORING. THEY HAVE NO PASSION LEFT F'EACH UTHA, EXCEPT F'MAYBE PASSIONATE DISLIKE...
HE TOLE ME HE'D HAD AN AFFAIR WITH A SOCIAL WORKER BACK HERE B'FAW HE LEFT. SHE STILL WORKS IN YOUAH OFFICE AS A MATTER OF FACT. SHE GOES OUT WEST T' SEE HIM EVERY ONCE IN A WHILE. HE SAYS THEY LOVE EACH UTHA...
HE'S GOING CRAZY BECAUSE HE DOESN'T KNOW WHAT T'DO. HE'D LIKE T' LEAVE HIS WIFE BUT HE'S GOT TWO KIDS. HE'S SEEIN' A SHRINK THREE TIMES A WEEK!
DOES HIS WIFE KNOW ABOUT THIS? SHE'LL TAKE HIM FOR EVERY PENNY IF SHE DIVORCES HIM. I KNOW THE TYPE.
YEAH, SHE WOULD.. SHE KNOWS ABOUT IT TOO, BUT SHE'D STILL RATHER STAY MARRIED... AFTA ALL, HE'S A LAWYA, AND HE MAKES BIG MON-EY NOW. THAT'S A BIG DEAL TO HER. SHE EXPECTS MAR-RIAGE TO BE LOUSY.
DID HE TELL YOU ANYTHING ABOUT THIS SOCIAL WORKER? DID HE DESCRIBE 'ER?
YEAH, HER NAME IS SHARON, SHE'S —
WAIT A MINIT! SHARON! I KNOW A SOCIAL WORKER NAMED SHARON THAT FITS THAT DESCRIPTION PERFECTLY. BUT WHAT WOULD SHE SEE IN YER BROTHER??
SHE'S ACTIVE. SHE'S INTO BACK-PACKING AN' STUFF LIKE THAT. SHE'S INTO ECO-LOGY. SHE'S ACTUALLY INTER-ESTED IN THINGS. YER BROTHER'S SLUGGISH. ALL HE CARES ABOUT IS MAKIN' MONEY. HIS IDEA OF A STRENUOUS TIME IS TO WATCH A FOOTBALL GAME ON T.V.

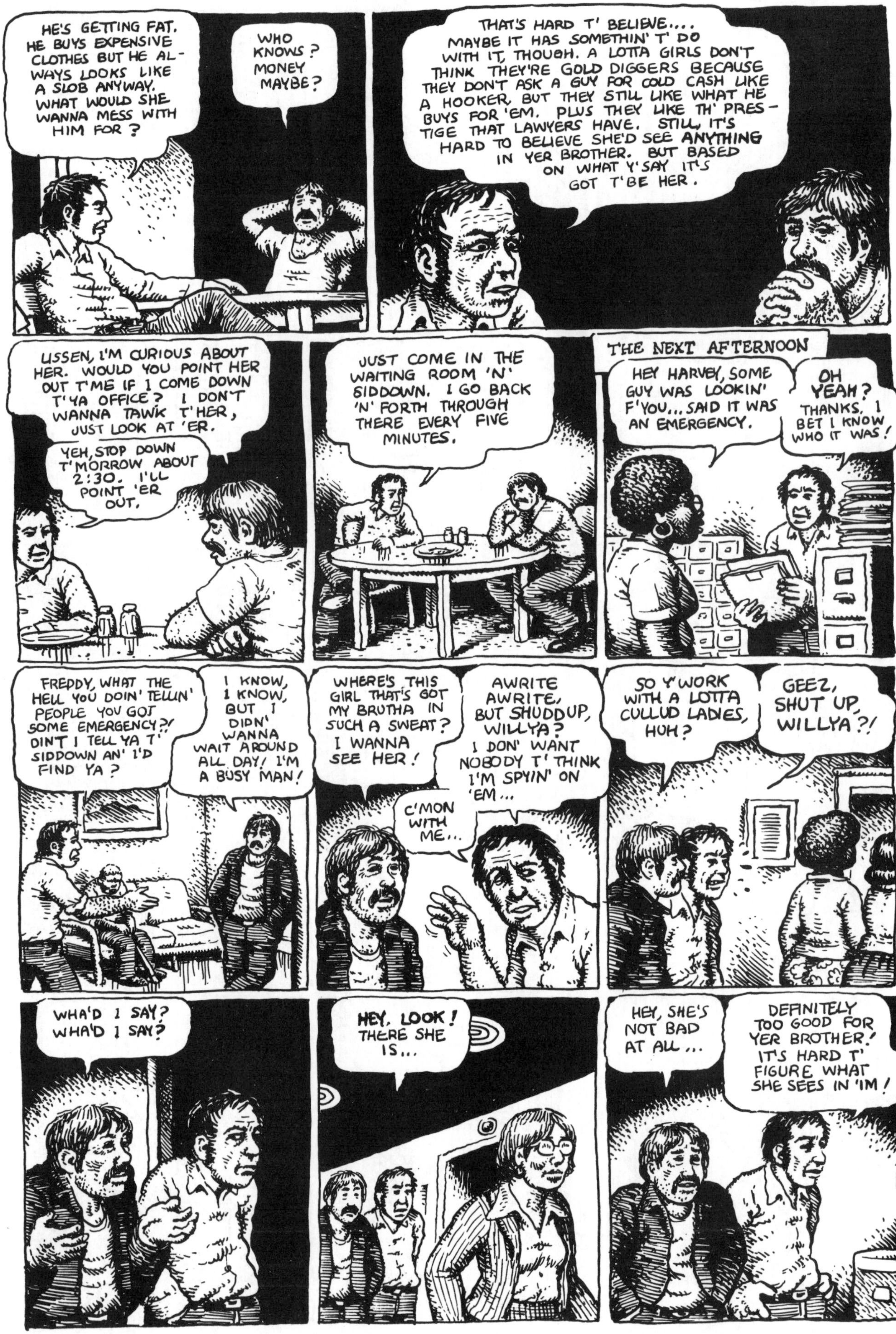

HE'S GETTING FAT. HE BUYS EXPENSIVE CLOTHES BUT HE ALWAYS LOOKS LIKE A SLOB ANYWAY. WHAT WOULD SHE WANNA MESS WITH HIM FOR?
WHO KNOWS? MONEY MAYBE?
THAT'S HARD T' BELIEVE.... MAYBE IT HAS SOMETHIN' T' DO WITH IT, THOUGH. A LOTTA GIRLS DON'T THINK THEY'RE GOLD DIGGERS BECAUSE THEY DON'T ASK A GUY FOR COLD CASH LIKE A HOOKER, BUT THEY STILL LIKE WHAT HE BUYS FOR 'EM. PLUS THEY LIKE TH' PRESTIGE THAT LAWYERS HAVE. STILL, IT'S HARD TO BELIEVE SHE'D SEE ANYTHING IN YER BROTHER. BUT BASED ON WHAT Y'SAY IT'S GOT T'BE HER.
LISSEN, I'M CURIOUS ABOUT HER. WOULD YOU POINT HER OUT T'ME IF I COME DOWN T'YA OFFICE? I DON'T WANNA TAWK T'HER, JUST LOOK AT 'ER.
YEH, STOP DOWN T'MORROW ABOUT 2:30. I'LL POINT 'ER OUT.
JUST COME IN THE WAITING ROOM 'N' SIDDOWN. I GO BACK 'N' FORTH THROUGH THERE EVERY FIVE MINUTES.
THE NEXT AFTERNOON
HEY HARVEY, SOME GUY WAS LOOKIN' F'YOU... SAID IT WAS AN EMERGENCY.
OH YEAH? THANKS. I BET I KNOW WHO IT WAS!
FREDDY, WHAT THE HELL YOU DOIN' TELLIN' PEOPLE YOU GOT SOME EMERGENCY?! DIN'T I TELL YA T' SIDDOWN AN' I'D FIND YA?
I KNOW, I KNOW, BUT I DIDN' WANNA WAIT AROUND ALL DAY! I'M A BUSY MAN!
WHERE'S THIS GIRL THAT'S GOT MY BRUTHA IN SUCH A SWEAT? I WANNA SEE HER!
AWRITE AWRITE, BUT SHUDDUP, WILLYA? I DON' WANT NOBODY T' THINK I'M SPYIN' ON 'EM...
C'MON WITH ME...
SO Y'WORK WITH A LOTTA CULLUD LADIES, HUH?
GEEZ, SHUT UP, WILLYA?!
WHA'D I SAY? WHA'D I SAY?
HEY, LOOK! THERE SHE IS...
HEY, SHE'S NOT BAD AT ALL...
DEFINITELY TOO GOOD FOR YER BROTHER! IT'S HARD T' FIGURE WHAT SHE SEES IN 'IM!

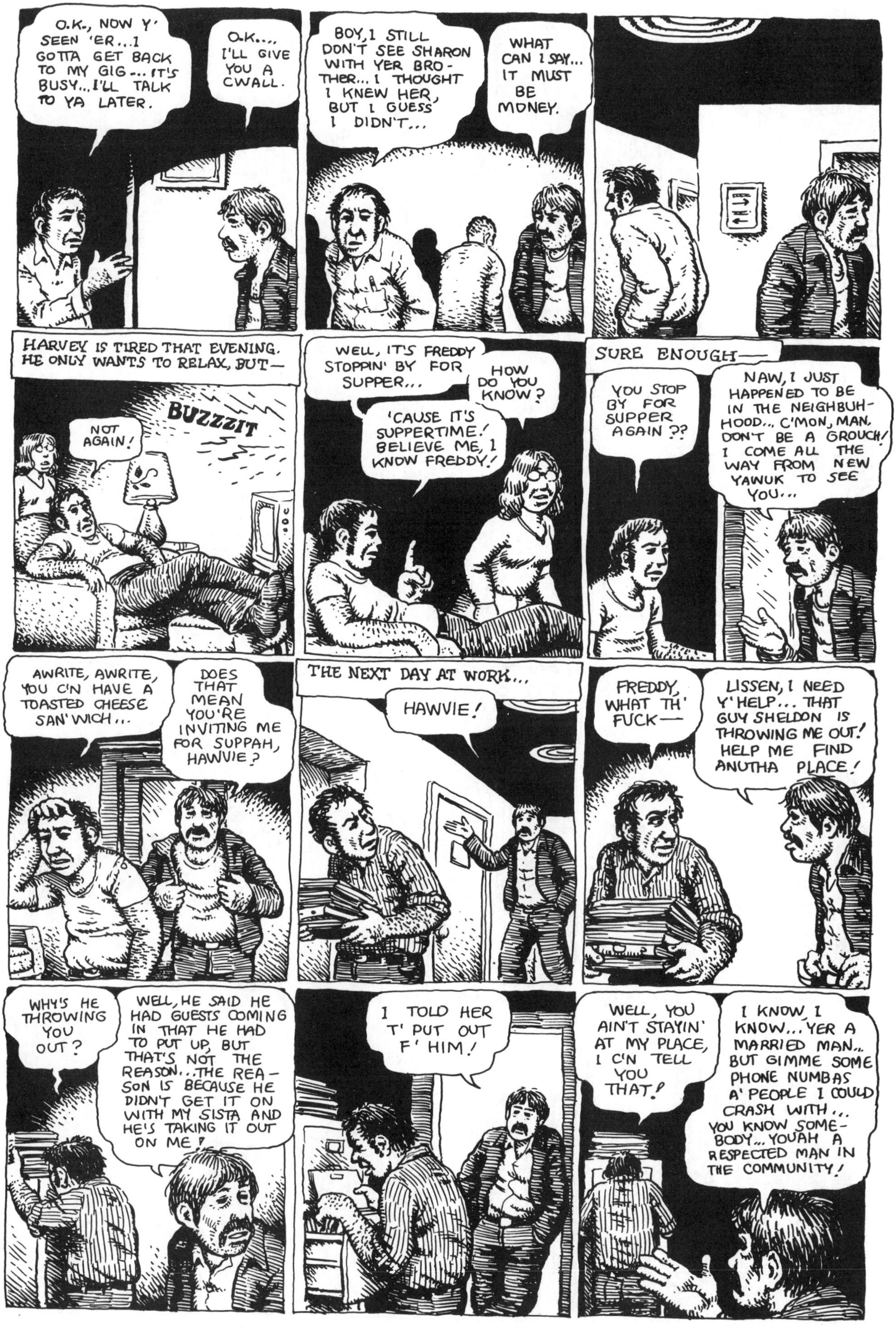
O.K., NOW Y' SEEN 'ER...I GOTTA GET BACK TO MY GIG...IT'S BUSY...I'LL TALK TO YA LATER.
O.K.... I'LL GIVE YOU A CWALL.
BOY, I STILL DON'T SEE SHARON WITH YER BROTHER...I THOUGHT I KNEW HER, BUT I GUESS I DIDN'T...
WHAT CAN I SAY... IT MUST BE MONEY.
HARVEY IS TIRED THAT EVENING. HE ONLY WANTS TO RELAX, BUT—
BUZZZIT
NOT AGAIN!
WELL, IT'S FREDDY STOPPIN' BY FOR SUPPER...
HOW DO YOU KNOW?
'CAUSE IT'S SUPPERTIME! BELIEVE ME, I KNOW FREDDY!
SURE ENOUGH—
YOU STOP BY FOR SUPPER AGAIN??
NAW, I JUST HAPPENED TO BE IN THE NEIGHBUHHOOD... C'MON, MAN, DON'T BE A GROUCH! I COME ALL THE WAY FROM NEW YAWUK TO SEE YOU...
AWRITE, AWRITE, YOU C'N HAVE A TOASTED CHEESE SAN'WICH...
DOES THAT MEAN YOU'RE INVITING ME FOR SUPPAH, HAWVIE?
THE NEXT DAY AT WORK...
HAWVIE!
FREDDY, WHAT TH' FUCK—
LISSEN, I NEED Y'HELP... THAT GUY SHELDON IS THROWING ME OUT! HELP ME FIND ANUTHA PLACE!
WHY'S HE THROWING YOU OUT?
WELL, HE SAID HE HAD GUESTS COMING IN THAT HE HAD TO PUT UP, BUT THAT'S NOT THE REASON...THE REASON IS BECAUSE HE DIDN'T GET IT ON WITH MY SISTA AND HE'S TAKING IT OUT ON ME!
I TOLD HER T' PUT OUT F' HIM!
WELL, YOU AIN'T STAYIN' AT MY PLACE, I C'N TELL YOU THAT!
I KNOW, I KNOW... YER A MARRIED MAN... BUT GIMME SOME PHONE NUMBAS A' PEOPLE I COULD CRASH WITH... YOU KNOW SOMEBODY... YOUAH A RESPECTED MAN IN THE COMMUNITY!

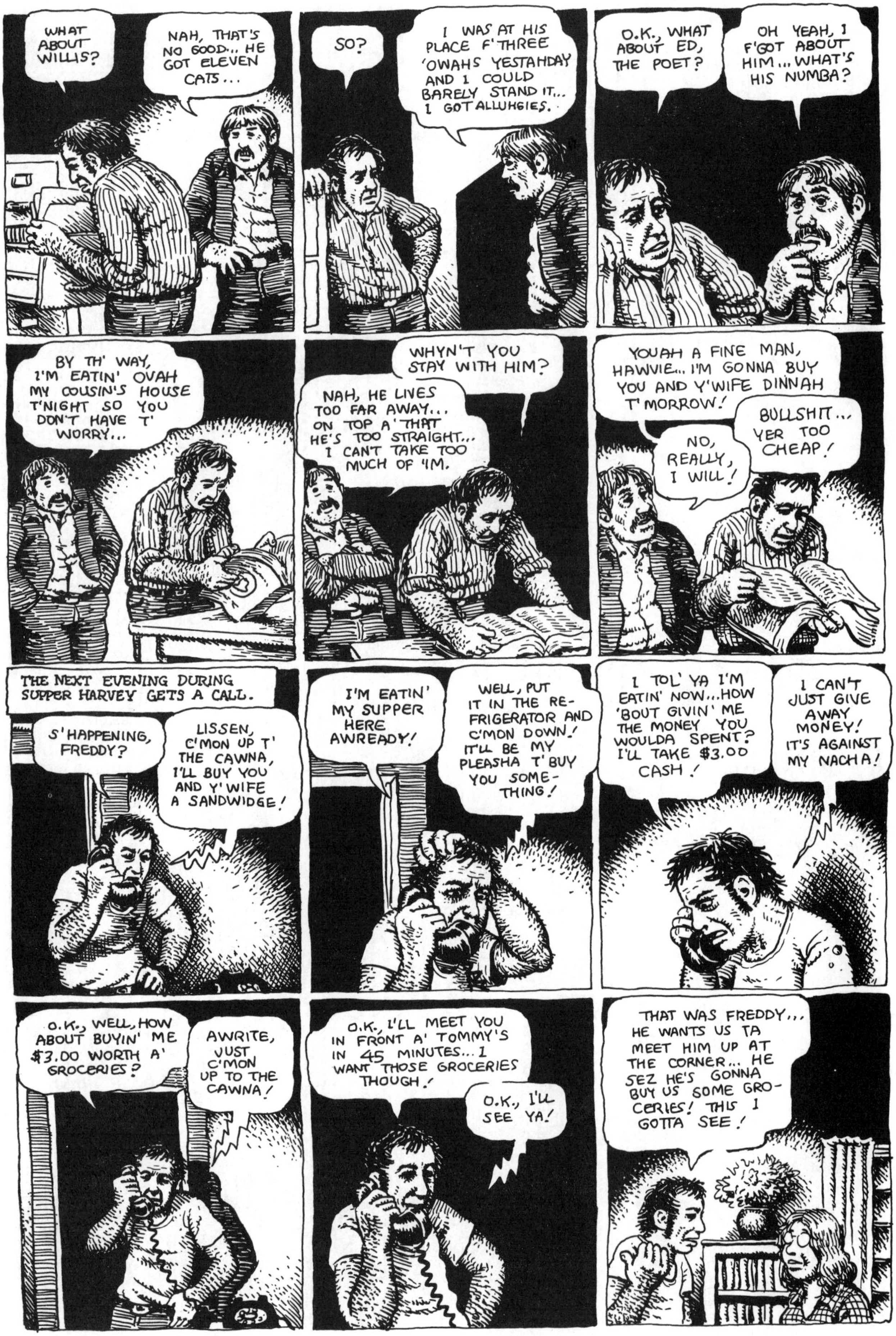
WHAT ABOUT WILLIS?
NAH, THAT'S NO GOOD... HE GOT ELEVEN CATS...
SO?
I WAS AT HIS PLACE F' THREE 'OWAHS YESTAHDAY AND I COULD BARELY STAND IT... I GOT ALLUHGIES.
O.K., WHAT ABOUT ED, THE POET?
OH YEAH, I F'GOT ABOUT HIM... WHAT'S HIS NUMBA?
BY TH' WAY, I'M EATIN' OVAH MY COUSIN'S HOUSE T'NIGHT SO YOU DON'T HAVE T' WORRY...
WHYN'T YOU STAY WITH HIM?
NAH, HE LIVES TOO FAR AWAY... ON TOP A' THAT HE'S TOO STRAIGHT... I CAN'T TAKE TOO MUCH OF 'IM.
YOUAH A FINE MAN, HAWVIE... I'M GONNA BUY YOU AND Y'WIFE DINNAH T'MORROW!
NO, REALLY, I WILL!
BULLSHIT... YER TOO CHEAP!
THE NEXT EVENING DURING SUPPER HARVEY GETS A CALL.
S'HAPPENING, FREDDY?
LISSEN, C'MON UP T' THE CAWNA, I'LL BUY YOU AND Y'WIFE A SANDWIDGE!
I'M EATIN' MY SUPPER HERE AWREADY!
WELL, PUT IT IN THE RE-FRIGERATOR AND C'MON DOWN! IT'LL BE MY PLEASHA T'BUY YOU SOME-THING!
I TOL' YA I'M EATIN' NOW... HOW 'BOUT GIVIN' ME THE MONEY YOU WOULDA SPENT? I'LL TAKE $3.00 CASH!
I CAN'T JUST GIVE AWAY MONEY! IT'S AGAINST MY NACHA!
O.K., WELL, HOW ABOUT BUYIN' ME $3.00 WORTH A' GROCERIES?
AWRITE, JUST C'MON UP TO THE CAWNA!
O.K., I'LL MEET YOU IN FRONT A' TOMMY'S IN 45 MINUTES... I WANT THOSE GROCERIES THOUGH!
O.K., I'LL SEE YA!
THAT WAS FREDDY... HE WANTS US TA MEET HIM UP AT THE CORNER... HE SEZ HE'S GONNA BUY US SOME GRO-CERIES! THIS I GOTTA SEE!

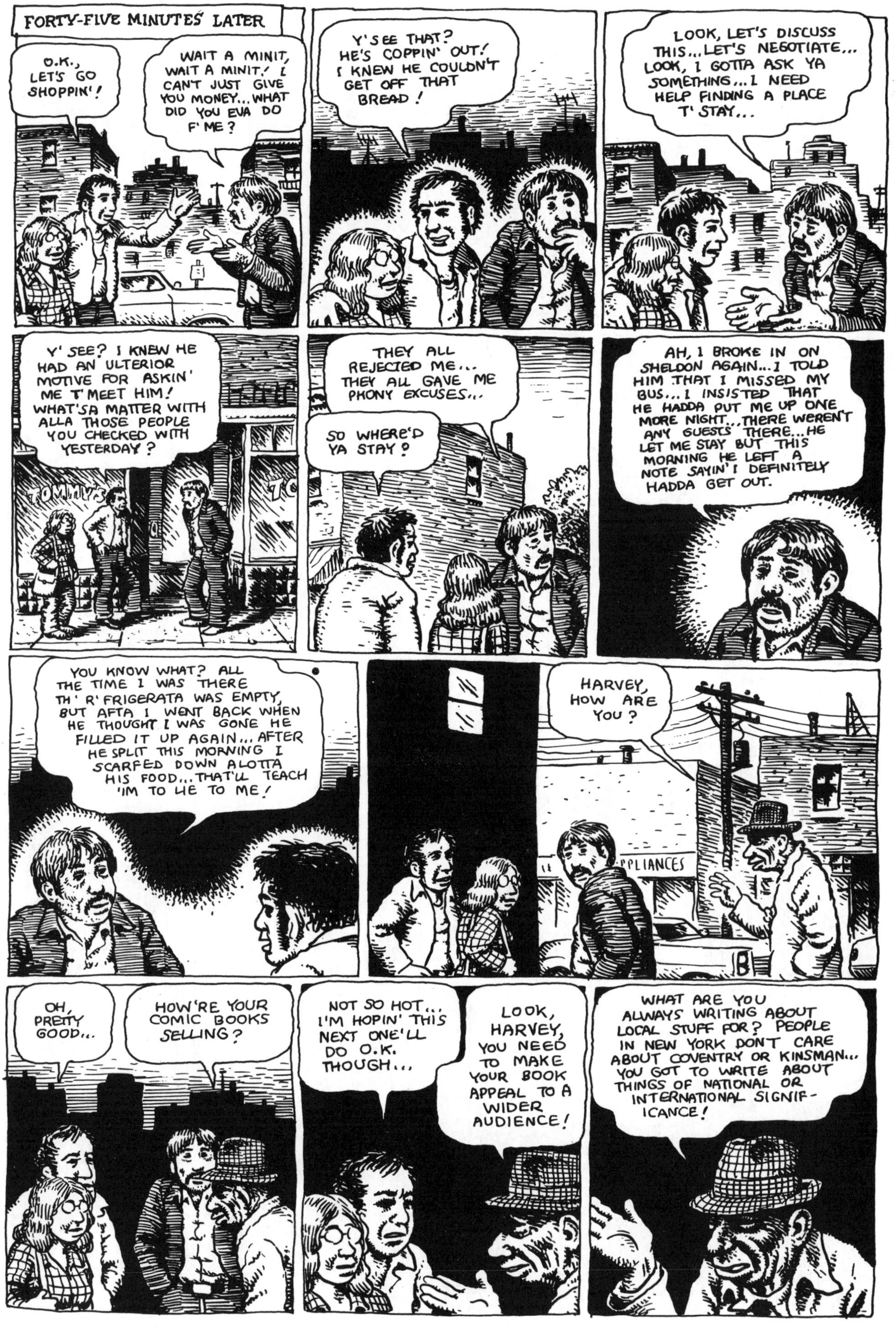
FORTY-FIVE MINUTES LATER
O.K., LET'S GO SHOPPIN'!
WAIT A MINIT, WAIT A MINIT! I CAN'T JUST GIVE YOU MONEY... WHAT DID YOU EVA DO F'ME?
Y'SEE THAT? HE'S COPPIN' OUT! I KNEW HE COULDN'T GET OFF THAT BREAD!
LOOK, LET'S DISCUSS THIS... LET'S NEGOTIATE... LOOK, I GOTTA ASK YA SOMETHING... I NEED HELP FINDING A PLACE T' STAY...
Y' SEE? I KNEW HE HAD AN ULTERIOR MOTIVE FOR ASKIN' ME T'MEET HIM! WHAT'SA MATTER WITH ALLA THOSE PEOPLE YOU CHECKED WITH YESTERDAY?
TOMMY'S
THEY ALL REJECTED ME... THEY ALL GAVE ME PHONY EXCUSES...
SO WHERE'D YA STAY?
AH, I BROKE IN ON SHELDON AGAIN... I TOLD HIM THAT I MISSED MY BUS... I INSISTED THAT HE HADDA PUT ME UP ONE MORE NIGHT... THERE WEREN'T ANY GUESTS THERE... HE LET ME STAY BUT THIS MORNING HE LEFT A NOTE SAYIN' I DEFINITELY HADDA GET OUT.
YOU KNOW WHAT? ALL THE TIME I WAS THERE TH' R'FRIGERATA WAS EMPTY, BUT AFTA I WENT BACK WHEN HE THOUGHT I WAS GONE HE FILLED IT UP AGAIN... AFTER HE SPLIT THIS MORNING I SCARFED DOWN ALOTTA HIS FOOD... THAT'LL TEACH 'IM TO LIE TO ME!
HARVEY, HOW ARE YOU?
PPLIANCES
OH, PRETTY GOOD...
HOW'RE YOUR COMIC BOOKS SELLING?
NOT SO HOT... I'M HOPIN' THIS NEXT ONE'LL DO O.K. THOUGH...
LOOK, HARVEY, YOU NEED TO MAKE YOUR BOOK APPEAL TO A WIDER AUDIENCE!
WHAT ARE YOU ALWAYS WRITING ABOUT LOCAL STUFF FOR? PEOPLE IN NEW YORK DON'T CARE ABOUT COVENTRY OR KINSMAN... YOU GOT TO WRITE ABOUT THINGS OF NATIONAL OR INTERNATIONAL SIGNIF-ICANCE!

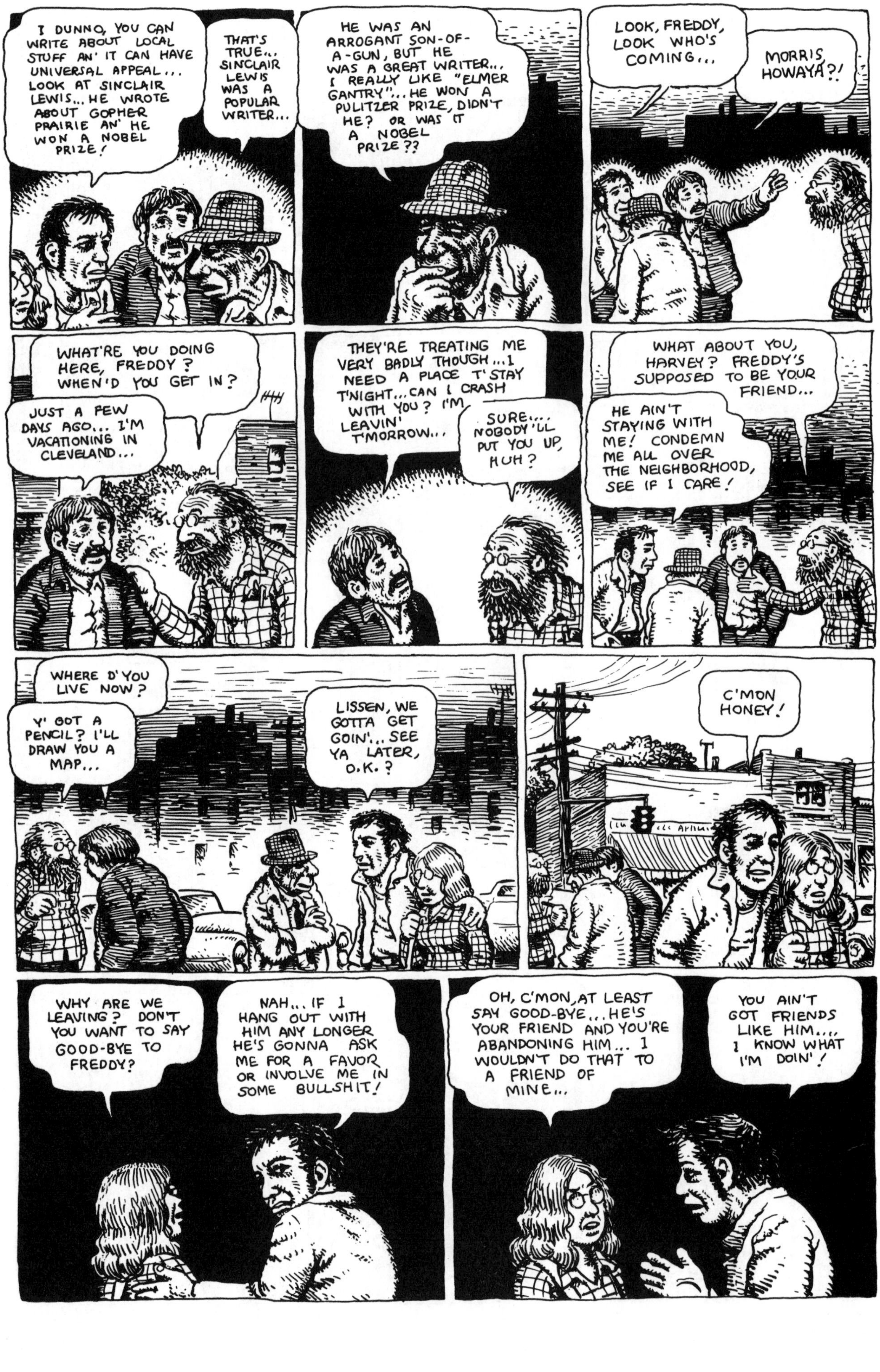
I DUNNO, YOU CAN WRITE ABOUT LOCAL STUFF AN' IT CAN HAVE UNIVERSAL APPEAL... LOOK AT SINCLAIR LEWIS... HE WROTE ABOUT GOPHER PRAIRIE AN' HE WON A NOBEL PRIZE!
THAT'S TRUE... SINCLAIR LEWIS WAS A POPULAR WRITER...
HE WAS AN ARROGANT SON-OF-A-GUN, BUT HE WAS A GREAT WRITER... I REALLY LIKE "ELMER GANTRY"... HE WON A PULITZER PRIZE, DIDN'T HE? OR WAS IT A NOBEL PRIZE??
LOOK, FREDDY, LOOK WHO'S COMING...
MORRIS HOWAYA?!
WHAT'RE YOU DOING HERE, FREDDY? WHEN'D YOU GET IN?
JUST A FEW DAYS AGO... I'M VACATIONING IN CLEVELAND...
THEY'RE TREATING ME VERY BADLY THOUGH... I NEED A PLACE T' STAY T'NIGHT... CAN I CRASH WITH YOU? I'M LEAVIN' T'MORROW...
SURE... NOBODY'LL PUT YOU UP, HUH?
WHAT ABOUT YOU, HARVEY? FREDDY'S SUPPOSED TO BE YOUR FRIEND...
HE AIN'T STAYING WITH ME! CONDEMN ME ALL OVER THE NEIGHBORHOOD, SEE IF I CARE!
WHERE D'YOU LIVE NOW?
Y' GOT A PENCIL? I'LL DRAW YOU A MAP...
LISSEN, WE GOTTA GET GOIN'... SEE YA LATER, O.K.?
C'MON HONEY!
WHY ARE WE LEAVING? DON'T YOU WANT TO SAY GOOD-BYE TO FREDDY?
NAH... IF I HANG OUT WITH HIM ANY LONGER HE'S GONNA ASK ME FOR A FAVOR OR INVOLVE ME IN SOME BULLSHIT!
OH, C'MON, AT LEAST SAY GOOD-BYE... HE'S YOUR FRIEND AND YOU'RE ABANDONING HIM... I WOULDN'T DO THAT TO A FRIEND OF MINE...
YOU AIN'T GOT FRIENDS LIKE HIM... I KNOW WHAT I'M DOIN'!

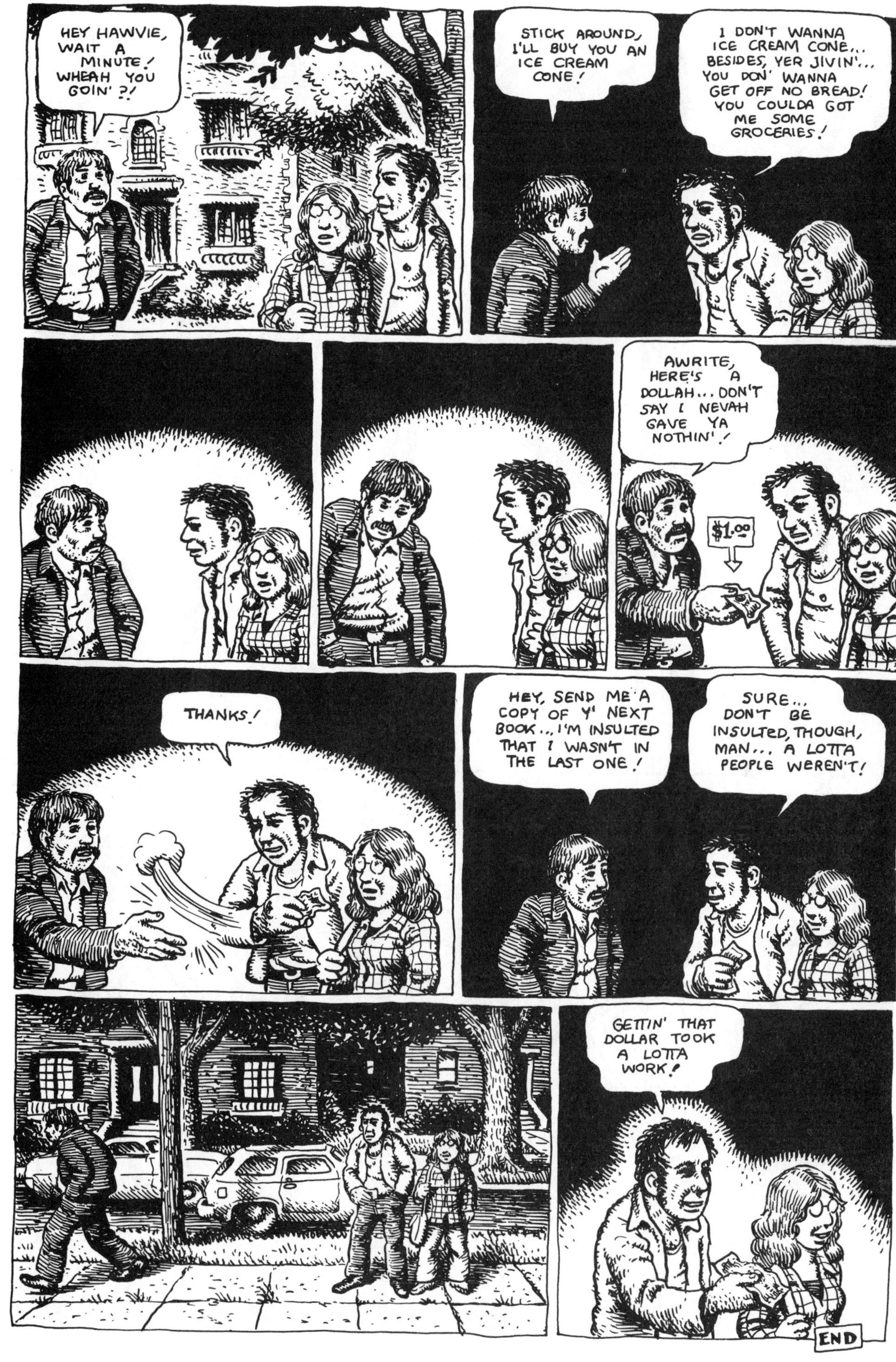
HEY HAWVIE, WAIT A MINUTE! WHEAH YOU GOIN' ?!
STICK AROUND, I'LL BUY YOU AN ICE CREAM CONE!
I DON'T WANNA ICE CREAM CONE... BESIDES, YER JIVIN'... YOU DON' WANNA GET OFF NO BREAD! YOU COULDA GOT ME SOME GROCERIES!
AWRITE, HERE'S A DOLLAH... DON'T SAY I NEVAH GAVE YA NOTHIN'!
$1.00
THANKS!
HEY, SEND ME A COPY OF Y' NEXT BOOK..., I'M INSULTED THAT I WASN'T IN THE LAST ONE!
SURE... DON'T BE INSULTED, THOUGH, MAN... A LOTTA PEOPLE WEREN'T!
GETTIN' THAT DOLLAR TOOK A LOTTA WORK!
END

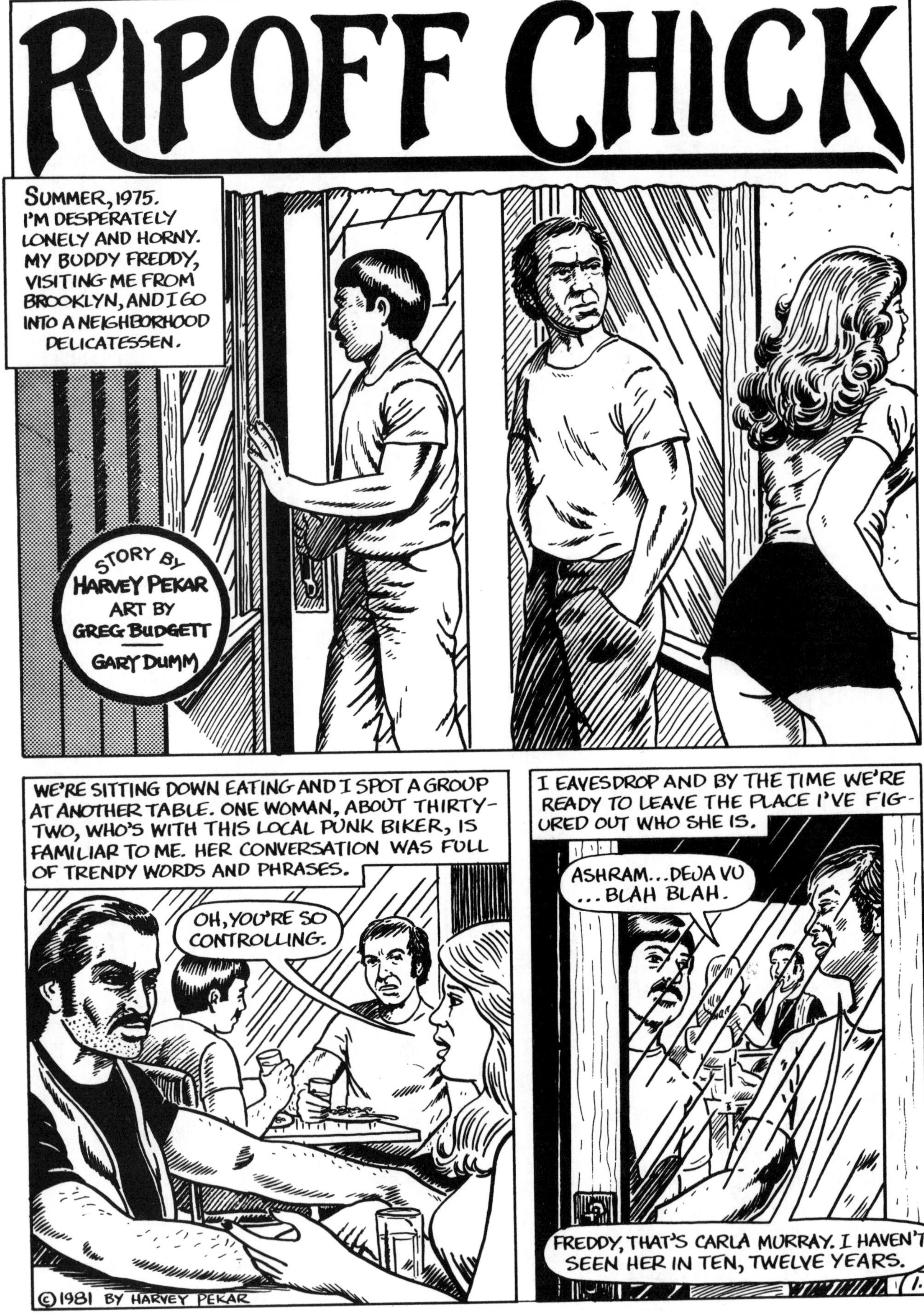
RIPOFF CHICK
SUMMER, 1975. I'M DESPERATELY LONELY AND HORNY. MY BUDDY FREDDY, VISITING ME FROM BROOKLYN, AND I GO INTO A NEIGHBORHOOD DELICATESSEN.
STORY BY HARVEY PEKAR ART BY GREG BUDGETT GARY DUMM
WE'RE SITTING DOWN EATING AND I SPOT A GROUP AT ANOTHER TABLE. ONE WOMAN, ABOUT THIRTY-TWO, WHO'S WITH THIS LOCAL PUNK BIKER, IS FAMILIAR TO ME. HER CONVERSATION WAS FULL OF TRENDY WORDS AND PHRASES.
OH, YOU'RE SO CONTROLLING.
©1981 BY HARVEY PEKAR
I EAVESDROP AND BY THE TIME WE'RE READY TO LEAVE THE PLACE I'VE FIGURED OUT WHO SHE IS.
ASHRAM... DEJA VU ... BLAH BLAH.
FREDDY, THAT'S CARLA MURRAY. I HAVEN'T SEEN HER IN TEN, TWELVE YEARS.
1.

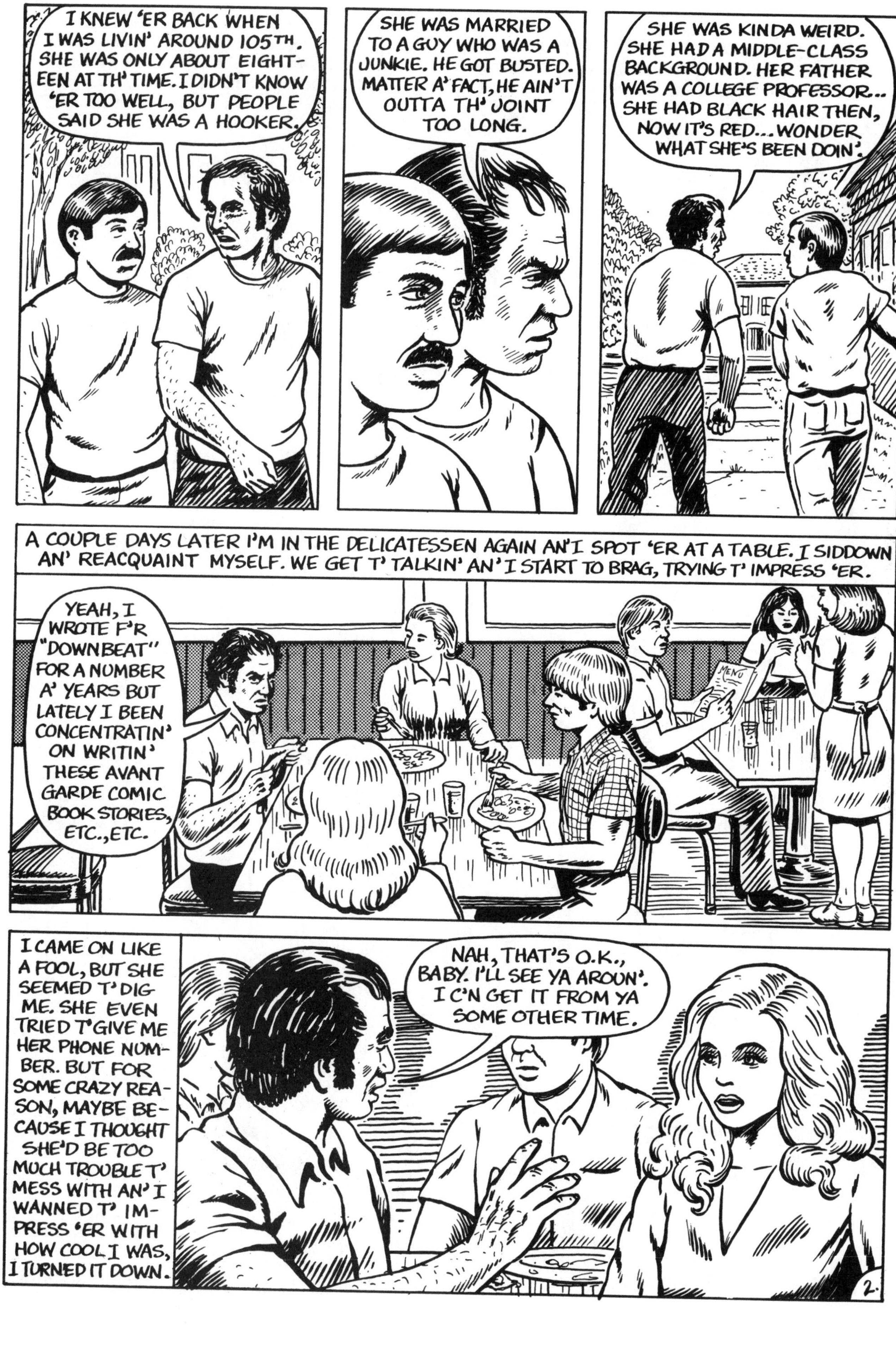
I KNEW 'ER BACK WHEN I WAS LIVIN' AROUND 105TH. SHE WAS ONLY ABOUT EIGHTEEN AT TH' TIME. I DIDN'T KNOW 'ER TOO WELL, BUT PEOPLE SAID SHE WAS A HOOKER.
SHE WAS MARRIED TO A GUY WHO WAS A JUNKIE. HE GOT BUSTED. MATTER A' FACT, HE AIN'T OUTTA TH' JOINT TOO LONG.
SHE WAS KINDA WEIRD. SHE HAD A MIDDLE-CLASS BACKGROUND. HER FATHER WAS A COLLEGE PROFESSOR... SHE HAD BLACK HAIR THEN, NOW IT'S RED... WONDER WHAT SHE'S BEEN DOIN'.
A COUPLE DAYS LATER I'M IN THE DELICATESSEN AGAIN AN' I SPOT 'ER AT A TABLE. I SIDDOWN AN' REACQUAINT MYSELF. WE GET T' TALKIN' AN' I START TO BRAG, TRYING T' IMPRESS 'ER.
YEAH, I WROTE F'R "DOWNBEAT" FOR A NUMBER A' YEARS BUT LATELY I BEEN CONCENTRATIN' ON WRITIN' THESE AVANT GARDE COMIC BOOK STORIES, ETC., ETC.
MENU
I CAME ON LIKE A FOOL, BUT SHE SEEMED T' DIG ME. SHE EVEN TRIED T' GIVE ME HER PHONE NUMBER. BUT FOR SOME CRAZY REASON, MAYBE BECAUSE I THOUGHT SHE'D BE TOO MUCH TROUBLE T' MESS WITH AN' I WANNED T' IMPRESS 'ER WITH HOW COOL I WAS, I TURNED IT DOWN.
NAH, THAT'S O.K., BABY. I'LL SEE YA AROUN'. I C'N GET IT FROM YA SOME OTHER TIME.
2.

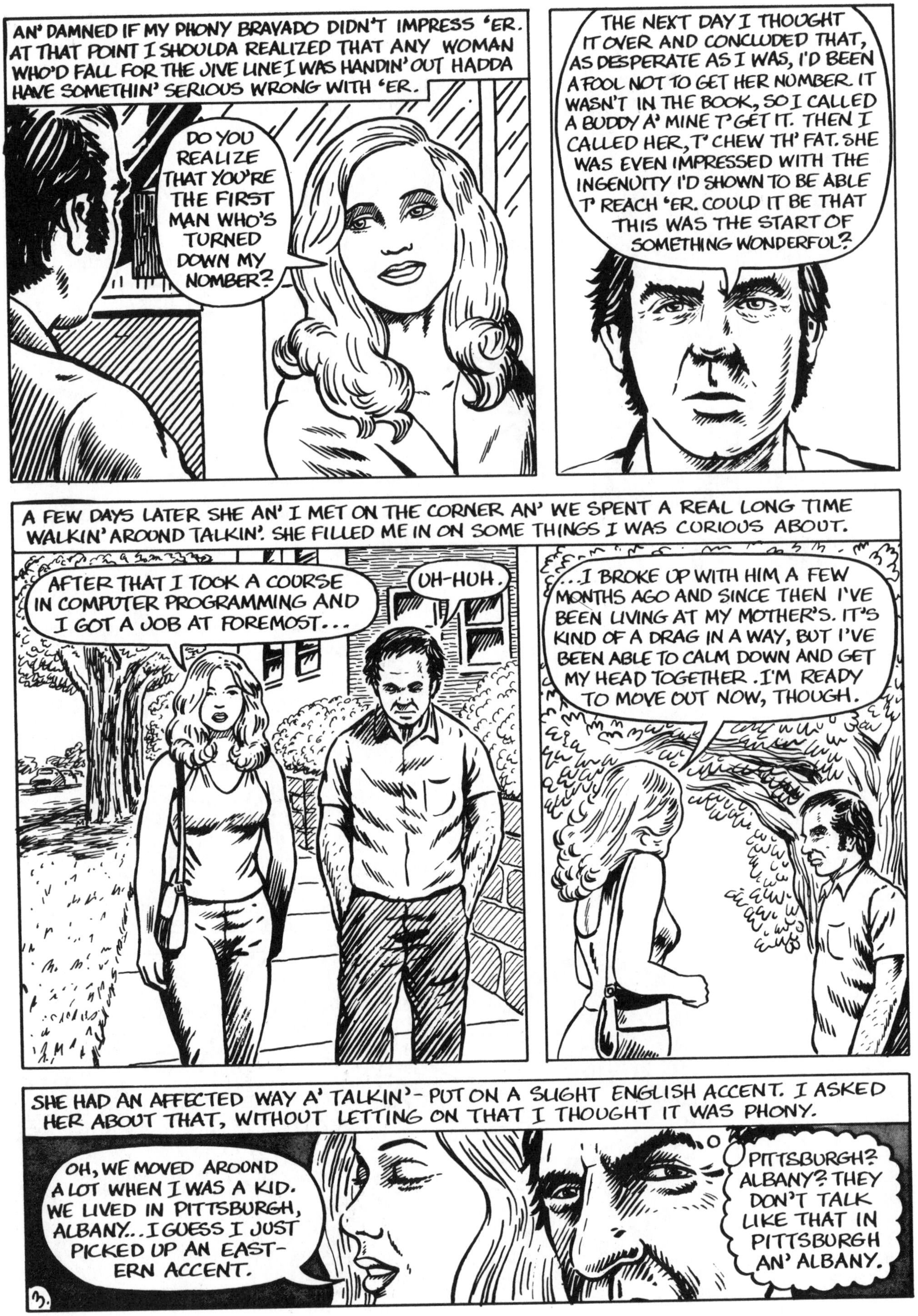

AN' DAMNED IF MY PHONY BRAVADO DIDN'T IMPRESS 'ER. AT THAT POINT I SHOULDA REALIZED THAT ANY WOMAN WHO'D FALL FOR THE JIVE LINE I WAS HANDIN' OUT HADDA HAVE SOMETHIN' SERIOUS WRONG WITH 'ER.
DO YOU REALIZE THAT YOU'RE THE FIRST MAN WHO'S TURNED DOWN MY NUMBER?
THE NEXT DAY I THOUGHT IT OVER AND CONCLUDED THAT, AS DESPERATE AS I WAS, I'D BEEN A FOOL NOT TO GET HER NUMBER. IT WASN'T IN THE BOOK, SO I CALLED A BUDDY A' MINE T' GET IT. THEN I CALLED HER, T' CHEW TH' FAT. SHE WAS EVEN IMPRESSED WITH THE INGENUITY I'D SHOWN TO BE ABLE T' REACH 'ER. COULD IT BE THAT THIS WAS THE START OF SOMETHING WONDERFUL?
A FEW DAYS LATER SHE AN' I MET ON THE CORNER AN' WE SPENT A REAL LONG TIME WALKIN' AROUND TALKIN'. SHE FILLED ME IN ON SOME THINGS I WAS CURIOUS ABOUT.
AFTER THAT I TOOK A COURSE IN COMPUTER PROGRAMMING AND I GOT A JOB AT FOREMOST...
UH-HUH.
...I BROKE UP WITH HIM A FEW MONTHS AGO AND SINCE THEN I'VE BEEN LIVING AT MY MOTHER'S. IT'S KIND OF A DRAG IN A WAY, BUT I'VE BEEN ABLE TO CALM DOWN AND GET MY HEAD TOGETHER. I'M READY TO MOVE OUT NOW, THOUGH.
SHE HAD AN AFFECTED WAY A' TALKIN' - PUT ON A SLIGHT ENGLISH ACCENT. I ASKED HER ABOUT THAT, WITHOUT LETTING ON THAT I THOUGHT IT WAS PHONY.
OH, WE MOVED AROUND A LOT WHEN I WAS A KID. WE LIVED IN PITTSBURGH, ALBANY... I GUESS I JUST PICKED UP AN EAST-ERN ACCENT.
PITTSBURGH? ALBANY? THEY DON'T TALK LIKE THAT IN PITTSBURGH AN' ALBANY.
3.

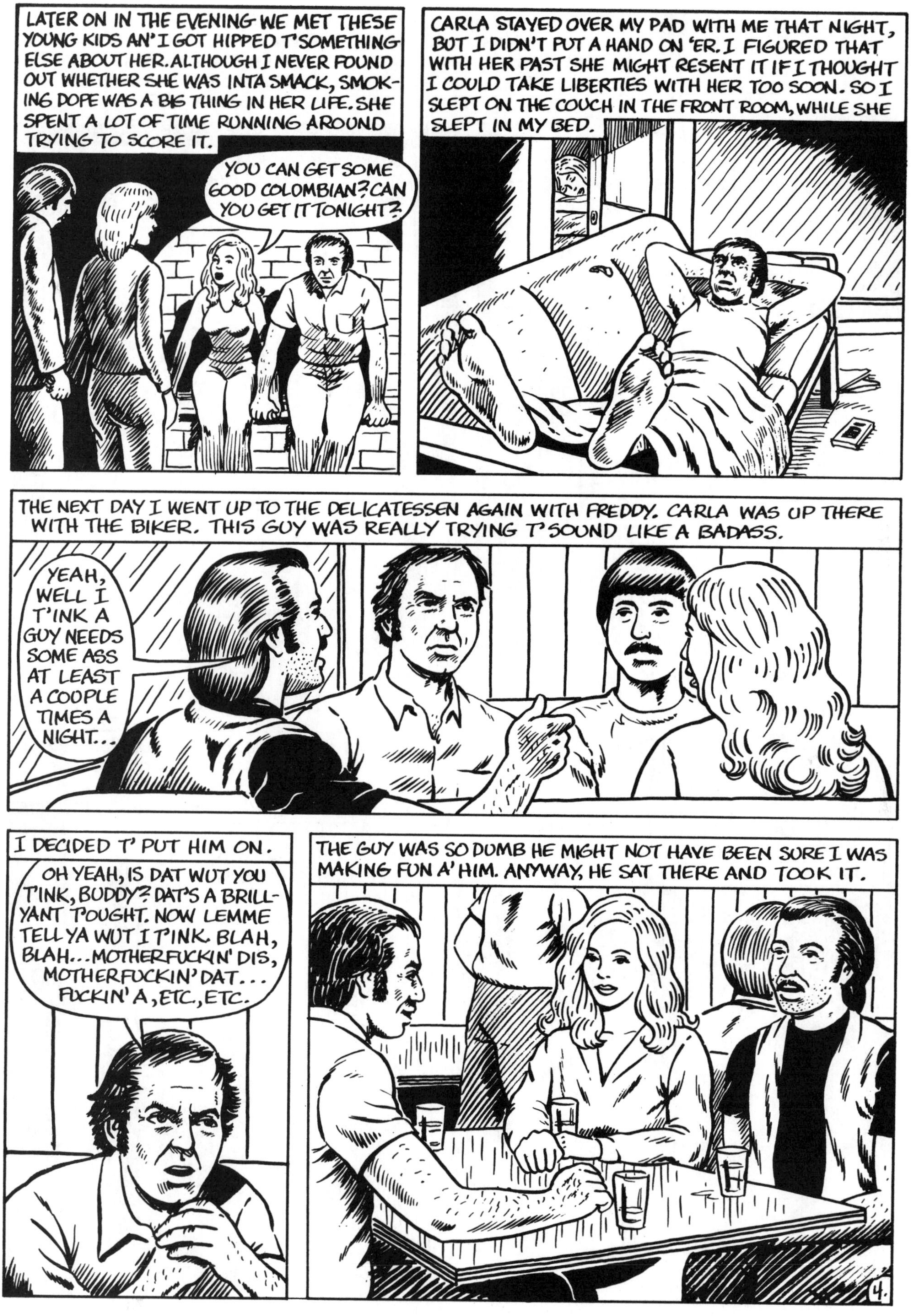

LATER ON IN THE EVENING WE MET THESE YOUNG KIDS AN' I GOT HIPPED T'SOMETHING ELSE ABOUT HER. ALTHOUGH I NEVER FOUND OUT WHETHER SHE WAS INTA SMACK, SMOKING DOPE WAS A BIG THING IN HER LIFE. SHE SPENT A LOT OF TIME RUNNING AROUND TRYING TO SCORE IT.
YOU CAN GET SOME GOOD COLOMBIAN? CAN YOU GET IT TONIGHT?
CARLA STAYED OVER MY PAD WITH ME THAT NIGHT, BUT I DIDN'T PUT A HAND ON 'ER. I FIGURED THAT WITH HER PAST SHE MIGHT RESENT IT IF I THOUGHT I COULD TAKE LIBERTIES WITH HER TOO SOON. SO I SLEPT ON THE COUCH IN THE FRONT ROOM, WHILE SHE SLEPT IN MY BED.
THE NEXT DAY I WENT UP TO THE DELICATESSEN AGAIN WITH FREDDY. CARLA WAS UP THERE WITH THE BIKER. THIS GUY WAS REALLY TRYING T'SOUND LIKE A BADASS.
YEAH, WELL I T'INK A GUY NEEDS SOME ASS AT LEAST A COUPLE TIMES A NIGHT...
I DECIDED T' PUT HIM ON.
OH YEAH, IS DAT WUT YOU T'INK, BUDDY? DAT'S A BRILLYANT T'OUGHT. NOW LEMME TELL YA WUT I T'INK. BLAH, BLAH... MOTHERFUCKIN' DIS, MOTHERFUCKIN' DAT... FUCKIN' A, ETC., ETC.
THE GUY WAS SO DUMB HE MIGHT NOT HAVE BEEN SURE I WAS MAKING FUN A' HIM. ANYWAY, HE SAT THERE AND TOOK IT.
4.

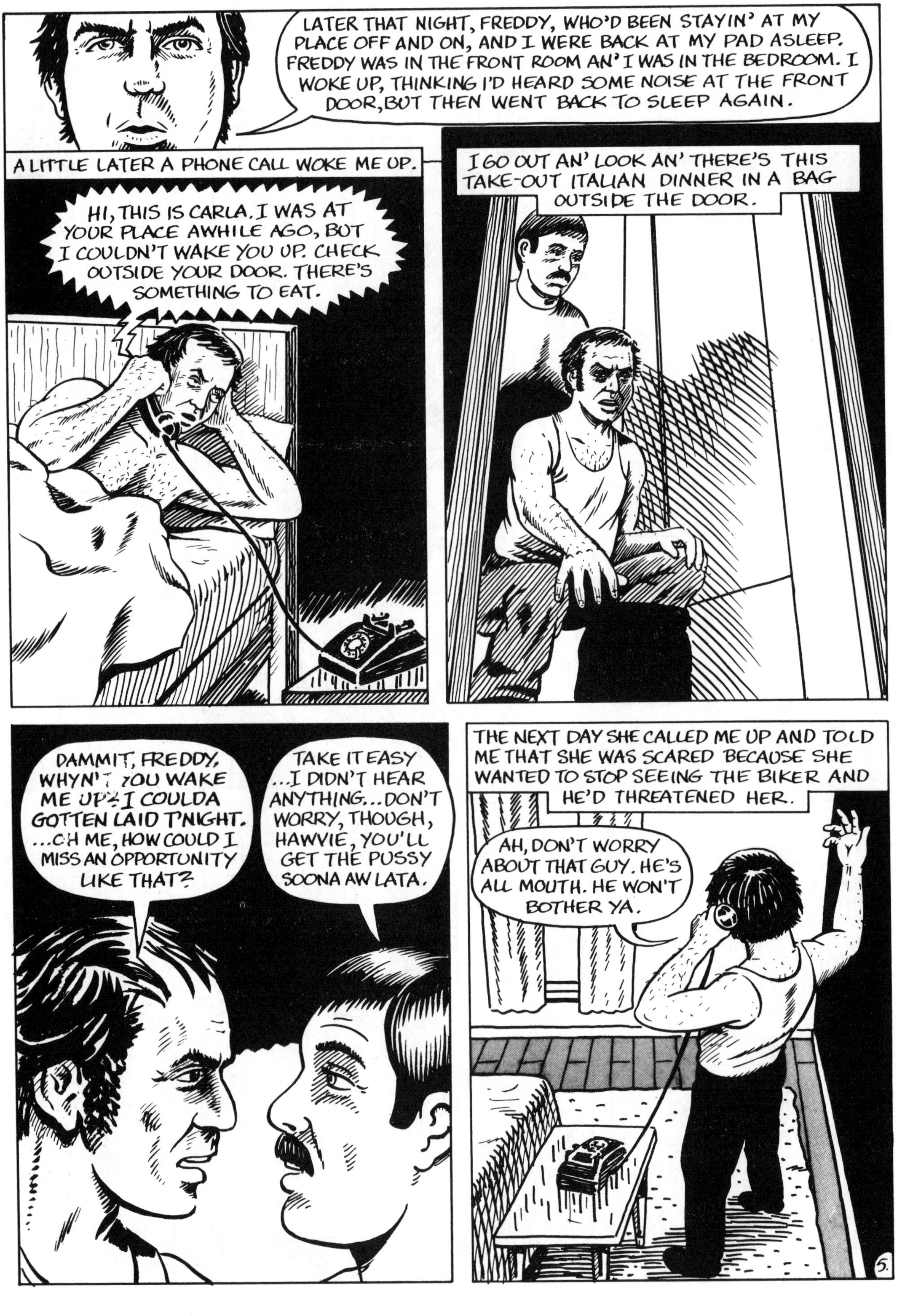
LATER THAT NIGHT, FREDDY, WHO'D BEEN STAYIN' AT MY PLACE OFF AND ON, AND I WERE BACK AT MY PAD ASLEEP. FREDDY WAS IN THE FRONT ROOM AN' I WAS IN THE BEDROOM. I WOKE UP, THINKING I'D HEARD SOME NOISE AT THE FRONT DOOR, BUT THEN WENT BACK TO SLEEP AGAIN.
A LITTLE LATER A PHONE CALL WOKE ME UP.
HI, THIS IS CARLA. I WAS AT YOUR PLACE AWHILE AGO, BUT I COULDN'T WAKE YOU UP. CHECK OUTSIDE YOUR DOOR. THERE'S SOMETHING TO EAT.
I GO OUT AN' LOOK AN' THERE'S THIS TAKE-OUT ITALIAN DINNER IN A BAG OUTSIDE THE DOOR.
DAMMIT, FREDDY, WHYN'T YOU WAKE ME UP? I COULDA GOTTEN LAID T'NIGHT. ...OH ME, HOW COULD I MISS AN OPPORTUNITY LIKE THAT?
TAKE IT EASY ...I DIDN'T HEAR ANYTHING... DON'T WORRY, THOUGH, HAWVIE, YOU'LL GET THE PUSSY SOONA AW LATA.
THE NEXT DAY SHE CALLED ME UP AND TOLD ME THAT SHE WAS SCARED BECAUSE SHE WANTED TO STOP SEEING THE BIKER AND HE'D THREATENED HER.
AH, DON'T WORRY ABOUT THAT GUY. HE'S ALL MOUTH. HE WON'T BOTHER YA.

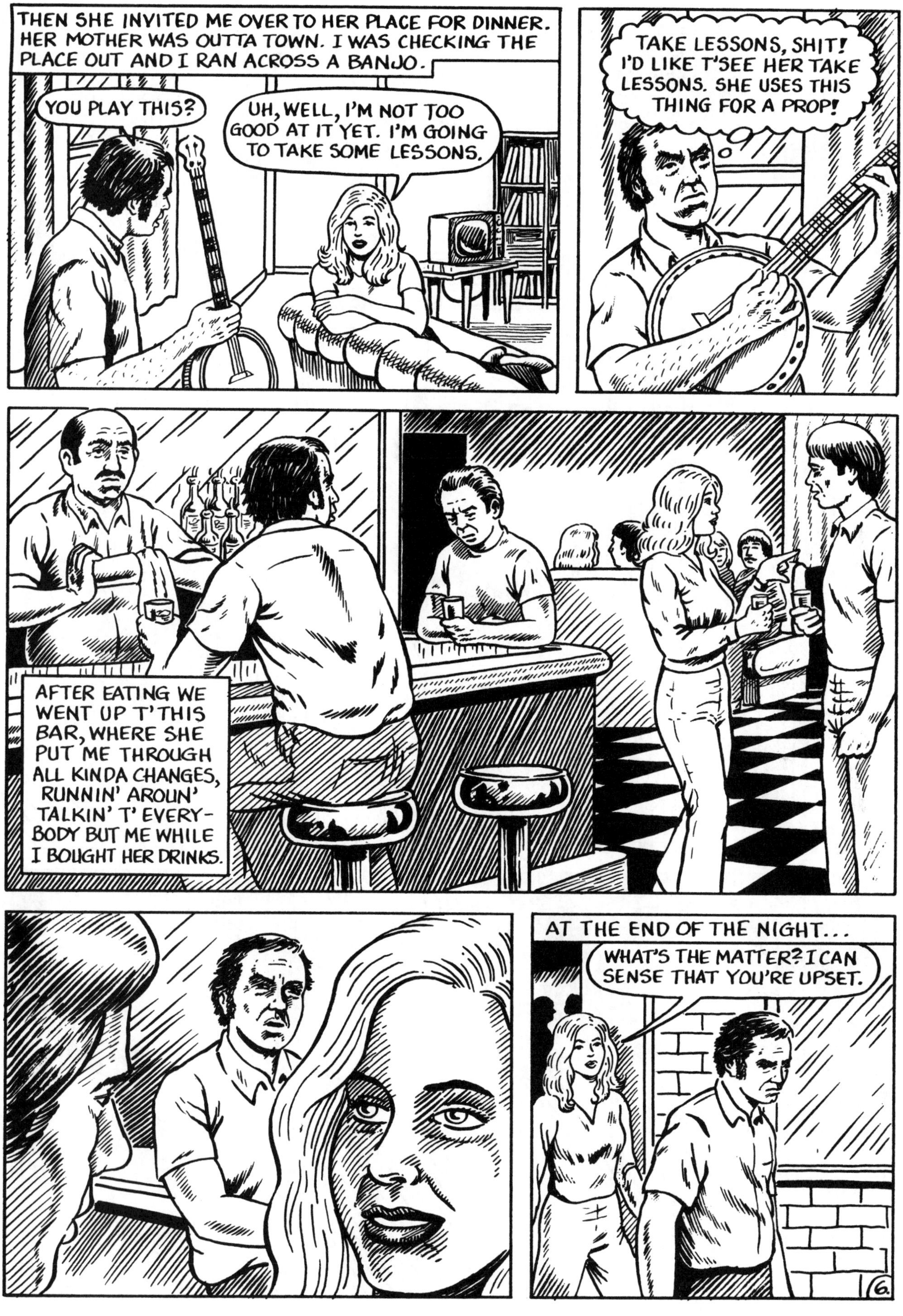
THEN SHE INVITED ME OVER TO HER PLACE FOR DINNER. HER MOTHER WAS OUTTA TOWN. I WAS CHECKING THE PLACE OUT AND I RAN ACROSS A BANJO.
YOU PLAY THIS?
UH, WELL, I'M NOT TOO GOOD AT IT YET. I'M GOING TO TAKE SOME LESSONS.
TAKE LESSONS, SHIT! I'D LIKE T'SEE HER TAKE LESSONS. SHE USES THIS THING FOR A PROP!
AFTER EATING WE WENT UP T'THIS BAR, WHERE SHE PUT ME THROUGH ALL KINDA CHANGES, RUNNIN' AROUN' TALKIN' T' EVERY-BODY BUT ME WHILE I BOUGHT HER DRINKS.
AT THE END OF THE NIGHT...
WHAT'S THE MATTER? I CAN SENSE THAT YOU'RE UPSET.
6

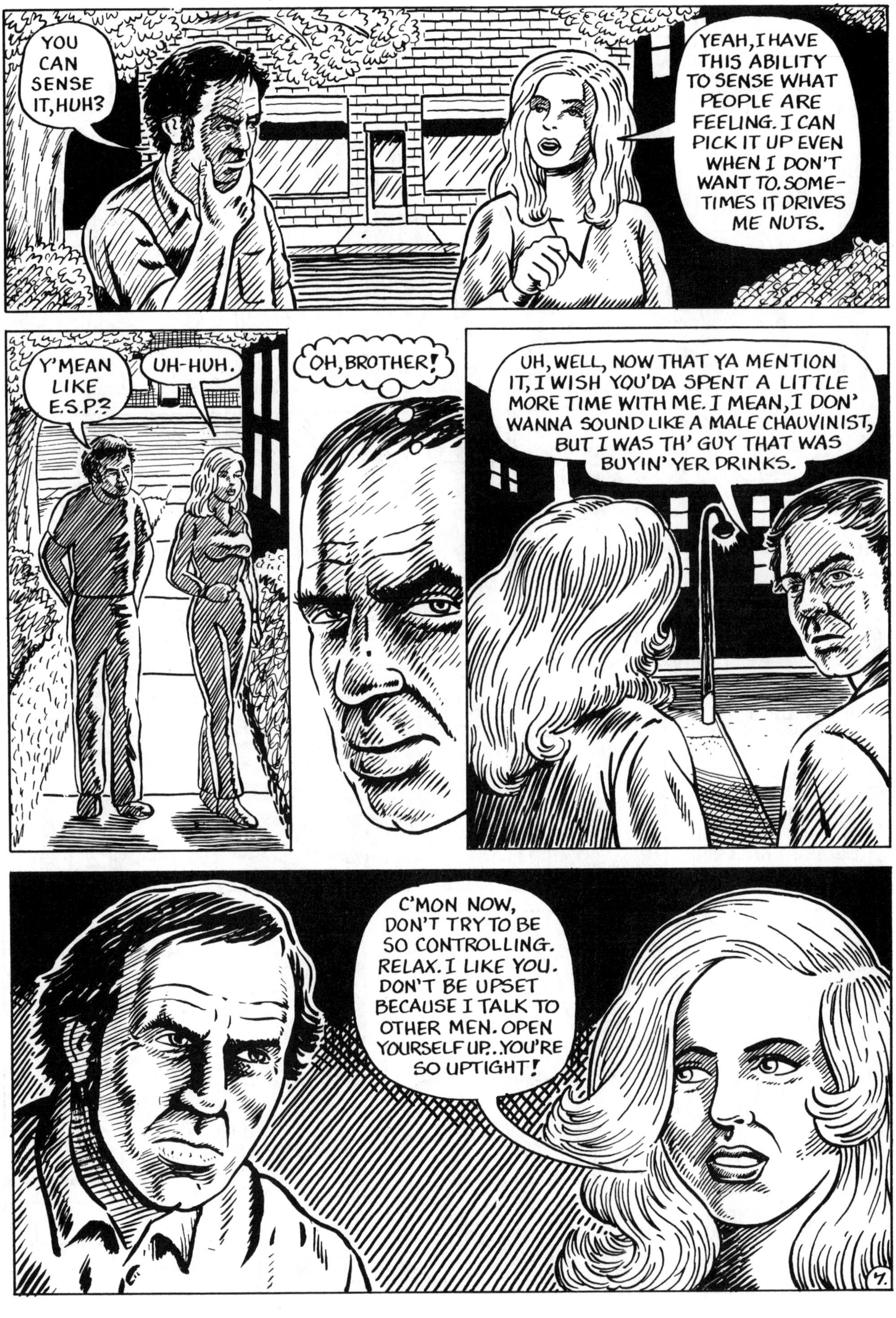
YOU CAN SENSE IT, HUH?
YEAH, I HAVE THIS ABILITY TO SENSE WHAT PEOPLE ARE FEELING. I CAN PICK IT UP EVEN WHEN I DON'T WANT TO. SOMETIMES IT DRIVES ME NUTS.
Y'MEAN LIKE E.S.P.?
UH-HUH.
OH, BROTHER!
UH, WELL, NOW THAT YA MENTION IT, I WISH YOU'DA SPENT A LITTLE MORE TIME WITH ME. I MEAN, I DON' WANNA SOUND LIKE A MALE CHAUVINIST, BUT I WAS TH' GUY THAT WAS BUYIN' YER DRINKS.
C'MON NOW, DON'T TRY TO BE SO CONTROLLING. RELAX. I LIKE YOU. DON'T BE UPSET BECAUSE I TALK TO OTHER MEN. OPEN YOURSELF UP.. YOU'RE SO UPTIGHT!

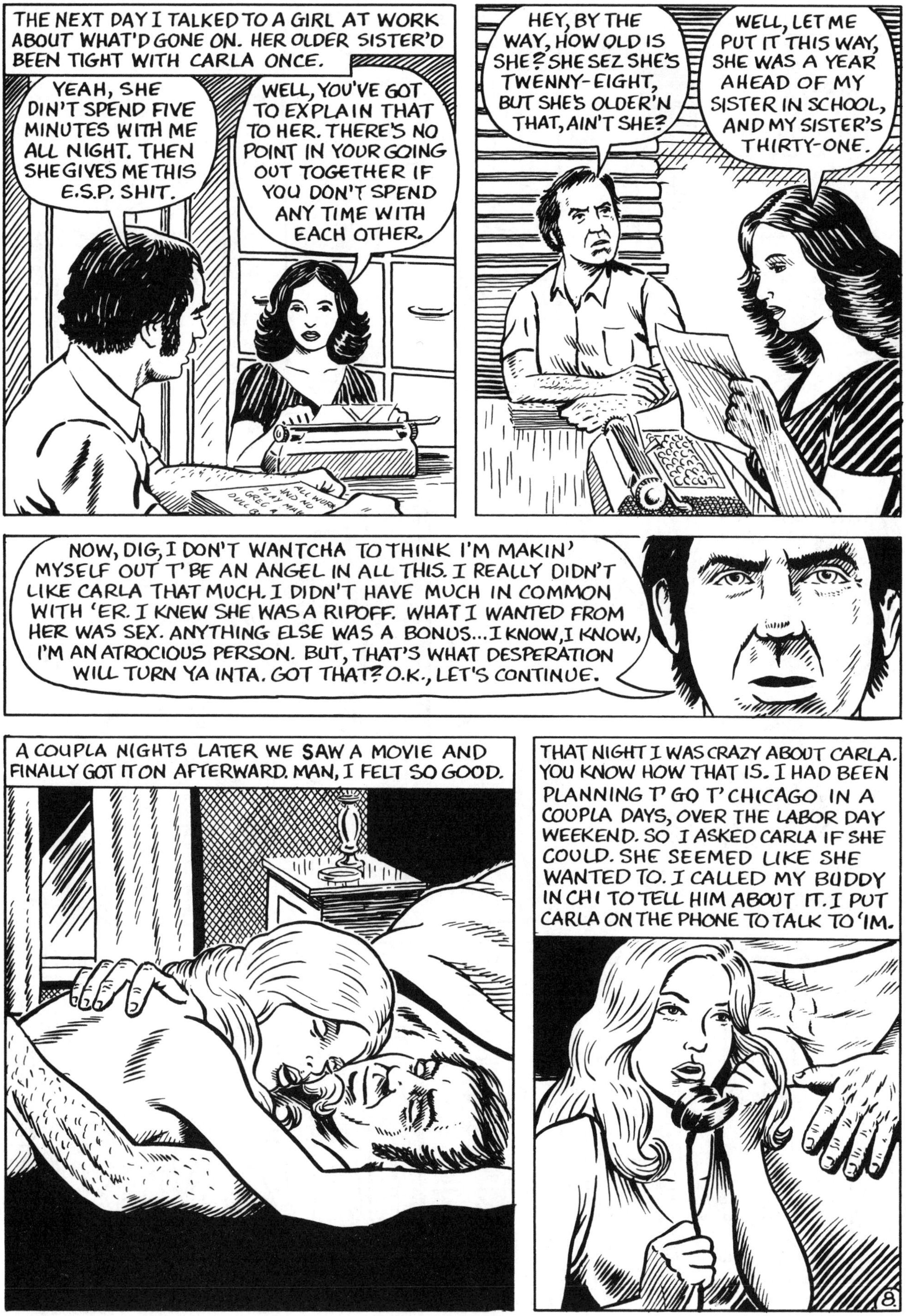

THE NEXT DAY I TALKED TO A GIRL AT WORK ABOUT WHAT'D GONE ON. HER OLDER SISTER'D BEEN TIGHT WITH CARLA ONCE.
YEAH, SHE DIN'T SPEND FIVE MINUTES WITH ME ALL NIGHT. THEN SHE GIVES ME THIS E.S.P. SHIT.
WELL, YOU'VE GOT TO EXPLAIN THAT TO HER. THERE'S NO POINT IN YOUR GOING OUT TOGETHER IF YOU DON'T SPEND ANY TIME WITH EACH OTHER.
HEY, BY THE WAY, HOW OLD IS SHE? SHE SEZ SHE'S TWENNY-EIGHT, BUT SHE'S OLDER'N THAT, AIN'T SHE?
WELL, LET ME PUT IT THIS WAY, SHE WAS A YEAR AHEAD OF MY SISTER IN SCHOOL, AND MY SISTER'S THIRTY-ONE.
NOW, DIG, I DON'T WANTCHA TO THINK I'M MAKIN' MYSELF OUT T'BE AN ANGEL IN ALL THIS. I REALLY DIDN'T LIKE CARLA THAT MUCH. I DIDN'T HAVE MUCH IN COMMON WITH 'ER. I KNEW SHE WAS A RIPOFF. WHAT I WANTED FROM HER WAS SEX. ANYTHING ELSE WAS A BONUS... I KNOW, I KNOW, I'M AN ATROCIOUS PERSON. BUT, THAT'S WHAT DESPERATION WILL TURN YA INTA. GOT THAT? O.K., LET'S CONTINUE.
A COUPLA NIGHTS LATER WE SAW A MOVIE AND FINALLY GOT IT ON AFTERWARD. MAN, I FELT SO GOOD.
THAT NIGHT I WAS CRAZY ABOUT CARLA. YOU KNOW HOW THAT IS. I HAD BEEN PLANNING T' GO T' CHICAGO IN A COUPLA DAYS, OVER THE LABOR DAY WEEKEND. SO I ASKED CARLA IF SHE COULD. SHE SEEMED LIKE SHE WANTED TO. I CALLED MY BUDDY IN CHI TO TELL HIM ABOUT IT. I PUT CARLA ON THE PHONE TO TALK TO 'IM.
8

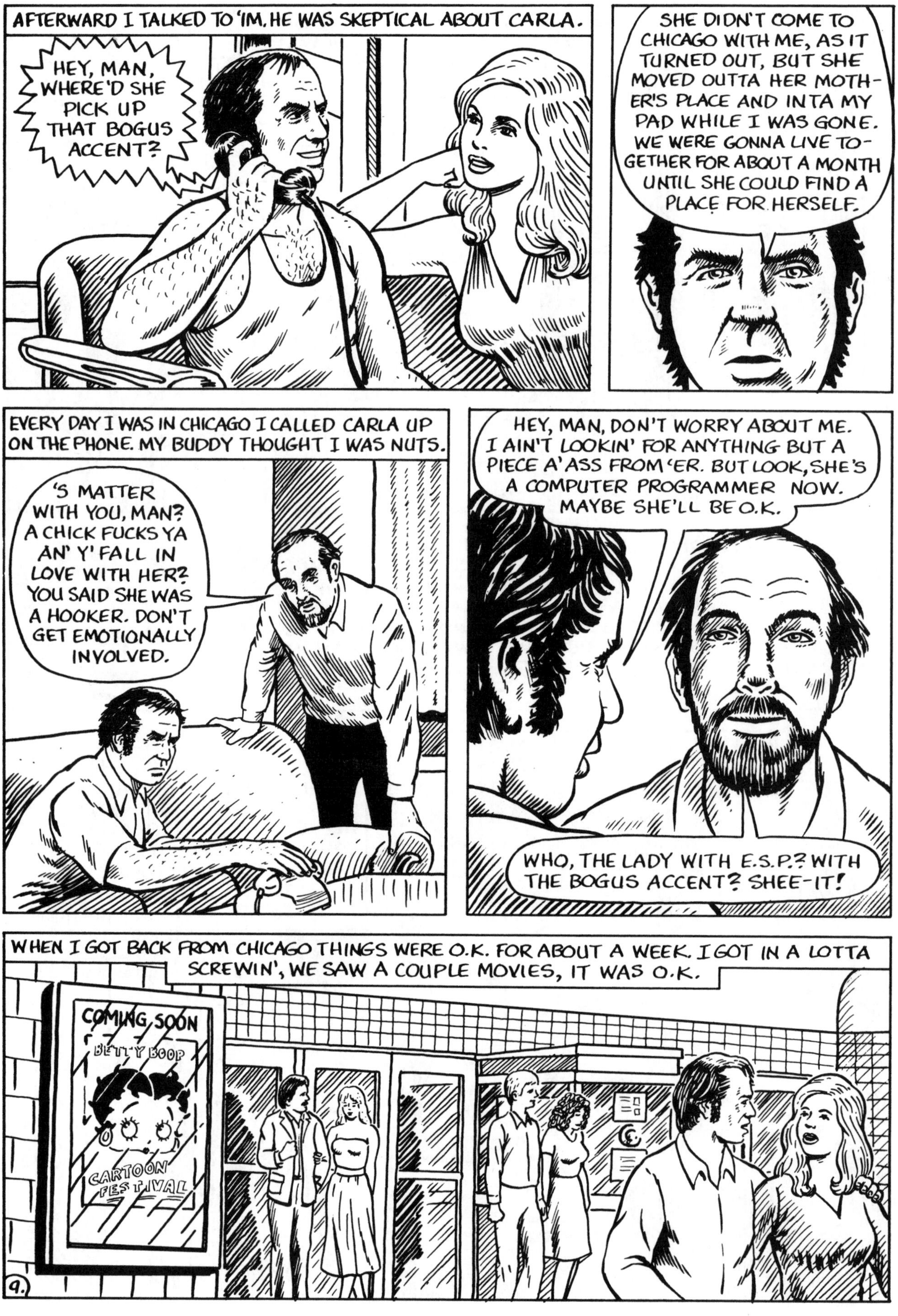

AFTERWARD I TALKED TO 'IM, HE WAS SKEPTICAL ABOUT CARLA.
HEY, MAN, WHERE'D SHE PICK UP THAT BOGUS ACCENT?
SHE DIDN'T COME TO CHICAGO WITH ME, AS IT TURNED OUT, BUT SHE MOVED OUTTA HER MOTHER'S PLACE AND INTA MY PAD WHILE I WAS GONE. WE WERE GONNA LIVE TOGETHER FOR ABOUT A MONTH UNTIL SHE COULD FIND A PLACE FOR HERSELF.
EVERY DAY I WAS IN CHICAGO I CALLED CARLA UP ON THE PHONE. MY BUDDY THOUGHT I WAS NUTS.
'S MATTER WITH YOU, MAN? A CHICK FUCKS YA AN' Y' FALL IN LOVE WITH HER? YOU SAID SHE WAS A HOOKER. DON'T GET EMOTIONALLY INVOLVED.
HEY, MAN, DON'T WORRY ABOUT ME. I AIN'T LOOKIN' FOR ANYTHING BUT A PIECE A' ASS FROM 'ER. BUT LOOK, SHE'S A COMPUTER PROGRAMMER NOW. MAYBE SHE'LL BE O.K.
WHO, THE LADY WITH E.S.P.? WITH THE BOGUS ACCENT? SHEE-IT!
WHEN I GOT BACK FROM CHICAGO THINGS WERE O.K. FOR ABOUT A WEEK. I GOT IN A LOTTA SCREWIN', WE SAW A COUPLE MOVIES, IT WAS O.K.
COMING SOON
BETTY BOOP
CARTOON FESTIVAL
9.

BUT THEN THEY TURNED SOUR. FIRST, SHE STOPPED COMIN' HOME AFTER WORK. I DON'T KNOW WHERE SHE WENT, BUT USUALLY I'D FIND 'ER BACK UP ON THE CORNER, AROUN' TEN OR ELEVEN O'CLOCK, OFTEN TRYIN' T' SCORE SOME DOPE.

EVEN THOUGH SHE MADE MORE MONEY THAN ME, SHE WAS FOREVER HITTING ON ME FOR BREAD, EVEN FOR PARKIN' TICKETS, WHICH SHE ALWAYS GOT BE- CAUSE SHE WAS TOO LAZY TO MOVE HER CAR OUTTA THESE ZONES WHERE YOU COULD ONLY PARK FOR A LIM- ITED TIME.

ONE DAY I WAS SUPPOSED T' MEET HER T' GO TO A MOVIE. SHE DIDN'T SHOW, SO I WENT WITH ANOTHER GIRL. THEN I GOT WORRIED THAT I HADN'T WAITED LONG ENOUGH, SO I GAVE THE GIRL I WAS WITH SOME EXCUSE AN' CUT OUT ON HER T' GO BACK HOME. THINGS WERE GETTIN' CRAZY.

IT'S A GOOD THING I DID, THOUGH. CARLA HAD JUST BEEN AT MY PAD AND HAD LEFT THE WATER DRIPPING IN THE BATHROOM SINK WHILE IT WAS STOPPED UP. IT WAS ABOUT TO OVERFLOW. GOD KNOWS WHAT WOULDA HAPPENED IN AN HOUR. AND MY LANDLADY LIVED JUST UNDERNEATH ME!

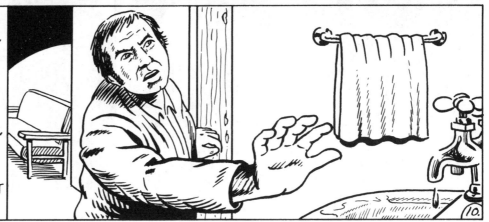

10.

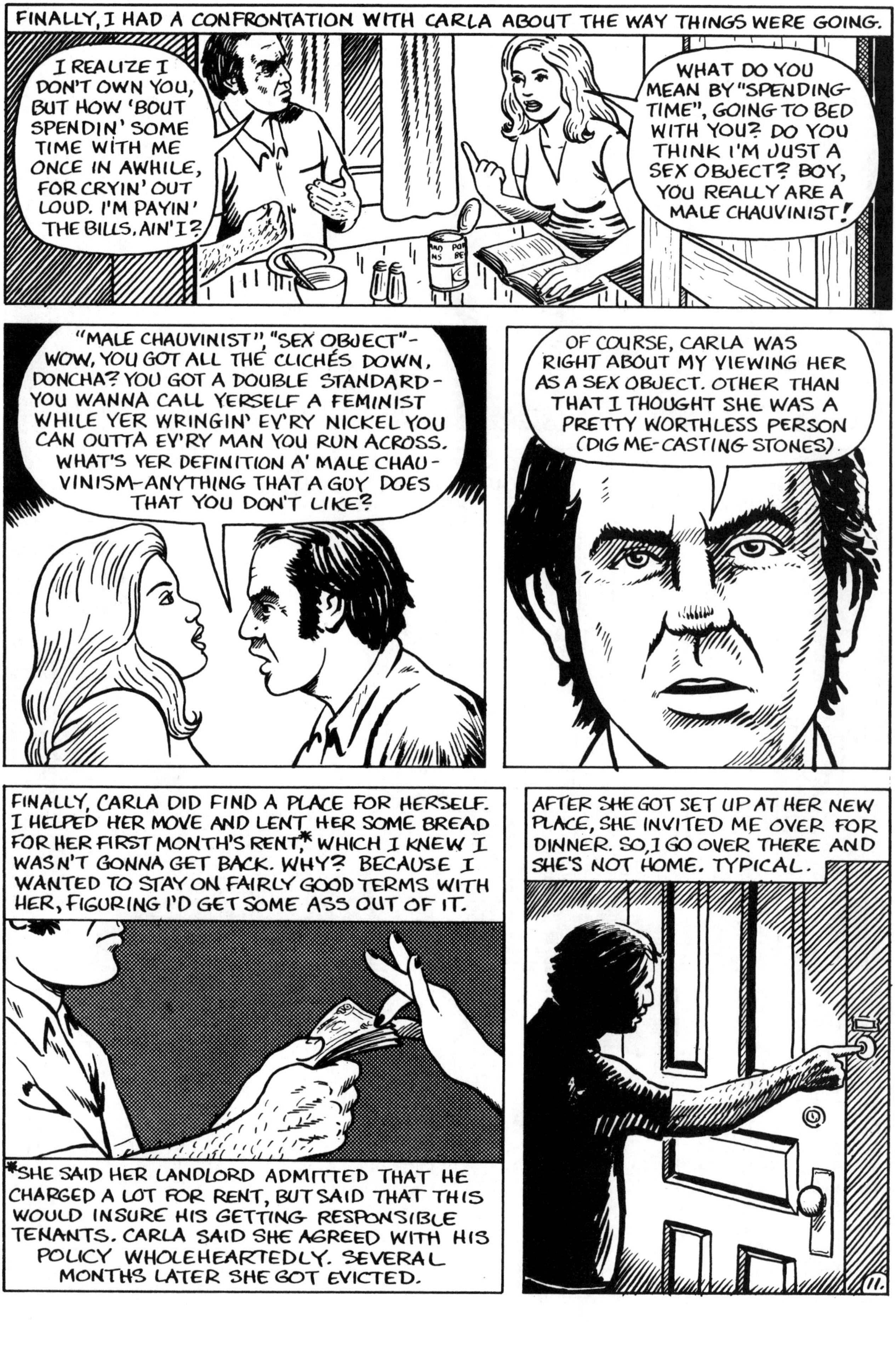
FINALLY, I HAD A CONFRONTATION WITH CARLA ABOUT THE WAY THINGS WERE GOING.
I REALIZE I DON'T OWN YOU, BUT HOW 'BOUT SPENDIN' SOME TIME WITH ME ONCE IN AWHILE, FOR CRYIN' OUT LOUD. I'M PAYIN' THE BILLS, AIN'T I?
WHAT DO YOU MEAN BY "SPENDING TIME", GOING TO BED WITH YOU? DO YOU THINK I'M JUST A SEX OBJECT? BOY, YOU REALLY ARE A MALE CHAUVINIST!
"MALE CHAUVINIST", "SEX OBJECT"- WOW, YOU GOT ALL THE CLICHÉS DOWN, DONCHA? YOU GOT A DOUBLE STANDARD- YOU WANNA CALL YERSELF A FEMINIST WHILE YER WRINGIN' EV'RY NICKEL YOU CAN OUTTA EV'RY MAN YOU RUN ACROSS. WHAT'S YER DEFINITION A' MALE CHAUVINISM- ANYTHING THAT A GUY DOES THAT YOU DON'T LIKE?
OF COURSE, CARLA WAS RIGHT ABOUT MY VIEWING HER AS A SEX OBJECT. OTHER THAN THAT I THOUGHT SHE WAS A PRETTY WORTHLESS PERSON (DIG ME- CASTING STONES)
FINALLY, CARLA DID FIND A PLACE FOR HERSELF. I HELPED HER MOVE AND LENT HER SOME BREAD FOR HER FIRST MONTH'S RENT,* WHICH I KNEW I WASN'T GONNA GET BACK. WHY? BECAUSE I WANTED TO STAY ON FAIRLY GOOD TERMS WITH HER, FIGURING I'D GET SOME ASS OUT OF IT.
*SHE SAID HER LANDLORD ADMITTED THAT HE CHARGED A LOT FOR RENT, BUT SAID THAT THIS WOULD INSURE HIS GETTING RESPONSIBLE TENANTS. CARLA SAID SHE AGREED WITH HIS POLICY WHOLEHEARTEDLY. SEVERAL MONTHS LATER SHE GOT EVICTED.
AFTER SHE GOT SET UP AT HER NEW PLACE, SHE INVITED ME OVER FOR DINNER. SO, I GO OVER THERE AND SHE'S NOT HOME. TYPICAL.
11.

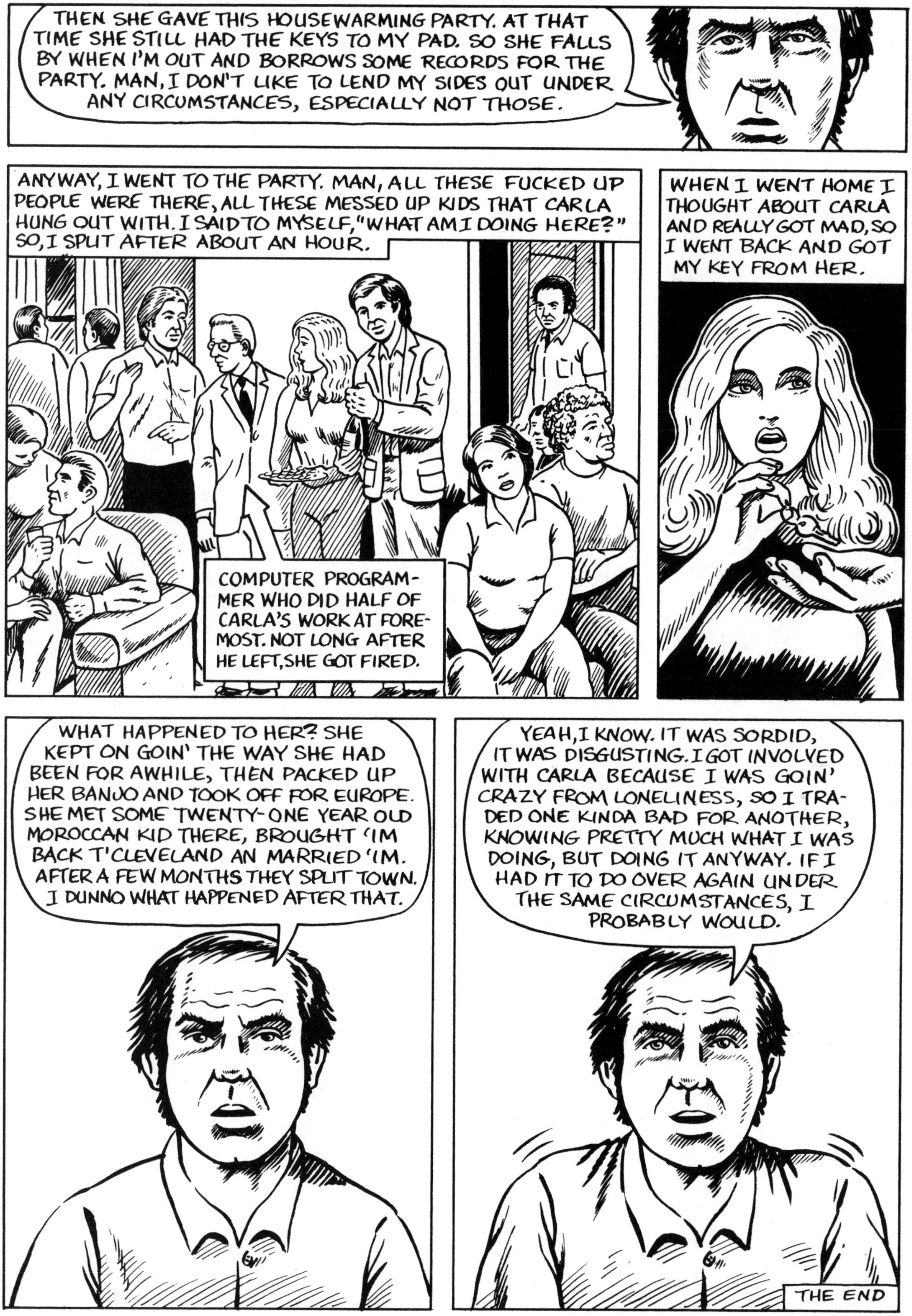
THEN SHE GAVE THIS HOUSEWARMING PARTY. AT THAT TIME SHE STILL HAD THE KEYS TO MY PAD. SO SHE FALLS BY WHEN I'M OUT AND BORROWS SOME RECORDS FOR THE PARTY. MAN, I DON'T LIKE TO LEND MY SIDES OUT UNDER ANY CIRCUMSTANCES, ESPECIALLY NOT THOSE.
ANYWAY, I WENT TO THE PARTY. MAN, ALL THESE FUCKED UP PEOPLE WERE THERE, ALL THESE MESSED UP KIDS THAT CARLA HUNG OUT WITH. I SAID TO MYSELF, "WHAT AM I DOING HERE?" SO, I SPLIT AFTER ABOUT AN HOUR.
COMPUTER PROGRAMMER WHO DID HALF OF CARLA'S WORK AT FOREMOST. NOT LONG AFTER HE LEFT, SHE GOT FIRED.
WHEN I WENT HOME I THOUGHT ABOUT CARLA AND REALLY GOT MAD, SO I WENT BACK AND GOT MY KEY FROM HER.
WHAT HAPPENED TO HER? SHE KEPT ON GOIN' THE WAY SHE HAD BEEN FOR AWHILE, THEN PACKED UP HER BANJO AND TOOK OFF FOR EUROPE. SHE MET SOME TWENTY-ONE YEAR OLD MOROCCAN KID THERE, BROUGHT 'IM BACK T'CLEVELAND AN MARRIED 'IM. AFTER A FEW MONTHS THEY SPLIT TOWN. I DUNNO WHAT HAPPENED AFTER THAT.
YEAH, I KNOW. IT WAS SORDID, IT WAS DISGUSTING. I GOT INVOLVED WITH CARLA BECAUSE I WAS GOIN' CRAZY FROM LONELINESS, SO I TRADED ONE KINDA BAD FOR ANOTHER, KNOWING PRETTY MUCH WHAT I WAS DOING, BUT DOING IT ANYWAY. IF I HAD IT TO DO OVER AGAIN UNDER THE SAME CIRCUMSTANCES, I PROBABLY WOULD.
THE END

ONE GOOD TURN DESERVES ANOTHER

STORY BY HARVEY PEKAR
ILLUSTRATED BY GERRY SHAMRAY

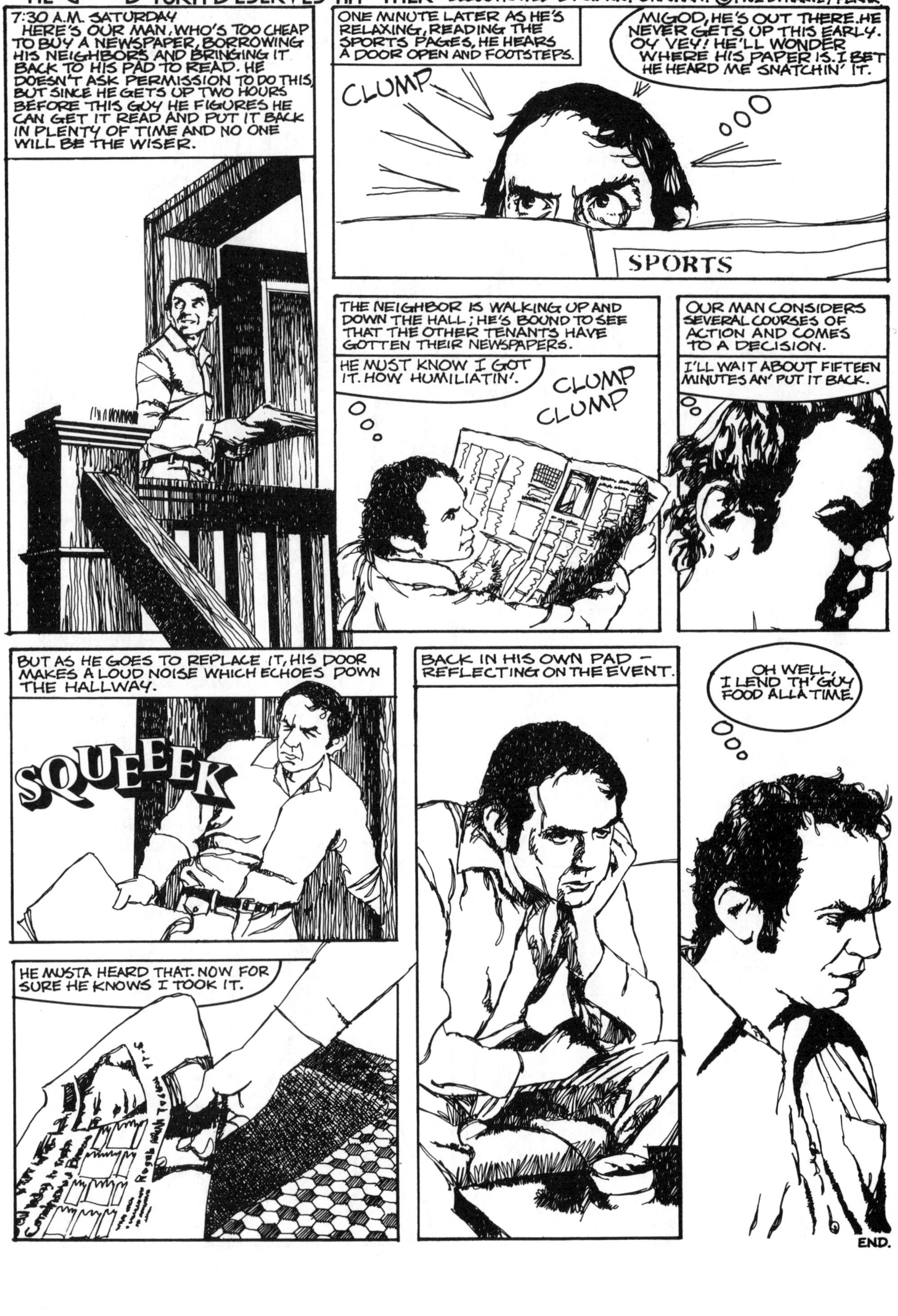

7:30 A.M. SATURDAY
HERE'S OUR MAN, WHO'S TOO CHEAP TO BUY A NEWSPAPER, BORROWING HIS NEIGHBORS AND BRINGING IT BACK TO HIS PAD TO READ. HE DOESN'T ASK PERMISSION TO DO THIS, BUT SINCE HE GETS UP TWO HOURS BEFORE THIS GUY HE FIGURES HE CAN GET IT READ AND PUT IT BACK IN PLENTY OF TIME AND NO ONE WILL BE THE WISER.
ONE MINUTE LATER AS HE'S RELAXING, READING THE SPORTS PAGES, HE HEARS A DOOR OPEN AND FOOTSTEPS.
CLUMP
MIGOD, HE'S OUT THERE. HE NEVER GETS UP THIS EARLY. OY VEY! HE'LL WONDER WHERE HIS PAPER IS. I BET HE HEARD ME SNATCHIN' IT.
SPORTS
THE NEIGHBOR IS WALKING UP AND DOWN THE HALL; HE'S BOUND TO SEE THAT THE OTHER TENANTS HAVE GOTTEN THEIR NEWSPAPERS.
HE MUST KNOW I GOT IT. HOW HUMILIATIN'.
CLUMP
CLUMP
OUR MAN CONSIDERS SEVERAL COURSES OF ACTION AND COMES TO A DECISION.
I'LL WAIT ABOUT FIFTEEN MINUTES AN' PUT IT BACK.
BUT AS HE GOES TO REPLACE IT, HIS DOOR MAKES A LOUD NOISE WHICH ECHOES DOWN THE HALLWAY.
SQUEEEK
HE MUSTA HEARD THAT. NOW FOR SURE HE KNOWS I TOOK IT.
BACK IN HIS OWN PAD - REFLECTING ON THE EVENT.
OH WELL, I LEND TH' GUY FOOD ALLA TIME.
END.

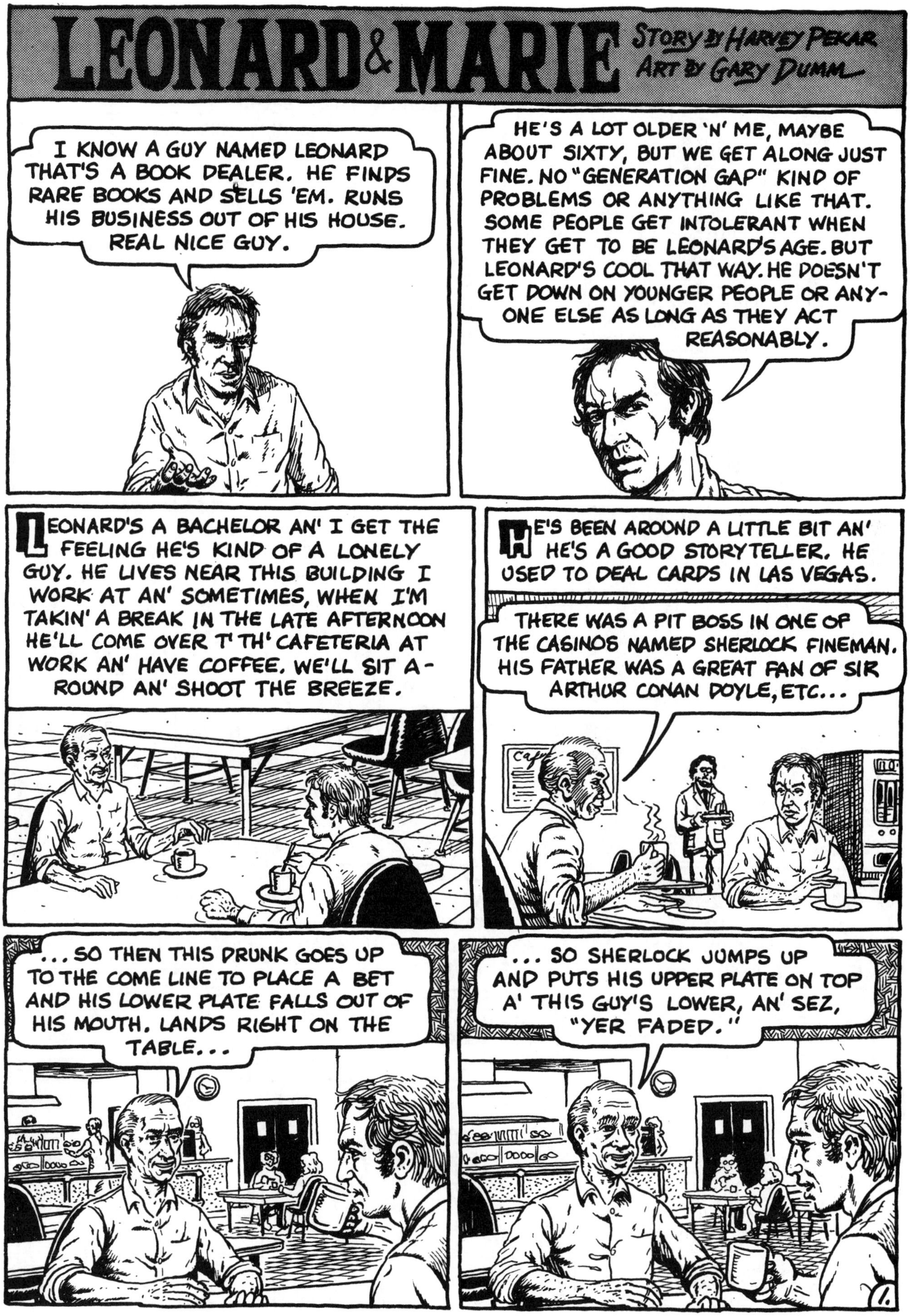
LEONARD & MARIE
STORY BY HARVEY PEKAR
ART BY GARY DUMM
I KNOW A GUY NAMED LEONARD THAT'S A BOOK DEALER. HE FINDS RARE BOOKS AND SELLS 'EM. RUNS HIS BUSINESS OUT OF HIS HOUSE. REAL NICE GUY.
HE'S A LOT OLDER 'N' ME, MAYBE ABOUT SIXTY, BUT WE GET ALONG JUST FINE. NO "GENERATION GAP" KIND OF PROBLEMS OR ANYTHING LIKE THAT. SOME PEOPLE GET INTOLERANT WHEN THEY GET TO BE LEONARD'S AGE. BUT LEONARD'S COOL THAT WAY. HE DOESN'T GET DOWN ON YOUNGER PEOPLE OR ANYONE ELSE AS LONG AS THEY ACT REASONABLY.
LEONARD'S A BACHELOR AN' I GET THE FEELING HE'S KIND OF A LONELY GUY. HE LIVES NEAR THIS BUILDING I WORK AT AN' SOMETIMES, WHEN I'M TAKIN' A BREAK IN THE LATE AFTERNOON HE'LL COME OVER T' TH' CAFETERIA AT WORK AN' HAVE COFFEE. WE'LL SIT AROUND AN' SHOOT THE BREEZE.
HE'S BEEN AROUND A LITTLE BIT AN' HE'S A GOOD STORYTELLER. HE USED TO DEAL CARDS IN LAS VEGAS.
THERE WAS A PIT BOSS IN ONE OF THE CASINOS NAMED SHERLOCK FINEMAN. HIS FATHER WAS A GREAT FAN OF SIR ARTHUR CONAN DOYLE, ETC...
... SO THEN THIS DRUNK GOES UP TO THE COME LINE TO PLACE A BET AND HIS LOWER PLATE FALLS OUT OF HIS MOUTH. LANDS RIGHT ON THE TABLE...
... SO SHERLOCK JUMPS UP AND PUTS HIS UPPER PLATE ON TOP A' THIS GUY'S LOWER, AN' SEZ, "YER FADED."
1.

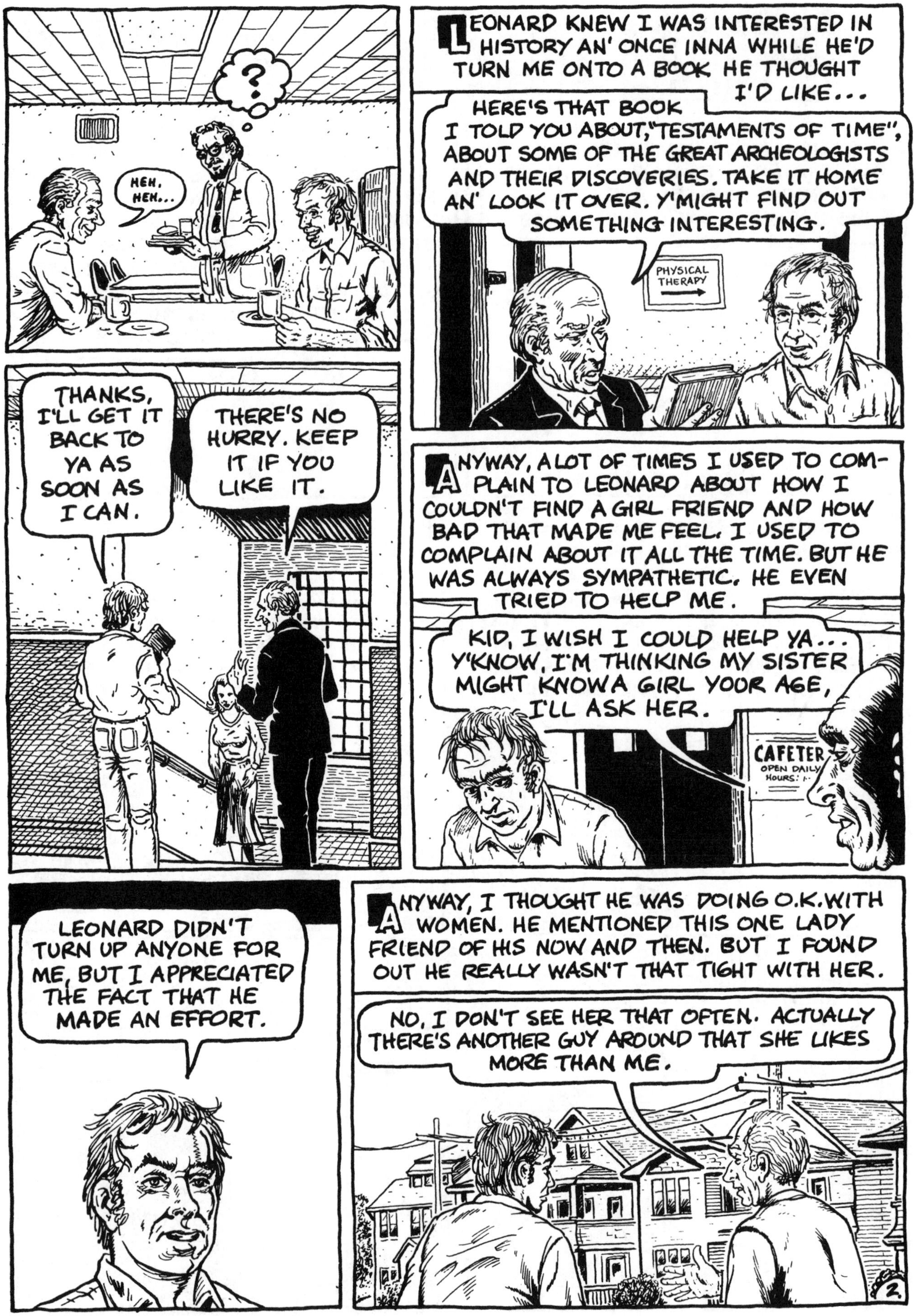

?
HEH, HEH...
LEONARD KNEW I WAS INTERESTED IN HISTORY AN' ONCE INNA WHILE HE'D TURN ME ONTO A BOOK HE THOUGHT I'D LIKE...
HERE'S THAT BOOK I TOLD YOU ABOUT, "TESTAMENTS OF TIME", ABOUT SOME OF THE GREAT ARCHEOLOGISTS AND THEIR DISCOVERIES. TAKE IT HOME AN' LOOK IT OVER. Y'MIGHT FIND OUT SOMETHING INTERESTING.
PHYSICAL THERAPY
THANKS, I'LL GET IT BACK TO YA AS SOON AS I CAN.
THERE'S NO HURRY. KEEP IT IF YOU LIKE IT.
ANYWAY, A LOT OF TIMES I USED TO COMPLAIN TO LEONARD ABOUT HOW I COULDN'T FIND A GIRL FRIEND AND HOW BAD THAT MADE ME FEEL. I USED TO COMPLAIN ABOUT IT ALL THE TIME. BUT HE WAS ALWAYS SYMPATHETIC. HE EVEN TRIED TO HELP ME.
KID, I WISH I COULD HELP YA... Y'KNOW, I'M THINKING MY SISTER MIGHT KNOW A GIRL YOUR AGE, I'LL ASK HER.
CAFETER
OPEN DAILY
HOURS:
LEONARD DIDN'T TURN UP ANYONE FOR ME, BUT I APPRECIATED THE FACT THAT HE MADE AN EFFORT.
ANYWAY, I THOUGHT HE WAS DOING O.K. WITH WOMEN. HE MENTIONED THIS ONE LADY FRIEND OF HIS NOW AND THEN. BUT I FOUND OUT HE REALLY WASN'T THAT TIGHT WITH HER.
NO, I DON'T SEE HER THAT OFTEN. ACTUALLY THERE'S ANOTHER GUY AROUND THAT SHE LIKES MORE THAN ME.
2.

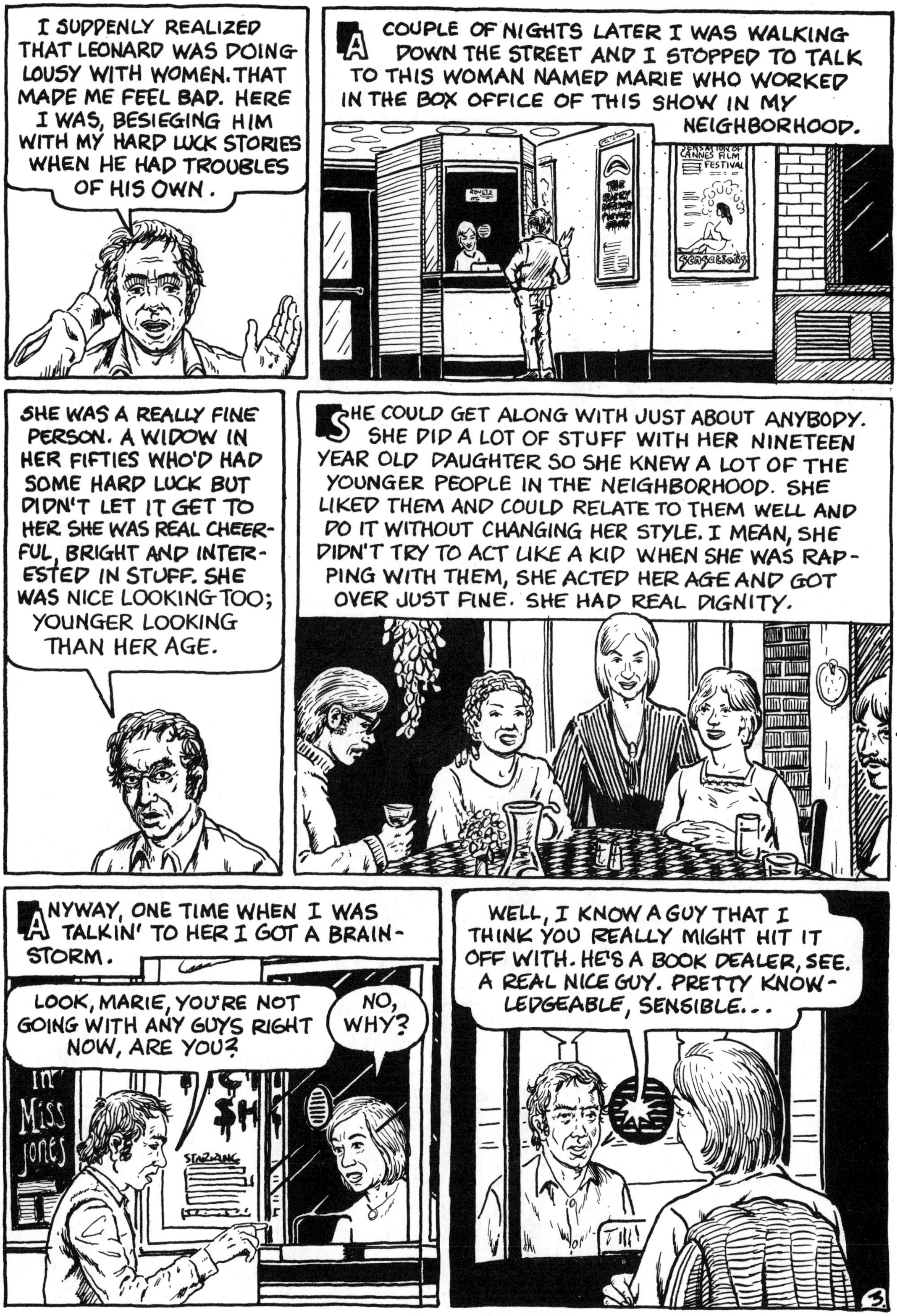
I SUDDENLY REALIZED THAT LEONARD WAS DOING LOUSY WITH WOMEN. THAT MADE ME FEEL BAD. HERE I WAS, BESIEGING HIM WITH MY HARD LUCK STORIES WHEN HE HAD TROUBLES OF HIS OWN.
A COUPLE OF NIGHTS LATER I WAS WALKING DOWN THE STREET AND I STOPPED TO TALK TO THIS WOMAN NAMED MARIE WHO WORKED IN THE BOX OFFICE OF THIS SHOW IN MY NEIGHBORHOOD.
SENSATION OF CANNES FILM FESTIVAL
SHE WAS A REALLY FINE PERSON. A WIDOW IN HER FIFTIES WHO'D HAD SOME HARD LUCK BUT DIDN'T LET IT GET TO HER SHE WAS REAL CHEERFUL, BRIGHT AND INTERESTED IN STUFF. SHE WAS NICE LOOKING TOO; YOUNGER LOOKING THAN HER AGE.
SHE COULD GET ALONG WITH JUST ABOUT ANYBODY. SHE DID A LOT OF STUFF WITH HER NINETEEN YEAR OLD DAUGHTER SO SHE KNEW A LOT OF THE YOUNGER PEOPLE IN THE NEIGHBORHOOD. SHE LIKED THEM AND COULD RELATE TO THEM WELL AND DO IT WITHOUT CHANGING HER STYLE. I MEAN, SHE DIDN'T TRY TO ACT LIKE A KID WHEN SHE WAS RAPPING WITH THEM, SHE ACTED HER AGE AND GOT OVER JUST FINE. SHE HAD REAL DIGNITY.
ANYWAY, ONE TIME WHEN I WAS TALKIN' TO HER I GOT A BRAINSTORM.
LOOK, MARIE, YOU'RE NOT GOING WITH ANY GUYS RIGHT NOW, ARE YOU?
NO, WHY?
Miss Jones
STARRING
WELL, I KNOW A GUY THAT I THINK YOU REALLY MIGHT HIT IT OFF WITH. HE'S A BOOK DEALER, SEE. A REAL NICE GUY. PRETTY KNOWLEDGEABLE, SENSIBLE...
3.

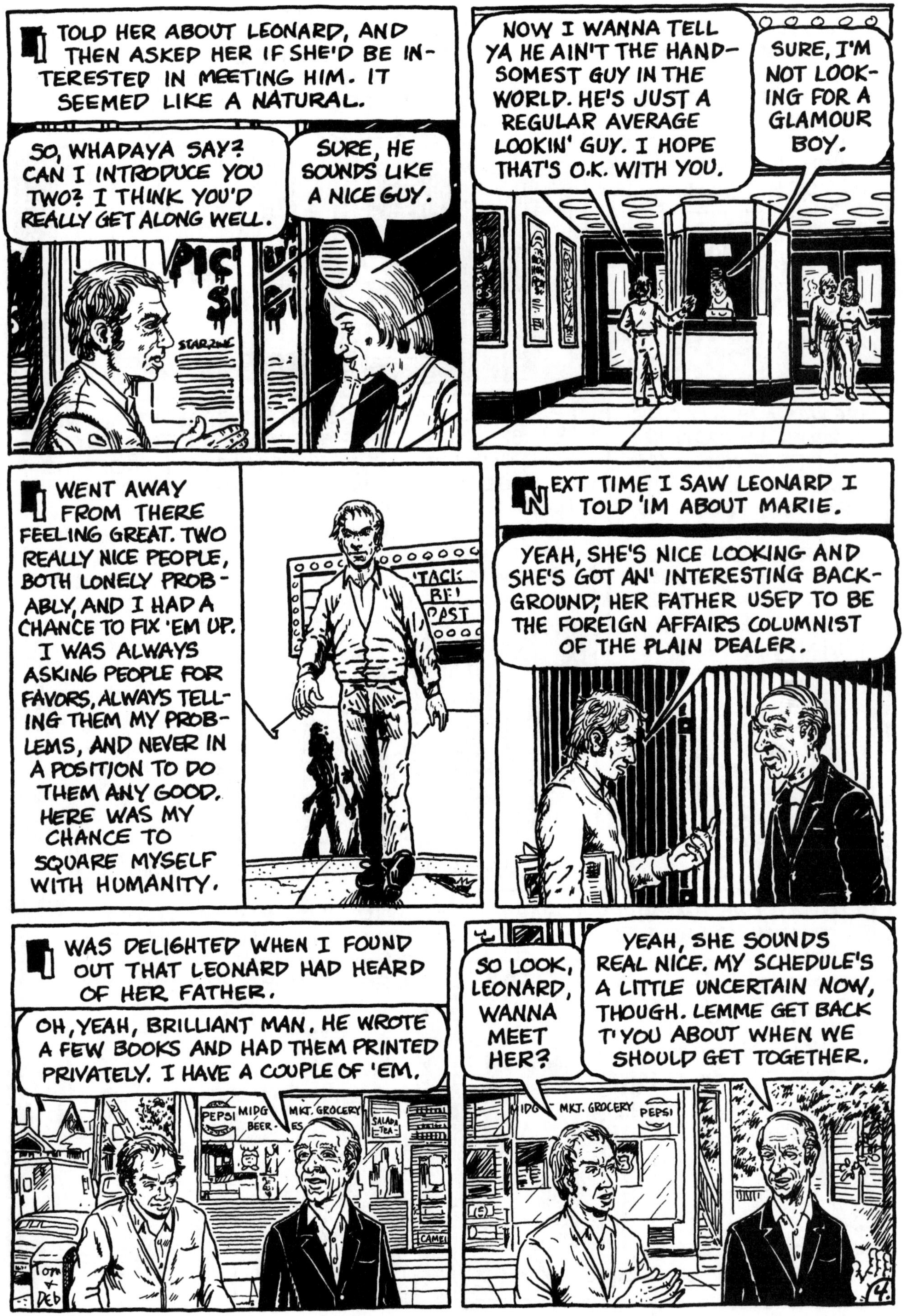
I TOLD HER ABOUT LEONARD, AND THEN ASKED HER IF SHE'D BE INTERESTED IN MEETING HIM. IT SEEMED LIKE A NATURAL.
SO, WHADAYA SAY? CAN I INTRODUCE YOU TWO? I THINK YOU'D REALLY GET ALONG WELL.
SURE, HE SOUNDS LIKE A NICE GUY.
NOW I WANNA TELL YA HE AIN'T THE HANDSOMEST GUY IN THE WORLD. HE'S JUST A REGULAR AVERAGE LOOKIN' GUY. I HOPE THAT'S O.K. WITH YOU.
SURE, I'M NOT LOOKING FOR A GLAMOUR BOY.
I WENT AWAY FROM THERE FEELING GREAT. TWO REALLY NICE PEOPLE, BOTH LONELY PROBABLY, AND I HAD A CHANCE TO FIX 'EM UP. I WAS ALWAYS ASKING PEOPLE FOR FAVORS, ALWAYS TELLING THEM MY PROBLEMS, AND NEVER IN A POSITION TO DO THEM ANY GOOD. HERE WAS MY CHANCE TO SQUARE MYSELF WITH HUMANITY.
NEXT TIME I SAW LEONARD I TOLD 'IM ABOUT MARIE.
YEAH, SHE'S NICE LOOKING AND SHE'S GOT AN' INTERESTING BACKGROUND; HER FATHER USED TO BE THE FOREIGN AFFAIRS COLUMNIST OF THE PLAIN DEALER.
I WAS DELIGHTED WHEN I FOUND OUT THAT LEONARD HAD HEARD OF HER FATHER.
OH, YEAH, BRILLIANT MAN. HE WROTE A FEW BOOKS AND HAD THEM PRINTED PRIVATELY. I HAVE A COUPLE OF 'EM.
PEPSI
MIDG
BEER
MKT. GROCERY
SALADA TEA
CAMEL
Tom + Deb
SO LOOK, LEONARD, WANNA MEET HER?
YEAH, SHE SOUNDS REAL NICE. MY SCHEDULE'S A LITTLE UNCERTAIN NOW, THOUGH. LEMME GET BACK T'YOU ABOUT WHEN WE SHOULD GET TOGETHER.
MIDG
MKT. GROCERY
PEPSI
4.

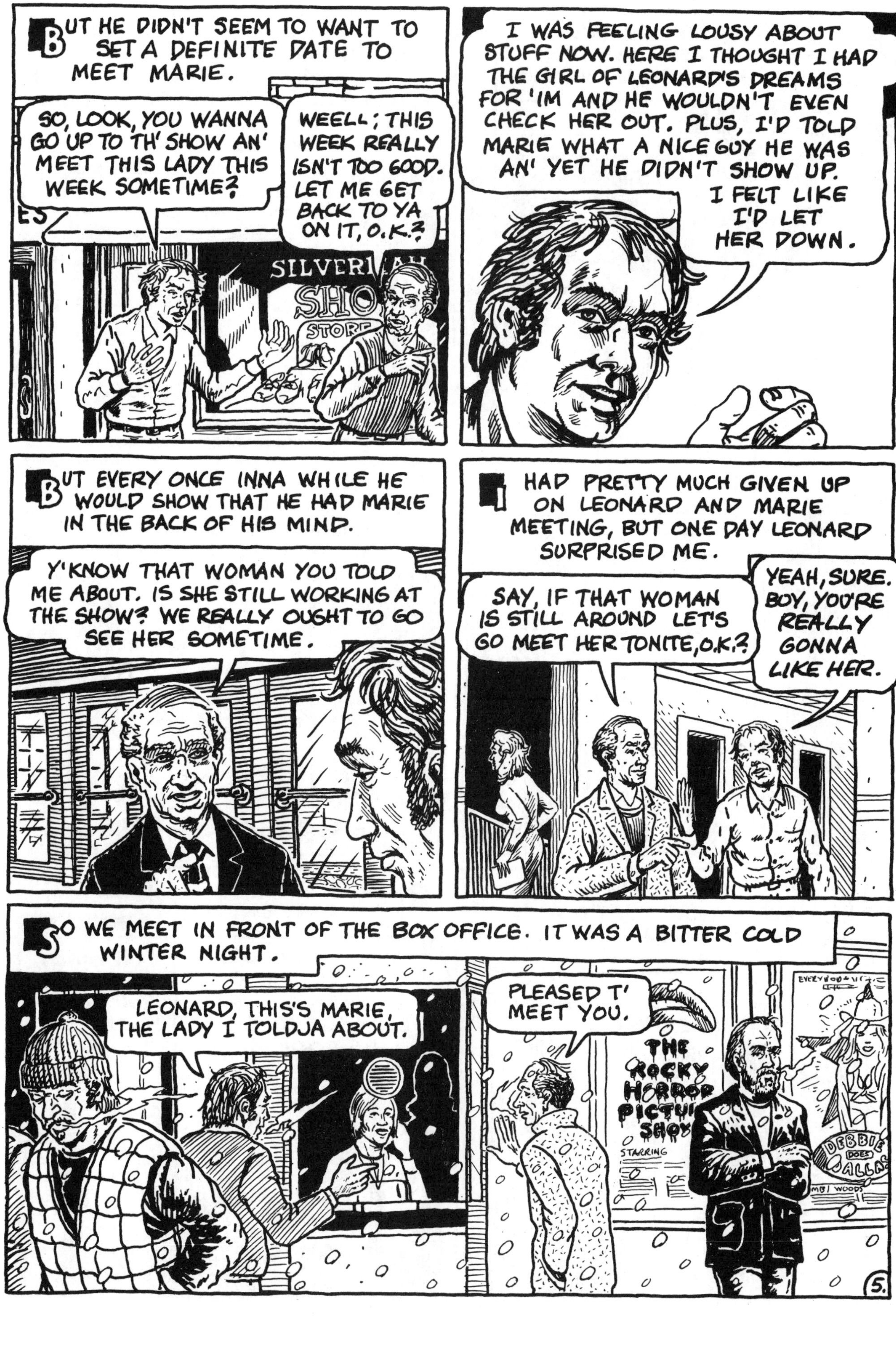
BUT HE DIDN'T SEEM TO WANT TO SET A DEFINITE DATE TO MEET MARIE.
SO, LOOK, YOU WANNA GO UP TO TH' SHOW AN' MEET THIS LADY THIS WEEK SOMETIME?
WEELL; THIS WEEK REALLY ISN'T TOO GOOD. LET ME GET BACK TO YA ON IT, O.K.?
SILVERLAKE
SHOE STORE
I WAS FEELING LOUSY ABOUT STUFF NOW. HERE I THOUGHT I HAD THE GIRL OF LEONARD'S DREAMS FOR 'IM AND HE WOULDN'T EVEN CHECK HER OUT. PLUS, I'D TOLD MARIE WHAT A NICE GUY HE WAS AN' YET HE DIDN'T SHOW UP.
I FELT LIKE I'D LET HER DOWN.
BUT EVERY ONCE INNA WHILE HE WOULD SHOW THAT HE HAD MARIE IN THE BACK OF HIS MIND.
Y'KNOW THAT WOMAN YOU TOLD ME ABOUT. IS SHE STILL WORKING AT THE SHOW? WE REALLY OUGHT TO GO SEE HER SOMETIME.
I HAD PRETTY MUCH GIVEN UP ON LEONARD AND MARIE MEETING, BUT ONE DAY LEONARD SURPRISED ME.
SAY, IF THAT WOMAN IS STILL AROUND LET'S GO MEET HER TONITE, O.K.?
YEAH, SURE. BOY, YOU'RE REALLY GONNA LIKE HER.
SO WE MEET IN FRONT OF THE BOX OFFICE. IT WAS A BITTER COLD WINTER NIGHT.
LEONARD, THIS'S MARIE, THE LADY I TOLDJA ABOUT.
PLEASED T' MEET YOU.
THE ROCKY HORROR PICTURE SHOW
STARRING
DEBBIE DOES DALLAS
5.

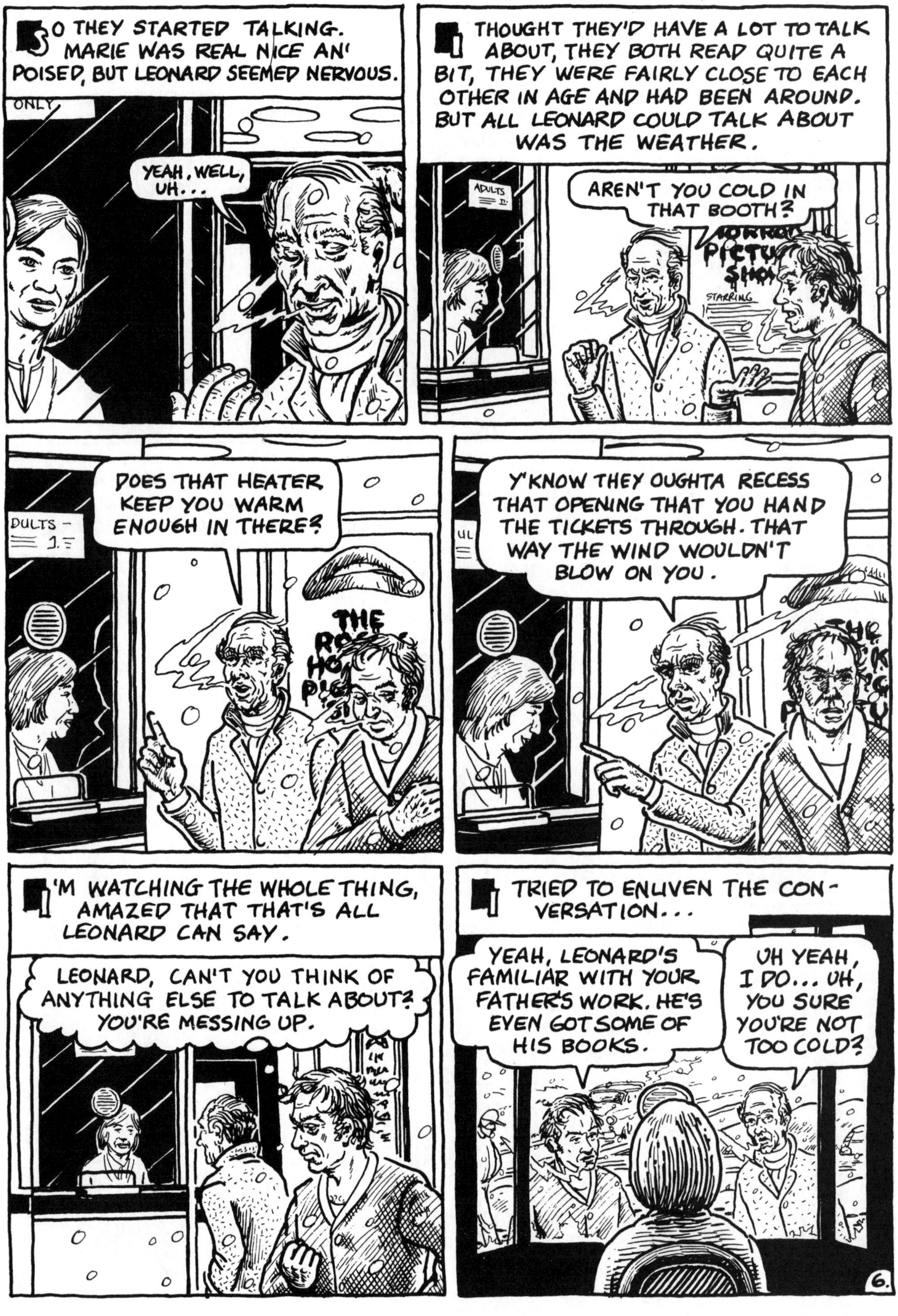
SO THEY STARTED TALKING. MARIE WAS REAL NICE AN' POISED, BUT LEONARD SEEMED NERVOUS.
YEAH, WELL, UH...
I THOUGHT THEY'D HAVE A LOT TO TALK ABOUT, THEY BOTH READ QUITE A BIT, THEY WERE FAIRLY CLOSE TO EACH OTHER IN AGE AND HAD BEEN AROUND. BUT ALL LEONARD COULD TALK ABOUT WAS THE WEATHER.
AREN'T YOU COLD IN THAT BOOTH?
DOES THAT HEATER KEEP YOU WARM ENOUGH IN THERE?
Y'KNOW THEY OUGHTA RECESS THAT OPENING THAT YOU HAND THE TICKETS THROUGH. THAT WAY THE WIND WOULDN'T BLOW ON YOU.
I'M WATCHING THE WHOLE THING, AMAZED THAT THAT'S ALL LEONARD CAN SAY.
LEONARD, CAN'T YOU THINK OF ANYTHING ELSE TO TALK ABOUT? YOU'RE MESSING UP.
I TRIED TO ENLIVEN THE CONVERSATION...
YEAH, LEONARD'S FAMILIAR WITH YOUR FATHER'S WORK. HE'S EVEN GOT SOME OF HIS BOOKS.
UH YEAH, I DO... UH, YOU SURE YOU'RE NOT TOO COLD?
6.

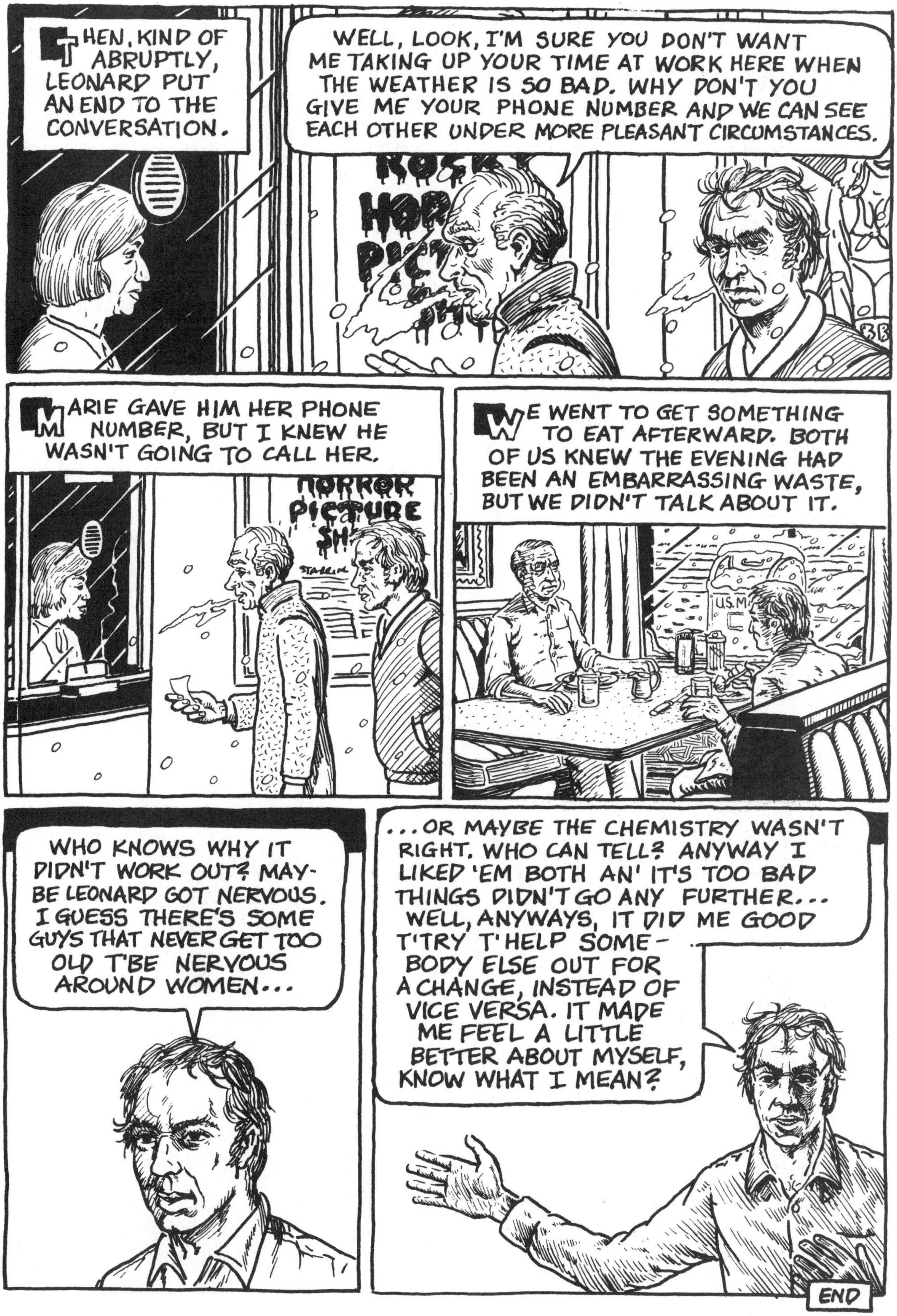
THEN, KIND OF ABRUPTLY, LEONARD PUT AN END TO THE CONVERSATION.
WELL, LOOK, I'M SURE YOU DON'T WANT ME TAKING UP YOUR TIME AT WORK HERE WHEN THE WEATHER IS SO BAD. WHY DON'T YOU GIVE ME YOUR PHONE NUMBER AND WE CAN SEE EACH OTHER UNDER MORE PLEASANT CIRCUMSTANCES.
MARIE GAVE HIM HER PHONE NUMBER, BUT I KNEW HE WASN'T GOING TO CALL HER.
HORROR PICTURE
WE WENT TO GET SOMETHING TO EAT AFTERWARD. BOTH OF US KNEW THE EVENING HAD BEEN AN EMBARRASSING WASTE, BUT WE DIDN'T TALK ABOUT IT.
WHO KNOWS WHY IT DIDN'T WORK OUT? MAYBE LEONARD GOT NERVOUS. I GUESS THERE'S SOME GUYS THAT NEVER GET TOO OLD T'BE NERVOUS AROUND WOMEN...
...OR MAYBE THE CHEMISTRY WASN'T RIGHT. WHO CAN TELL? ANYWAY I LIKED 'EM BOTH AN' IT'S TOO BAD THINGS DIDN'T GO ANY FURTHER... WELL, ANYWAYS, IT DID ME GOOD T'TRY T'HELP SOMEBODY ELSE OUT FOR A CHANGE, INSTEAD OF VICE VERSA. IT MADE ME FEEL A LITTLE BETTER ABOUT MYSELF, KNOW WHAT I MEAN?
END

NOAH'S ARK

STORY BY HARVEY PEKAR
ILLUSTRATED BY GERRY SHAMRAY

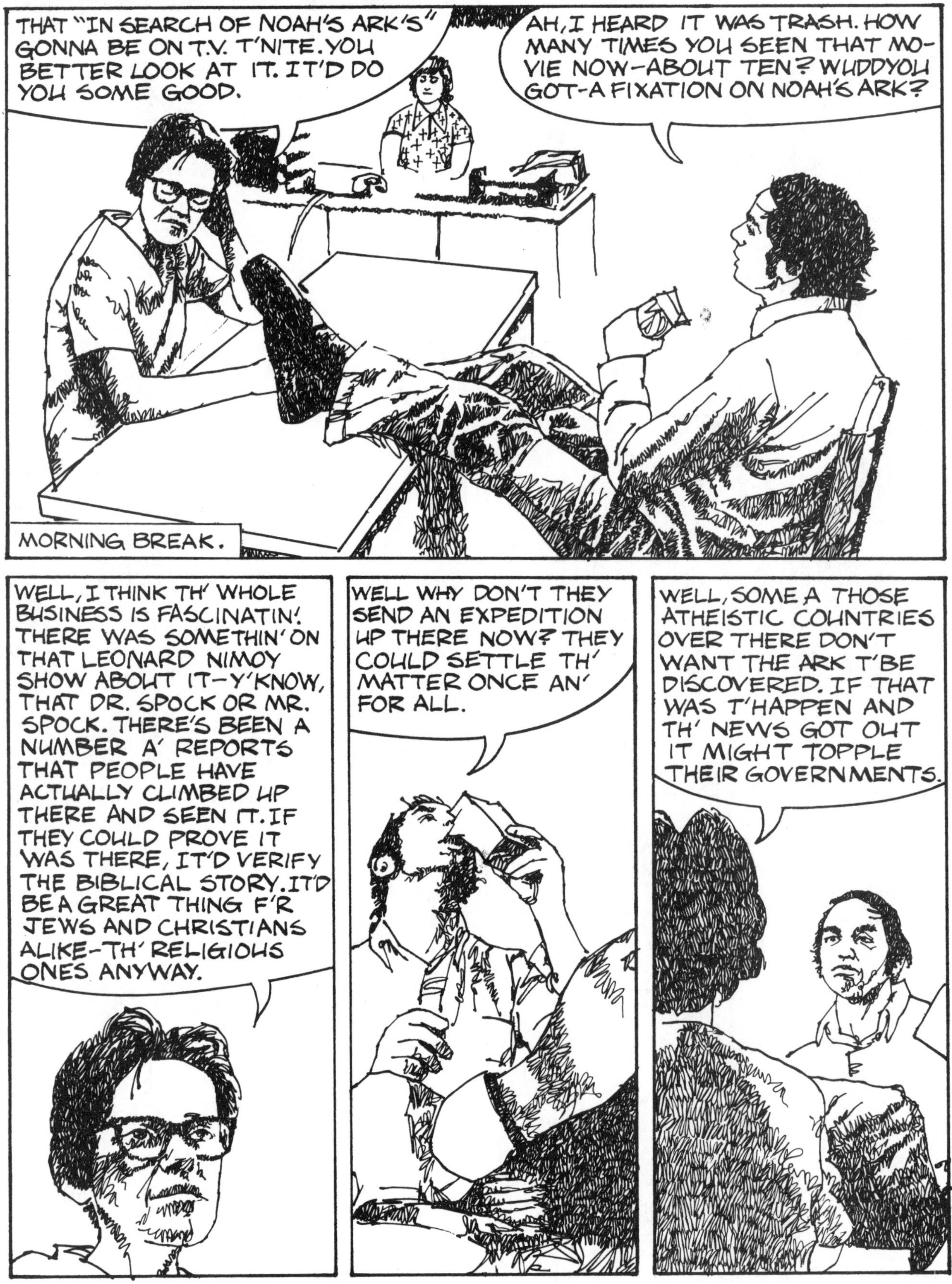
THAT "IN SEARCH OF NOAH'S ARK'S" GONNA BE ON T.V. T'NITE. YOU BETTER LOOK AT IT. IT'D DO YOU SOME GOOD.
AH, I HEARD IT WAS TRASH. HOW MANY TIMES YOU SEEN THAT MOVIE NOW–ABOUT TEN? WUDDYOU GOT–A FIXATION ON NOAH'S ARK?
MORNING BREAK.
WELL, I THINK TH' WHOLE BUSINESS IS FASCINATIN'. THERE WAS SOMETHIN' ON THAT LEONARD NIMOY SHOW ABOUT IT–Y'KNOW, THAT DR. SPOCK OR MR. SPOCK. THERE'S BEEN A NUMBER A' REPORTS THAT PEOPLE HAVE ACTUALLY CLIMBED UP THERE AND SEEN IT. IF THEY COULD PROVE IT WAS THERE, IT'D VERIFY THE BIBLICAL STORY. IT'D BE A GREAT THING F'R JEWS AND CHRISTIANS ALIKE–TH' RELIGIOUS ONES ANYWAY.
WELL WHY DON'T THEY SEND AN EXPEDITION UP THERE NOW? THEY COULD SETTLE TH' MATTER ONCE AN' FOR ALL.
WELL, SOME A THOSE ATHEISTIC COUNTRIES OVER THERE DON'T WANT THE ARK T'BE DISCOVERED. IF THAT WAS T'HAPPEN AND TH' NEWS GOT OUT IT MIGHT TOPPLE THEIR GOVERNMENTS.

IF THE ARK IS SUPPOSED TO BE ANY PLACE IT AIN'T IN NO ATHEISTIC COUNTRY. IT AIN'T IN RUSSIA. IT'S SUPPOSED TO BE ON MT. ARARAT, IN TURKEY. TURKEY AIN'T NO ATHEISTIC COUNTRY, IT'S MUSLIM.

WELL, I DON'T KNOW WHAT GOVERNMENT THAT PART A' TH' WORLD IS UNDER NOW. IF Y'WANT T'KNOW MORE ABOUT THAT STUFF TH' PERSON T'ASK IS WILLIAM F. BUCKLEY OR SOMEONE A' THAT ILK. HE'S PECULIAR, BUT HE'S A BRILLIANT MAN.

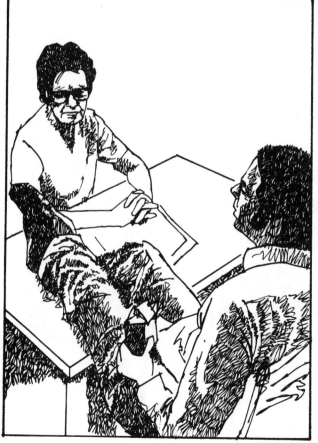

SAY, WOULDJA MIND PUTTIN' YER FEET DOWN? I'M EXPECTIN' TH' BOSS IN ANY MINUTE NOW AN' HE'LL HIT THE CEILING IF HE SEES YOU SPRAWLED OUT LIKE THAT.

Class Antagonism

STORY BY HARVEY PEKAR ILLUSTRATED BY GERRY SHAMRAY

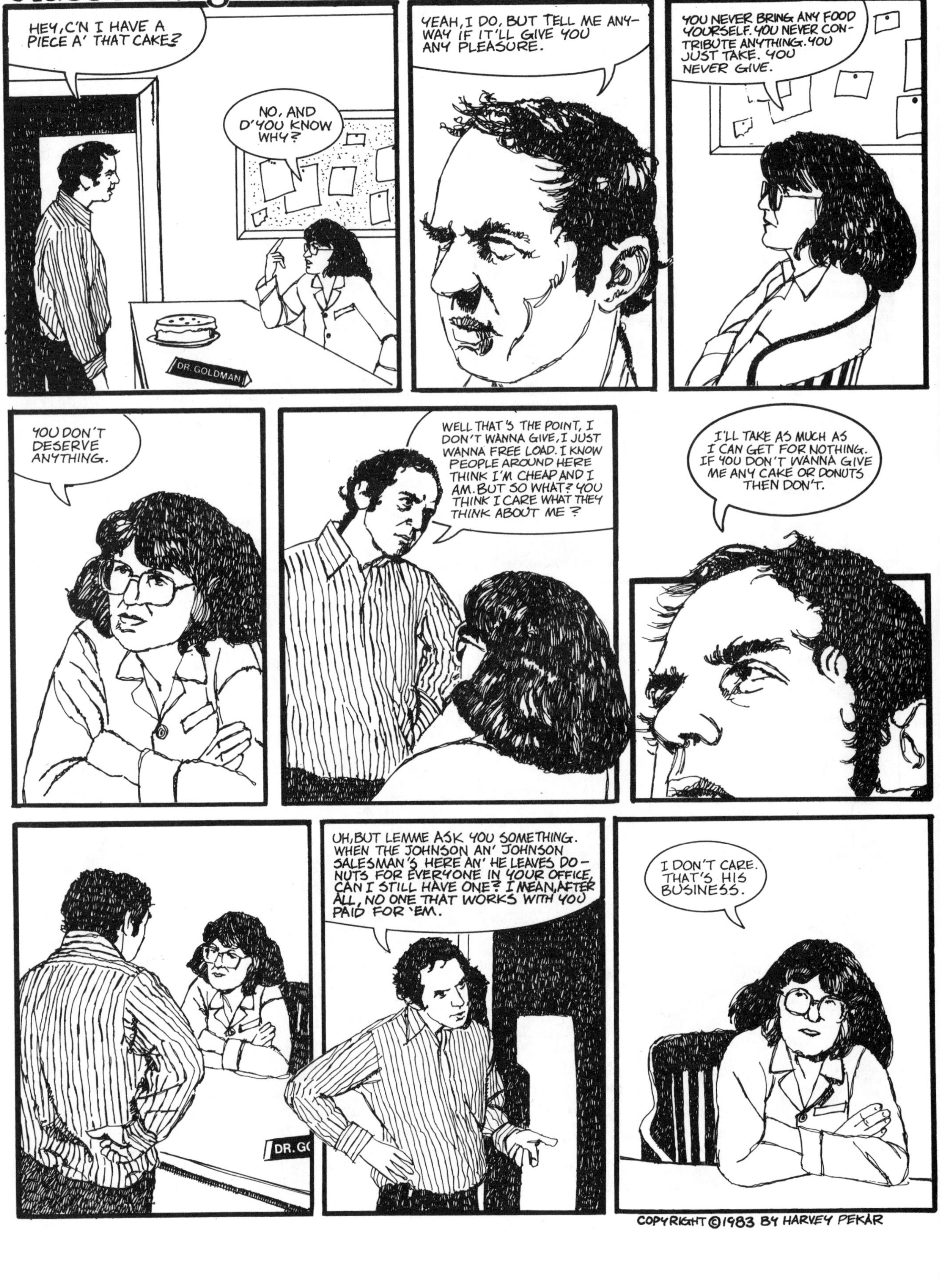
HEY, C'N I HAVE A PIECE A' THAT CAKE?
NO, AND D'YOU KNOW WHY?
DR. GOLDMAN
YEAH, I DO, BUT TELL ME ANYWAY IF IT'LL GIVE YOU ANY PLEASURE.
YOU NEVER BRING ANY FOOD YOURSELF. YOU NEVER CONTRIBUTE ANYTHING. YOU JUST TAKE. YOU NEVER GIVE.
YOU DON'T DESERVE ANYTHING.
WELL THAT'S THE POINT, I DON'T WANNA GIVE, I JUST WANNA FREE LOAD. I KNOW PEOPLE AROUND HERE THINK I'M CHEAP AND I AM. BUT SO WHAT? YOU THINK I CARE WHAT THEY THINK ABOUT ME?
I'LL TAKE AS MUCH AS I CAN GET FOR NOTHING. IF YOU DON'T WANNA GIVE ME ANY CAKE OR DONUTS THEN DON'T.
UH, BUT LEMME ASK YOU SOMETHING. WHEN THE JOHNSON AN' JOHNSON SALESMAN'S HERE AN' HE LEAVES DONUTS FOR EVERYONE IN YOUR OFFICE, CAN I STILL HAVE ONE? I MEAN, AFTER ALL, NO ONE THAT WORKS WITH YOU PAID FOR 'EM.
DR. GO
I DON'T CARE. THAT'S HIS BUSINESS.

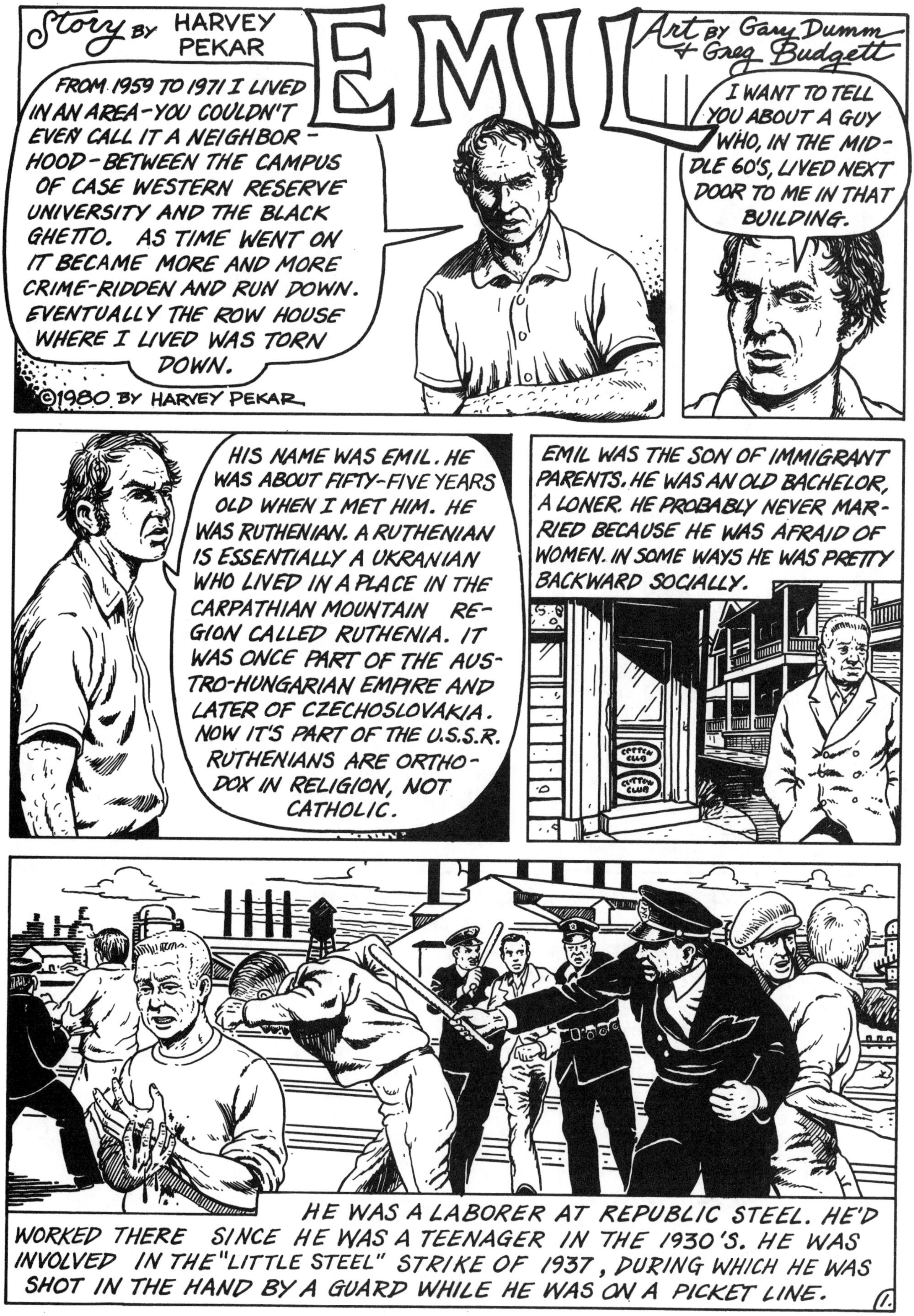
Story by HARVEY PEKAR
EMIL
Art by Gary Dumm + Greg Budgett
FROM 1959 TO 1971 I LIVED IN AN AREA - YOU COULDN'T EVEN CALL IT A NEIGHBORHOOD - BETWEEN THE CAMPUS OF CASE WESTERN RESERVE UNIVERSITY AND THE BLACK GHETTO. AS TIME WENT ON IT BECAME MORE AND MORE CRIME-RIDDEN AND RUN DOWN. EVENTUALLY THE ROW HOUSE WHERE I LIVED WAS TORN DOWN.
©1980 BY HARVEY PEKAR
I WANT TO TELL YOU ABOUT A GUY WHO, IN THE MIDDLE 60'S, LIVED NEXT DOOR TO ME IN THAT BUILDING.
HIS NAME WAS EMIL. HE WAS ABOUT FIFTY-FIVE YEARS OLD WHEN I MET HIM. HE WAS RUTHENIAN. A RUTHENIAN IS ESSENTIALLY A UKRANIAN WHO LIVED IN A PLACE IN THE CARPATHIAN MOUNTAIN REGION CALLED RUTHENIA. IT WAS ONCE PART OF THE AUSTRO-HUNGARIAN EMPIRE AND LATER OF CZECHOSLOVAKIA. NOW IT'S PART OF THE U.S.S.R. RUTHENIANS ARE ORTHODOX IN RELIGION, NOT CATHOLIC.
EMIL WAS THE SON OF IMMIGRANT PARENTS. HE WAS AN OLD BACHELOR, A LONER. HE PROBABLY NEVER MARRIED BECAUSE HE WAS AFRAID OF WOMEN. IN SOME WAYS HE WAS PRETTY BACKWARD SOCIALLY.
HE WAS A LABORER AT REPUBLIC STEEL. HE'D WORKED THERE SINCE HE WAS A TEENAGER IN THE 1930'S. HE WAS INVOLVED IN THE "LITTLE STEEL" STRIKE OF 1937, DURING WHICH HE WAS SHOT IN THE HAND BY A GUARD WHILE HE WAS ON A PICKET LINE.
1.

HE WAS IN THE ARMY DURING THE SECOND WORLD WAR, BUT AFTER THAT HE WENT BACK TO HIS JOB AT REPUBLIC AND TO LIVING WITH HIS FAMILY.

HE LIVED IN A POOR, WHITE NEIGHBORHOOD OF CLEVELAND BORDERING THE STEEL MILLS.

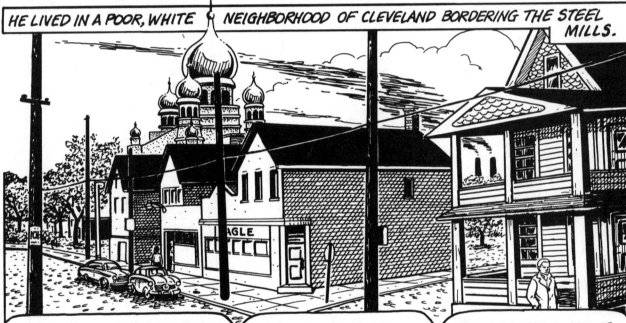

EMIL TOLD ME THAT WHEN HE WAS A YOUNG MAN HE'D BELONGED TO THE COMMUNIST PARTY. HE WAS NO INTELLECTUAL, BUT I GUESS HE WAS PRETTY IDEALISTIC AT ONE TIME. HE WAS ALSO A MEMBER OF THE NAACP FOR AWHILE.

ANYWAY, FOR SOME REASON EMIL DECIDED TO MOVE AWAY FROM HIS FAMILY AND GET A PLACE OF HIS OWN. HE WAS OVER FIFTY WHEN HE DID THIS.

THE GUY WAS MAKING GOOD MONEY AT REPUBLIC, HE HAD NO EXPENSES TO SPEAK OF, HE COULD HAVE LIVED A LOT OF PLACES.

2.

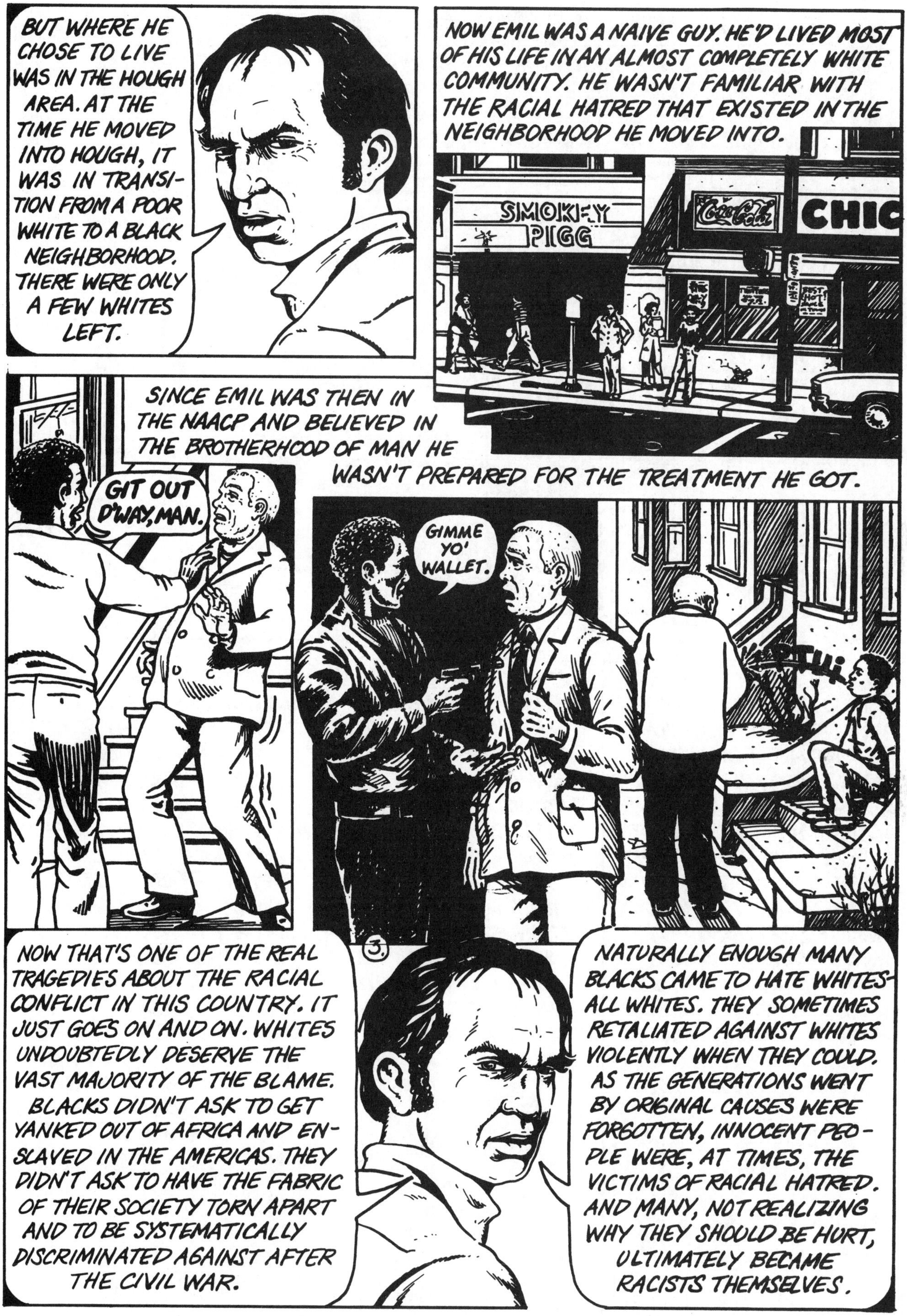

BUT WHERE HE CHOSE TO LIVE WAS IN THE HOUGH AREA. AT THE TIME HE MOVED INTO HOUGH, IT WAS IN TRANSITION FROM A POOR WHITE TO A BLACK NEIGHBORHOOD. THERE WERE ONLY A FEW WHITES LEFT.
NOW EMIL WAS A NAIVE GUY. HE'D LIVED MOST OF HIS LIFE IN AN ALMOST COMPLETELY WHITE COMMUNITY. HE WASN'T FAMILIAR WITH THE RACIAL HATRED THAT EXISTED IN THE NEIGHBORHOOD HE MOVED INTO.
SMOKEY PIGG
Coca-Cola
CHIC
SINCE EMIL WAS THEN IN THE NAACP AND BELIEVED IN THE BROTHERHOOD OF MAN HE WASN'T PREPARED FOR THE TREATMENT HE GOT.
GIT OUT D'WAY, MAN.
GIMME YO' WALLET.
PTUI
NOW THAT'S ONE OF THE REAL TRAGEDIES ABOUT THE RACIAL CONFLICT IN THIS COUNTRY. IT JUST GOES ON AND ON. WHITES UNDOUBTEDLY DESERVE THE VAST MAJORITY OF THE BLAME. BLACKS DIDN'T ASK TO GET YANKED OUT OF AFRICA AND ENSLAVED IN THE AMERICAS. THEY DIDN'T ASK TO HAVE THE FABRIC OF THEIR SOCIETY TORN APART AND TO BE SYSTEMATICALLY DISCRIMINATED AGAINST AFTER THE CIVIL WAR.
3.
NATURALLY ENOUGH MANY BLACKS CAME TO HATE WHITES - ALL WHITES. THEY SOMETIMES RETALIATED AGAINST WHITES VIOLENTLY WHEN THEY COULD. AS THE GENERATIONS WENT BY ORIGINAL CAUSES WERE FORGOTTEN, INNOCENT PEOPLE WERE, AT TIMES, THE VICTIMS OF RACIAL HATRED. AND MANY, NOT REALIZING WHY THEY SHOULD BE HURT, ULTIMATELY BECAME RACISTS THEMSELVES.

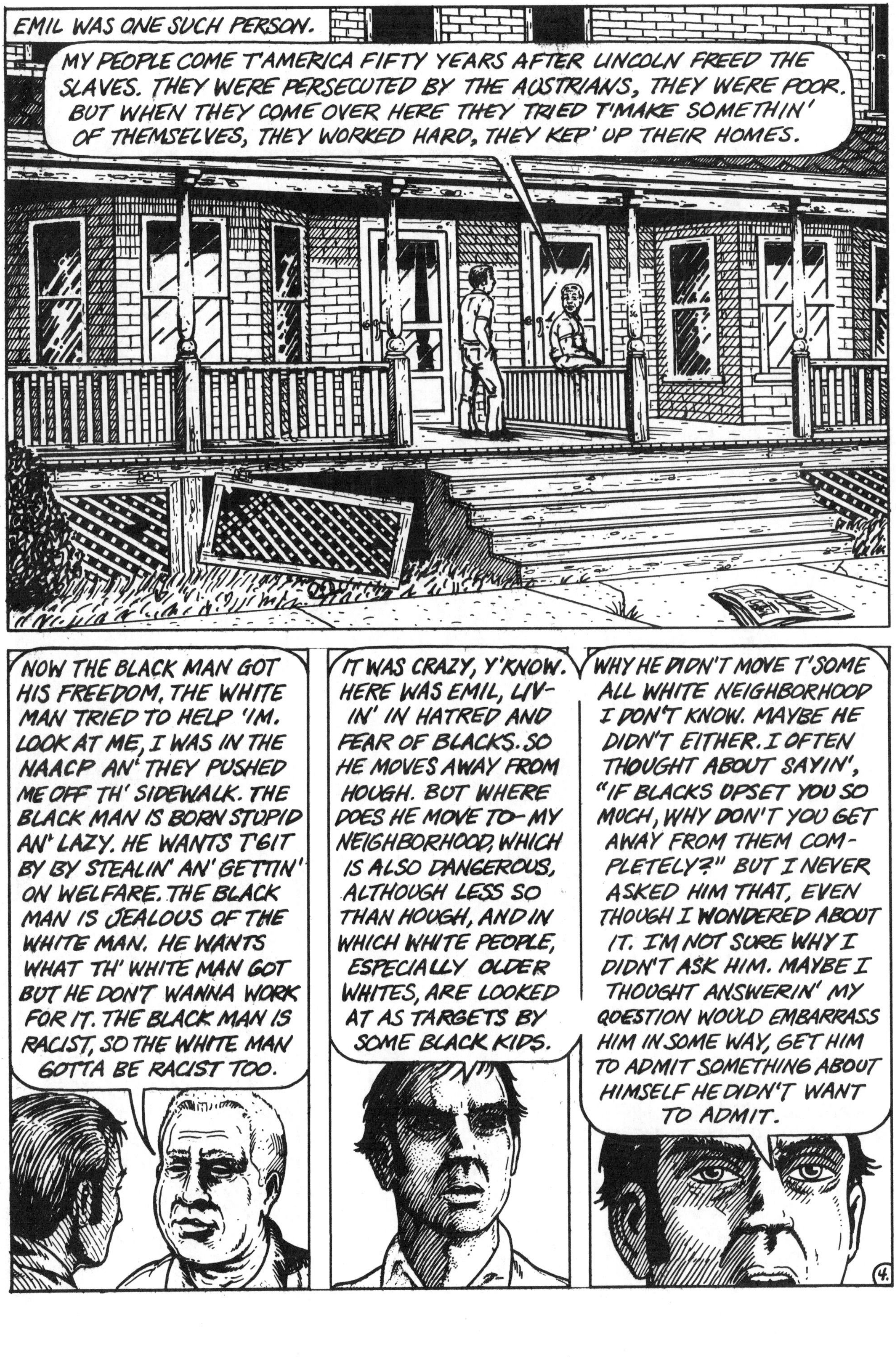
EMIL WAS ONE SUCH PERSON.
MY PEOPLE COME T'AMERICA FIFTY YEARS AFTER LINCOLN FREED THE SLAVES. THEY WERE PERSECUTED BY THE AUSTRIANS, THEY WERE POOR. BUT WHEN THEY COME OVER HERE THEY TRIED T'MAKE SOMETHIN' OF THEMSELVES, THEY WORKED HARD, THEY KEP' UP THEIR HOMES.
NOW THE BLACK MAN GOT HIS FREEDOM, THE WHITE MAN TRIED TO HELP 'IM. LOOK AT ME, I WAS IN THE NAACP AN' THEY PUSHED ME OFF TH' SIDEWALK. THE BLACK MAN IS BORN STUPID AN' LAZY. HE WANTS T'GIT BY BY STEALIN' AN' GETTIN' ON WELFARE. THE BLACK MAN IS JEALOUS OF THE WHITE MAN. HE WANTS WHAT TH' WHITE MAN GOT BUT HE DON'T WANNA WORK FOR IT. THE BLACK MAN IS RACIST, SO THE WHITE MAN GOTTA BE RACIST TOO.
IT WAS CRAZY, Y'KNOW. HERE WAS EMIL, LIVIN' IN HATRED AND FEAR OF BLACKS. SO HE MOVES AWAY FROM HOUGH. BUT WHERE DOES HE MOVE TO- MY NEIGHBORHOOD, WHICH IS ALSO DANGEROUS, ALTHOUGH LESS SO THAN HOUGH, AND IN WHICH WHITE PEOPLE, ESPECIALLY OLDER WHITES, ARE LOOKED AT AS TARGETS BY SOME BLACK KIDS.
WHY HE DIDN'T MOVE T'SOME ALL WHITE NEIGHBORHOOD I DON'T KNOW. MAYBE HE DIDN'T EITHER. I OFTEN THOUGHT ABOUT SAYIN', "IF BLACKS UPSET YOU SO MUCH, WHY DON'T YOU GET AWAY FROM THEM COMPLETELY?" BUT I NEVER ASKED HIM THAT, EVEN THOUGH I WONDERED ABOUT IT. I'M NOT SURE WHY I DIDN'T ASK HIM. MAYBE I THOUGHT ANSWERIN' MY QUESTION WOULD EMBARRASS HIM IN SOME WAY, GET HIM TO ADMIT SOMETHING ABOUT HIMSELF HE DIDN'T WANT TO ADMIT.
4.

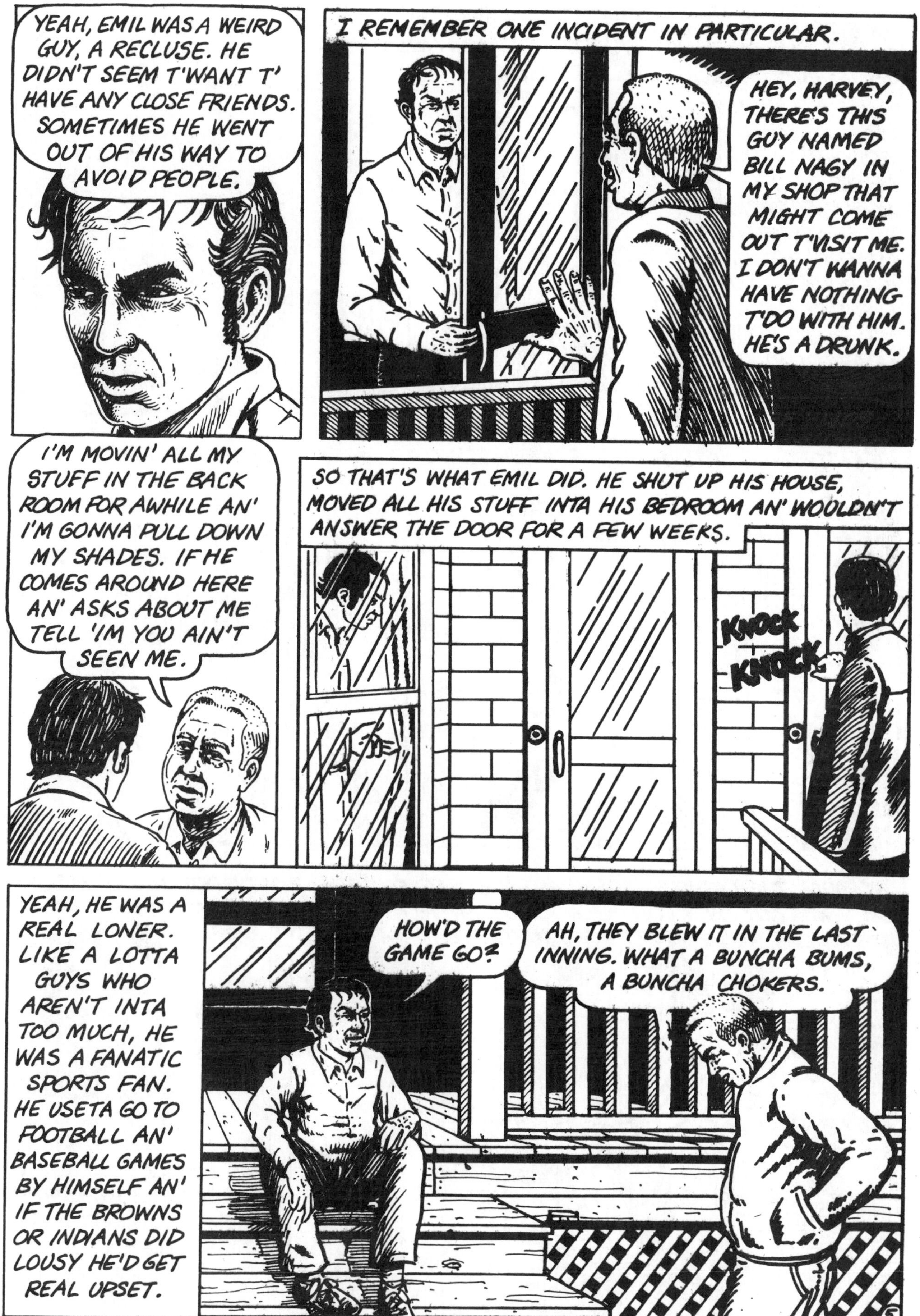
YEAH, EMIL WAS A WEIRD GUY, A RECLUSE. HE DIDN'T SEEM T'WANT T' HAVE ANY CLOSE FRIENDS. SOMETIMES HE WENT OUT OF HIS WAY TO AVOID PEOPLE.
I REMEMBER ONE INCIDENT IN PARTICULAR.
HEY, HARVEY, THERE'S THIS GUY NAMED BILL NAGY IN MY SHOP THAT MIGHT COME OUT T'VISIT ME. I DON'T WANNA HAVE NOTHING T'DO WITH HIM. HE'S A DRUNK.
I'M MOVIN' ALL MY STUFF IN THE BACK ROOM FOR AWHILE AN' I'M GONNA PULL DOWN MY SHADES. IF HE COMES AROUND HERE AN' ASKS ABOUT ME TELL 'IM YOU AIN'T SEEN ME.
SO THAT'S WHAT EMIL DID. HE SHUT UP HIS HOUSE, MOVED ALL HIS STUFF INTA HIS BEDROOM AN' WOULDN'T ANSWER THE DOOR FOR A FEW WEEKS.
KNOCK
KNOCK
YEAH, HE WAS A REAL LONER. LIKE A LOTTA GUYS WHO AREN'T INTA TOO MUCH, HE WAS A FANATIC SPORTS FAN. HE USETA GO TO FOOTBALL AN' BASEBALL GAMES BY HIMSELF AN' IF THE BROWNS OR INDIANS DID LOUSY HE'D GET REAL UPSET.
HOW'D THE GAME GO?
AH, THEY BLEW IT IN THE LAST INNING. WHAT A BUNCHA BUMS, A BUNCHA CHOKERS.
5.

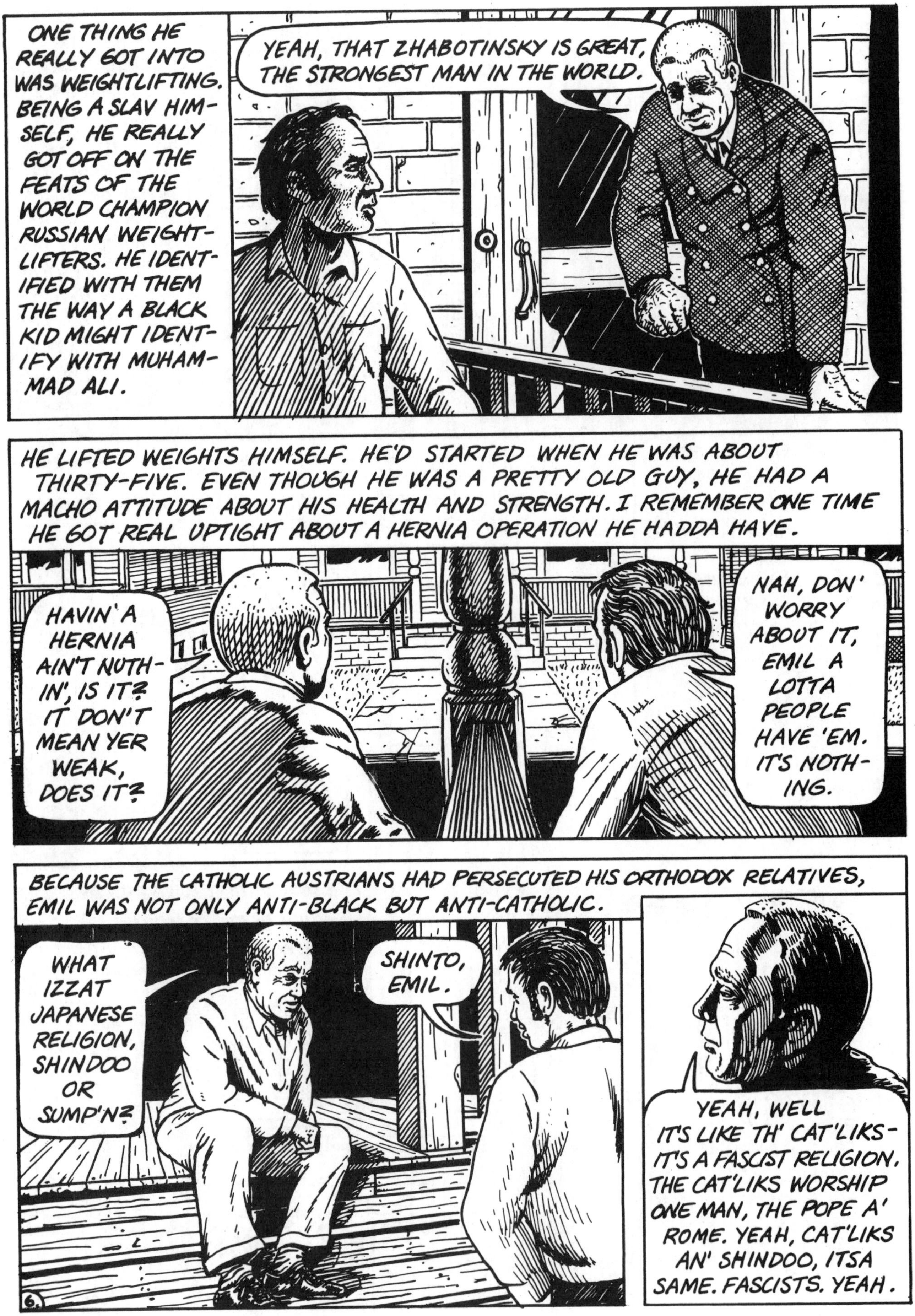

ONE THING HE REALLY GOT INTO WAS WEIGHTLIFTING. BEING A SLAV HIMSELF, HE REALLY GOT OFF ON THE FEATS OF THE WORLD CHAMPION RUSSIAN WEIGHTLIFTERS. HE IDENTIFIED WITH THEM THE WAY A BLACK KID MIGHT IDENTIFY WITH MUHAMMAD ALI.
YEAH, THAT ZHABOTINSKY IS GREAT, THE STRONGEST MAN IN THE WORLD.
HE LIFTED WEIGHTS HIMSELF. HE'D STARTED WHEN HE WAS ABOUT THIRTY-FIVE. EVEN THOUGH HE WAS A PRETTY OLD GUY, HE HAD A MACHO ATTITUDE ABOUT HIS HEALTH AND STRENGTH. I REMEMBER ONE TIME HE GOT REAL UPTIGHT ABOUT A HERNIA OPERATION HE HADDA HAVE.
HAVIN' A HERNIA AIN'T NUTHIN', IS IT? IT DON'T MEAN YER WEAK, DOES IT?
NAH, DON' WORRY ABOUT IT, EMIL A LOTTA PEOPLE HAVE 'EM. IT'S NOTHING.
BECAUSE THE CATHOLIC AUSTRIANS HAD PERSECUTED HIS ORTHODOX RELATIVES, EMIL WAS NOT ONLY ANTI-BLACK BUT ANTI-CATHOLIC.
WHAT IZZAT JAPANESE RELIGION, SHINDOO OR SUMP'N?
SHINTO, EMIL.
YEAH, WELL IT'S LIKE TH' CAT'LIKS - IT'S A FASCIST RELIGION. THE CAT'LIKS WORSHIP ONE MAN, THE POPE A' ROME. YEAH, CAT'LIKS AN' SHINDOO, ITSA SAME. FASCISTS. YEAH.
6.

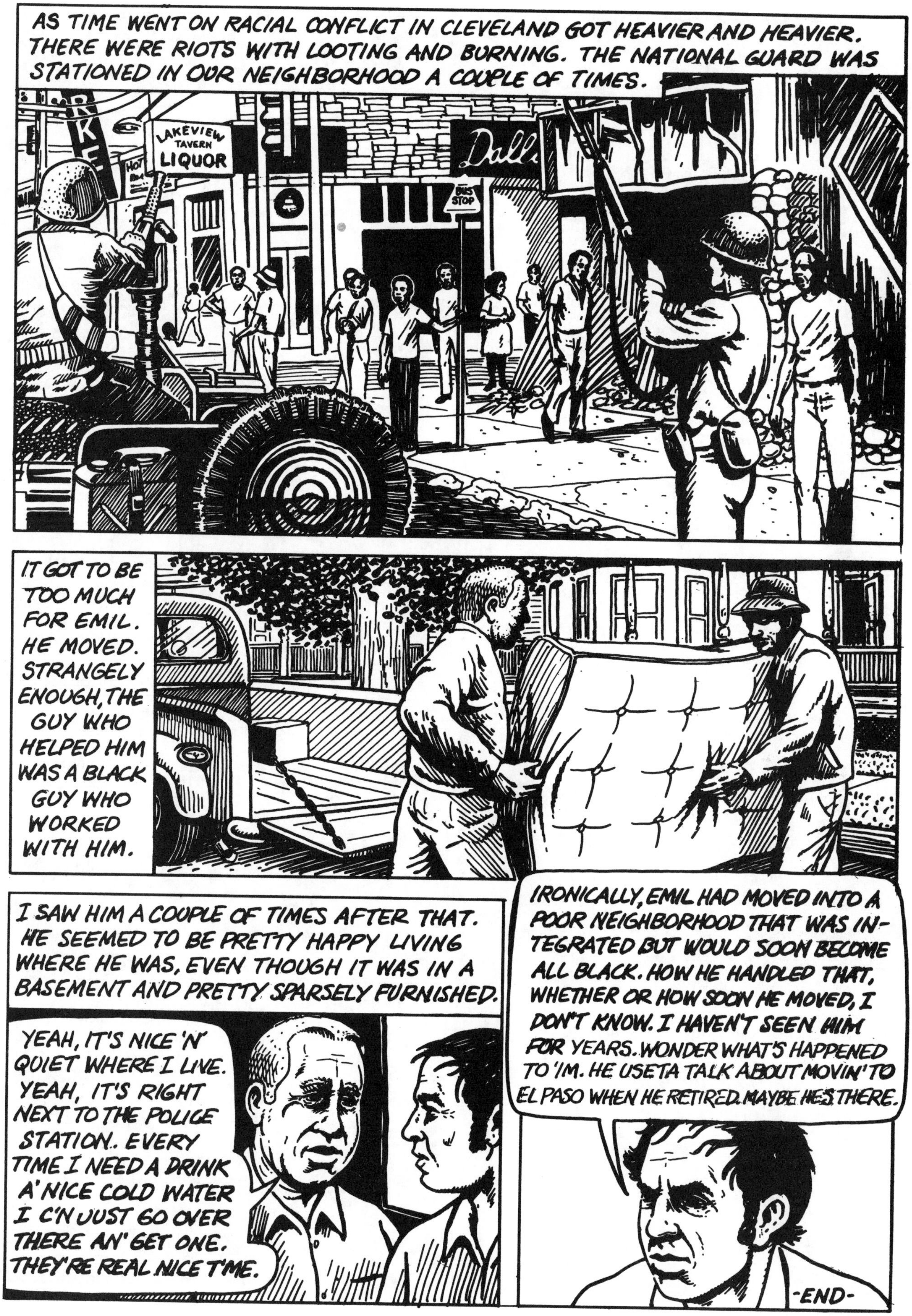
AS TIME WENT ON RACIAL CONFLICT IN CLEVELAND GOT HEAVIER AND HEAVIER. THERE WERE RIOTS WITH LOOTING AND BURNING. THE NATIONAL GUARD WAS STATIONED IN OUR NEIGHBORHOOD A COUPLE OF TIMES.
LAKEVIEW TAVERN LIQUOR
BUS STOP
IT GOT TO BE TOO MUCH FOR EMIL. HE MOVED. STRANGELY ENOUGH, THE GUY WHO HELPED HIM WAS A BLACK GUY WHO WORKED WITH HIM.
I SAW HIM A COUPLE OF TIMES AFTER THAT. HE SEEMED TO BE PRETTY HAPPY LIVING WHERE HE WAS, EVEN THOUGH IT WAS IN A BASEMENT AND PRETTY SPARSELY FURNISHED.
YEAH, IT'S NICE 'N' QUIET WHERE I LIVE. YEAH, IT'S RIGHT NEXT TO THE POLICE STATION.. EVERY TIME I NEED A DRINK A' NICE COLD WATER I C'N JUST GO OVER THERE AN' GET ONE. THEY'RE REAL NICE T'ME.
IRONICALLY, EMIL HAD MOVED INTO A POOR NEIGHBORHOOD THAT WAS INTEGRATED BUT WOULD SOON BECOME ALL BLACK. HOW HE HANDLED THAT, WHETHER OR HOW SOON HE MOVED, I DON'T KNOW. I HAVEN'T SEEN HIM FOR YEARS. WONDER WHAT'S HAPPENED TO 'IM. HE USETA TALK ABOUT MOVIN' TO EL PASO WHEN HE RETIRED. MAYBE HE'S THERE.
-END-

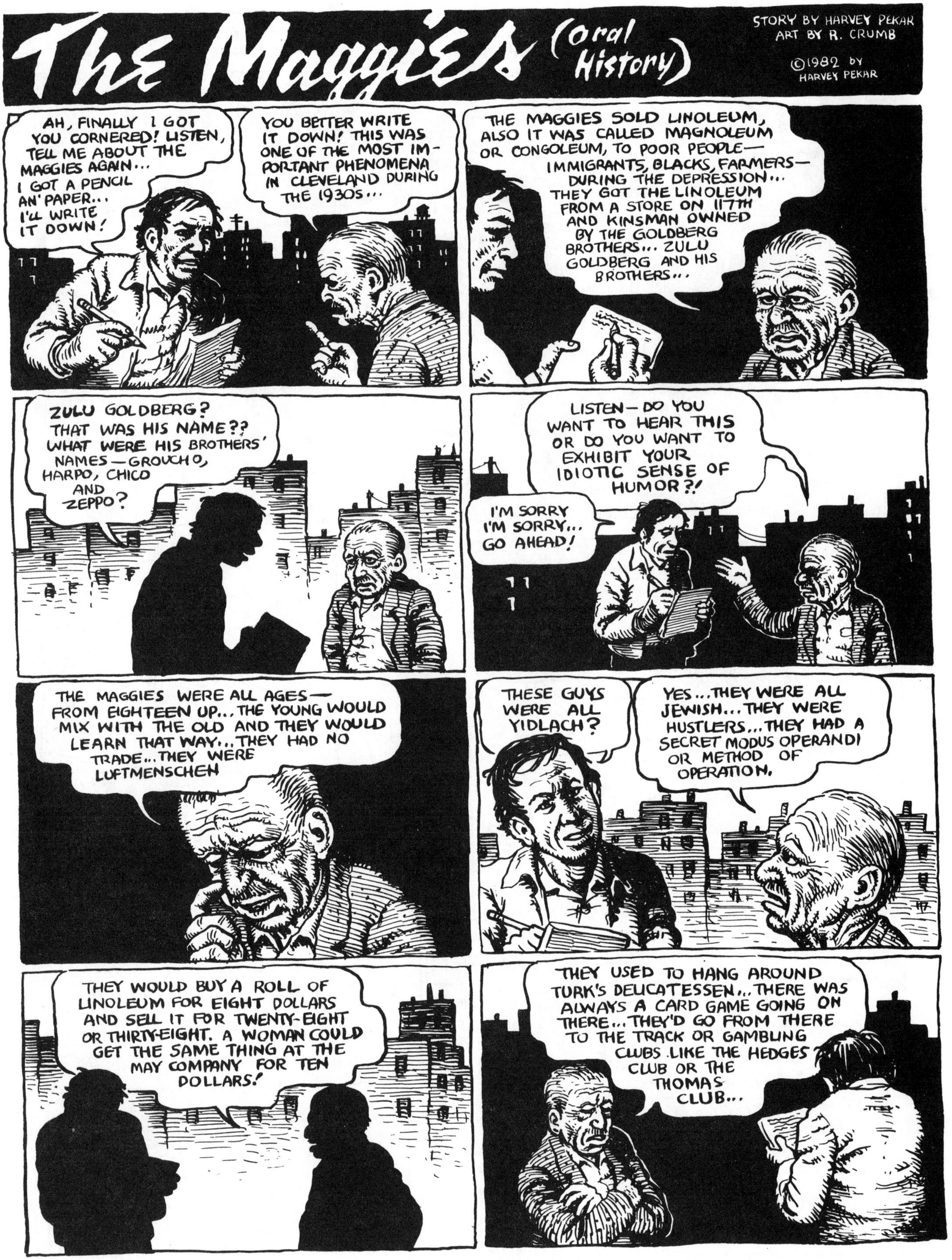
The Maggies (oral history)
STORY BY HARVEY PEKAR
ART BY R. CRUMB
©1982 BY HARVEY PEKAR
AH, FINALLY I GOT YOU CORNERED! LISTEN, TELL ME ABOUT THE MAGGIES AGAIN... I GOT A PENCIL AN' PAPER... I'LL WRITE IT DOWN!
YOU BETTER WRITE IT DOWN! THIS WAS ONE OF THE MOST IMPORTANT PHENOMENA IN CLEVELAND DURING THE 1930S...
THE MAGGIES SOLD LINOLEUM, ALSO IT WAS CALLED MAGNOLEUM OR CONGOLEUM, TO POOR PEOPLE— IMMIGRANTS, BLACKS, FARMERS— DURING THE DEPRESSION... THEY GOT THE LINOLEUM FROM A STORE ON 117TH AND KINSMAN OWNED BY THE GOLDBERG BROTHERS... ZULU GOLDBERG AND HIS BROTHERS...
ZULU GOLDBERG? THAT WAS HIS NAME?? WHAT WERE HIS BROTHERS' NAMES—GROUCHO, HARPO, CHICO AND ZEPPO?
LISTEN—DO YOU WANT TO HEAR THIS OR DO YOU WANT TO EXHIBIT YOUR IDIOTIC SENSE OF HUMOR?!
I'M SORRY I'M SORRY... GO AHEAD!
THE MAGGIES WERE ALL AGES— FROM EIGHTEEN UP... THE YOUNG WOULD MIX WITH THE OLD AND THEY WOULD LEARN THAT WAY... THEY HAD NO TRADE... THEY WERE LUFTMENSCHEN
THESE GUYS WERE ALL YIDLACH?
YES... THEY WERE ALL JEWISH... THEY WERE HUSTLERS... THEY HAD A SECRET MODUS OPERANDI OR METHOD OF OPERATION.
THEY WOULD BUY A ROLL OF LINOLEUM FOR EIGHT DOLLARS AND SELL IT FOR TWENTY-EIGHT OR THIRTY-EIGHT. A WOMAN COULD GET THE SAME THING AT THE MAY COMPANY FOR TEN DOLLARS!
THEY USED TO HANG AROUND TURK'S DELICATESSEN... THERE WAS ALWAYS A CARD GAME GOING ON THERE... THEY'D GO FROM THERE TO THE TRACK OR GAMBLING CLUBS LIKE THE HEDGES CLUB OR THE THOMAS CLUB...

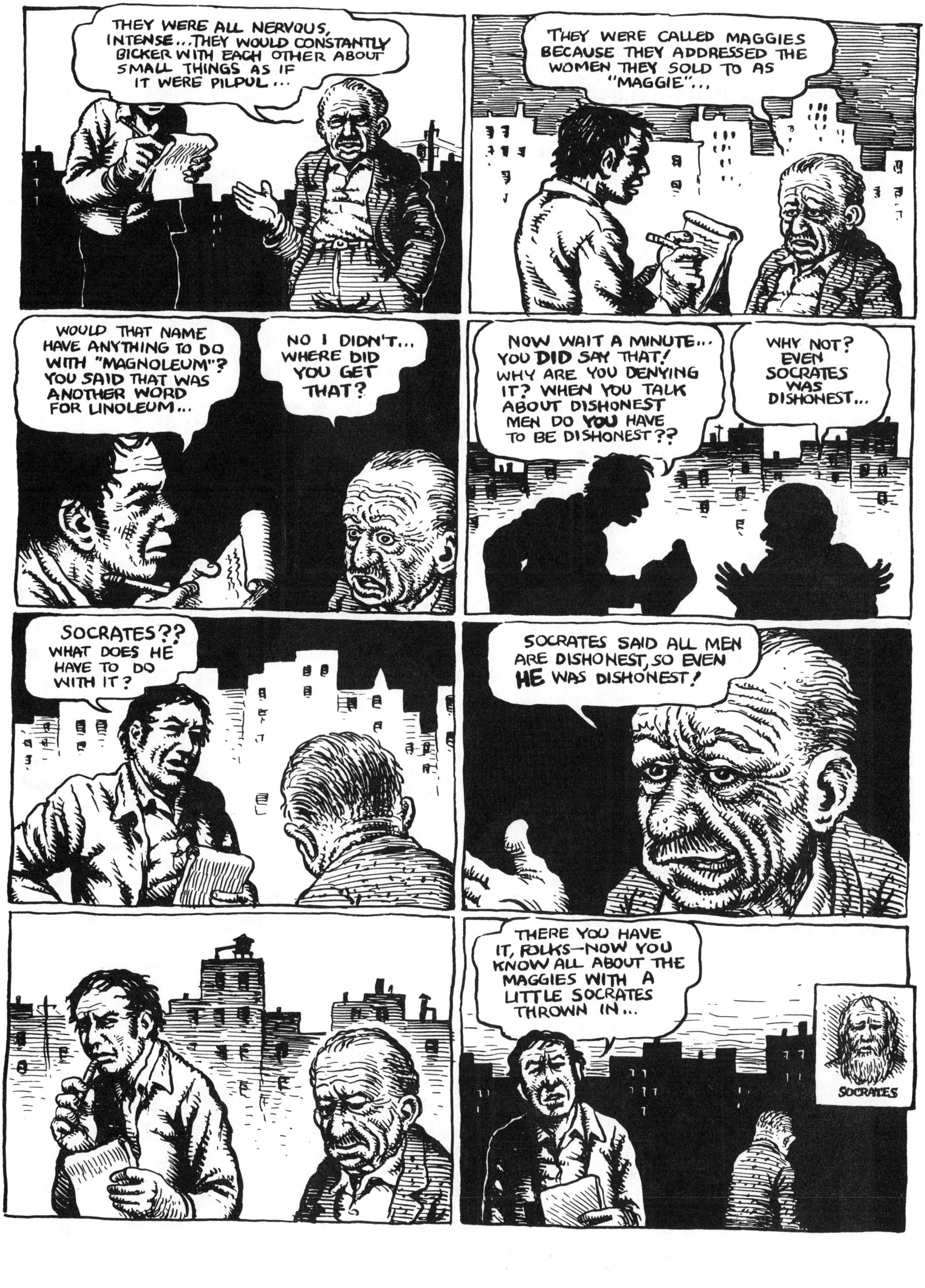
THEY WERE ALL NERVOUS, INTENSE... THEY WOULD CONSTANTLY BICKER WITH EACH OTHER ABOUT SMALL THINGS AS IF IT WERE PILPUL...
THEY WERE CALLED MAGGIES BECAUSE THEY ADDRESSED THE WOMEN THEY SOLD TO AS "MAGGIE"...
WOULD THAT NAME HAVE ANYTHING TO DO WITH "MAGNOLEUM"? YOU SAID THAT WAS ANOTHER WORD FOR LINOLEUM...
NO I DIDN'T... WHERE DID YOU GET THAT?
NOW WAIT A MINUTE... YOU **DID** SAY THAT! WHY ARE YOU DENYING IT? WHEN YOU TALK ABOUT DISHONEST MEN DO **YOU** HAVE TO BE DISHONEST??
WHY NOT? EVEN SOCRATES WAS DISHONEST...
SOCRATES?? WHAT DOES HE HAVE TO DO WITH IT?
SOCRATES SAID ALL MEN ARE DISHONEST, SO EVEN **HE** WAS DISHONEST!
THERE YOU HAVE IT, FOLKS—NOW YOU KNOW ALL ABOUT THE MAGGIES WITH A LITTLE SOCRATES THROWN IN...
SOCRATES

KAPARRA

STORY BY HARVEY PEKAR
ILLUSTRATED BY GERRY SHAMRAY

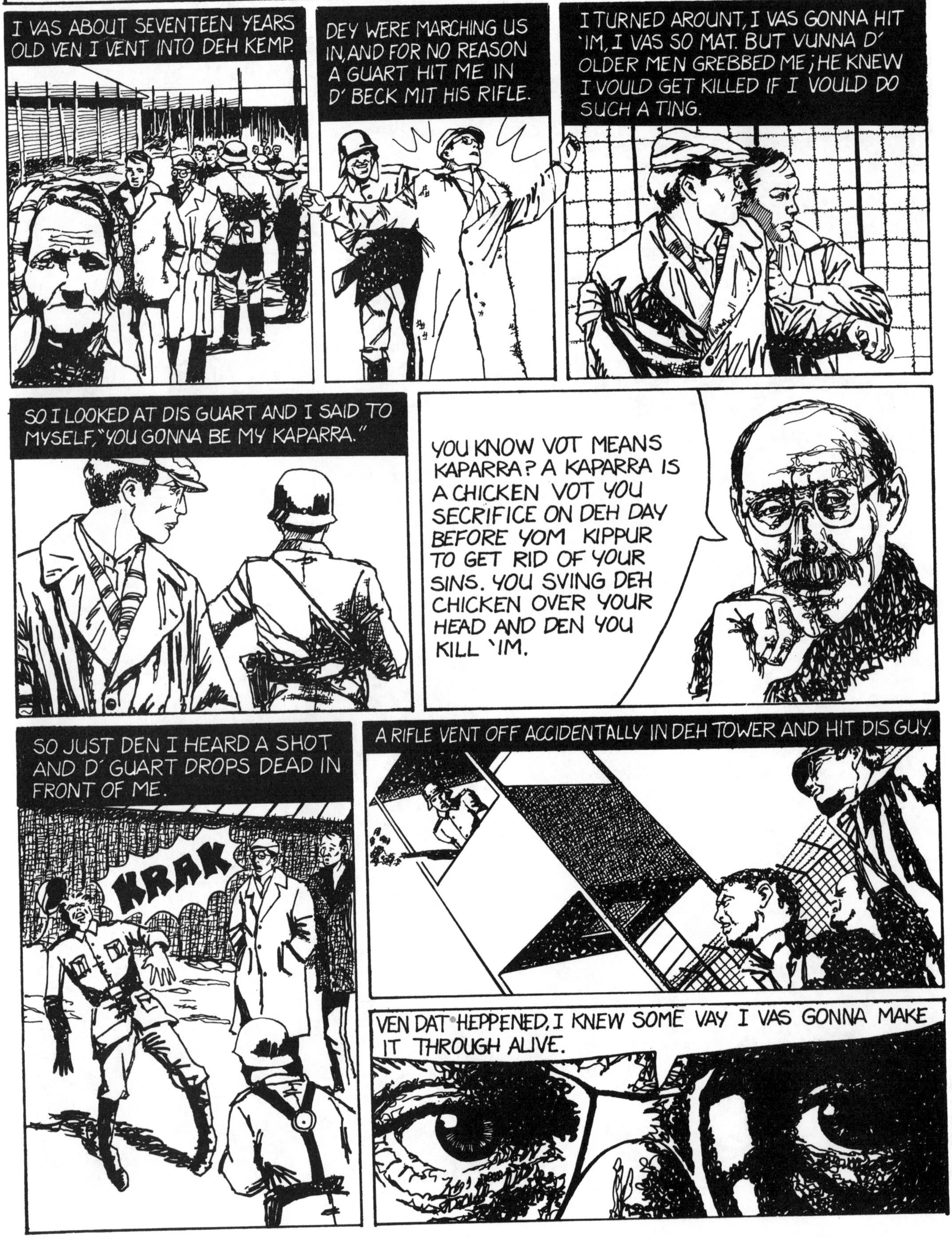
I VAS ABOUT SEVENTEEN YEARS OLD VEN I VENT INTO DEH KEMP.
DEY WERE MARCHING US IN, AND FOR NO REASON A GUART HIT ME IN D' BECK MIT HIS RIFLE.
I TURNED AROUNT, I VAS GONNA HIT 'IM, I VAS SO MAT. BUT VUNNA D' OLDER MEN GREBBED ME; HE KNEW I VOULD GET KILLED IF I VOULD DO SUCH A TING.
SO I LOOKED AT DIS GUART AND I SAID TO MYSELF, "YOU GONNA BE MY KAPARRA."
YOU KNOW VOT MEANS KAPARRA? A KAPARRA IS A CHICKEN VOT YOU SECRIFICE ON DEH DAY BEFORE YOM KIPPUR TO GET RID OF YOUR SINS. YOU SVING DEH CHICKEN OVER YOUR HEAD AND DEN YOU KILL 'IM.
SO JUST DEN I HEARD A SHOT AND D' GUART DROPS DEAD IN FRONT OF ME.
KRAK
A RIFLE VENT OFF ACCIDENTALLY IN DEH TOWER AND HIT DIS GUY.
VEN DAT HEPPENED, I KNEW SOME VAY I VAS GONNA MAKE IT THROUGH ALIVE.

AMERICAN SPLENDOR ASSAULTS THE MEDIA

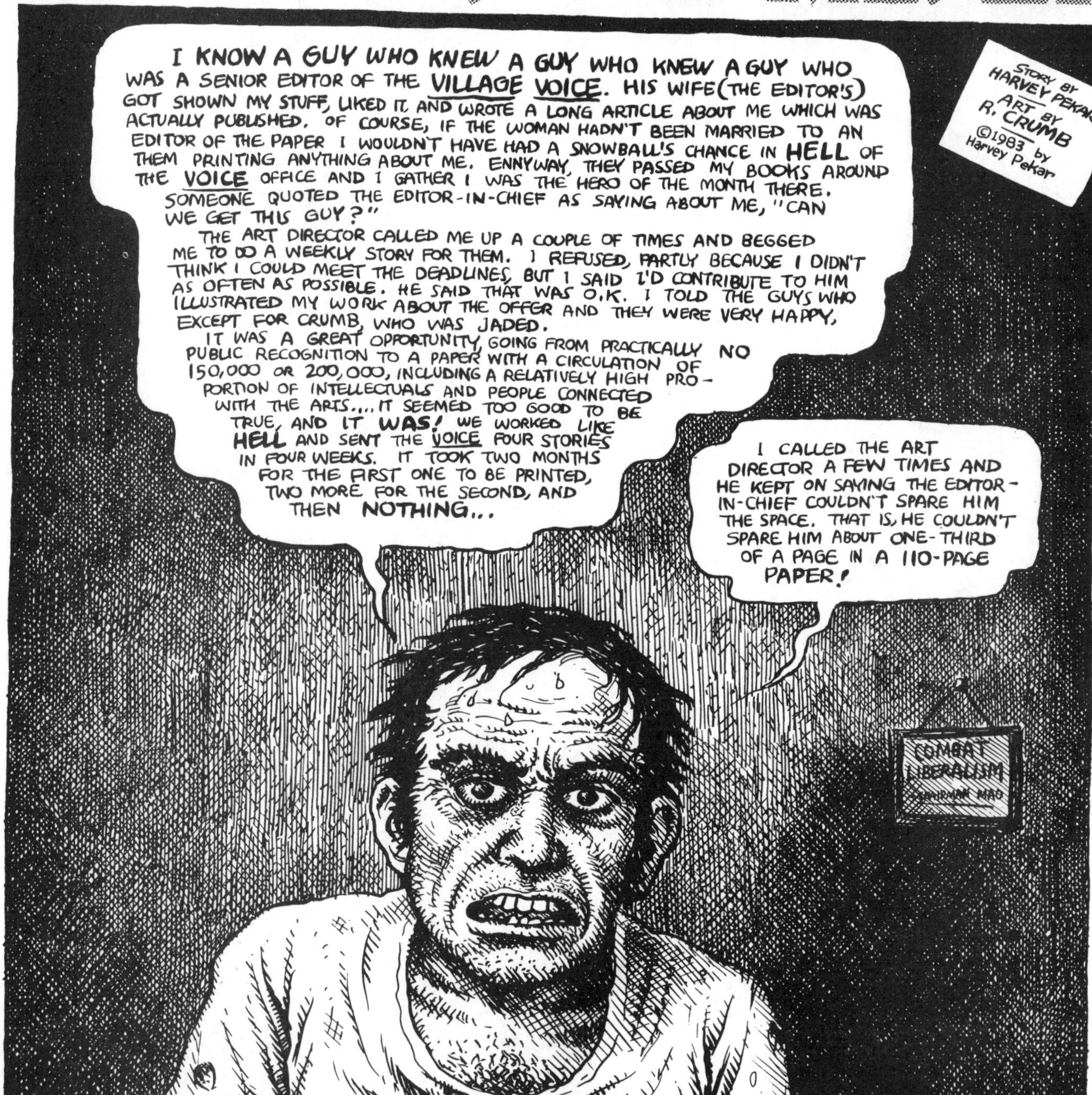
STORY BY HARVEY PEKAR ART BY R. CRUMB ©1983 by Harvey Pekar
I KNOW A GUY WHO KNEW A GUY WHO KNEW A GUY WHO WAS A SENIOR EDITOR OF THE VILLAGE VOICE. HIS WIFE (THE EDITOR'S) GOT SHOWN MY STUFF, LIKED IT, AND WROTE A LONG ARTICLE ABOUT ME WHICH WAS ACTUALLY PUBLISHED. OF COURSE, IF THE WOMAN HADN'T BEEN MARRIED TO AN EDITOR OF THE PAPER I WOULDN'T HAVE HAD A SNOWBALL'S CHANCE IN HELL OF THEM PRINTING ANYTHING ABOUT ME. ENNYWAY, THEY PASSED MY BOOKS AROUND THE VOICE OFFICE AND I GATHER I WAS THE HERO OF THE MONTH THERE. SOMEONE QUOTED THE EDITOR-IN-CHIEF AS SAYING ABOUT ME, "CAN WE GET THIS GUY?" THE ART DIRECTOR CALLED ME UP A COUPLE OF TIMES AND BEGGED ME TO DO A WEEKLY STORY FOR THEM. I REFUSED, PARTLY BECAUSE I DIDN'T THINK I COULD MEET THE DEADLINES, BUT I SAID I'D CONTRIBUTE TO HIM AS OFTEN AS POSSIBLE. HE SAID THAT WAS O.K. I TOLD THE GUYS WHO ILLUSTRATED MY WORK ABOUT THE OFFER AND THEY WERE VERY HAPPY, EXCEPT FOR CRUMB, WHO WAS JADED. IT WAS A GREAT OPPORTUNITY, GOING FROM PRACTICALLY NO PUBLIC RECOGNITION TO A PAPER WITH A CIRCULATION OF 150,000 OR 200,000, INCLUDING A RELATIVELY HIGH PROPORTION OF INTELLECTUALS AND PEOPLE CONNECTED WITH THE ARTS.... IT SEEMED TOO GOOD TO BE TRUE, AND IT WAS! WE WORKED LIKE HELL AND SENT THE VOICE FOUR STORIES IN FOUR WEEKS. IT TOOK TWO MONTHS FOR THE FIRST ONE TO BE PRINTED, TWO MORE FOR THE SECOND, AND THEN NOTHING...
I CALLED THE ART DIRECTOR A FEW TIMES AND HE KEPT ON SAYING THE EDITOR-IN-CHIEF COULDN'T SPARE HIM THE SPACE. THAT IS, HE COULDN'T SPARE HIM ABOUT ONE-THIRD OF A PAGE IN A 110-PAGE PAPER!
COMBAT LIBERALISM

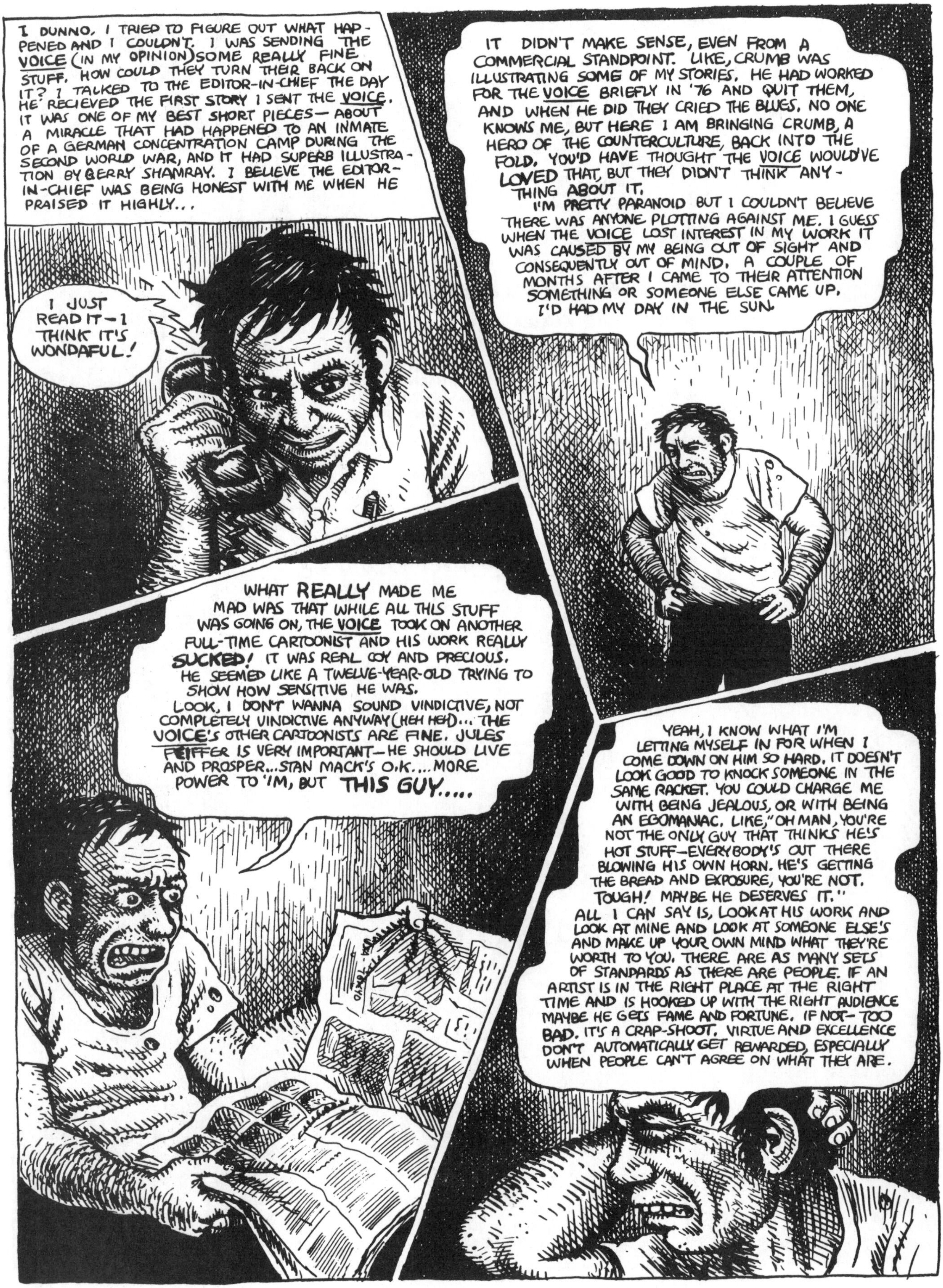
I DUNNO, I TRIED TO FIGURE OUT WHAT HAPPENED AND I COULDN'T. I WAS SENDING THE VOICE (IN MY OPINION) SOME REALLY FINE STUFF. HOW COULD THEY TURN THEIR BACK ON IT? I TALKED TO THE EDITOR-IN-CHIEF THE DAY HE RECIEVED THE FIRST STORY I SENT THE VOICE. IT WAS ONE OF MY BEST SHORT PIECES— ABOUT A MIRACLE THAT HAD HAPPENED TO AN INMATE OF A GERMAN CONCENTRATION CAMP DURING THE SECOND WORLD WAR, AND IT HAD SUPERB ILLUSTRATION BY GERRY SHAMRAY. I BELIEVE THE EDITOR-IN-CHIEF WAS BEING HONEST WITH ME WHEN HE PRAISED IT HIGHLY...
I JUST READ IT— I THINK IT'S WONDAFUL!
IT DIDN'T MAKE SENSE, EVEN FROM A COMMERCIAL STANDPOINT. LIKE, CRUMB WAS ILLUSTRATING SOME OF MY STORIES. HE HAD WORKED FOR THE VOICE BRIEFLY IN '76 AND QUIT THEM, AND WHEN HE DID THEY CRIED THE BLUES. NO ONE KNOWS ME, BUT HERE I AM BRINGING CRUMB, A HERO OF THE COUNTERCULTURE, BACK INTO THE FOLD. YOU'D HAVE THOUGHT THE VOICE WOULD'VE LOVED THAT, BUT THEY DIDN'T THINK ANYTHING ABOUT IT. I'M PRETTY PARANOID BUT I COULDN'T BELIEVE THERE WAS ANYONE PLOTTING AGAINST ME. I GUESS WHEN THE VOICE LOST INTEREST IN MY WORK IT WAS CAUSED BY MY BEING OUT OF SIGHT AND CONSEQUENTLY OUT OF MIND. A COUPLE OF MONTHS AFTER I CAME TO THEIR ATTENTION SOMETHING OR SOMEONE ELSE CAME UP. I'D HAD MY DAY IN THE SUN.
WHAT REALLY MADE ME MAD WAS THAT WHILE ALL THIS STUFF WAS GOING ON, THE VOICE TOOK ON ANOTHER FULL-TIME CARTOONIST AND HIS WORK REALLY SUCKED! IT WAS REAL COY AND PRECIOUS. HE SEEMED LIKE A TWELVE-YEAR-OLD TRYING TO SHOW HOW SENSITIVE HE WAS. LOOK, I DON'T WANNA SOUND VINDICTIVE, NOT COMPLETELY VINDICTIVE ANYWAY (HEH HEH)... THE VOICE'S OTHER CARTOONISTS ARE FINE. JULES FEIFFER IS VERY IMPORTANT— HE SHOULD LIVE AND PROSPER... STAN MACK'S O.K. ... MORE POWER TO 'IM, BUT THIS GUY.....
YEAH, I KNOW WHAT I'M LETTING MYSELF IN FOR WHEN I COME DOWN ON HIM SO HARD. IT DOESN'T LOOK GOOD TO KNOCK SOMEONE IN THE SAME RACKET. YOU COULD CHARGE ME WITH BEING JEALOUS, OR WITH BEING AN EGOMANIAC. LIKE, "OH MAN, YOU'RE NOT THE ONLY GUY THAT THINKS HE'S HOT STUFF— EVERYBODY'S OUT THERE BLOWING HIS OWN HORN. HE'S GETTING THE BREAD AND EXPOSURE, YOU'RE NOT. TOUGH! MAYBE HE DESERVES IT." ALL I CAN SAY IS, LOOK AT HIS WORK AND LOOK AT MINE AND LOOK AT SOMEONE ELSE'S AND MAKE UP YOUR OWN MIND WHAT THEY'RE WORTH TO YOU. THERE ARE AS MANY SETS OF STANDARDS AS THERE ARE PEOPLE. IF AN ARTIST IS IN THE RIGHT PLACE AT THE RIGHT TIME AND IS HOOKED UP WITH THE RIGHT AUDIENCE MAYBE HE GETS FAME AND FORTUNE. IF NOT— TOO BAD. IT'S A CRAP-SHOOT. VIRTUE AND EXCELLENCE DON'T AUTOMATICALLY GET REWARDED, ESPECIALLY WHEN PEOPLE CAN'T AGREE ON WHAT THEY ARE.

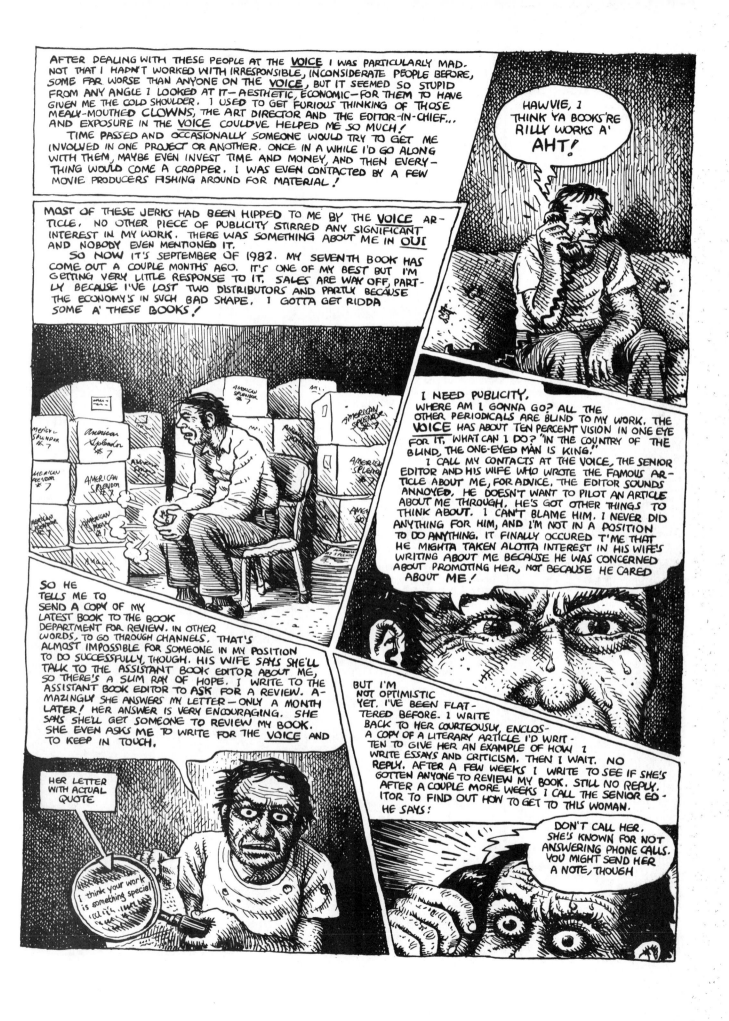

AFTER DEALING WITH THESE PEOPLE AT THE VOICE I WAS PARTICULARLY MAD. NOT THAT I HADN'T WORKED WITH IRRESPONSIBLE, INCONSIDERATE PEOPLE BEFORE, SOME FAR WORSE THAN ANYONE ON THE VOICE, BUT IT SEEMED SO STUPID FROM ANY ANGLE I LOOKED AT IT— AESTHETIC, ECONOMIC—FOR THEM TO HAVE GIVEN ME THE COLD SHOULDER. I USED TO GET FURIOUS THINKING OF THOSE MEALY-MOUTHED CLOWNS, THE ART DIRECTOR AND THE EDITOR-IN-CHIEF... AND EXPOSURE IN THE VOICE COULD'VE HELPED ME SO MUCH!

TIME PASSED AND OCCASIONALLY SOMEONE WOULD TRY TO GET ME INVOLVED IN ONE PROJECT OR ANOTHER. ONCE IN A WHILE I'D GO ALONG WITH THEM, MAYBE EVEN INVEST TIME AND MONEY, AND THEN EVERY-THING WOULD COME A CROPPER. I WAS EVEN CONTACTED BY A FEW MOVIE PRODUCERS FISHING AROUND FOR MATERIAL!

MOST OF THESE JERKS HAD BEEN HIPPED TO ME BY THE VOICE AR-TICLE. NO OTHER PIECE OF PUBLICITY STIRRED ANY SIGNIFICANT INTEREST IN MY WORK. THERE WAS SOMETHING ABOUT ME IN OUI AND NOBODY EVEN MENTIONED IT.

SO NOW IT'S SEPTEMBER OF 1982. MY SEVENTH BOOK HAS COME OUT A COUPLE MONTHS AGO. IT'S ONE OF MY BEST BUT I'M GETTING VERY LITTLE RESPONSE TO IT. SALES ARE WAY OFF, PART-LY BECAUSE I'VE LOST TWO DISTRIBUTORS AND PARTLY BECAUSE THE ECONOMY'S IN SUCH BAD SHAPE. I GOTTA GET RIDDA SOME A' THESE BOOKS!

HAWVIE, I THINK YA BOOKS'RE RILLY WORKS A' AHT!

I NEED PUBLICITY. WHERE AM I GONNA GO? ALL THE OTHER PERIODICALS ARE BLIND TO MY WORK. THE VOICE HAS ABOUT TEN PERCENT VISION IN ONE EYE FOR IT, WHAT CAN I DO? "IN THE COUNTRY OF THE BLIND, THE ONE-EYED MAN IS KING."

I CALL MY CONTACTS AT THE VOICE, THE SENIOR EDITOR AND HIS WIFE WHO WROTE THE FAMOUS AR-TICLE ABOUT ME, FOR ADVICE. THE EDITOR SOUNDS ANNOYED. HE DOESN'T WANT TO PILOT AN ARTICLE ABOUT ME THROUGH. HE'S GOT OTHER THINGS TO THINK ABOUT. I CAN'T BLAME HIM. I NEVER DID ANYTHING FOR HIM, AND I'M NOT IN A POSITION TO DO ANYTHING. IT FINALLY OCCURED T'ME THAT HE MIGHTA TAKEN ALOTTA INTEREST IN HIS WIFE'S WRITING ABOUT ME BECAUSE HE WAS CONCERNED ABOUT PROMOTING HER, NOT BECAUSE HE CARED ABOUT ME!

SO HE TELLS ME TO SEND A COPY OF MY LATEST BOOK TO THE BOOK DEPARTMENT FOR REVIEW. IN OTHER WORDS, TO GO THROUGH CHANNELS. THAT'S ALMOST IMPOSSIBLE FOR SOMEONE IN MY POSITION TO DO SUCCESSFULLY, THOUGH. HIS WIFE SAYS SHE'LL TALK TO THE ASSISTANT BOOK EDITOR ABOUT ME, SO THERE'S A SLIM RAY OF HOPE. I WRITE TO THE ASSISTANT BOOK EDITOR TO ASK FOR A REVIEW. A-MAZINGLY SHE ANSWERS MY LETTER — ONLY A MONTH LATER! HER ANSWER IS VERY ENCOURAGING. SHE SAYS SHE'LL GET SOMEONE TO REVIEW MY BOOK. SHE EVEN ASKS ME TO WRITE FOR THE VOICE AND TO KEEP IN TOUCH.

HER LETTER WITH ACTUAL QUOTE

I think your work is something special

BUT I'M NOT OPTIMISTIC YET. I'VE BEEN FLAT-TERED BEFORE. I WRITE BACK TO HER COURTEOUSLY, ENCLOS-A COPY OF A LITERARY ARTICLE I'D WRIT-TEN TO GIVE HER AN EXAMPLE OF HOW I WRITE ESSAYS AND CRITICISM. THEN I WAIT. NO REPLY. AFTER A FEW WEEKS I WRITE TO SEE IF SHE'S GOTTEN ANYONE TO REVIEW MY BOOK. STILL NO REPLY. AFTER A COUPLE MORE WEEKS I CALL THE SENIOR ED-ITOR TO FIND OUT HOW TO GET TO THIS WOMAN. HE SAYS:

DON'T CALL HER. SHE'S KNOWN FOR NOT ANSWERING PHONE CALLS. YOU MIGHT SEND HER A NOTE, THOUGH

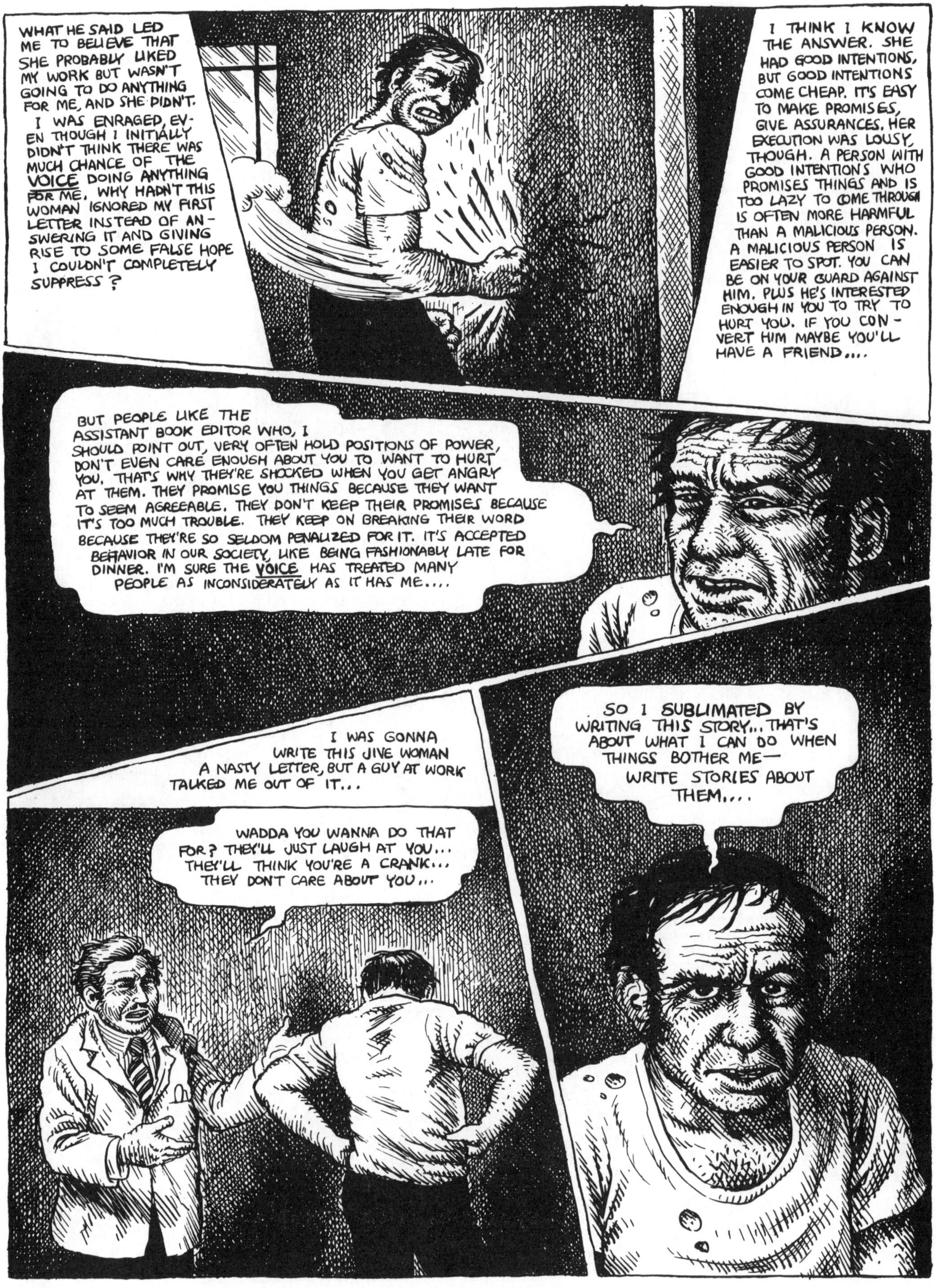
WHAT HE SAID LED ME TO BELIEVE THAT SHE PROBABLY LIKED MY WORK BUT WASN'T GOING TO DO ANYTHING FOR ME, AND SHE DIDN'T. I WAS ENRAGED, EVEN THOUGH I INITIALLY DIDN'T THINK THERE WAS MUCH CHANCE OF THE VOICE DOING ANYTHING FOR ME. WHY HADN'T THIS WOMAN IGNORED MY FIRST LETTER INSTEAD OF ANSWERING IT AND GIVING RISE TO SOME FALSE HOPE I COULDN'T COMPLETELY SUPPRESS?
I THINK I KNOW THE ANSWER. SHE HAD GOOD INTENTIONS, BUT GOOD INTENTIONS COME CHEAP. IT'S EASY TO MAKE PROMISES, GIVE ASSURANCES. HER EXECUTION WAS LOUSY, THOUGH. A PERSON WITH GOOD INTENTIONS WHO PROMISES THINGS AND IS TOO LAZY TO COME THROUGH IS OFTEN MORE HARMFUL THAN A MALICIOUS PERSON. A MALICIOUS PERSON IS EASIER TO SPOT. YOU CAN BE ON YOUR GUARD AGAINST HIM. PLUS HE'S INTERESTED ENOUGH IN YOU TO TRY TO HURT YOU. IF YOU CONVERT HIM MAYBE YOU'LL HAVE A FRIEND....
BUT PEOPLE LIKE THE ASSISTANT BOOK EDITOR WHO, I SHOULD POINT OUT, VERY OFTEN HOLD POSITIONS OF POWER, DON'T EVEN CARE ENOUGH ABOUT YOU TO WANT TO HURT YOU. THAT'S WHY THEY'RE SHOCKED WHEN YOU GET ANGRY AT THEM. THEY PROMISE YOU THINGS BECAUSE THEY WANT TO SEEM AGREEABLE. THEY DON'T KEEP THEIR PROMISES BECAUSE IT'S TOO MUCH TROUBLE. THEY KEEP ON BREAKING THEIR WORD BECAUSE THEY'RE SO SELDOM PENALIZED FOR IT. IT'S ACCEPTED BEHAVIOR IN OUR SOCIETY, LIKE BEING FASHIONABLY LATE FOR DINNER. I'M SURE THE VOICE HAS TREATED MANY PEOPLE AS INCONSIDERATELY AS IT HAS ME....
I WAS GONNA WRITE THIS JIVE WOMAN A NASTY LETTER, BUT A GUY AT WORK TALKED ME OUT OF IT...
WADDA YOU WANNA DO THAT FOR? THEY'LL JUST LAUGH AT YOU... THEY'LL THINK YOU'RE A CRANK... THEY DON'T CARE ABOUT YOU...
SO I SUBLIMATED BY WRITING THIS STORY... THAT'S ABOUT WHAT I CAN DO WHEN THINGS BOTHER ME— WRITE STORIES ABOUT THEM....

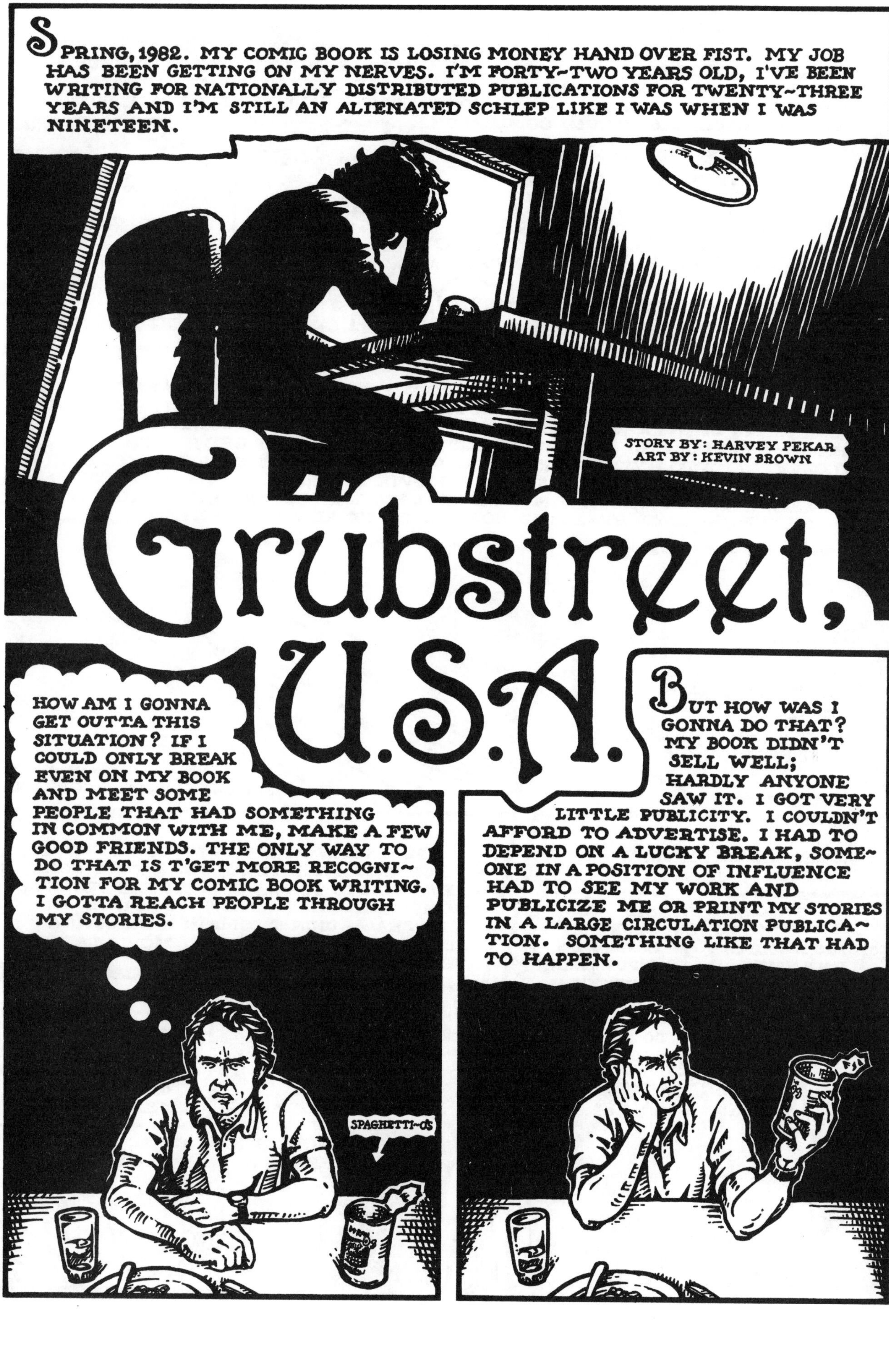
SPRING, 1982. MY COMIC BOOK IS LOSING MONEY HAND OVER FIST. MY JOB HAS BEEN GETTING ON MY NERVES. I'M FORTY-TWO YEARS OLD, I'VE BEEN WRITING FOR NATIONALLY DISTRIBUTED PUBLICATIONS FOR TWENTY-THREE YEARS AND I'M STILL AN ALIENATED SCHLEP LIKE I WAS WHEN I WAS NINETEEN.
STORY BY: HARVEY PEKAR
ART BY: KEVIN BROWN
Grubstreet, U.S.A.
HOW AM I GONNA GET OUTTA THIS SITUATION? IF I COULD ONLY BREAK EVEN ON MY BOOK AND MEET SOME PEOPLE THAT HAD SOMETHING IN COMMON WITH ME, MAKE A FEW GOOD FRIENDS. THE ONLY WAY TO DO THAT IS T'GET MORE RECOGNITION FOR MY COMIC BOOK WRITING. I GOTTA REACH PEOPLE THROUGH MY STORIES.
SPAGHETTI-OS
BUT HOW WAS I GONNA DO THAT? MY BOOK DIDN'T SELL WELL; HARDLY ANYONE SAW IT. I GOT VERY LITTLE PUBLICITY. I COULDN'T AFFORD TO ADVERTISE. I HAD TO DEPEND ON A LUCKY BREAK, SOMEONE IN A POSITION OF INFLUENCE HAD TO SEE MY WORK AND PUBLICIZE ME OR PRINT MY STORIES IN A LARGE CIRCULATION PUBLICATION. SOMETHING LIKE THAT HAD TO HAPPEN.

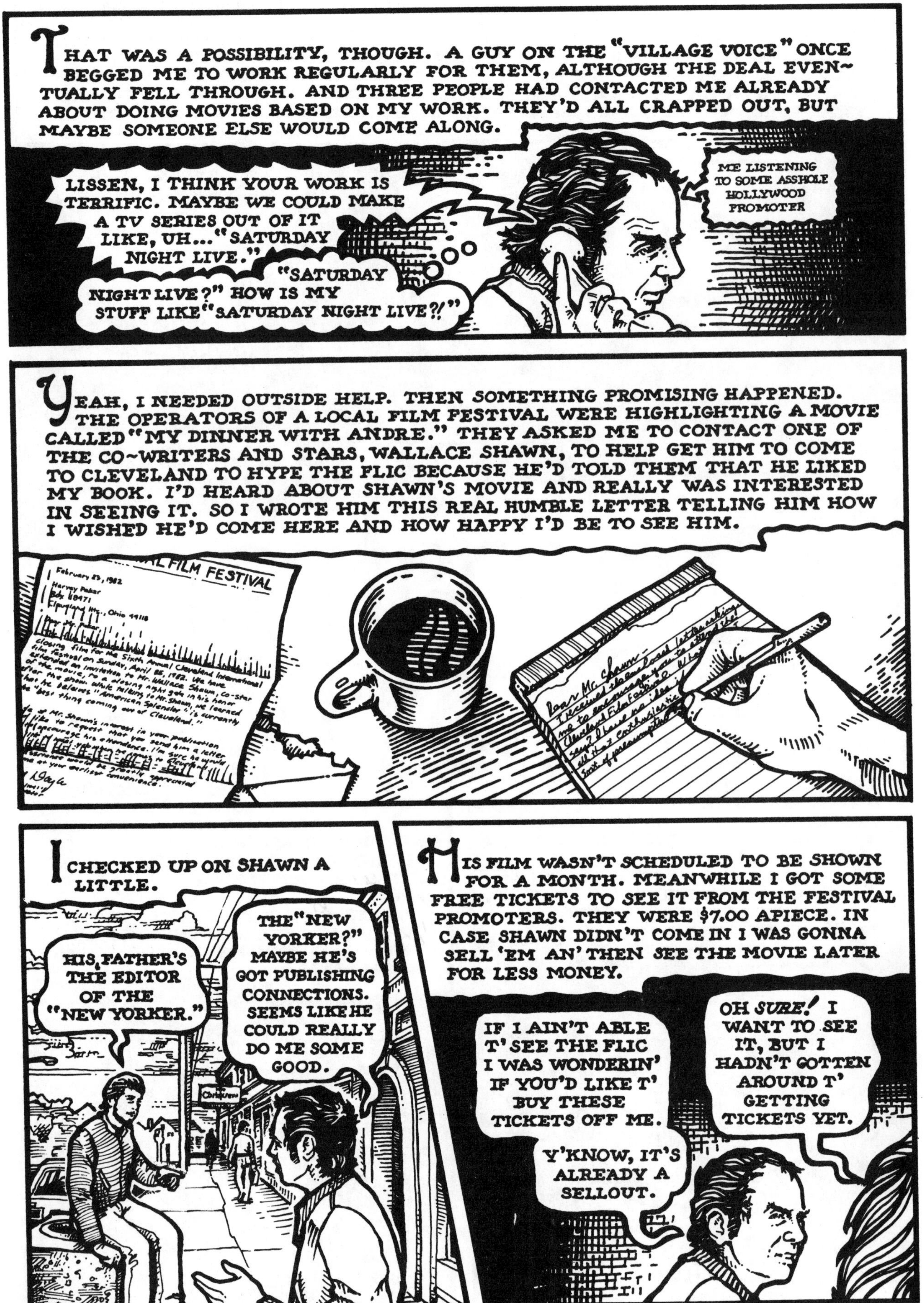
THAT WAS A POSSIBILITY, THOUGH. A GUY ON THE "VILLAGE VOICE" ONCE BEGGED ME TO WORK REGULARLY FOR THEM, ALTHOUGH THE DEAL EVENTUALLY FELL THROUGH. AND THREE PEOPLE HAD CONTACTED ME ALREADY ABOUT DOING MOVIES BASED ON MY WORK. THEY'D ALL CRAPPED OUT, BUT MAYBE SOMEONE ELSE WOULD COME ALONG.
ME LISTENING TO SOME ASSHOLE HOLLYWOOD PROMOTER
LISSEN, I THINK YOUR WORK IS TERRIFIC. MAYBE WE COULD MAKE A TV SERIES OUT OF IT LIKE, UH..."SATURDAY NIGHT LIVE."
"SATURDAY NIGHT LIVE?" HOW IS MY STUFF LIKE "SATURDAY NIGHT LIVE?!"
YEAH, I NEEDED OUTSIDE HELP. THEN SOMETHING PROMISING HAPPENED. THE OPERATORS OF A LOCAL FILM FESTIVAL WERE HIGHLIGHTING A MOVIE CALLED "MY DINNER WITH ANDRE." THEY ASKED ME TO CONTACT ONE OF THE CO~WRITERS AND STARS, WALLACE SHAWN, TO HELP GET HIM TO COME TO CLEVELAND TO HYPE THE FLIC BECAUSE HE'D TOLD THEM THAT HE LIKED MY BOOK. I'D HEARD ABOUT SHAWN'S MOVIE AND REALLY WAS INTERESTED IN SEEING IT. SO I WROTE HIM THIS REAL HUMBLE LETTER TELLING HIM HOW I WISHED HE'D COME HERE AND HOW HAPPY I'D BE TO SEE HIM.
FILM FESTIVAL
I CHECKED UP ON SHAWN A LITTLE.
HIS FATHER'S THE EDITOR OF THE "NEW YORKER."
THE "NEW YORKER?" MAYBE HE'S GOT PUBLISHING CONNECTIONS. SEEMS LIKE HE COULD REALLY DO ME SOME GOOD.
HIS FILM WASN'T SCHEDULED TO BE SHOWN FOR A MONTH. MEANWHILE I GOT SOME FREE TICKETS TO SEE IT FROM THE FESTIVAL PROMOTERS. THEY WERE $7.00 APIECE. IN CASE SHAWN DIDN'T COME IN I WAS GONNA SELL 'EM AN' THEN SEE THE MOVIE LATER FOR LESS MONEY.
IF I AIN'T ABLE T' SEE THE FLIC I WAS WONDERIN' IF YOU'D LIKE T' BUY THESE TICKETS OFF ME.
Y'KNOW, IT'S ALREADY A SELLOUT.
OH SURE! I WANT TO SEE IT, BUT I HADN'T GOTTEN AROUND T' GETTING TICKETS YET.

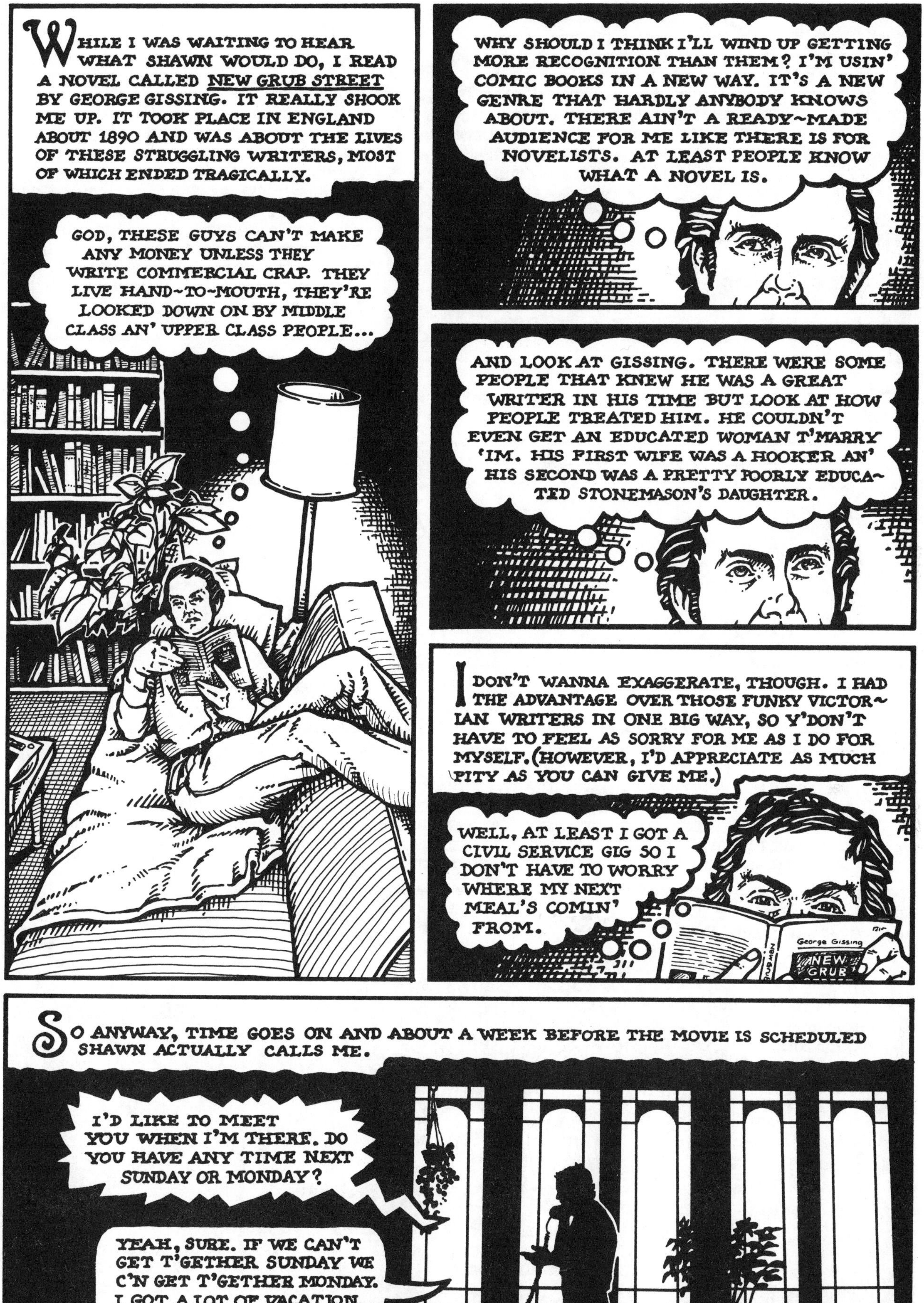
WHILE I WAS WAITING TO HEAR WHAT SHAWN WOULD DO, I READ A NOVEL CALLED NEW GRUB STREET BY GEORGE GISSING. IT REALLY SHOOK ME UP. IT TOOK PLACE IN ENGLAND ABOUT 1890 AND WAS ABOUT THE LIVES OF THESE STRUGGLING WRITERS, MOST OF WHICH ENDED TRAGICALLY.
GOD, THESE GUYS CAN'T MAKE ANY MONEY UNLESS THEY WRITE COMMERCIAL CRAP. THEY LIVE HAND-TO-MOUTH, THEY'RE LOOKED DOWN ON BY MIDDLE CLASS AN' UPPER CLASS PEOPLE...
WHY SHOULD I THINK I'LL WIND UP GETTING MORE RECOGNITION THAN THEM? I'M USIN' COMIC BOOKS IN A NEW WAY. IT'S A NEW GENRE THAT HARDLY ANYBODY KNOWS ABOUT. THERE AIN'T A READY-MADE AUDIENCE FOR ME LIKE THERE IS FOR NOVELISTS. AT LEAST PEOPLE KNOW WHAT A NOVEL IS.
AND LOOK AT GISSING. THERE WERE SOME PEOPLE THAT KNEW HE WAS A GREAT WRITER IN HIS TIME BUT LOOK AT HOW PEOPLE TREATED HIM. HE COULDN'T EVEN GET AN EDUCATED WOMAN T'MARRY 'IM. HIS FIRST WIFE WAS A HOOKER AN' HIS SECOND WAS A PRETTY POORLY EDUCATED STONEMASON'S DAUGHTER.
I DON'T WANNA EXAGGERATE, THOUGH. I HAD THE ADVANTAGE OVER THOSE FUNKY VICTORIAN WRITERS IN ONE BIG WAY, SO Y'DON'T HAVE TO FEEL AS SORRY FOR ME AS I DO FOR MYSELF. (HOWEVER, I'D APPRECIATE AS MUCH PITY AS YOU CAN GIVE ME.)
WELL, AT LEAST I GOT A CIVIL SERVICE GIG SO I DON'T HAVE TO WORRY WHERE MY NEXT MEAL'S COMIN' FROM.
George Gissing
NEW GRUB
SO ANYWAY, TIME GOES ON AND ABOUT A WEEK BEFORE THE MOVIE IS SCHEDULED SHAWN ACTUALLY CALLS ME.
I'D LIKE TO MEET YOU WHEN I'M THERE. DO YOU HAVE ANY TIME NEXT SUNDAY OR MONDAY?
YEAH, SURE. IF WE CAN'T GET T'GETHER SUNDAY WE C'N GET T'GETHER MONDAY. I GOT A LOT OF VACATION TIME I C'N USE.

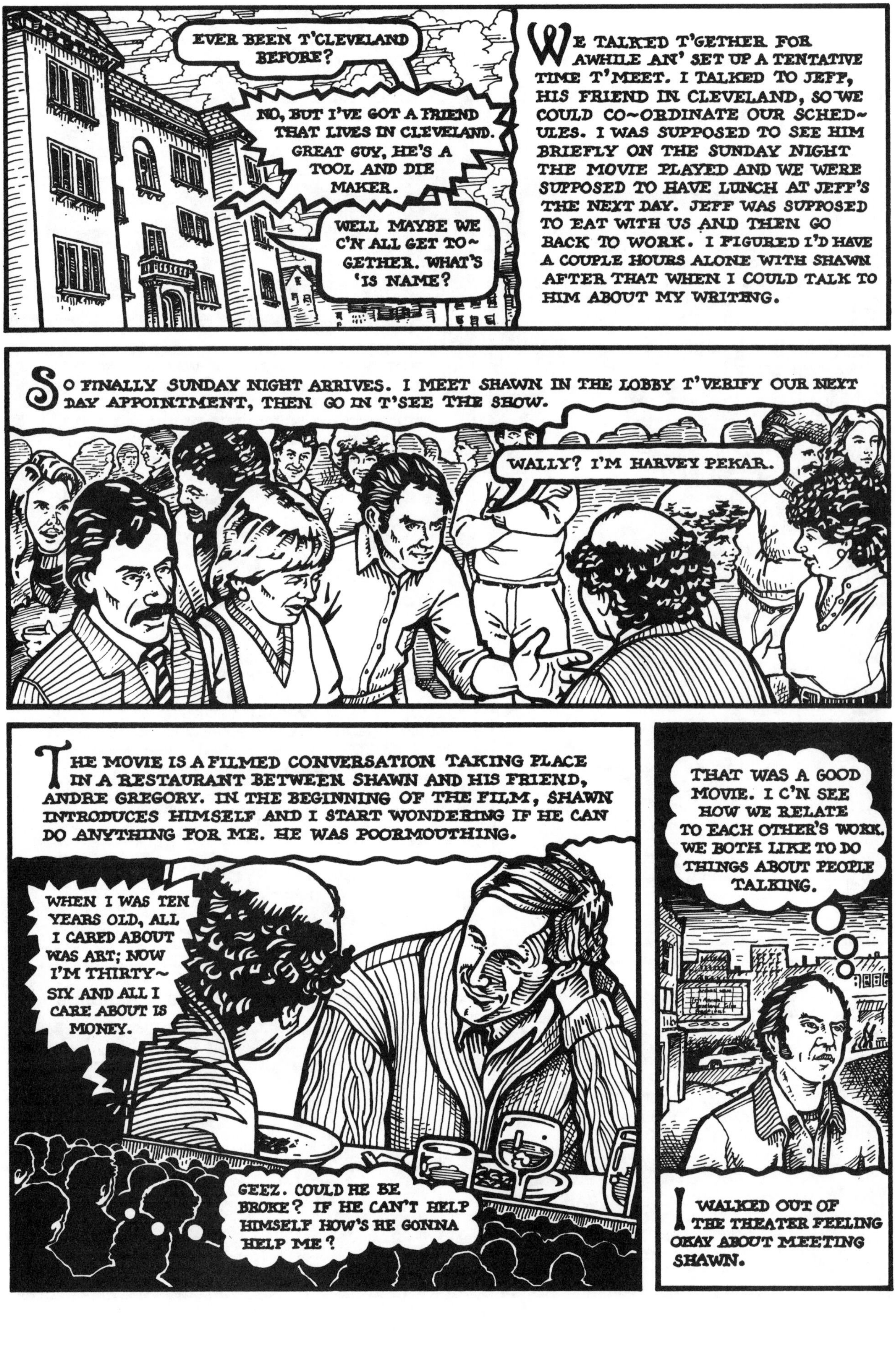
EVER BEEN T'CLEVELAND BEFORE?
NO, BUT I'VE GOT A FRIEND THAT LIVES IN CLEVELAND. GREAT GUY, HE'S A TOOL AND DIE MAKER.
WELL MAYBE WE C'N ALL GET TO~GETHER. WHAT'S 'IS NAME?
WE TALKED T'GETHER FOR AWHILE AN' SET UP A TENTATIVE TIME T'MEET. I TALKED TO JEFF, HIS FRIEND IN CLEVELAND, SO WE COULD CO~ORDINATE OUR SCHED~ULES. I WAS SUPPOSED TO SEE HIM BRIEFLY ON THE SUNDAY NIGHT THE MOVIE PLAYED AND WE WERE SUPPOSED TO HAVE LUNCH AT JEFF'S THE NEXT DAY. JEFF WAS SUPPOSED TO EAT WITH US AND THEN GO BACK TO WORK. I FIGURED I'D HAVE A COUPLE HOURS ALONE WITH SHAWN AFTER THAT WHEN I COULD TALK TO HIM ABOUT MY WRITING.
SO FINALLY SUNDAY NIGHT ARRIVES. I MEET SHAWN IN THE LOBBY T'VERIFY OUR NEXT DAY APPOINTMENT, THEN GO IN T'SEE THE SHOW.
WALLY? I'M HARVEY PEKAR.
THE MOVIE IS A FILMED CONVERSATION TAKING PLACE IN A RESTAURANT BETWEEN SHAWN AND HIS FRIEND, ANDRE GREGORY. IN THE BEGINNING OF THE FILM, SHAWN INTRODUCES HIMSELF AND I START WONDERING IF HE CAN DO ANYTHING FOR ME. HE WAS POORMOUTHING.
WHEN I WAS TEN YEARS OLD, ALL I CARED ABOUT WAS ART; NOW I'M THIRTY~SIX AND ALL I CARE ABOUT IS MONEY.
GEEZ. COULD HE BE BROKE? IF HE CAN'T HELP HIMSELF HOW'S HE GONNA HELP ME?
THAT WAS A GOOD MOVIE. I C'N SEE HOW WE RELATE TO EACH OTHER'S WORK. WE BOTH LIKE TO DO THINGS ABOUT PEOPLE TALKING.
I WALKED OUT OF THE THEATER FEELING OKAY ABOUT MEETING SHAWN.

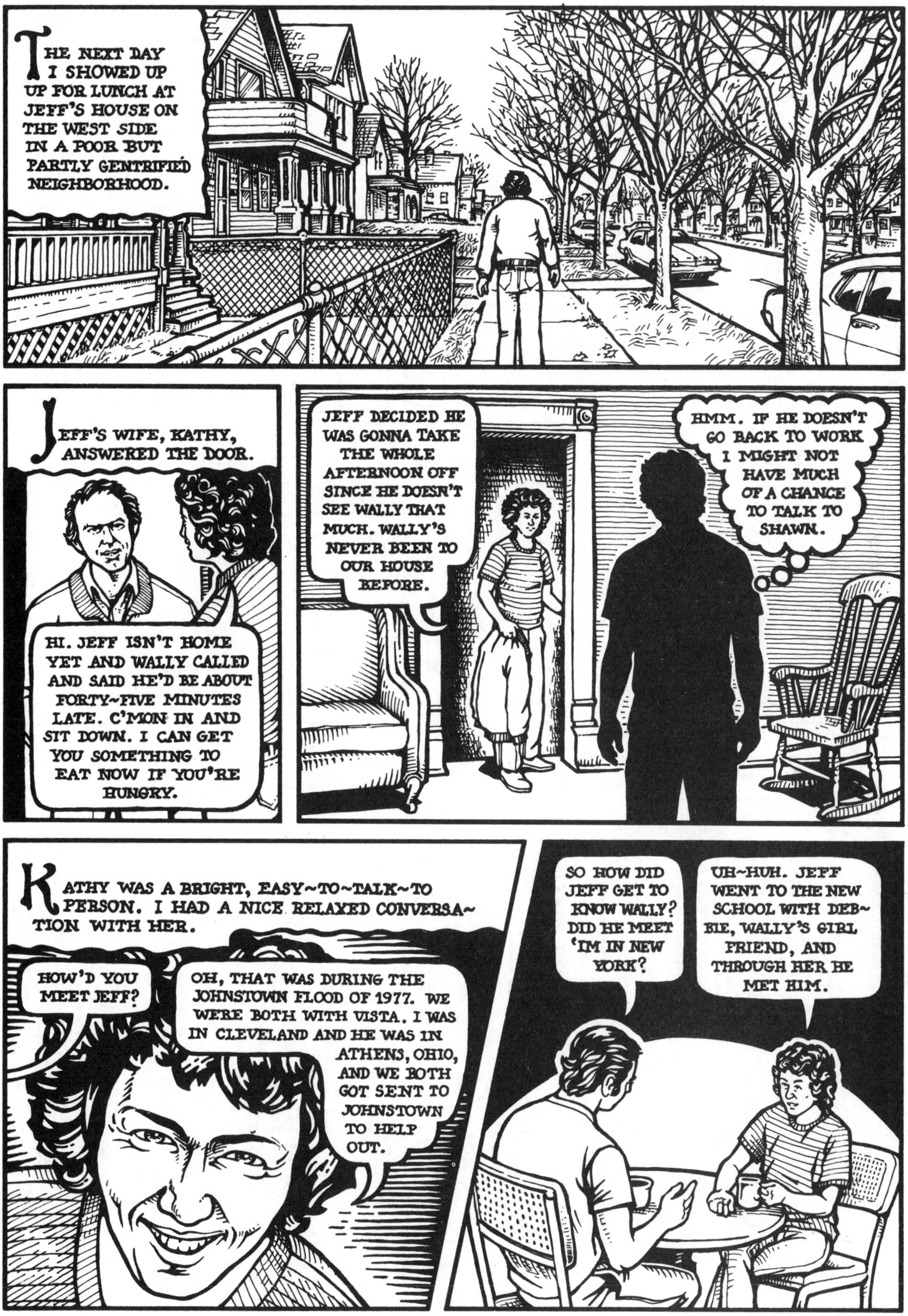
THE NEXT DAY I SHOWED UP UP FOR LUNCH AT JEFF'S HOUSE ON THE WEST SIDE IN A POOR BUT PARTLY GENTRIFIED NEIGHBORHOOD.
JEFF'S WIFE, KATHY, ANSWERED THE DOOR.
HI. JEFF ISN'T HOME YET AND WALLY CALLED AND SAID HE'D BE ABOUT FORTY~FIVE MINUTES LATE. C'MON IN AND SIT DOWN. I CAN GET YOU SOMETHING TO EAT NOW IF YOU'RE HUNGRY.
JEFF DECIDED HE WAS GONNA TAKE THE WHOLE AFTERNOON OFF SINCE HE DOESN'T SEE WALLY THAT MUCH. WALLY'S NEVER BEEN TO OUR HOUSE BEFORE.
HMM. IF HE DOESN'T GO BACK TO WORK I MIGHT NOT HAVE MUCH OF A CHANCE TO TALK TO SHAWN.
KATHY WAS A BRIGHT, EASY~TO~TALK~TO PERSON. I HAD A NICE RELAXED CONVERSA~TION WITH HER.
HOW'D YOU MEET JEFF?
OH, THAT WAS DURING THE JOHNSTOWN FLOOD OF 1977. WE WERE BOTH WITH VISTA. I WAS IN CLEVELAND AND HE WAS IN ATHENS, OHIO, AND WE BOTH GOT SENT TO JOHNSTOWN TO HELP OUT.
SO HOW DID JEFF GET TO KNOW WALLY? DID HE MEET 'IM IN NEW YORK?
UH~HUH. JEFF WENT TO THE NEW SCHOOL WITH DEB~BIE, WALLY'S GIRL FRIEND, AND THROUGH HER HE MET HIM.

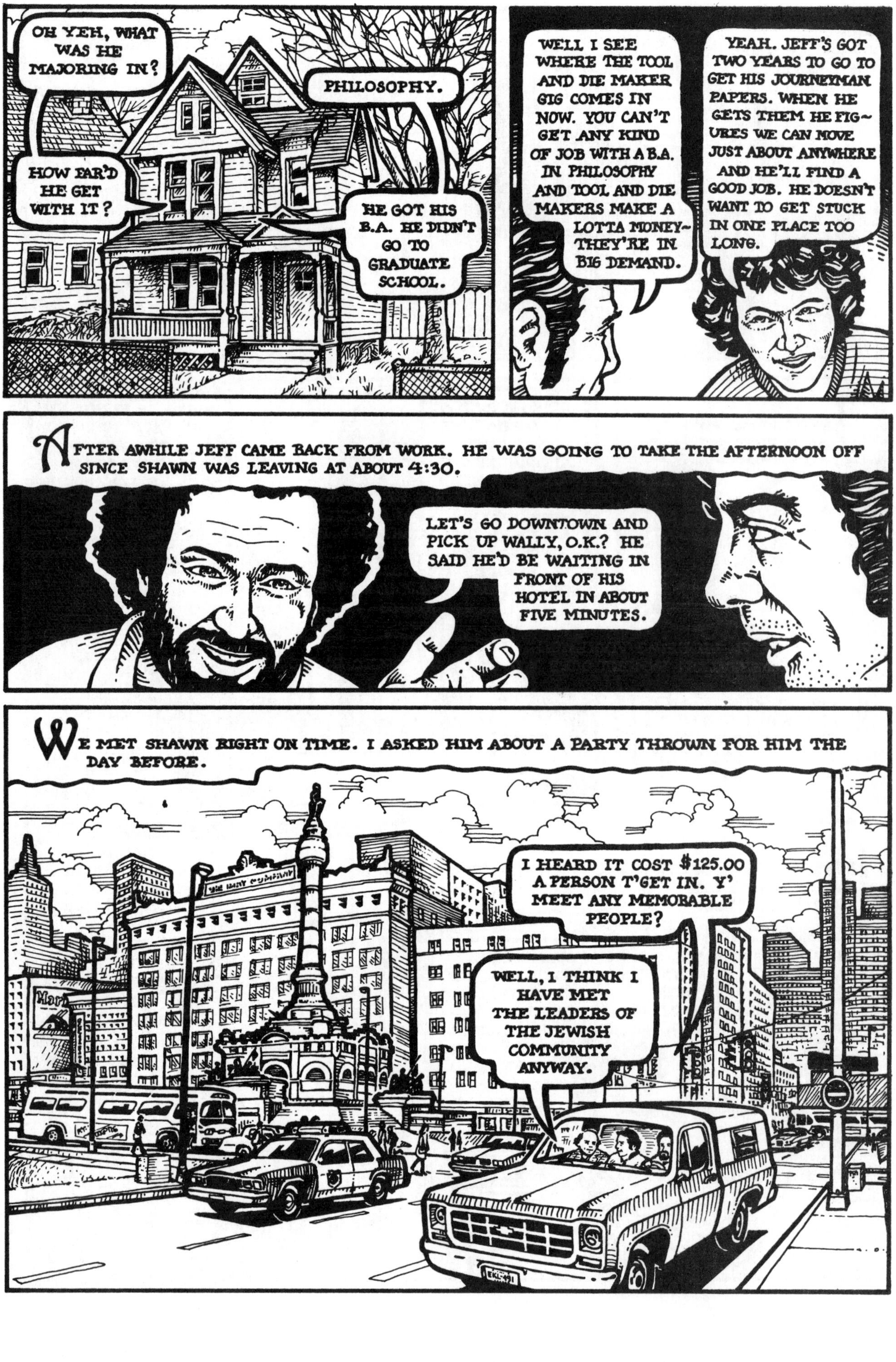
OH YEH, WHAT WAS HE MAJORING IN?
PHILOSOPHY.
HOW FAR'D HE GET WITH IT?
HE GOT HIS B.A. HE DIDN'T GO TO GRADUATE SCHOOL.
WELL I SEE WHERE THE TOOL AND DIE MAKER GIG COMES IN NOW. YOU CAN'T GET ANY KIND OF JOB WITH A B.A. IN PHILOSOPHY AND TOOL AND DIE MAKERS MAKE A LOTTA MONEY- THEY'RE IN BIG DEMAND.
YEAH. JEFF'S GOT TWO YEARS TO GO TO GET HIS JOURNEYMAN PAPERS. WHEN HE GETS THEM HE FIG- URES WE CAN MOVE JUST ABOUT ANYWHERE AND HE'LL FIND A GOOD JOB. HE DOESN'T WANT TO GET STUCK IN ONE PLACE TOO LONG.
AFTER AWHILE JEFF CAME BACK FROM WORK. HE WAS GOING TO TAKE THE AFTERNOON OFF SINCE SHAWN WAS LEAVING AT ABOUT 4:30.
LET'S GO DOWNTOWN AND PICK UP WALLY, O.K.? HE SAID HE'D BE WAITING IN FRONT OF HIS HOTEL IN ABOUT FIVE MINUTES.
WE MET SHAWN RIGHT ON TIME. I ASKED HIM ABOUT A PARTY THROWN FOR HIM THE DAY BEFORE.
I HEARD IT COST $125.00 A PERSON T'GET IN. Y' MEET ANY MEMORABLE PEOPLE?
WELL, I THINK I HAVE MET THE LEADERS OF THE JEWISH COMMUNITY ANYWAY.

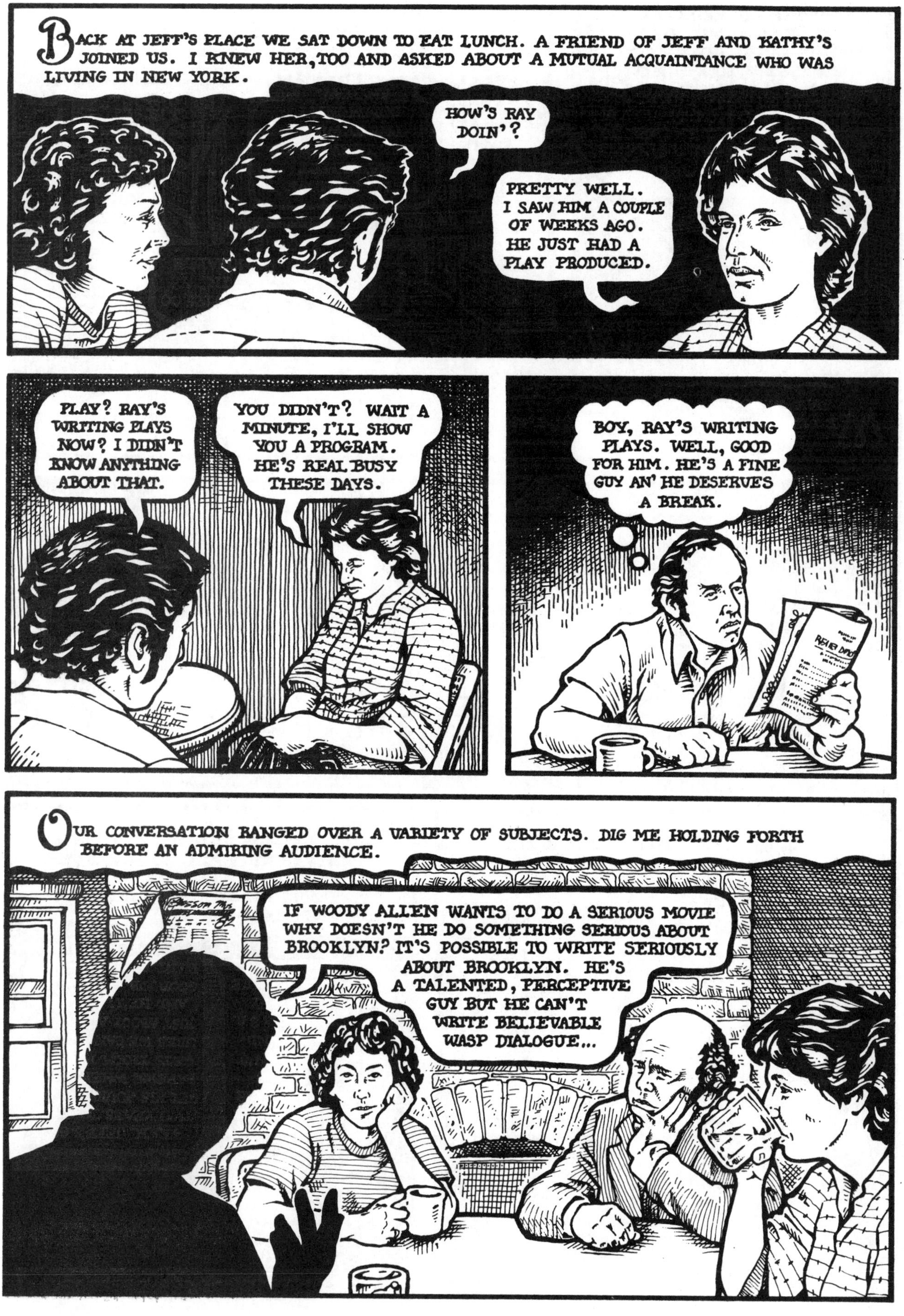
BACK AT JEFF'S PLACE WE SAT DOWN TO EAT LUNCH. A FRIEND OF JEFF AND KATHY'S JOINED US. I KNEW HER, TOO AND ASKED ABOUT A MUTUAL ACQUAINTANCE WHO WAS LIVING IN NEW YORK.
HOW'S RAY DOIN'?
PRETTY WELL. I SAW HIM A COUPLE OF WEEKS AGO. HE JUST HAD A PLAY PRODUCED.
PLAY? RAY'S WRITING PLAYS NOW? I DIDN'T KNOW ANYTHING ABOUT THAT.
YOU DIDN'T? WAIT A MINUTE, I'LL SHOW YOU A PROGRAM. HE'S REAL BUSY THESE DAYS.
BOY, RAY'S WRITING PLAYS. WELL, GOOD FOR HIM. HE'S A FINE GUY AN' HE DESERVES A BREAK.
OUR CONVERSATION RANGED OVER A VARIETY OF SUBJECTS. DIG ME HOLDING FORTH BEFORE AN ADMIRING AUDIENCE.
IF WOODY ALLEN WANTS TO DO A SERIOUS MOVIE WHY DOESN'T HE DO SOMETHING SERIOUS ABOUT BROOKLYN? IT'S POSSIBLE TO WRITE SERIOUSLY ABOUT BROOKLYN. HE'S A TALENTED, PERCEPTIVE GUY BUT HE CAN'T WRITE BELIEVABLE WASP DIALOGUE...

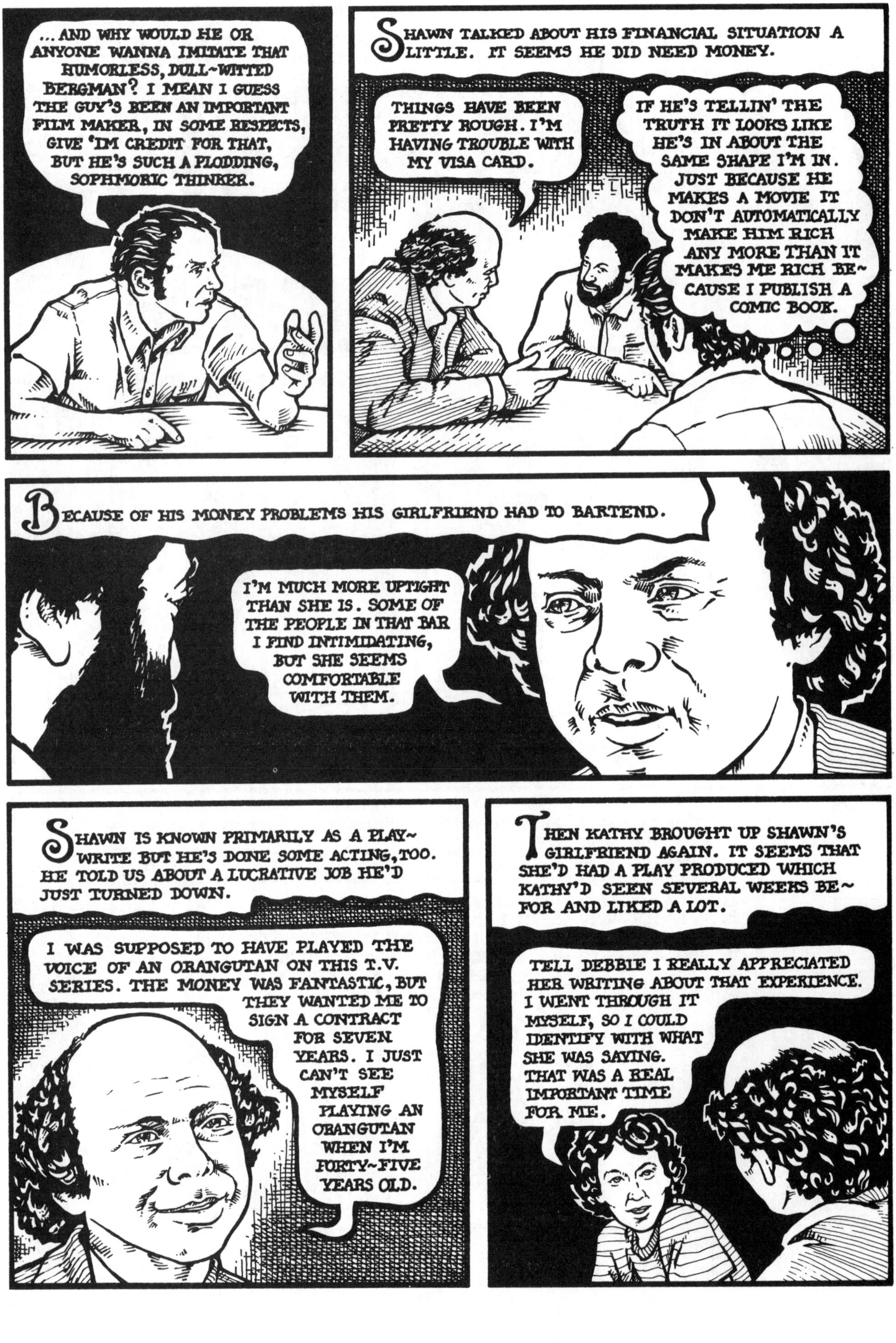
...AND WHY WOULD HE OR ANYONE WANNA IMITATE THAT HUMORLESS, DULL~WITTED BERGMAN? I MEAN I GUESS THE GUY'S BEEN AN IMPORTANT FILM MAKER, IN SOME RESPECTS, GIVE 'IM CREDIT FOR THAT, BUT HE'S SUCH A PLODDING, SOPHMORIC THINKER.
SHAWN TALKED ABOUT HIS FINANCIAL SITUATION A LITTLE. IT SEEMS HE DID NEED MONEY.
THINGS HAVE BEEN PRETTY ROUGH. I'M HAVING TROUBLE WITH MY VISA CARD.
IF HE'S TELLIN' THE TRUTH IT LOOKS LIKE HE'S IN ABOUT THE SAME SHAPE I'M IN. JUST BECAUSE HE MAKES A MOVIE IT DON'T AUTOMATICALLY MAKE HIM RICH ANY MORE THAN IT MAKES ME RICH BE~CAUSE I PUBLISH A COMIC BOOK.
BECAUSE OF HIS MONEY PROBLEMS HIS GIRLFRIEND HAD TO BARTEND.
I'M MUCH MORE UPTIGHT THAN SHE IS. SOME OF THE PEOPLE IN THAT BAR I FIND INTIMIDATING, BUT SHE SEEMS COMFORTABLE WITH THEM.
SHAWN IS KNOWN PRIMARILY AS A PLAY~WRITE BUT HE'S DONE SOME ACTING, TOO. HE TOLD US ABOUT A LUCRATIVE JOB HE'D JUST TURNED DOWN.
I WAS SUPPOSED TO HAVE PLAYED THE VOICE OF AN ORANGUTAN ON THIS T.V. SERIES. THE MONEY WAS FANTASTIC, BUT THEY WANTED ME TO SIGN A CONTRACT FOR SEVEN YEARS. I JUST CAN'T SEE MYSELF PLAYING AN ORANGUTAN WHEN I'M FORTY~FIVE YEARS OLD.
THEN KATHY BROUGHT UP SHAWN'S GIRLFRIEND AGAIN. IT SEEMS THAT SHE'D HAD A PLAY PRODUCED WHICH KATHY'D SEEN SEVERAL WEEKS BE~FOR AND LIKED A LOT.
TELL DEBBIE I REALLY APPRECIATED HER WRITING ABOUT THAT EXPERIENCE. I WENT THROUGH IT MYSELF, SO I COULD IDENTIFY WITH WHAT SHE WAS SAYING. THAT WAS A REAL IMPORTANT TIME FOR ME.

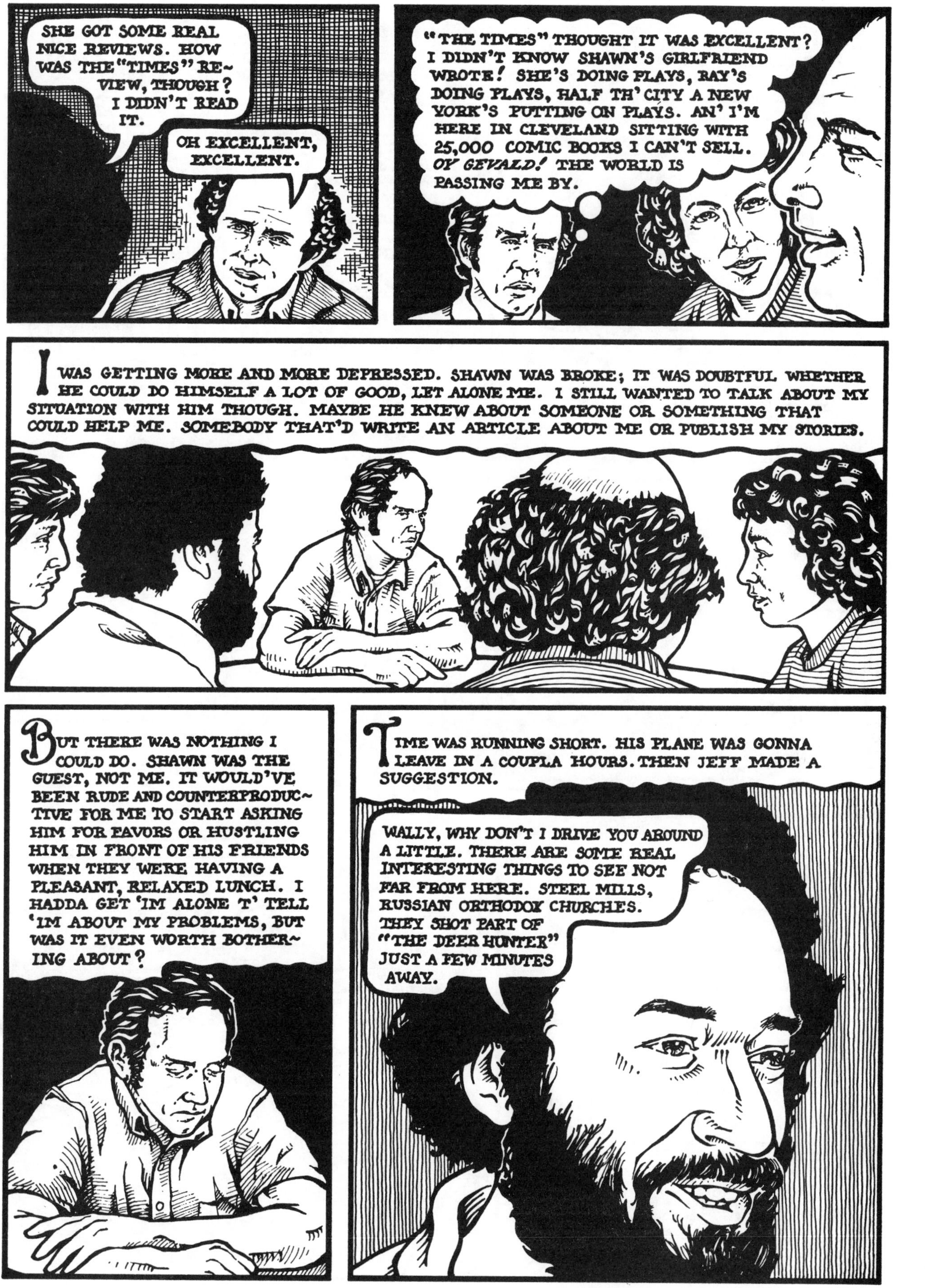
SHE GOT SOME REAL NICE REVIEWS. HOW WAS THE "TIMES" RE~VIEW, THOUGH? I DIDN'T READ IT.
OH EXCELLENT, EXCELLENT.
"THE TIMES" THOUGHT IT WAS EXCELLENT? I DIDN'T KNOW SHAWN'S GIRLFRIEND WROTE! SHE'S DOING PLAYS, RAY'S DOING PLAYS, HALF TH' CITY A NEW YORK'S PUTTING ON PLAYS. AN' I'M HERE IN CLEVELAND SITTING WITH 25,000 COMIC BOOKS I CAN'T SELL. OY GEVALD! THE WORLD IS PASSING ME BY.
I WAS GETTING MORE AND MORE DEPRESSED. SHAWN WAS BROKE; IT WAS DOUBTFUL WHETHER HE COULD DO HIMSELF A LOT OF GOOD, LET ALONE ME. I STILL WANTED TO TALK ABOUT MY SITUATION WITH HIM THOUGH. MAYBE HE KNEW ABOUT SOMEONE OR SOMETHING THAT COULD HELP ME. SOMEBODY THAT'D WRITE AN ARTICLE ABOUT ME OR PUBLISH MY STORIES.
BUT THERE WAS NOTHING I COULD DO. SHAWN WAS THE GUEST, NOT ME. IT WOULD'VE BEEN RUDE AND COUNTERPRODUC~TIVE FOR ME TO START ASKING HIM FOR FAVORS OR HUSTLING HIM IN FRONT OF HIS FRIENDS WHEN THEY WERE HAVING A PLEASANT, RELAXED LUNCH. I HADDA GET 'IM ALONE T' TELL 'IM ABOUT MY PROBLEMS, BUT WAS IT EVEN WORTH BOTHER~ING ABOUT?
TIME WAS RUNNING SHORT. HIS PLANE WAS GONNA LEAVE IN A COUPLA HOURS. THEN JEFF MADE A SUGGESTION.
WALLY, WHY DON'T I DRIVE YOU AROUND A LITTLE. THERE ARE SOME REAL INTERESTING THINGS TO SEE NOT FAR FROM HERE. STEEL MILLS, RUSSIAN ORTHODOX CHURCHES. THEY SHOT PART OF "THE DEER HUNTER" JUST A FEW MINUTES AWAY.

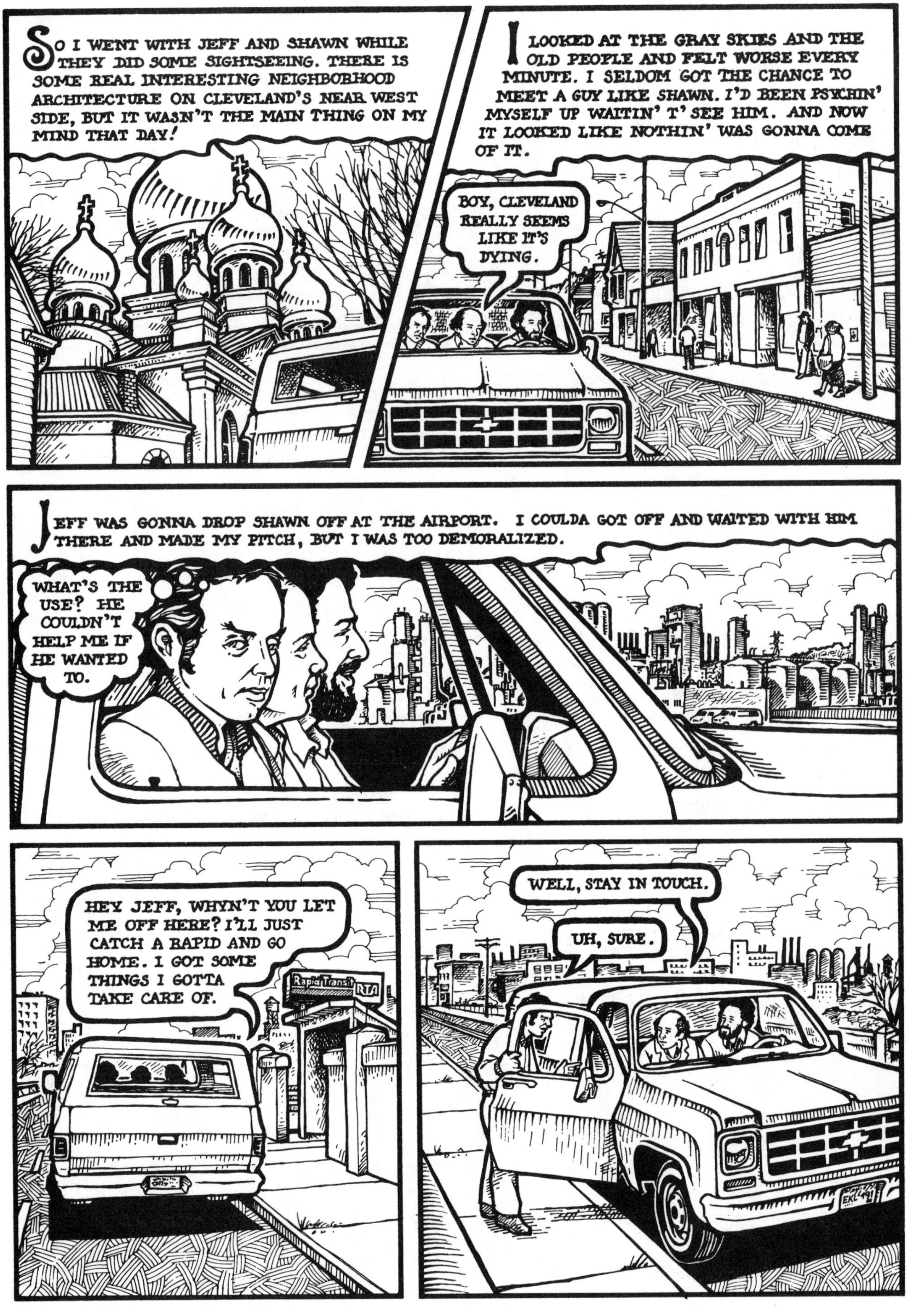
So I went with Jeff and Shawn while they did some sightseeing. There is some real interesting neighborhood architecture on Cleveland's near west side, but it wasn't the main thing on my mind that day!
I looked at the gray skies and the old people and felt worse every minute. I seldom got the chance to meet a guy like Shawn. I'd been psychin' myself up waitin' t' see him. And now it looked like nothin' was gonna come of it.
Boy, Cleveland really seems like it's dying.
Jeff was gonna drop Shawn off at the airport. I coulda got off and waited with him there and made my pitch, but I was too demoralized.
What's the use? He couldn't help me if he wanted to.
Hey Jeff, whyn't you let me off here? I'll just catch a rapid and go home. I got some things I gotta take care of.
Rapid Transit RTA
Well, stay in touch.
Uh, sure.

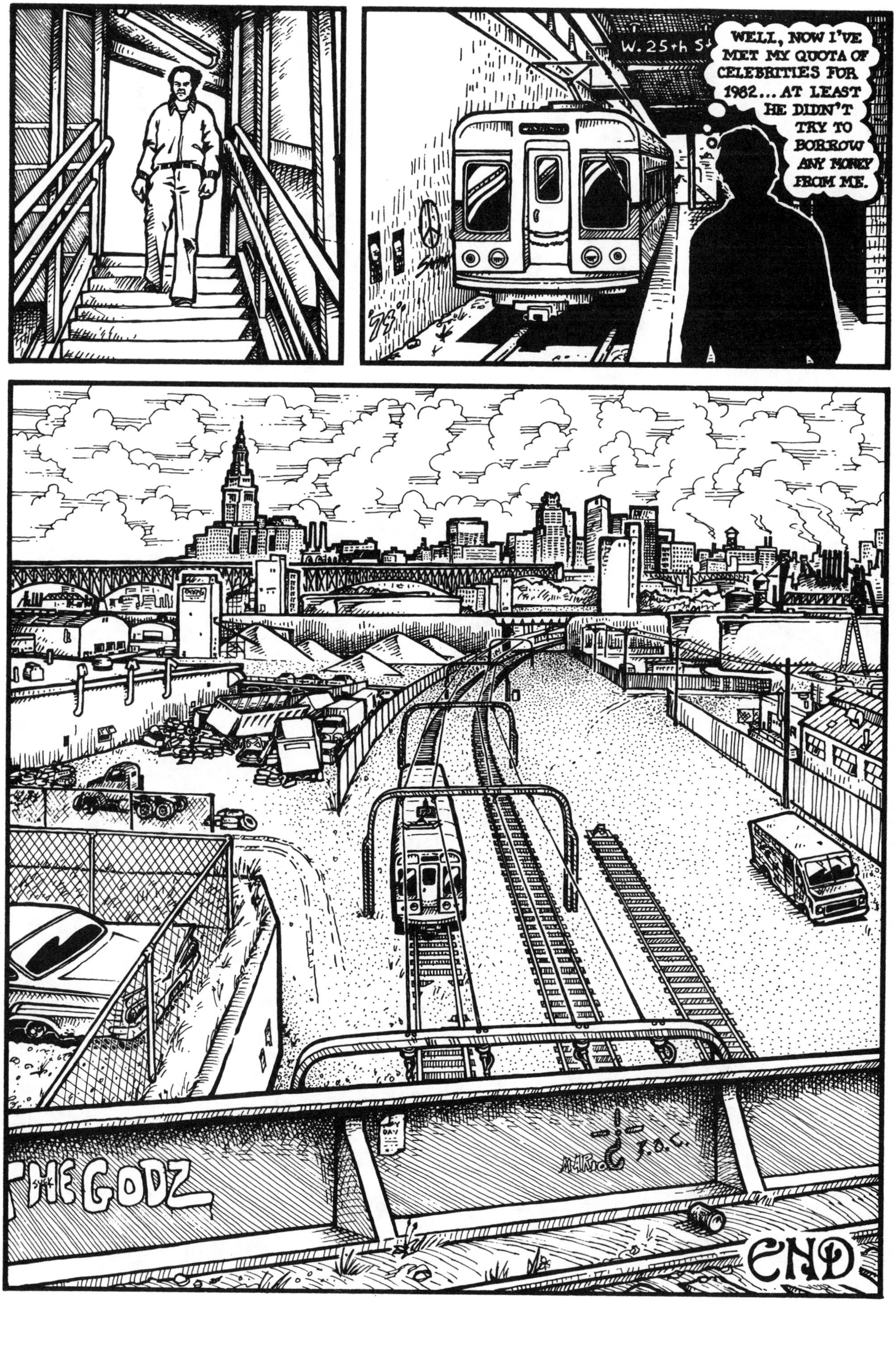
W. 25th St
WELL, NOW I'VE MET MY QUOTA OF CELEBRITIES FOR 1982... AT LEAST HE DIDN'T TRY TO BORROW ANY MONEY FROM ME.
THE GODZ
END

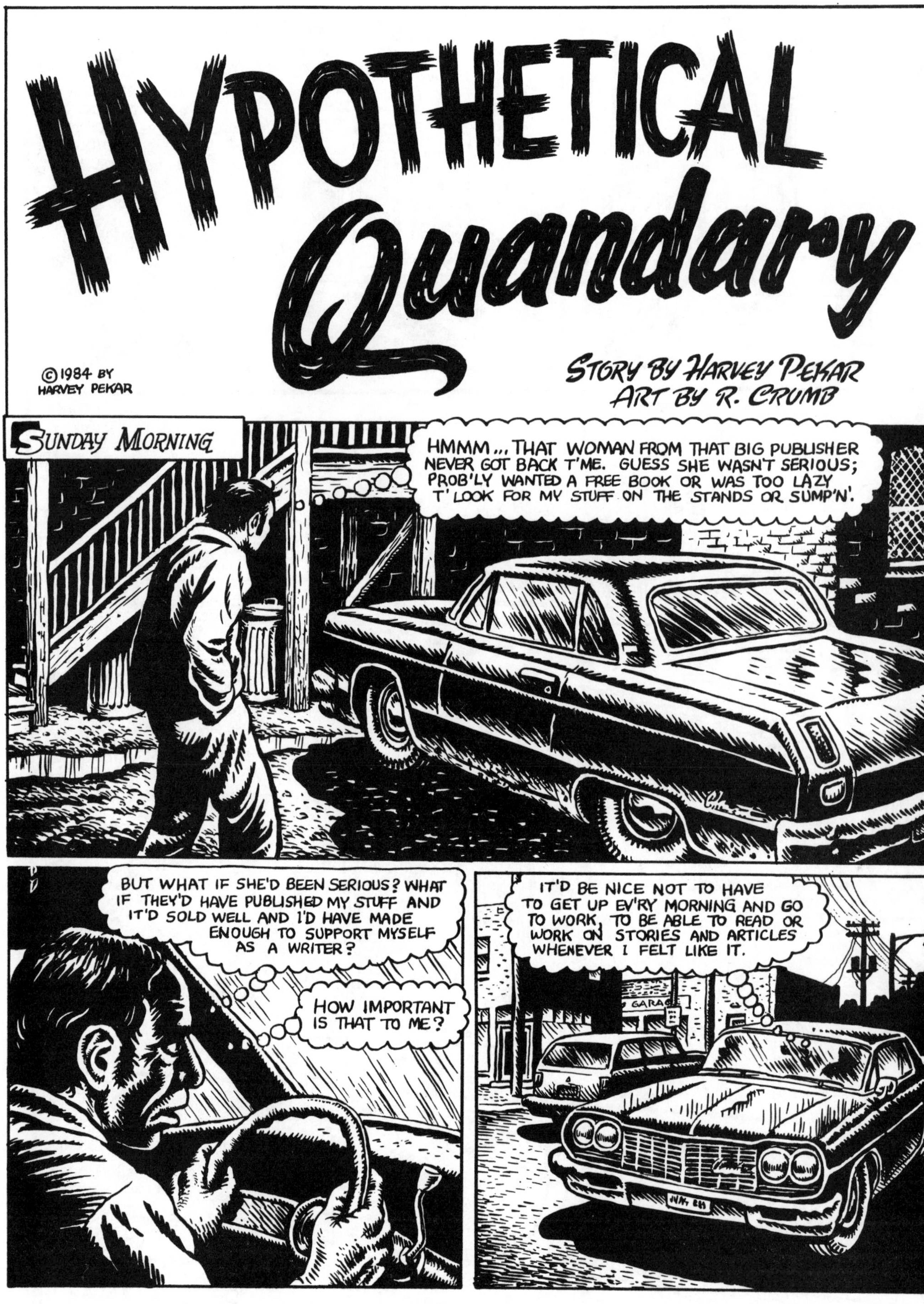
HYPOTHETICAL Quandary
©1984 BY HARVEY PEKAR
STORY BY HARVEY PEKAR
ART BY R. CRUMB
SUNDAY MORNING
HMMM... THAT WOMAN FROM THAT BIG PUBLISHER NEVER GOT BACK T'ME. GUESS SHE WASN'T SERIOUS; PROB'LY WANTED A FREE BOOK OR WAS TOO LAZY T' LOOK FOR MY STUFF ON THE STANDS OR SUMP'N'.
BUT WHAT IF SHE'D BEEN SERIOUS? WHAT IF THEY'D HAVE PUBLISHED MY STUFF AND IT'D SOLD WELL AND I'D HAVE MADE ENOUGH TO SUPPORT MYSELF AS A WRITER?
HOW IMPORTANT IS THAT TO ME?
IT'D BE NICE NOT TO HAVE TO GET UP EV'RY MORNING AND GO TO WORK, TO BE ABLE TO READ OR WORK ON STORIES AND ARTICLES WHENEVER I FELT LIKE IT.

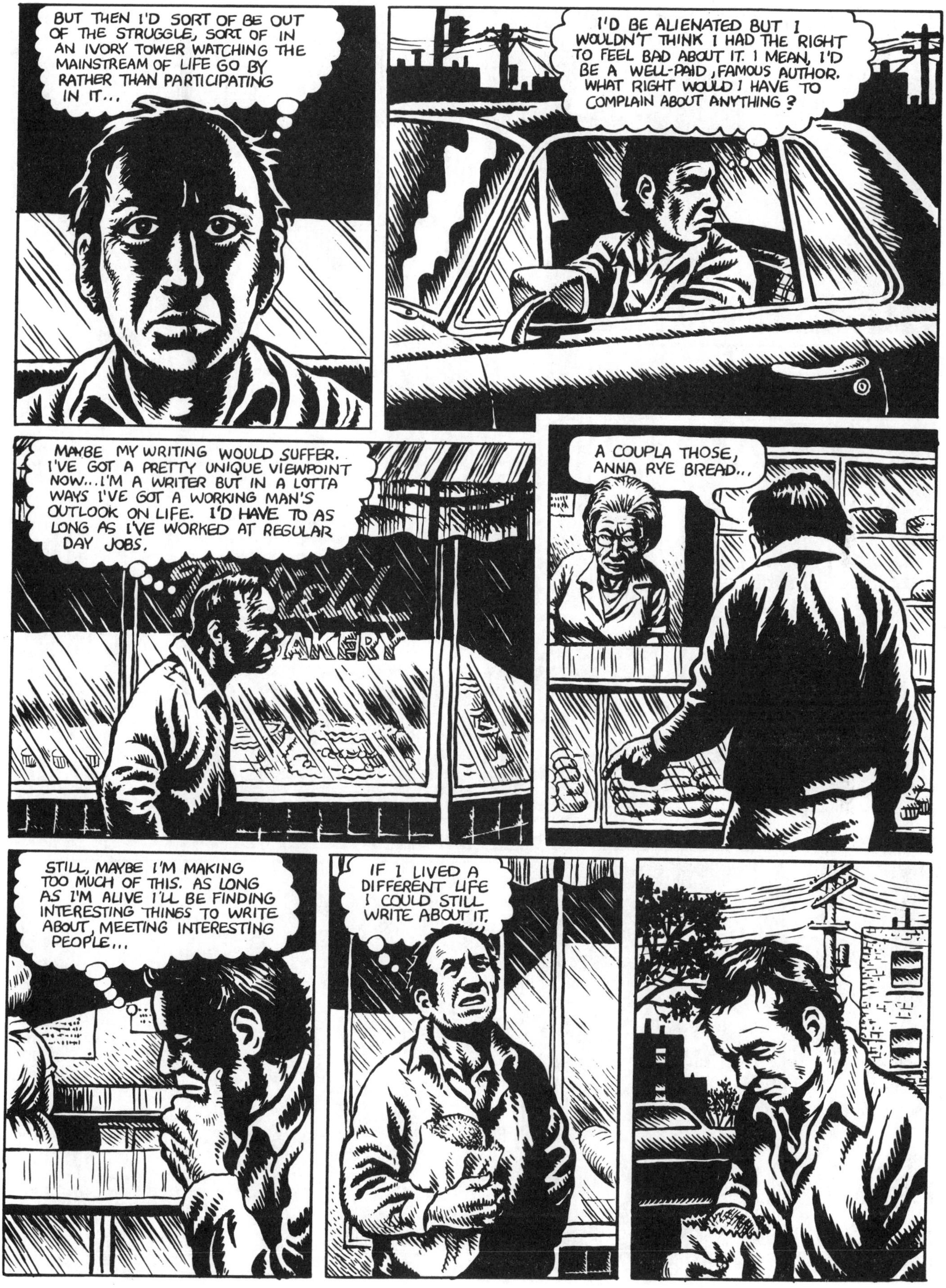

BUT THEN I'D SORT OF BE OUT OF THE STRUGGLE, SORT OF IN AN IVORY TOWER WATCHING THE MAINSTREAM OF LIFE GO BY RATHER THAN PARTICIPATING IN IT...
I'D BE ALIENATED BUT I WOULDN'T THINK I HAD THE RIGHT TO FEEL BAD ABOUT IT. I MEAN, I'D BE A WELL-PAID, FAMOUS AUTHOR. WHAT RIGHT WOULD I HAVE TO COMPLAIN ABOUT ANYTHING?
MAYBE MY WRITING WOULD SUFFER. I'VE GOT A PRETTY UNIQUE VIEWPOINT NOW...I'M A WRITER BUT IN A LOTTA WAYS I'VE GOT A WORKING MAN'S OUTLOOK ON LIFE. I'D HAVE TO AS LONG AS I'VE WORKED AT REGULAR DAY JOBS.
AKERY
A COUPLA THOSE, ANNA RYE BREAD...
STILL, MAYBE I'M MAKING TOO MUCH OF THIS. AS LONG AS I'M ALIVE I'LL BE FINDING INTERESTING THINGS TO WRITE ABOUT, MEETING INTERESTING PEOPLE...
IF I LIVED A DIFFERENT LIFE I COULD STILL WRITE ABOUT IT.

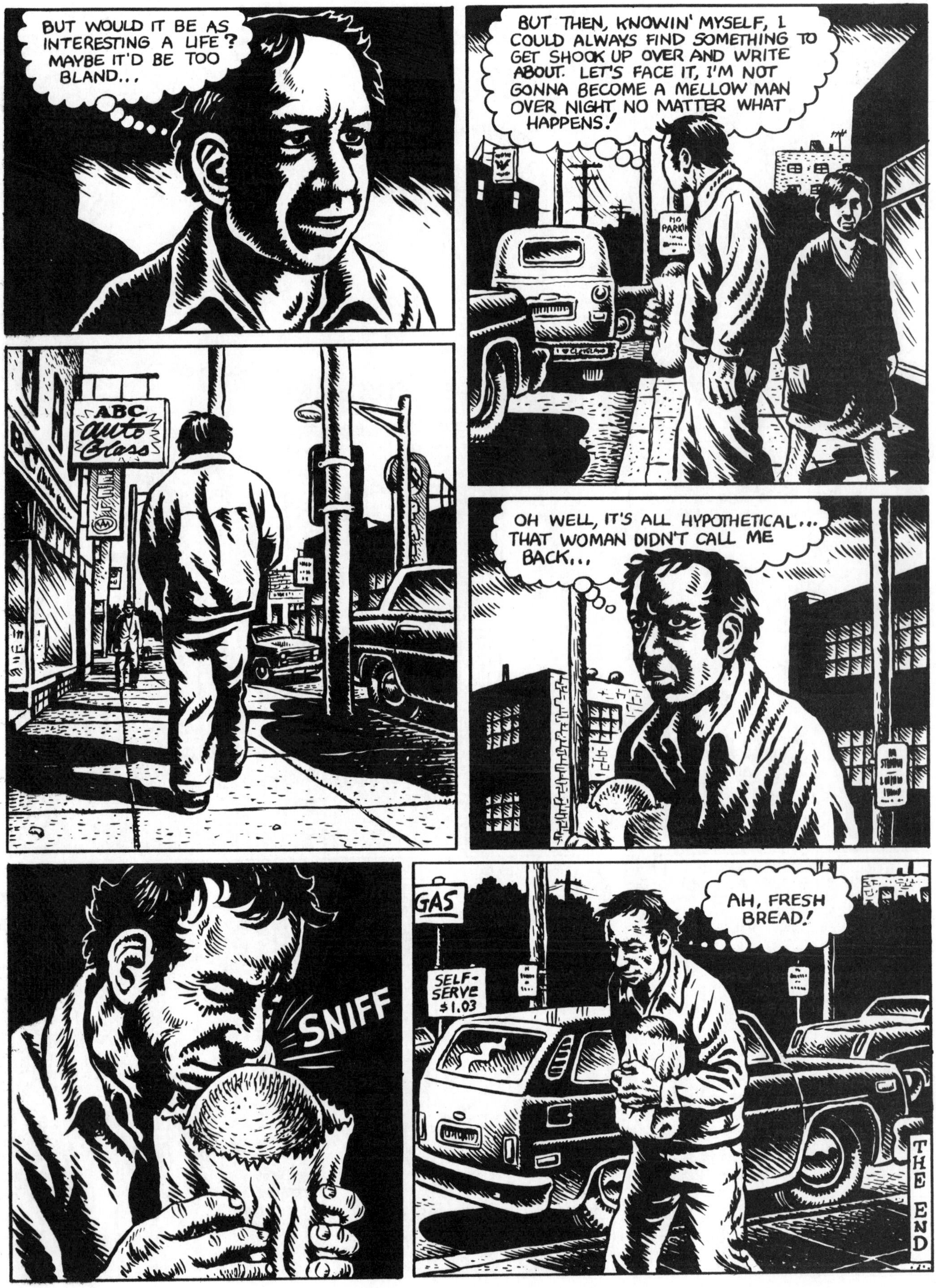
BUT WOULD IT BE AS INTERESTING A LIFE? MAYBE IT'D BE TOO BLAND...
BUT THEN, KNOWIN' MYSELF, I COULD ALWAYS FIND SOMETHING TO GET SHOOK UP OVER AND WRITE ABOUT. LET'S FACE IT, I'M NOT GONNA BECOME A MELLOW MAN OVER NIGHT, NO MATTER WHAT HAPPENS!
ABC auto Glass
OH WELL, IT'S ALL HYPOTHETICAL... THAT WOMAN DIDN'T CALL ME BACK...
SNIFF
GAS
SELF-SERVE $1.03
AH, FRESH BREAD!
THE END

FROM OFF THE STREETS OF CLEVELAND COMES...

More AMERICAN SPLENDOR

THE LIFE AND TIMES OF HARVEY PEKAR

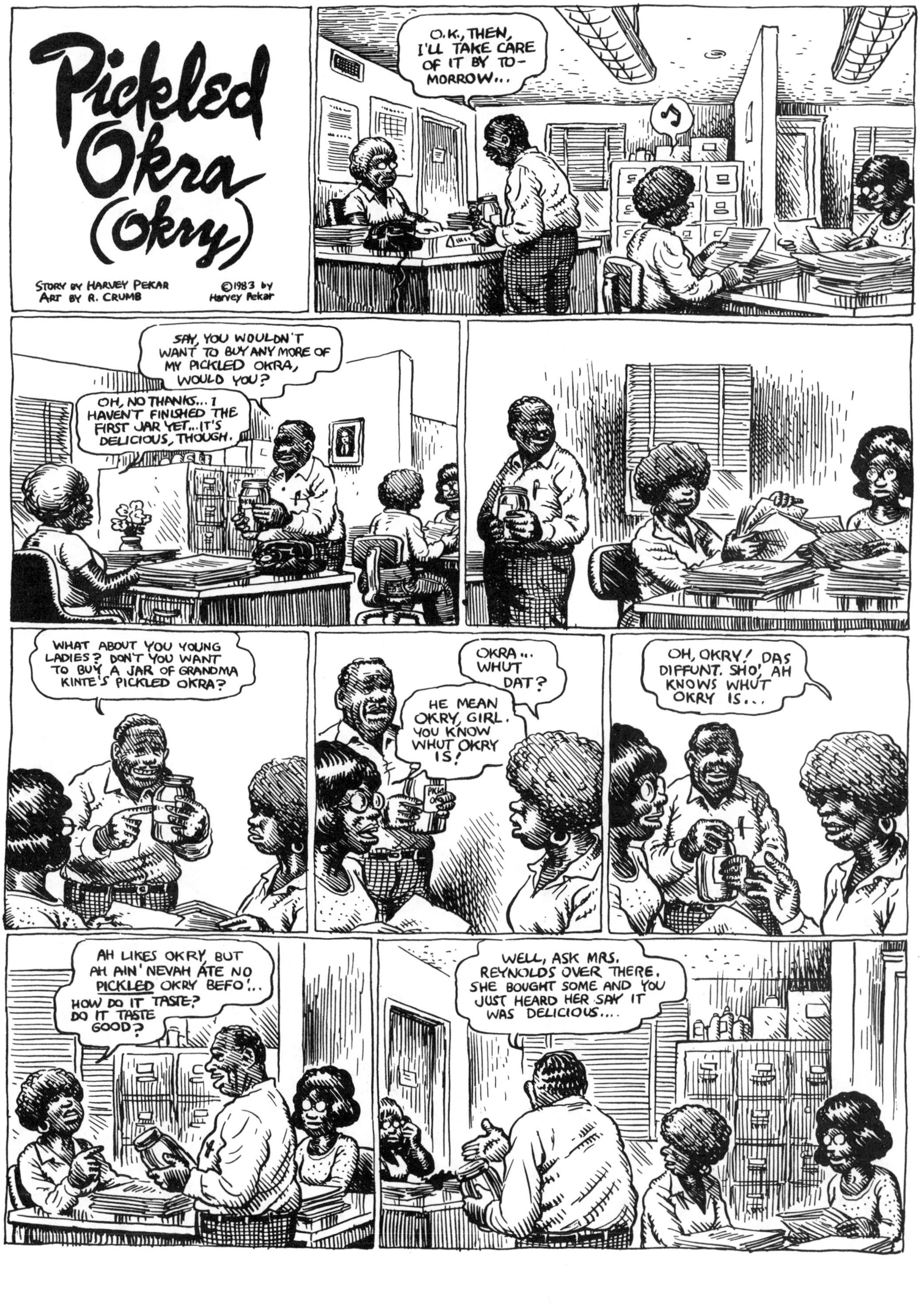
Pickled Okra (Okry)
STORY BY HARVEY PEKAR
ART BY R. CRUMB
©1983 by Harvey Pekar
O.K., THEN, I'LL TAKE CARE OF IT BY TO-MORROW...
♪
SAY, YOU WOULDN'T WANT TO BUY ANY MORE OF MY PICKLED OKRA, WOULD YOU?
OH, NO THANKS... I HAVEN'T FINISHED THE FIRST JAR YET... IT'S DELICIOUS, THOUGH.
WHAT ABOUT YOU YOUNG LADIES? DON'T YOU WANT TO BUY A JAR OF GRANDMA KINTE'S PICKLED OKRA?
OKRA... WHUT DAT?
HE MEAN OKRY, GIRL. YOU KNOW WHUT OKRY IS!
OH, OKRY! DAS DIFFUNT. SHO', AH KNOWS WHUT OKRY IS...
AH LIKES OKRY, BUT AH AIN' NEVAH ÁTE NO PICKLED OKRY BEFO'!.. HOW DO IT TASTE? DO IT TASTE GOOD?
WELL, ASK MRS. REYNOLDS OVER THERE. SHE BOUGHT SOME AND YOU JUST HEARD HER SAY IT WAS DELICIOUS....

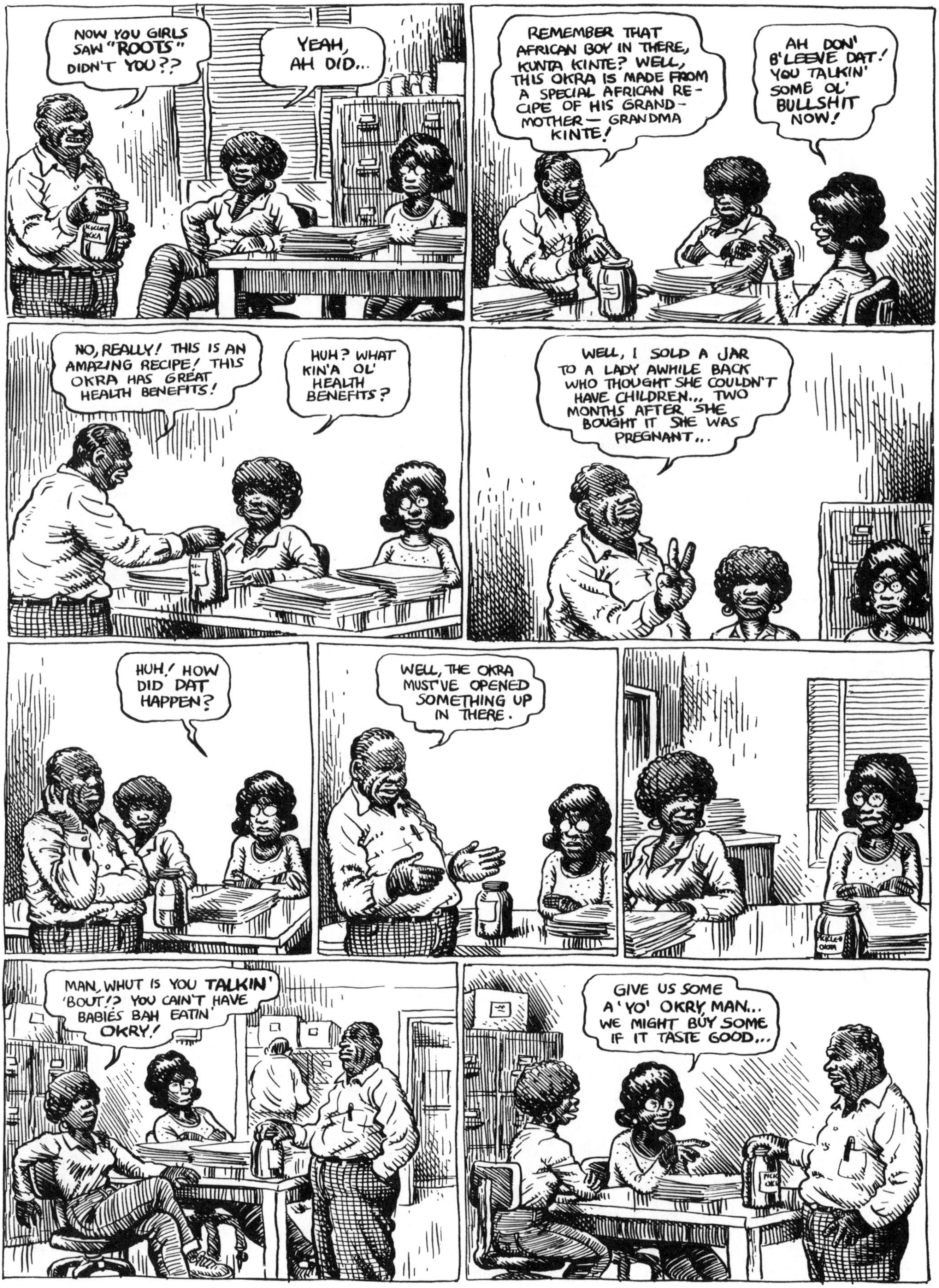
NOW YOU GIRLS SAW "ROOTS" DIDN'T YOU??
YEAH, AH DID...
REMEMBER THAT AFRICAN BOY IN THERE, KUNTA KINTE? WELL, THIS OKRA IS MADE FROM A SPECIAL AFRICAN RECIPE OF HIS GRANDMOTHER — GRANDMA KINTE!
AH DON' B'LEEVE DAT! YOU TALKIN' SOME OL' BULLSHIT NOW!
NO, REALLY! THIS IS AN AMAZING RECIPE! THIS OKRA HAS GREAT HEALTH BENEFITS!
HUH? WHAT KIN'A OL' HEALTH BENEFITS?
WELL, I SOLD A JAR TO A LADY AWHILE BACK WHO THOUGHT SHE COULDN'T HAVE CHILDREN... TWO MONTHS AFTER SHE BOUGHT IT SHE WAS PREGNANT...
HUH! HOW DID DAT HAPPEN?
WELL, THE OKRA MUST'VE OPENED SOMETHING UP IN THERE.
MAN, WHUT IS YOU TALKIN' 'BOUT!? YOU CAIN'T HAVE BABIES BAH EATIN' OKRY!
GIVE US SOME A 'YO' OKRY, MAN... WE MIGHT BUY SOME IF IT TASTE GOOD...

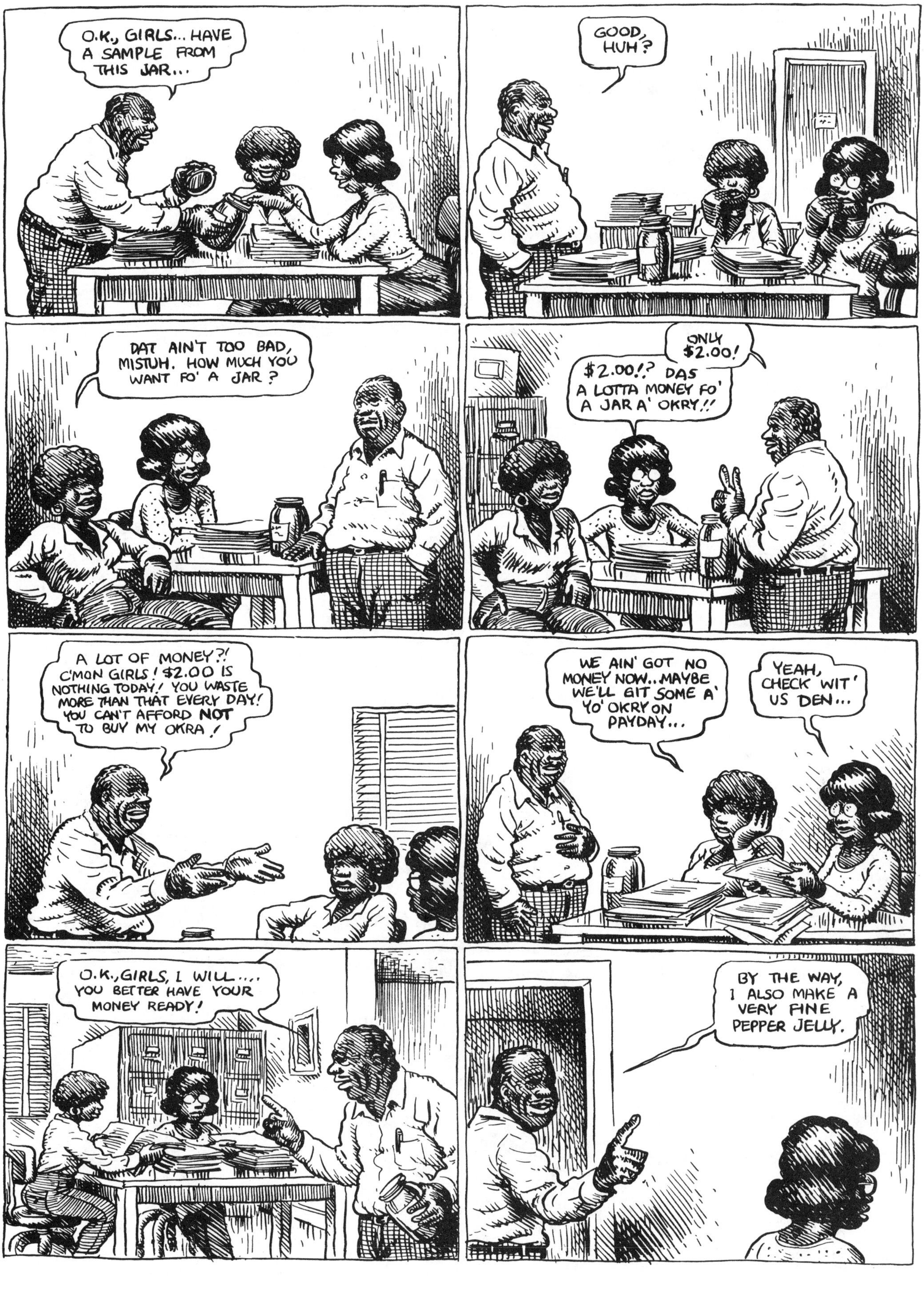
O.K., GIRLS... HAVE A SAMPLE FROM THIS JAR...
GOOD, HUH?
DAT AIN'T TOO BAD, MISTUH. HOW MUCH YOU WANT FO' A JAR?
ONLY $2.00!
$2.00!? DAS A LOTTA MONEY FO' A JAR A' OKRY!!
A LOT OF MONEY?! C'MON GIRLS! $2.00 IS NOTHING TODAY! YOU WASTE MORE THAN THAT EVERY DAY! YOU CAN'T AFFORD NOT TO BUY MY OKRA!
WE AIN' GOT NO MONEY NOW.. MAYBE WE'LL GIT SOME A' YO' OKRY ON PAYDAY...
YEAH, CHECK WIT' US DEN...
O.K., GIRLS, I WILL.... YOU BETTER HAVE YOUR MONEY READY!
BY THE WAY, I ALSO MAKE A VERY FINE PEPPER JELLY.

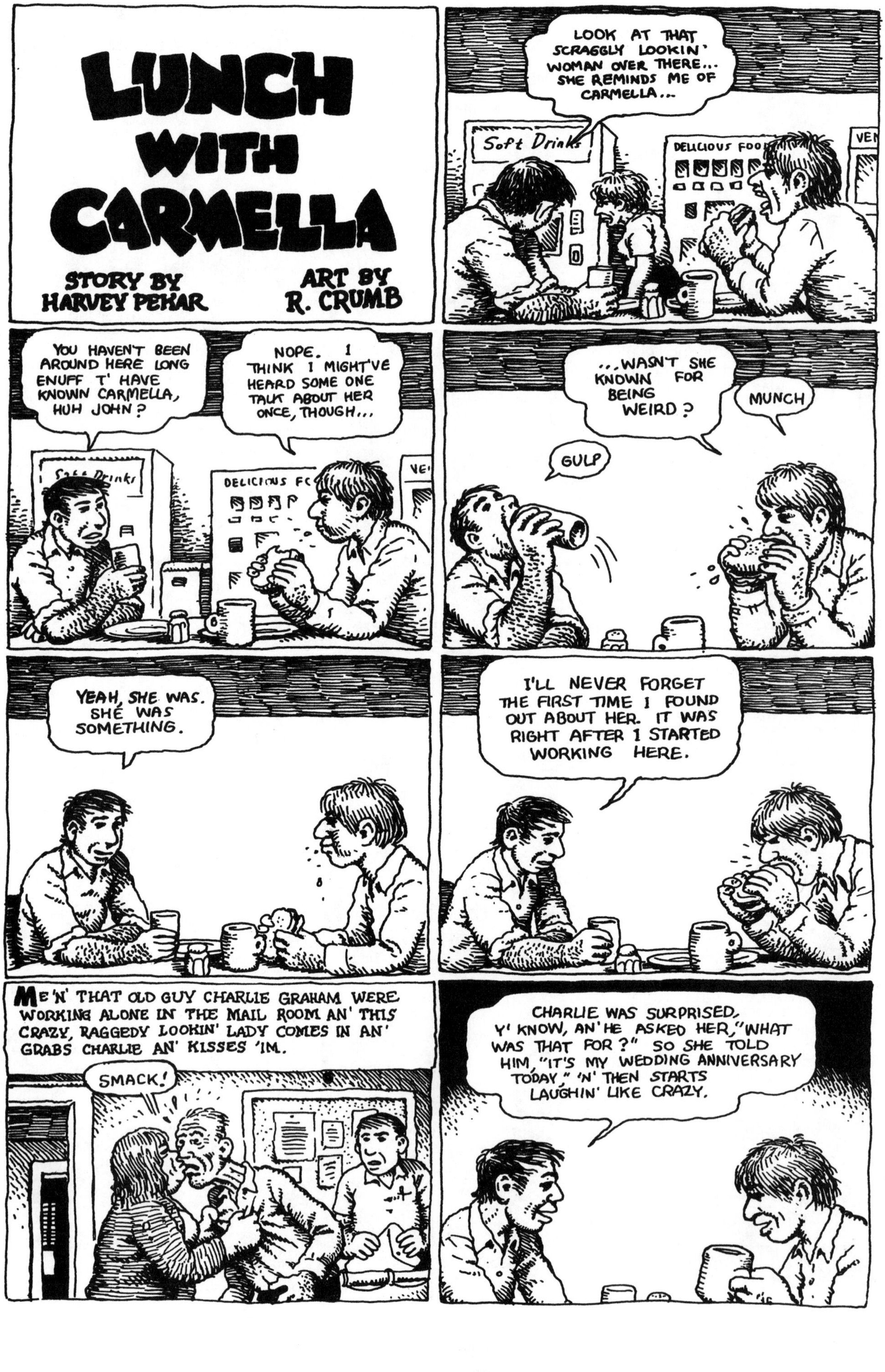
LUNCH WITH CARMELLA
STORY BY HARVEY PEKAR
ART BY R. CRUMB
LOOK AT THAT SCRAGGLY LOOKIN' WOMAN OVER THERE... SHE REMINDS ME OF CARMELLA...
Soft Drinks
DELICIOUS FOO
VEN
YOU HAVEN'T BEEN AROUND HERE LONG ENUFF T' HAVE KNOWN CARMELLA, HUH JOHN?
NOPE. I THINK I MIGHT'VE HEARD SOME ONE TALK ABOUT HER ONCE, THOUGH...
...WASN'T SHE KNOWN FOR BEING WEIRD?
MUNCH
GULP
YEAH, SHE WAS. SHE WAS SOMETHING.
I'LL NEVER FORGET THE FIRST TIME I FOUND OUT ABOUT HER. IT WAS RIGHT AFTER I STARTED WORKING HERE.
ME 'N' THAT OLD GUY CHARLIE GRAHAM WERE WORKING ALONE IN THE MAIL ROOM AN' THIS CRAZY, RAGGEDY LOOKIN' LADY COMES IN AN' GRABS CHARLIE AN' KISSES 'IM.
SMACK!
CHARLIE WAS SURPRISED, Y' KNOW, AN' HE ASKED HER, "WHAT WAS THAT FOR?" SO SHE TOLD HIM, "IT'S MY WEDDING ANNIVERSARY TODAY," 'N' THEN STARTS LAUGHIN' LIKE CRAZY.

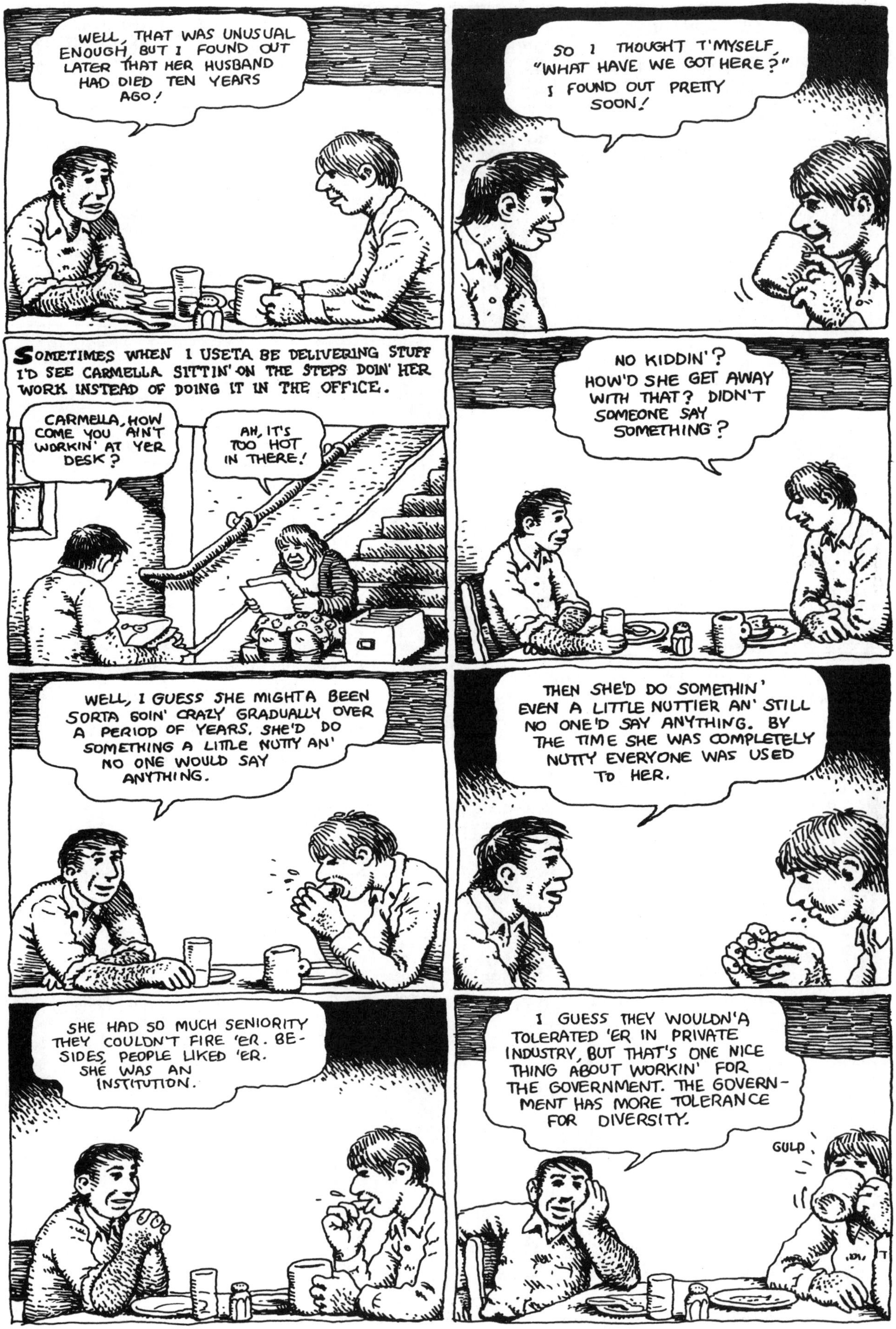
WELL, THAT WAS UNUSUAL ENOUGH, BUT I FOUND OUT LATER THAT HER HUSBAND HAD DIED TEN YEARS AGO!
SO I THOUGHT T'MYSELF, "WHAT HAVE WE GOT HERE?" I FOUND OUT PRETTY SOON!
SOMETIMES WHEN I USETA BE DELIVERING STUFF I'D SEE CARMELLA SITTIN' ON THE STEPS DOIN' HER WORK INSTEAD OF DOING IT IN THE OFFICE.
CARMELLA, HOW COME YOU AIN'T WORKIN' AT YER DESK?
AH, IT'S TOO HOT IN THERE!
NO KIDDIN'? HOW'D SHE GET AWAY WITH THAT? DIDN'T SOMEONE SAY SOMETHING?
WELL, I GUESS SHE MIGHTA BEEN SORTA GOIN' CRAZY GRADUALLY OVER A PERIOD OF YEARS. SHE'D DO SOMETHING A LITTLE NUTTY AN' NO ONE WOULD SAY ANYTHING.
THEN SHE'D DO SOMETHIN' EVEN A LITTLE NUTTIER AN' STILL NO ONE'D SAY ANYTHING. BY THE TIME SHE WAS COMPLETELY NUTTY EVERYONE WAS USED TO HER.
SHE HAD SO MUCH SENIORITY THEY COULDN'T FIRE 'ER. BESIDES, PEOPLE LIKED 'ER. SHE WAS AN INSTITUTION.
I GUESS THEY WOULDN'A TOLERATED 'ER IN PRIVATE INDUSTRY, BUT THAT'S ONE NICE THING ABOUT WORKIN' FOR THE GOVERNMENT. THE GOVERNMENT HAS MORE TOLERANCE FOR DIVERSITY.
GULP

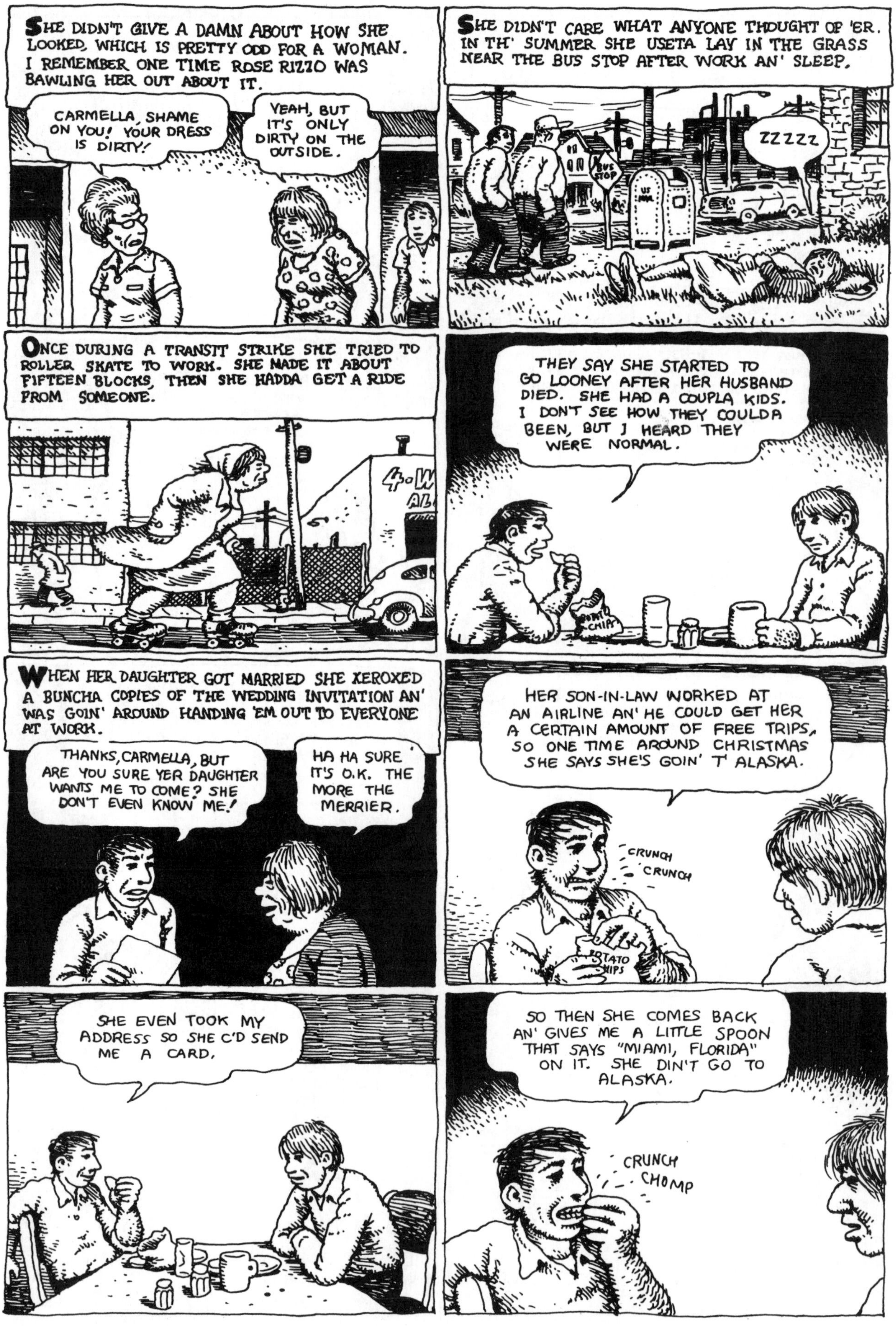
SHE DIDN'T GIVE A DAMN ABOUT HOW SHE LOOKED, WHICH IS PRETTY ODD FOR A WOMAN. I REMEMBER ONE TIME ROSE RIZZO WAS BAWLING HER OUT ABOUT IT.
CARMELLA, SHAME ON YOU! YOUR DRESS IS DIRTY!
YEAH, BUT IT'S ONLY DIRTY ON THE OUTSIDE.
SHE DIDN'T CARE WHAT ANYONE THOUGHT OF 'ER. IN TH' SUMMER SHE USETA LAY IN THE GRASS NEAR THE BUS STOP AFTER WORK AN' SLEEP.
BUS STOP
ZZZZZ
ONCE DURING A TRANSIT STRIKE SHE TRIED TO ROLLER SKATE TO WORK. SHE MADE IT ABOUT FIFTEEN BLOCKS, THEN SHE HADDA GET A RIDE FROM SOMEONE.
THEY SAY SHE STARTED TO GO LOONEY AFTER HER HUSBAND DIED. SHE HAD A COUPLA KIDS. I DON'T SEE HOW THEY COULDA BEEN, BUT I HEARD THEY WERE NORMAL.
WHEN HER DAUGHTER GOT MARRIED SHE XEROXED A BUNCHA COPIES OF THE WEDDING INVITATION AN' WAS GOIN' AROUND HANDING 'EM OUT TO EVERYONE AT WORK.
THANKS, CARMELLA, BUT ARE YOU SURE YER DAUGHTER WANTS ME TO COME? SHE DON'T EVEN KNOW ME!
HA HA SURE IT'S O.K. THE MORE THE MERRIER.
HER SON-IN-LAW WORKED AT AN AIRLINE AN' HE COULD GET HER A CERTAIN AMOUNT OF FREE TRIPS, SO ONE TIME AROUND CHRISTMAS SHE SAYS SHE'S GOIN' T' ALASKA.
CRUNCH
CRUNCH
SHE EVEN TOOK MY ADDRESS SO SHE C'D SEND ME A CARD.
SO THEN SHE COMES BACK AN' GIVES ME A LITTLE SPOON THAT SAYS "MIAMI, FLORIDA" ON IT. SHE DIN'T GO TO ALASKA.
CRUNCH
CHOMP

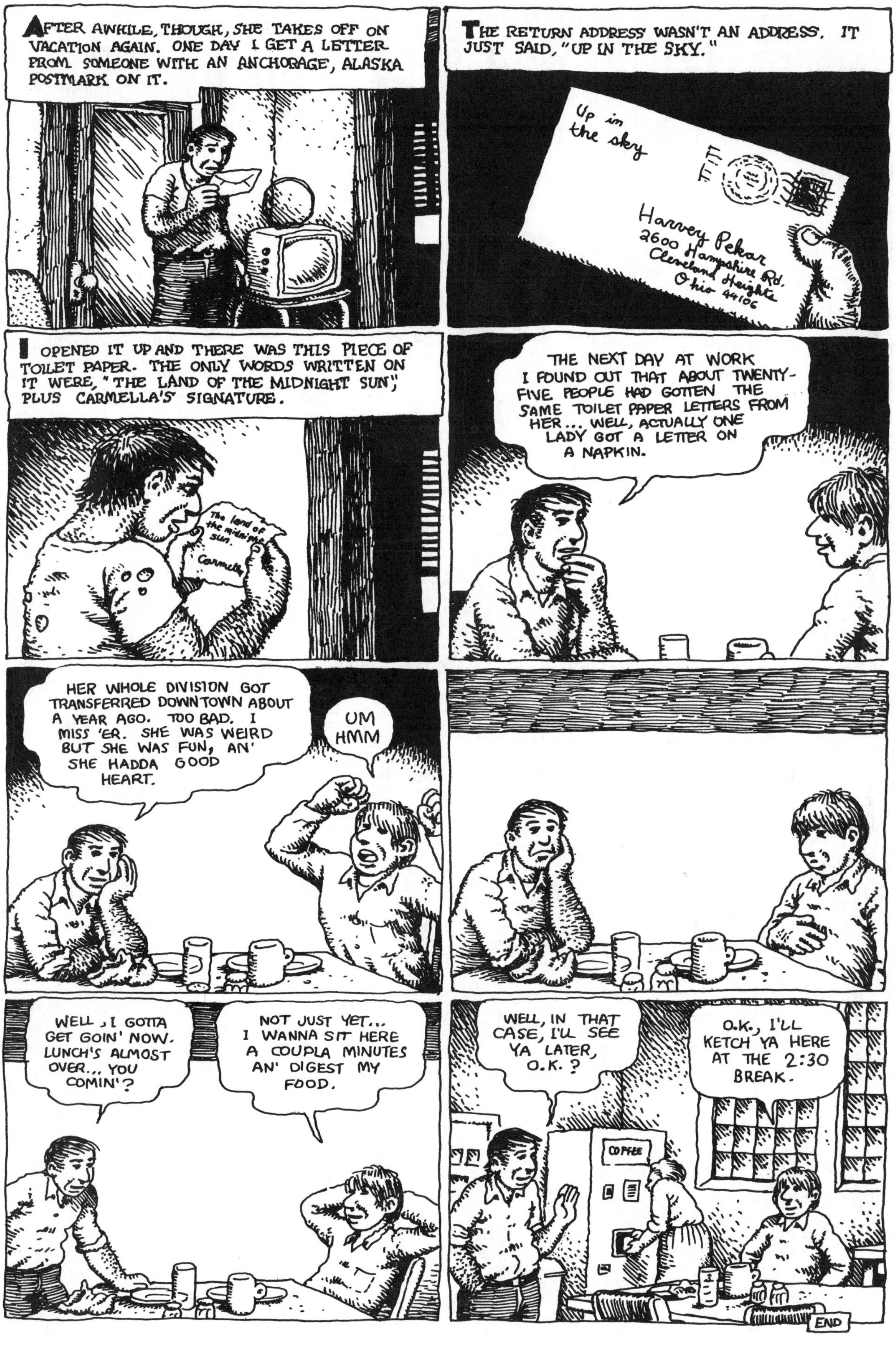
AFTER AWHILE, THOUGH, SHE TAKES OFF ON VACATION AGAIN. ONE DAY I GET A LETTER FROM SOMEONE WITH AN ANCHORAGE, ALASKA POSTMARK ON IT.
THE RETURN ADDRESS WASN'T AN ADDRESS. IT JUST SAID, "UP IN THE SKY."
Up in the sky
Harvey Pekar
2600 Hampshire Rd.
Cleveland Heights
Ohio 44106
I OPENED IT UP AND THERE WAS THIS PIECE OF TOILET PAPER. THE ONLY WORDS WRITTEN ON IT WERE, "THE LAND OF THE MIDNIGHT SUN", PLUS CARMELLA'S SIGNATURE.
The land of the midnight sun.
Carmella
THE NEXT DAY AT WORK I FOUND OUT THAT ABOUT TWENTY-FIVE PEOPLE HAD GOTTEN THE SAME TOILET PAPER LETTERS FROM HER... WELL, ACTUALLY ONE LADY GOT A LETTER ON A NAPKIN.
HER WHOLE DIVISION GOT TRANSFERRED DOWNTOWN ABOUT A YEAR AGO. TOO BAD. I MISS 'ER. SHE WAS WEIRD BUT SHE WAS FUN, AN' SHE HADDA GOOD HEART.
UM HMM
WELL, I GOTTA GET GOIN' NOW. LUNCH'S ALMOST OVER... YOU COMIN'?
NOT JUST YET... I WANNA SIT HERE A COUPLA MINUTES AN' DIGEST MY FOOD.
WELL, IN THAT CASE, I'LL SEE YA LATER, O.K.?
O.K., I'LL KETCH YA HERE AT THE 2:30 BREAK.
COFFEE
END

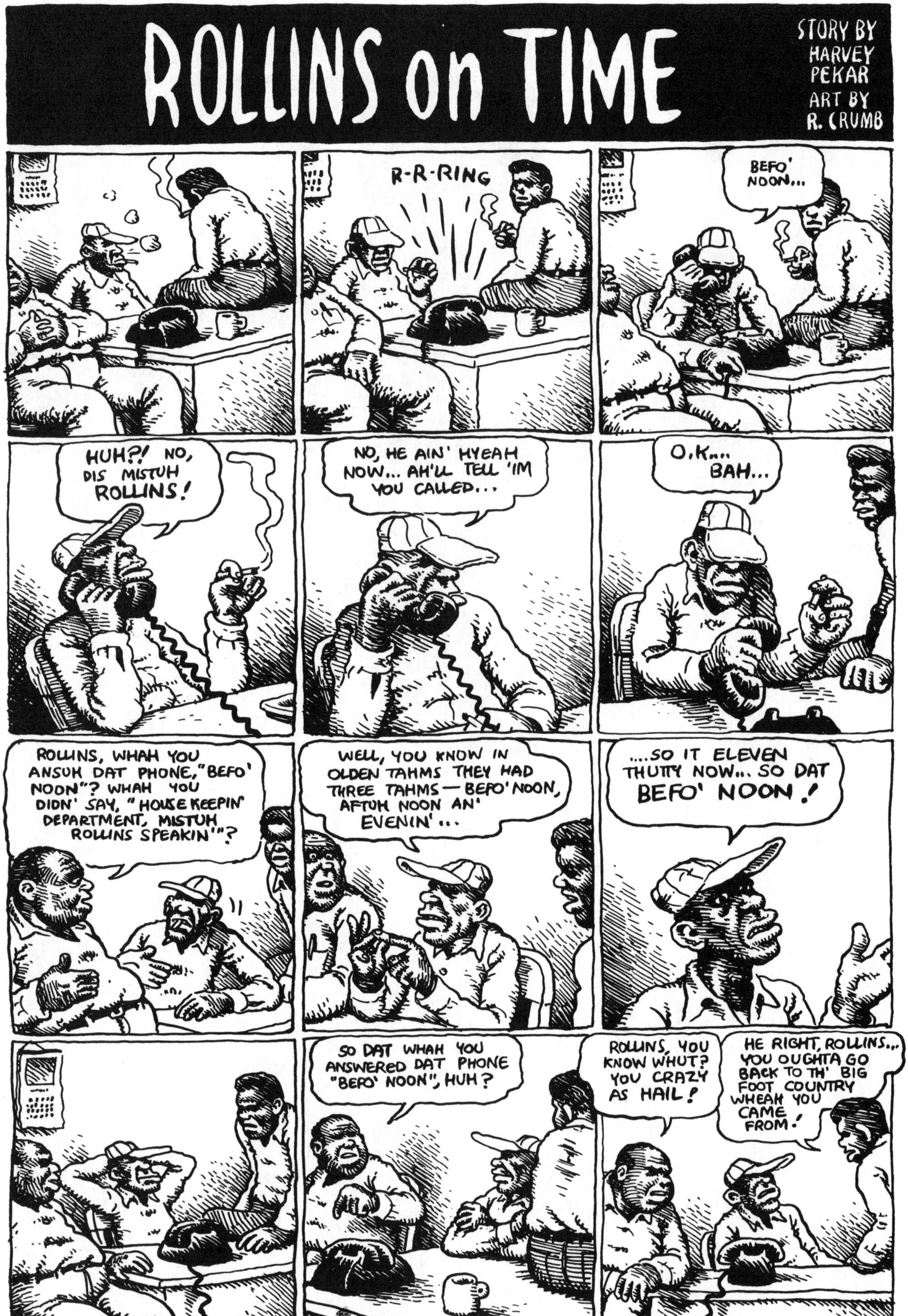
ROLLINS on TIME
STORY BY HARVEY PEKAR
ART BY R. CRUMB
R-R-RING
BEFO' NOON...
HUH?! NO, DIS MISTUH ROLLINS!
NO, HE AIN' HYEAH NOW... AH'LL TELL 'IM YOU CALLED...
O.K... BAH...
ROLLINS, WHAH YOU ANSUH DAT PHONE, "BEFO' NOON"? WHAH YOU DIDN' SAY, "HOUSE KEEPIN' DEPARTMENT, MISTUH ROLLINS SPEAKIN'"?
WELL, YOU KNOW IN OLDEN TAHMS THEY HAD THREE TAHMS — BEFO' NOON, AFTUH NOON AN' EVENIN'...
....SO IT ELEVEN THUTTY NOW... SO DAT BEFO' NOON!
SO DAT WHAH YOU ANSWERED DAT PHONE "BEFO' NOON", HUH?
ROLLINS, YOU KNOW WHUT? YOU CRAZY AS HAIL!
HE RIGHT, ROLLINS... YOU OUGHTA GO BACK TO TH' BIG FOOT COUNTRY WHEAH YOU CAME FROM!

VISUALIZE, ACTUALIZE, REALIZE

STORY BY HARVEY PEKAR
ART BY R. CRUMB

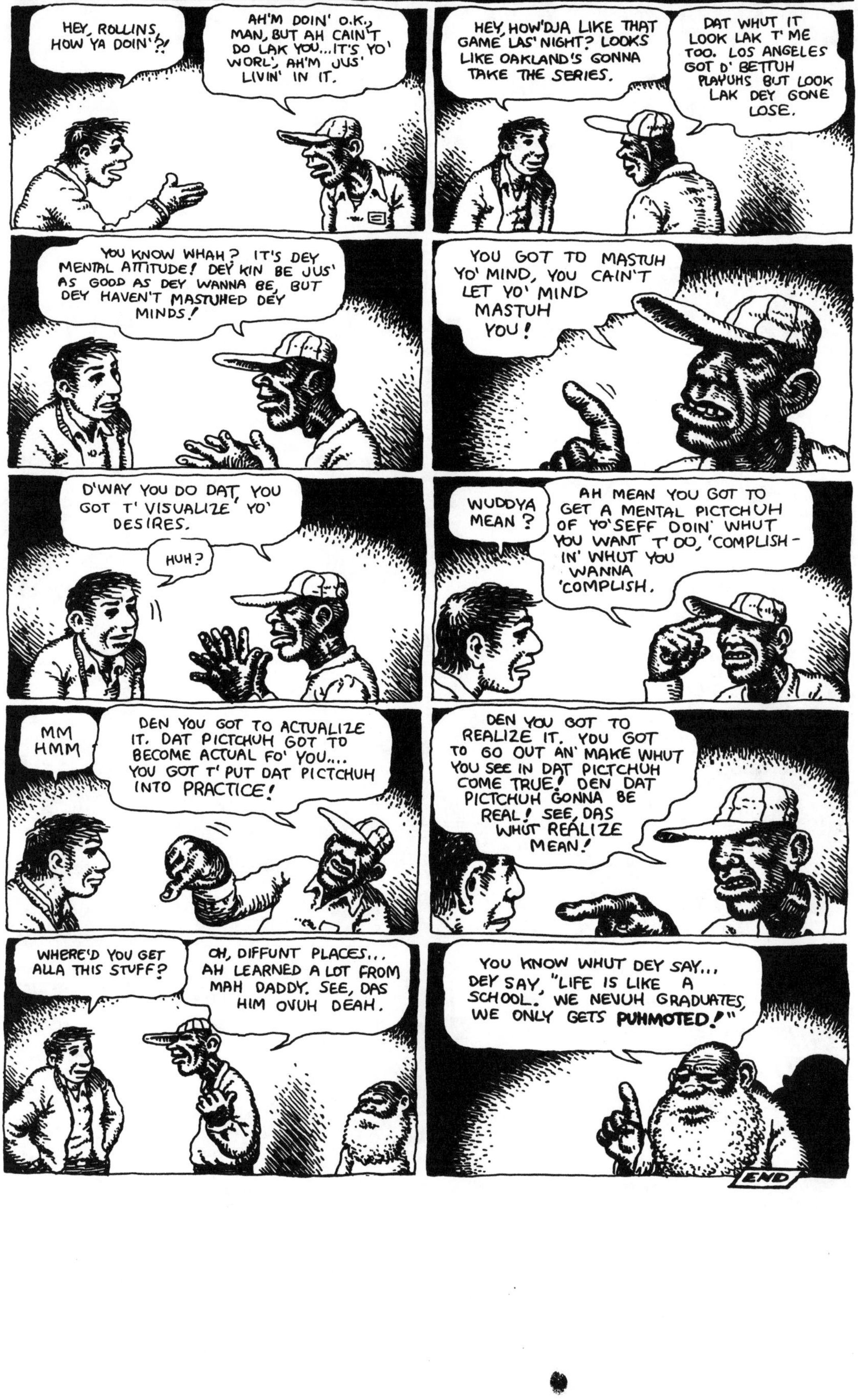

HEY, ROLLINS, HOW YA DOIN'?!
AH'M DOIN' O.K., MAN, BUT AH CAIN'T DO LAK YOU...IT'S YO' WORL', AH'M JUS' LIVIN' IN IT.
HEY, HOW'DJA LIKE THAT GAME LAS' NIGHT? LOOKS LIKE OAKLAND'S GONNA TAKE THE SERIES.
DAT WHUT IT LOOK LAK T' ME TOO. LOS ANGELES GOT D' BETTUH PLAYUHS BUT LOOK LAK DEY GONE LOSE.
YOU KNOW WHAH? IT'S DEY MENTAL ATTITUDE! DEY KIN BE JUS' AS GOOD AS DEY WANNA BE, BUT DEY HAVEN'T MASTUHED DEY MINDS!
YOU GOT TO MASTUH YO' MIND, YOU CAIN'T LET YO' MIND MASTUH YOU!
D'WAY YOU DO DAT, YOU GOT T' VISUALIZE YO' DESIRES.
HUH?
WUDDYA MEAN?
AH MEAN YOU GOT TO GET A MENTAL PICTCHUH OF YO'SEFF DOIN' WHUT YOU WANT T' DO, 'COMPLISH-IN' WHUT YOU WANNA 'COMPLISH.
MM HMM
DEN YOU GOT TO ACTUALIZE IT. DAT PICTCHUH GOT TO BECOME ACTUAL FO' YOU... YOU GOT T' PUT DAT PICTCHUH INTO PRACTICE!
DEN YOU GOT TO REALIZE IT. YOU GOT TO GO OUT AN' MAKE WHUT YOU SEE IN DAT PICTCHUH COME TRUE! DEN DAT PICTCHUH GONNA BE REAL! SEE, DAS WHUT REALIZE MEAN!
WHERE'D YOU GET ALLA THIS STUFF?
OH, DIFFUNT PLACES... AH LEARNED A LOT FROM MAH DADDY. SEE, DAS HIM OVUH DEAH.
YOU KNOW WHUT DEY SAY... DEY SAY, "LIFE IS LIKE A SCHOOL. WE NEVUH GRADUATES, WE ONLY GETS PUHMOTED!"
END

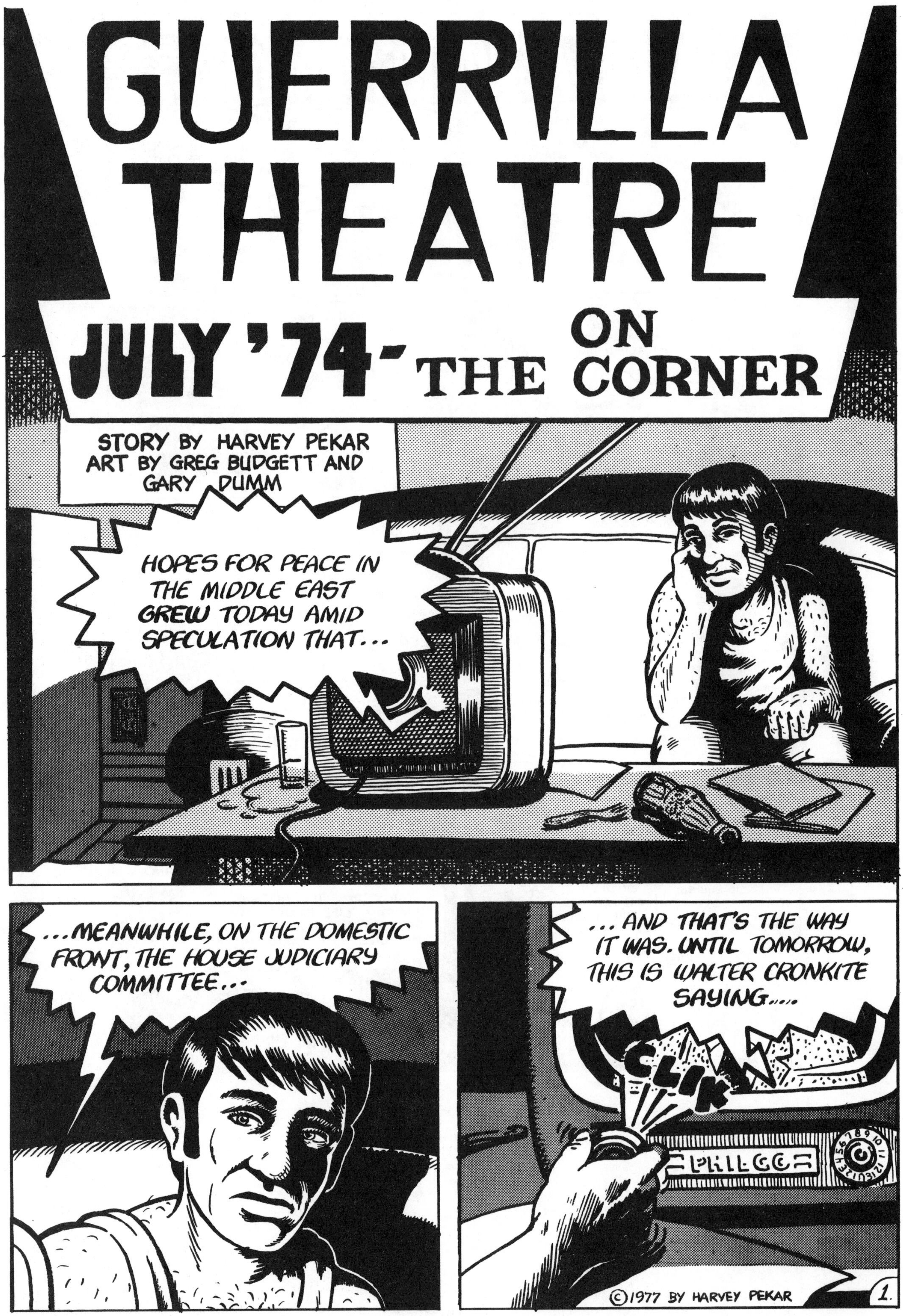
GUERRILLA THEATRE
JULY '74 - ON THE CORNER
STORY BY HARVEY PEKAR ART BY GREG BUDGETT AND GARY DUMM
HOPES FOR PEACE IN THE MIDDLE EAST GREW TODAY AMID SPECULATION THAT...
...MEANWHILE, ON THE DOMESTIC FRONT, THE HOUSE JUDICIARY COMMITTEE...
...AND THAT'S THE WAY IT WAS. UNTIL TOMORROW, THIS IS WALTER CRONKITE SAYING.....
CLIK
PHILCO
©1977 BY HARVEY PEKAR
1.

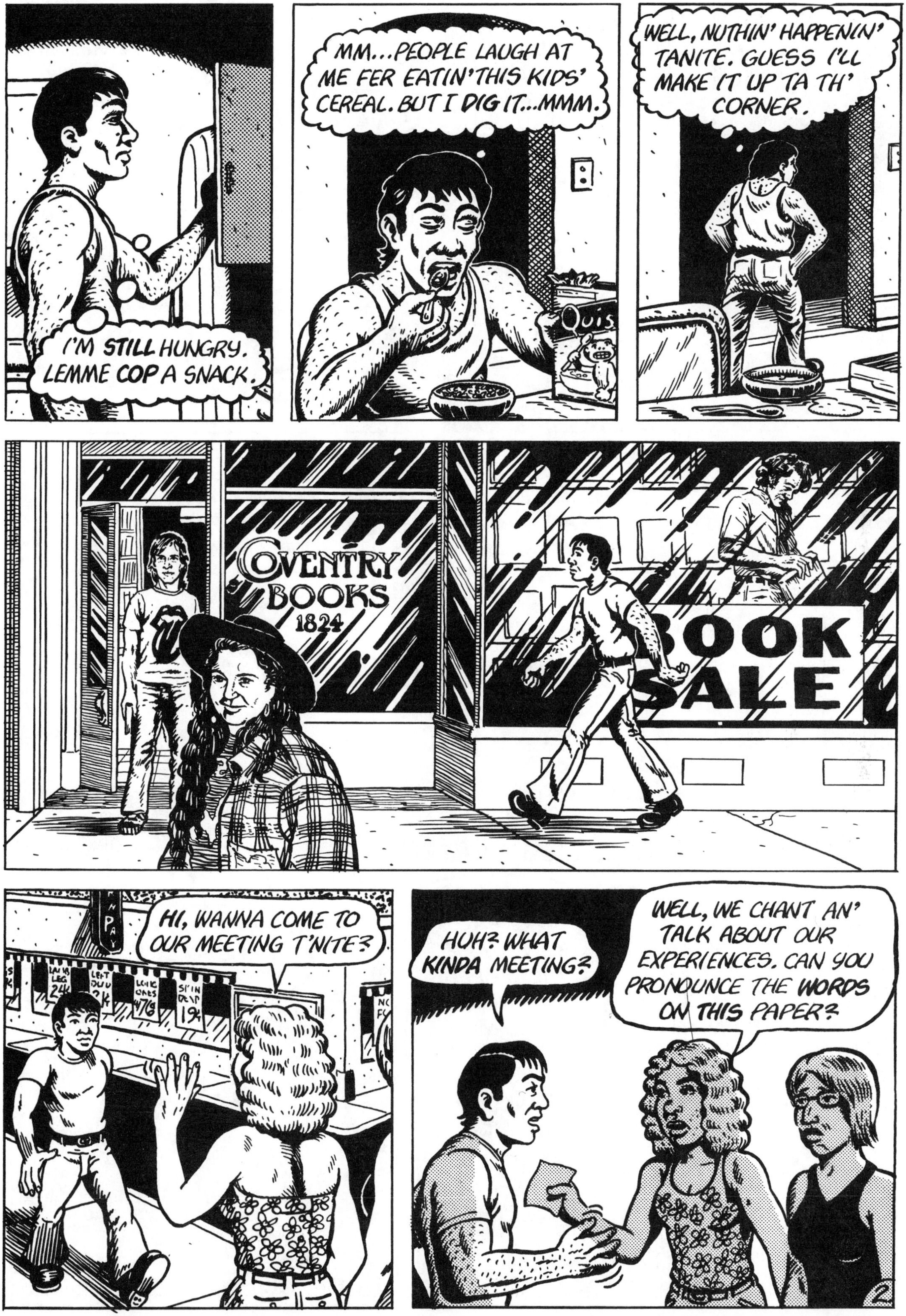
I'M STILL HUNGRY. LEMME COP A SNACK.
MM...PEOPLE LAUGH AT ME FER EATIN' THIS KIDS' CEREAL. BUT I DIG IT...MMM.
Quis
WELL, NUTHIN' HAPPENIN' TANITE. GUESS I'LL MAKE IT UP TA TH' CORNER.
COVENTRY BOOKS 1824
BOOK SALE
HI, WANNA COME TO OUR MEETING T'NITE?
HUH? WHAT KINDA MEETING?
WELL, WE CHANT AN' TALK ABOUT OUR EXPERIENCES. CAN YOU PRONOUNCE THE WORDS ON THIS PAPER?

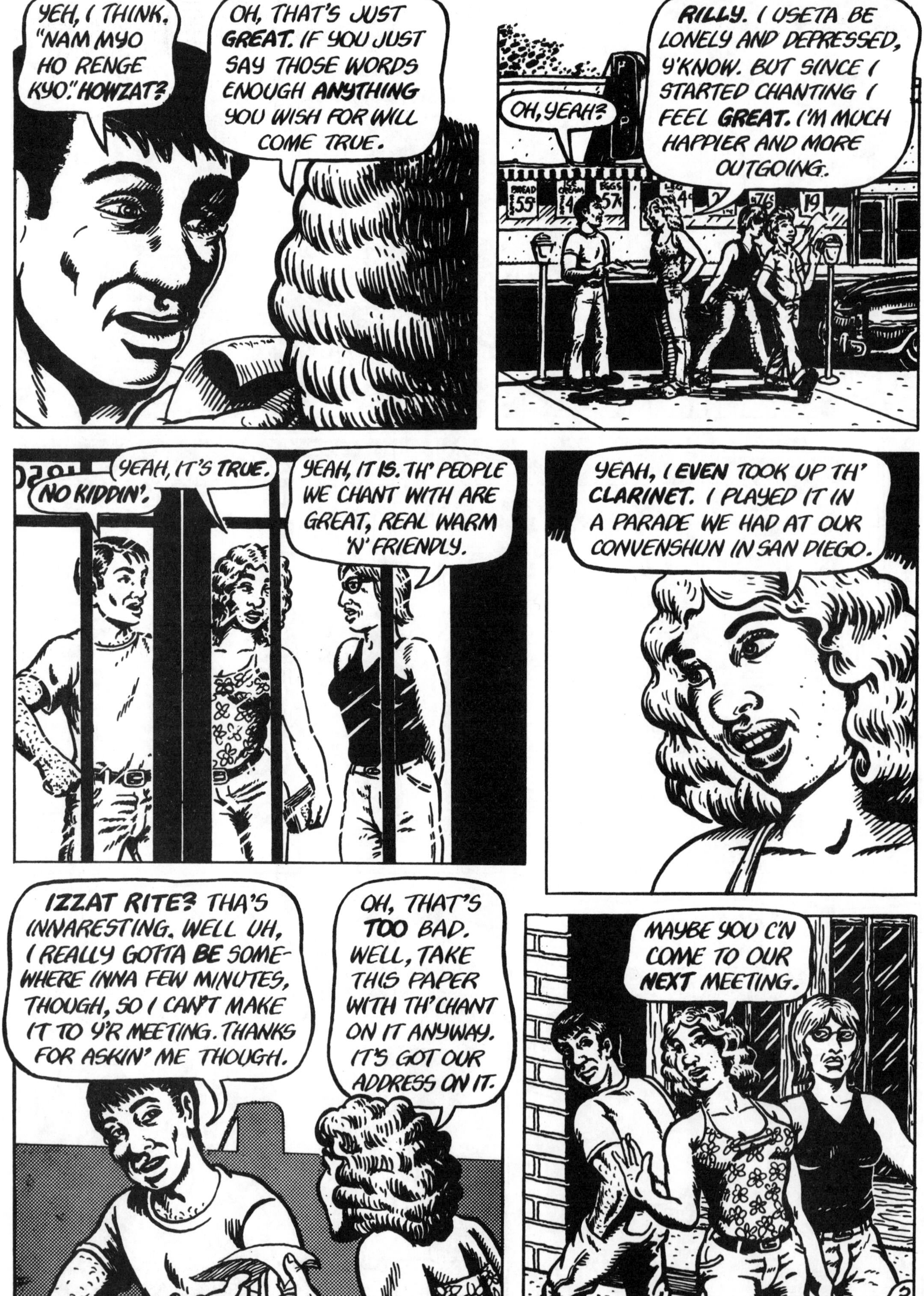

YEH, I THINK. "NAM MYO HO RENGE KYO." HOWZAT?
OH, THAT'S JUST GREAT. IF YOU JUST SAY THOSE WORDS ENOUGH ANYTHING YOU WISH FOR WILL COME TRUE.
OH, YEAH?
RILLY. I USETA BE LONELY AND DEPRESSED, Y'KNOW. BUT SINCE I STARTED CHANTING I FEEL GREAT. I'M MUCH HAPPIER AND MORE OUTGOING.
BREAD 55¢
EGGS 57¢
NO KIDDIN'.
YEAH, IT'S TRUE.
YEAH, IT IS. TH' PEOPLE WE CHANT WITH ARE GREAT, REAL WARM 'N' FRIENDLY.
YEAH, I EVEN TOOK UP TH' CLARINET. I PLAYED IT IN A PARADE WE HAD AT OUR CONVENSHUN IN SAN DIEGO.
IZZAT RITE? THA'S INNARESTING. WELL UH, I REALLY GOTTA BE SOMEWHERE INNA FEW MINUTES, THOUGH, SO I CAN'T MAKE IT TO Y'R MEETING. THANKS FOR ASKIN' ME THOUGH.
OH, THAT'S TOO BAD. WELL, TAKE THIS PAPER WITH TH' CHANT ON IT ANYWAY. IT'S GOT OUR ADDRESS ON IT.
MAYBE YOU C'N COME TO OUR NEXT MEETING.

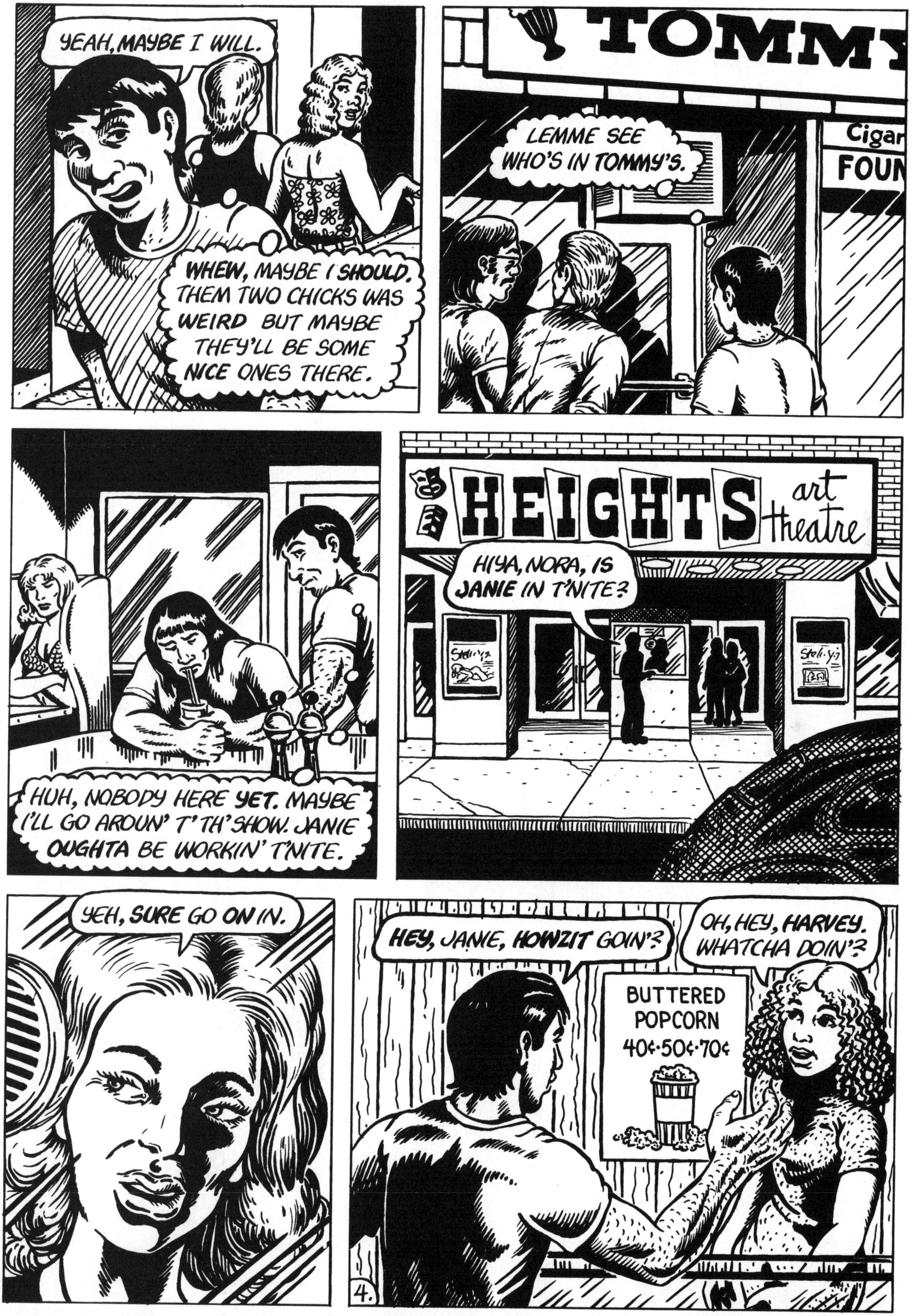
YEAH, MAYBE I WILL.
WHEW, MAYBE I SHOULD. THEM TWO CHICKS WAS WEIRD BUT MAYBE THEY'LL BE SOME NICE ONES THERE.
TOMMY
Cigar
FOUN
LEMME SEE WHO'S IN TOMMY'S.
HUH, NOBODY HERE YET. MAYBE I'LL GO AROUN' T' TH' SHOW. JANIE OUGHTA BE WORKIN' T'NITE.
HEIGHTS art theatre
HIYA, NORA, IS JANIE IN T'NITE?
YEH, SURE GO ON IN.
HEY, JANIE, HOWZIT GOIN'?
OH, HEY, HARVEY. WHATCHA DOIN'?
BUTTERED POPCORN 40¢·50¢·70¢
4.

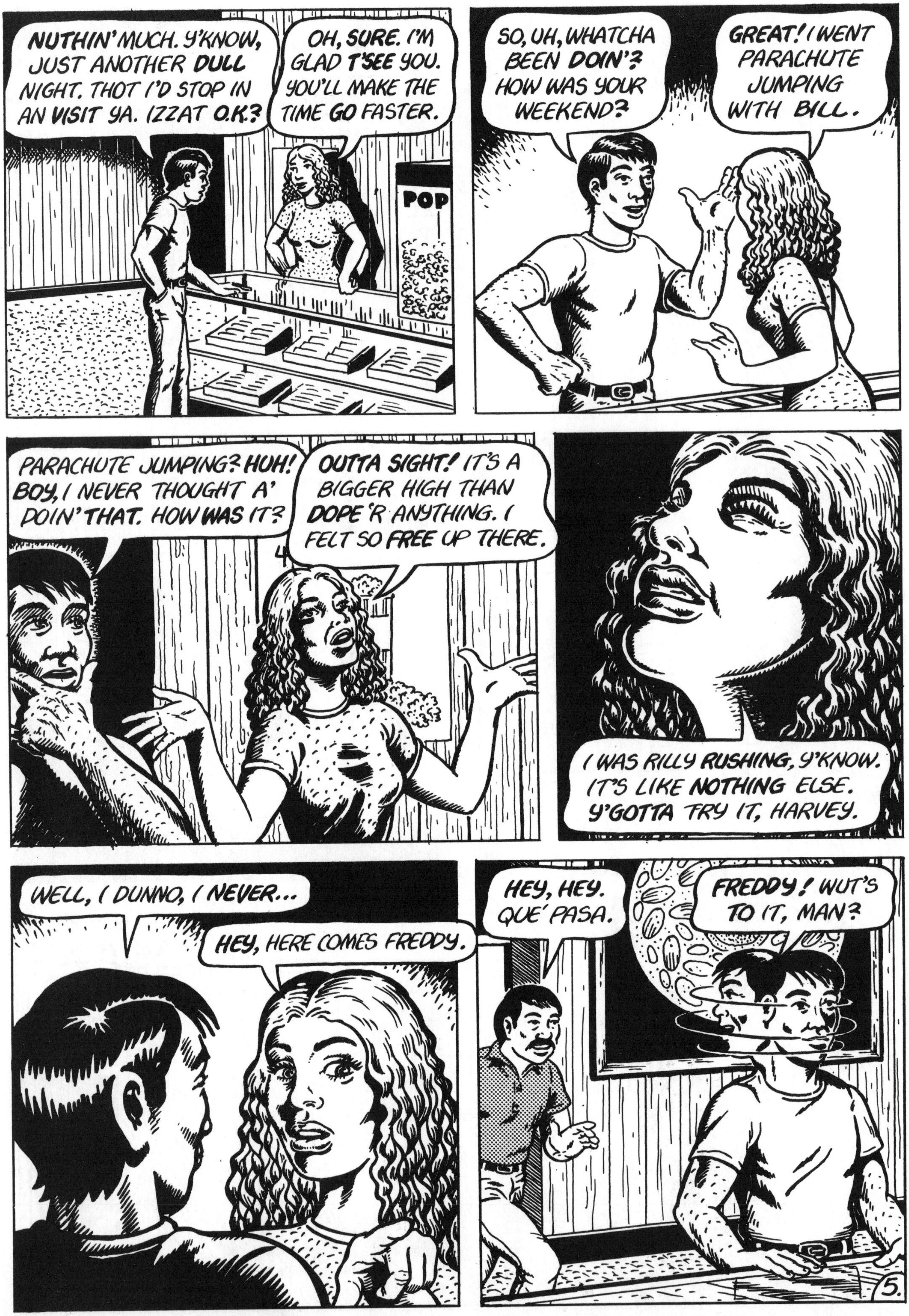
NUTHIN' MUCH. Y'KNOW, JUST ANOTHER DULL NIGHT. THOT I'D STOP IN AN VISIT YA. IZZAT O.K.?
OH, SURE. I'M GLAD T'SEE YOU. YOU'LL MAKE THE TIME GO FASTER.
POP
SO, UH, WHATCHA BEEN DOIN'? HOW WAS YOUR WEEKEND?
GREAT! I WENT PARACHUTE JUMPING WITH BILL.
PARACHUTE JUMPING? HUH! BOY, I NEVER THOUGHT A' DOIN' THAT. HOW WAS IT?
OUTTA SIGHT! IT'S A BIGGER HIGH THAN DOPE 'R ANYTHING. I FELT SO FREE UP THERE.
I WAS RILLY RUSHING, Y'KNOW. IT'S LIKE NOTHING ELSE. Y'GOTTA TRY IT, HARVEY.
WELL, I DUNNO, I NEVER...
HEY, HERE COMES FREDDY.
HEY, HEY. QUE' PASA.
FREDDY! WUT'S TO IT, MAN?

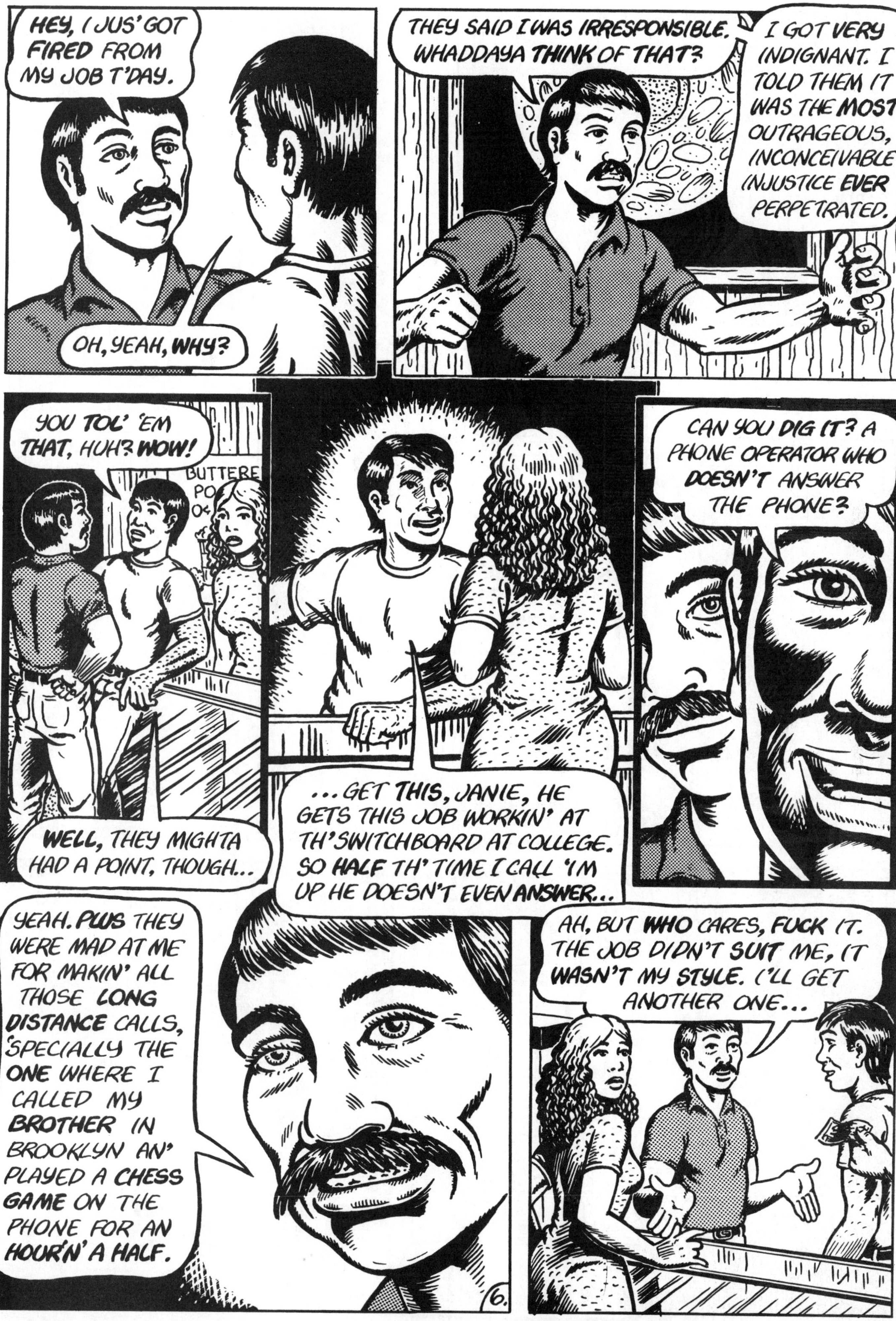
HEY, I JUS' GOT FIRED FROM MY JOB T'DAY.
OH, YEAH, WHY?
THEY SAID I WAS IRRESPONSIBLE. WHADDAYA THINK OF THAT?
I GOT VERY INDIGNANT. I TOLD THEM IT WAS THE MOST OUTRAGEOUS, INCONCEIVABLE INJUSTICE EVER PERPETRATED.
YOU TOL' 'EM THAT, HUH? WOW!
BUTTERE PO
WELL, THEY MIGHTA HAD A POINT, THOUGH...
...GET THIS, JANIE, HE GETS THIS JOB WORKIN' AT TH' SWITCHBOARD AT COLLEGE. SO HALF TH' TIME I CALL 'IM UP HE DOESN'T EVEN ANSWER...
CAN YOU DIG IT? A PHONE OPERATOR WHO DOESN'T ANSWER THE PHONE?
YEAH. PLUS THEY WERE MAD AT ME FOR MAKIN' ALL THOSE LONG DISTANCE CALLS, 'SPECIALLY THE ONE WHERE I CALLED MY BROTHER IN BROOKLYN AN' PLAYED A CHESS GAME ON THE PHONE FOR AN HOUR'N' A HALF.
6.
AH, BUT WHO CARES, FUCK IT. THE JOB DIDN'T SUIT ME, IT WASN'T MY STYLE. I'LL GET ANOTHER ONE...

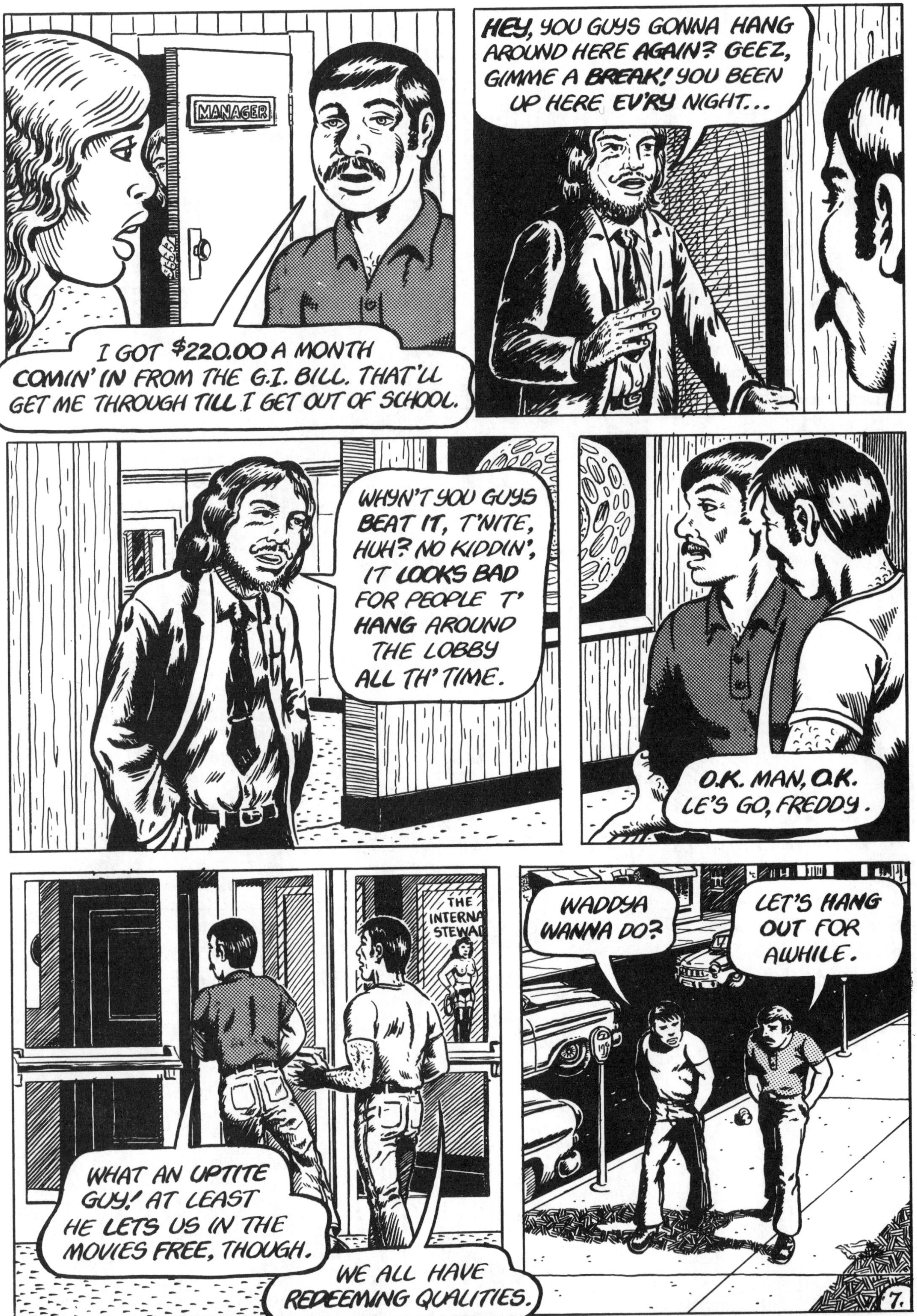
MANAGER
I GOT $220.00 A MONTH COMIN' IN FROM THE G.I. BILL. THAT'LL GET ME THROUGH TILL I GET OUT OF SCHOOL.
HEY, YOU GUYS GONNA HANG AROUND HERE AGAIN? GEEZ, GIMME A BREAK! YOU BEEN UP HERE EV'RY NIGHT...
WHYN'T YOU GUYS BEAT IT, T'NITE, HUH? NO KIDDIN', IT LOOKS BAD FOR PEOPLE T' HANG AROUND THE LOBBY ALL TH' TIME.
O.K. MAN, O.K. LE'S GO, FREDDY.
THE INTERNA STEWA
WHAT AN UPTITE GUY! AT LEAST HE LETS US IN THE MOVIES FREE, THOUGH.
WE ALL HAVE REDEEMING QUALITIES.
WADDYA WANNA DO?
LET'S HANG OUT FOR AWHILE.
7.

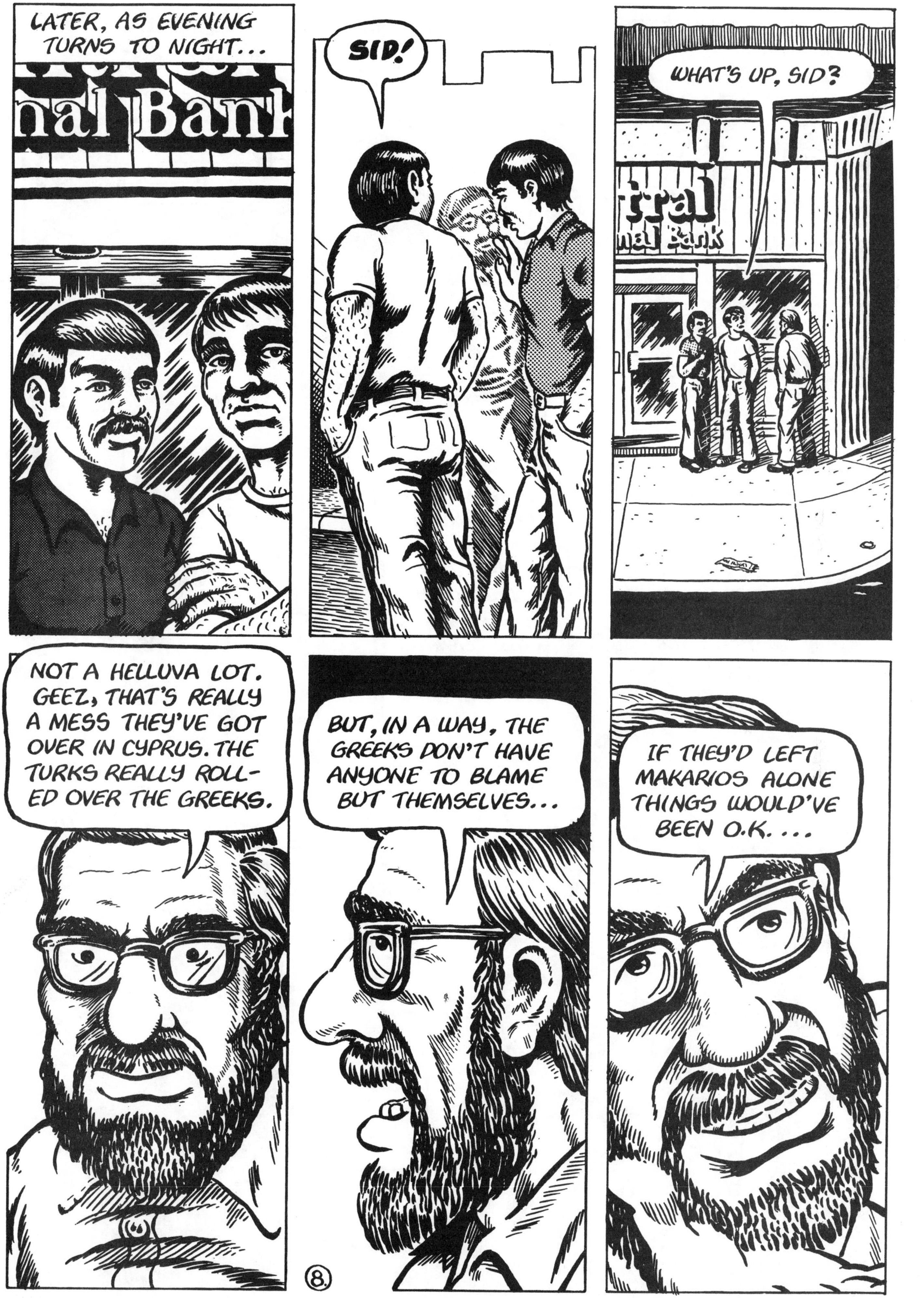
LATER, AS EVENING TURNS TO NIGHT...
nal Bank
SID!
tral
nal Bank
WHAT'S UP, SID?
NOT A HELLUVA LOT. GEEZ, THAT'S REALLY A MESS THEY'VE GOT OVER IN CYPRUS. THE TURKS REALLY ROLL-ED OVER THE GREEKS.
BUT, IN A WAY, THE GREEKS DON'T HAVE ANYONE TO BLAME BUT THEMSELVES...
IF THEY'D LEFT MAKARIOS ALONE THINGS WOULD'VE BEEN O.K. ...

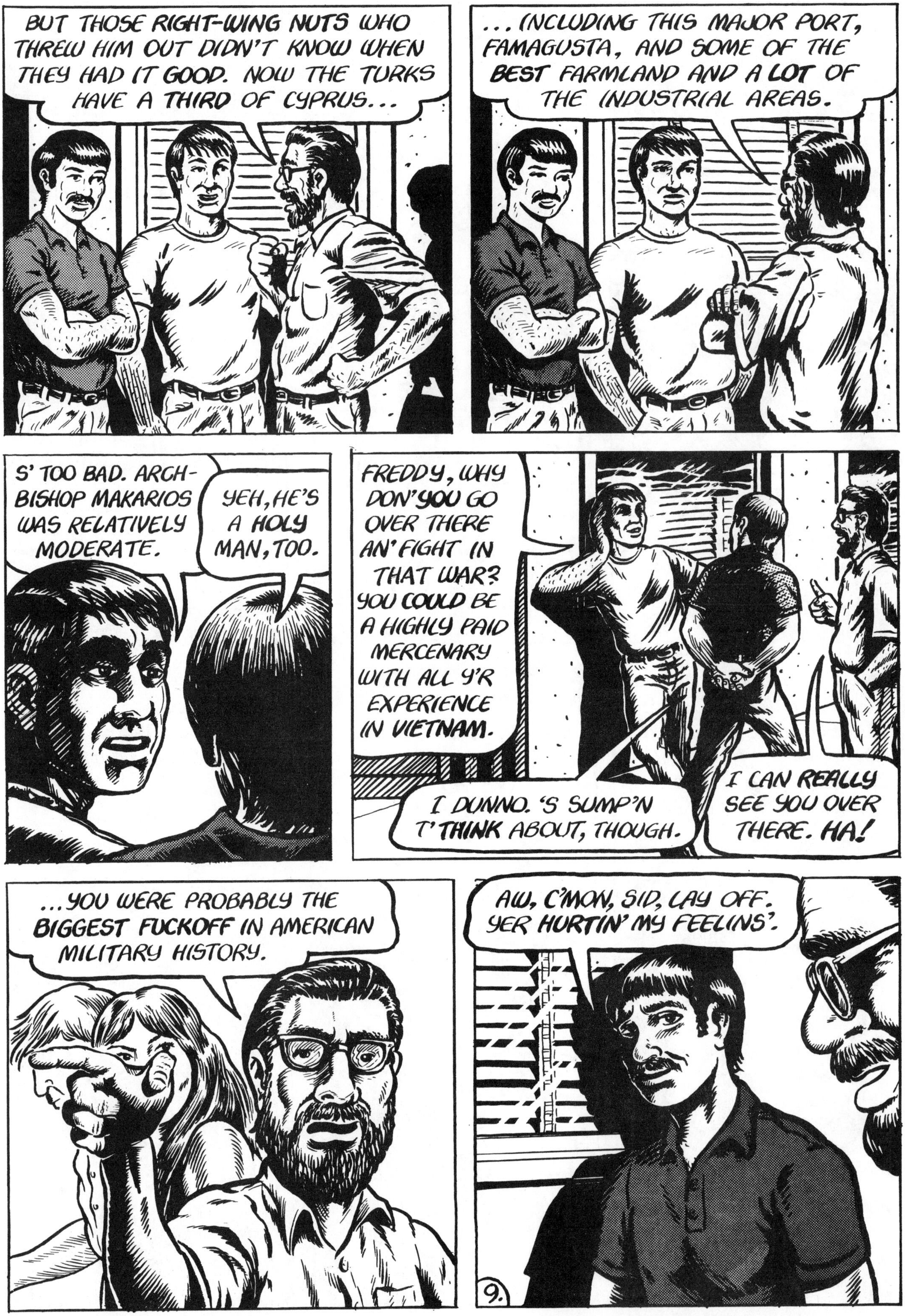
BUT THOSE RIGHT-WING NUTS WHO THREW HIM OUT DIDN'T KNOW WHEN THEY HAD IT GOOD. NOW THE TURKS HAVE A THIRD OF CYPRUS...
...INCLUDING THIS MAJOR PORT, FAMAGUSTA, AND SOME OF THE BEST FARMLAND AND A LOT OF THE INDUSTRIAL AREAS.
S' TOO BAD. ARCH-BISHOP MAKARIOS WAS RELATIVELY MODERATE.
YEH, HE'S A HOLY MAN, TOO.
FREDDY, WHY DON' YOU GO OVER THERE AN' FIGHT IN THAT WAR? YOU COULD BE A HIGHLY PAID MERCENARY WITH ALL Y'R EXPERIENCE IN VIETNAM.
I DUNNO. 'S SUMP'N T' THINK ABOUT, THOUGH.
I CAN REALLY SEE YOU OVER THERE. HA!
...YOU WERE PROBABLY THE BIGGEST FUCKOFF IN AMERICAN MILITARY HISTORY.
AW, C'MON, SID, LAY OFF. YER HURTIN' MY FEELINS'.
9.

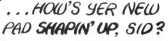

...HOW'S YER NEW PAD SHAPIN' UP, SID?

PRETTY GOOD. HEY, THAT REMINDS ME, WILL YOU GUYS GIMME A HAND MOVING A COUPLE CHAIRS AND A RUG...

I STILL HAVEN'T GOTTEN OVER THIS DETACHED RETINA THING. TH' DOCTOR DOESN'T EVEN WANT ME WALKING AROUND, LET ALONE MOVING FURNITURE.

SURE, 'S O.K WITH ME.

WHERE'S TH' STUFF AT?

IT'S OVER ON WALTER'S FRONT PORCH I SAW HIM AT IRV'S THE OTHER NIGHT AND HE SAID HE WAS GETTING RID OF THEM, SO I ASKED IF I COULD HAVE 'EM AND HE SAID "SURE".

C'MON, I'LL DRIVE US OVER TO WALTER'S.

10.

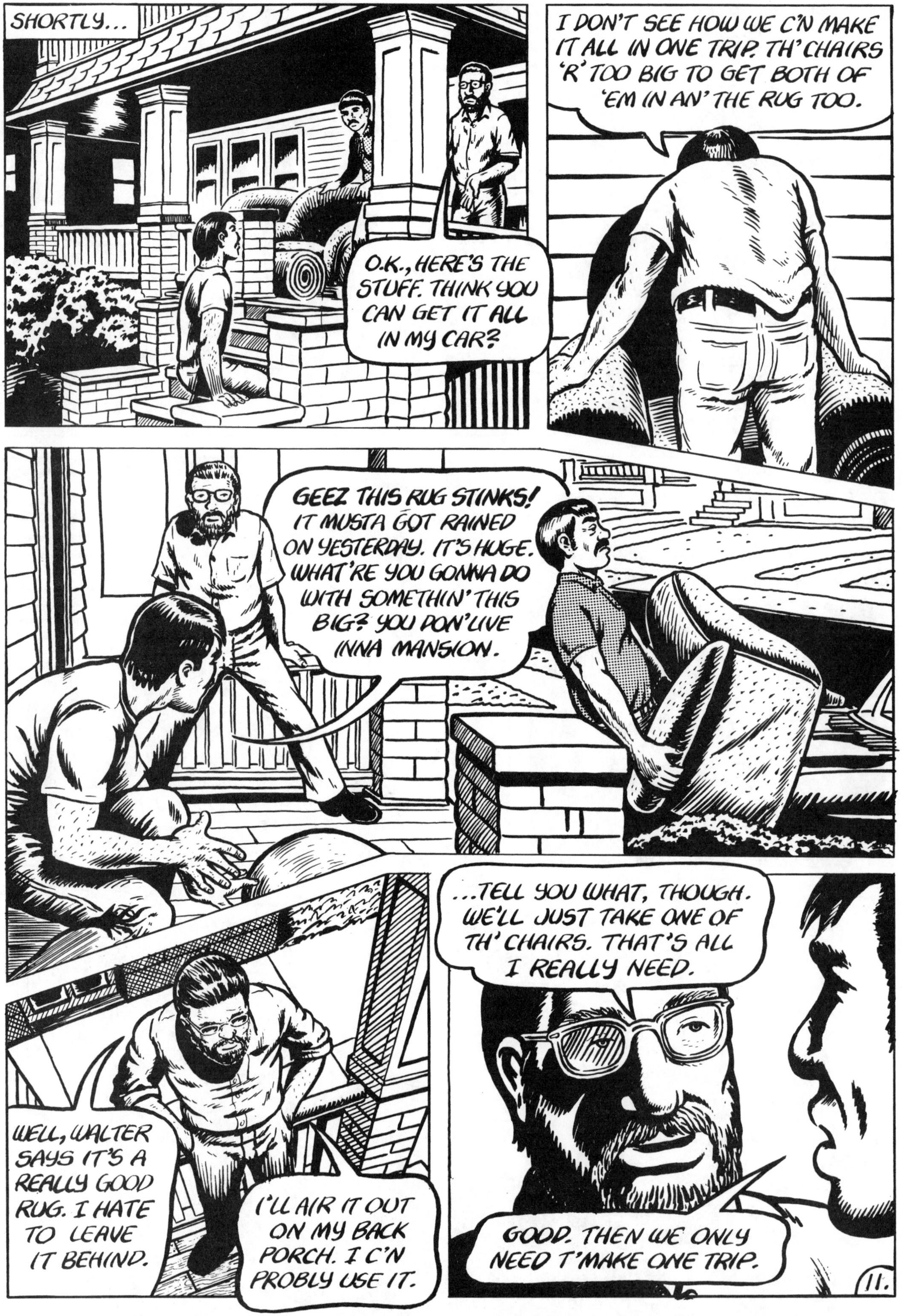
SHORTLY...
O.K., HERE'S THE STUFF. THINK YOU CAN GET IT ALL IN MY CAR?
I DON'T SEE HOW WE C'N MAKE IT ALL IN ONE TRIP. TH' CHAIRS 'R' TOO BIG TO GET BOTH OF 'EM IN AN' THE RUG TOO.
GEEZ THIS RUG STINKS! IT MUSTA GOT RAINED ON YESTERDAY. IT'S HUGE. WHAT'RE YOU GONNA DO WITH SOMETHIN' THIS BIG? YOU DON'LIVE INNA MANSION.
WELL, WALTER SAYS IT'S A REALLY GOOD RUG. I HATE TO LEAVE IT BEHIND.
I'LL AIR IT OUT ON MY BACK PORCH. I C'N PROBLY USE IT.
...TELL YOU WHAT, THOUGH. WE'LL JUST TAKE ONE OF TH' CHAIRS. THAT'S ALL I REALLY NEED.
GOOD. THEN WE ONLY NEED T'MAKE ONE TRIP.
11.

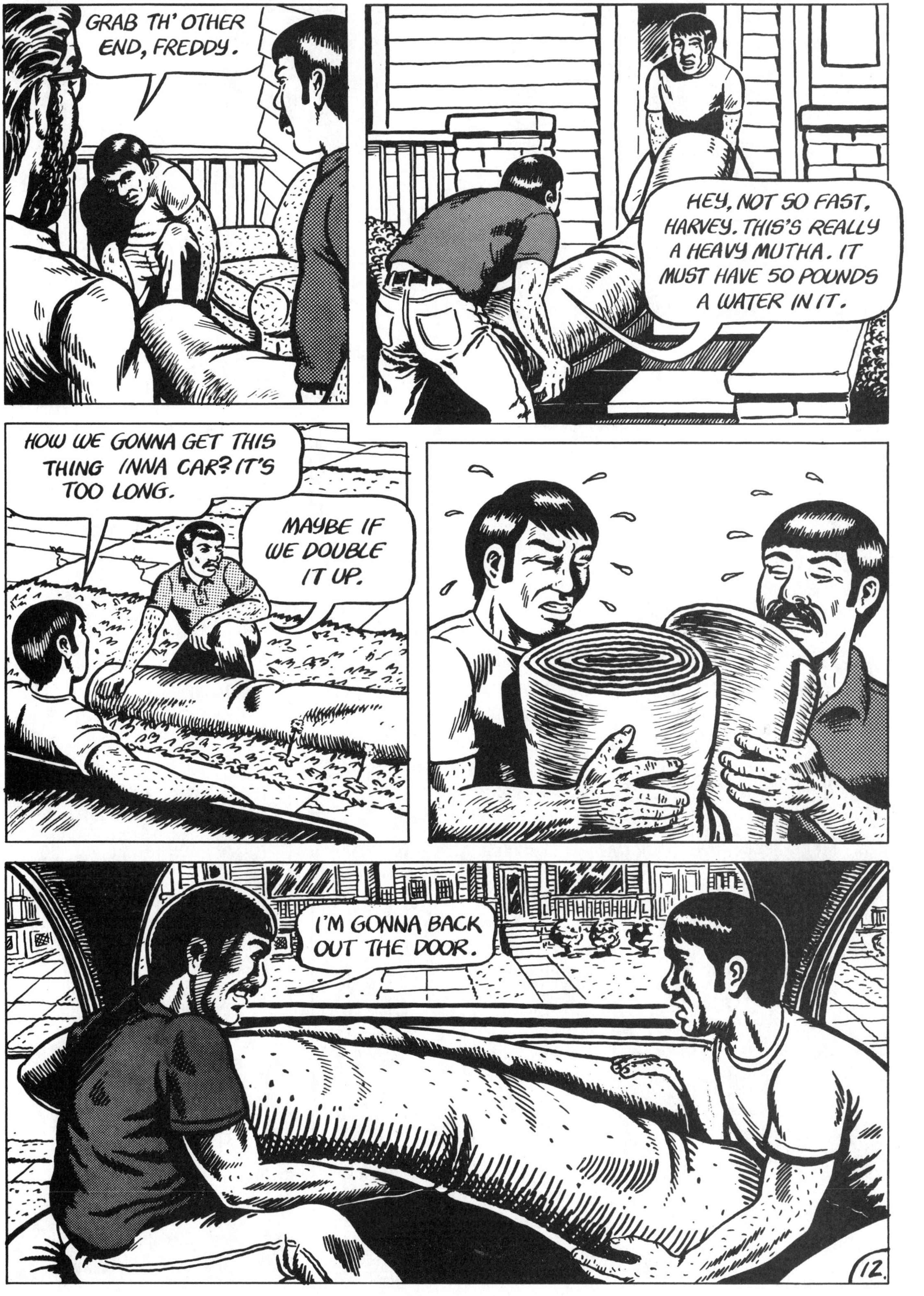
GRAB TH' OTHER END, FREDDY.
HEY, NOT SO FAST, HARVEY. THIS'S REALLY A HEAVY MUTHA. IT MUST HAVE 50 POUNDS A WATER IN IT.
HOW WE GONNA GET THIS THING INNA CAR? IT'S TOO LONG.
MAYBE IF WE DOUBLE IT UP.
I'M GONNA BACK OUT THE DOOR.
12.

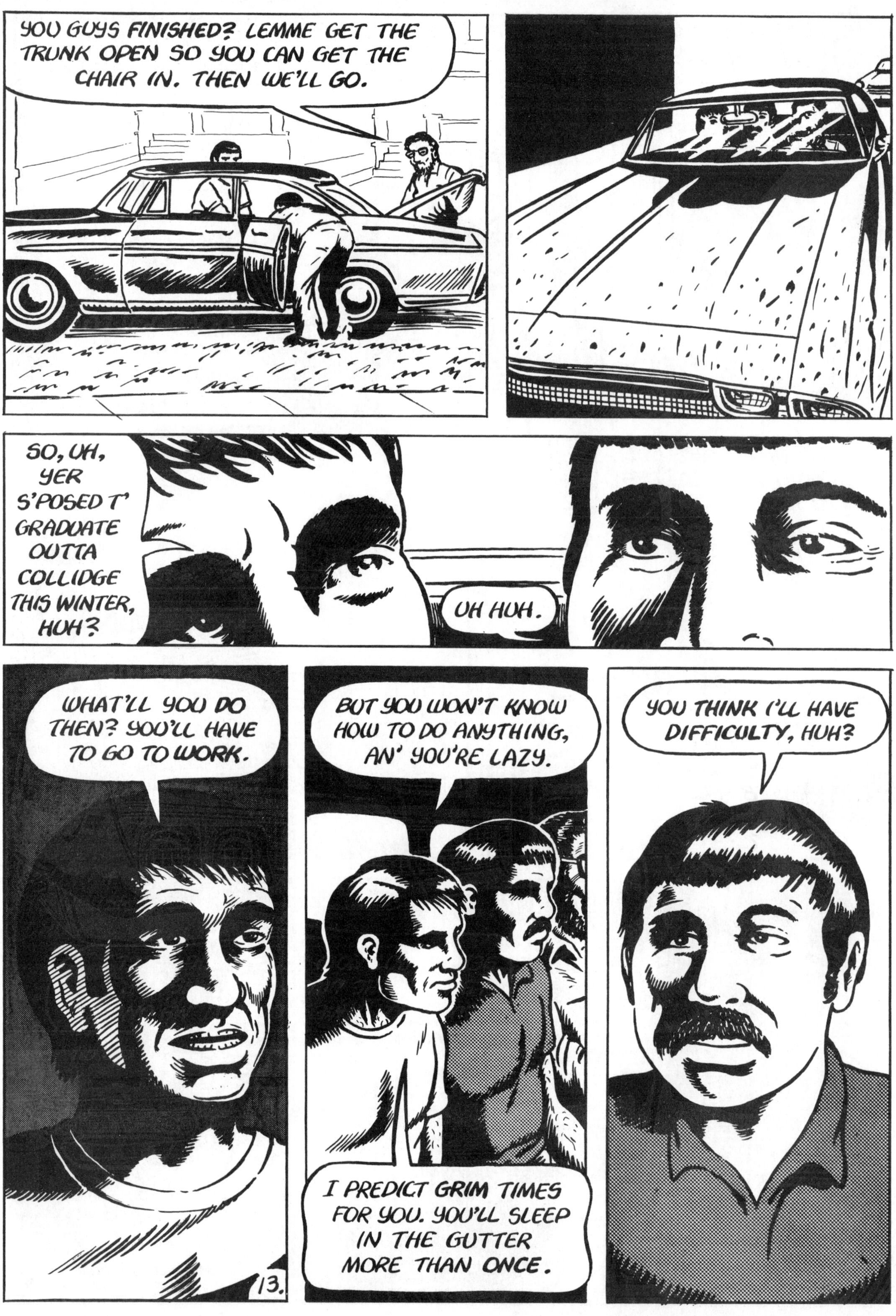
YOU GUYS FINISHED? LEMME GET THE TRUNK OPEN SO YOU CAN GET THE CHAIR IN. THEN WE'LL GO.
SO, UH, YER S'POSED T' GRADUATE OUTTA COLLIDGE THIS WINTER, HUH?
UH HUH.
WHAT'LL YOU DO THEN? YOU'LL HAVE TO GO TO WORK.
BUT YOU WON'T KNOW HOW TO DO ANYTHING, AN' YOU'RE LAZY.
I PREDICT GRIM TIMES FOR YOU. YOU'LL SLEEP IN THE GUTTER MORE THAN ONCE.
YOU THINK I'LL HAVE DIFFICULTY, HUH?
13.

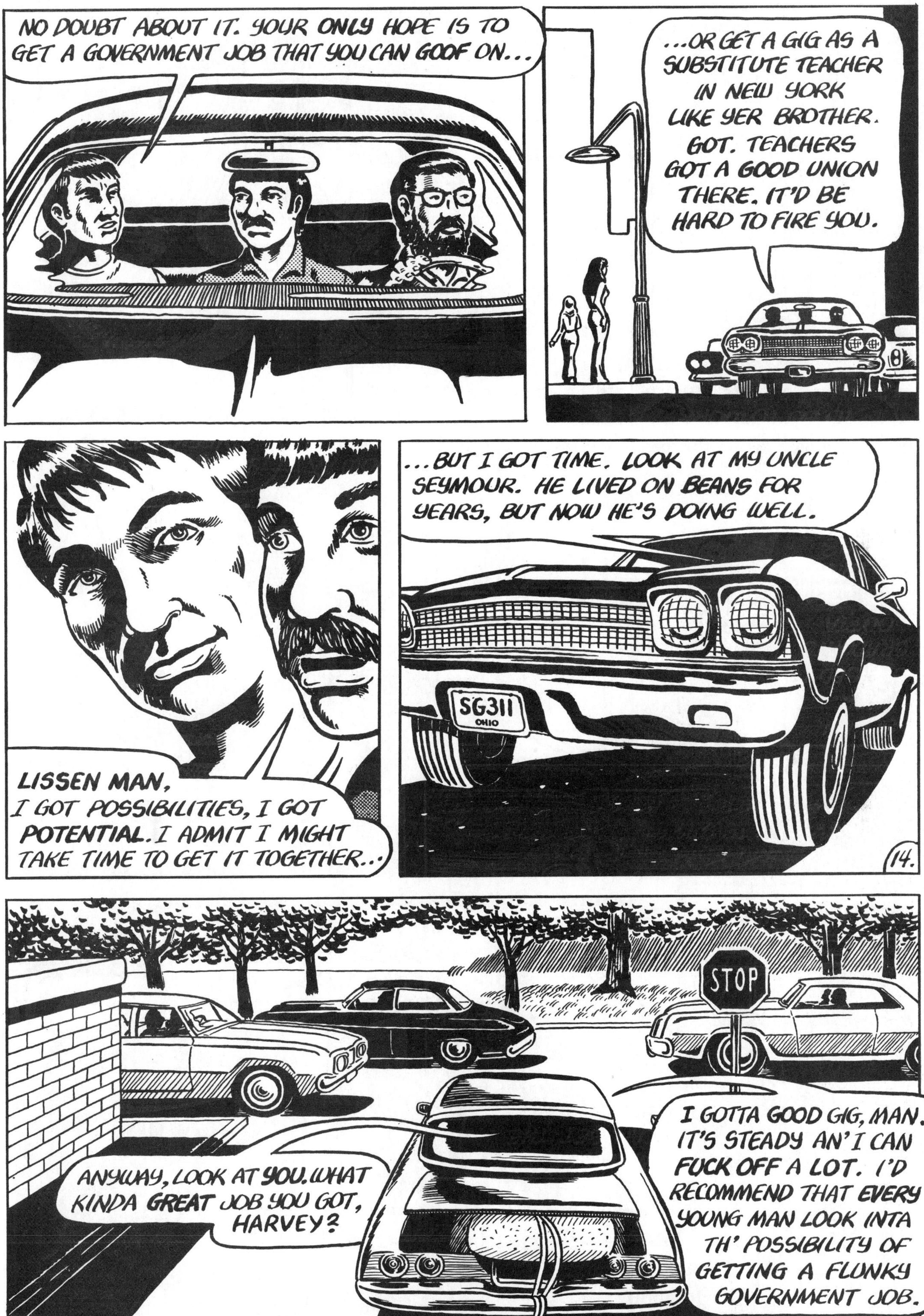
NO DOUBT ABOUT IT. YOUR ONLY HOPE IS TO GET A GOVERNMENT JOB THAT YOU CAN GOOF ON...
...OR GET A GIG AS A SUBSTITUTE TEACHER IN NEW YORK LIKE YER BROTHER. GOT. TEACHERS GOT A GOOD UNION THERE. IT'D BE HARD TO FIRE YOU.
LISSEN MAN, I GOT POSSIBILITIES, I GOT POTENTIAL. I ADMIT I MIGHT TAKE TIME TO GET IT TOGETHER...
...BUT I GOT TIME. LOOK AT MY UNCLE SEYMOUR. HE LIVED ON BEANS FOR YEARS, BUT NOW HE'S DOING WELL.
SG311
OHIO
14.
STOP
ANYWAY, LOOK AT YOU. WHAT KINDA GREAT JOB YOU GOT, HARVEY?
I GOTTA GOOD GIG, MAN. IT'S STEADY AN' I CAN FUCK OFF A LOT. I'D RECOMMEND THAT EVERY YOUNG MAN LOOK INTA TH' POSSIBILITY OF GETTING A FLUNKY GOVERNMENT JOB.

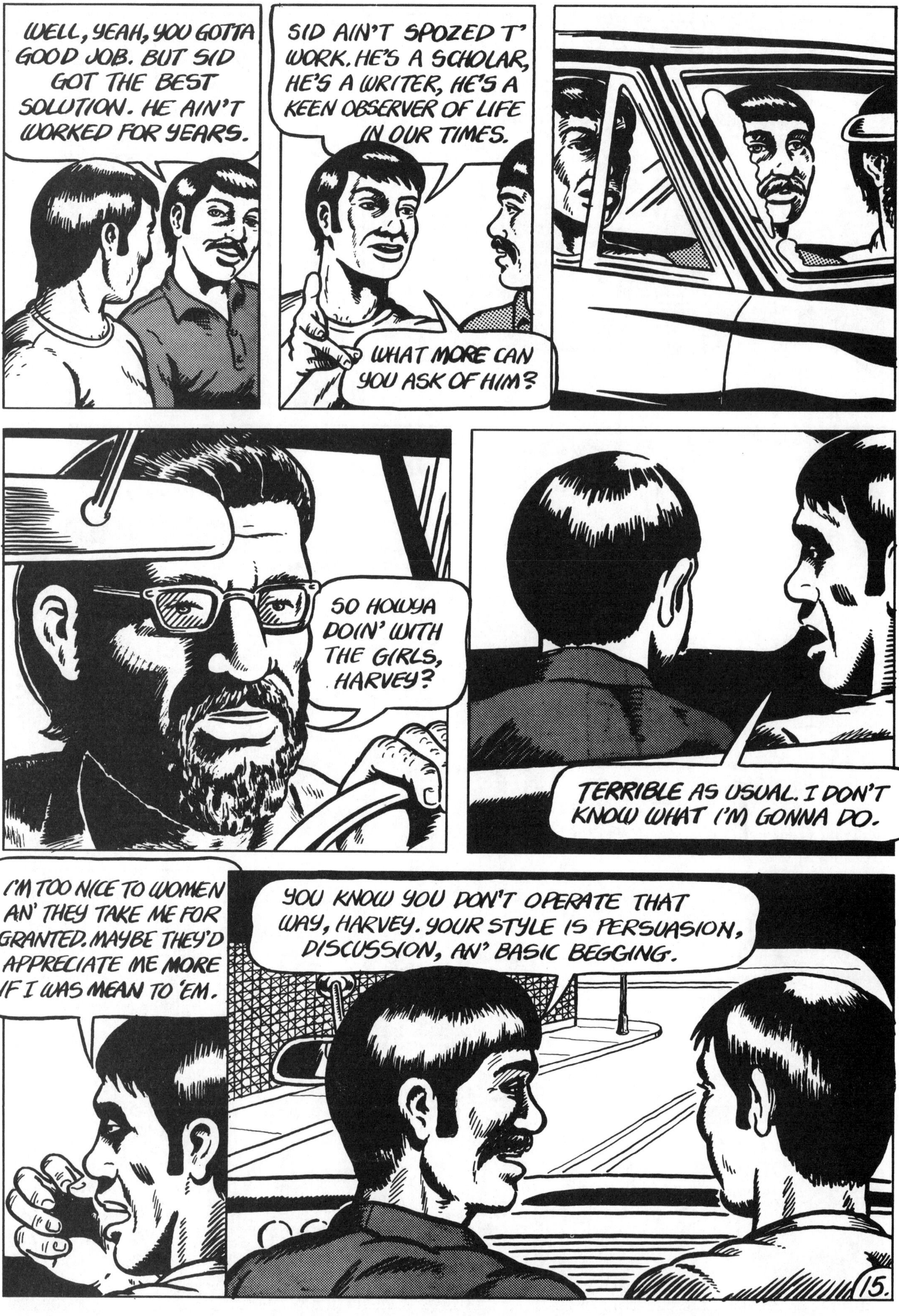
WELL, YEAH, YOU GOTTA GOOD JOB. BUT SID GOT THE BEST SOLUTION. HE AIN'T WORKED FOR YEARS.
SID AIN'T SPOZED T' WORK. HE'S A SCHOLAR, HE'S A WRITER, HE'S A KEEN OBSERVER OF LIFE IN OUR TIMES.
WHAT MORE CAN YOU ASK OF HIM?
SO HOWYA DOIN' WITH THE GIRLS, HARVEY?
TERRIBLE AS USUAL. I DON'T KNOW WHAT I'M GONNA DO.
I'M TOO NICE TO WOMEN AN' THEY TAKE ME FOR GRANTED. MAYBE THEY'D APPRECIATE ME MORE IF I WAS MEAN TO 'EM.
YOU KNOW YOU DON'T OPERATE THAT WAY, HARVEY. YOUR STYLE IS PERSUASION, DISCUSSION, AN' BASIC BEGGING.
15.

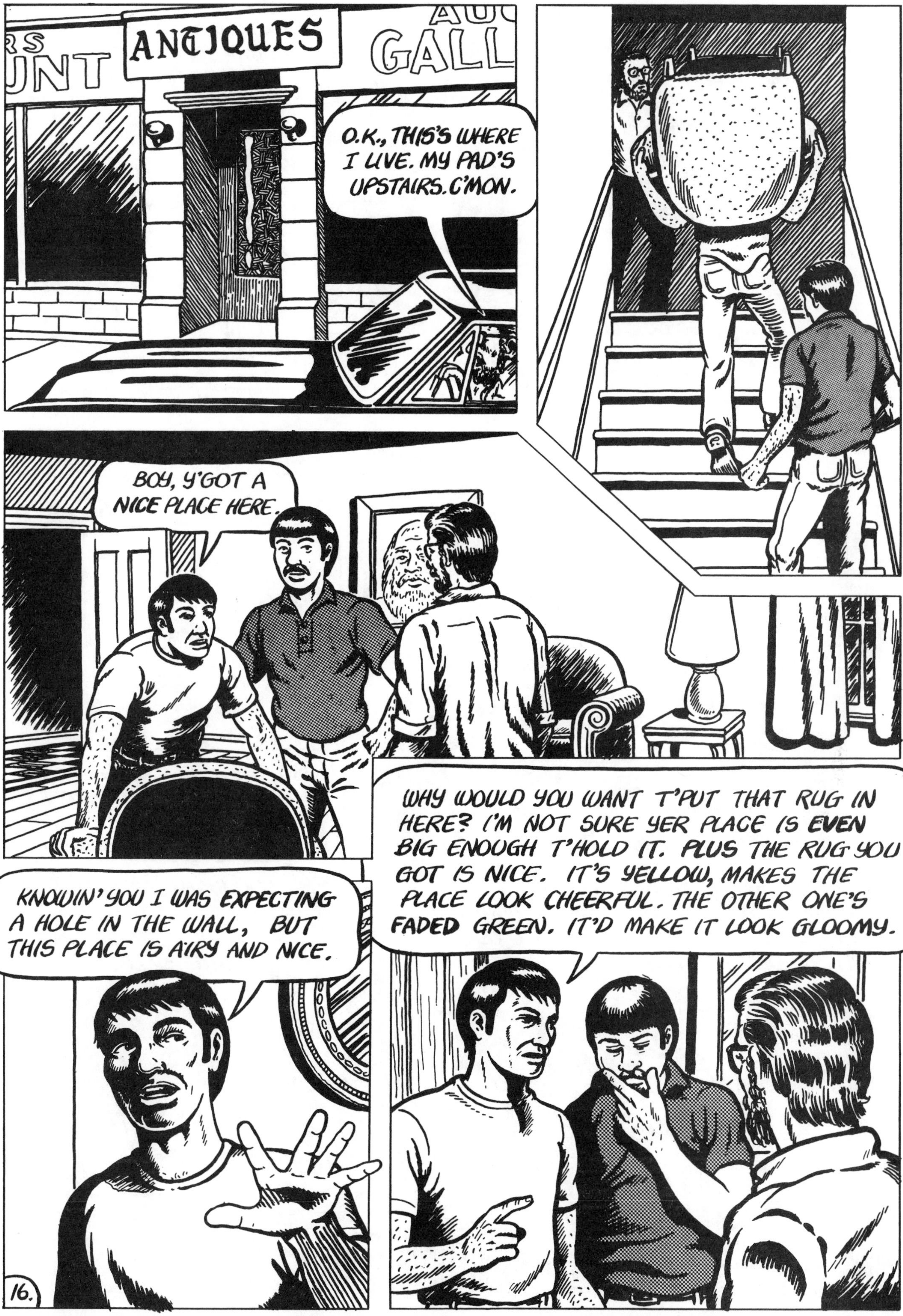
ANTIQUES
GALL
O.K., THIS'S WHERE I LIVE. MY PAD'S UPSTAIRS. C'MON.
BOY, Y'GOT A NICE PLACE HERE.
WHY WOULD YOU WANT T'PUT THAT RUG IN HERE? I'M NOT SURE YER PLACE IS EVEN BIG ENOUGH T'HOLD IT. PLUS THE RUG YOU GOT IS NICE. IT'S YELLOW, MAKES THE PLACE LOOK CHEERFUL. THE OTHER ONE'S FADED GREEN. IT'D MAKE IT LOOK GLOOMY.
KNOWIN' YOU I WAS EXPECTING A HOLE IN THE WALL, BUT THIS PLACE IS AIRY AND NICE.

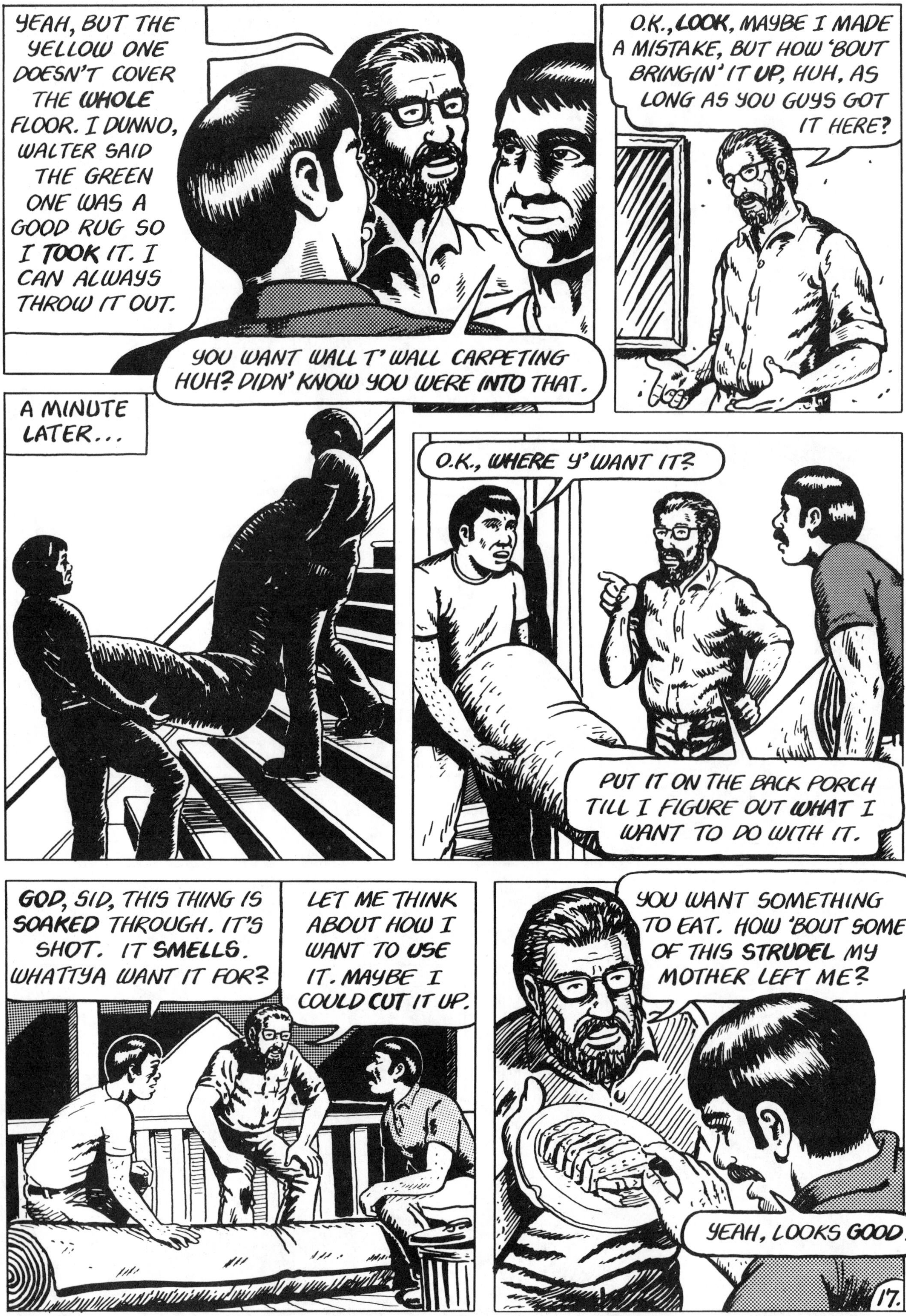
YEAH, BUT THE YELLOW ONE DOESN'T COVER THE WHOLE FLOOR. I DUNNO, WALTER SAID THE GREEN ONE WAS A GOOD RUG SO I TOOK IT. I CAN ALWAYS THROW IT OUT.
YOU WANT WALL T' WALL CARPETING HUH? DIDN' KNOW YOU WERE INTO THAT.
O.K., LOOK, MAYBE I MADE A MISTAKE, BUT HOW 'BOUT BRINGIN' IT UP, HUH, AS LONG AS YOU GUYS GOT IT HERE?
A MINUTE LATER...
O.K., WHERE Y' WANT IT?
PUT IT ON THE BACK PORCH TILL I FIGURE OUT WHAT I WANT TO DO WITH IT.
GOD, SID, THIS THING IS SOAKED THROUGH. IT'S SHOT. IT SMELLS. WHATTYA WANT IT FOR?
LET ME THINK ABOUT HOW I WANT TO USE IT. MAYBE I COULD CUT IT UP.
YOU WANT SOMETHING TO EAT. HOW 'BOUT SOME OF THIS STRUDEL MY MOTHER LEFT ME?
YEAH, LOOKS GOOD.
17.

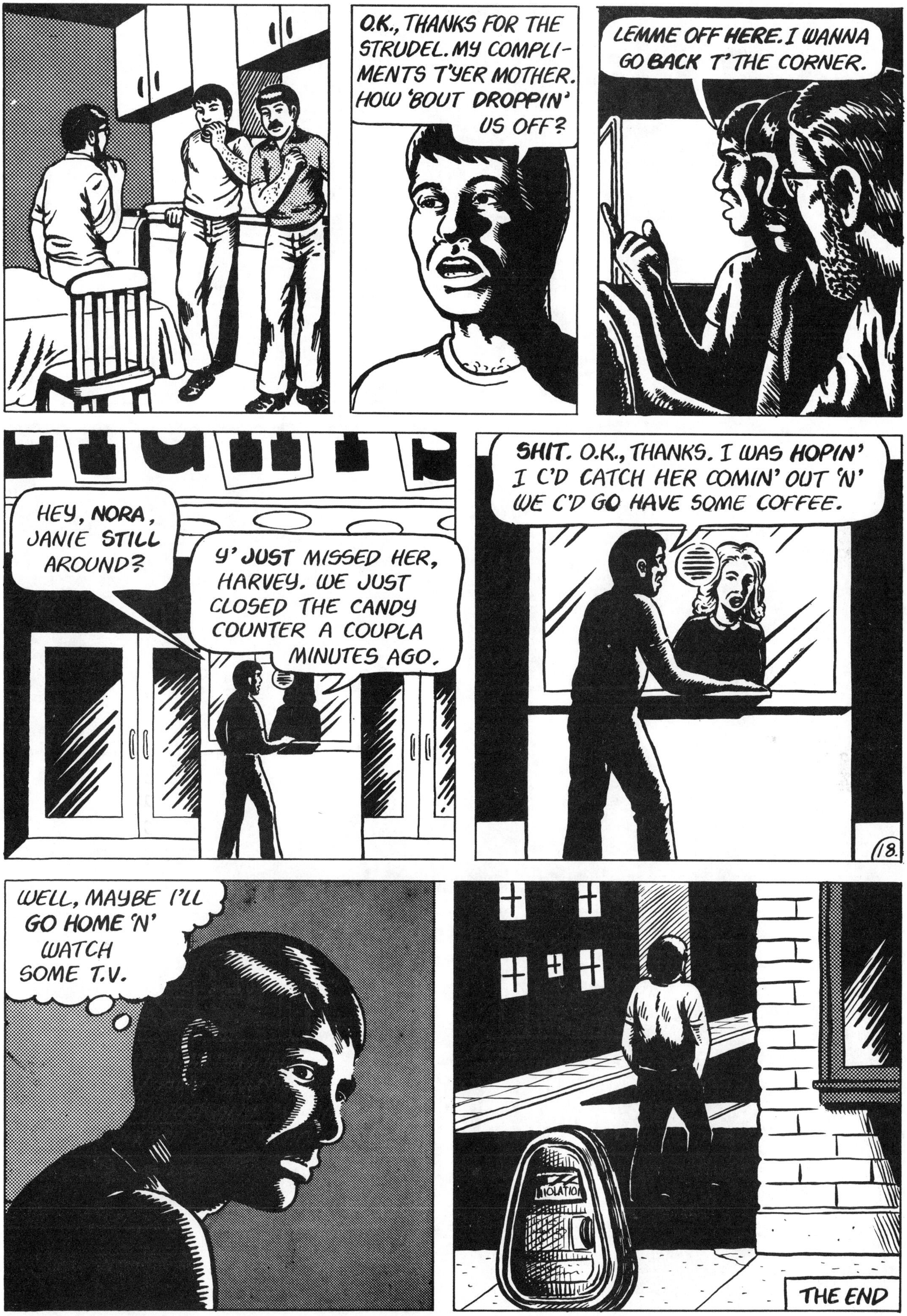
O.K., THANKS FOR THE STRUDEL. MY COMPLIMENTS T'YER MOTHER. HOW 'BOUT DROPPIN' US OFF?
LEMME OFF HERE. I WANNA GO BACK T' THE CORNER.
HEY, NORA, JANIE STILL AROUND?
Y' JUST MISSED HER, HARVEY. WE JUST CLOSED THE CANDY COUNTER A COUPLA MINUTES AGO.
SHIT. O.K., THANKS. I WAS HOPIN' I C'D CATCH HER COMIN' OUT 'N' WE C'D GO HAVE SOME COFFEE.
WELL, MAYBE I'LL GO HOME 'N' WATCH SOME T.V.
VIOLATION
THE END

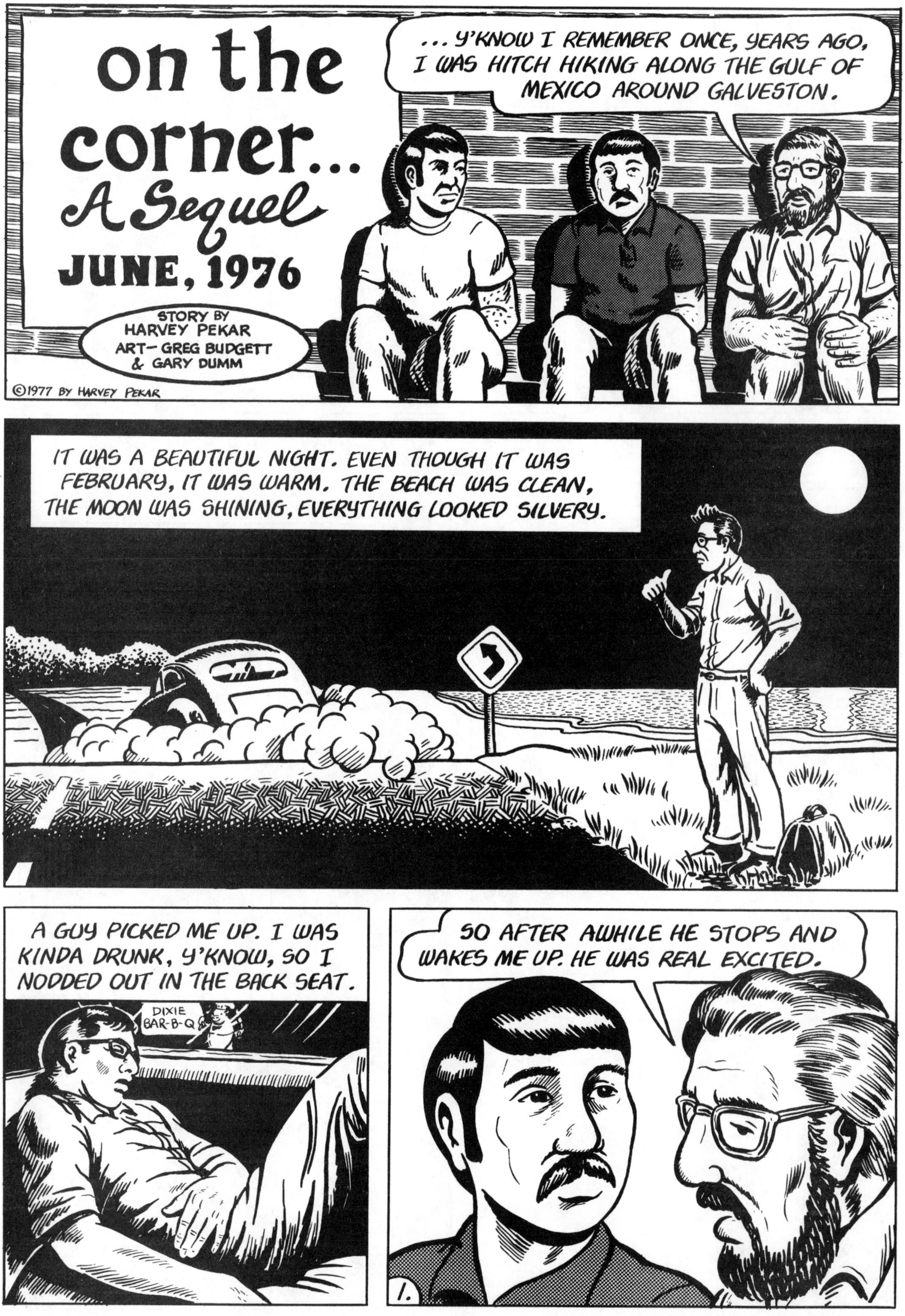
on the corner... A Sequel
JUNE, 1976
STORY BY HARVEY PEKAR
ART— GREG BUDGETT & GARY DUMM
©1977 BY HARVEY PEKAR
...Y'KNOW I REMEMBER ONCE, YEARS AGO, I WAS HITCH HIKING ALONG THE GULF OF MEXICO AROUND GALVESTON.
IT WAS A BEAUTIFUL NIGHT. EVEN THOUGH IT WAS FEBRUARY, IT WAS WARM. THE BEACH WAS CLEAN, THE MOON WAS SHINING, EVERYTHING LOOKED SILVERY.
A GUY PICKED ME UP. I WAS KINDA DRUNK, Y'KNOW, SO I NODDED OUT IN THE BACK SEAT.
DIXIE BAR-B-Q
SO AFTER AWHILE HE STOPS AND WAKES ME UP. HE WAS REAL EXCITED.
1.

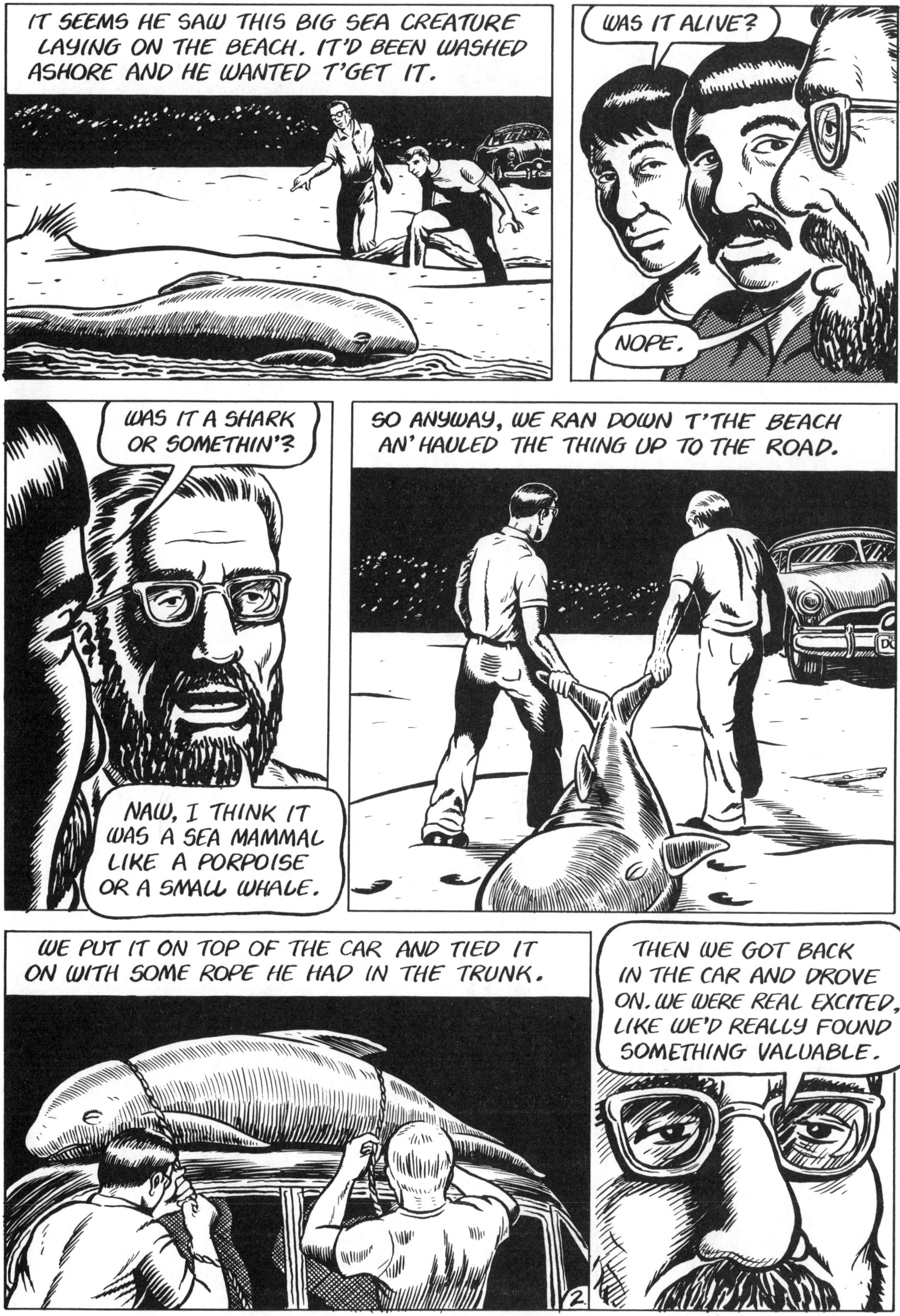
IT SEEMS HE SAW THIS BIG SEA CREATURE LAYING ON THE BEACH. IT'D BEEN WASHED ASHORE AND HE WANTED T'GET IT.
WAS IT ALIVE?
NOPE.
WAS IT A SHARK OR SOMETHIN'?
NAW, I THINK IT WAS A SEA MAMMAL LIKE A PORPOISE OR A SMALL WHALE.
SO ANYWAY, WE RAN DOWN T'THE BEACH AN' HAULED THE THING UP TO THE ROAD.
WE PUT IT ON TOP OF THE CAR AND TIED IT ON WITH SOME ROPE HE HAD IN THE TRUNK.
THEN WE GOT BACK IN THE CAR AND DROVE ON. WE WERE REAL EXCITED, LIKE WE'D REALLY FOUND SOMETHING VALUABLE.
2.

I FELL RIGHT BACK TO SLEEP, BUT ABOUT AN HOUR LATER THE GUY WAKES ME UP AGAIN.

THE THING ON THE CAR WAS STINKING. MAN, IT WAS REEKING. WE COULDN'T BREATHE.

SO WE UNTIED IT AN' DUMPED IT ALONG THE SIDE OF THE ROAD. THEN WE DROVE AWAY WONDERING WHY IN HELL WE'D GOTTEN SO EXCITED BY IT IN THE FIRST PLACE. I WAS DRUNK AND THE WHOLE THING SEEMED LIKE A FANTASY TO ME.

WHATEVER HAPPENED TO THAT RUG?

I HATE T'TELL YOU THIS, BUT I LEFT IT OUT ON THE BACK PORCH FOR A WEEK AND THEN I THREW IT OUT.

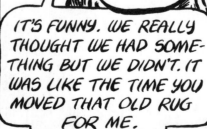

IT'S FUNNY. WE REALLY THOUGHT WE HAD SOMETHING BUT WE DIDN'T. IT WAS LIKE THE TIME YOU MOVED THAT OLD RUG FOR ME.

3.

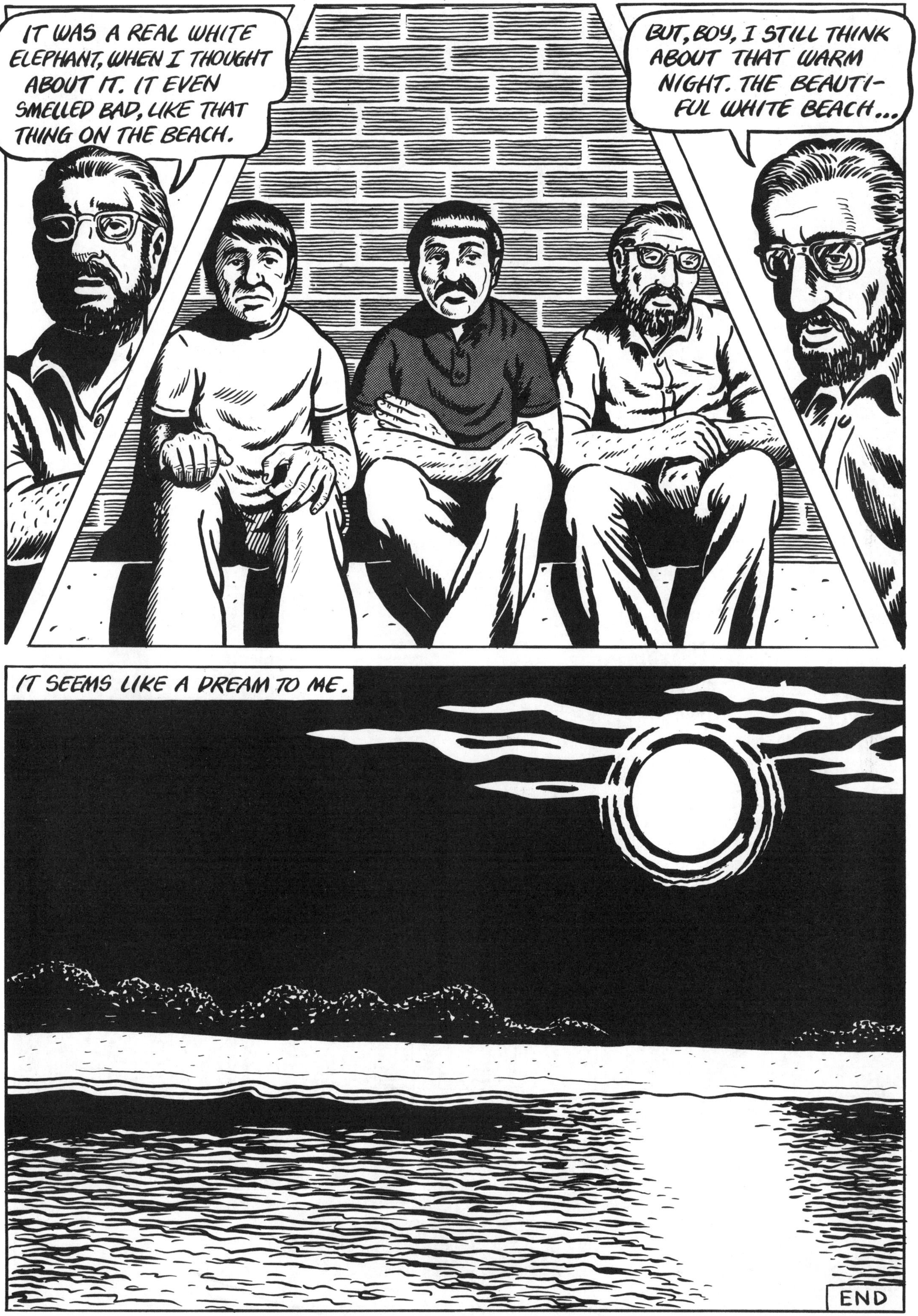
IT WAS A REAL WHITE ELEPHANT, WHEN I THOUGHT ABOUT IT. IT EVEN SMELLED BAD, LIKE THAT THING ON THE BEACH.
BUT, BOY, I STILL THINK ABOUT THAT WARM NIGHT. THE BEAUTIFUL WHITE BEACH...
IT SEEMS LIKE A DREAM TO ME.
END

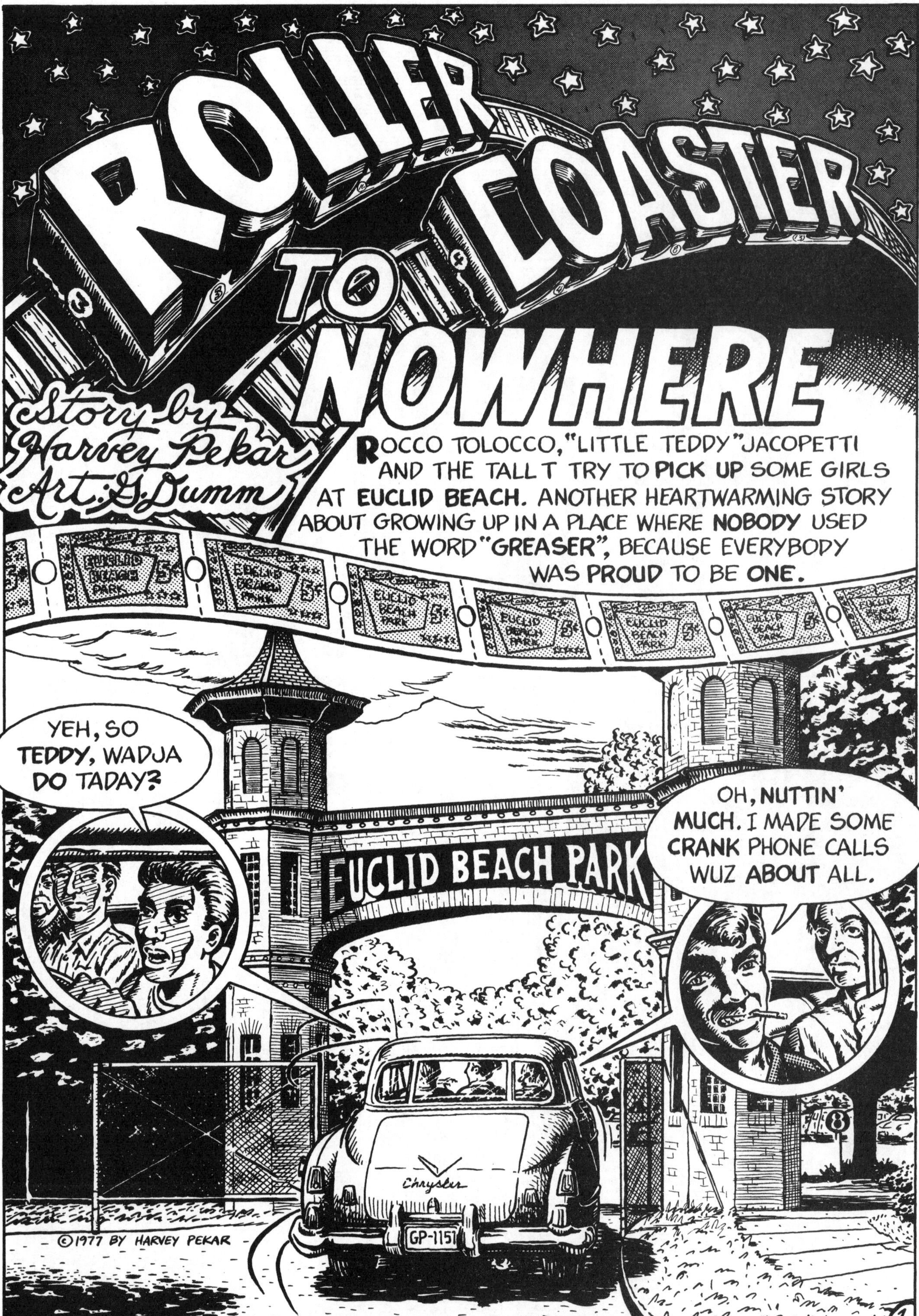

ROLLER COASTER TO NOWHERE
Story by Harvey Pekar
Art: G. Dumm
ROCCO TOLOCCO, "LITTLE TEDDY" JACOPETTI AND THE TALL T TRY TO PICK UP SOME GIRLS AT EUCLID BEACH. ANOTHER HEARTWARMING STORY ABOUT GROWING UP IN A PLACE WHERE NOBODY USED THE WORD "GREASER", BECAUSE EVERYBODY WAS PROUD TO BE ONE.
YEH, SO TEDDY, WADJA DO TADAY?
EUCLID BEACH PARK
OH, NUTTIN' MUCH. I MADE SOME CRANK PHONE CALLS WUZ ABOUT ALL.
GP-1151
©1977 BY HARVEY PEKAR

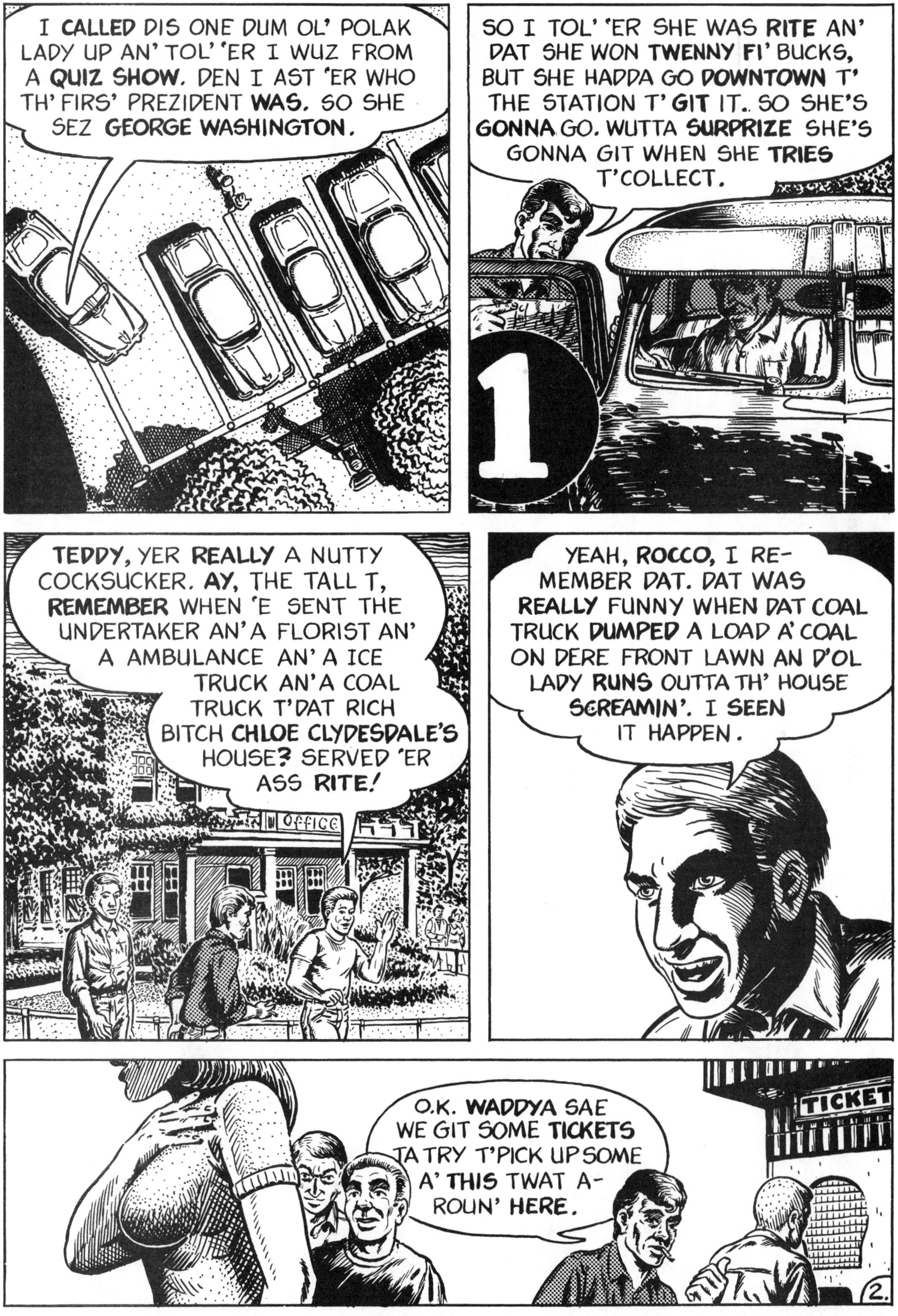
I CALLED DIS ONE DUM OL' POLAK LADY UP AN' TOL' 'ER I WUZ FROM A QUIZ SHOW. DEN I AST 'ER WHO TH' FIRS' PREZIDENT WAS. SO SHE SEZ GEORGE WASHINGTON.
SO I TOL' 'ER SHE WAS RITE AN' DAT SHE WON TWENNY FI' BUCKS, BUT SHE HADDA GO DOWNTOWN T' THE STATION T' GIT IT.. SO SHE'S GONNA GO. WUTTA SURPRIZE SHE'S GONNA GIT WHEN SHE TRIES T'COLLECT.
1
TEDDY, YER REALLY A NUTTY COCKSUCKER. AY, THE TALL T, REMEMBER WHEN 'E SENT THE UNDERTAKER AN' A FLORIST AN' A AMBULANCE AN' A ICE TRUCK AN' A COAL TRUCK T'DAT RICH BITCH CHLOE CLYDESDALE'S HOUSE? SERVED 'ER ASS RITE!
Office
YEAH, ROCCO, I RE-MEMBER DAT. DAT WAS REALLY FUNNY WHEN DAT COAL TRUCK DUMPED A LOAD A' COAL ON DERE FRONT LAWN AN D'OL LADY RUNS OUTTA TH' HOUSE SCREAMIN'. I SEEN IT HAPPEN.
O.K. WADDYA SAE WE GIT SOME TICKETS TA TRY T'PICK UP SOME A' THIS TWAT A-ROUN' HERE.
TICKET
2.

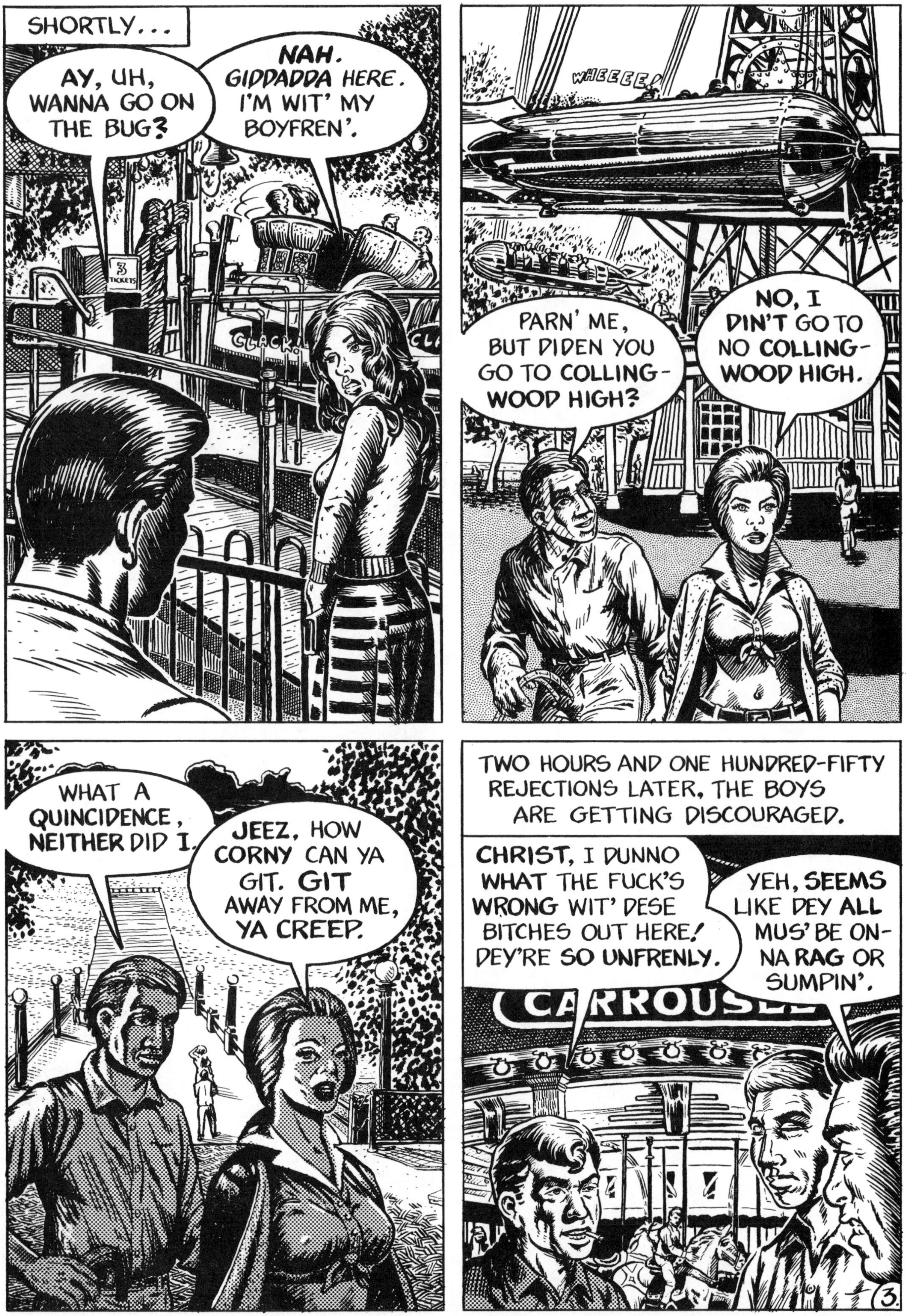
SHORTLY...
AY, UH, WANNA GO ON THE BUG?
NAH. GIDDADDA HERE. I'M WIT' MY BOYFREN'.
3 TICKETS
CLACK
WHEEEEE!
PARN' ME, BUT DIDEN YOU GO TO COLLING-WOOD HIGH?
NO, I DIN'T GO TO NO COLLING-WOOD HIGH.
WHAT A QUINCIDENCE, NEITHER DID I.
JEEZ, HOW CORNY CAN YA GIT. GIT AWAY FROM ME, YA CREEP.
TWO HOURS AND ONE HUNDRED-FIFTY REJECTIONS LATER, THE BOYS ARE GETTING DISCOURAGED.
CHRIST, I DUNNO WHAT THE FUCK'S WRONG WIT' DESE BITCHES OUT HERE! DEY'RE SO UNFRENLY.
YEH, SEEMS LIKE DEY ALL MUS' BE ON-NA RAG OR SUMPIN'.
CARROUSEL
3.

I DUNNO WUTS WIT' EM EITHER, BUT I'M GITTIN' **SICK** A' FUCKIN' A-ROUN' HERE. I'M GOIN' TA GIT SUM **POPCORN** AN' WALK AROUN' FOR A-WHILE. I'LL **MEET** YOU GUYS OVER HERE IN **TEN MINITS.**

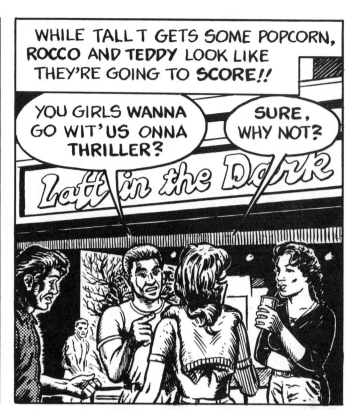

WHILE **TALL T** GETS SOME POPCORN, **ROCCO** AND **TEDDY** LOOK LIKE THEY'RE GOING TO **SCORE!!**

YOU GIRLS WANNA GO WIT'US ONNA **THRILLER?**

SURE, WHY NOT?

Latt'in the Dark

I CAN'T BELIEVE IT. THEY'RE **AKSHULLY** GONNA GO **WIT'US.**

WELL, 'AT JUS' SHOWS YA, PERSISTENCE PAYS OFF.

Flying Turns *Flying Turns*

THE **TALL T** SEES THE FOUR GETTING ON THE RIDE AND RUNS AFTER THEM, PANICKY...

AY, WUT ABOUT **ME?** HOW'M I SPOZED TA GIT HOME T'NITE IF YOU FOUR TAKE OFF IN **ROCCO'S** CAR? THERE AIN' NO BUSSES RUNNIN' FROM **HERE** THIS LATE.

ROCCO AND **TEDDY** ATTEMPT TO REASSURE HIM...

DON' WORRY T, WE'LL FIN' YA A GIRL. DESE GIRLS PROBLY GOT **ANOTHER** GIRL FREN'. THEN WE'LL **ALL** GO HOME.

YEAH, WE'LL GIT YA HOME. (LIKE **SHIT!**)

4.

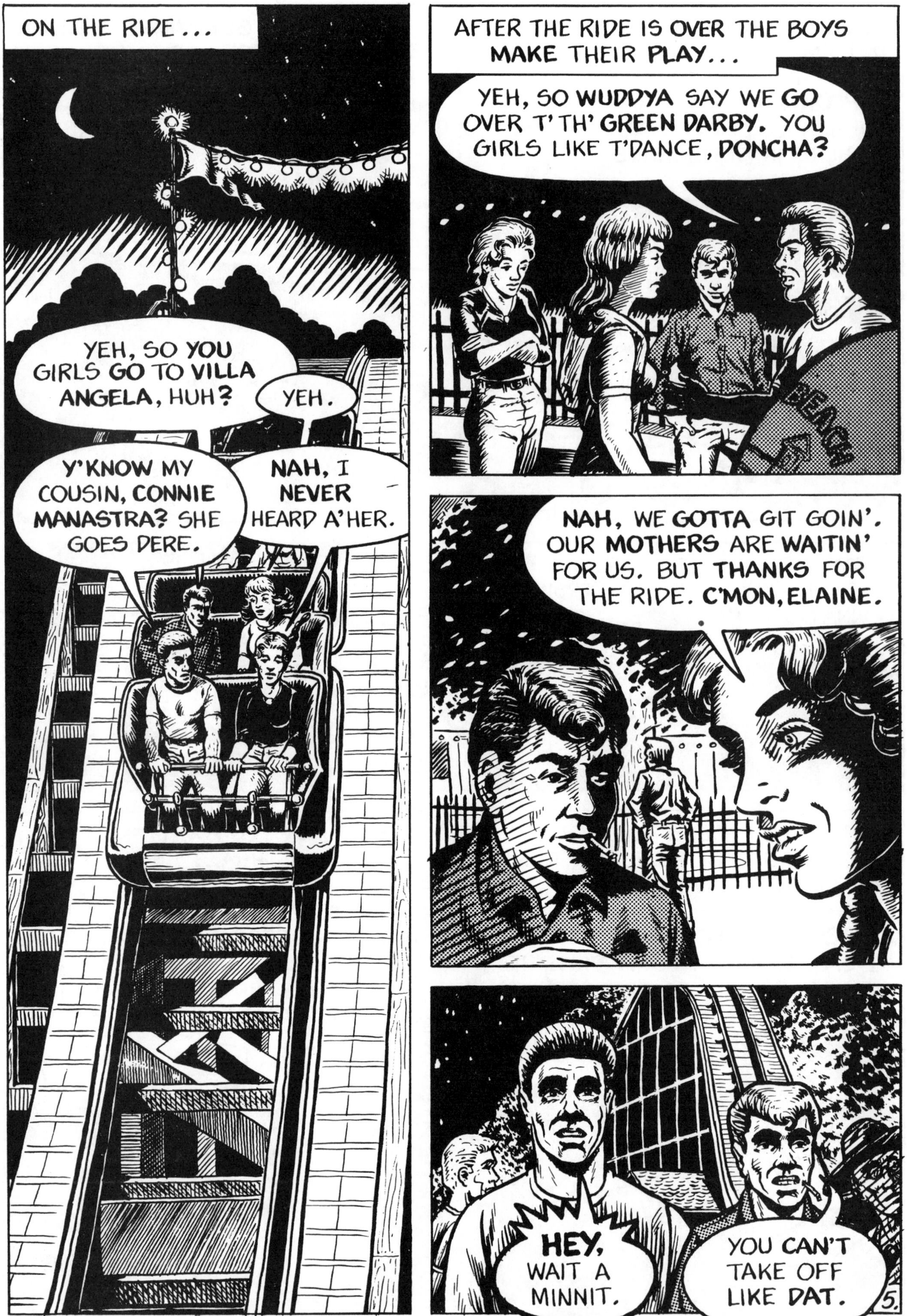
ON THE RIDE...
YEH, SO YOU GIRLS GO TO VILLA ANGELA, HUH?
YEH.
Y'KNOW MY COUSIN, CONNIE MANASTRA? SHE GOES DERE.
NAH, I NEVER HEARD A'HER.
AFTER THE RIDE IS OVER THE BOYS MAKE THEIR PLAY...
YEH, SO WUDDYA SAY WE GO OVER T' TH' GREEN DARBY. YOU GIRLS LIKE T'DANCE, DONCHA?
BEACH
NAH, WE GOTTA GIT GOIN'. OUR MOTHERS ARE WAITIN' FOR US. BUT THANKS FOR THE RIDE. C'MON, ELAINE.
HEY, WAIT A MINNIT.
YOU CAN'T TAKE OFF LIKE DAT.

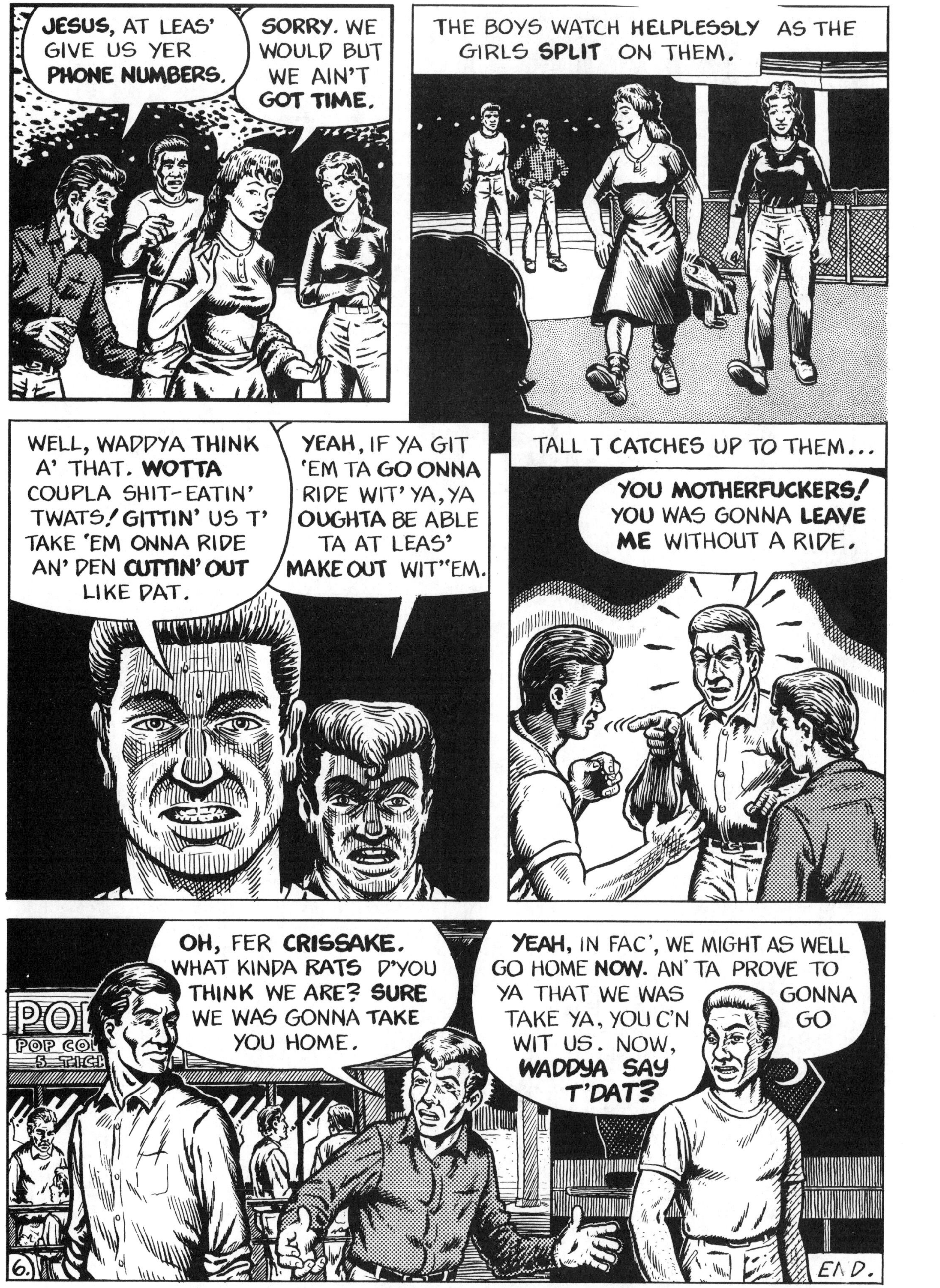
JESUS, AT LEAS' GIVE US YER PHONE NUMBERS.
SORRY. WE WOULD BUT WE AIN'T GOT TIME.
THE BOYS WATCH HELPLESSLY AS THE GIRLS SPLIT ON THEM.
WELL, WADDYA THINK A' THAT. WOTTA COUPLA SHIT-EATIN' TWATS! GITTIN' US T' TAKE 'EM ONNA RIDE AN' DEN CUTTIN' OUT LIKE DAT.
YEAH, IF YA GIT 'EM TA GO ONNA RIDE WIT' YA, YA OUGHTA BE ABLE TA AT LEAS' MAKE OUT WIT''EM.
TALL T CATCHES UP TO THEM...
YOU MOTHERFUCKERS! YOU WAS GONNA LEAVE ME WITHOUT A RIDE.
OH, FER CRISSAKE. WHAT KINDA RATS D'YOU THINK WE ARE? SURE WE WAS GONNA TAKE YOU HOME.
YEAH, IN FAC', WE MIGHT AS WELL GO HOME NOW. AN' TA PROVE TO YA THAT WE WAS GONNA TAKE YA, YOU C'N GO WIT US. NOW, WADDYA SAY T'DAT?
6.
END.

STORY WRITTEN BY HARVEY PEKAR IN JUNE, 1972

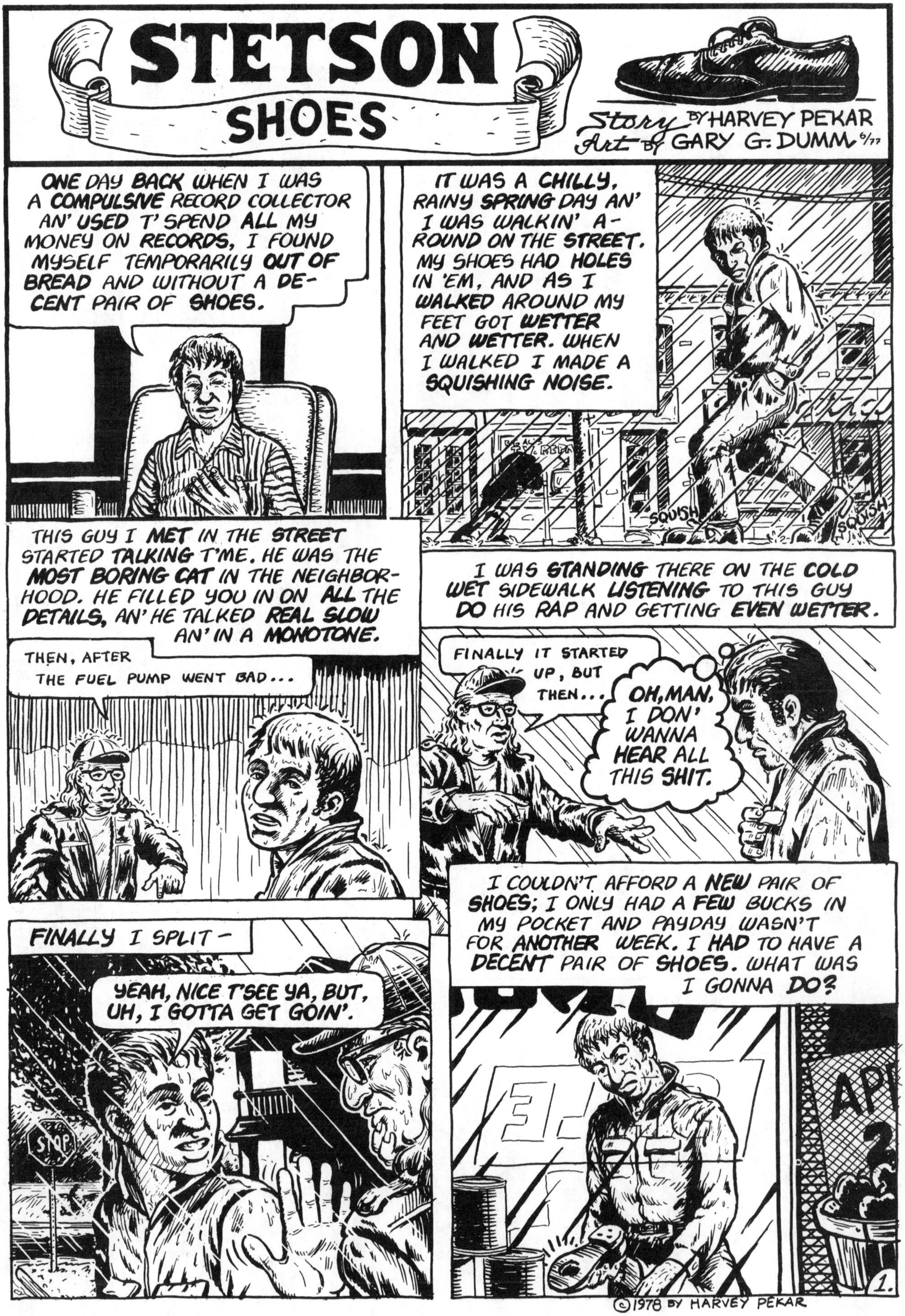
STETSON SHOES
Story BY HARVEY PEKAR
Art BY GARY G. DUMM 6/77
ONE DAY BACK WHEN I WAS A COMPULSIVE RECORD COLLECTOR AN' USED T' SPEND ALL MY MONEY ON RECORDS, I FOUND MYSELF TEMPORARILY OUT OF BREAD AND WITHOUT A DECENT PAIR OF SHOES.
IT WAS A CHILLY, RAINY SPRING DAY AN' I WAS WALKIN' AROUND ON THE STREET. MY SHOES HAD HOLES IN 'EM, AND AS I WALKED AROUND MY FEET GOT WETTER AND WETTER. WHEN I WALKED I MADE A SQUISHING NOISE.
SQUISH
SQUISH
THIS GUY I MET IN THE STREET STARTED TALKING T'ME. HE WAS THE MOST BORING CAT IN THE NEIGHBORHOOD. HE FILLED YOU IN ON ALL THE DETAILS, AN' HE TALKED REAL SLOW AN' IN A MONOTONE.
THEN, AFTER THE FUEL PUMP WENT BAD...
I WAS STANDING THERE ON THE COLD WET SIDEWALK LISTENING TO THIS GUY DO HIS RAP AND GETTING EVEN WETTER.
FINALLY IT STARTED UP, BUT THEN...
OH, MAN, I DON' WANNA HEAR ALL THIS SHIT.
FINALLY I SPLIT -
YEAH, NICE T'SEE YA, BUT, UH, I GOTTA GET GOIN'.
STOP
I COULDN'T AFFORD A NEW PAIR OF SHOES; I ONLY HAD A FEW BUCKS IN MY POCKET AND PAYDAY WASN'T FOR ANOTHER WEEK. I HAD TO HAVE A DECENT PAIR OF SHOES. WHAT WAS I GONNA DO?
1.

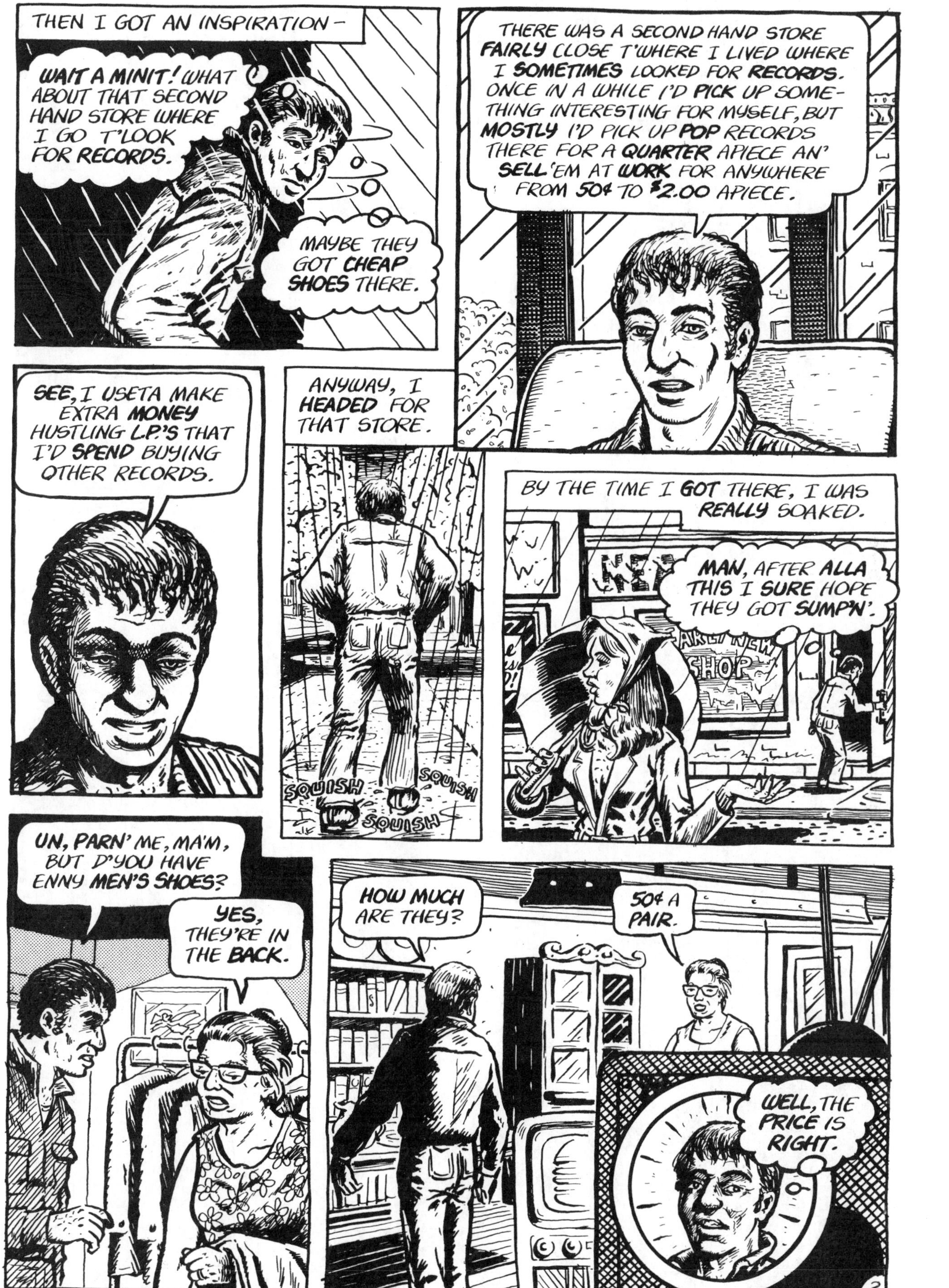
THEN I GOT AN INSPIRATION—
WAIT A MINIT! WHAT ABOUT THAT SECOND HAND STORE WHERE I GO T'LOOK FOR RECORDS.
MAYBE THEY GOT CHEAP SHOES THERE.
THERE WAS A SECOND HAND STORE FAIRLY CLOSE T'WHERE I LIVED WHERE I SOMETIMES LOOKED FOR RECORDS. ONCE IN A WHILE I'D PICK UP SOMETHING INTERESTING FOR MYSELF, BUT MOSTLY I'D PICK UP POP RECORDS THERE FOR A QUARTER APIECE AN' SELL 'EM AT WORK FOR ANYWHERE FROM 50¢ TO $2.00 APIECE.
SEE, I USETA MAKE EXTRA MONEY HUSTLING L.P.'S THAT I'D SPEND BUYING OTHER RECORDS.
ANYWAY, I HEADED FOR THAT STORE.
SQUISH SQUISH SQUISH
BY THE TIME I GOT THERE, I WAS REALLY SOAKED.
MAN, AFTER ALLA THIS I SURE HOPE THEY GOT SUMP'N'.
SHOP
UH, PARN' ME, MA'M, BUT D'YOU HAVE ENNY MEN'S SHOES?
YES, THEY'RE IN THE BACK.
HOW MUCH ARE THEY?
50¢ A PAIR.
WELL, THE PRICE IS RIGHT.
2.

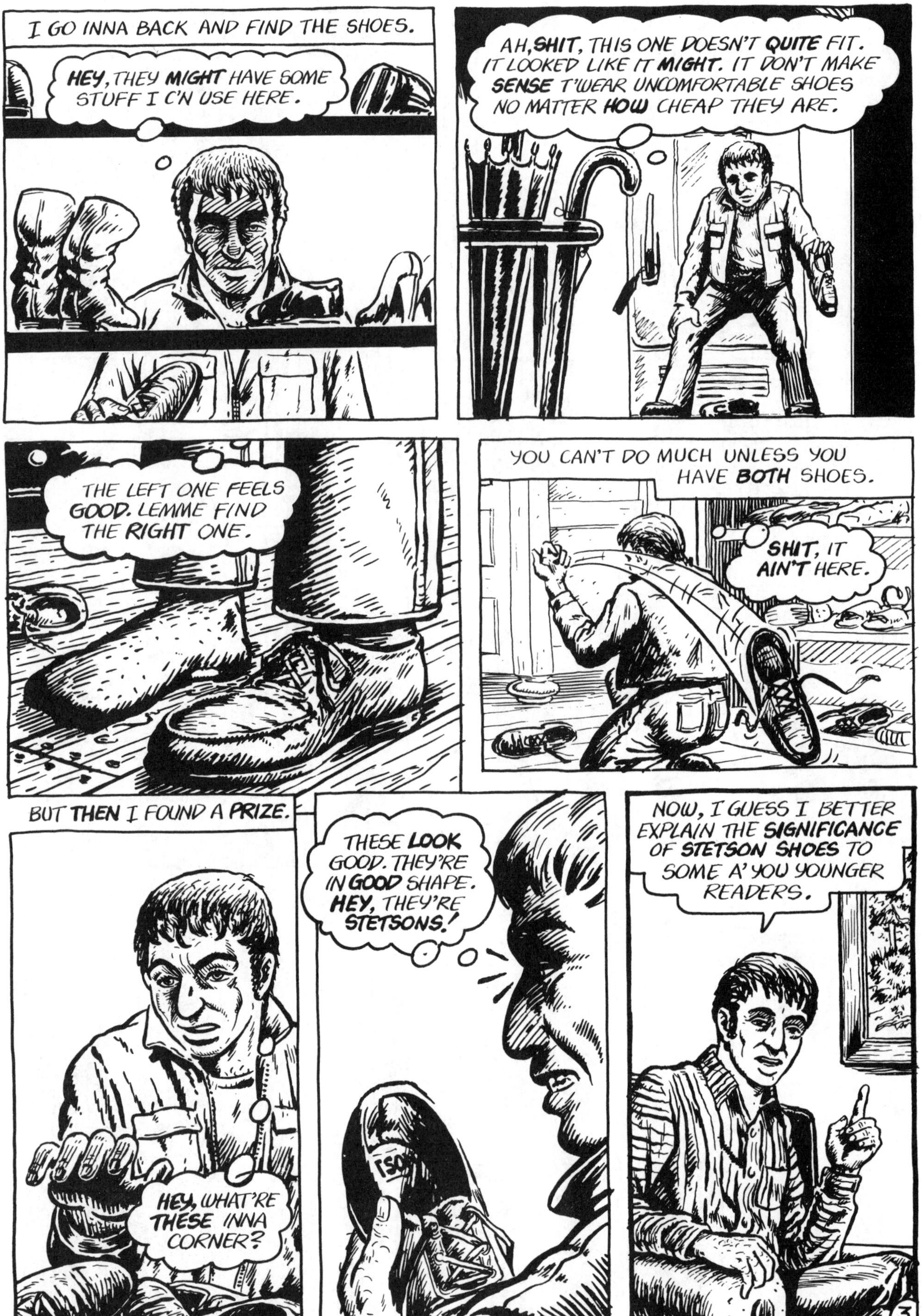

I GO INNA BACK AND FIND THE SHOES.
HEY, THEY MIGHT HAVE SOME STUFF I C'N USE HERE.
AH, SHIT, THIS ONE DOESN'T QUITE FIT. IT LOOKED LIKE IT MIGHT. IT DON'T MAKE SENSE T'WEAR UNCOMFORTABLE SHOES NO MATTER HOW CHEAP THEY ARE.
THE LEFT ONE FEELS GOOD. LEMME FIND THE RIGHT ONE.
YOU CAN'T DO MUCH UNLESS YOU HAVE BOTH SHOES.
SHIT, IT AIN'T HERE.
BUT THEN I FOUND A PRIZE.
HEY, WHAT'RE THESE INNA CORNER?
THESE LOOK GOOD. THEY'RE IN GOOD SHAPE. HEY, THEY'RE STETSONS!
NOW, I GUESS I BETTER EXPLAIN THE SIGNIFICANCE OF STETSON SHOES TO SOME A' YOU YOUNGER READERS.
3.

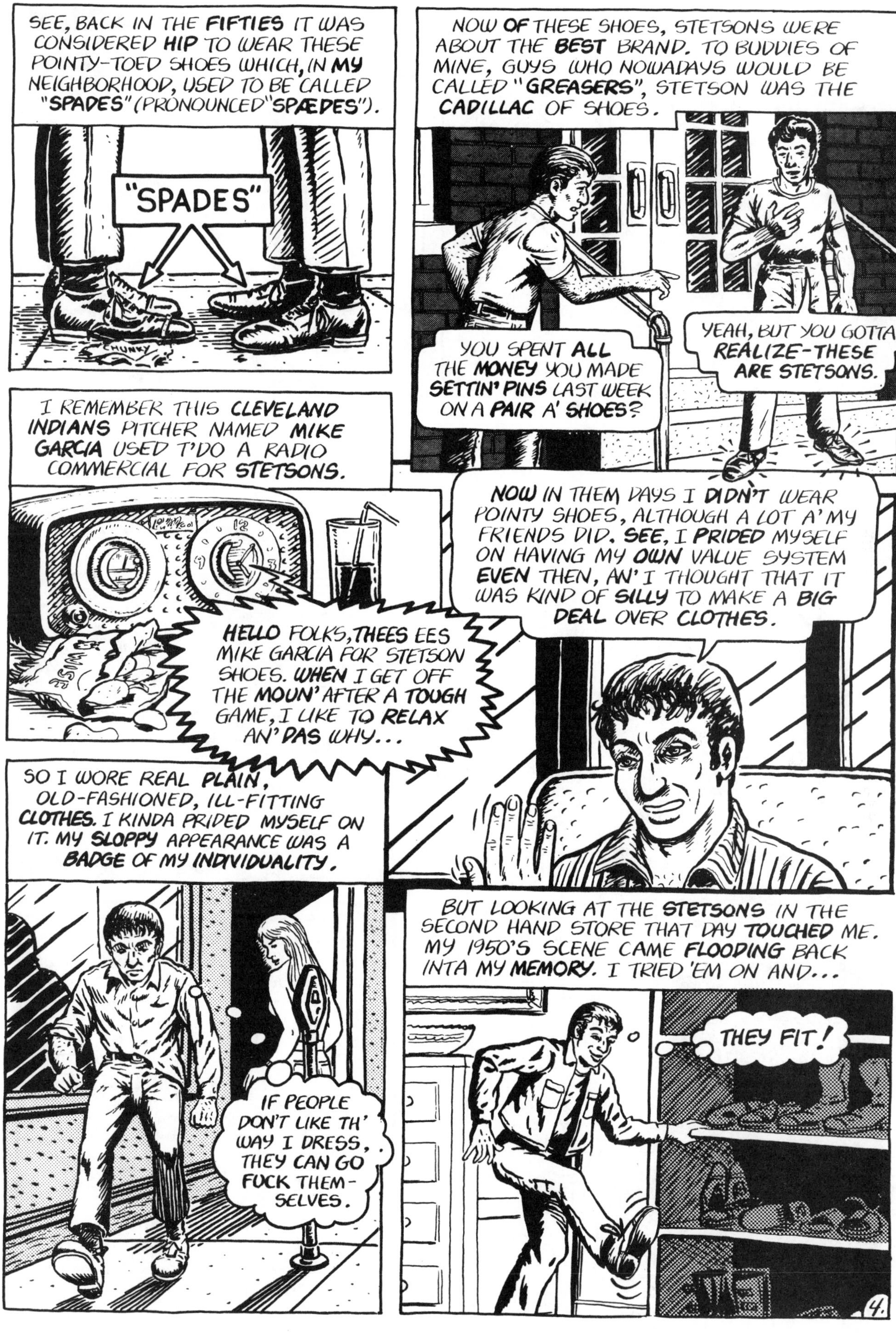
SEE, BACK IN THE FIFTIES IT WAS CONSIDERED HIP TO WEAR THESE POINTY-TOED SHOES WHICH, IN MY NEIGHBORHOOD, USED TO BE CALLED "SPADES" (PRONOUNCED "SPÆDES").
"SPADES"
CHUNKY
NOW OF THESE SHOES, STETSONS WERE ABOUT THE BEST BRAND. TO BUDDIES OF MINE, GUYS WHO NOWADAYS WOULD BE CALLED "GREASERS", STETSON WAS THE CADILLAC OF SHOES.
YOU SPENT ALL THE MONEY YOU MADE SETTIN' PINS LAST WEEK ON A PAIR A' SHOES?
YEAH, BUT YOU GOTTA REALIZE-THESE ARE STETSONS.
I REMEMBER THIS CLEVELAND INDIANS PITCHER NAMED MIKE GARCIA USED T'DO A RADIO COMMERCIAL FOR STETSONS.
WISE
HELLO FOLKS, THEES EES MIKE GARCIA FOR STETSON SHOES. WHEN I GET OFF THE MOUN' AFTER A TOUGH GAME, I LIKE TO RELAX AN' DAS WHY...
NOW IN THEM DAYS I DIDN'T WEAR POINTY SHOES, ALTHOUGH A LOT A' MY FRIENDS DID. SEE, I PRIDED MYSELF ON HAVING MY OWN VALUE SYSTEM EVEN THEN, AN' I THOUGHT THAT IT WAS KIND OF SILLY TO MAKE A BIG DEAL OVER CLOTHES.
SO I WORE REAL PLAIN, OLD-FASHIONED, ILL-FITTING CLOTHES. I KINDA PRIDED MYSELF ON IT. MY SLOPPY APPEARANCE WAS A BADGE OF MY INDIVIDUALITY.
IF PEOPLE DON'T LIKE TH' WAY I DRESS, THEY CAN GO FUCK THEM-SELVES.
BUT LOOKING AT THE STETSONS IN THE SECOND HAND STORE THAT DAY TOUCHED ME. MY 1950'S SCENE CAME FLOODING BACK INTA MY MEMORY. I TRIED 'EM ON AND...
THEY FIT!

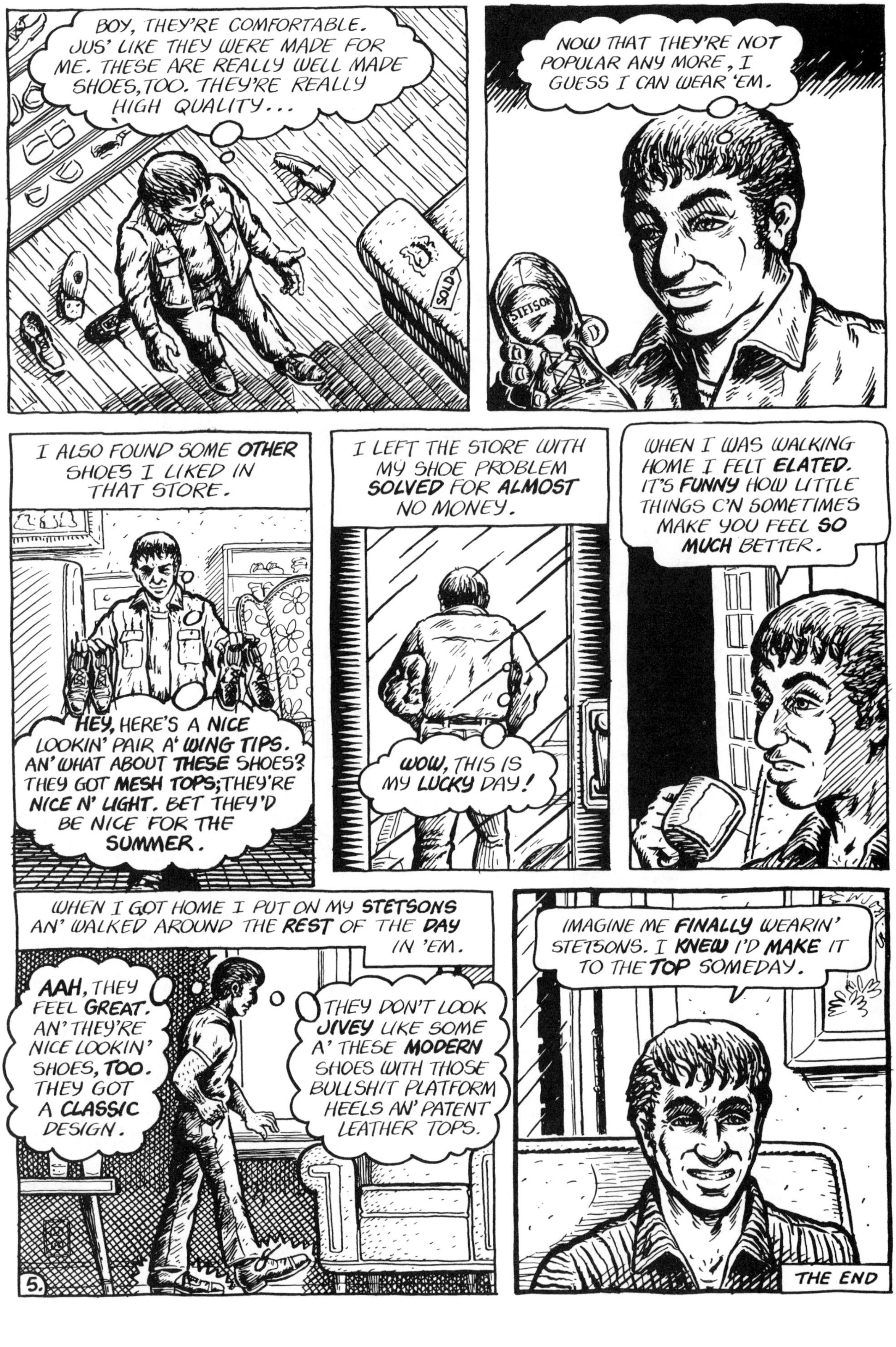
BOY, THEY'RE COMFORTABLE. JUS' LIKE THEY WERE MADE FOR ME. THESE ARE REALLY WELL MADE SHOES, TOO. THEY'RE REALLY HIGH QUALITY...
SOLD
NOW THAT THEY'RE NOT POPULAR ANY MORE, I GUESS I CAN WEAR 'EM.
STETSON
I ALSO FOUND SOME OTHER SHOES I LIKED IN THAT STORE.
HEY, HERE'S A NICE LOOKIN' PAIR A' WING TIPS. AN' WHAT ABOUT THESE SHOES? THEY GOT MESH TOPS; THEY'RE NICE N' LIGHT. BET THEY'D BE NICE FOR THE SUMMER.
I LEFT THE STORE WITH MY SHOE PROBLEM SOLVED FOR ALMOST NO MONEY.
WOW, THIS IS MY LUCKY DAY!
WHEN I WAS WALKING HOME I FELT ELATED. IT'S FUNNY HOW LITTLE THINGS C'N SOMETIMES MAKE YOU FEEL SO MUCH BETTER.
WHEN I GOT HOME I PUT ON MY STETSONS AN' WALKED AROUND THE REST OF THE DAY IN 'EM.
AAH, THEY FEEL GREAT. AN' THEY'RE NICE LOOKIN' SHOES, TOO. THEY GOT A CLASSIC DESIGN.
THEY DON'T LOOK JIVEY LIKE SOME A' THESE MODERN SHOES WITH THOSE BULLSHIT PLATFORM HEELS AN' PATENT LEATHER TOPS.
IMAGINE ME FINALLY WEARIN' STETSONS. I KNEW I'D MAKE IT TO THE TOP SOMEDAY.
THE END
5.

MRS. ROOSEVELT AND THE YOUNG QUEEN OF GREECE

HIYA, LOUIE, HOWYA...

SHH, SHH, LISTEN T' THIS GUY. HE REALLY KNOWS WHAT HE'S TALKIN' ABOUT.

...WHY, UH, THE YOUNG QUEEN OF GREECE WAS OVER HERE ON A STATE VISIT...THIS WAS DURING THE TRUMAN ADMINISTRATION...

STORY BY HARVEY PEKAR
ART BY GARY DUMM & GREG BUDGETT

© 1980 by HARVEY PEKAR

...AND MRS. ROOSEVELT INVITED THE YOUNG QUEEN OF GREECE TO STAY WITH HER IN NEW YORK CITY - IN HER GREENWICH VILLAGE APARTMENT, YOU KNOW - AS PART OF HER VACATION.

WHILE SHE WAS THERE, MRS. ROOSEVELT COOKED FOR THE YOUNG QUEEN OF GREECE. SHE COOKED SUCH HOMELY THINGS AS BACON AND EGGS, HOMINY GRITS AND BAKED BEANS.

SHE DIDN'T WASH ANY DISHES. SHE WAS A WEALTHY WOMAN.

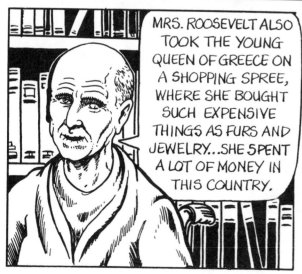

MRS. ROOSEVELT ALSO TOOK THE YOUNG QUEEN OF GREECE ON A SHOPPING SPREE, WHERE SHE BOUGHT SUCH EXPENSIVE THINGS AS FURS AND JEWELRY...SHE SPENT A LOT OF MONEY IN THIS COUNTRY.

1.

LEAVE IT TO MRS. ROOSEVELT TO KNOW WHAT TO DO.

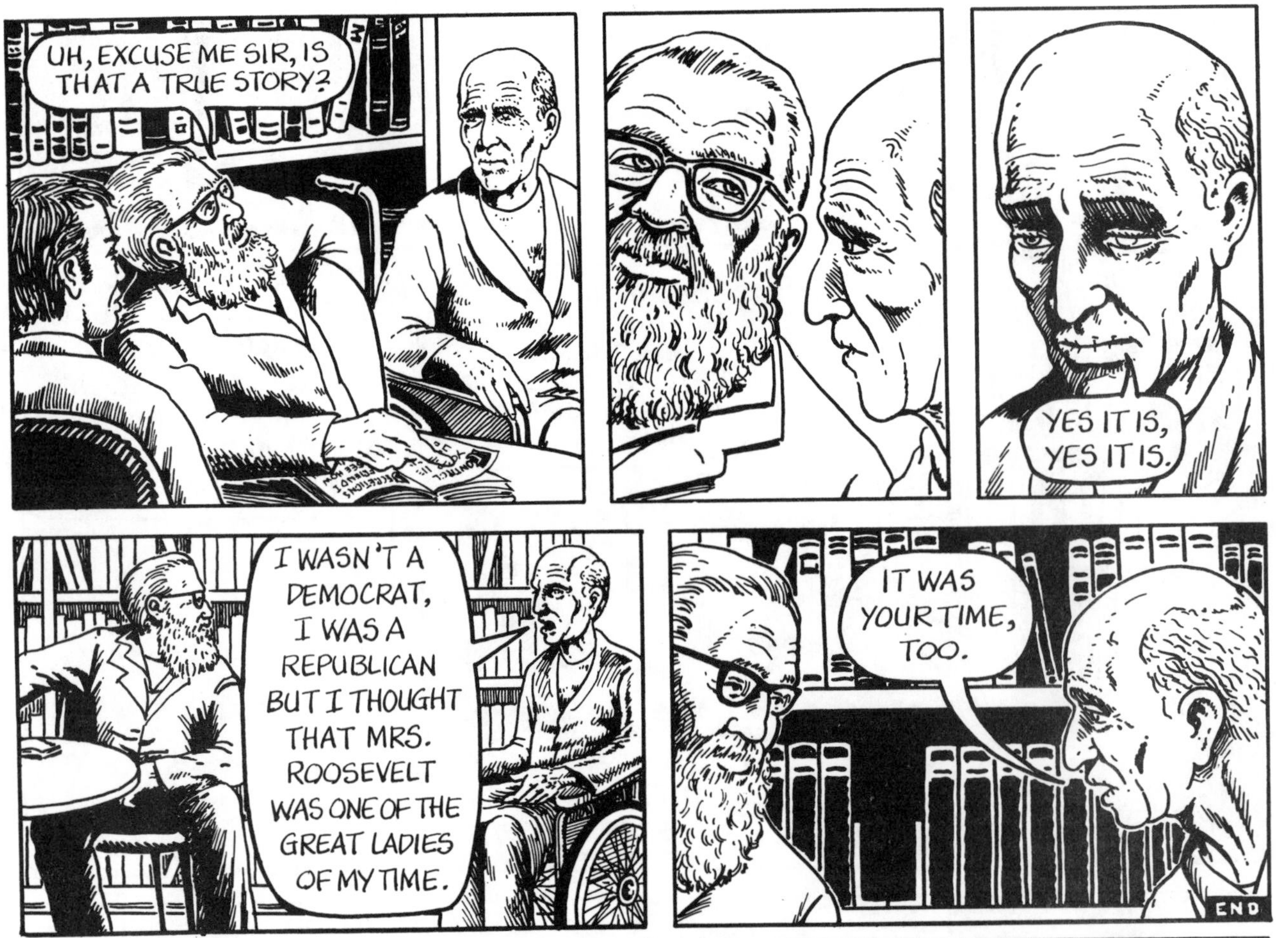
UH, EXCUSE ME SIR, IS THAT A TRUE STORY?
YES IT IS, YES IT IS.
I WASN'T A DEMOCRAT, I WAS A REPUBLICAN BUT I THOUGHT THAT MRS. ROOSEVELT WAS ONE OF THE GREAT LADIES OF MY TIME.
IT WAS YOUR TIME, TOO.
END

BUSMAN'S HOLIDAY

STORY BY HARVEY PEKAR ART BY GREG BUDGETT & GARY DUMM

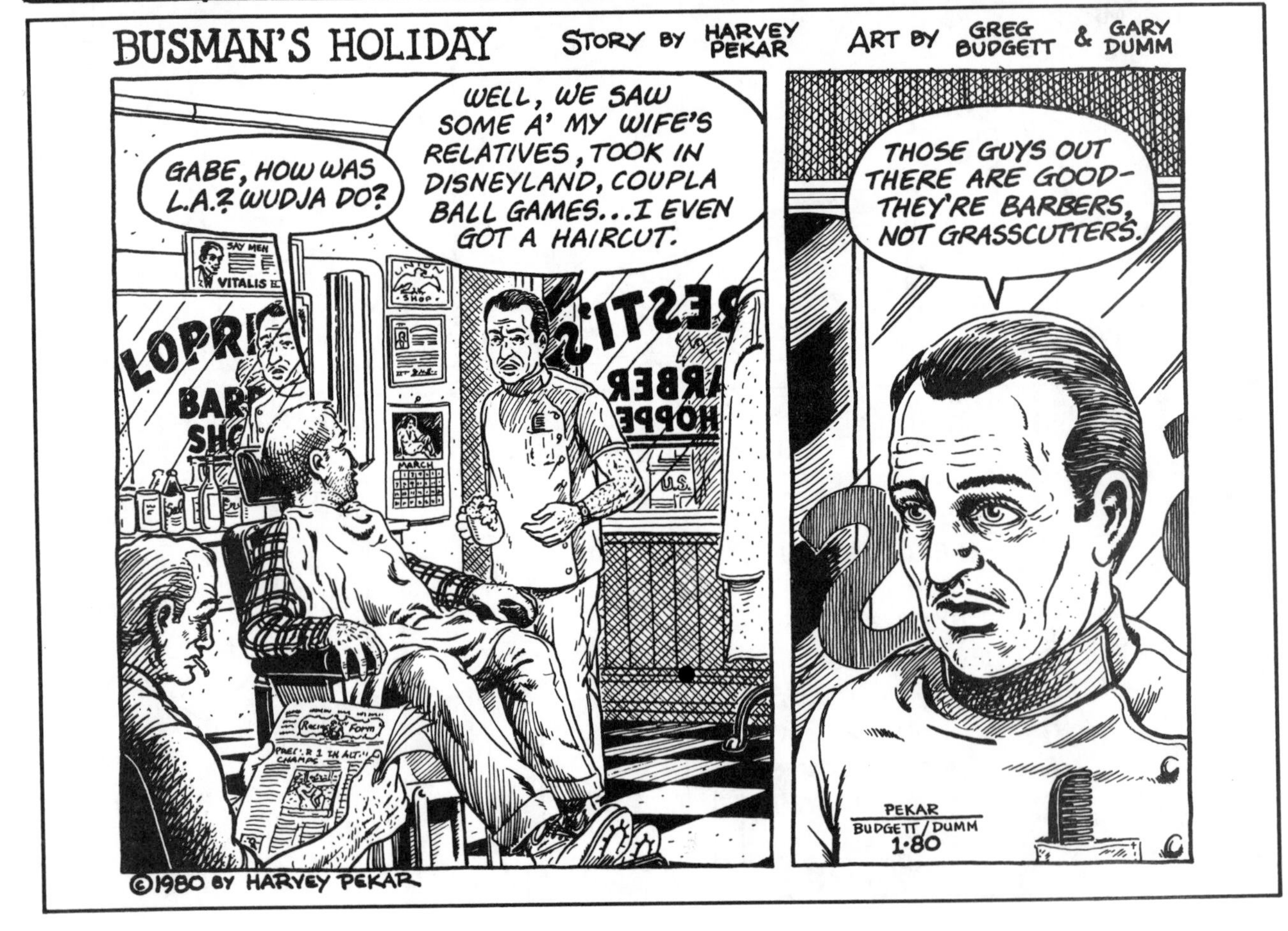
GABE, HOW WAS L.A.? WUDJA DO?
WELL, WE SAW SOME A' MY WIFE'S RELATIVES, TOOK IN DISNEYLAND, COUPLA BALL GAMES...I EVEN GOT A HAIRCUT.
THOSE GUYS OUT THERE ARE GOOD-THEY'RE BARBERS, NOT GRASSCUTTERS.
SAY MEN
VITALIS
PEKAR
BUDGETT/DUMM
1·80

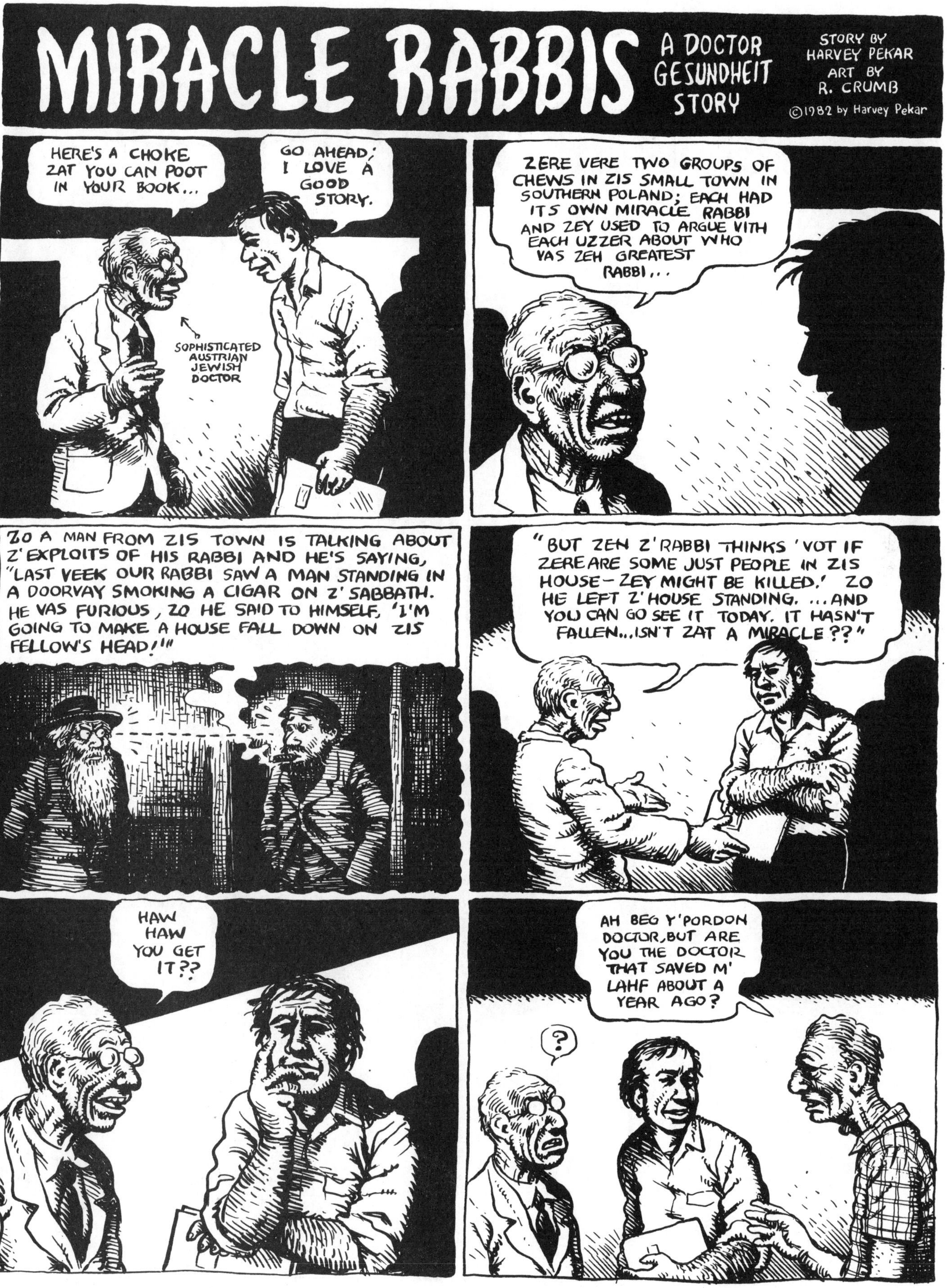
MIRACLE RABBIS
A DOCTOR GESUNDHEIT STORY
STORY BY HARVEY PEKAR
ART BY R. CRUMB
©1982 by Harvey Pekar
HERE'S A CHOKE ZAT YOU CAN POOT IN YOUR BOOK...
GO AHEAD; I LOVE A GOOD STORY.
SOPHISTICATED AUSTRIAN JEWISH DOCTOR
ZERE VERE TWO GROUPS OF CHEWS IN ZIS SMALL TOWN IN SOUTHERN POLAND; EACH HAD ITS OWN MIRACLE RABBI AND ZEY USED TO ARGUE VITH EACH UZZER ABOUT WHO VAS ZEH GREATEST RABBI...
ZO A MAN FROM ZIS TOWN IS TALKING ABOUT Z' EXPLOITS OF HIS RABBI AND HE'S SAYING, "LAST VEEK OUR RABBI SAW A MAN STANDING IN A DOORVAY SMOKING A CIGAR ON Z' SABBATH. HE VAS FURIOUS, ZO HE SAID TO HIMSELF, 'I'M GOING TO MAKE A HOUSE FALL DOWN ON ZIS FELLOW'S HEAD!'"
"BUT ZEN Z'RABBI THINKS 'VOT IF ZERE ARE SOME JUST PEOPLE IN ZIS HOUSE— ZEY MIGHT BE KILLED.' ZO HE LEFT Z' HOUSE STANDING. ...AND YOU CAN GO SEE IT TODAY. IT HASN'T FALLEN... ISN'T ZAT A MIRACLE??"
HAW HAW YOU GET IT??
AH BEG Y'PORDON DOCTOR, BUT ARE YOU THE DOCTOR THAT SAVED M' LAHF ABOUT A YEAR AGO?
?

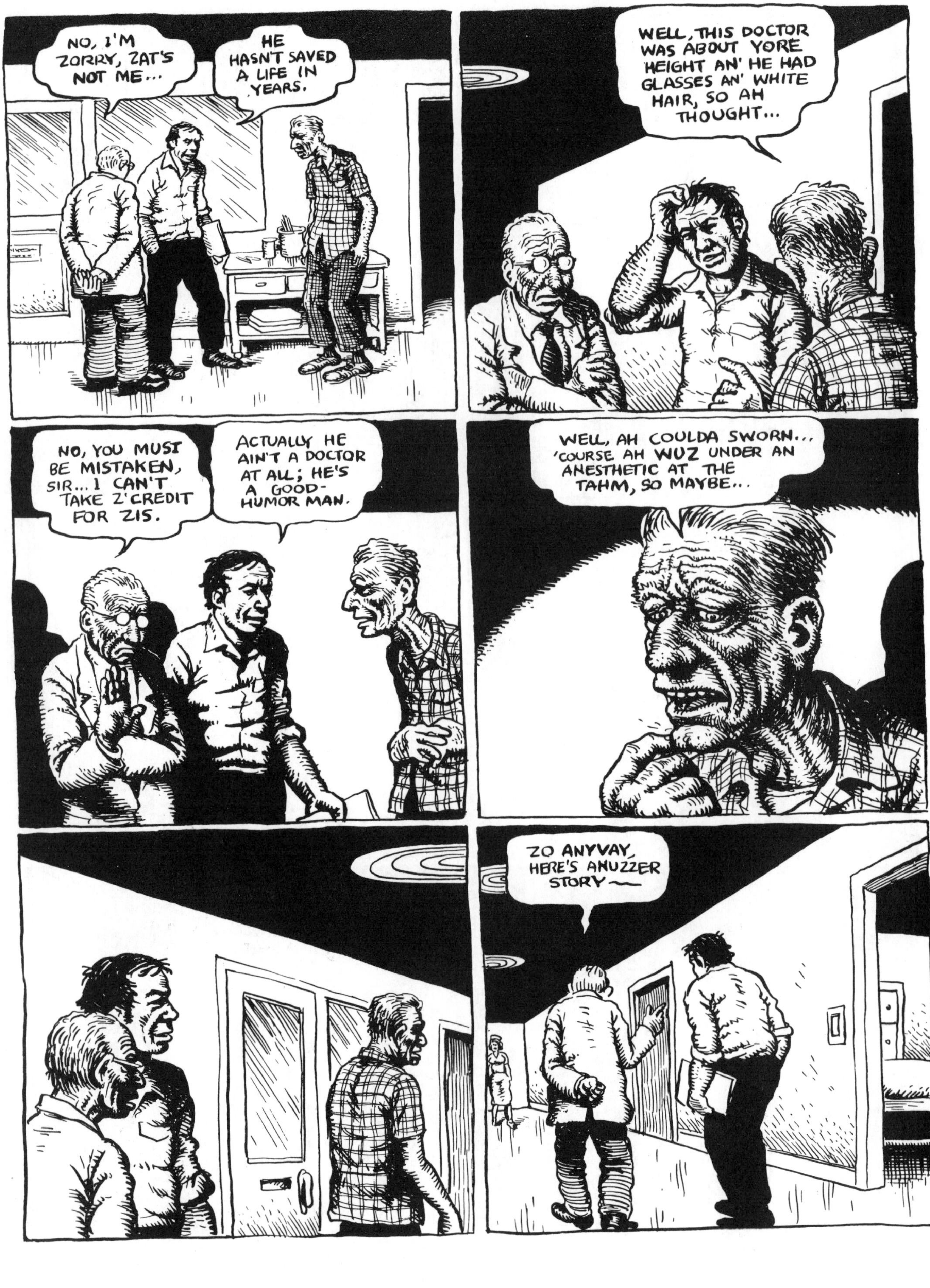
NO, I'M ZORRY, ZAT'S NOT ME...
HE HASN'T SAVED A LIFE IN YEARS.
WELL, THIS DOCTOR WAS ABOUT YORE HEIGHT AN' HE HAD GLASSES AN' WHITE HAIR, SO AH THOUGHT...
NO, YOU MUST BE MISTAKEN, SIR... I CAN'T TAKE Z'CREDIT FOR ZIS.
ACTUALLY HE AIN'T A DOCTOR AT ALL; HE'S A GOOD-HUMOR MAN.
WELL, AH COULDA SWORN... 'COURSE AH WUZ UNDER AN ANESTHETIC AT THE TAHM, SO MAYBE...
ZO ANYVAY, HERE'S ANUZZER STORY ~~

An Everyday Horror Story

story by harvey pekar – illustrated by gerry shamray

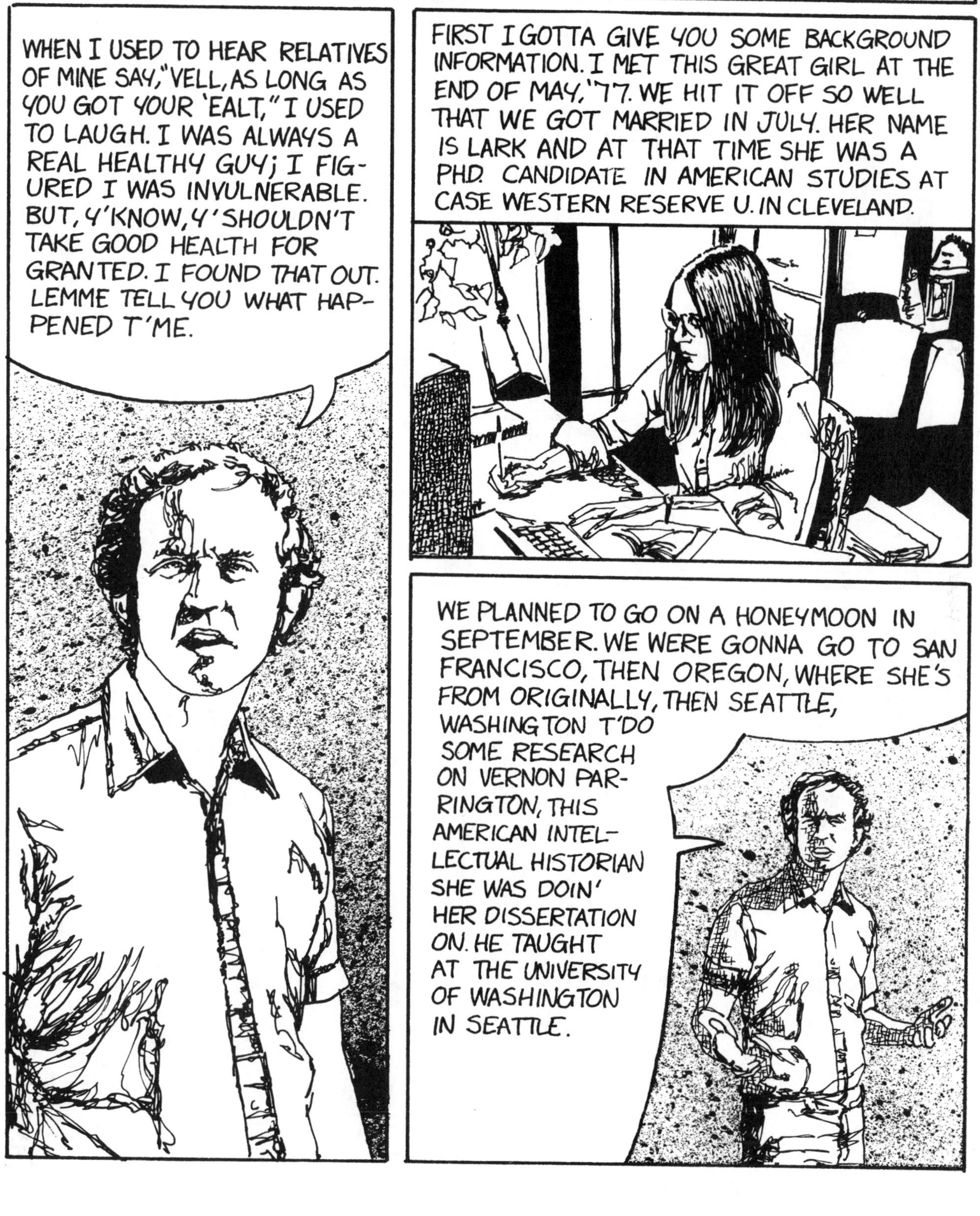
WHEN I USED TO HEAR RELATIVES OF MINE SAY, "VELL, AS LONG AS YOU GOT YOUR 'EALT," I USED TO LAUGH. I WAS ALWAYS A REAL HEALTHY GUY; I FIGURED I WAS INVULNERABLE. BUT, Y'KNOW, Y'SHOULDN'T TAKE GOOD HEALTH FOR GRANTED. I FOUND THAT OUT. LEMME TELL YOU WHAT HAPPENED T'ME.
FIRST I GOTTA GIVE YOU SOME BACKGROUND INFORMATION. I MET THIS GREAT GIRL AT THE END OF MAY, '77. WE HIT IT OFF SO WELL THAT WE GOT MARRIED IN JULY. HER NAME IS LARK AND AT THAT TIME SHE WAS A PHD. CANDIDATE IN AMERICAN STUDIES AT CASE WESTERN RESERVE U. IN CLEVELAND.
WE PLANNED TO GO ON A HONEYMOON IN SEPTEMBER. WE WERE GONNA GO TO SAN FRANCISCO, THEN OREGON, WHERE SHE'S FROM ORIGINALLY, THEN SEATTLE, WASHINGTON T'DO SOME RESEARCH ON VERNON PARRINGTON, THIS AMERICAN INTELLECTUAL HISTORIAN SHE WAS DOIN' HER DISSERTATION ON. HE TAUGHT AT THE UNIVERSITY OF WASHINGTON IN SEATTLE.

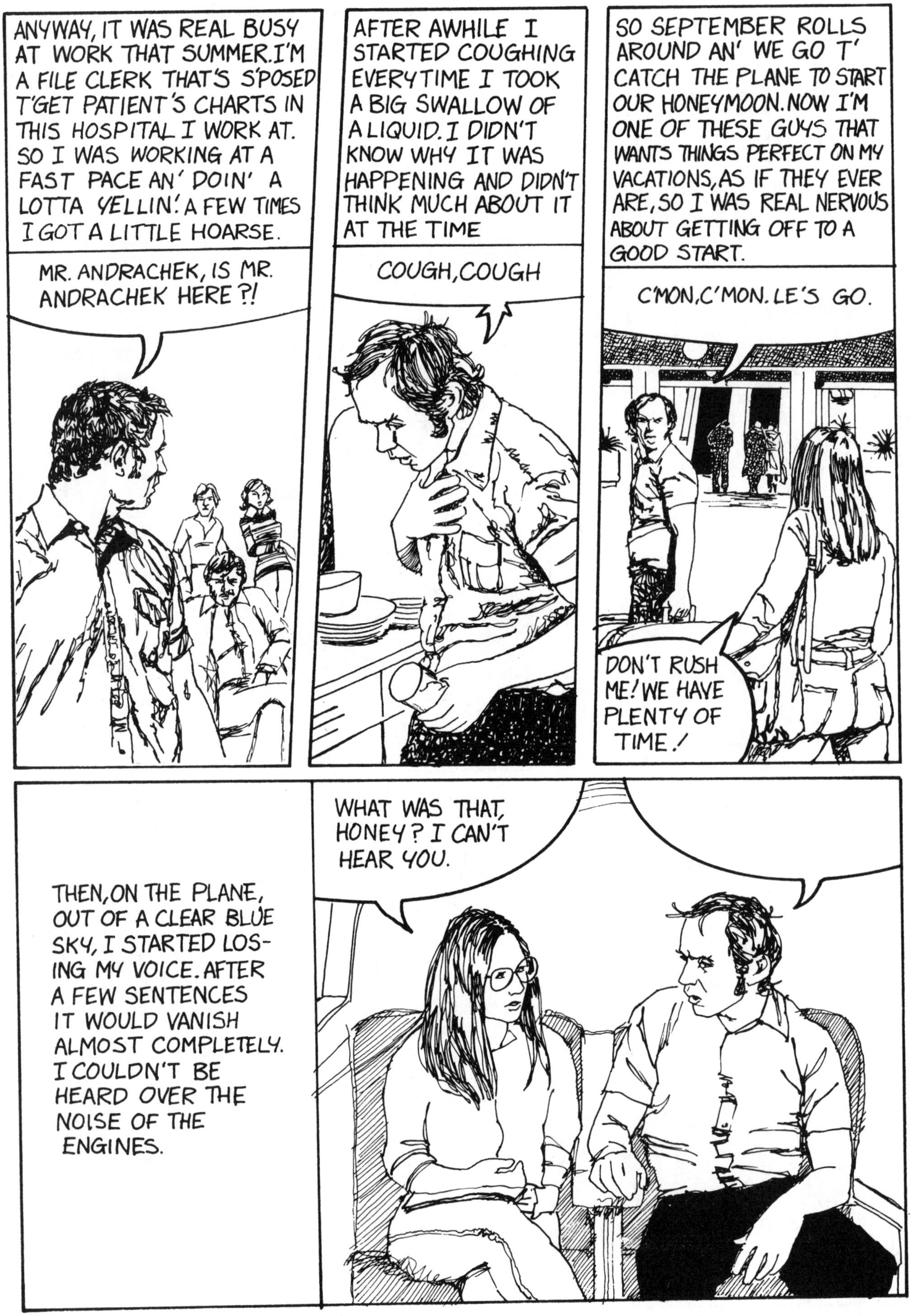
ANYWAY, IT WAS REAL BUSY AT WORK THAT SUMMER. I'M A FILE CLERK THAT'S S'POSED T'GET PATIENT'S CHARTS IN THIS HOSPITAL I WORK AT. SO I WAS WORKING AT A FAST PACE AN' DOIN' A LOTTA YELLIN'. A FEW TIMES I GOT A LITTLE HOARSE.
MR. ANDRACHEK, IS MR. ANDRACHEK HERE?!
AFTER AWHILE I STARTED COUGHING EVERYTIME I TOOK A BIG SWALLOW OF A LIQUID. I DIDN'T KNOW WHY IT WAS HAPPENING AND DIDN'T THINK MUCH ABOUT IT AT THE TIME
COUGH, COUGH
SO SEPTEMBER ROLLS AROUND AN' WE GO T' CATCH THE PLANE TO START OUR HONEYMOON. NOW I'M ONE OF THESE GUYS THAT WANTS THINGS PERFECT ON MY VACATIONS, AS IF THEY EVER ARE, SO I WAS REAL NERVOUS ABOUT GETTING OFF TO A GOOD START.
C'MON, C'MON. LE'S GO.
DON'T RUSH ME! WE HAVE PLENTY OF TIME!
THEN, ON THE PLANE, OUT OF A CLEAR BLUE SKY, I STARTED LOSING MY VOICE. AFTER A FEW SENTENCES IT WOULD VANISH ALMOST COMPLETELY. I COULDN'T BE HEARD OVER THE NOISE OF THE ENGINES.
WHAT WAS THAT, HONEY? I CAN'T HEAR YOU.

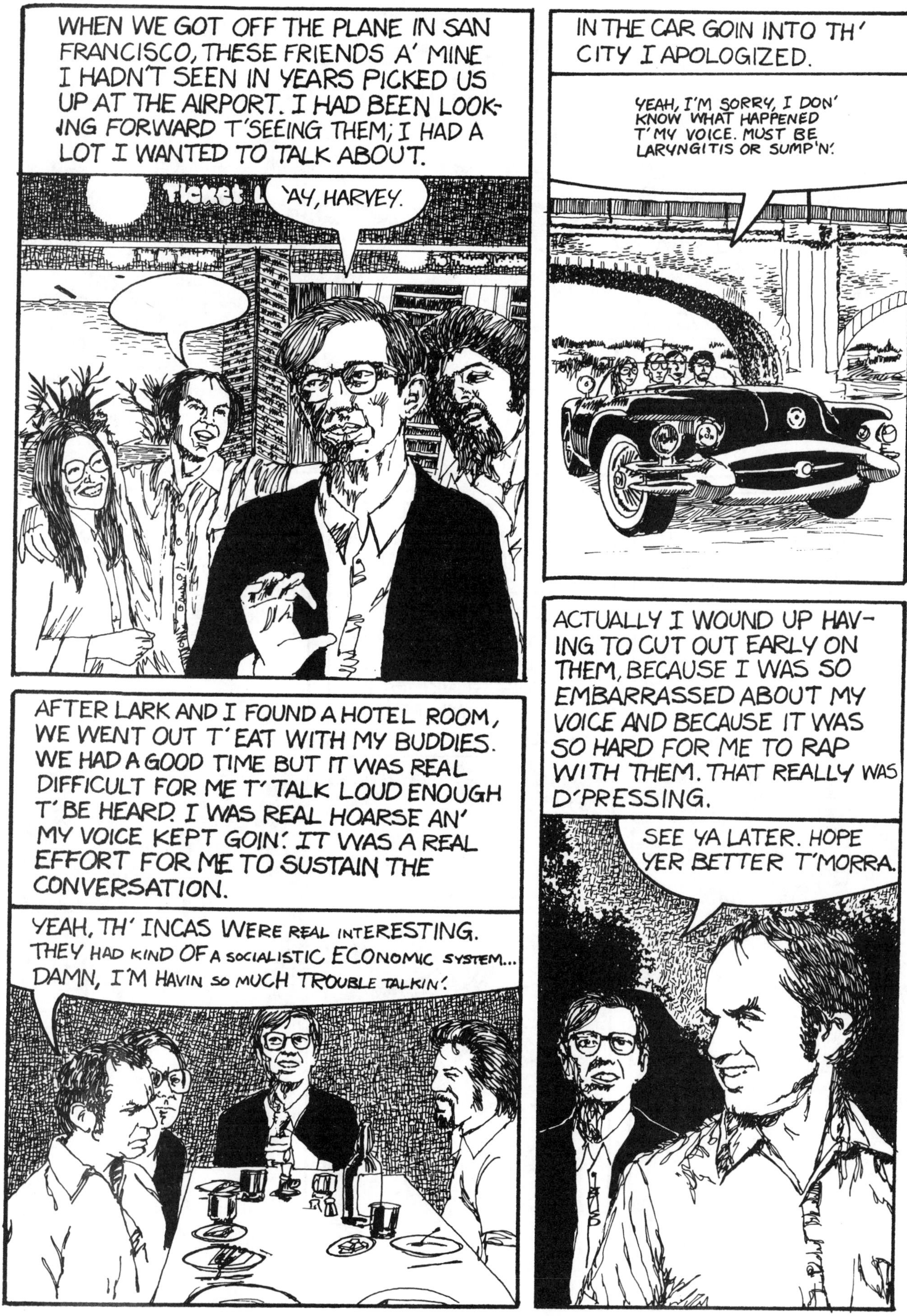
WHEN WE GOT OFF THE PLANE IN SAN FRANCISCO, THESE FRIENDS A' MINE I HADN'T SEEN IN YEARS PICKED US UP AT THE AIRPORT. I HAD BEEN LOOKING FORWARD T'SEEING THEM; I HAD A LOT I WANTED TO TALK ABOUT.
Ticket L
'AY, HARVEY.
IN THE CAR GOIN INTO TH' CITY I APOLOGIZED.
YEAH, I'M SORRY, I DON' KNOW WHAT HAPPENED T'MY VOICE. MUST BE LARYNGITIS OR SUMP'N'.
AFTER LARK AND I FOUND A HOTEL ROOM, WE WENT OUT T'EAT WITH MY BUDDIES. WE HAD A GOOD TIME BUT IT WAS REAL DIFFICULT FOR ME T'TALK LOUD ENOUGH T'BE HEARD. I WAS REAL HOARSE AN' MY VOICE KEPT GOIN'. IT WAS A REAL EFFORT FOR ME TO SUSTAIN THE CONVERSATION.
YEAH, TH' INCAS WERE REAL INTERESTING. THEY HAD KIND OF A SOCIALISTIC ECONOMIC SYSTEM... DAMN, I'M HAVIN SO MUCH TROUBLE TALKIN'.
ACTUALLY I WOUND UP HAVING TO CUT OUT EARLY ON THEM, BECAUSE I WAS SO EMBARRASSED ABOUT MY VOICE AND BECAUSE IT WAS SO HARD FOR ME TO RAP WITH THEM. THAT REALLY WAS D'PRESSING.
SEE YA LATER. HOPE YER BETTER T'MORRA.

I DID SOME REAL INTER-
ESTING THINGS IN SAN
FRANCISCO, BUT MY ENJOY-
MENT WAS MARRED BY MY
INABILITY TO TALK ABOUT
THINGS WHILE I WAS DOING
THEM. I SAW ART LANDE, A
JAZZ PIANIST I REALLY
LIKED, AT A CLUB. I WANTED
T' TALK T' HIM DURING A
BREAK, BUT I DECIDED NOT
TO BECAUSE I THOUGHT
HE MIGHT NOT BE ABLE T'
HEAR ME ABOVE THE CROWD
NOISE.

AT FIRST I WAS JUST
ANNOYED BY MY SPEECH
DIFFICULTIES. EVERY NIGHT
I'D GO TO SLEEP THINKING
I JUST HAD LARYNGITIS
AND WOULD BE OK WHEN
I WOKE UP. BUT THINGS
DIDN'T GET MUCH BETTER.
AFTER A COUPLE A' DAYS
I STARTED T' WORRY.

THEN IT CAME TIME T'
HEAD NORTH. WE RODE
THE TRAIN FROM SAN
FRANCISCO TO SALEM,
OREGON. IT TOOK 18
HOURS AND WAS A DRAG.
I COULDN'T SLEEP. I WAS
SWEATING, STINKING; I
COULD FEEL MY BEARD
POP OUT.

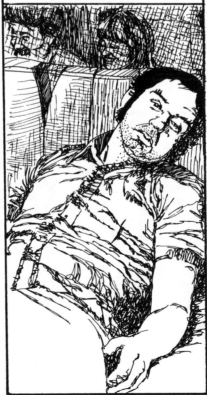

WHEN WE GOT OFF IN SA-
LEM, I WAS TIRED AND
FUNKY AND FELT APPRE-
HENSIVE ABOUT MEETING
LARK'S SISTER.

HONEY, THIS IS APRIL.

HI, GLAD T' MEETCHA. SORRY
ABOUT THE WAY I SOUND. I
GOT LARYNGITIS THAT JUS'
WON'T QUIT.

BEING IN OREGON FOR THE FIRST TIME WAS A TREMENDOUS EXPERIENCE. THE NORTHWEST QUARTER OF OREGON HAS TO BE, SQUARE MILE FOR SQUARE MILE, ONE OF THE MOST BEAUTIFUL AND GEOGRAPHICALLY VARIED REGIONS IN THE WORLD. I SAW SEACOAST, THE COLUMBIA RIVER, WATERFALLS, RAINFORESTS, LAVA FIELDS, MOUNTAINS, RICH FARMLAND AND EVEN SEMI-ARID HILL COUNTRY, ALL WITHIN ABOUT A 135 MILE RADIUS OF SALEM.

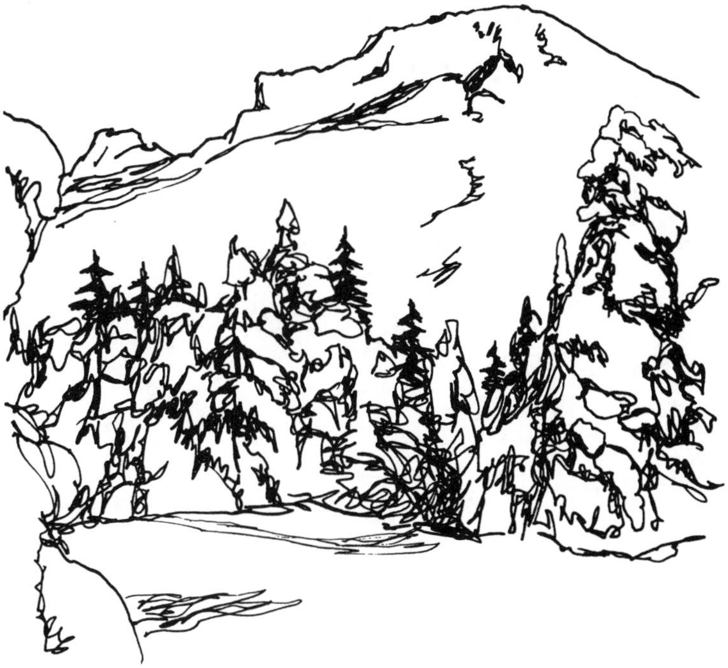

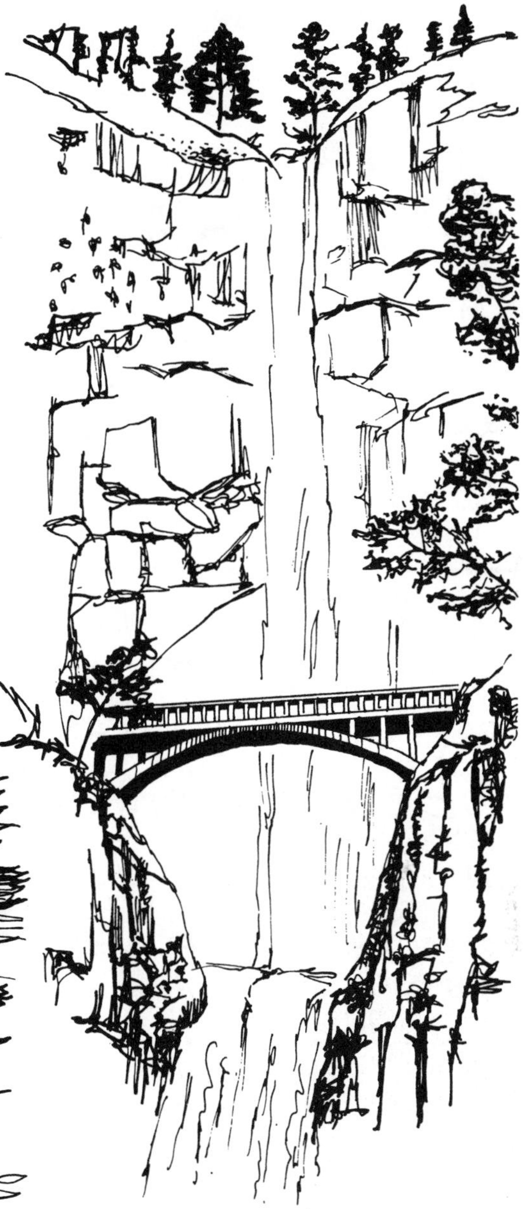

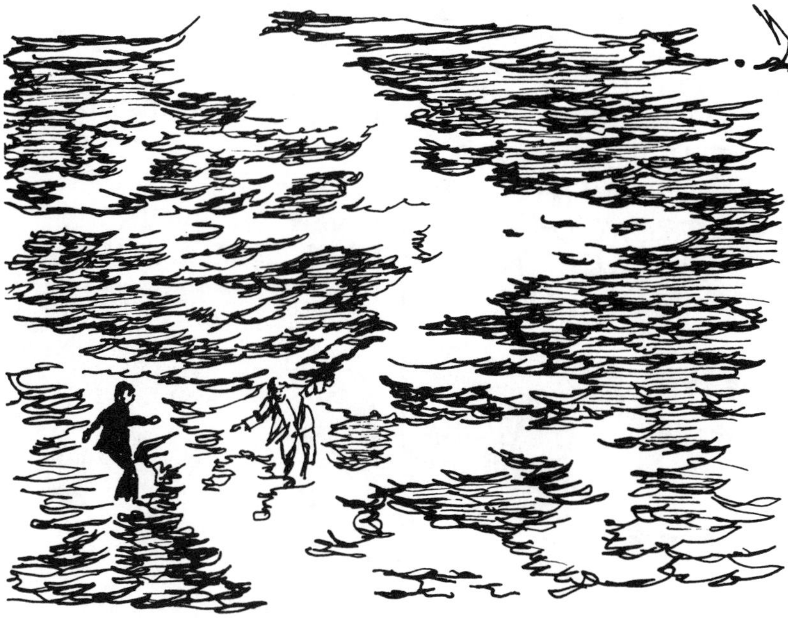

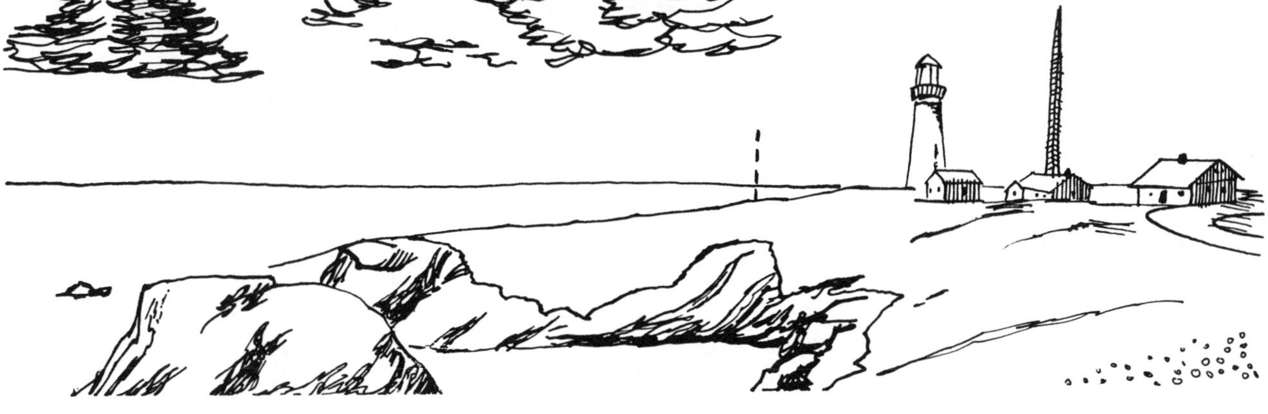

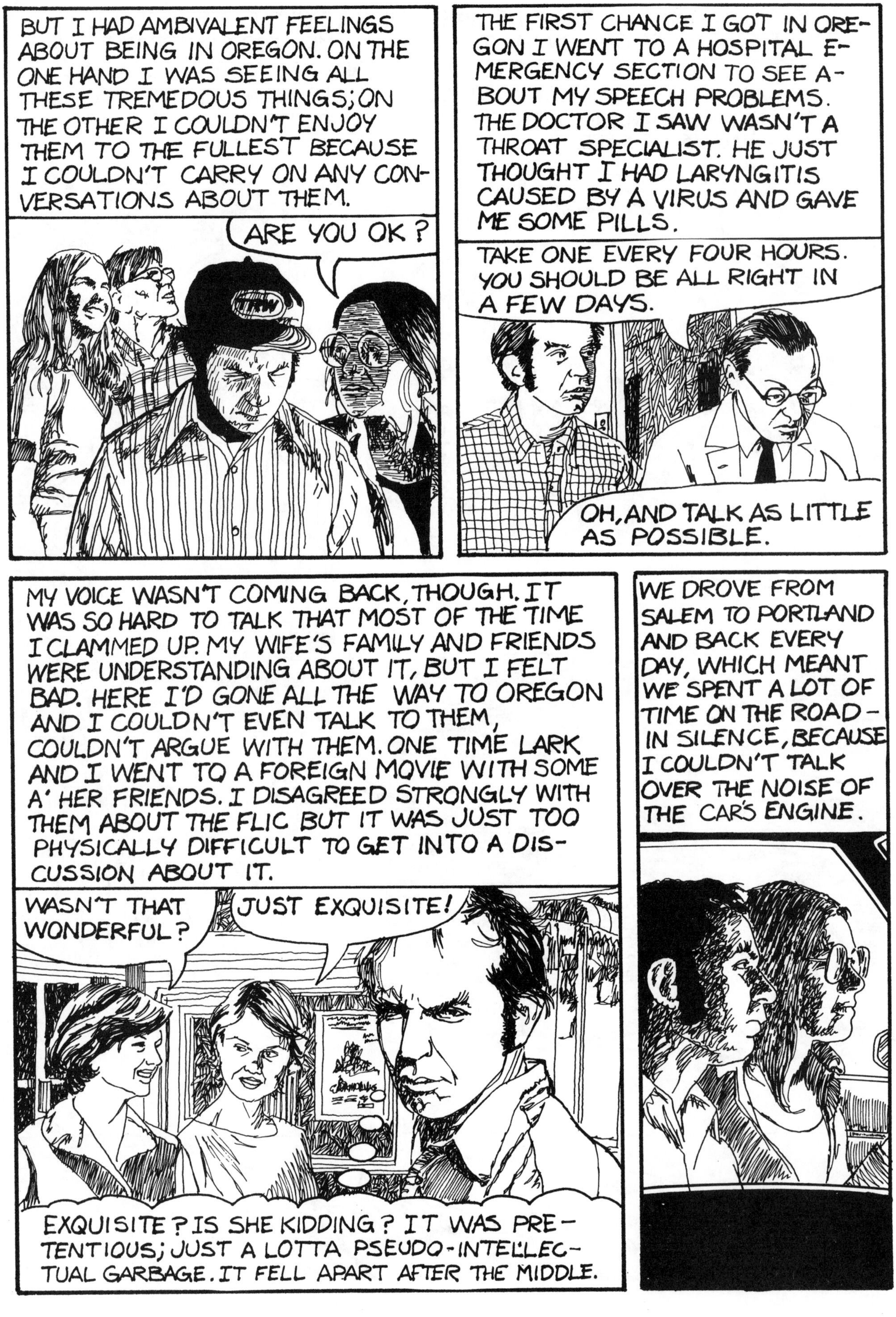
BUT I HAD AMBIVALENT FEELINGS ABOUT BEING IN OREGON. ON THE ONE HAND I WAS SEEING ALL THESE TREMEDOUS THINGS; ON THE OTHER I COULDN'T ENJOY THEM TO THE FULLEST BECAUSE I COULDN'T CARRY ON ANY CONVERSATIONS ABOUT THEM.
ARE YOU OK ?
THE FIRST CHANCE I GOT IN OREGON I WENT TO A HOSPITAL EMERGENCY SECTION TO SEE ABOUT MY SPEECH PROBLEMS. THE DOCTOR I SAW WASN'T A THROAT SPECIALIST. HE JUST THOUGHT I HAD LARYNGITIS CAUSED BY A VIRUS AND GAVE ME SOME PILLS.
TAKE ONE EVERY FOUR HOURS. YOU SHOULD BE ALL RIGHT IN A FEW DAYS.
OH, AND TALK AS LITTLE AS POSSIBLE.
MY VOICE WASN'T COMING BACK, THOUGH. IT WAS SO HARD TO TALK THAT MOST OF THE TIME I CLAMMED UP. MY WIFE'S FAMILY AND FRIENDS WERE UNDERSTANDING ABOUT IT, BUT I FELT BAD. HERE I'D GONE ALL THE WAY TO OREGON AND I COULDN'T EVEN TALK TO THEM, COULDN'T ARGUE WITH THEM. ONE TIME LARK AND I WENT TO A FOREIGN MOVIE WITH SOME A' HER FRIENDS. I DISAGREED STRONGLY WITH THEM ABOUT THE FLIC BUT IT WAS JUST TOO PHYSICALLY DIFFICULT TO GET INTO A DISCUSSION ABOUT IT.
WASN'T THAT WONDERFUL?
JUST EXQUISITE!
EXQUISITE? IS SHE KIDDING? IT WAS PRETENTIOUS; JUST A LOTTA PSEUDO-INTELLECTUAL GARBAGE. IT FELL APART AFTER THE MIDDLE.
WE DROVE FROM SALEM TO PORTLAND AND BACK EVERY DAY, WHICH MEANT WE SPENT A LOT OF TIME ON THE ROAD - IN SILENCE, BECAUSE I COULDN'T TALK OVER THE NOISE OF THE CAR'S ENGINE.

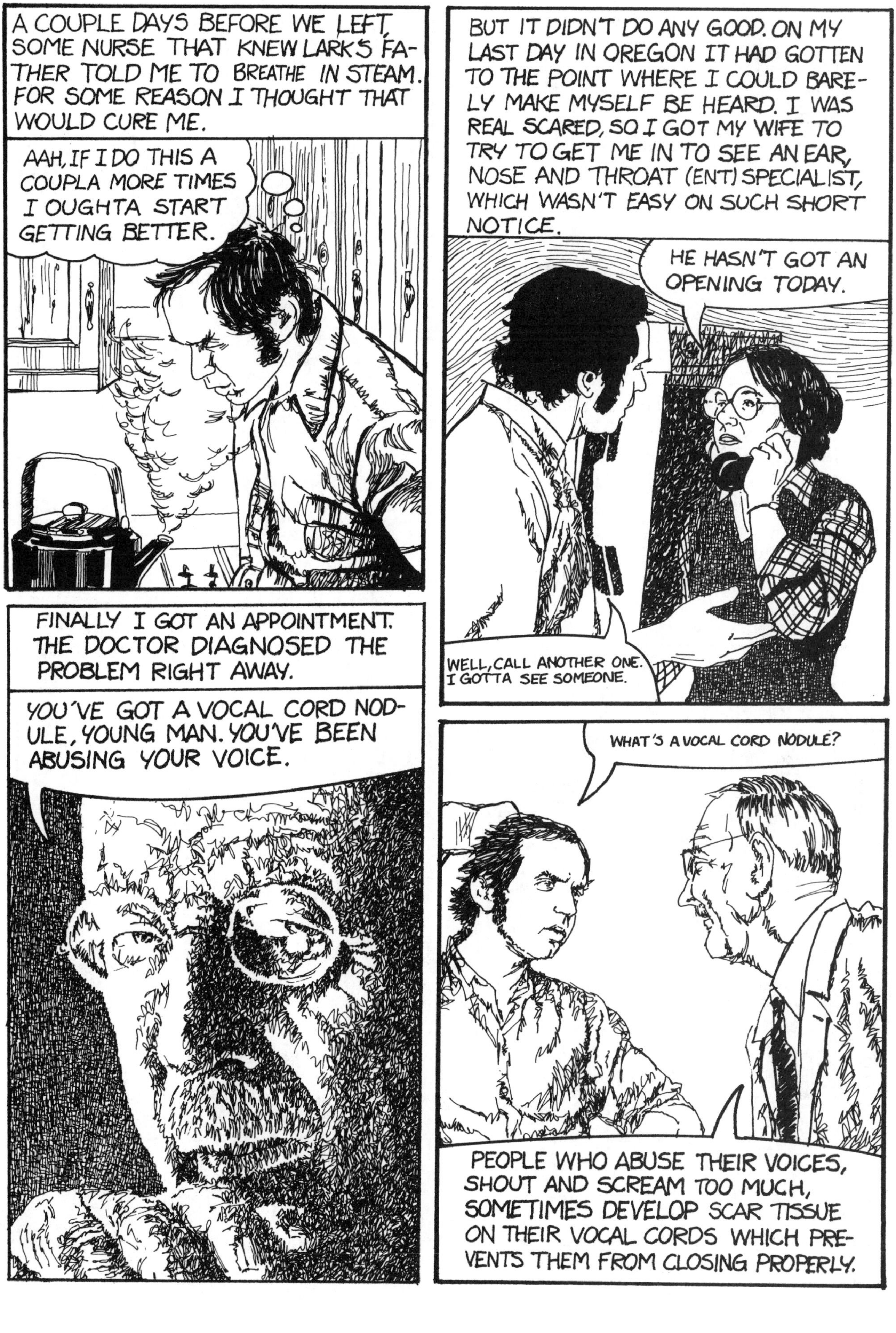
A COUPLE DAYS BEFORE WE LEFT, SOME NURSE THAT KNEW LARK'S FATHER TOLD ME TO BREATHE IN STEAM. FOR SOME REASON I THOUGHT THAT WOULD CURE ME.
AAH, IF I DO THIS A COUPLA MORE TIMES I OUGHTA START GETTING BETTER.
BUT IT DIDN'T DO ANY GOOD. ON MY LAST DAY IN OREGON IT HAD GOTTEN TO THE POINT WHERE I COULD BARELY MAKE MYSELF BE HEARD. I WAS REAL SCARED, SO I GOT MY WIFE TO TRY TO GET ME IN TO SEE AN EAR, NOSE AND THROAT (ENT) SPECIALIST, WHICH WASN'T EASY ON SUCH SHORT NOTICE.
HE HASN'T GOT AN OPENING TODAY.
WELL, CALL ANOTHER ONE. I GOTTA SEE SOMEONE.
FINALLY I GOT AN APPOINTMENT. THE DOCTOR DIAGNOSED THE PROBLEM RIGHT AWAY.
YOU'VE GOT A VOCAL CORD NODULE, YOUNG MAN. YOU'VE BEEN ABUSING YOUR VOICE.
WHAT'S A VOCAL CORD NODULE?
PEOPLE WHO ABUSE THEIR VOICES, SHOUT AND SCREAM TOO MUCH, SOMETIMES DEVELOP SCAR TISSUE ON THEIR VOCAL CORDS WHICH PREVENTS THEM FROM CLOSING PROPERLY.

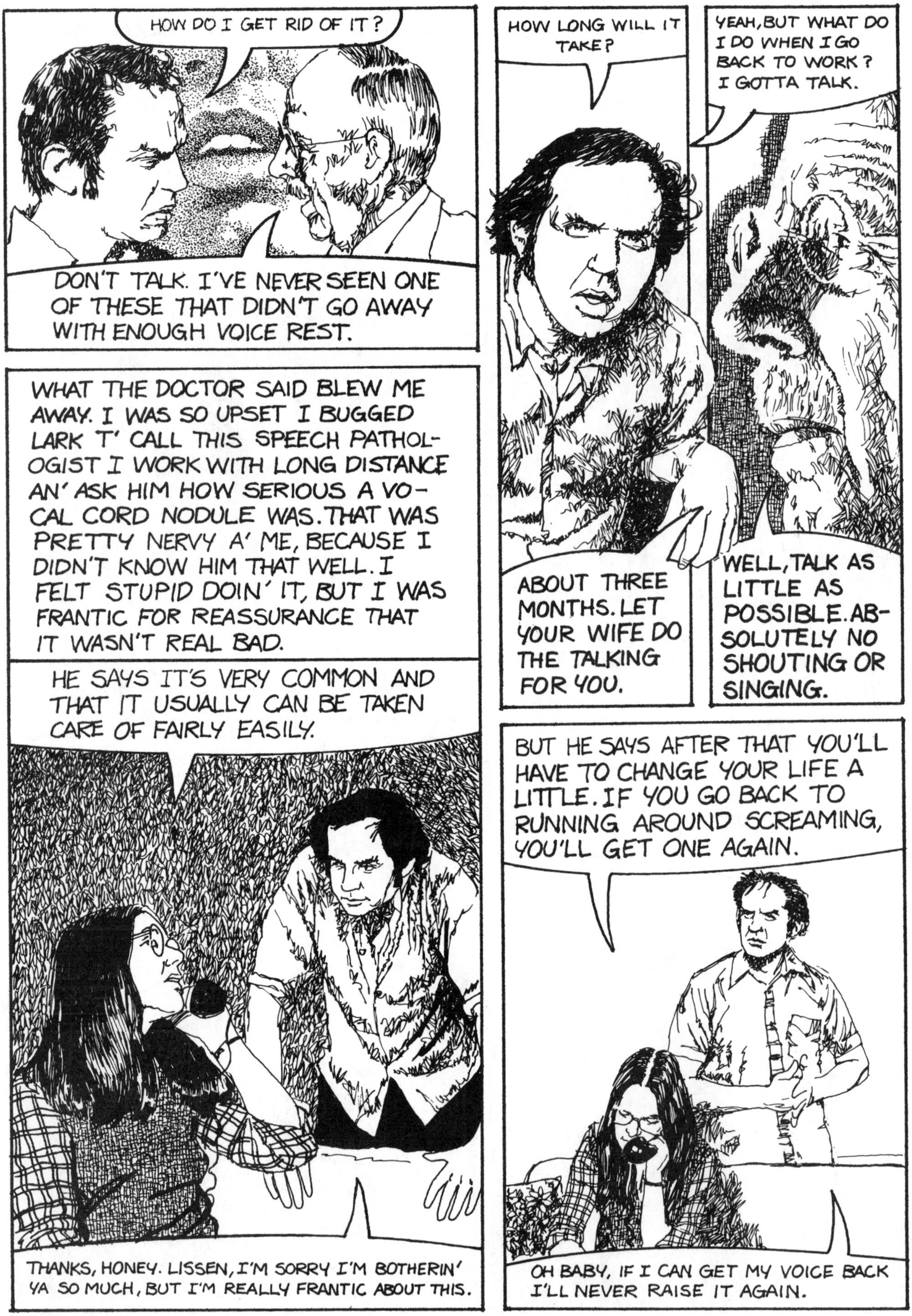
HOW DO I GET RID OF IT?
DON'T TALK. I'VE NEVER SEEN ONE OF THESE THAT DIDN'T GO AWAY WITH ENOUGH VOICE REST.
HOW LONG WILL IT TAKE?
ABOUT THREE MONTHS. LET YOUR WIFE DO THE TALKING FOR YOU.
YEAH, BUT WHAT DO I DO WHEN I GO BACK TO WORK? I GOTTA TALK.
WELL, TALK AS LITTLE AS POSSIBLE. ABSOLUTELY NO SHOUTING OR SINGING.
WHAT THE DOCTOR SAID BLEW ME AWAY. I WAS SO UPSET I BUGGED LARK T' CALL THIS SPEECH PATHOLOGIST I WORK WITH LONG DISTANCE AN' ASK HIM HOW SERIOUS A VOCAL CORD NODULE WAS. THAT WAS PRETTY NERVY A' ME, BECAUSE I DIDN'T KNOW HIM THAT WELL. I FELT STUPID DOIN' IT, BUT I WAS FRANTIC FOR REASSURANCE THAT IT WASN'T REAL BAD.
HE SAYS IT'S VERY COMMON AND THAT IT USUALLY CAN BE TAKEN CARE OF FAIRLY EASILY.
THANKS, HONEY. LISSEN, I'M SORRY I'M BOTHERIN' YA SO MUCH, BUT I'M REALLY FRANTIC ABOUT THIS.
BUT HE SAYS AFTER THAT YOU'LL HAVE TO CHANGE YOUR LIFE A LITTLE. IF YOU GO BACK TO RUNNING AROUND SCREAMING, YOU'LL GET ONE AGAIN.
OH BABY, IF I CAN GET MY VOICE BACK I'LL NEVER RAISE IT AGAIN.

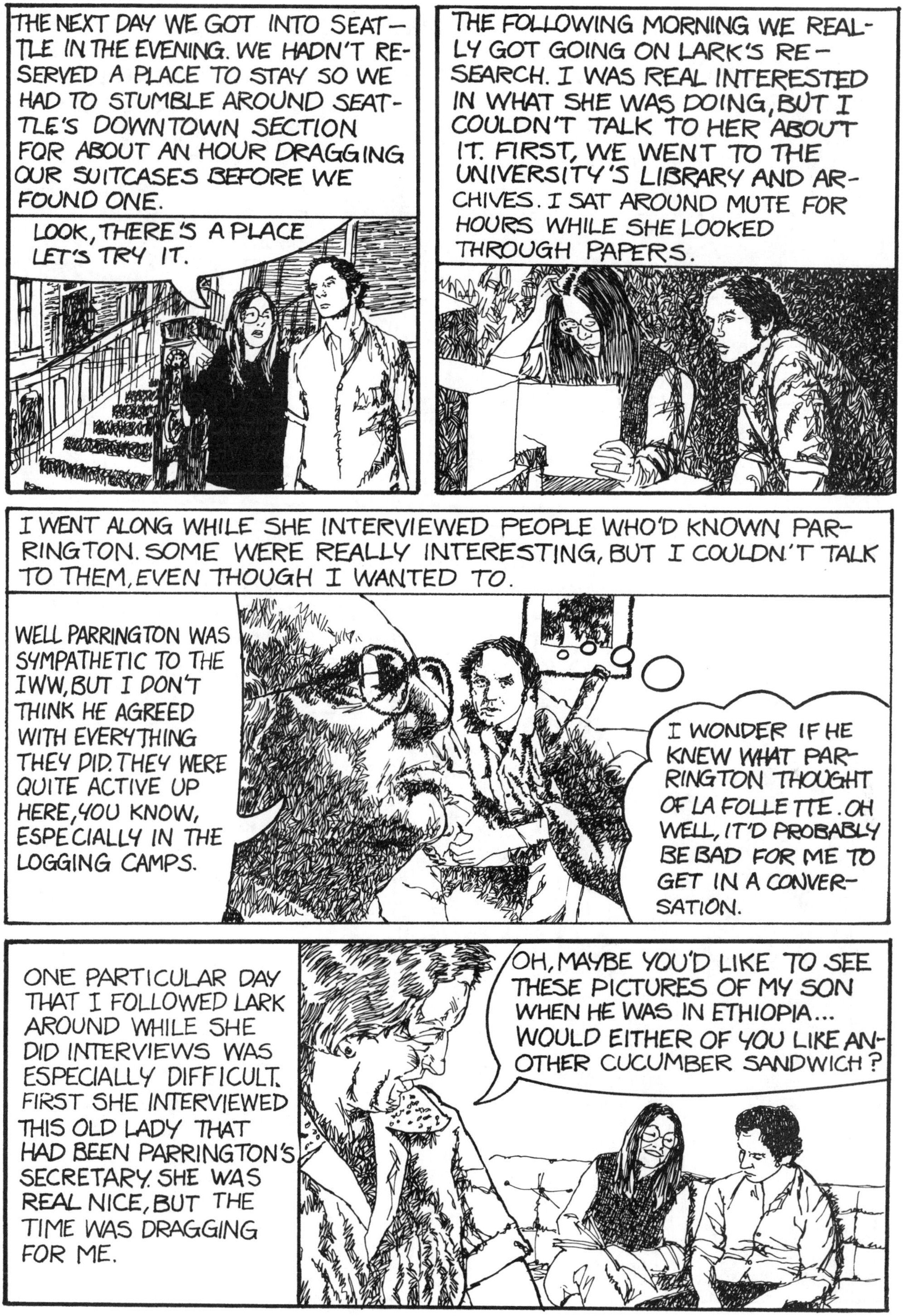
THE NEXT DAY WE GOT INTO SEATTLE IN THE EVENING. WE HADN'T RESERVED A PLACE TO STAY SO WE HAD TO STUMBLE AROUND SEATTLE'S DOWNTOWN SECTION FOR ABOUT AN HOUR DRAGGING OUR SUITCASES BEFORE WE FOUND ONE.
LOOK, THERE'S A PLACE LET'S TRY IT.
THE FOLLOWING MORNING WE REALLY GOT GOING ON LARK'S RESEARCH. I WAS REAL INTERESTED IN WHAT SHE WAS DOING, BUT I COULDN'T TALK TO HER ABOUT IT. FIRST, WE WENT TO THE UNIVERSITY'S LIBRARY AND ARCHIVES. I SAT AROUND MUTE FOR HOURS WHILE SHE LOOKED THROUGH PAPERS.
I WENT ALONG WHILE SHE INTERVIEWED PEOPLE WHO'D KNOWN PARRINGTON. SOME WERE REALLY INTERESTING, BUT I COULDN'T TALK TO THEM, EVEN THOUGH I WANTED TO.
WELL PARRINGTON WAS SYMPATHETIC TO THE IWW, BUT I DON'T THINK HE AGREED WITH EVERYTHING THEY DID. THEY WERE QUITE ACTIVE UP HERE, YOU KNOW, ESPECIALLY IN THE LOGGING CAMPS.
I WONDER IF HE KNEW WHAT PARRINGTON THOUGHT OF LA FOLLETTE. OH WELL, IT'D PROBABLY BE BAD FOR ME TO GET IN A CONVERSATION.
ONE PARTICULAR DAY THAT I FOLLOWED LARK AROUND WHILE SHE DID INTERVIEWS WAS ESPECIALLY DIFFICULT. FIRST SHE INTERVIEWED THIS OLD LADY THAT HAD BEEN PARRINGTON'S SECRETARY. SHE WAS REAL NICE, BUT THE TIME WAS DRAGGING FOR ME.
OH, MAYBE YOU'D LIKE TO SEE THESE PICTURES OF MY SON WHEN HE WAS IN ETHIOPIA... WOULD EITHER OF YOU LIKE ANOTHER CUCUMBER SANDWICH?

RIGHT AFTER THAT WE SAW A RETIRED PROFESSOR FOR A FEW HOURS. I WAS REALLY GETTING IMPATIENT BY THEN.

YOU'VE SHOULD'VE SEEN THE CONDITIONS IN THE LOGGING CAMPS IN THOSE DAYS. YOU YOUNG PEOPLE DON'T KNOW HOW EASY YOU HAVE IT.

CAN'T THIS OLD GEEZER SHUT UP FOR A MINIT?

AFTER WE GOT OUT OF HIS HOUSE IT WAS LATE AND UNSEASONABLY COLD. I WAS WORRIED ABOUT BUSES STILL RUNNING AT THAT HOUR.

SHIT, I'M SO TIRED A' TRAVELIN' ON BUSES, PLANES, TRAINS. I'LL BE SO HAPPY T'GET HOME!

IT WAS SO HARD FOR ME TO TALK. IT SEEMED LIKE I HAD TO PUSH SO HARD JUST TO MAKE A SQUEAK. I'D WALK ALONG THE STREET AND LOOK AT PEOPLE TALKING TO EACH OTHER LIKE IT WAS NOTHING AND I'D BE AMAZED.

BLAH BLAH

SO THEN HE SAID

BLAH BLAH

IZZAT RIGHT?

HOW DO THEY DO IT?

I STARTED HAVING TO WRITE NOTES TO MY WIFE TO COMMUNICATE. I CARRIED THESE MEMO PADS AROUND WITH ME. AFTER A FEW DAYS OF THAT I GOT CRAZY. I THOUGHT I WAS NEVER GONNA GET WELL. I WROTE LARK THIS NOTE:

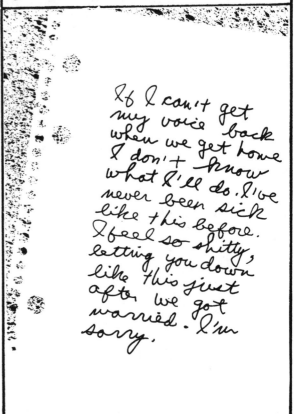

If I can't get my voice back when we get home I don't know what I'll do. I've never been sick like this before. I feel so shitty, letting you down like this just after we got married. I'm sorry.

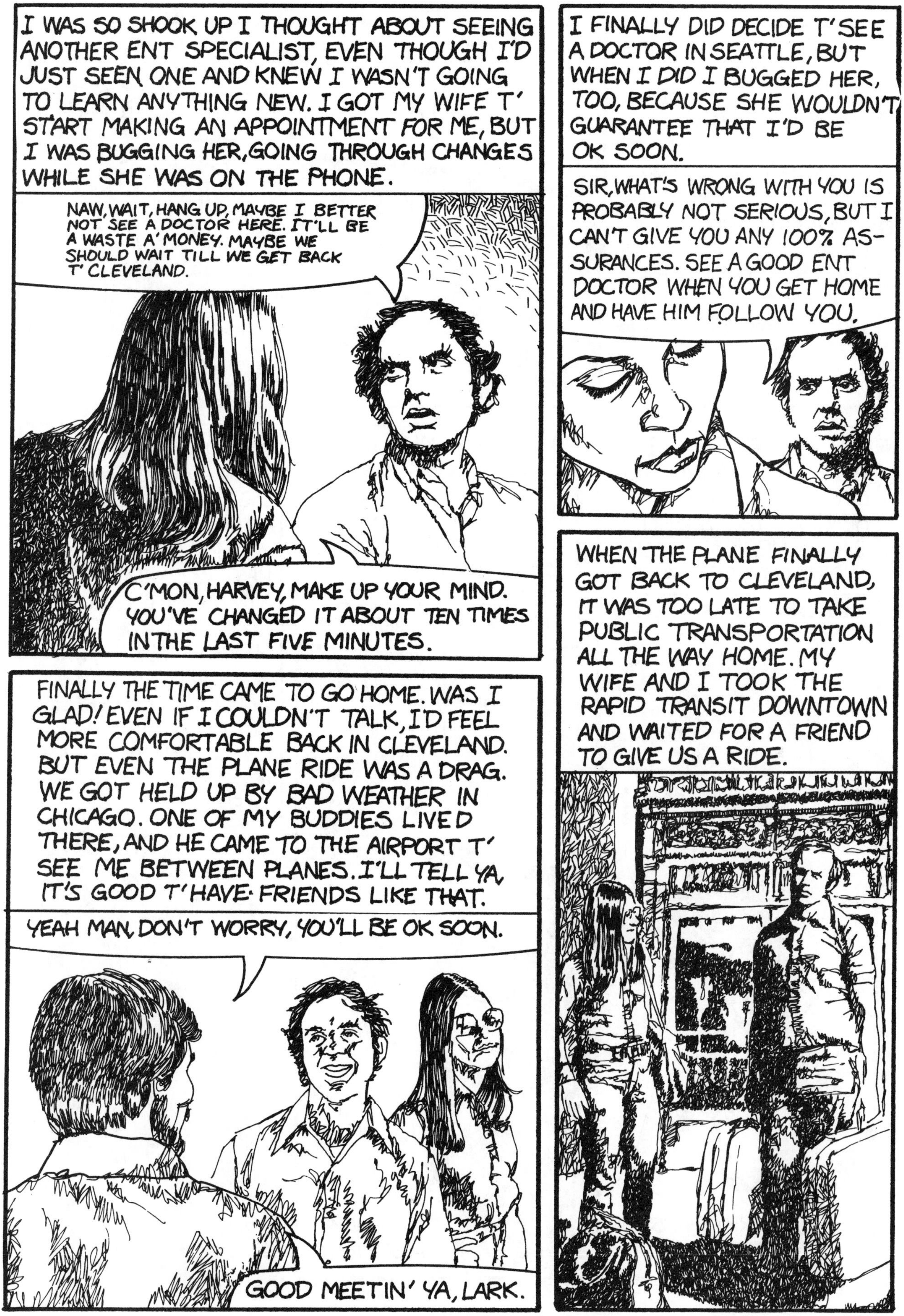
I WAS SO SHOOK UP I THOUGHT ABOUT SEEING ANOTHER ENT SPECIALIST, EVEN THOUGH I'D JUST SEEN ONE AND KNEW I WASN'T GOING TO LEARN ANYTHING NEW. I GOT MY WIFE T' START MAKING AN APPOINTMENT FOR ME, BUT I WAS BUGGING HER, GOING THROUGH CHANGES WHILE SHE WAS ON THE PHONE.
NAW, WAIT, HANG UP, MAYBE I BETTER NOT SEE A DOCTOR HERE. IT'LL BE A WASTE A' MONEY. MAYBE WE SHOULD WAIT TILL WE GET BACK T' CLEVELAND.
C'MON, HARVEY, MAKE UP YOUR MIND. YOU'VE CHANGED IT ABOUT TEN TIMES IN THE LAST FIVE MINUTES.
I FINALLY DID DECIDE T' SEE A DOCTOR IN SEATTLE, BUT WHEN I DID I BUGGED HER, TOO, BECAUSE SHE WOULDN'T GUARANTEE THAT I'D BE OK SOON.
SIR, WHAT'S WRONG WITH YOU IS PROBABLY NOT SERIOUS, BUT I CAN'T GIVE YOU ANY 100% ASSURANCES. SEE A GOOD ENT DOCTOR WHEN YOU GET HOME AND HAVE HIM FOLLOW YOU.
FINALLY THE TIME CAME TO GO HOME. WAS I GLAD! EVEN IF I COULDN'T TALK, I'D FEEL MORE COMFORTABLE BACK IN CLEVELAND. BUT EVEN THE PLANE RIDE WAS A DRAG. WE GOT HELD UP BY BAD WEATHER IN CHICAGO. ONE OF MY BUDDIES LIVED THERE, AND HE CAME TO THE AIRPORT T' SEE ME BETWEEN PLANES. I'LL TELL YA, IT'S GOOD T' HAVE FRIENDS LIKE THAT.
YEAH MAN, DON'T WORRY, YOU'LL BE OK SOON.
GOOD MEETIN' YA, LARK.
WHEN THE PLANE FINALLY GOT BACK TO CLEVELAND, IT WAS TOO LATE TO TAKE PUBLIC TRANSPORTATION ALL THE WAY HOME. MY WIFE AND I TOOK THE RAPID TRANSIT DOWNTOWN AND WAITED FOR A FRIEND TO GIVE US A RIDE.

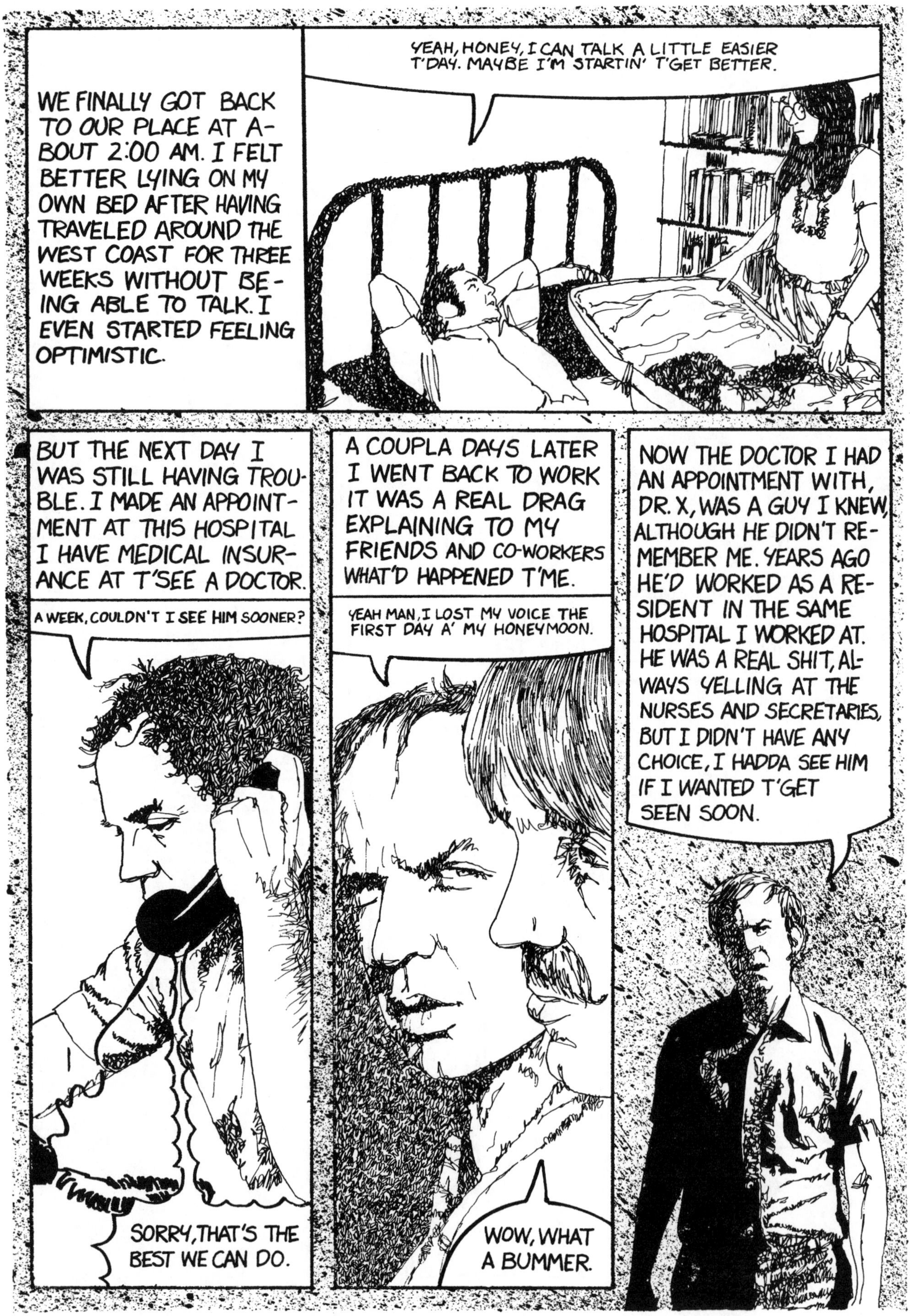
WE FINALLY GOT BACK TO OUR PLACE AT ABOUT 2:00 AM. I FELT BETTER LYING ON MY OWN BED AFTER HAVING TRAVELED AROUND THE WEST COAST FOR THREE WEEKS WITHOUT BEING ABLE TO TALK. I EVEN STARTED FEELING OPTIMISTIC.
YEAH, HONEY, I CAN TALK A LITTLE EASIER T'DAY. MAYBE I'M STARTIN' T'GET BETTER.
BUT THE NEXT DAY I WAS STILL HAVING TROUBLE. I MADE AN APPOINTMENT AT THIS HOSPITAL I HAVE MEDICAL INSURANCE AT T'SEE A DOCTOR.
A WEEK, COULDN'T I SEE HIM SOONER?
SORRY, THAT'S THE BEST WE CAN DO.
A COUPLA DAYS LATER I WENT BACK TO WORK IT WAS A REAL DRAG EXPLAINING TO MY FRIENDS AND CO-WORKERS WHAT'D HAPPENED T'ME.
YEAH MAN, I LOST MY VOICE THE FIRST DAY A' MY HONEYMOON.
WOW, WHAT A BUMMER.
NOW THE DOCTOR I HAD AN APPOINTMENT WITH, DR. X, WAS A GUY I KNEW, ALTHOUGH HE DIDN'T REMEMBER ME. YEARS AGO HE'D WORKED AS A RESIDENT IN THE SAME HOSPITAL I WORKED AT. HE WAS A REAL SHIT, ALWAYS YELLING AT THE NURSES AND SECRETARIES, BUT I DIDN'T HAVE ANY CHOICE, I HADDA SEE HIM IF I WANTED T'GET SEEN SOON.

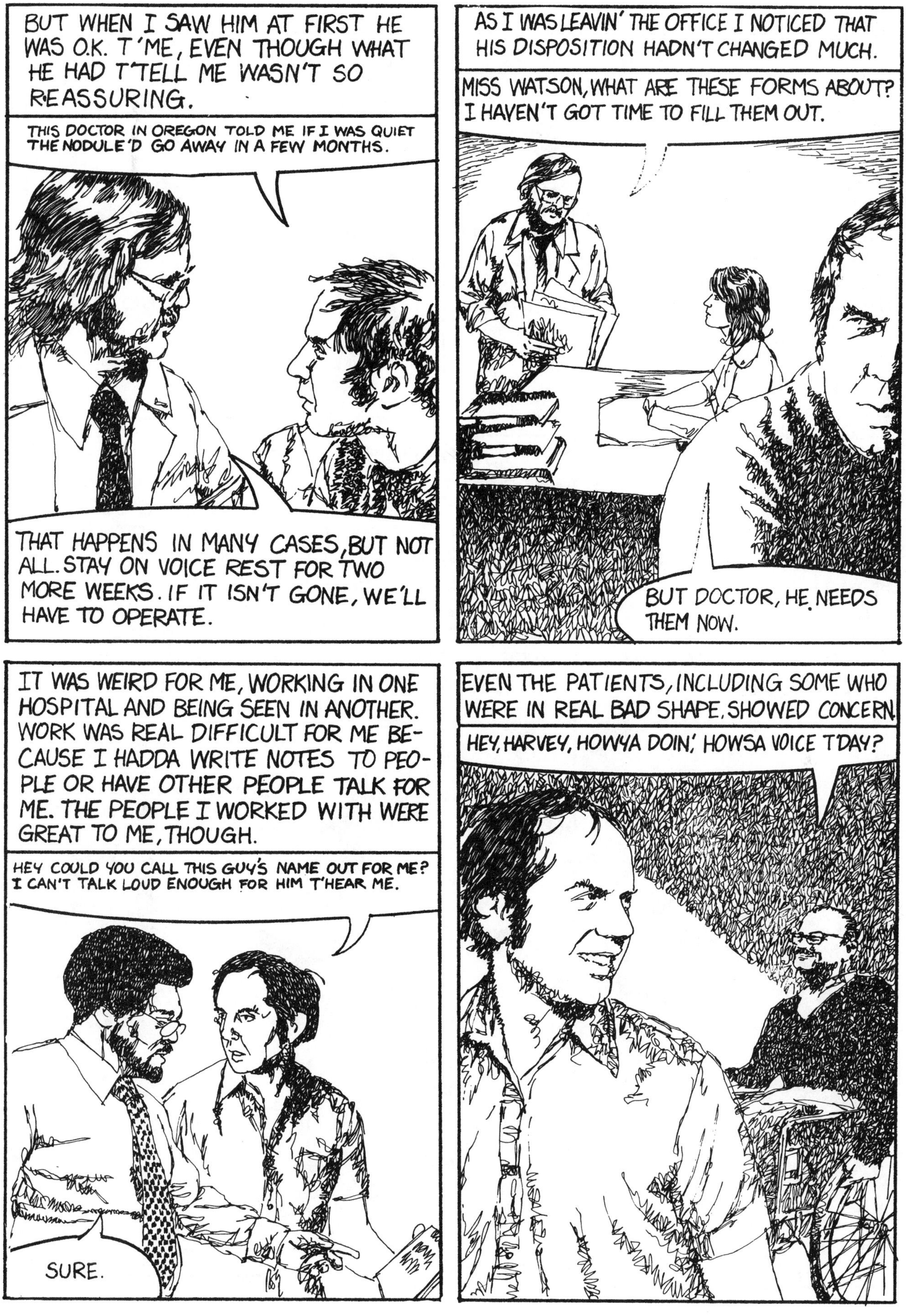
BUT WHEN I SAW HIM AT FIRST HE WAS O.K. T'ME, EVEN THOUGH WHAT HE HAD T'TELL ME WASN'T SO REASSURING.
THIS DOCTOR IN OREGON TOLD ME IF I WAS QUIET THE NODULE'D GO AWAY IN A FEW MONTHS.
THAT HAPPENS IN MANY CASES, BUT NOT ALL. STAY ON VOICE REST FOR TWO MORE WEEKS. IF IT ISN'T GONE, WE'LL HAVE TO OPERATE.
AS I WAS LEAVIN' THE OFFICE I NOTICED THAT HIS DISPOSITION HADN'T CHANGED MUCH.
MISS WATSON, WHAT ARE THESE FORMS ABOUT? I HAVEN'T GOT TIME TO FILL THEM OUT.
BUT DOCTOR, HE NEEDS THEM NOW.
IT WAS WEIRD FOR ME, WORKING IN ONE HOSPITAL AND BEING SEEN IN ANOTHER. WORK WAS REAL DIFFICULT FOR ME BECAUSE I HADDA WRITE NOTES TO PEOPLE OR HAVE OTHER PEOPLE TALK FOR ME. THE PEOPLE I WORKED WITH WERE GREAT TO ME, THOUGH.
HEY COULD YOU CALL THIS GUY'S NAME OUT FOR ME? I CAN'T TALK LOUD ENOUGH FOR HIM T'HEAR ME.
SURE.
EVEN THE PATIENTS, INCLUDING SOME WHO WERE IN REAL BAD SHAPE, SHOWED CONCERN.
HEY, HARVEY, HOWYA DOIN', HOWSA VOICE T'DAY?

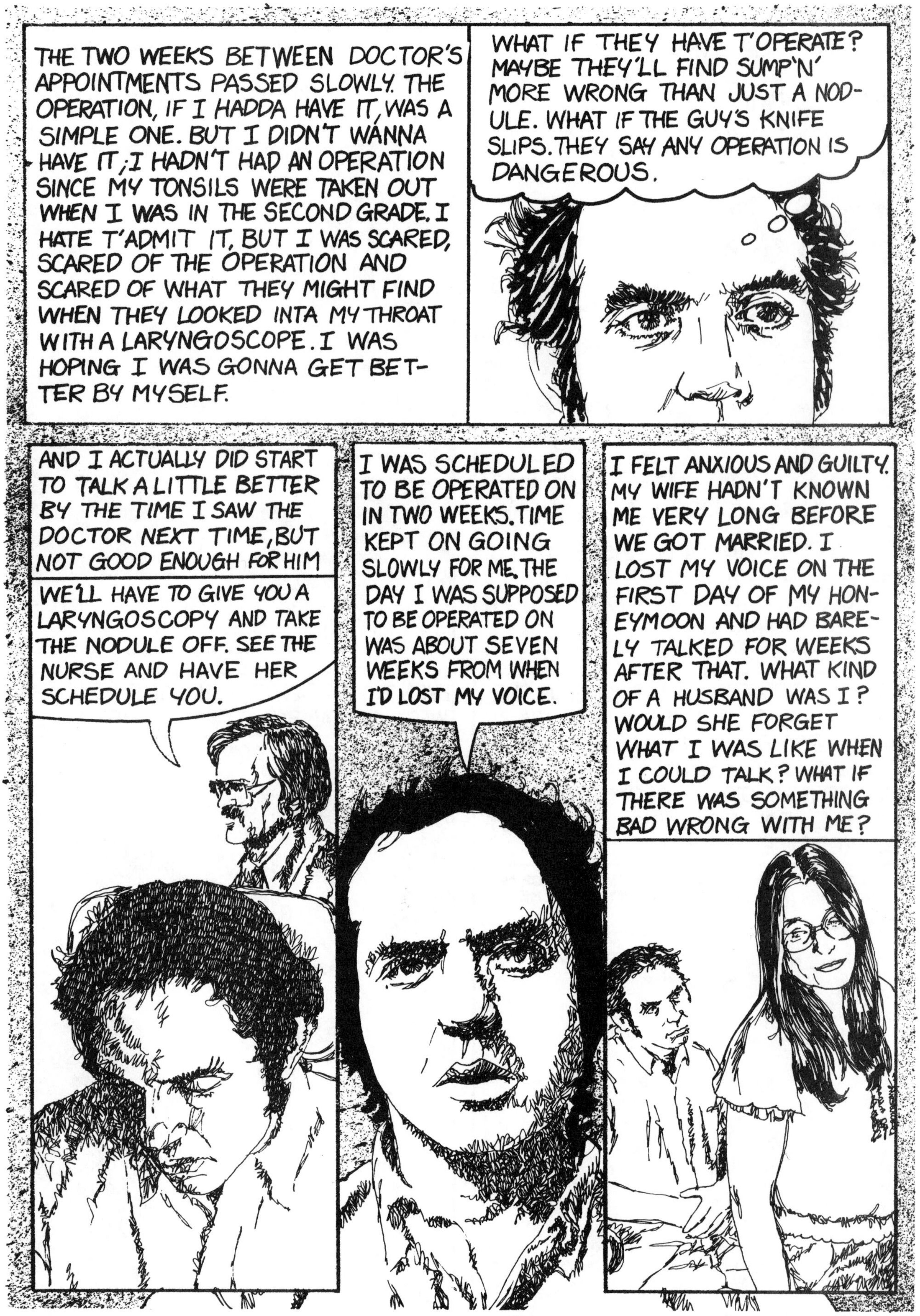
THE TWO WEEKS BETWEEN DOCTOR'S APPOINTMENTS PASSED SLOWLY. THE OPERATION, IF I HADDA HAVE IT, WAS A SIMPLE ONE. BUT I DIDN'T WANNA HAVE IT; I HADN'T HAD AN OPERATION SINCE MY TONSILS WERE TAKEN OUT WHEN I WAS IN THE SECOND GRADE. I HATE T'ADMIT IT, BUT I WAS SCARED, SCARED OF THE OPERATION AND SCARED OF WHAT THEY MIGHT FIND WHEN THEY LOOKED INTA MY THROAT WITH A LARYNGOSCOPE. I WAS HOPING I WAS GONNA GET BETTER BY MYSELF.
WHAT IF THEY HAVE T'OPERATE? MAYBE THEY'LL FIND SUMP'N' MORE WRONG THAN JUST A NODULE. WHAT IF THE GUY'S KNIFE SLIPS. THEY SAY ANY OPERATION IS DANGEROUS.
AND I ACTUALLY DID START TO TALK A LITTLE BETTER BY THE TIME I SAW THE DOCTOR NEXT TIME, BUT NOT GOOD ENOUGH FOR HIM
WE'LL HAVE TO GIVE YOU A LARYNGOSCOPY AND TAKE THE NODULE OFF. SEE THE NURSE AND HAVE HER SCHEDULE YOU.
I WAS SCHEDULED TO BE OPERATED ON IN TWO WEEKS. TIME KEPT ON GOING SLOWLY FOR ME. THE DAY I WAS SUPPOSED TO BE OPERATED ON WAS ABOUT SEVEN WEEKS FROM WHEN I'D LOST MY VOICE.
I FELT ANXIOUS AND GUILTY. MY WIFE HADN'T KNOWN ME VERY LONG BEFORE WE GOT MARRIED. I LOST MY VOICE ON THE FIRST DAY OF MY HONEYMOON AND HAD BARELY TALKED FOR WEEKS AFTER THAT. WHAT KIND OF A HUSBAND WAS I? WOULD SHE FORGET WHAT I WAS LIKE WHEN I COULD TALK? WHAT IF THERE WAS SOMETHING BAD WRONG WITH ME?

FINALLY THE TIME CAME. I REMEMBER DRIVING INTO THE HOSPITAL ON A GRAY NOVEMBER MORNING.

THE PEOPLE AT THE HOSPITAL WERE NICE. THEY PUT ME AT EASE.

NO KIDDING, THIS OPERATION IS NOTHING TO WORRY ABOUT. IT'LL BE OVER IN FIVE MINUTES. YOU'LL BE ABLE TO TALK IN A WEEK.

THE OPERATION **WAS** OVER REAL FAST AND I WENT HOME THAT AFTERNOON. EVERYTHING WENT SMOOTHLY. I WAS SUPPOSED TO KEEP QUIET FOR ANOTHER WEEK AND THEN SEE THE DOCTOR.

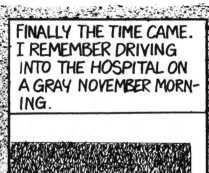

AFTER THE OPERATION LARK SEEMED FAIRLY OPTIMISTIC. AFTER ALL, I WAS SUPPOSED TO BE VASTLY IMPROVED IN JUST 7 DAYS.

IT'S BEEN A REAL ORDEAL, BUT THINGS OUGHT TO BE GETTING BACK TO NORMAL BY NEXT FRIDAY.

BUT I WAS STILL WORRIED. EVERY DAY DURING THAT WEEK I'D SAY A LITTLE SOMETHING JUST TO SEE HOW I WAS DOING. I COULD TALK, BUT IT WAS STILL DIFFICULT.

TESTING, TESTING, HOW DO YOU SOUND TODAY, MAN?

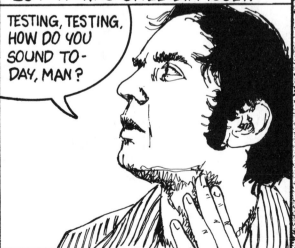

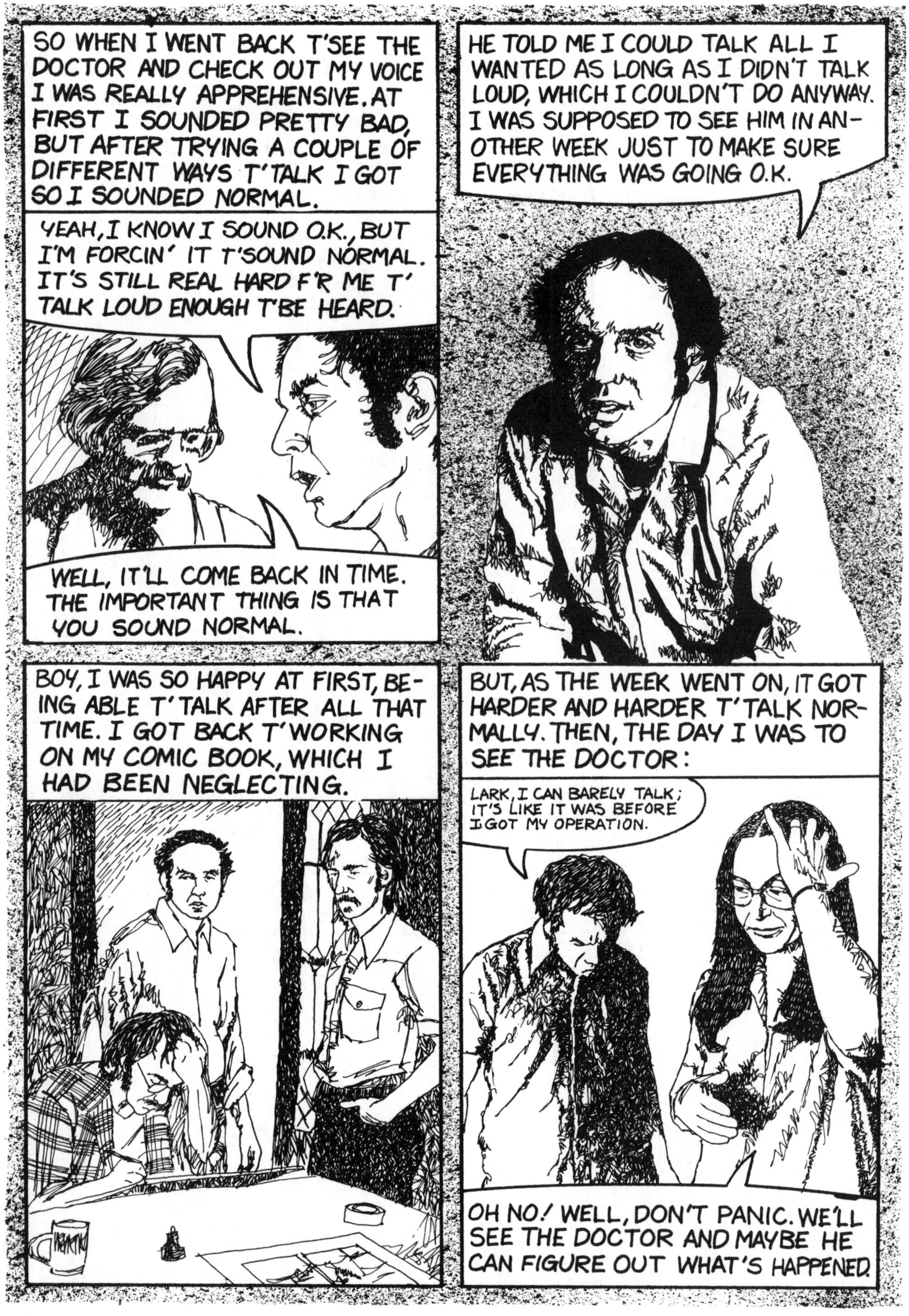

SO WHEN I WENT BACK T'SEE THE DOCTOR AND CHECK OUT MY VOICE I WAS REALLY APPREHENSIVE. AT FIRST I SOUNDED PRETTY BAD, BUT AFTER TRYING A COUPLE OF DIFFERENT WAYS T'TALK I GOT SO I SOUNDED NORMAL.
YEAH, I KNOW I SOUND O.K., BUT I'M FORCIN' IT T'SOUND NORMAL. IT'S STILL REAL HARD F'R ME T' TALK LOUD ENOUGH T'BE HEARD.
WELL, IT'LL COME BACK IN TIME. THE IMPORTANT THING IS THAT YOU SOUND NORMAL.
HE TOLD ME I COULD TALK ALL I WANTED AS LONG AS I DIDN'T TALK LOUD, WHICH I COULDN'T DO ANYWAY. I WAS SUPPOSED TO SEE HIM IN AN-OTHER WEEK JUST TO MAKE SURE EVERYTHING WAS GOING O.K.
BOY, I WAS SO HAPPY AT FIRST, BE-ING ABLE T'TALK AFTER ALL THAT TIME. I GOT BACK T'WORKING ON MY COMIC BOOK, WHICH I HAD BEEN NEGLECTING.
BUT, AS THE WEEK WENT ON, IT GOT HARDER AND HARDER T'TALK NOR-MALLY. THEN, THE DAY I WAS TO SEE THE DOCTOR:
LARK, I CAN BARELY TALK; IT'S LIKE IT WAS BEFORE I GOT MY OPERATION.
OH NO! WELL, DON'T PANIC. WE'LL SEE THE DOCTOR AND MAYBE HE CAN FIGURE OUT WHAT'S HAPPENED.

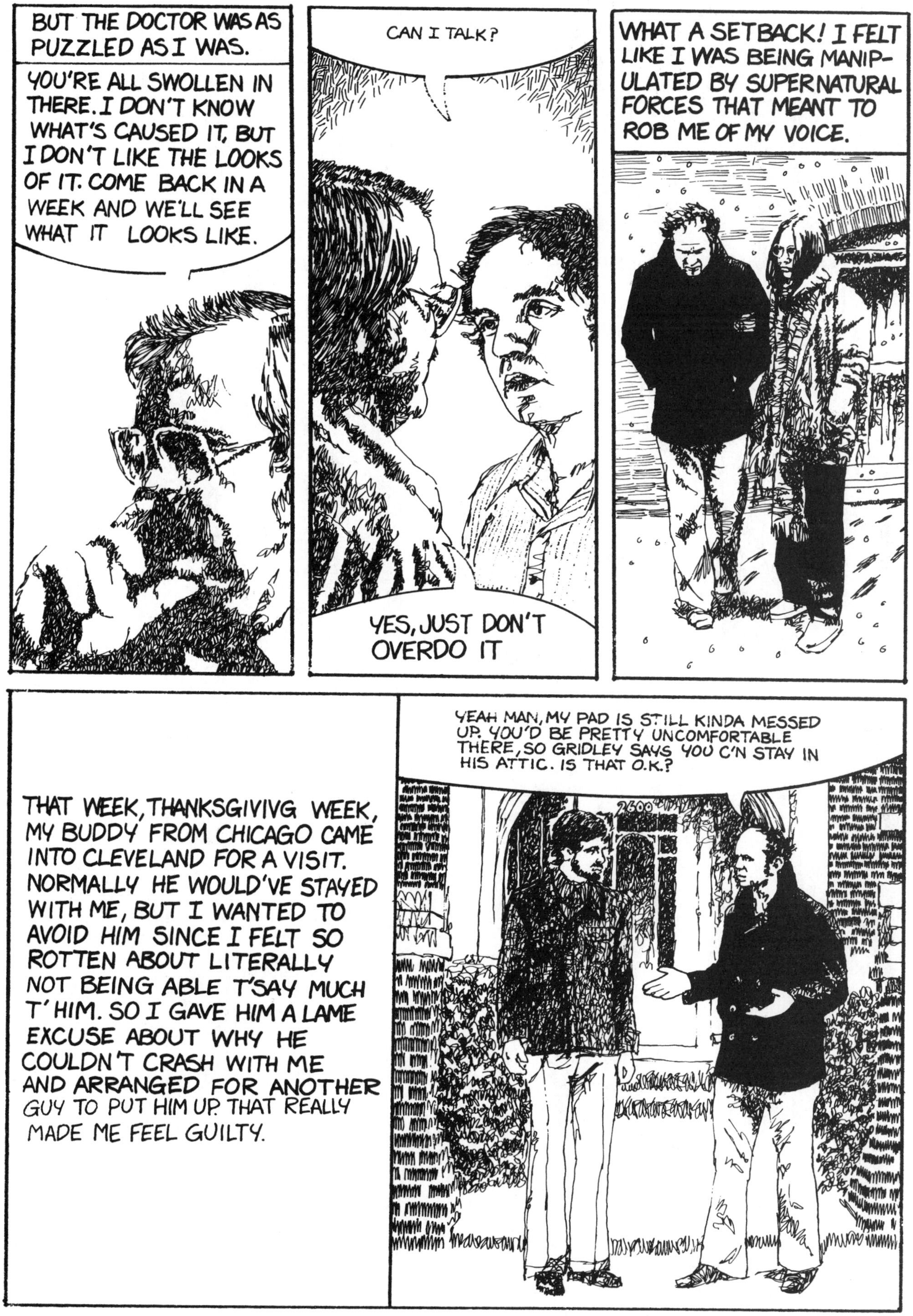
BUT THE DOCTOR WAS AS PUZZLED AS I WAS.
YOU'RE ALL SWOLLEN IN THERE. I DON'T KNOW WHAT'S CAUSED IT, BUT I DON'T LIKE THE LOOKS OF IT. COME BACK IN A WEEK AND WE'LL SEE WHAT IT LOOKS LIKE.
CAN I TALK?
YES, JUST DON'T OVERDO IT
WHAT A SETBACK! I FELT LIKE I WAS BEING MANIPULATED BY SUPERNATURAL FORCES THAT MEANT TO ROB ME OF MY VOICE.
THAT WEEK, THANKSGIVIVG WEEK, MY BUDDY FROM CHICAGO CAME INTO CLEVELAND FOR A VISIT. NORMALLY HE WOULD'VE STAYED WITH ME, BUT I WANTED TO AVOID HIM SINCE I FELT SO ROTTEN ABOUT LITERALLY NOT BEING ABLE T'SAY MUCH T' HIM. SO I GAVE HIM A LAME EXCUSE ABOUT WHY HE COULDN'T CRASH WITH ME AND ARRANGED FOR ANOTHER GUY TO PUT HIM UP. THAT REALLY MADE ME FEEL GUILTY.
YEAH MAN, MY PAD IS STILL KINDA MESSED UP. YOU'D BE PRETTY UNCOMFORTABLE THERE, SO GRIDLEY SAYS YOU C'N STAY IN HIS ATTIC. IS THAT O.K.?
2600

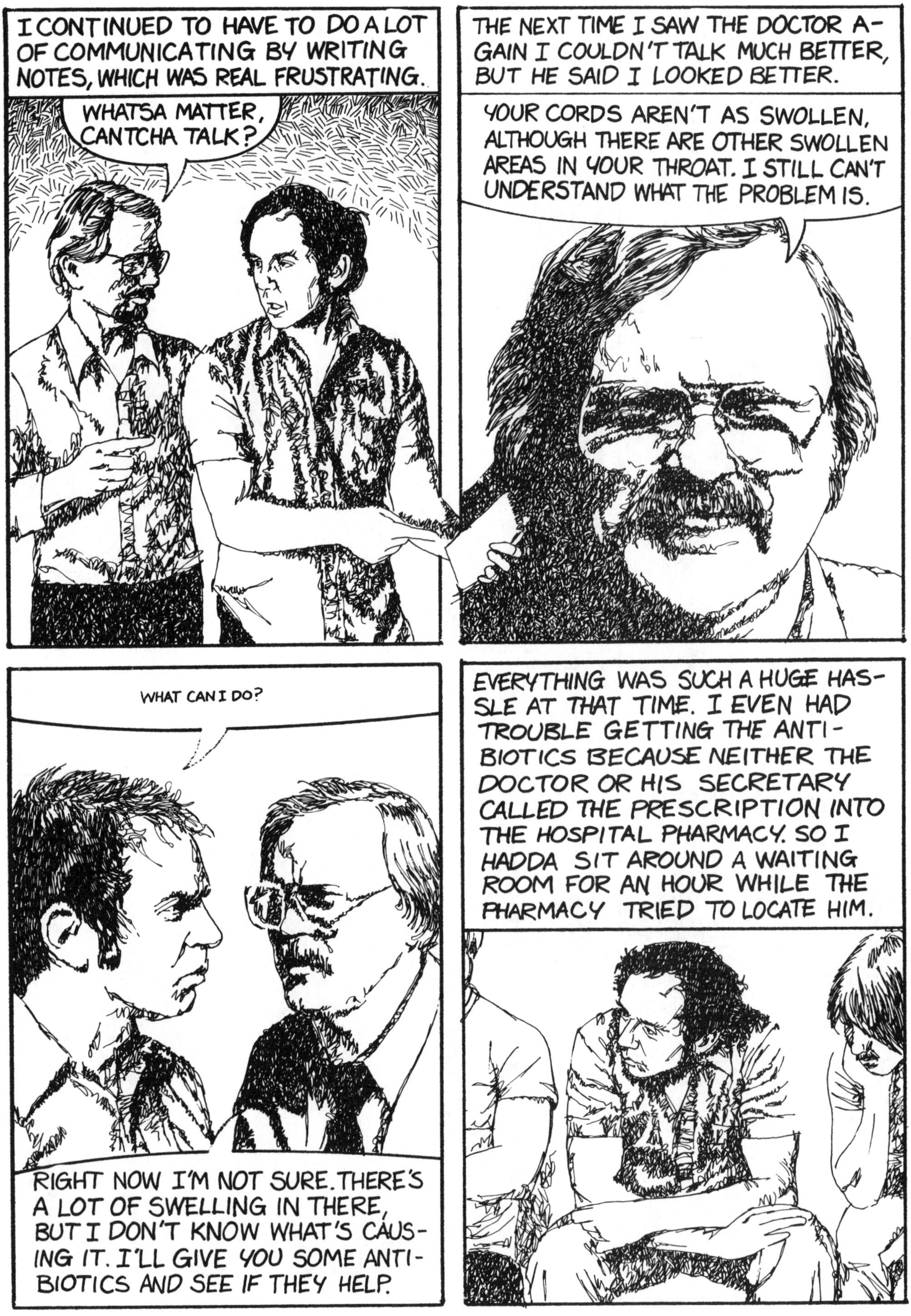
I CONTINUED TO HAVE TO DO A LOT OF COMMUNICATING BY WRITING NOTES, WHICH WAS REAL FRUSTRATING.
WHATSA MATTER, CANTCHA TALK?
THE NEXT TIME I SAW THE DOCTOR A-GAIN I COULDN'T TALK MUCH BETTER, BUT HE SAID I LOOKED BETTER.
YOUR CORDS AREN'T AS SWOLLEN, ALTHOUGH THERE ARE OTHER SWOLLEN AREAS IN YOUR THROAT. I STILL CAN'T UNDERSTAND WHAT THE PROBLEM IS.
WHAT CAN I DO?
RIGHT NOW I'M NOT SURE. THERE'S A LOT OF SWELLING IN THERE, BUT I DON'T KNOW WHAT'S CAUS-ING IT. I'LL GIVE YOU SOME ANTI-BIOTICS AND SEE IF THEY HELP.
EVERYTHING WAS SUCH A HUGE HAS-SLE AT THAT TIME. I EVEN HAD TROUBLE GETTING THE ANTI-BIOTICS BECAUSE NEITHER THE DOCTOR OR HIS SECRETARY CALLED THE PRESCRIPTION INTO THE HOSPITAL PHARMACY. SO I HADDA SIT AROUND A WAITING ROOM FOR AN HOUR WHILE THE PHARMACY TRIED TO LOCATE HIM.

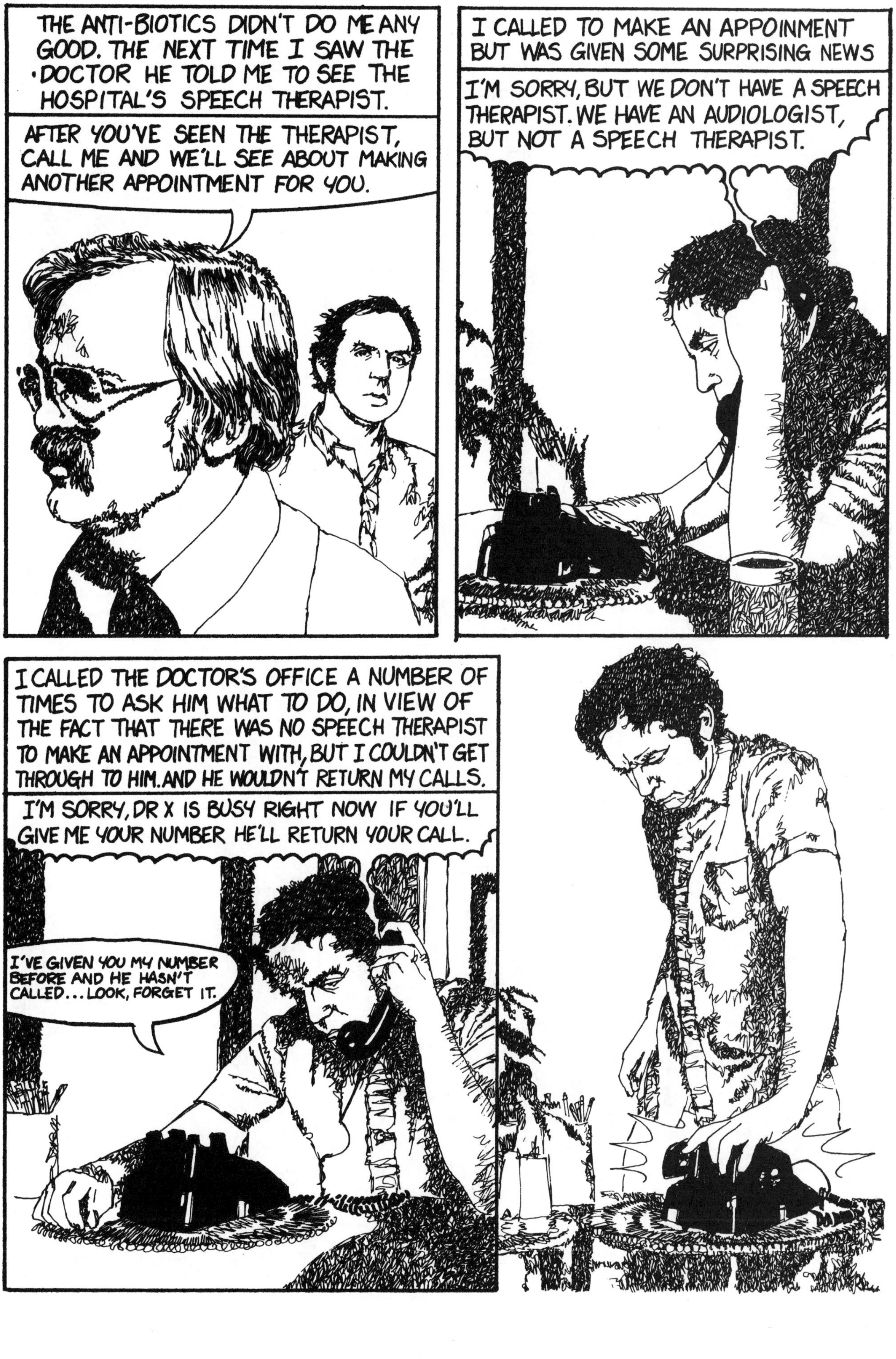
THE ANTI-BIOTICS DIDN'T DO ME ANY GOOD. THE NEXT TIME I SAW THE DOCTOR HE TOLD ME TO SEE THE HOSPITAL'S SPEECH THERAPIST.
AFTER YOU'VE SEEN THE THERAPIST, CALL ME AND WE'LL SEE ABOUT MAKING ANOTHER APPOINTMENT FOR YOU.
I CALLED TO MAKE AN APPOINMENT BUT WAS GIVEN SOME SURPRISING NEWS
I'M SORRY, BUT WE DON'T HAVE A SPEECH THERAPIST. WE HAVE AN AUDIOLOGIST, BUT NOT A SPEECH THERAPIST.
I CALLED THE DOCTOR'S OFFICE A NUMBER OF TIMES TO ASK HIM WHAT TO DO, IN VIEW OF THE FACT THAT THERE WAS NO SPEECH THERAPIST TO MAKE AN APPOINTMENT WITH, BUT I COULDN'T GET THROUGH TO HIM. AND HE WOULDN'T RETURN MY CALLS.
I'M SORRY, DR X IS BUSY RIGHT NOW IF YOU'LL GIVE ME YOUR NUMBER HE'LL RETURN YOUR CALL.
I'VE GIVEN YOU MY NUMBER BEFORE AND HE HASN'T CALLED... LOOK, FORGET IT.

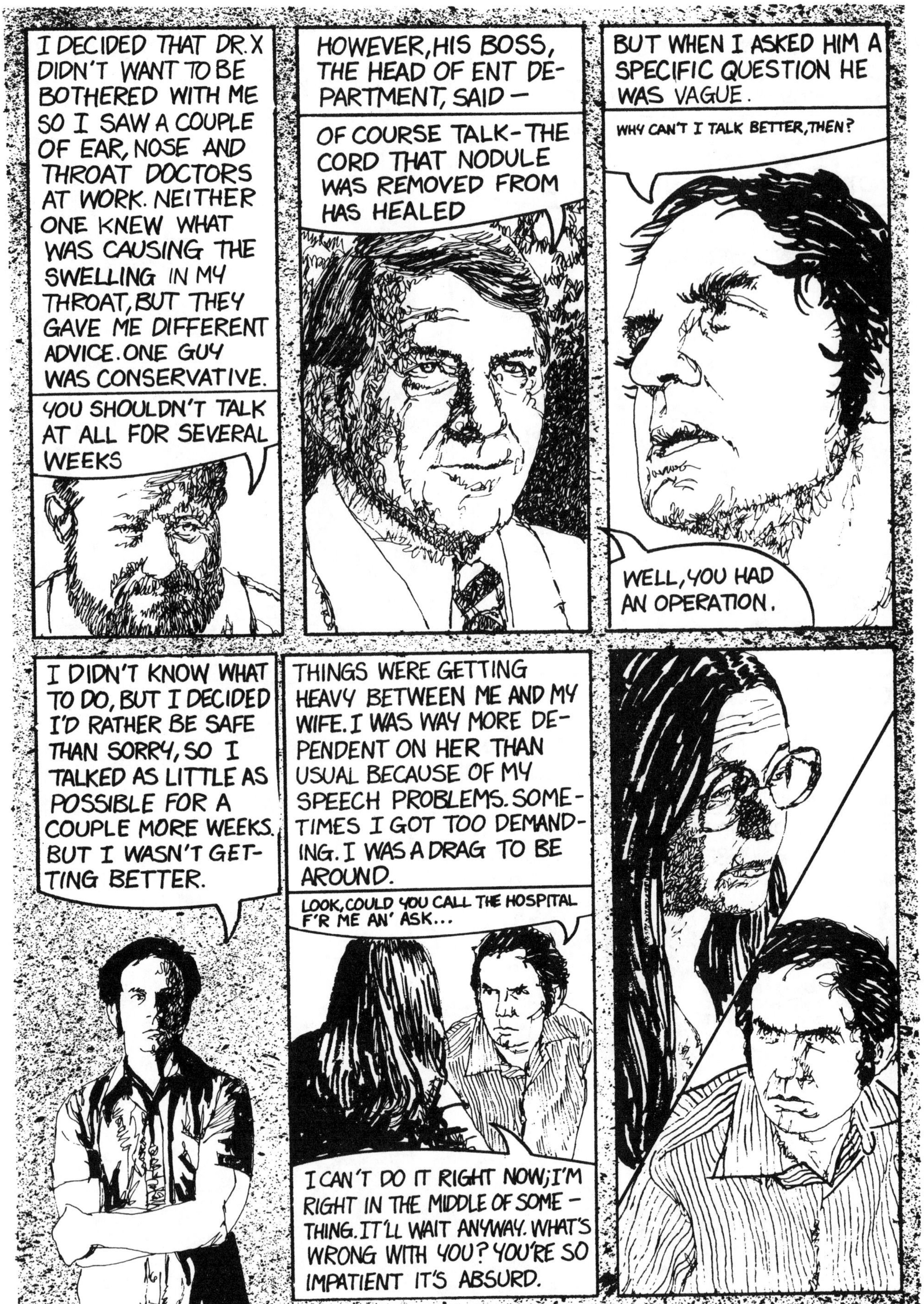
I DECIDED THAT DR. X DIDN'T WANT TO BE BOTHERED WITH ME SO I SAW A COUPLE OF EAR, NOSE AND THROAT DOCTORS AT WORK. NEITHER ONE KNEW WHAT WAS CAUSING THE SWELLING IN MY THROAT, BUT THEY GAVE ME DIFFERENT ADVICE. ONE GUY WAS CONSERVATIVE.
YOU SHOULDN'T TALK AT ALL FOR SEVERAL WEEKS
HOWEVER, HIS BOSS, THE HEAD OF ENT DEPARTMENT, SAID —
OF COURSE TALK - THE CORD THAT NODULE WAS REMOVED FROM HAS HEALED
BUT WHEN I ASKED HIM A SPECIFIC QUESTION HE WAS VAGUE.
WHY CAN'T I TALK BETTER, THEN?
WELL, YOU HAD AN OPERATION.
I DIDN'T KNOW WHAT TO DO, BUT I DECIDED I'D RATHER BE SAFE THAN SORRY, SO I TALKED AS LITTLE AS POSSIBLE FOR A COUPLE MORE WEEKS. BUT I WASN'T GETTING BETTER.
THINGS WERE GETTING HEAVY BETWEEN ME AND MY WIFE. I WAS WAY MORE DEPENDENT ON HER THAN USUAL BECAUSE OF MY SPEECH PROBLEMS. SOMETIMES I GOT TOO DEMANDING. I WAS A DRAG TO BE AROUND.
LOOK, COULD YOU CALL THE HOSPITAL F'R ME AN' ASK...
I CAN'T DO IT RIGHT NOW; I'M RIGHT IN THE MIDDLE OF SOMETHING. IT'LL WAIT ANYWAY. WHAT'S WRONG WITH YOU? YOU'RE SO IMPATIENT IT'S ABSURD.

I GOT INTO A SELF-PITY TRIP REAL BAD AND CONTINUED TO WRITE MY WIFE MAUDLIN NOTES.

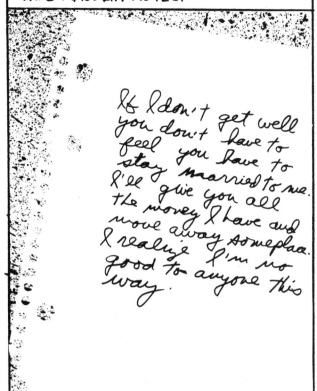

If I don't get well you don't have to feel you have to stay married to me. I'll give you all the money I have and move away someplace. I realize I'm no good to anyone this way.

THAT MADE HER FURIOUS.

WHAT'S THE MATTER WITH YOU, FEELING SORRY FOR YOURSELF LIKE THAT? MY FATHER'S HAD A HEART CONDITION SINCE HE WAS A CHILD AND HE NEVER GAVE UP THE WAY YOU ARE. WHAT'S WRONG WITH YOU IS VERY INCONVENIENT BUT IT'S TEMPORARY. YOU'LL GET YOUR VOICE BACK. FOR NOW TRY TO MAKE THE BEST OF IT!

I WAS REAL SELF-CONSCIOUS ABOUT MY SPEECH PROBLEM. I'D WORKED IN A HOSPITAL A LONG TIME AND I'D SEEN PATIENTS THAT I REGARDED AS MORE OR LESS NORMAL GET DISABLED BY THINGS LIKE STROKES. I WONDERED IF PEOPLE LOOKED AT ME AS IF I WERE A CRIPPLE. I COULD ESPECIALLY SYMPATHIZE NOW WITH STROKE VICTIMS WHO COULD THINK AS WELL AS EVER BUT COULDN'T TALK.

FINALLY I FLIPPED. I THOUGHT THAT THE HOSPITAL WHERE I WAS OPERATED ON HAD BETTER GET SOMEONE, IF NOT DR. X THEN SOMEONE ELSE, TO TAKE CARE OF MY THROAT. AFTER ALL, I WAS PAYING THEM INSURANCE. SO I CALLED THEM UP.

LOOK, I HAVEN'T BEEN ABLE TO TALK NORMALLY IN MONTHS. I WANNA SEE SOMEONE ABOUT THIS. IT'S RIDICULOUS.

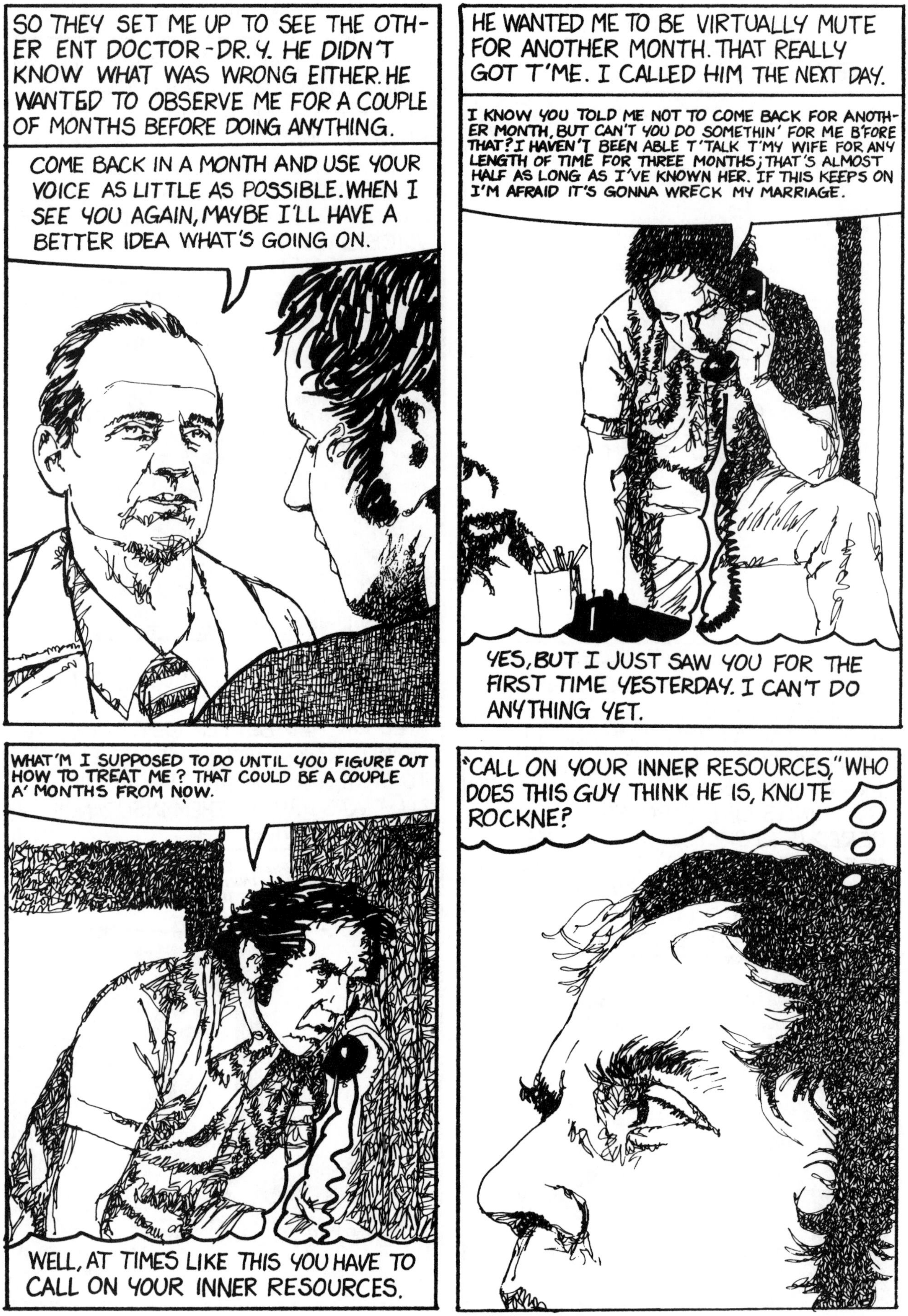
SO THEY SET ME UP TO SEE THE OTHER ENT DOCTOR-DR. Y. HE DIDN'T KNOW WHAT WAS WRONG EITHER. HE WANTED TO OBSERVE ME FOR A COUPLE OF MONTHS BEFORE DOING ANYTHING.
COME BACK IN A MONTH AND USE YOUR VOICE AS LITTLE AS POSSIBLE. WHEN I SEE YOU AGAIN, MAYBE I'LL HAVE A BETTER IDEA WHAT'S GOING ON.
HE WANTED ME TO BE VIRTUALLY MUTE FOR ANOTHER MONTH. THAT REALLY GOT T'ME. I CALLED HIM THE NEXT DAY.
I KNOW YOU TOLD ME NOT TO COME BACK FOR ANOTHER MONTH, BUT CAN'T YOU DO SOMETHIN' FOR ME B'FORE THAT? I HAVEN'T BEEN ABLE T'TALK T'MY WIFE FOR ANY LENGTH OF TIME FOR THREE MONTHS; THAT'S ALMOST HALF AS LONG AS I'VE KNOWN HER. IF THIS KEEPS ON I'M AFRAID IT'S GONNA WRECK MY MARRIAGE.
YES, BUT I JUST SAW YOU FOR THE FIRST TIME YESTERDAY. I CAN'T DO ANYTHING YET.
WHAT'M I SUPPOSED TO DO UNTIL YOU FIGURE OUT HOW TO TREAT ME? THAT COULD BE A COUPLE A' MONTHS FROM NOW.
WELL, AT TIMES LIKE THIS YOU HAVE TO CALL ON YOUR INNER RESOURCES.
"CALL ON YOUR INNER RESOURCES," WHO DOES THIS GUY THINK HE IS, KNUTE ROCKNE?

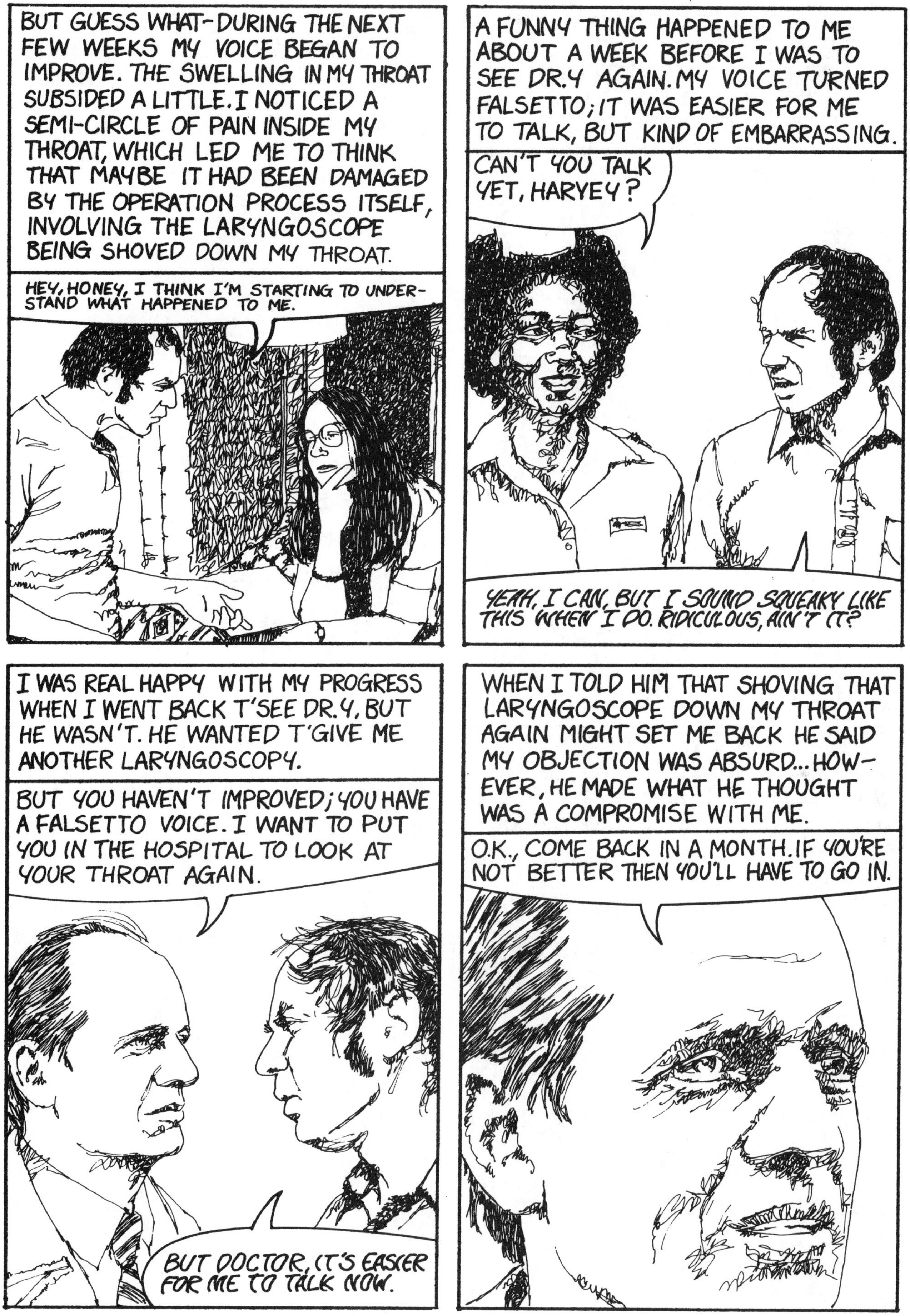
BUT GUESS WHAT- DURING THE NEXT FEW WEEKS MY VOICE BEGAN TO IMPROVE. THE SWELLING IN MY THROAT SUBSIDED A LITTLE. I NOTICED A SEMI-CIRCLE OF PAIN INSIDE MY THROAT, WHICH LED ME TO THINK THAT MAYBE IT HAD BEEN DAMAGED BY THE OPERATION PROCESS ITSELF, INVOLVING THE LARYNGOSCOPE BEING SHOVED DOWN MY THROAT.
HEY, HONEY, I THINK I'M STARTING TO UNDERSTAND WHAT HAPPENED TO ME.
A FUNNY THING HAPPENED TO ME ABOUT A WEEK BEFORE I WAS TO SEE DR. Y AGAIN. MY VOICE TURNED FALSETTO; IT WAS EASIER FOR ME TO TALK, BUT KIND OF EMBARRASSING.
CAN'T YOU TALK YET, HARVEY?
YEAH, I CAN, BUT I SOUND SQUEAKY LIKE THIS WHEN I DO. RIDICULOUS, AIN'T IT?
I WAS REAL HAPPY WITH MY PROGRESS WHEN I WENT BACK T'SEE DR. Y, BUT HE WASN'T. HE WANTED T'GIVE ME ANOTHER LARYNGOSCOPY.
BUT YOU HAVEN'T IMPROVED; YOU HAVE A FALSETTO VOICE. I WANT TO PUT YOU IN THE HOSPITAL TO LOOK AT YOUR THROAT AGAIN.
BUT DOCTOR, IT'S EASIER FOR ME TO TALK NOW.
WHEN I TOLD HIM THAT SHOVING THAT LARYNGOSCOPE DOWN MY THROAT AGAIN MIGHT SET ME BACK HE SAID MY OBJECTION WAS ABSURD... HOWEVER, HE MADE WHAT HE THOUGHT WAS A COMPROMISE WITH ME.
O.K., COME BACK IN A MONTH. IF YOU'RE NOT BETTER THEN YOU'LL HAVE TO GO IN.

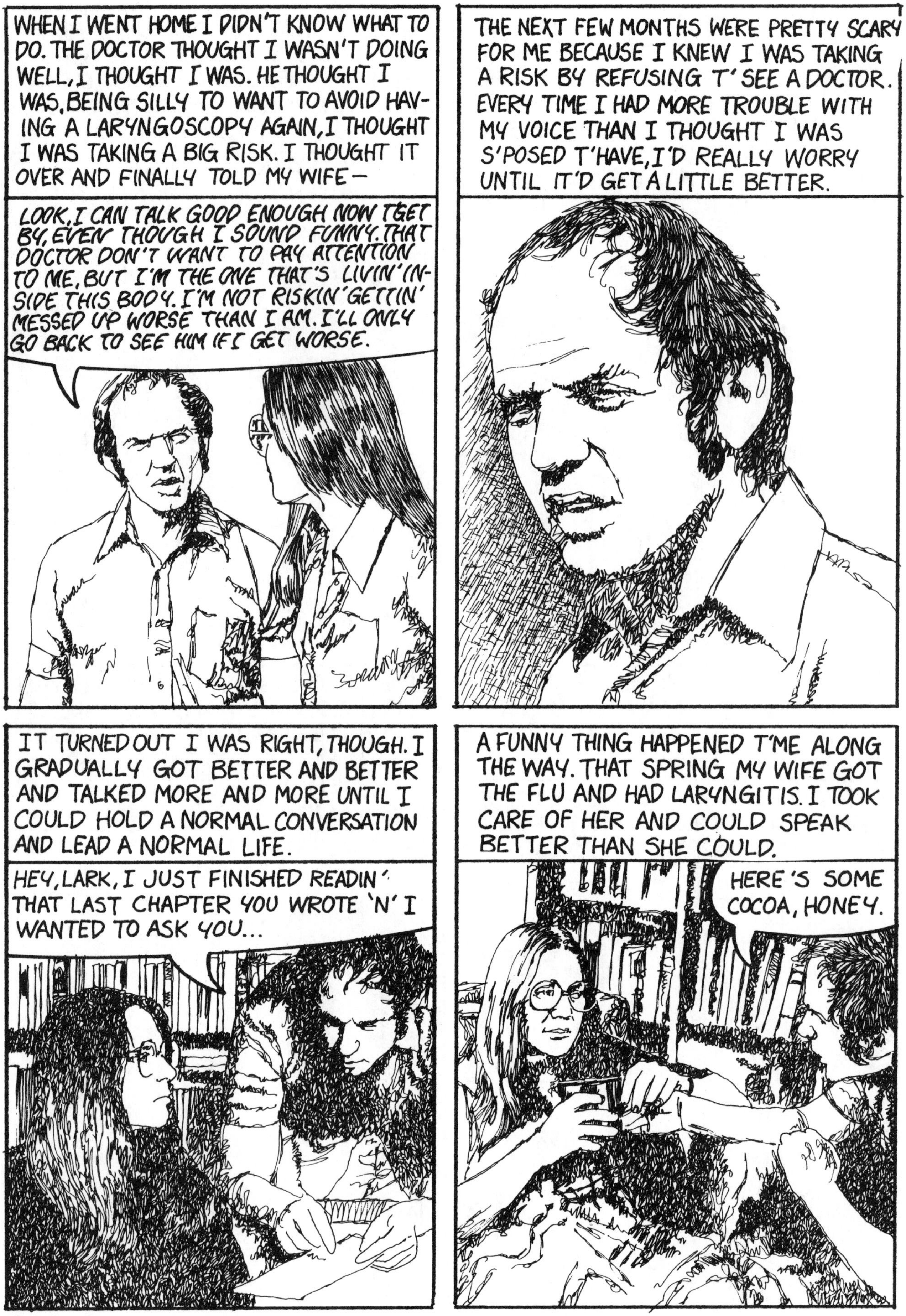
WHEN I WENT HOME I DIDN'T KNOW WHAT TO DO. THE DOCTOR THOUGHT I WASN'T DOING WELL, I THOUGHT I WAS. HE THOUGHT I WAS BEING SILLY TO WANT TO AVOID HAVING A LARYNGOSCOPY AGAIN, I THOUGHT I WAS TAKING A BIG RISK. I THOUGHT IT OVER AND FINALLY TOLD MY WIFE—
LOOK, I CAN TALK GOOD ENOUGH NOW T'GET BY, EVEN THOUGH I SOUND FUNNY. THAT DOCTOR DON'T WANT TO PAY ATTENTION TO ME, BUT I'M THE ONE THAT'S LIVIN' INSIDE THIS BODY. I'M NOT RISKIN' GETTIN' MESSED UP WORSE THAN I AM. I'LL ONLY GO BACK TO SEE HIM IF I GET WORSE.
THE NEXT FEW MONTHS WERE PRETTY SCARY FOR ME BECAUSE I KNEW I WAS TAKING A RISK BY REFUSING T' SEE A DOCTOR. EVERY TIME I HAD MORE TROUBLE WITH MY VOICE THAN I THOUGHT I WAS S'POSED T'HAVE, I'D REALLY WORRY UNTIL IT'D GET A LITTLE BETTER.
IT TURNED OUT I WAS RIGHT, THOUGH. I GRADUALLY GOT BETTER AND BETTER AND TALKED MORE AND MORE UNTIL I COULD HOLD A NORMAL CONVERSATION AND LEAD A NORMAL LIFE.
HEY, LARK, I JUST FINISHED READIN' THAT LAST CHAPTER YOU WROTE 'N' I WANTED TO ASK YOU...
A FUNNY THING HAPPENED T'ME ALONG THE WAY. THAT SPRING MY WIFE GOT THE FLU AND HAD LARYNGITIS. I TOOK CARE OF HER AND COULD SPEAK BETTER THAN SHE COULD.
HERE'S SOME COCOA, HONEY.

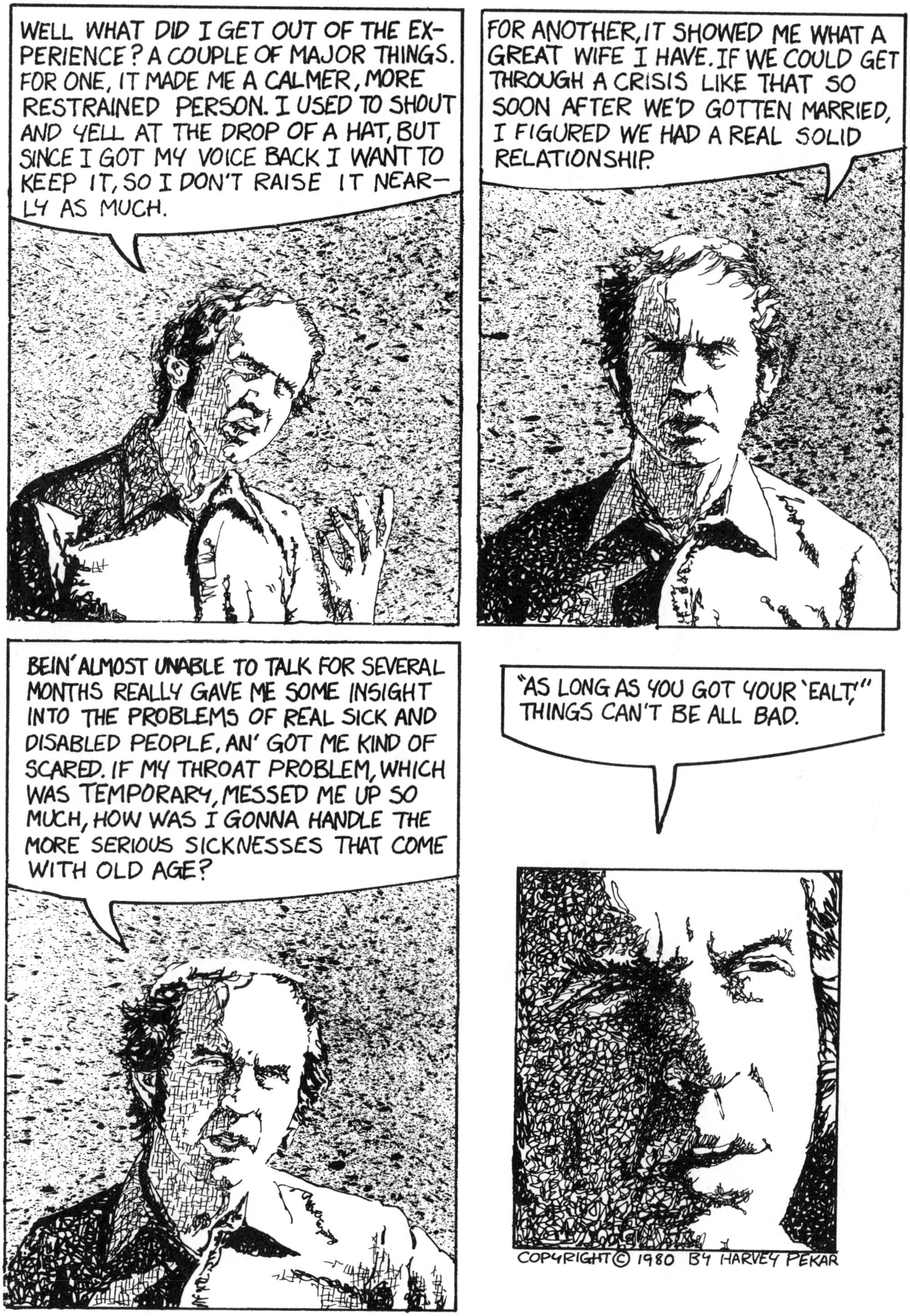
WELL WHAT DID I GET OUT OF THE EXPERIENCE? A COUPLE OF MAJOR THINGS. FOR ONE, IT MADE ME A CALMER, MORE RESTRAINED PERSON. I USED TO SHOUT AND YELL AT THE DROP OF A HAT, BUT SINCE I GOT MY VOICE BACK I WANT TO KEEP IT, SO I DON'T RAISE IT NEARLY AS MUCH.
FOR ANOTHER, IT SHOWED ME WHAT A GREAT WIFE I HAVE. IF WE COULD GET THROUGH A CRISIS LIKE THAT SO SOON AFTER WE'D GOTTEN MARRIED, I FIGURED WE HAD A REAL SOLID RELATIONSHIP.
BEIN' ALMOST UNABLE TO TALK FOR SEVERAL MONTHS REALLY GAVE ME SOME INSIGHT INTO THE PROBLEMS OF REAL SICK AND DISABLED PEOPLE, AN' GOT ME KIND OF SCARED. IF MY THROAT PROBLEM, WHICH WAS TEMPORARY, MESSED ME UP SO MUCH, HOW WAS I GONNA HANDLE THE MORE SERIOUS SICKNESSES THAT COME WITH OLD AGE?
"AS LONG AS YOU GOT YOUR 'EALT,'" THINGS CAN'T BE ALL BAD.
COPYRIGHT © 1980 BY HARVEY PEKAR

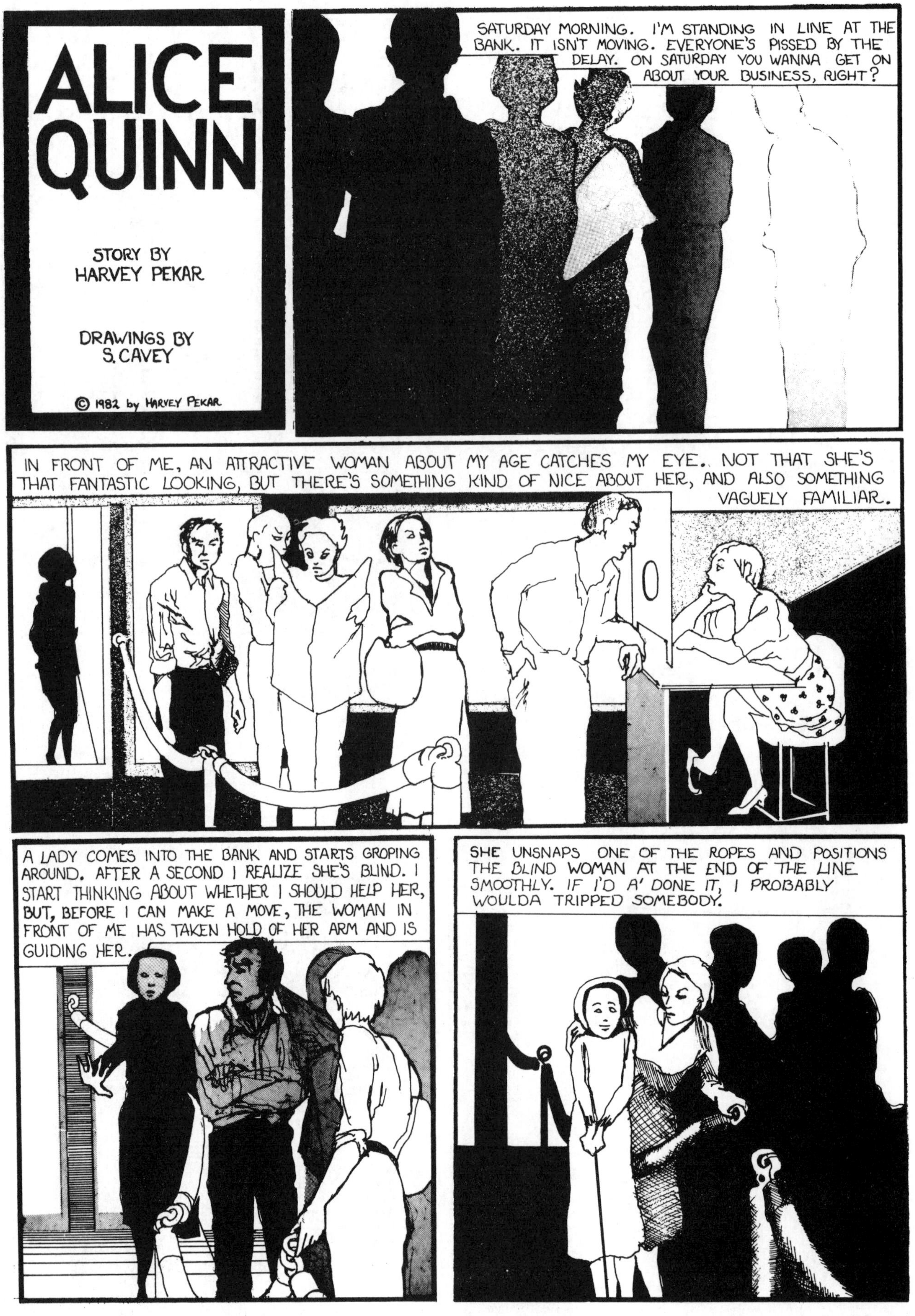
ALICE QUINN
STORY BY HARVEY PEKAR
DRAWINGS BY S. CAVEY
© 1982 by HARVEY PEKAR
SATURDAY MORNING. I'M STANDING IN LINE AT THE BANK. IT ISN'T MOVING. EVERYONE'S PISSED BY THE DELAY. ON SATURDAY YOU WANNA GET ON ABOUT YOUR BUSINESS, RIGHT?
IN FRONT OF ME, AN ATTRACTIVE WOMAN ABOUT MY AGE CATCHES MY EYE. NOT THAT SHE'S THAT FANTASTIC LOOKING, BUT THERE'S SOMETHING KIND OF NICE ABOUT HER, AND ALSO SOMETHING VAGUELY FAMILIAR.
A LADY COMES INTO THE BANK AND STARTS GROPING AROUND. AFTER A SECOND I REALIZE SHE'S BLIND. I START THINKING ABOUT WHETHER I SHOULD HELP HER, BUT, BEFORE I CAN MAKE A MOVE, THE WOMAN IN FRONT OF ME HAS TAKEN HOLD OF HER ARM AND IS GUIDING HER.
SHE UNSNAPS ONE OF THE ROPES AND POSITIONS THE BLIND WOMAN AT THE END OF THE LINE SMOOTHLY. IF I'D A' DONE IT, I PROBABLY WOULDA TRIPPED SOMEBODY.

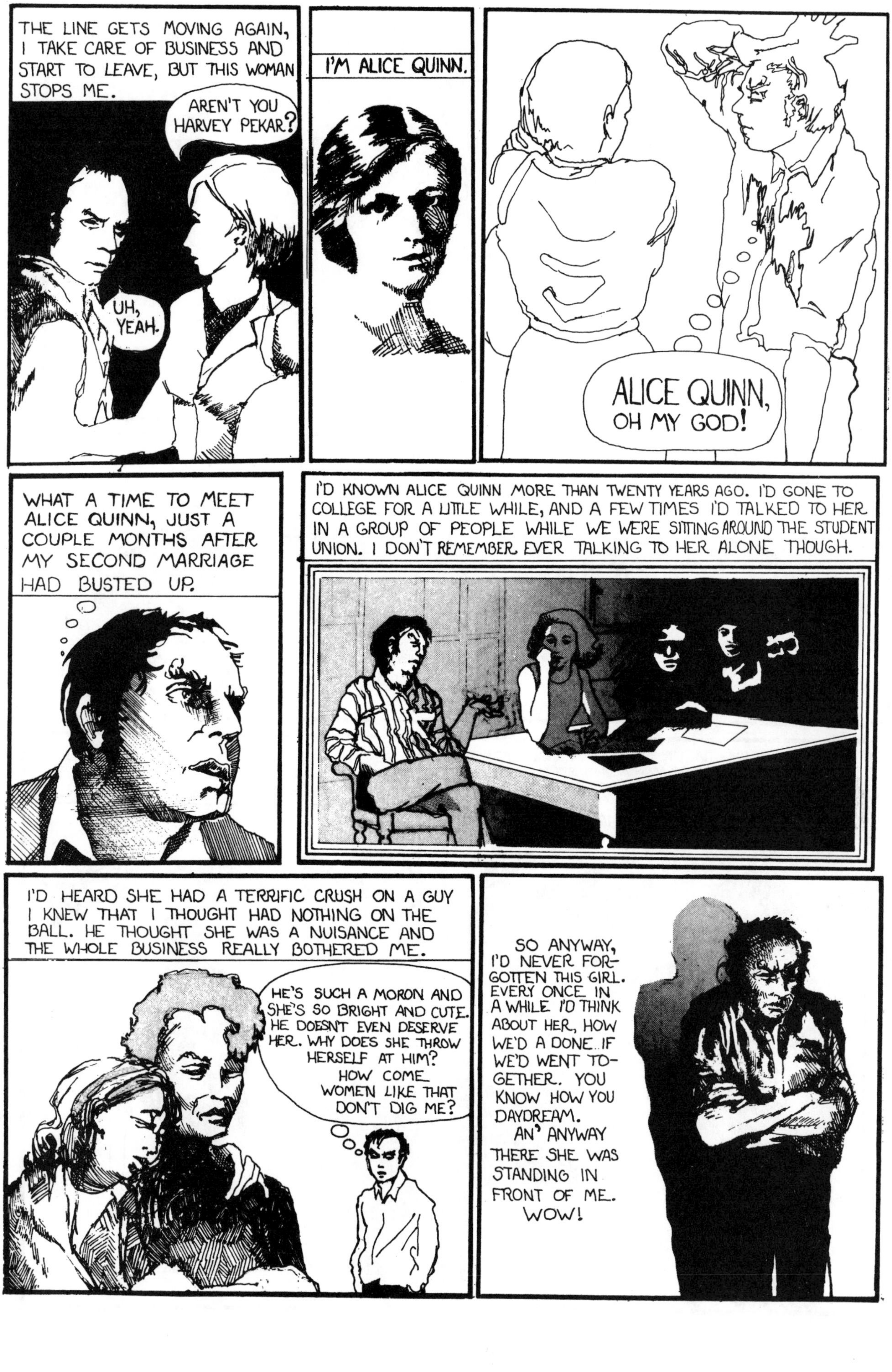

THE LINE GETS MOVING AGAIN, I TAKE CARE OF BUSINESS AND START TO LEAVE, BUT THIS WOMAN STOPS ME.
AREN'T YOU HARVEY PEKAR?
UH, YEAH.
I'M ALICE QUINN.
ALICE QUINN, OH MY GOD!
WHAT A TIME TO MEET ALICE QUINN, JUST A COUPLE MONTHS AFTER MY SECOND MARRIAGE HAD BUSTED UP.
I'D KNOWN ALICE QUINN MORE THAN TWENTY YEARS AGO. I'D GONE TO COLLEGE FOR A LITTLE WHILE, AND A FEW TIMES I'D TALKED TO HER IN A GROUP OF PEOPLE WHILE WE WERE SITTING AROUND THE STUDENT UNION. I DON'T REMEMBER EVER TALKING TO HER ALONE THOUGH.
I'D HEARD SHE HAD A TERRIFIC CRUSH ON A GUY I KNEW THAT I THOUGHT HAD NOTHING ON THE BALL. HE THOUGHT SHE WAS A NUISANCE AND THE WHOLE BUSINESS REALLY BOTHERED ME.
HE'S SUCH A MORON AND SHE'S SO BRIGHT AND CUTE. HE DOESN'T EVEN DESERVE HER. WHY DOES SHE THROW HERSELF AT HIM? HOW COME WOMEN LIKE THAT DON'T DIG ME?
SO ANYWAY, I'D NEVER FORGOTTEN THIS GIRL. EVERY ONCE IN A WHILE I'D THINK ABOUT HER, HOW WE'D A DONE IF WE'D WENT TOGETHER. YOU KNOW HOW YOU DAYDREAM.
AN' ANYWAY THERE SHE WAS STANDING IN FRONT OF ME. WOW!

SO WE GOT INTO THIS RAP TELLIN'
EACH OTHER WHAT WE'D BEEN UP
TO DURING THE PAST TWENNY
YEARS. AS SHE WAS TALKING
I WAS LOOKING AT HER HAND.
DAMMIT, SHE HAD ON A
WEDDING RING.

SO SHE SAYS SHE NEEDS T'GET HOME BUT SHE LIVES RIGHT
BY THE BANK AND INVITES ME TO FALL BY TO CONTINUE
OUR CONVERSATION. THAT WAS COOL BECAUSE PEOPLE
WERE EAVESDROPPING ON US IN THE BANK ANYWAY.

WE WENT BACK T' HER HOUSE—MAN, SHE KNEW ABOUT MY COMIC BOOKS AN' THAT I'D BEEN A
JAZZ CRITIC— IT REALLY MADE ME FEEL NICE. SHE EVEN HAD SOME OF MY COMICS.

WE GET BACK TO 'ER PLACE AN' SHE INTRO-
DUCES ME TO 'ER OL' MAN, WHO SEEMED LIKE
A NICE GUY. HE WAS A LOT OLDER THAN SHE
WAS OR ELSE HE'D AGED A LOT QUICKER.
ANYWAY, I LOOKED BETTER THAN HE DID AND
THAT MADE ME FEEL GOOD, YEAH, I KNOW,
ALL IS VANITY.

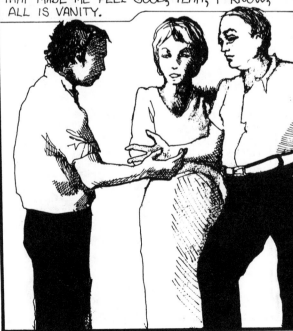

HE WAS JUST GOING AN' HE NEEDED
SOME BREAD AN' SHE GAVE HIM JUST
ABOUT EVERY CENT SHE HAD ON HER.

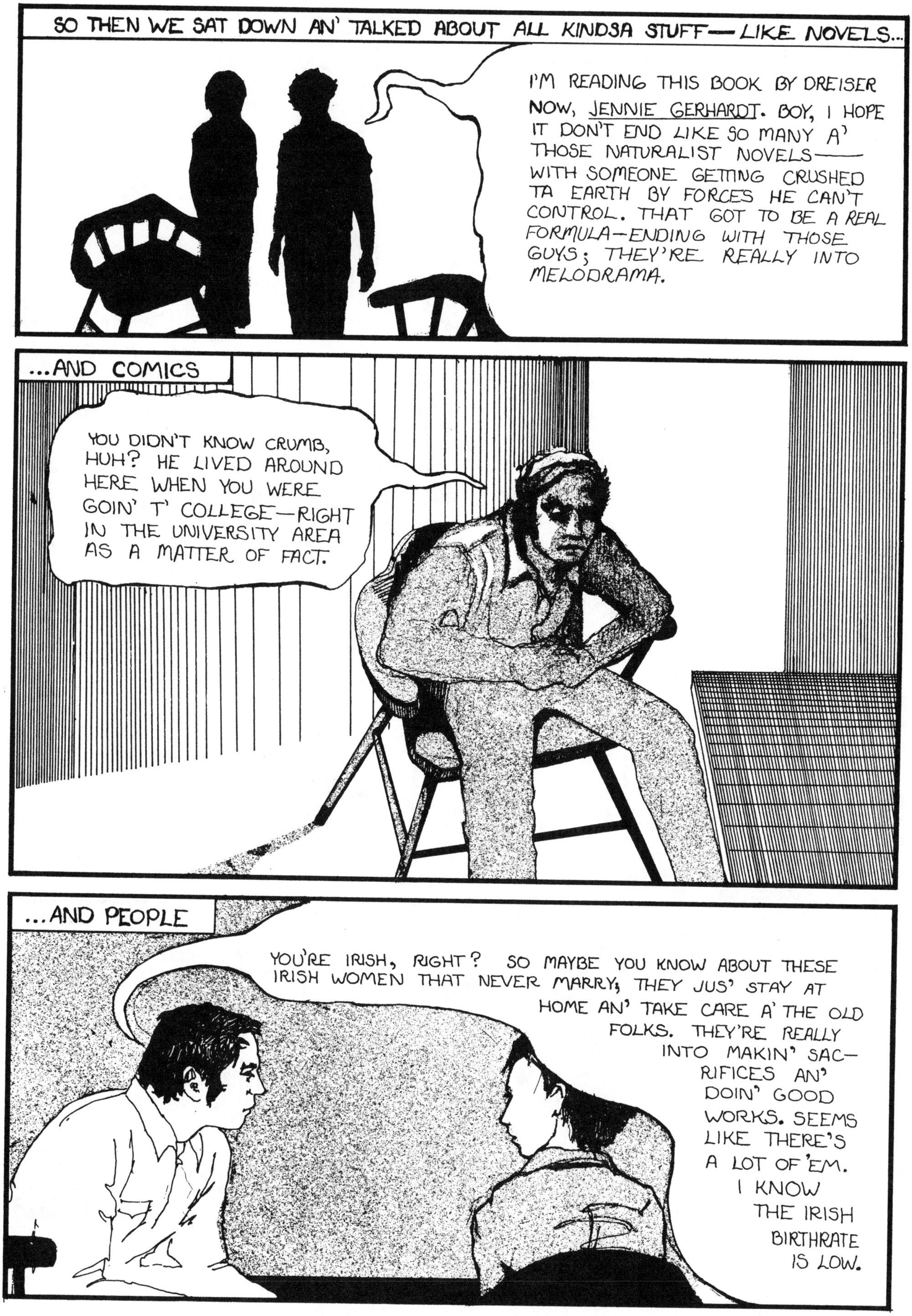
SO THEN WE SAT DOWN AN' TALKED ABOUT ALL KINDSA STUFF—LIKE NOVELS...
I'M READING THIS BOOK BY DREISER NOW, JENNIE GERHARDT. BOY, I HOPE IT DON'T END LIKE SO MANY A' THOSE NATURALIST NOVELS—WITH SOMEONE GETTING CRUSHED TA EARTH BY FORCES HE CAN'T CONTROL. THAT GOT TO BE A REAL FORMULA—ENDING WITH THOSE GUYS; THEY'RE REALLY INTO MELODRAMA.
...AND COMICS
YOU DIDN'T KNOW CRUMB, HUH? HE LIVED AROUND HERE WHEN YOU WERE GOIN' T' COLLEGE—RIGHT IN THE UNIVERSITY AREA AS A MATTER OF FACT.
...AND PEOPLE
YOU'RE IRISH, RIGHT? SO MAYBE YOU KNOW ABOUT THESE IRISH WOMEN THAT NEVER MARRY; THEY JUS' STAY AT HOME AN' TAKE CARE A' THE OLD FOLKS. THEY'RE REALLY INTO MAKIN' SACRIFICES AN' DOIN' GOOD WORKS. SEEMS LIKE THERE'S A LOT OF 'EM. I KNOW THE IRISH BIRTHRATE IS LOW.

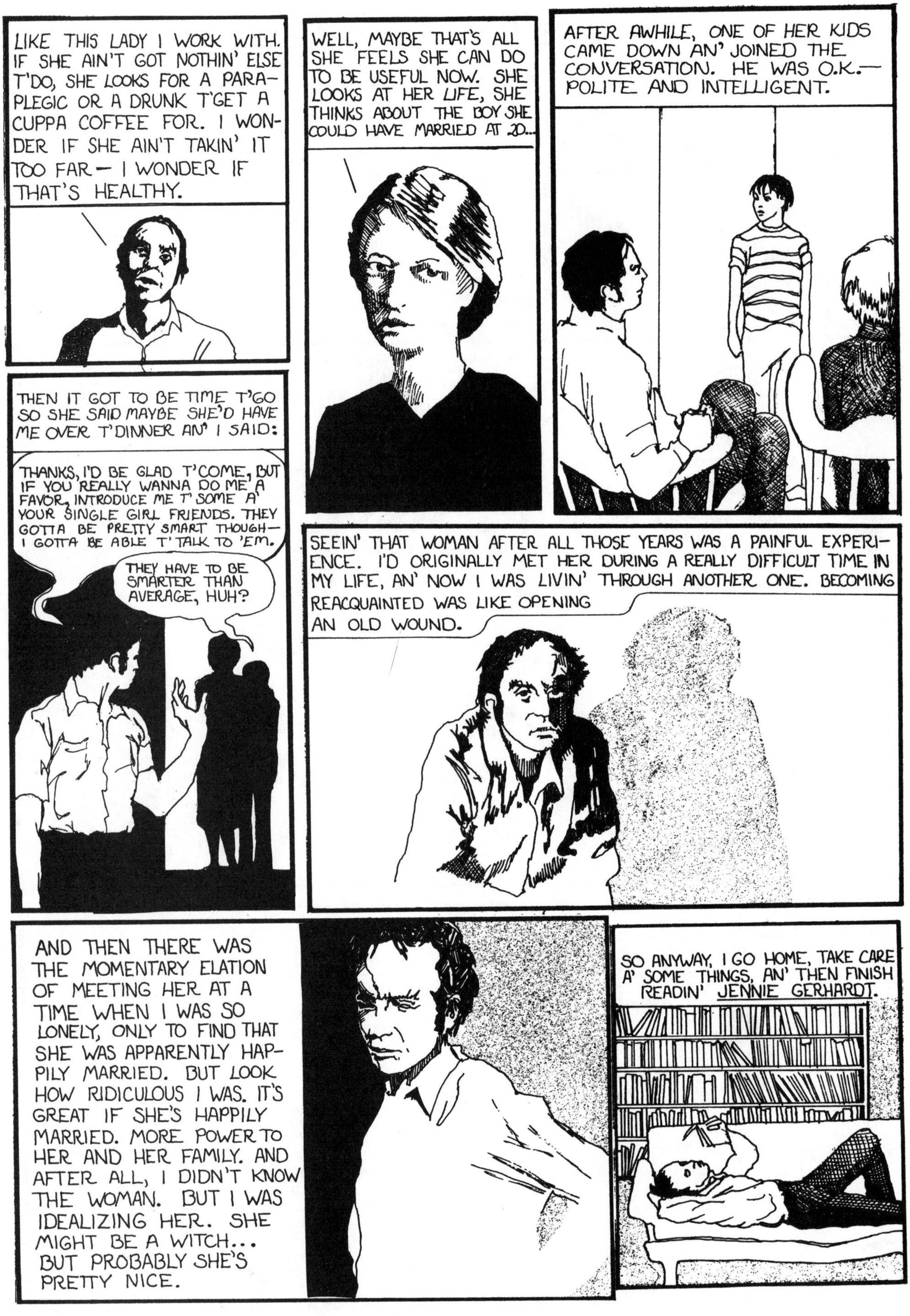
LIKE THIS LADY I WORK WITH. IF SHE AIN'T GOT NOTHIN' ELSE T'DO, SHE LOOKS FOR A PARAPLEGIC OR A DRUNK T'GET A CUPPA COFFEE FOR. I WONDER IF SHE AIN'T TAKIN' IT TOO FAR— I WONDER IF THAT'S HEALTHY.
WELL, MAYBE THAT'S ALL SHE FEELS SHE CAN DO TO BE USEFUL NOW. SHE LOOKS AT HER LIFE, SHE THINKS ABOUT THE BOY SHE COULD HAVE MARRIED AT 20...
AFTER AWHILE, ONE OF HER KIDS CAME DOWN AN' JOINED THE CONVERSATION. HE WAS O.K.— POLITE AND INTELLIGENT.
THEN IT GOT TO BE TIME T'GO SO SHE SAID MAYBE SHE'D HAVE ME OVER T'DINNER AN' I SAID:
THANKS, I'D BE GLAD T'COME, BUT IF YOU REALLY WANNA DO ME A FAVOR, INTRODUCE ME T' SOME A' YOUR SINGLE GIRL FRIENDS. THEY GOTTA BE PRETTY SMART THOUGH— I GOTTA BE ABLE T' TALK TO 'EM.
THEY HAVE TO BE SMARTER THAN AVERAGE, HUH?
SEEIN' THAT WOMAN AFTER ALL THOSE YEARS WAS A PAINFUL EXPERIENCE. I'D ORIGINALLY MET HER DURING A REALLY DIFFICULT TIME IN MY LIFE, AN' NOW I WAS LIVIN' THROUGH ANOTHER ONE. BECOMING REACQUAINTED WAS LIKE OPENING AN OLD WOUND.
AND THEN THERE WAS THE MOMENTARY ELATION OF MEETING HER AT A TIME WHEN I WAS SO LONELY, ONLY TO FIND THAT SHE WAS APPARENTLY HAPPILY MARRIED. BUT LOOK HOW RIDICULOUS I WAS. IT'S GREAT IF SHE'S HAPPILY MARRIED. MORE POWER TO HER AND HER FAMILY. AND AFTER ALL, I DIDN'T KNOW THE WOMAN. BUT I WAS IDEALIZING HER. SHE MIGHT BE A WITCH... BUT PROBABLY SHE'S PRETTY NICE.
SO ANYWAY, I GO HOME, TAKE CARE A' SOME THINGS, AN' THEN FINISH READIN' JENNIE GERHARDT.

IT TURNED OUT TO BE REAL GOOD, WAY BETTER THAN I EXPECTED. THE BOOK COVERS A NUM-
BER A' YEARS IN THE LIVES OF THESE TWO PEOPLE, LESTER KANE AN' JENNIE GERHARDT,
WHO WAS HIS MISTRESS. LESTER DIES IN THE END, BUT AT LEAST HE'S OLD AN' DIES A DIG-
NIFIED NATURAL DEATH; HE DON'T CROAK AS A PATHETIC BUM AN' GET BURIED IN POTTER'S FIELD
LIKE HURSTWOOD IN SISTER CARRIE.

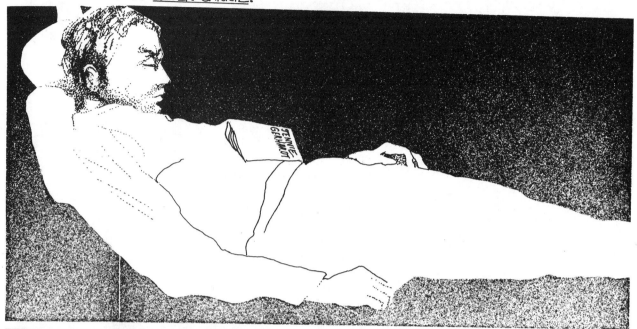

I WAS ALONE ALL
THAT WEEKEND. I
THOUGHT ABOUT
JENNIE GERHARDT
AN' ALICE QUINN
AN' DECADES
A' FACES RAN
THROUGH
MY MIND.
I FELT LIKE
CRYIN'; LIFE
SEEMED SO SWEET
AN' SO SAD AN'
SO HARD T' LET GO
OF IN THE END.

BUT THIS IS MONDAY.
I WENT T' WORK, HUS-
TLED SOME RECORDS,
CAME HOME AN' WROTE
THIS. T' NIGHT I'LL
FINISH A CONNECTICUT
YANKEE IN KING ARTHUR'S
COURT. LIFE GOES ON.
EVERY DAY IS A NEW DEAL.
KEEP WORKIN' AN' MAY-
BE SUMP'N'LL TURN UP.

END

I'll Be Forty-three on Friday (How I'm Living Now)

STORY BY HARVEY PEKAR
ILLUSTRATED BY GERRY SHAMRAY

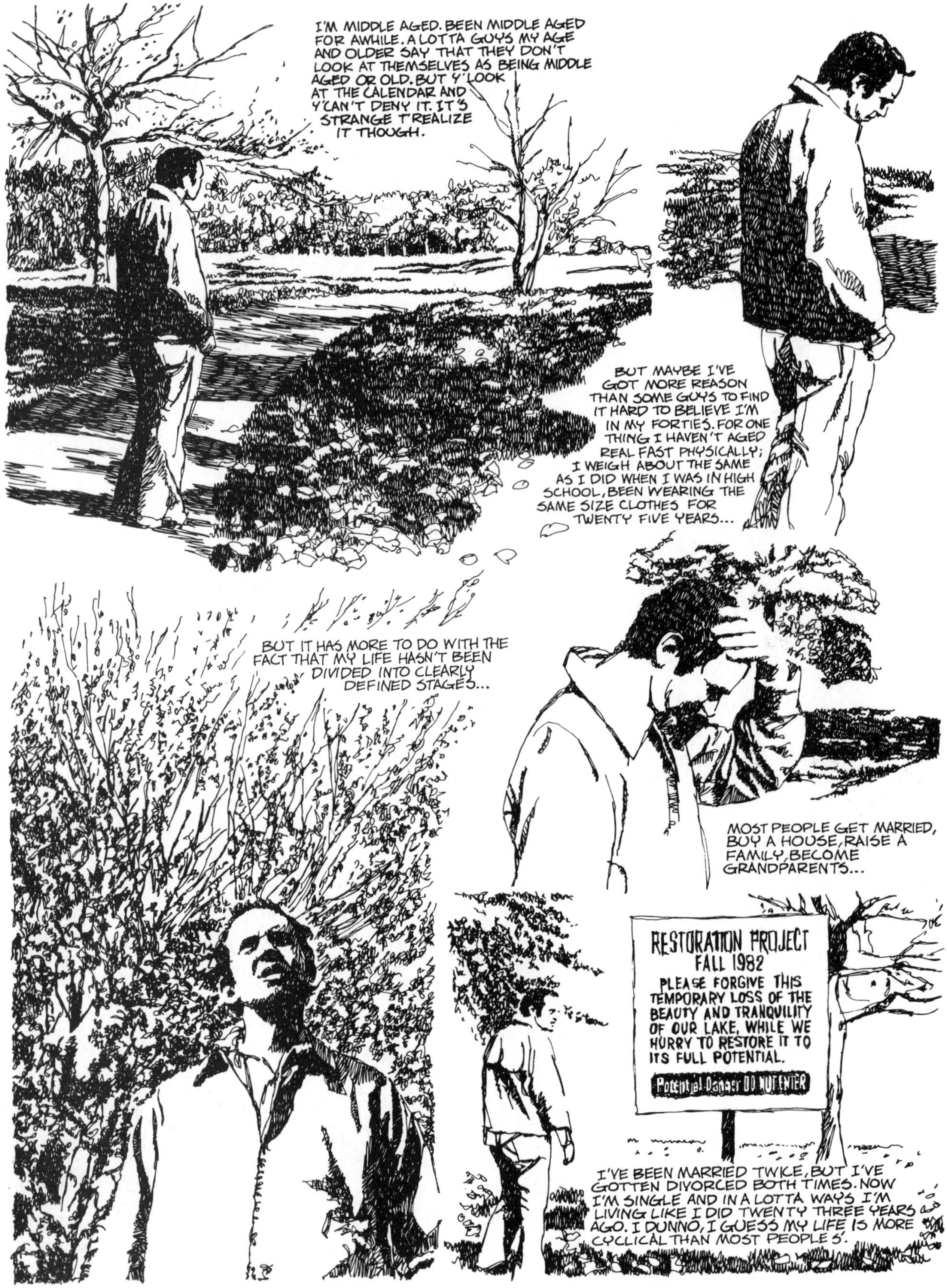
I'M MIDDLE AGED. BEEN MIDDLE AGED FOR AWHILE. A LOTTA GUYS MY AGE AND OLDER SAY THAT THEY DON'T LOOK AT THEMSELVES AS BEING MIDDLE AGED OR OLD. BUT Y'LOOK AT THE CALENDAR AND Y'CAN'T DENY IT. IT'S STRANGE T'REALIZE IT THOUGH.
BUT MAYBE I'VE GOT MORE REASON THAN SOME GUYS TO FIND IT HARD TO BELIEVE I'M IN MY FORTIES. FOR ONE THING I HAVEN'T AGED REAL FAST PHYSICALLY; I WEIGH ABOUT THE SAME AS I DID WHEN I WAS IN HIGH SCHOOL, BEEN WEARING THE SAME SIZE CLOTHES FOR TWENTY FIVE YEARS...
BUT IT HAS MORE TO DO WITH THE FACT THAT MY LIFE HASN'T BEEN DIVIDED INTO CLEARLY DEFINED STAGES...
MOST PEOPLE GET MARRIED, BUY A HOUSE, RAISE A FAMILY, BECOME GRANDPARENTS...
RESTORATION PROJECT
FALL 1982
PLEASE FORGIVE THIS TEMPORARY LOSS OF THE BEAUTY AND TRANQUILITY OF OUR LAKE, WHILE WE HURRY TO RESTORE IT TO ITS FULL POTENTIAL.
Potential Danger DO NOT ENTER
I'VE BEEN MARRIED TWICE, BUT I'VE GOTTEN DIVORCED BOTH TIMES. NOW I'M SINGLE AND IN A LOTTA WAYS I'M LIVING LIKE I DID TWENTY THREE YEARS AGO. I DUNNO, I GUESS MY LIFE IS MORE CYCLICAL THAN MOST PEOPLE'S.

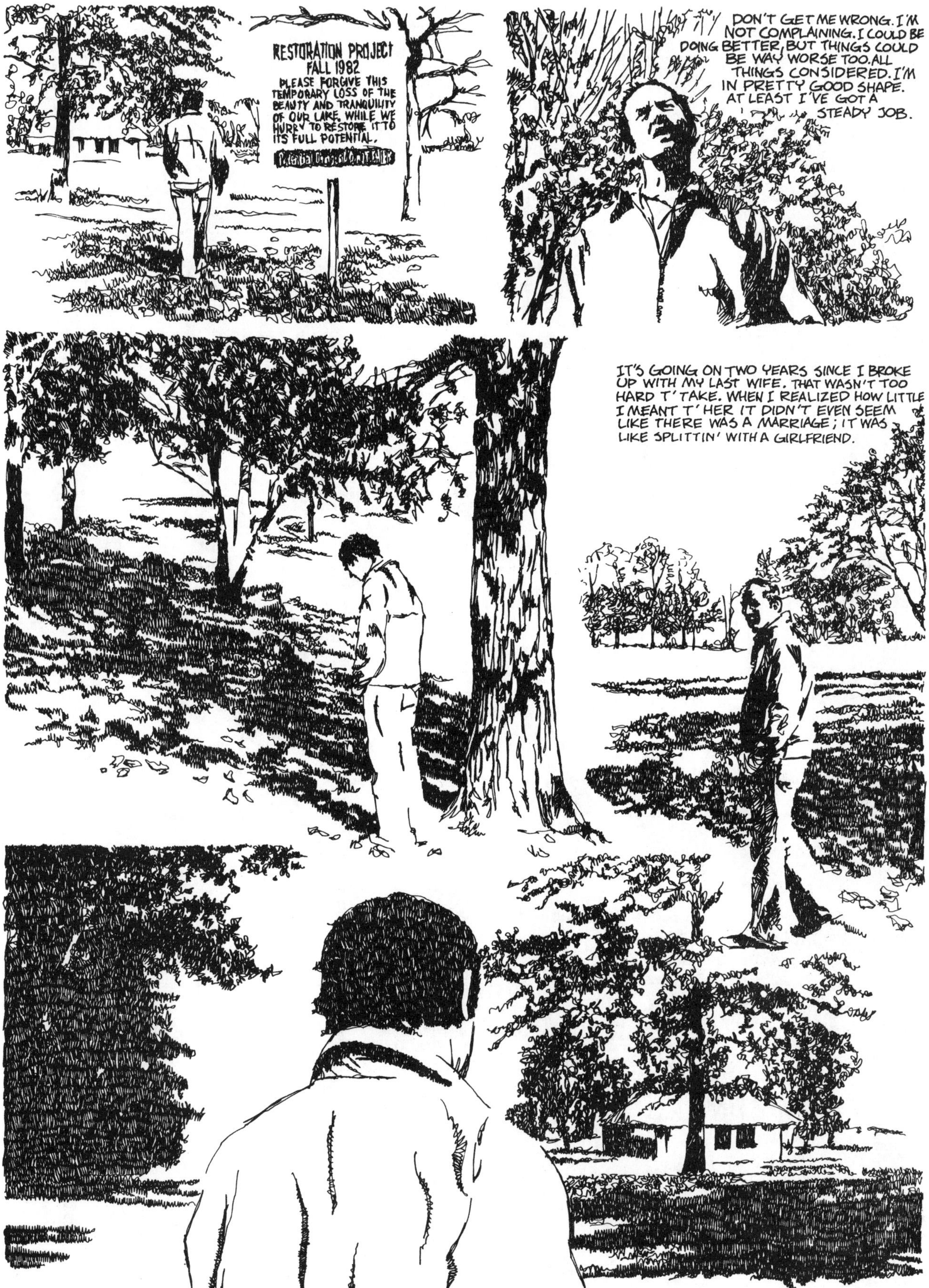
RESTORATION PROJECT
FALL 1982
PLEASE FORGIVE THIS TEMPORARY LOSS OF THE BEAUTY AND TRANQUILITY OF OUR LAKE WHILE WE HURRY TO RESTORE IT TO ITS FULL POTENTIAL.
DON'T GET ME WRONG. I'M NOT COMPLAINING. I COULD BE DOING BETTER, BUT THINGS COULD BE WAY WORSE TOO. ALL THINGS CONSIDERED, I'M IN PRETTY GOOD SHAPE. AT LEAST I'VE GOT A STEADY JOB.
IT'S GOING ON TWO YEARS SINCE I BROKE UP WITH MY LAST WIFE. THAT WASN'T TOO HARD T' TAKE. WHEN I REALIZED HOW LITTLE I MEANT T' HER IT DIDN'T EVEN SEEM LIKE THERE WAS A MARRIAGE; IT WAS LIKE SPLITTIN' WITH A GIRLFRIEND.

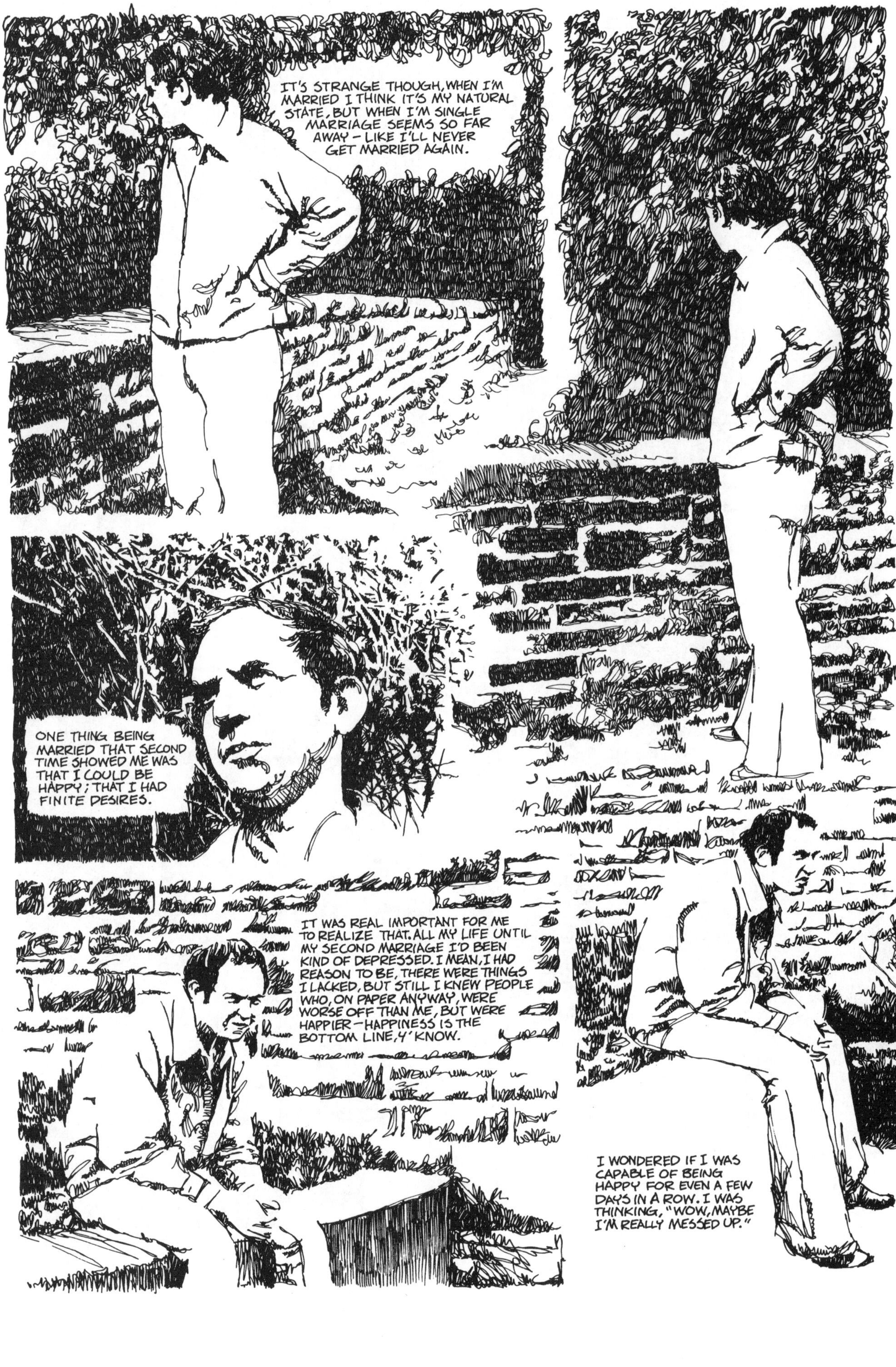
IT'S STRANGE THOUGH, WHEN I'M MARRIED I THINK IT'S MY NATURAL STATE, BUT WHEN I'M SINGLE MARRIAGE SEEMS SO FAR AWAY – LIKE I'LL NEVER GET MARRIED AGAIN.
ONE THING BEING MARRIED THAT SECOND TIME SHOWED ME WAS THAT I COULD BE HAPPY; THAT I HAD FINITE DESIRES.
IT WAS REAL IMPORTANT FOR ME TO REALIZE THAT. ALL MY LIFE UNTIL MY SECOND MARRIAGE I'D BEEN KIND OF DEPRESSED. I MEAN, I HAD REASON TO BE, THERE WERE THINGS I LACKED, BUT STILL I KNEW PEOPLE WHO, ON PAPER ANYWAY, WERE WORSE OFF THAN ME, BUT WERE HAPPIER – HAPPINESS IS THE BOTTOM LINE, Y'KNOW.
I WONDERED IF I WAS CAPABLE OF BEING HAPPY FOR EVEN A FEW DAYS IN A ROW. I WAS THINKING, "WOW, MAYBE I'M REALLY MESSED UP."

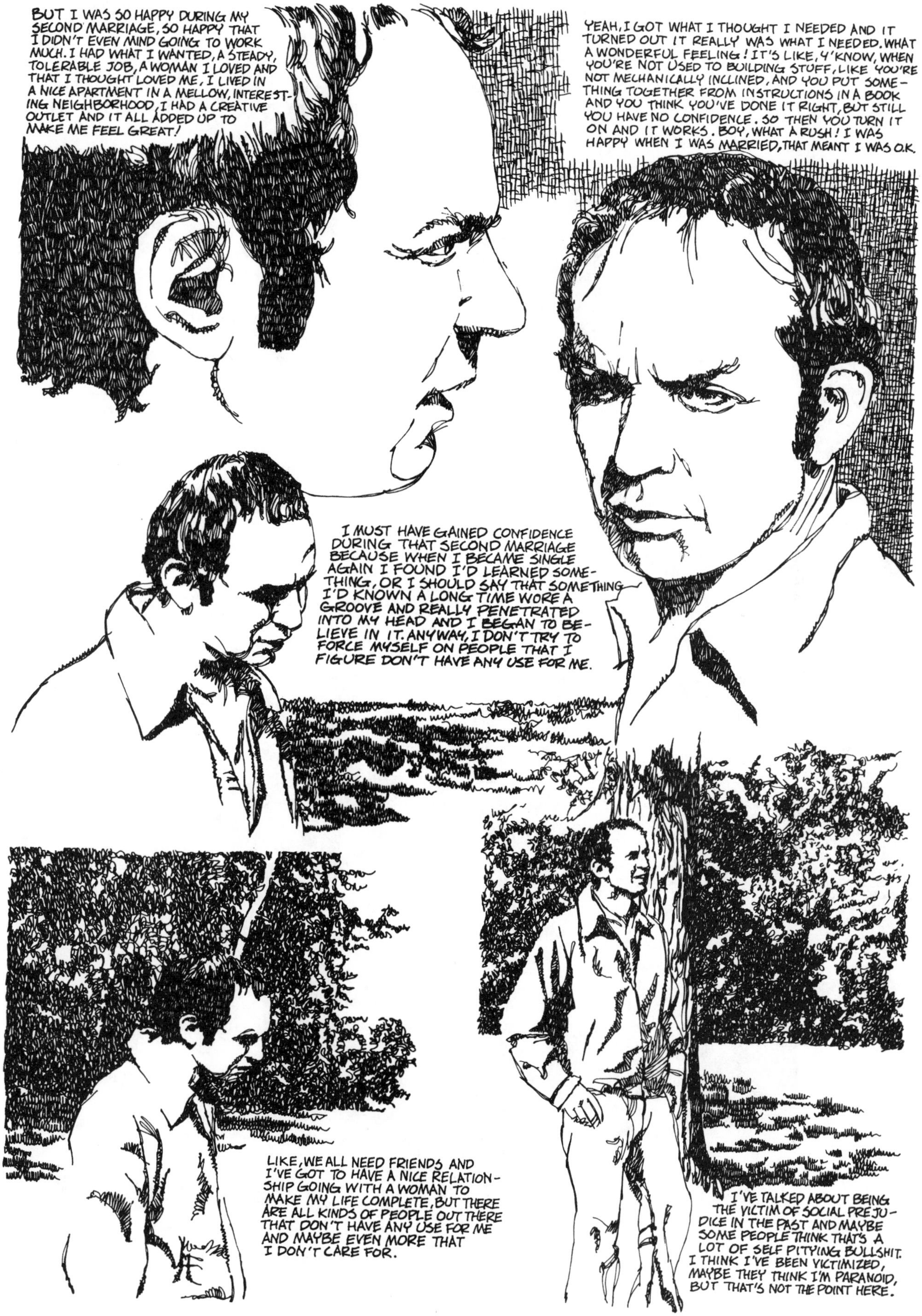
BUT I WAS SO HAPPY DURING MY SECOND MARRIAGE, SO HAPPY THAT I DIDN'T EVEN MIND GOING TO WORK MUCH. I HAD WHAT I WANTED, A STEADY, TOLERABLE JOB, A WOMAN I LOVED AND THAT I THOUGHT LOVED ME, I LIVED IN A NICE APARTMENT IN A MELLOW, INTERESTING NEIGHBORHOOD, I HAD A CREATIVE OUTLET AND IT ALL ADDED UP TO MAKE ME FEEL GREAT!
YEAH, I GOT WHAT I THOUGHT I NEEDED AND IT TURNED OUT IT REALLY WAS WHAT I NEEDED. WHAT A WONDERFUL FEELING! IT'S LIKE, Y'KNOW, WHEN YOU'RE NOT USED TO BUILDING STUFF, LIKE YOU'RE NOT MECHANICALLY INCLINED, AND YOU PUT SOMETHING TOGETHER FROM INSTRUCTIONS IN A BOOK AND YOU THINK YOU'VE DONE IT RIGHT, BUT STILL YOU HAVE NO CONFIDENCE. SO THEN YOU TURN IT ON AND IT WORKS. BOY, WHAT A RUSH! I WAS HAPPY WHEN I WAS MARRIED, THAT MEANT I WAS O.K.
I MUST HAVE GAINED CONFIDENCE DURING THAT SECOND MARRIAGE BECAUSE WHEN I BECAME SINGLE AGAIN I FOUND I'D LEARNED SOMETHING, OR I SHOULD SAY THAT SOMETHING I'D KNOWN A LONG TIME WORE A GROOVE AND REALLY PENETRATED INTO MY HEAD AND I BEGAN TO BELIEVE IN IT. ANYWAY, I DON'T TRY TO FORCE MYSELF ON PEOPLE THAT I FIGURE DON'T HAVE ANY USE FOR ME.
LIKE, WE ALL NEED FRIENDS AND I'VE GOT TO HAVE A NICE RELATIONSHIP GOING WITH A WOMAN TO MAKE MY LIFE COMPLETE, BUT THERE ARE ALL KINDS OF PEOPLE OUT THERE THAT DON'T HAVE ANY USE FOR ME AND MAYBE EVEN MORE THAT I DON'T CARE FOR.
I'VE TALKED ABOUT BEING THE VICTIM OF SOCIAL PREJUDICE IN THE PAST AND MAYBE SOME PEOPLE THINK THAT'S A LOT OF SELF PITYING BULLSHIT. I THINK I'VE BEEN VICTIMIZED, MAYBE THEY THINK I'M PARANOID, BUT THAT'S NOT THE POINT HERE.

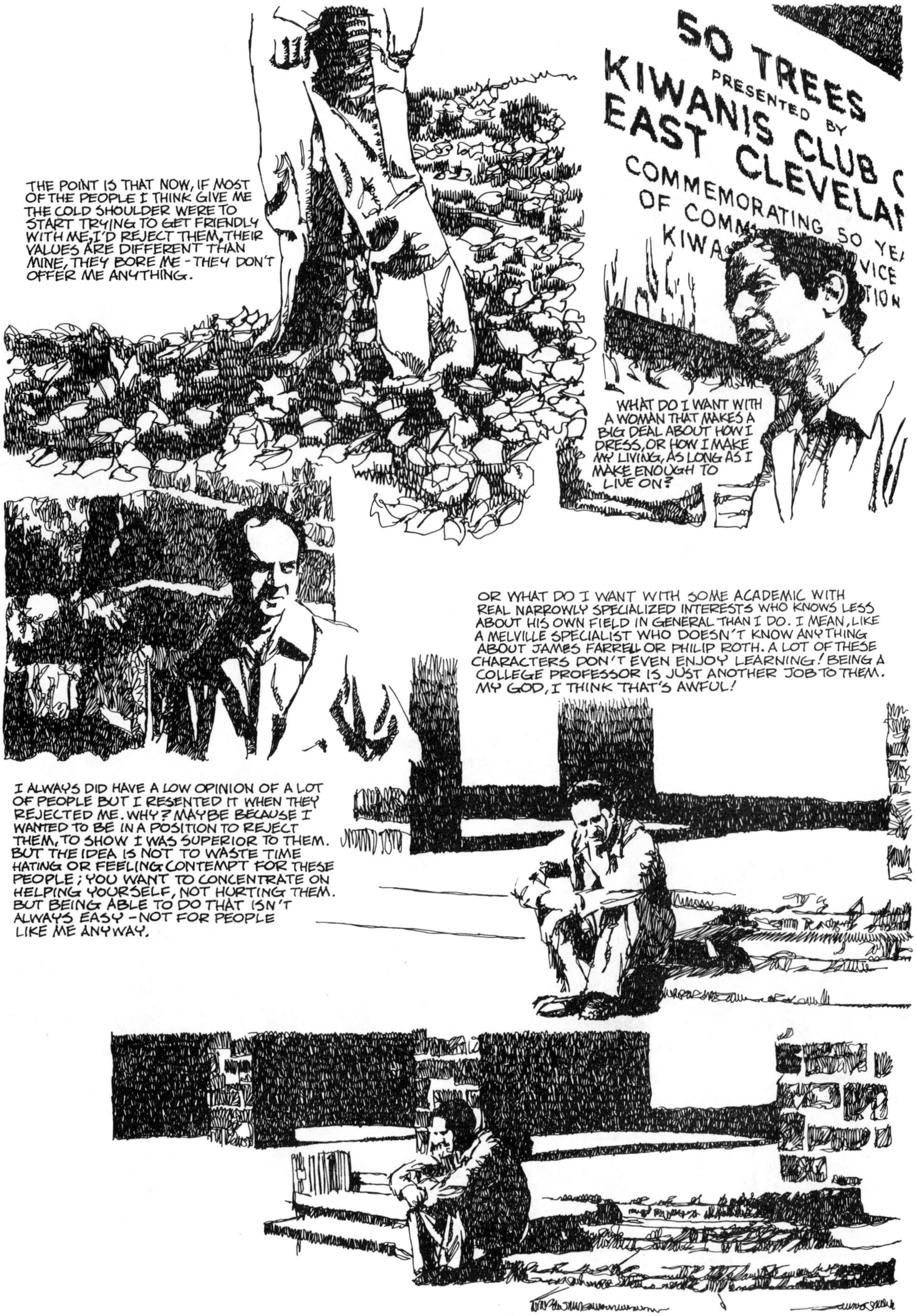
THE POINT IS THAT NOW, IF MOST OF THE PEOPLE I THINK GIVE ME THE COLD SHOULDER WERE TO START TRYING TO GET FRIENDLY WITH ME, I'D REJECT THEM. THEIR VALUES ARE DIFFERENT THAN MINE, THEY BORE ME - THEY DON'T OFFER ME ANYTHING.
50 TREES
PRESENTED BY
KIWANIS CLUB
EAST
COMMEMORATING
WHAT DO I WANT WITH A WOMAN THAT MAKES A BIG DEAL ABOUT HOW I DRESS, OR HOW I MAKE MY LIVING, AS LONG AS I MAKE ENOUGH TO LIVE ON?
OR WHAT DO I WANT WITH SOME ACADEMIC WITH REAL NARROWLY SPECIALIZED INTERESTS WHO KNOWS LESS ABOUT HIS OWN FIELD IN GENERAL THAN I DO. I MEAN, LIKE A MELVILLE SPECIALIST WHO DOESN'T KNOW ANYTHING ABOUT JAMES FARRELL OR PHILIP ROTH. A LOT OF THESE CHARACTERS DON'T EVEN ENJOY LEARNING! BEING A COLLEGE PROFESSOR IS JUST ANOTHER JOB TO THEM. MY GOD, I THINK THAT'S AWFUL!
I ALWAYS DID HAVE A LOW OPINION OF A LOT OF PEOPLE BUT I RESENTED IT WHEN THEY REJECTED ME. WHY? MAYBE BECAUSE I WANTED TO BE IN A POSITION TO REJECT THEM, TO SHOW I WAS SUPERIOR TO THEM. BUT THE IDEA IS NOT TO WASTE TIME HATING OR FEELING CONTEMPT FOR THESE PEOPLE; YOU WANT TO CONCENTRATE ON HELPING YOURSELF, NOT HURTING THEM. BUT BEING ABLE TO DO THAT ISN'T ALWAYS EASY - NOT FOR PEOPLE LIKE ME ANYWAY.

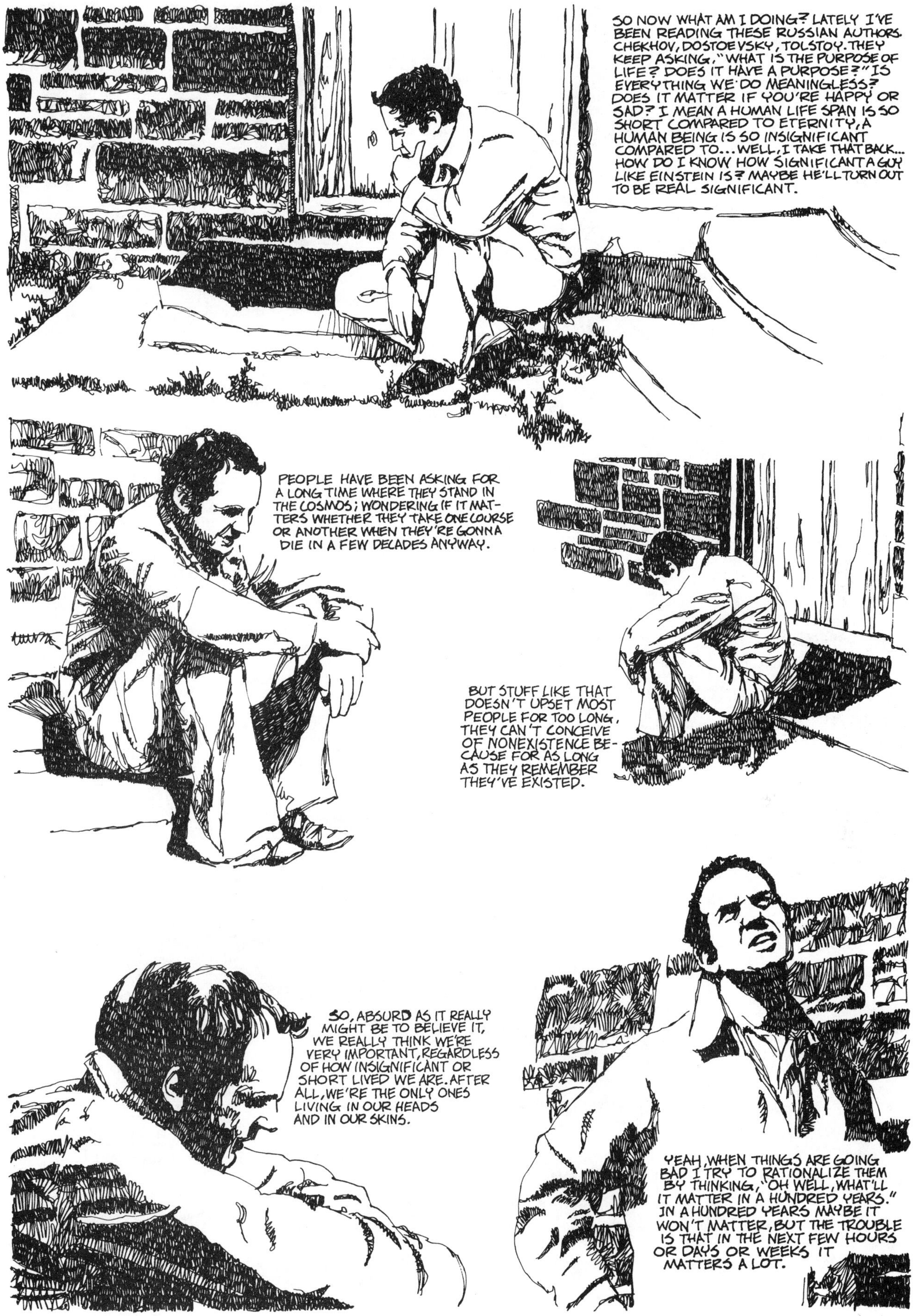
SO NOW WHAT AM I DOING? LATELY I'VE BEEN READING THESE RUSSIAN AUTHORS. CHEKHOV, DOSTOEVSKY, TOLSTOY. THEY KEEP ASKING, "WHAT IS THE PURPOSE OF LIFE? DOES IT HAVE A PURPOSE?" IS EVERYTHING WE DO MEANINGLESS? DOES IT MATTER IF YOU'RE HAPPY OR SAD? I MEAN A HUMAN LIFE SPAN IS SO SHORT COMPARED TO ETERNITY, A HUMAN BEING IS SO INSIGNIFICANT COMPARED TO... WELL, I TAKE THAT BACK... HOW DO I KNOW HOW SIGNIFICANT A GUY LIKE EINSTEIN IS? MAYBE HE'LL TURN OUT TO BE REAL SIGNIFICANT.
PEOPLE HAVE BEEN ASKING FOR A LONG TIME WHERE THEY STAND IN THE COSMOS; WONDERING IF IT MATTERS WHETHER THEY TAKE ONE COURSE OR ANOTHER WHEN THEY'RE GONNA DIE IN A FEW DECADES ANYWAY.
BUT STUFF LIKE THAT DOESN'T UPSET MOST PEOPLE FOR TOO LONG. THEY CAN'T CONCEIVE OF NONEXISTENCE BECAUSE FOR AS LONG AS THEY REMEMBER THEY'VE EXISTED.
SO, ABSURD AS IT REALLY MIGHT BE TO BELIEVE IT, WE REALLY THINK WE'RE VERY IMPORTANT, REGARDLESS OF HOW INSIGNIFICANT OR SHORT LIVED WE ARE. AFTER ALL, WE'RE THE ONLY ONES LIVING IN OUR HEADS AND IN OUR SKINS.
YEAH, WHEN THINGS ARE GOING BAD I TRY TO RATIONALIZE THEM BY THINKING, "OH WELL, WHAT'LL IT MATTER IN A HUNDRED YEARS." IN A HUNDRED YEARS MAYBE IT WON'T MATTER, BUT THE TROUBLE IS THAT IN THE NEXT FEW HOURS OR DAYS OR WEEKS IT MATTERS A LOT.

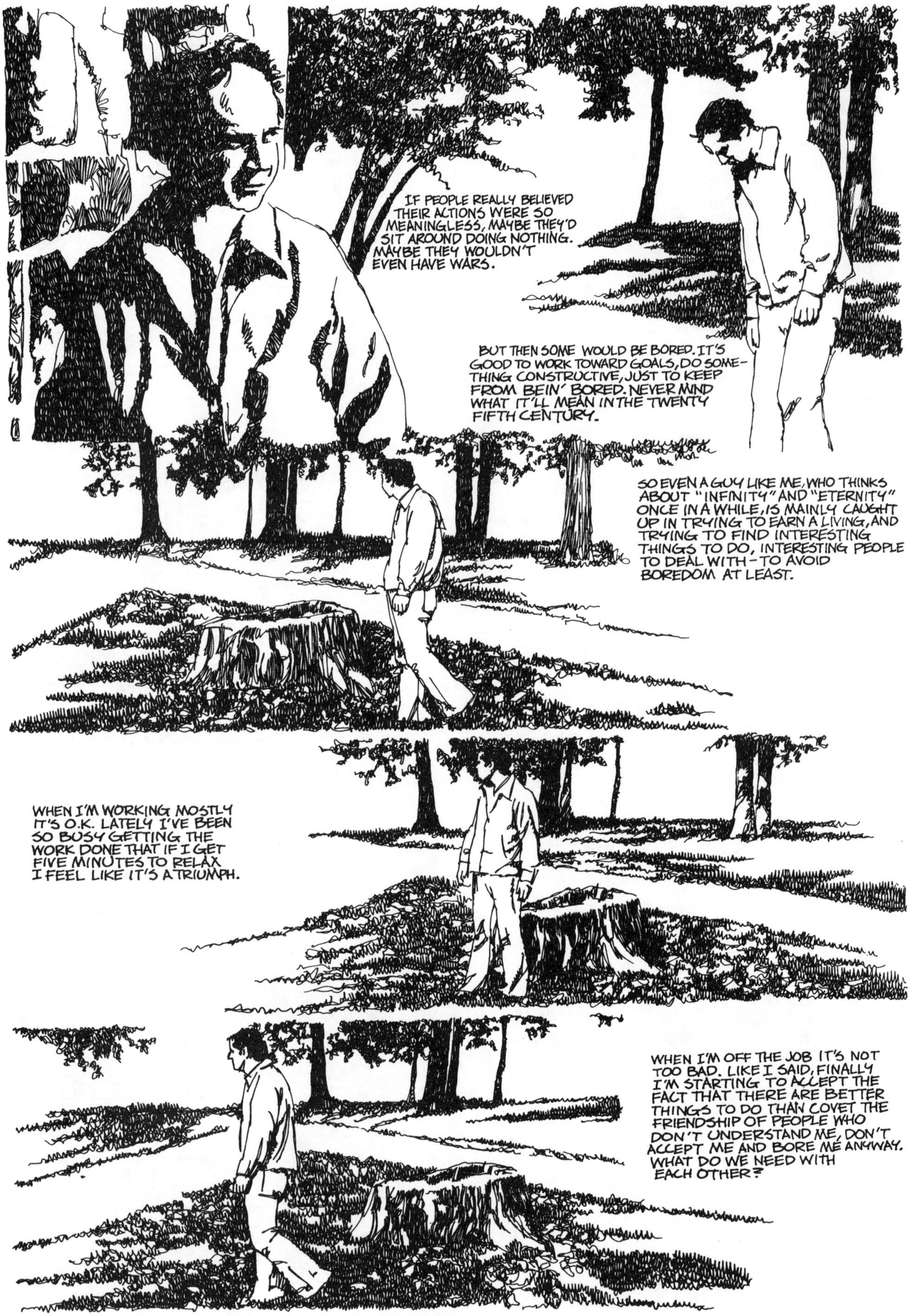

IF PEOPLE REALLY BELIEVED THEIR ACTIONS WERE SO MEANINGLESS, MAYBE THEY'D SIT AROUND DOING NOTHING. MAYBE THEY WOULDN'T EVEN HAVE WARS.
BUT THEN SOME WOULD BE BORED. IT'S GOOD TO WORK TOWARD GOALS, DO SOMETHING CONSTRUCTIVE, JUST TO KEEP FROM BEIN' BORED. NEVER MIND WHAT IT'LL MEAN IN THE TWENTY FIFTH CENTURY.
SO EVEN A GUY LIKE ME, WHO THINKS ABOUT "INFINITY" AND "ETERNITY" ONCE IN A WHILE, IS MAINLY CAUGHT UP IN TRYING TO EARN A LIVING, AND TRYING TO FIND INTERESTING THINGS TO DO, INTERESTING PEOPLE TO DEAL WITH - TO AVOID BOREDOM AT LEAST.
WHEN I'M WORKING MOSTLY IT'S O.K. LATELY I'VE BEEN SO BUSY GETTING THE WORK DONE THAT IF I GET FIVE MINUTES TO RELAX I FEEL LIKE IT'S A TRIUMPH.
WHEN I'M OFF THE JOB IT'S NOT TOO BAD. LIKE I SAID, FINALLY I'M STARTING TO ACCEPT THE FACT THAT THERE ARE BETTER THINGS TO DO THAN COVET THE FRIENDSHIP OF PEOPLE WHO DON'T UNDERSTAND ME, DON'T ACCEPT ME AND BORE ME ANYWAY. WHAT DO WE NEED WITH EACH OTHER?

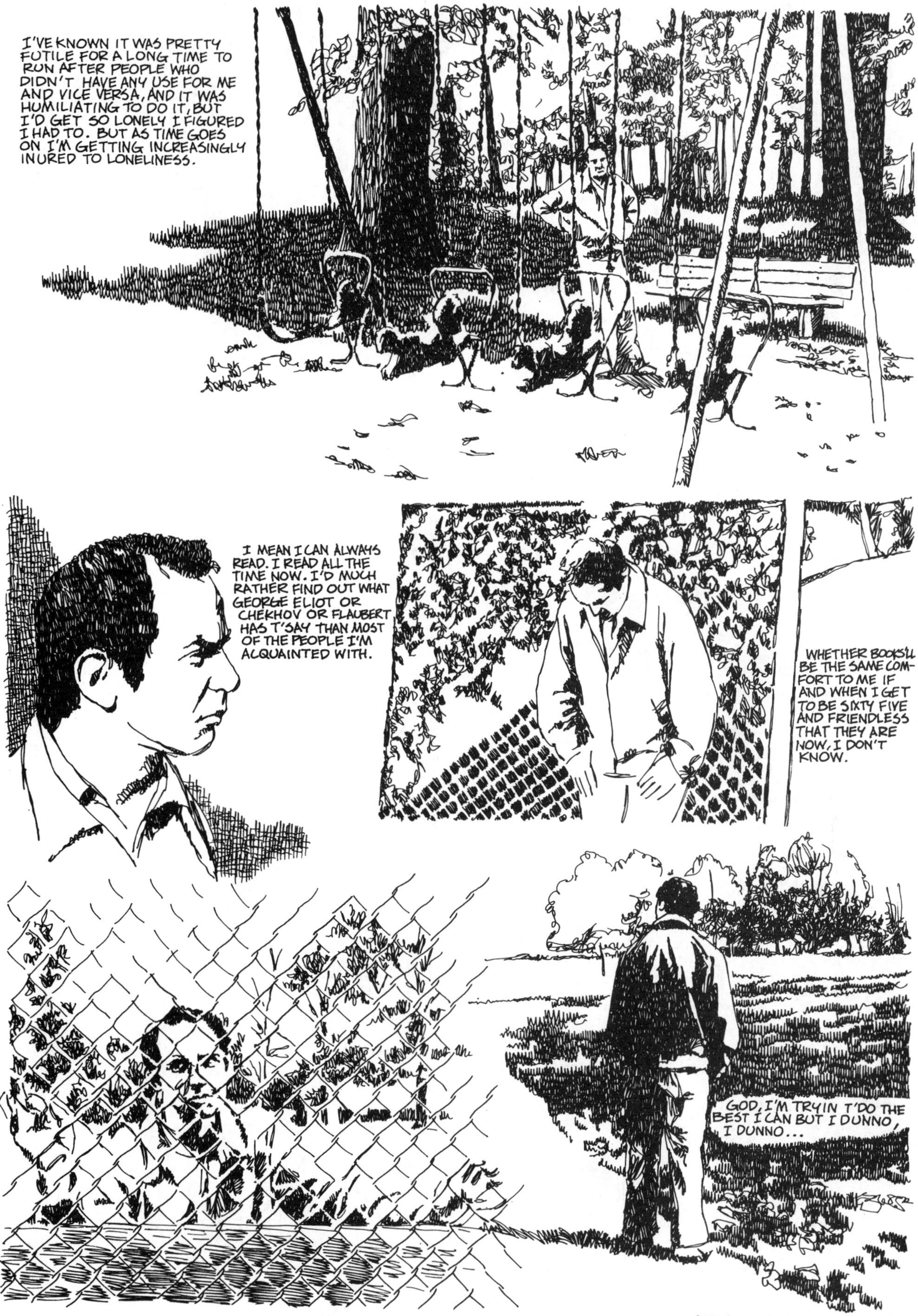
I'VE KNOWN IT WAS PRETTY FUTILE FOR A LONG TIME TO RUN AFTER PEOPLE WHO DIDN'T HAVE ANY USE FOR ME AND VICE VERSA, AND IT WAS HUMILIATING TO DO IT, BUT I'D GET SO LONELY I FIGURED I HAD TO. BUT AS TIME GOES ON I'M GETTING INCREASINGLY INURED TO LONELINESS.
I MEAN I CAN ALWAYS READ. I READ ALL THE TIME NOW. I'D MUCH RATHER FIND OUT WHAT GEORGE ELIOT OR CHEKHOV OR FLAUBERT HAS T'SAY THAN MOST OF THE PEOPLE I'M ACQUAINTED WITH.
WHETHER BOOKS'LL BE THE SAME COMFORT TO ME IF AND WHEN I GET TO BE SIXTY FIVE AND FRIENDLESS THAT THEY ARE NOW, I DON'T KNOW.
GOD, I'M TRYIN T'DO THE BEST I CAN BUT I DUNNO, I DUNNO...

story by
Harvey Pekar

drawings by
S. Cavey

ONE DAY I CAME HOME FROM WORK TO FIND A LETTER SUMMONING ME TO PERFORM A DUTY I DID NOT RELISH.

Mr. Harvey Pekar
2600 Hampshire Rd.
Cleveland Hts, Oh.

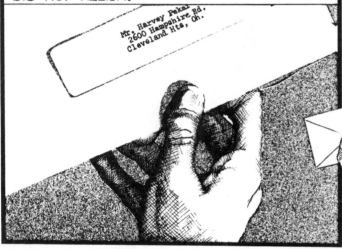

I WAS SUPPOSED TO DO JURY DUTY BEGINNING IN ABOUT TEN DAYS FROM WHEN I GOT THE SUMMONS.

I CONSIDERED THIS A BUMMER FOR SEVERAL REASONS. FOR ONE THING, I'D BE AWAY FROM MY JOB FOR TWO WEEKS. I'M NOT IN LOVE WITH MY GIG, BUT IT'S A STABLIZING ELEMENT IN MY LIFE. I HAVE ALMOST NOTHING TO DO WITH MY FAMILY AND I HAVE VERY FEW FRIENDS. WORKING AND DEALING WITH PEOPLE AT WORK, MANY OF WHOM I LIKE, PREVENTS ME FROM GETTING TOO LONELY AND HELPS ME KEEP THE RIGHT PERSPECTIVE ON THINGS; IT TENDS TO STOP ME FROM EXAGGERATING MY PROBLEMS.

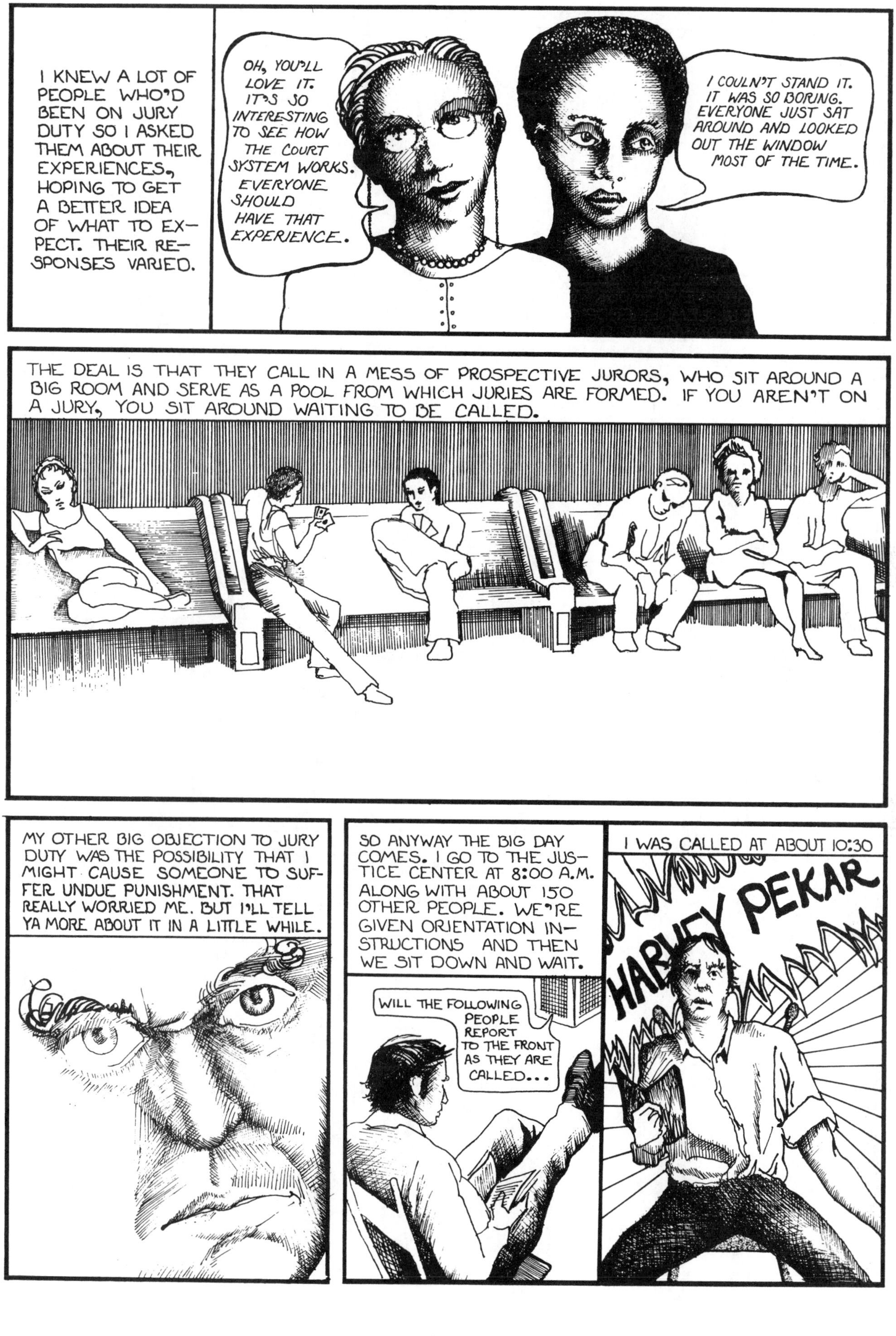
I KNEW A LOT OF PEOPLE WHO'D BEEN ON JURY DUTY SO I ASKED THEM ABOUT THEIR EXPERIENCES, HOPING TO GET A BETTER IDEA OF WHAT TO EXPECT. THEIR RESPONSES VARIED.
OH, YOU'LL LOVE IT. IT'S SO INTERESTING TO SEE HOW THE COURT SYSTEM WORKS. EVERYONE SHOULD HAVE THAT EXPERIENCE.
I COULN'T STAND IT. IT WAS SO BORING. EVERYONE JUST SAT AROUND AND LOOKED OUT THE WINDOW MOST OF THE TIME.
THE DEAL IS THAT THEY CALL IN A MESS OF PROSPECTIVE JURORS, WHO SIT AROUND A BIG ROOM AND SERVE AS A POOL FROM WHICH JURIES ARE FORMED. IF YOU AREN'T ON A JURY, YOU SIT AROUND WAITING TO BE CALLED.
MY OTHER BIG OBJECTION TO JURY DUTY WAS THE POSSIBILITY THAT I MIGHT CAUSE SOMEONE TO SUFFER UNDUE PUNISHMENT. THAT REALLY WORRIED ME. BUT I'LL TELL YA MORE ABOUT IT IN A LITTLE WHILE.
SO ANYWAY THE BIG DAY COMES. I GO TO THE JUSTICE CENTER AT 8:00 A.M. ALONG WITH ABOUT 150 OTHER PEOPLE. WE'RE GIVEN ORIENTATION INSTRUCTIONS AND THEN WE SIT DOWN AND WAIT.
WILL THE FOLLOWING PEOPLE REPORT TO THE FRONT AS THEY ARE CALLED...
I WAS CALLED AT ABOUT 10:30
HARVEY PEKAR

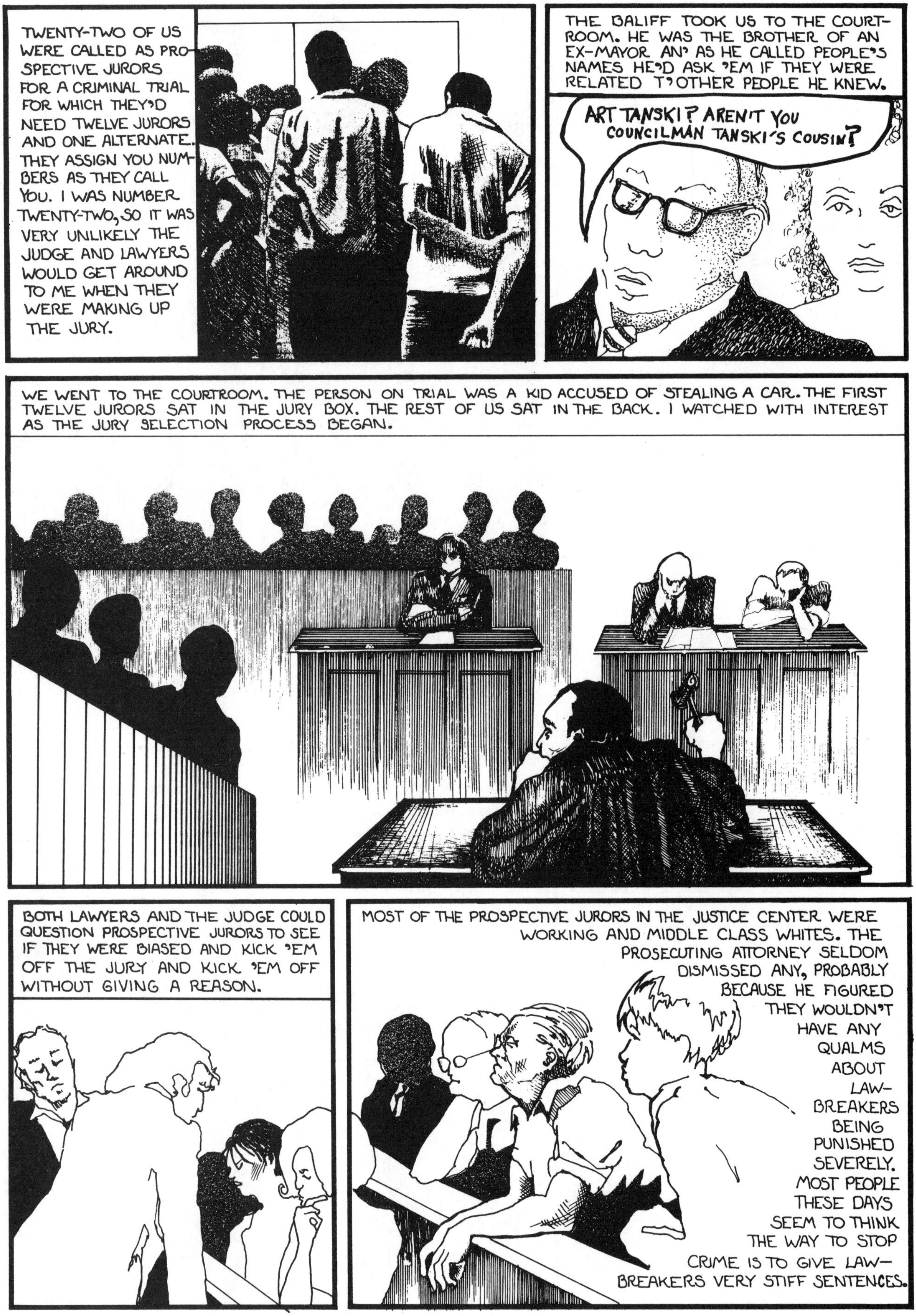
TWENTY-TWO OF US WERE CALLED AS PROSPECTIVE JURORS FOR A CRIMINAL TRIAL FOR WHICH THEY'D NEED TWELVE JURORS AND ONE ALTERNATE. THEY ASSIGN YOU NUMBERS AS THEY CALL YOU. I WAS NUMBER TWENTY-TWO, SO IT WAS VERY UNLIKELY THE JUDGE AND LAWYERS WOULD GET AROUND TO ME WHEN THEY WERE MAKING UP THE JURY.
THE BALIFF TOOK US TO THE COURTROOM. HE WAS THE BROTHER OF AN EX-MAYOR AN' AS HE CALLED PEOPLE'S NAMES HE'D ASK 'EM IF THEY WERE RELATED T'OTHER PEOPLE HE KNEW.
ART TANSKI? AREN'T YOU COUNCILMAN TANSKI'S COUSIN?
WE WENT TO THE COURTROOM. THE PERSON ON TRIAL WAS A KID ACCUSED OF STEALING A CAR. THE FIRST TWELVE JURORS SAT IN THE JURY BOX. THE REST OF US SAT IN THE BACK. I WATCHED WITH INTEREST AS THE JURY SELECTION PROCESS BEGAN.
BOTH LAWYERS AND THE JUDGE COULD QUESTION PROSPECTIVE JURORS TO SEE IF THEY WERE BIASED AND KICK 'EM OFF THE JURY AND KICK 'EM OFF WITHOUT GIVING A REASON.
MOST OF THE PROSPECTIVE JURORS IN THE JUSTICE CENTER WERE WORKING AND MIDDLE CLASS WHITES. THE PROSECUTING ATTORNEY SELDOM DISMISSED ANY, PROBABLY BECAUSE HE FIGURED THEY WOULDN'T HAVE ANY QUALMS ABOUT LAW-BREAKERS BEING PUNISHED SEVERELY. MOST PEOPLE THESE DAYS SEEM TO THINK THE WAY TO STOP CRIME IS TO GIVE LAW-BREAKERS VERY STIFF SENTENCES.

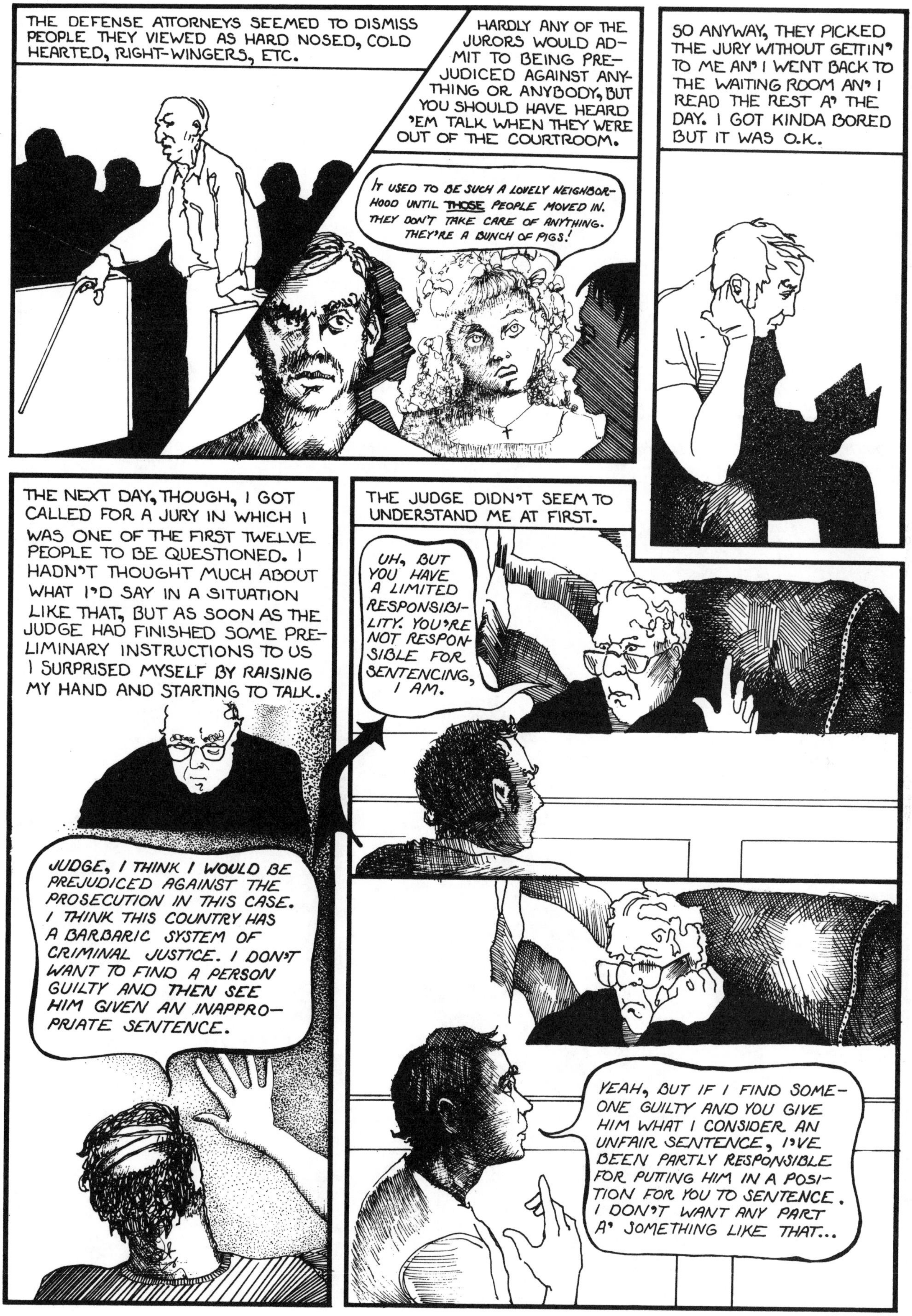
THE DEFENSE ATTORNEYS SEEMED TO DISMISS PEOPLE THEY VIEWED AS HARD NOSED, COLD HEARTED, RIGHT-WINGERS, ETC.
HARDLY ANY OF THE JURORS WOULD ADMIT TO BEING PREJUDICED AGAINST ANYTHING OR ANYBODY, BUT YOU SHOULD HAVE HEARD 'EM TALK WHEN THEY WERE OUT OF THE COURTROOM.
IT USED TO BE SUCH A LOVELY NEIGHBORHOOD UNTIL THOSE PEOPLE MOVED IN. THEY DON'T TAKE CARE OF ANYTHING. THEY'RE A BUNCH OF PIGS!
SO ANYWAY, THEY PICKED THE JURY WITHOUT GETTIN' TO ME AN' I WENT BACK TO THE WAITING ROOM AN' I READ THE REST A' THE DAY. I GOT KINDA BORED BUT IT WAS O.K.
THE NEXT DAY, THOUGH, I GOT CALLED FOR A JURY IN WHICH I WAS ONE OF THE FIRST TWELVE PEOPLE TO BE QUESTIONED. I HADN'T THOUGHT MUCH ABOUT WHAT I'D SAY IN A SITUATION LIKE THAT, BUT AS SOON AS THE JUDGE HAD FINISHED SOME PRELIMINARY INSTRUCTIONS TO US I SURPRISED MYSELF BY RAISING MY HAND AND STARTING TO TALK.
JUDGE, I THINK I WOULD BE PREJUDICED AGAINST THE PROSECUTION IN THIS CASE. I THINK THIS COUNTRY HAS A BARBARIC SYSTEM OF CRIMINAL JUSTICE. I DON'T WANT TO FIND A PERSON GUILTY AND THEN SEE HIM GIVEN AN INAPPROPRIATE SENTENCE.
THE JUDGE DIDN'T SEEM TO UNDERSTAND ME AT FIRST.
UH, BUT YOU HAVE A LIMITED RESPONSIBILITY. YOU'RE NOT RESPONSIBLE FOR SENTENCING, I AM.
YEAH, BUT IF I FIND SOMEONE GUILTY AND YOU GIVE HIM WHAT I CONSIDER AN UNFAIR SENTENCE, I'VE BEEN PARTLY RESPONSIBLE FOR PUTTING HIM IN A POSITION FOR YOU TO SENTENCE. I DON'T WANT ANY PART A' SOMETHING LIKE THAT...

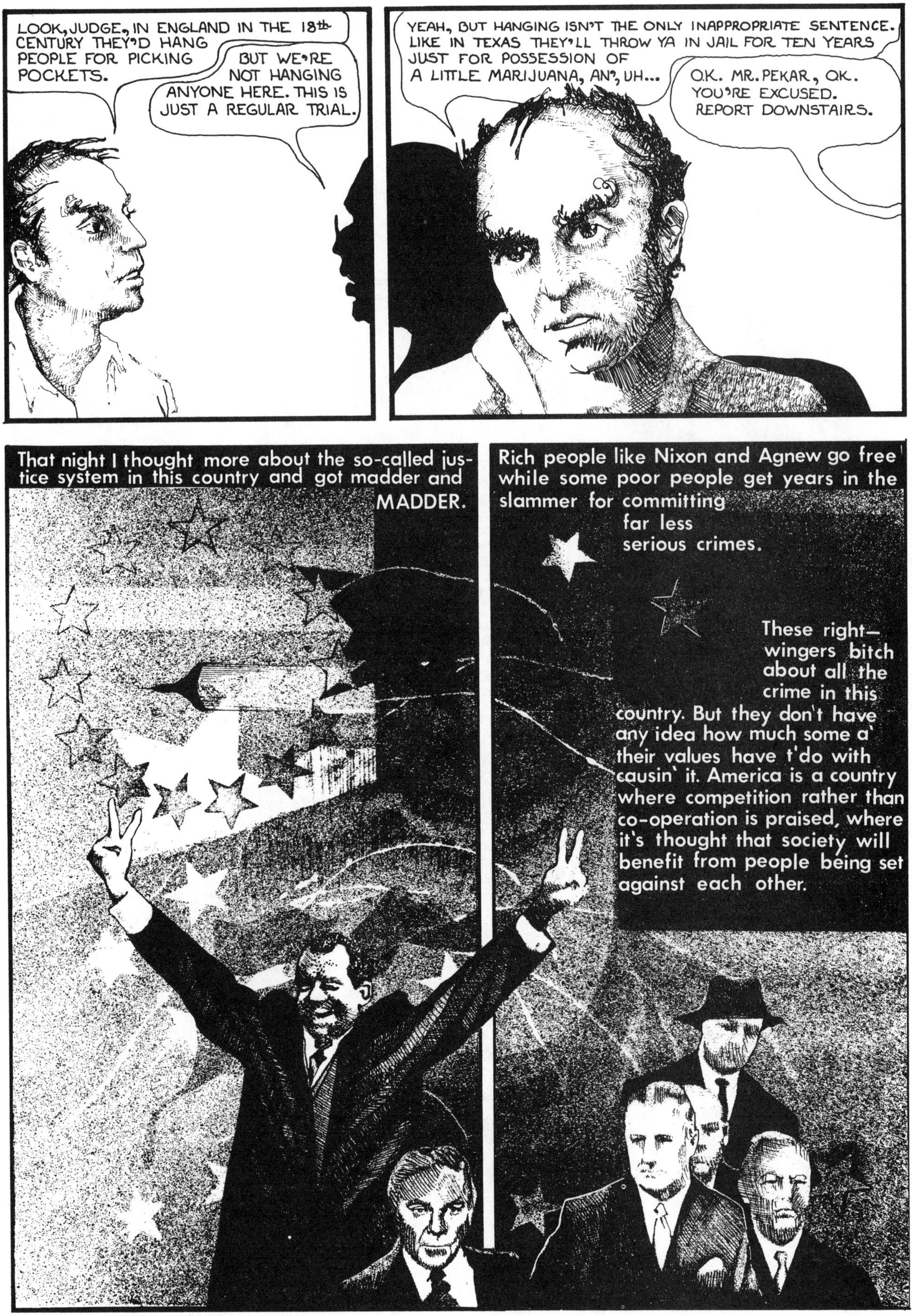
LOOK, JUDGE, IN ENGLAND IN THE 18th CENTURY THEY'D HANG PEOPLE FOR PICKING POCKETS.
BUT WE'RE NOT HANGING ANYONE HERE. THIS IS JUST A REGULAR TRIAL.
YEAH, BUT HANGING ISN'T THE ONLY INAPPROPRIATE SENTENCE. LIKE IN TEXAS THEY'LL THROW YA IN JAIL FOR TEN YEARS JUST FOR POSSESSION OF A LITTLE MARIJUANA, AN', UH...
O.K. MR. PEKAR, O.K. YOU'RE EXCUSED. REPORT DOWNSTAIRS.
That night I thought more about the so-called justice system in this country and got madder and MADDER.
Rich people like Nixon and Agnew go free while some poor people get years in the slammer for committing far less serious crimes.
These right-wingers bitch about all the crime in this country. But they don't have any idea how much some a' their values have t'do with causin' it. America is a country where competition rather than co-operation is praised, where it's thought that society will benefit from people being set against each other.

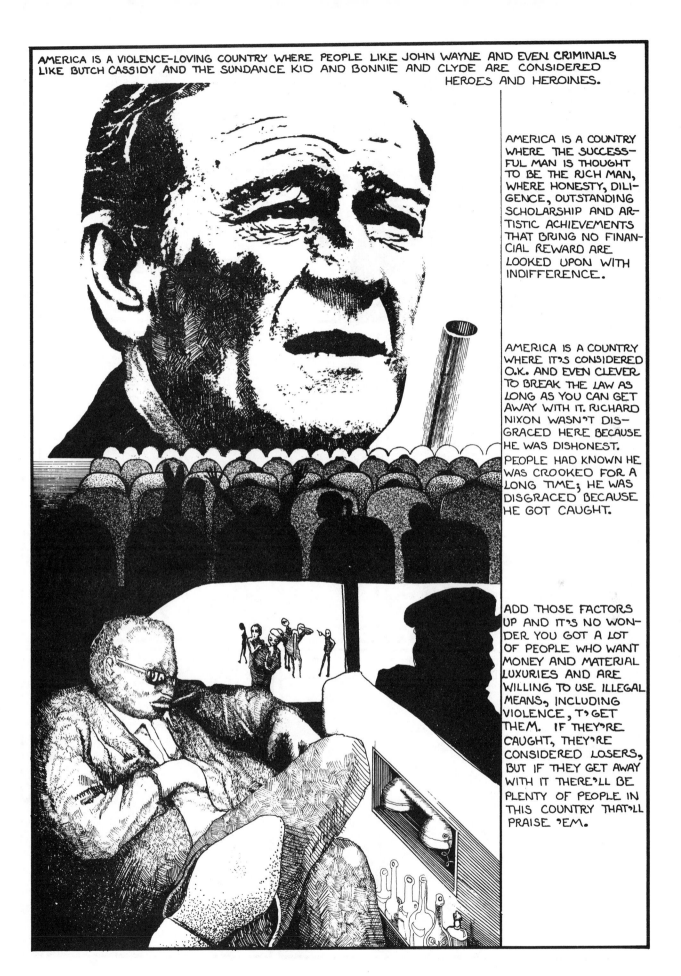

AMERICA IS A VIOLENCE-LOVING COUNTRY WHERE PEOPLE LIKE JOHN WAYNE AND EVEN CRIMINALS LIKE BUTCH CASSIDY AND THE SUNDANCE KID AND BONNIE AND CLYDE ARE CONSIDERED HEROES AND HEROINES.

AMERICA IS A COUNTRY WHERE THE SUCCESSFUL MAN IS THOUGHT TO BE THE RICH MAN, WHERE HONESTY, DILIGENCE, OUTSTANDING SCHOLARSHIP AND ARTISTIC ACHIEVEMENTS THAT BRING NO FINANCIAL REWARD ARE LOOKED UPON WITH INDIFFERENCE.

AMERICA IS A COUNTRY WHERE IT'S CONSIDERED O.K. AND EVEN CLEVER TO BREAK THE LAW AS LONG AS YOU CAN GET AWAY WITH IT. RICHARD NIXON WASN'T DISGRACED HERE BECAUSE HE WAS DISHONEST. PEOPLE HAD KNOWN HE WAS CROOKED FOR A LONG TIME; HE WAS DISGRACED BECAUSE HE GOT CAUGHT.

ADD THOSE FACTORS UP AND IT'S NO WONDER YOU GOT A LOT OF PEOPLE WHO WANT MONEY AND MATERIAL LUXURIES AND ARE WILLING TO USE ILLEGAL MEANS, INCLUDING VIOLENCE, T' GET THEM. IF THEY'RE CAUGHT, THEY'RE CONSIDERED LOSERS, BUT IF THEY GET AWAY WITH IT THERE'LL BE PLENTY OF PEOPLE IN THIS COUNTRY THAT'LL PRAISE 'EM.

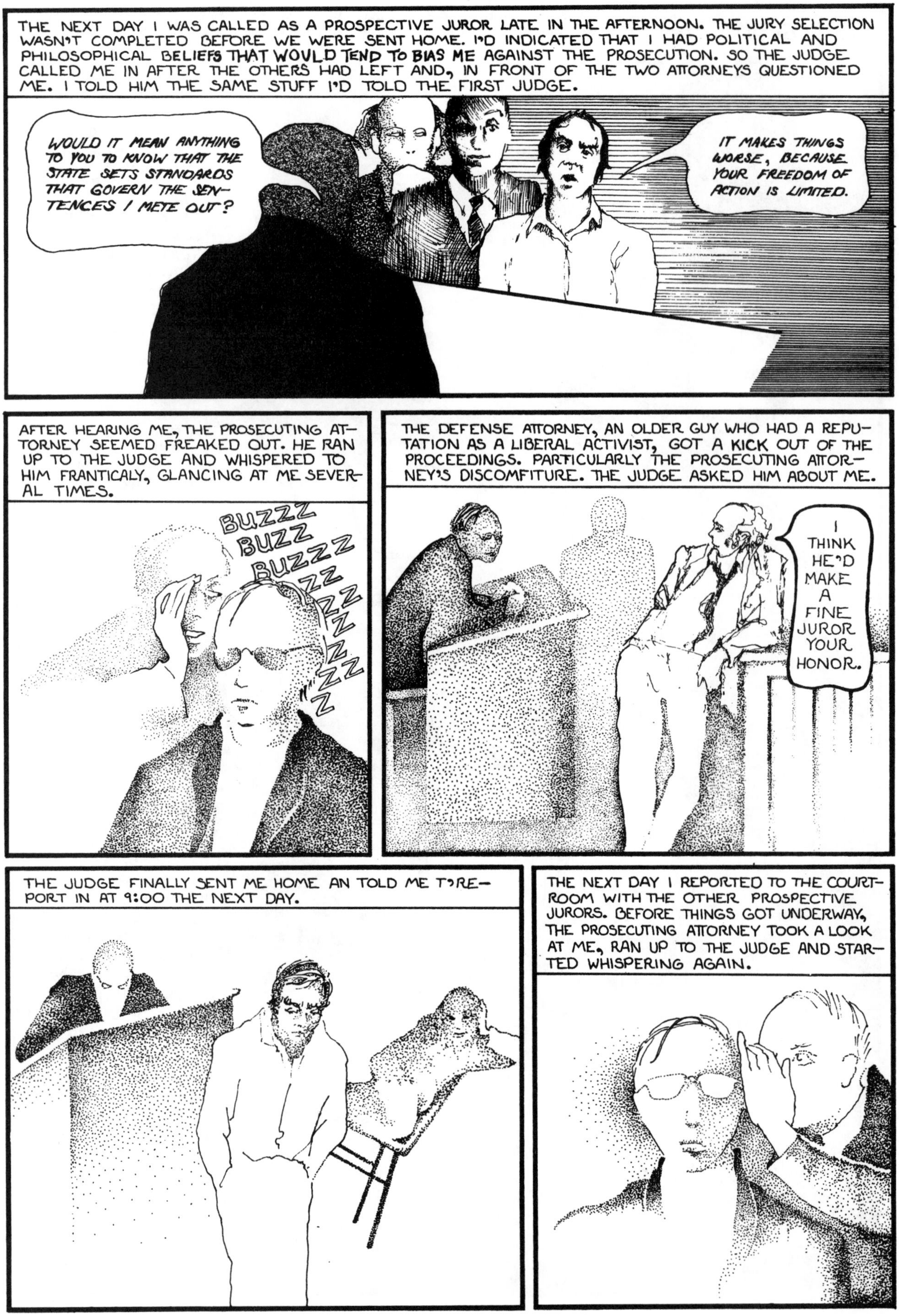
THE NEXT DAY I WAS CALLED AS A PROSPECTIVE JUROR LATE IN THE AFTERNOON. THE JURY SELECTION WASN'T COMPLETED BEFORE WE WERE SENT HOME. I'D INDICATED THAT I HAD POLITICAL AND PHILOSOPHICAL BELIEFS THAT WOULD TEND TO BIAS ME AGAINST THE PROSECUTION. SO THE JUDGE CALLED ME IN AFTER THE OTHERS HAD LEFT AND, IN FRONT OF THE TWO ATTORNEYS QUESTIONED ME. I TOLD HIM THE SAME STUFF I'D TOLD THE FIRST JUDGE.
WOULD IT MEAN ANYTHING TO YOU TO KNOW THAT THE STATE SETS STANDARDS THAT GOVERN THE SENTENCES I METE OUT?
IT MAKES THINGS WORSE, BECAUSE YOUR FREEDOM OF ACTION IS LIMITED.
AFTER HEARING ME, THE PROSECUTING ATTORNEY SEEMED FREAKED OUT. HE RAN UP TO THE JUDGE AND WHISPERED TO HIM FRANTICALY, GLANCING AT ME SEVERAL TIMES.
BUZZZ BUZZ BUZZZ ZZZZZZZZ
THE DEFENSE ATTORNEY, AN OLDER GUY WHO HAD A REPUTATION AS A LIBERAL ACTIVIST, GOT A KICK OUT OF THE PROCEEDINGS. PARTICULARLY THE PROSECUTING ATTORNEY'S DISCOMFITURE. THE JUDGE ASKED HIM ABOUT ME.
I THINK HE'D MAKE A FINE JUROR YOUR HONOR.
THE JUDGE FINALLY SENT ME HOME AN TOLD ME T'REPORT IN AT 9:00 THE NEXT DAY.
THE NEXT DAY I REPORTED TO THE COURTROOM WITH THE OTHER PROSPECTIVE JURORS. BEFORE THINGS GOT UNDERWAY, THE PROSECUTING ATTORNEY TOOK A LOOK AT ME, RAN UP TO THE JUDGE AND STARTED WHISPERING AGAIN.

A COUPLE OF MINUTES LATER A BALIFF CAME UP BEHIND ME.

MR. PEKAR, WOULD YOU COME WITH ME? YOU'VE BEEN EXCUSED.

I TOOK WHAT I WAS SAYING AND DOING VERY SERIOUSLY. AFTER JURY DUTY THAT DAY I REVIEWED MY WORDS AND ACTIONS WITH A FRIEND.

SEE, AFTER LOOKIN' AT IT FROM ALL ANGLES I THINK THIS IS THE ONLY THING THAT'S RIGHT FOR ME T'DO.

AS A JUROR Y'TAKE AN OATH T'DETERMINE T' TH' BEST OF YER ABILITY THE GUILT OR IN-NOCENCE OF THE DEFENDANT. BUT IF YOU 'N' THE OTHER JURORS FIND 'IM GUILTY, YER TURNIN' HIM OVER TO THE JUDGE FOR SENTENCING. SO MAYBE HE GOES T'JAIL. YOU KNOW WHAT JAILS 'R' LIKE — AMONG OTHER THINGS, THEY'RE SCHOOLS FOR CRIMINALS. MOST PEOPLE IN THIS COUNTRY DON'T CARE ABOUT REHABILITATING LAW-BREAKERS; THEY JUST WANT TO PUNISH 'EM AND GET 'EM OUTTA THE WAY.

AFTER THINKING EVERYTHING OVER AND BECOMING CON-VINCED THAT WHAT I WAS DOING WAS RIGHT, I BE-CAME ALMOST TRANQUIL. I WAS CALLED AS A PRO-SPECTIVE JUROR A COUPLE TIMES AFTER THAT AND BOTH TIMES WAS DIS-MISSED WITHOUT HAVING T'MAKE A SPEECH. MOSTLY I SAT AROUND AND READ. I FINISHED SOME NOVELS I'D BEEN WANTING T'GET TO AND IN THAT SENSE I USED MY TIME CONSTRUCTIVELY.

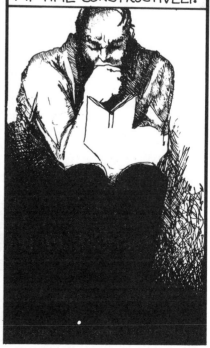

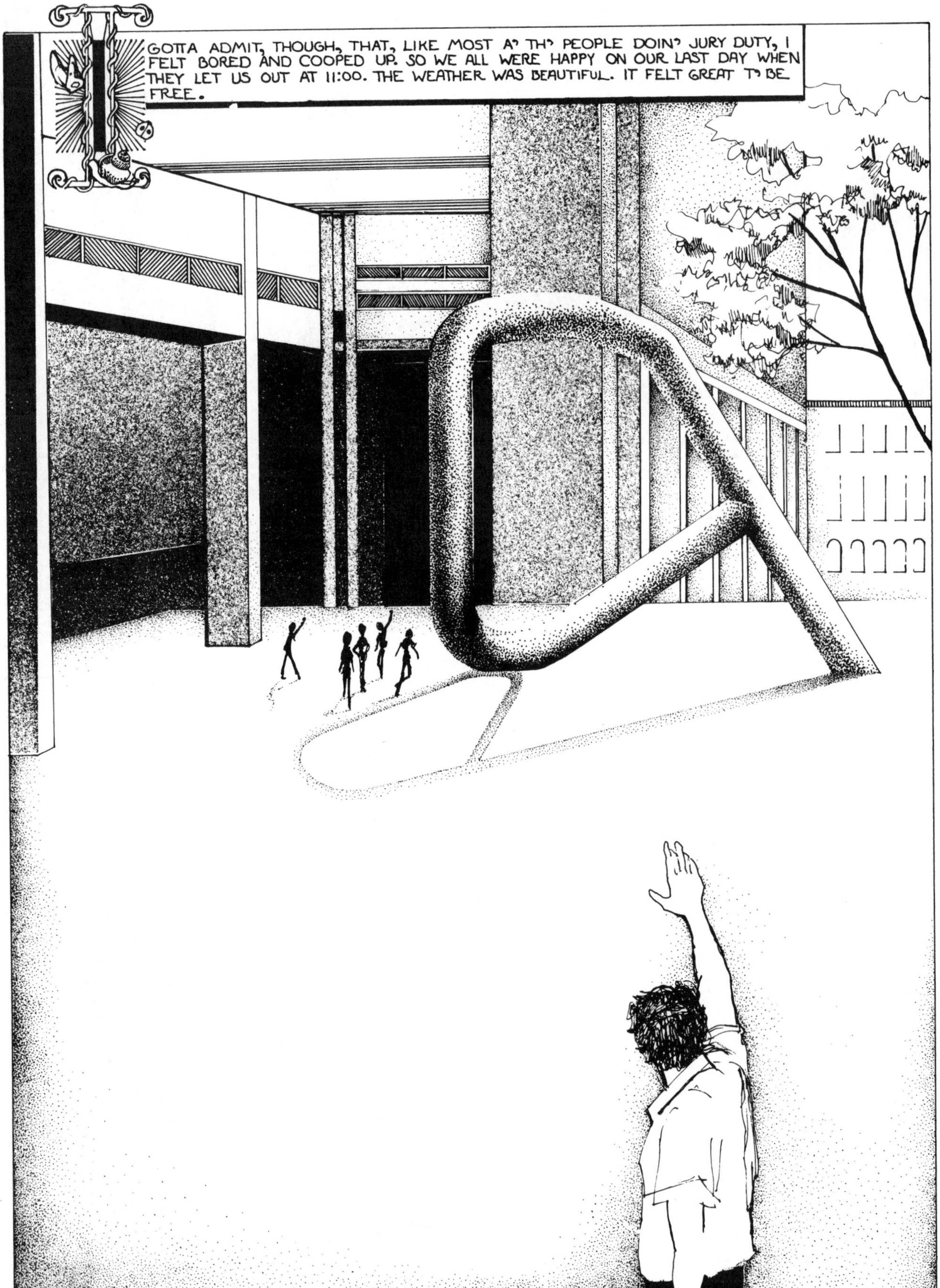
I GOTTA ADMIT, THOUGH, THAT, LIKE MOST A' TH' PEOPLE DOIN' JURY DUTY, I FELT BORED AND COOPED UP. SO WE ALL WERE HAPPY ON OUR LAST DAY WHEN THEY LET US OUT AT 11:00. THE WEATHER WAS BEAUTIFUL. IT FELT GREAT T' BE FREE.
END

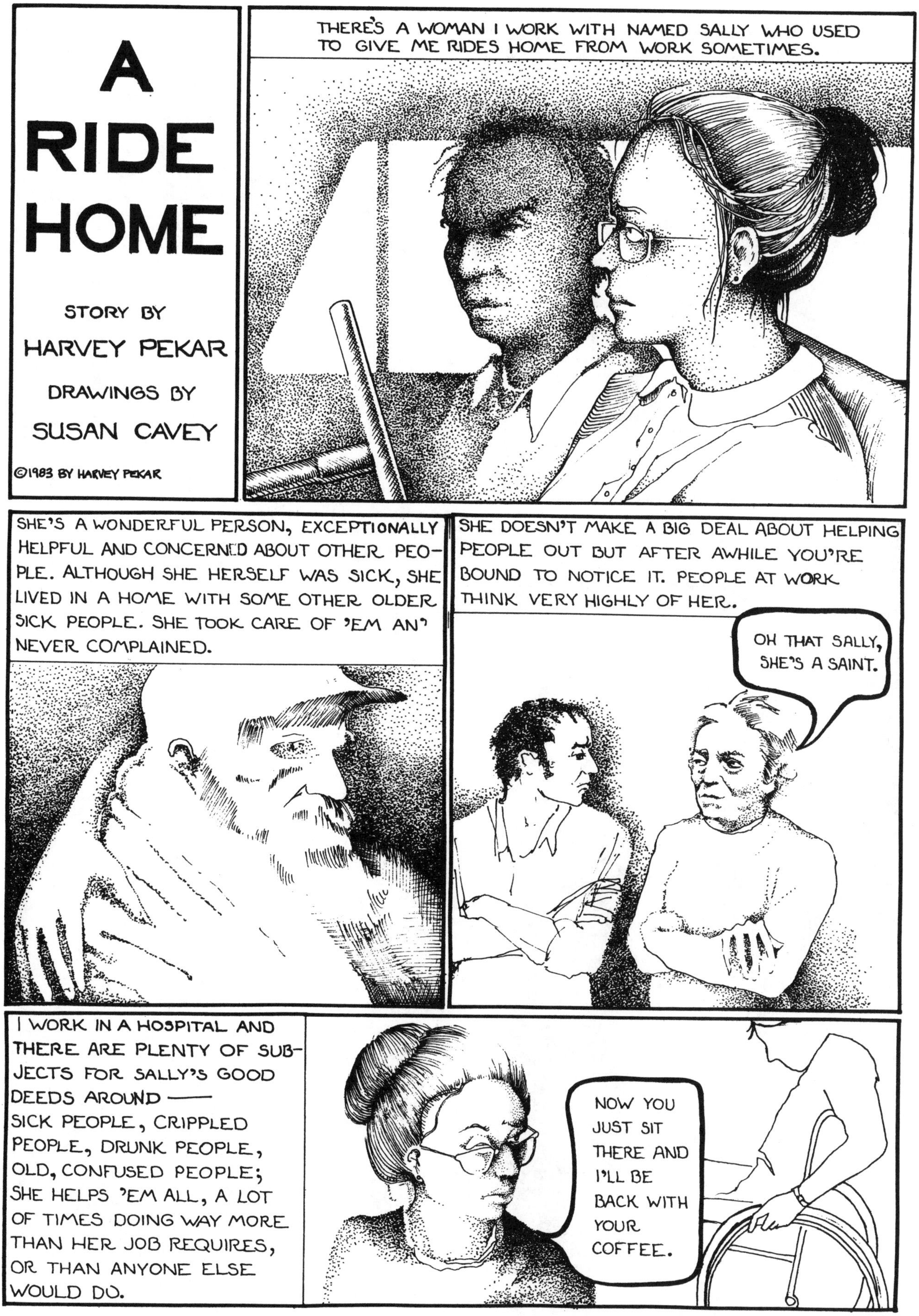
A RIDE HOME
STORY BY HARVEY PEKAR
DRAWINGS BY SUSAN CAVEY
©1983 BY HARVEY PEKAR
THERE'S A WOMAN I WORK WITH NAMED SALLY WHO USED TO GIVE ME RIDES HOME FROM WORK SOMETIMES.
SHE'S A WONDERFUL PERSON, EXCEPTIONALLY HELPFUL AND CONCERNED ABOUT OTHER PEOPLE. ALTHOUGH SHE HERSELF WAS SICK, SHE LIVED IN A HOME WITH SOME OTHER OLDER SICK PEOPLE. SHE TOOK CARE OF 'EM AN' NEVER COMPLAINED.
SHE DOESN'T MAKE A BIG DEAL ABOUT HELPING PEOPLE OUT BUT AFTER AWHILE YOU'RE BOUND TO NOTICE IT. PEOPLE AT WORK THINK VERY HIGHLY OF HER.
OH THAT SALLY, SHE'S A SAINT.
I WORK IN A HOSPITAL AND THERE ARE PLENTY OF SUBJECTS FOR SALLY'S GOOD DEEDS AROUND —— SICK PEOPLE, CRIPPLED PEOPLE, DRUNK PEOPLE, OLD, CONFUSED PEOPLE; SHE HELPS 'EM ALL, A LOT OF TIMES DOING WAY MORE THAN HER JOB REQUIRES, OR THAN ANYONE ELSE WOULD DO.
NOW YOU JUST SIT THERE AND I'LL BE BACK WITH YOUR COFFEE.

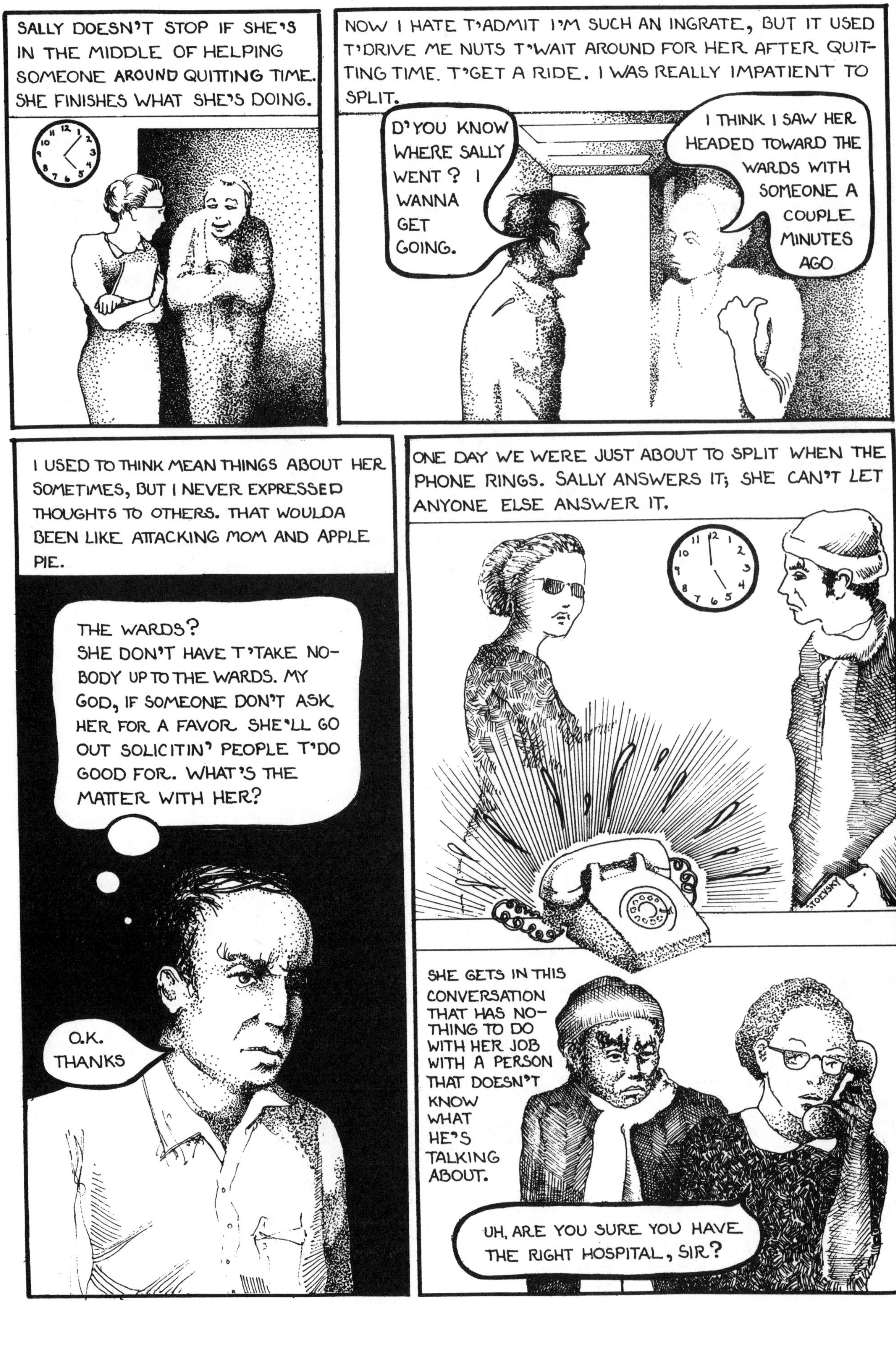
SALLY DOESN'T STOP IF SHE'S IN THE MIDDLE OF HELPING SOMEONE AROUND QUITTING TIME. SHE FINISHES WHAT SHE'S DOING.
NOW I HATE T'ADMIT I'M SUCH AN INGRATE, BUT IT USED T'DRIVE ME NUTS T'WAIT AROUND FOR HER AFTER QUITTING TIME. T'GET A RIDE. I WAS REALLY IMPATIENT TO SPLIT.
D'YOU KNOW WHERE SALLY WENT? I WANNA GET GOING.
I THINK I SAW HER HEADED TOWARD THE WARDS WITH SOMEONE A COUPLE MINUTES AGO
I USED TO THINK MEAN THINGS ABOUT HER SOMETIMES, BUT I NEVER EXPRESSED THOUGHTS TO OTHERS. THAT WOULDA BEEN LIKE ATTACKING MOM AND APPLE PIE.
THE WARDS? SHE DON'T HAVE T'TAKE NOBODY UP TO THE WARDS. MY GOD, IF SOMEONE DON'T ASK HER FOR A FAVOR SHE'LL GO OUT SOLICITIN' PEOPLE T'DO GOOD FOR. WHAT'S THE MATTER WITH HER?
O.K. THANKS
ONE DAY WE WERE JUST ABOUT TO SPLIT WHEN THE PHONE RINGS. SALLY ANSWERS IT; SHE CAN'T LET ANYONE ELSE ANSWER IT.
SHE GETS IN THIS CONVERSATION THAT HAS NOTHING TO DO WITH HER JOB WITH A PERSON THAT DOESN'T KNOW WHAT HE'S TALKING ABOUT.
UH, ARE YOU SURE YOU HAVE THE RIGHT HOSPITAL, SIR?

FINALLY, SHE TURNS THE CALL OVER TO SOMEONE ELSE. I THINK SHE'S GONNA LEAVE.

BUT THE OTHER PERSON DOESN'T UNDERSTAND THE CALLER EITHER.

SO SALLY TAKES OVER THE CALL AGAIN.

UH, WHEN DID THIS HAPPEN?

I'M SORRY, BUT YOU DON'T SEEM TO UNDERSTAND ME.

COULD YOU REPEAT THAT, SIR?

NOW IT'S 5:15 AND I'M FUMING. I'D BEEN ASHAMED TO COMPLAIN TO SALLY BEFORE. SHE WAS DOING ME THE FAVOR BY TAKING ME HOME. SHE HARDLY EVER MADE ME WAIT MORE THAN A COUPLE OF MINUTES.

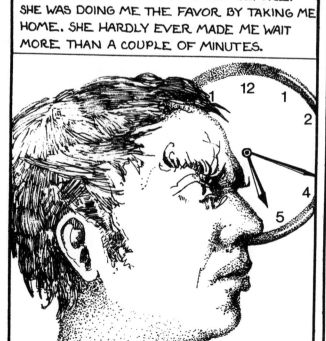

FINALLY, I EXPLODED, AND THREW DOWN A BOOK I WAS CARRYING.

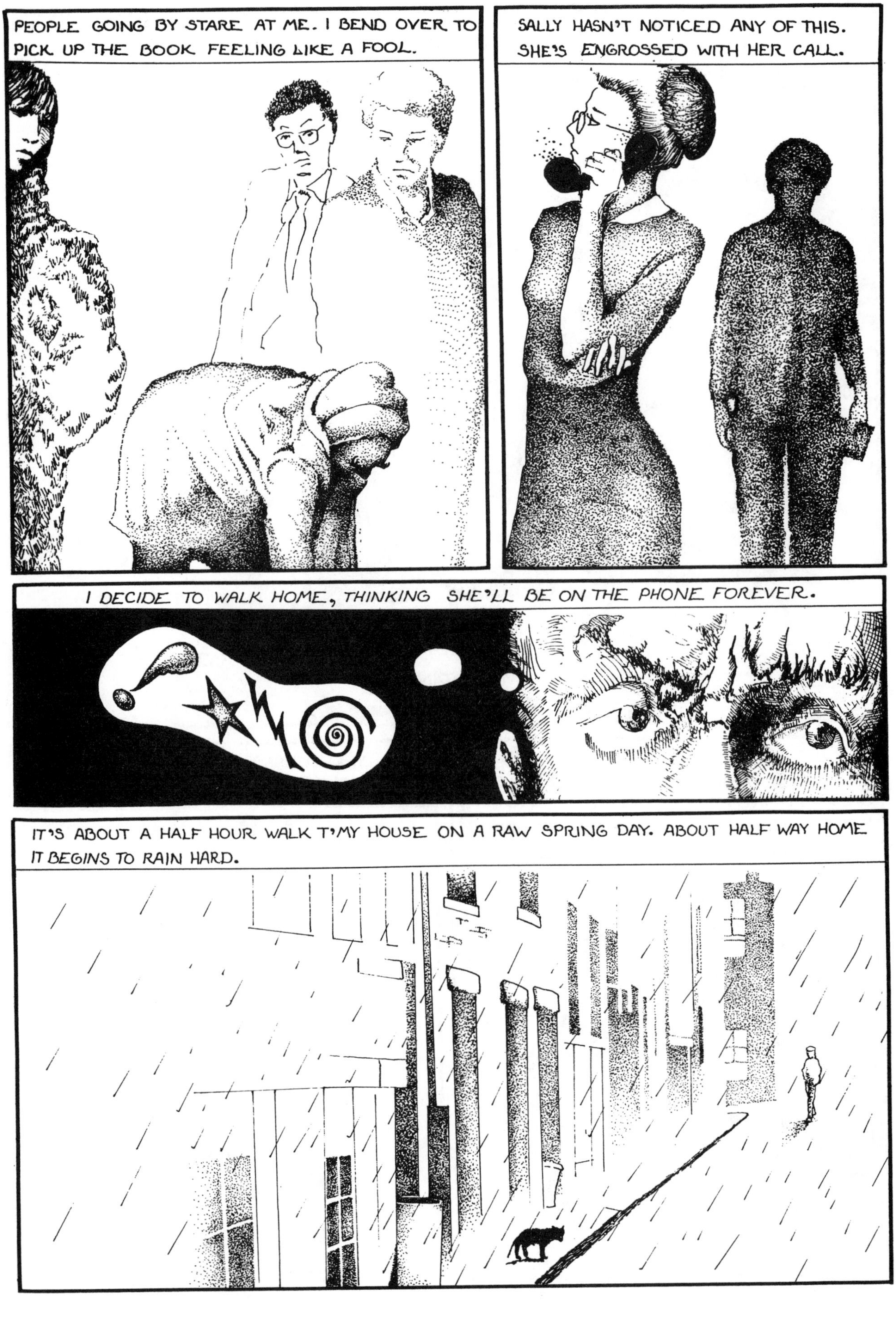
PEOPLE GOING BY STARE AT ME. I BEND OVER TO PICK UP THE BOOK FEELING LIKE A FOOL.
SALLY HASN'T NOTICED ANY OF THIS. SHE'S ENGROSSED WITH HER CALL.
I DECIDE TO WALK HOME, THINKING SHE'LL BE ON THE PHONE FOREVER.
IT'S ABOUT A HALF HOUR WALK T'MY HOUSE ON A RAW SPRING DAY. ABOUT HALF WAY HOME IT BEGINS TO RAIN HARD.

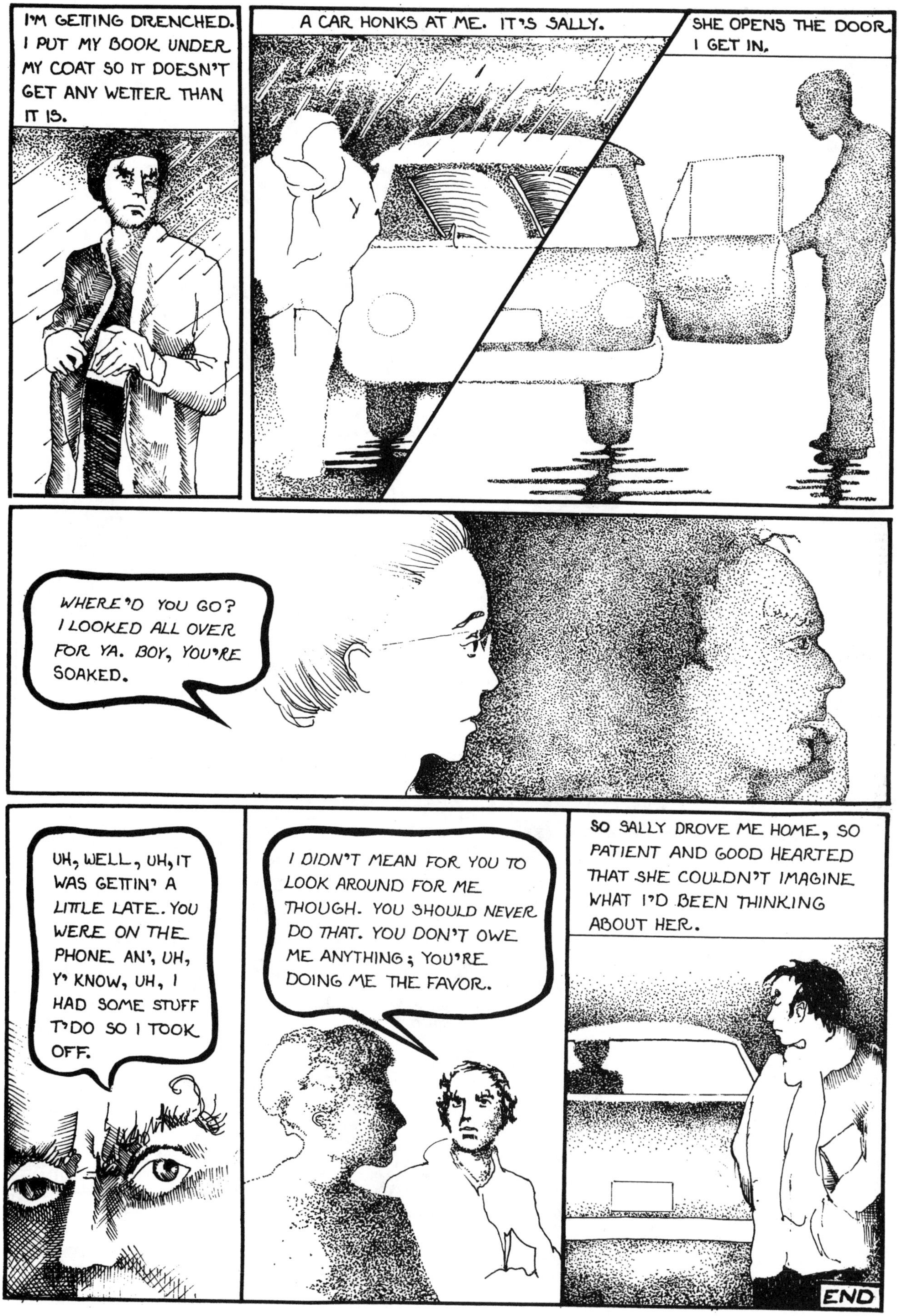
I'M GETTING DRENCHED. I PUT MY BOOK UNDER MY COAT SO IT DOESN'T GET ANY WETTER THAN IT IS.
A CAR HONKS AT ME. IT'S SALLY.
SHE OPENS THE DOOR. I GET IN.
WHERE'D YOU GO? I LOOKED ALL OVER FOR YA. BOY, YOU'RE SOAKED.
UH, WELL, UH, IT WAS GETTIN' A LITTLE LATE. YOU WERE ON THE PHONE AN', UH, Y' KNOW, UH, I HAD SOME STUFF T'DO SO I TOOK OFF.
I DIDN'T MEAN FOR YOU TO LOOK AROUND FOR ME THOUGH. YOU SHOULD NEVER DO THAT. YOU DON'T OWE ME ANYTHING; YOU'RE DOING ME THE FAVOR.
SO SALLY DROVE ME HOME, SO PATIENT AND GOOD HEARTED THAT SHE COULDN'T IMAGINE WHAT I'D BEEN THINKING ABOUT HER.
END

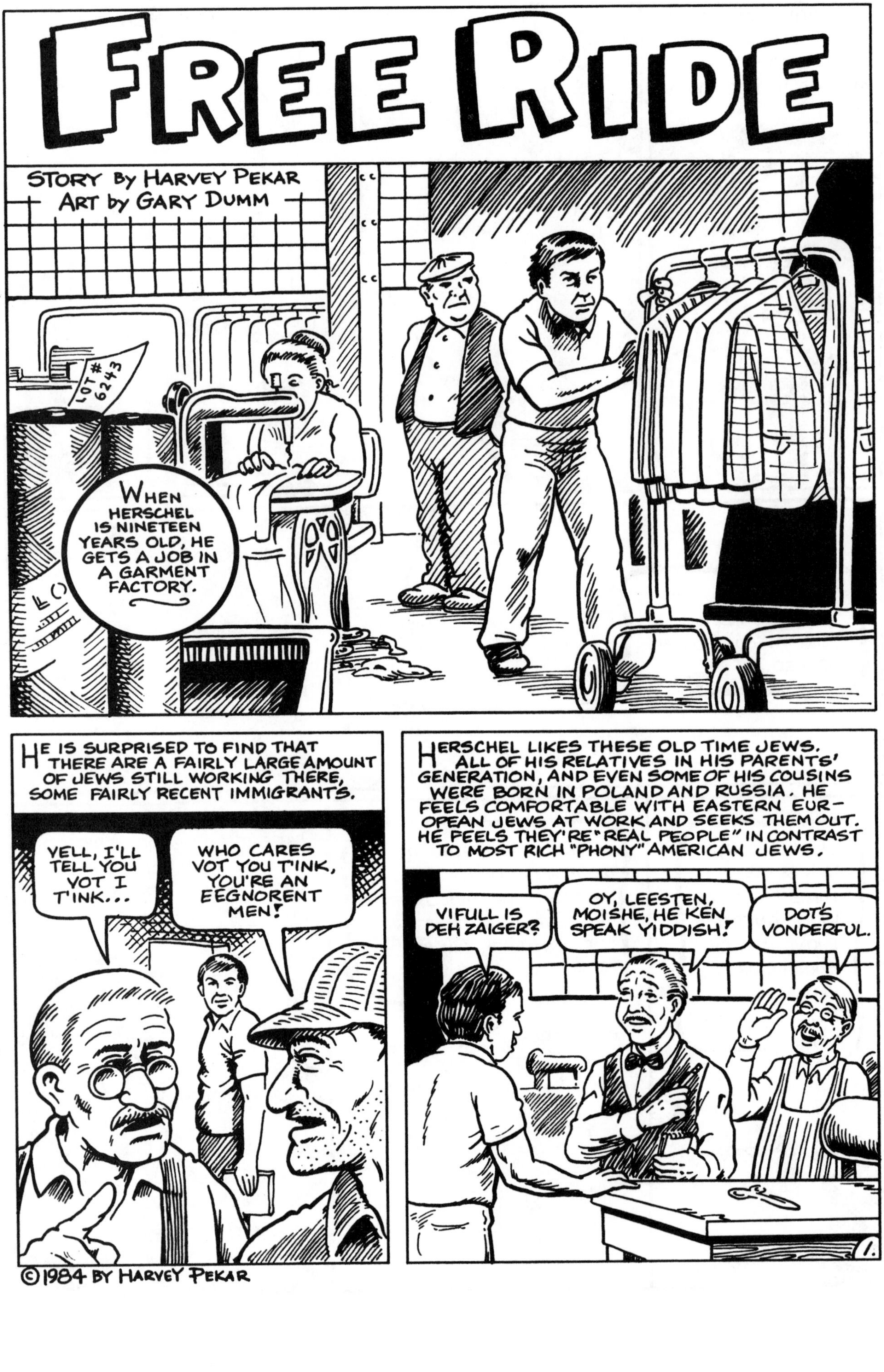
FREE RIDE
STORY BY HARVEY PEKAR
ART BY GARY DUMM
LOT # 6243
WHEN HERSCHEL IS NINETEEN YEARS OLD, HE GETS A JOB IN A GARMENT FACTORY.
HE IS SURPRISED TO FIND THAT THERE ARE A FAIRLY LARGE AMOUNT OF JEWS STILL WORKING THERE, SOME FAIRLY RECENT IMMIGRANTS.
YELL, I'LL TELL YOU VOT I T'INK...
WHO CARES VOT YOU T'INK, YOU'RE AN EEGNORENT MEN!
HERSCHEL LIKES THESE OLD TIME JEWS. ALL OF HIS RELATIVES IN HIS PARENTS' GENERATION, AND EVEN SOME OF HIS COUSINS WERE BORN IN POLAND AND RUSSIA. HE FEELS COMFORTABLE WITH EASTERN EUROPEAN JEWS AT WORK AND SEEKS THEM OUT. HE FEELS THEY'RE "REAL PEOPLE" IN CONTRAST TO MOST RICH "PHONY" AMERICAN JEWS.
VIFULL IS DEH ZAIGER?
OY, LEESTEN, MOISHE, HE KEN SPEAK YIDDISH!
DOT'S VONDERFUL.
1.

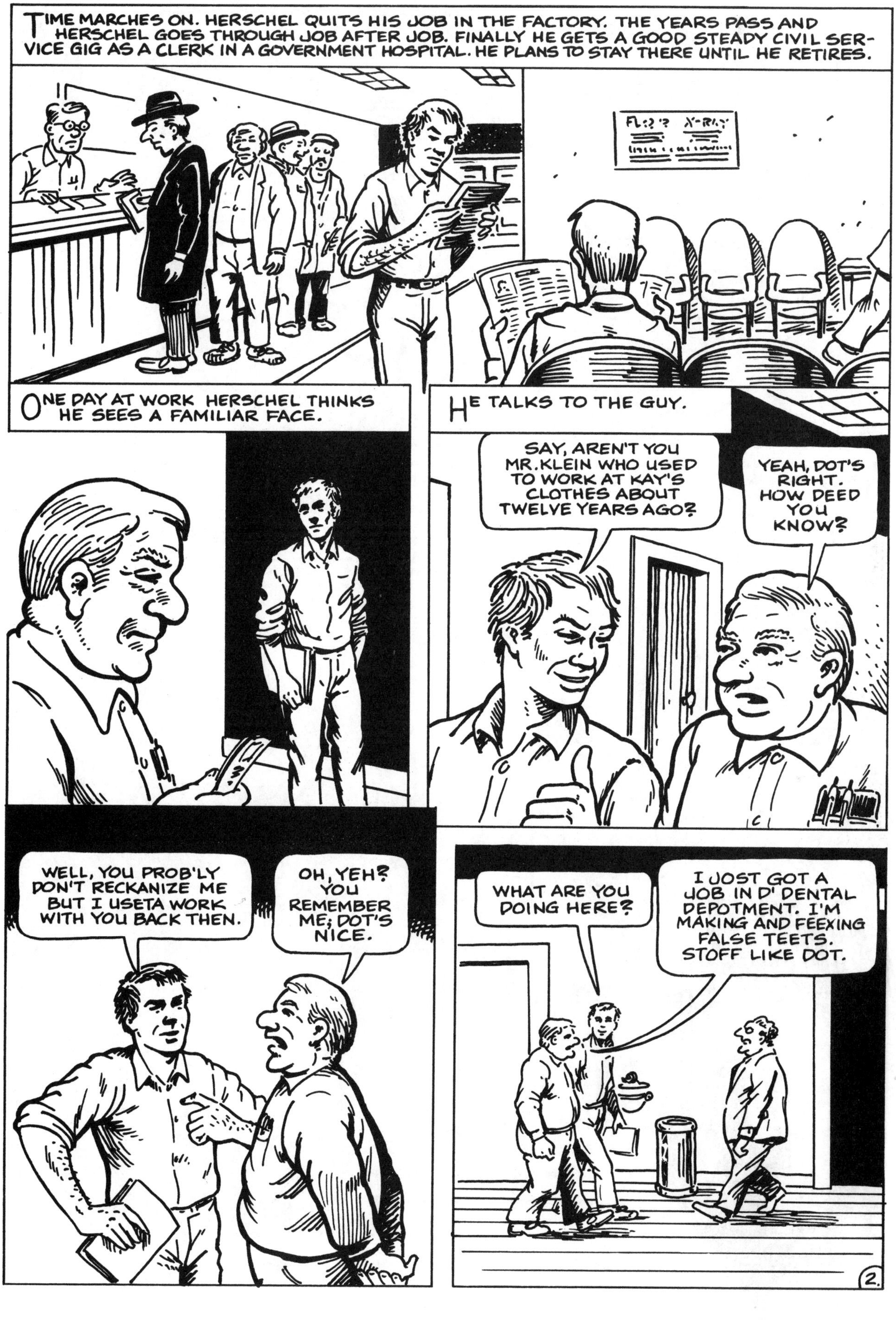
TIME MARCHES ON. HERSCHEL QUITS HIS JOB IN THE FACTORY. THE YEARS PASS AND HERSCHEL GOES THROUGH JOB AFTER JOB. FINALLY HE GETS A GOOD STEADY CIVIL SERVICE GIG AS A CLERK IN A GOVERNMENT HOSPITAL. HE PLANS TO STAY THERE UNTIL HE RETIRES.
ONE DAY AT WORK HERSCHEL THINKS HE SEES A FAMILIAR FACE.
HE TALKS TO THE GUY.
SAY, AREN'T YOU MR. KLEIN WHO USED TO WORK AT KAY'S CLOTHES ABOUT TWELVE YEARS AGO?
YEAH, DOT'S RIGHT. HOW DEED YOU KNOW?
WELL, YOU PROB'LY DON'T RECKANIZE ME BUT I USETA WORK WITH YOU BACK THEN.
OH, YEH? YOU REMEMBER ME; DOT'S NICE.
WHAT ARE YOU DOING HERE?
I JOST GOT A JOB IN D' DENTAL DEPOTMENT. I'M MAKING AND FEEXING FALSE TEETS. STOFF LIKE DOT.

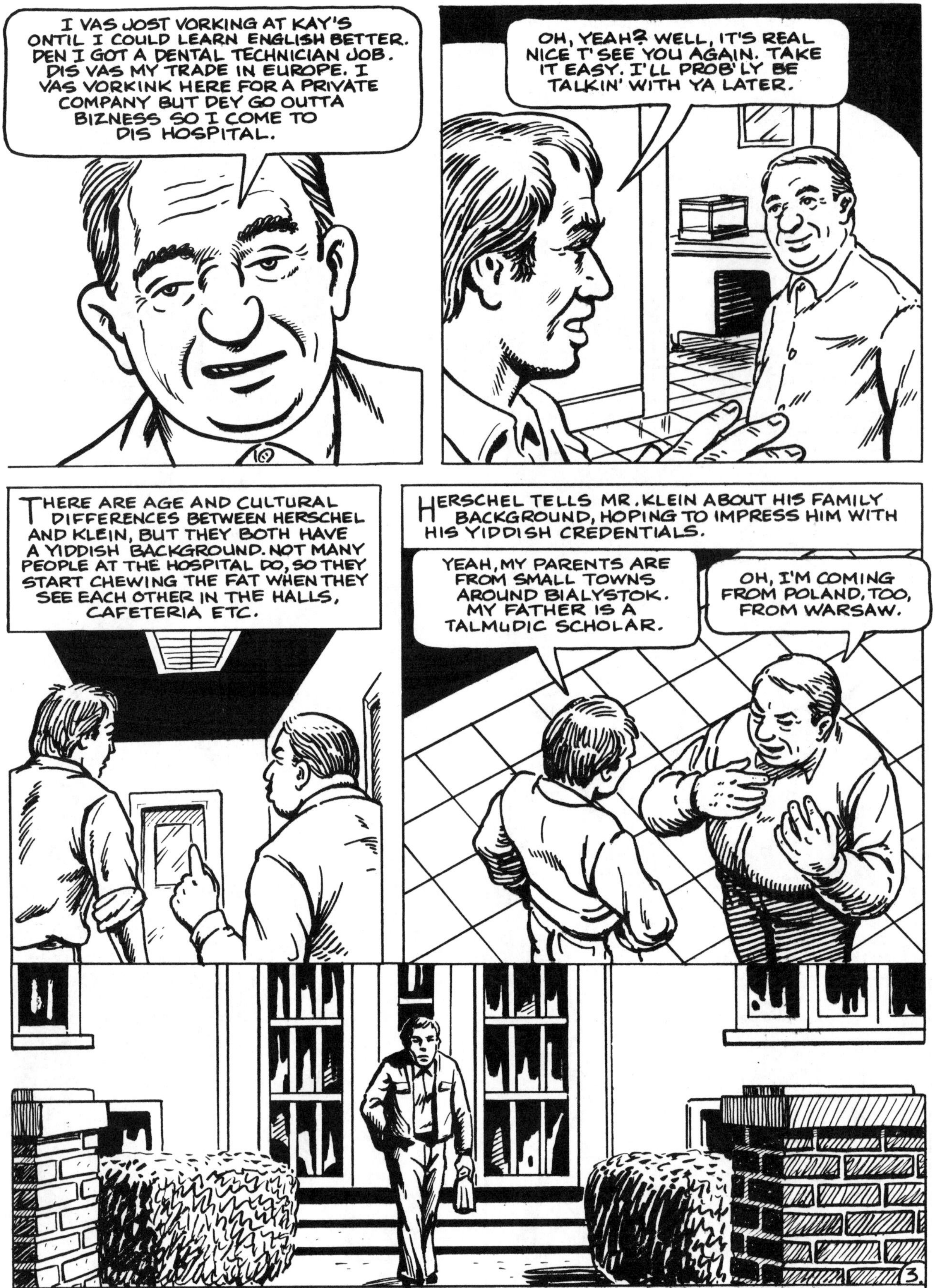
I VAS JOST VORKING AT KAY'S ONTIL I COULD LEARN ENGLISH BETTER. DEN I GOT A DENTAL TECHNICIAN JOB. DIS VAS MY TRADE IN EUROPE. I VAS VORKINK HERE FOR A PRIVATE COMPANY BUT DEY GO OUTTA BIZNESS SO I COME TO DIS HOSPITAL.
OH, YEAH? WELL, IT'S REAL NICE T' SEE YOU AGAIN. TAKE IT EASY. I'LL PROB'LY BE TALKIN' WITH YA LATER.
THERE ARE AGE AND CULTURAL DIFFERENCES BETWEEN HERSCHEL AND KLEIN, BUT THEY BOTH HAVE A YIDDISH BACKGROUND. NOT MANY PEOPLE AT THE HOSPITAL DO, SO THEY START CHEWING THE FAT WHEN THEY SEE EACH OTHER IN THE HALLS, CAFETERIA ETC.
HERSCHEL TELLS MR. KLEIN ABOUT HIS FAMILY BACKGROUND, HOPING TO IMPRESS HIM WITH HIS YIDDISH CREDENTIALS.
YEAH, MY PARENTS ARE FROM SMALL TOWNS AROUND BIALYSTOK. MY FATHER IS A TALMUDIC SCHOLAR.
OH, I'M COMING FROM POLAND, TOO, FROM WARSAW.
3.
NOW IT HAPPENS THAT HERSCHEL DOES NOT HAVE A CAR. HE STARTS OUT WALKING TO WORK EVERYDAY.

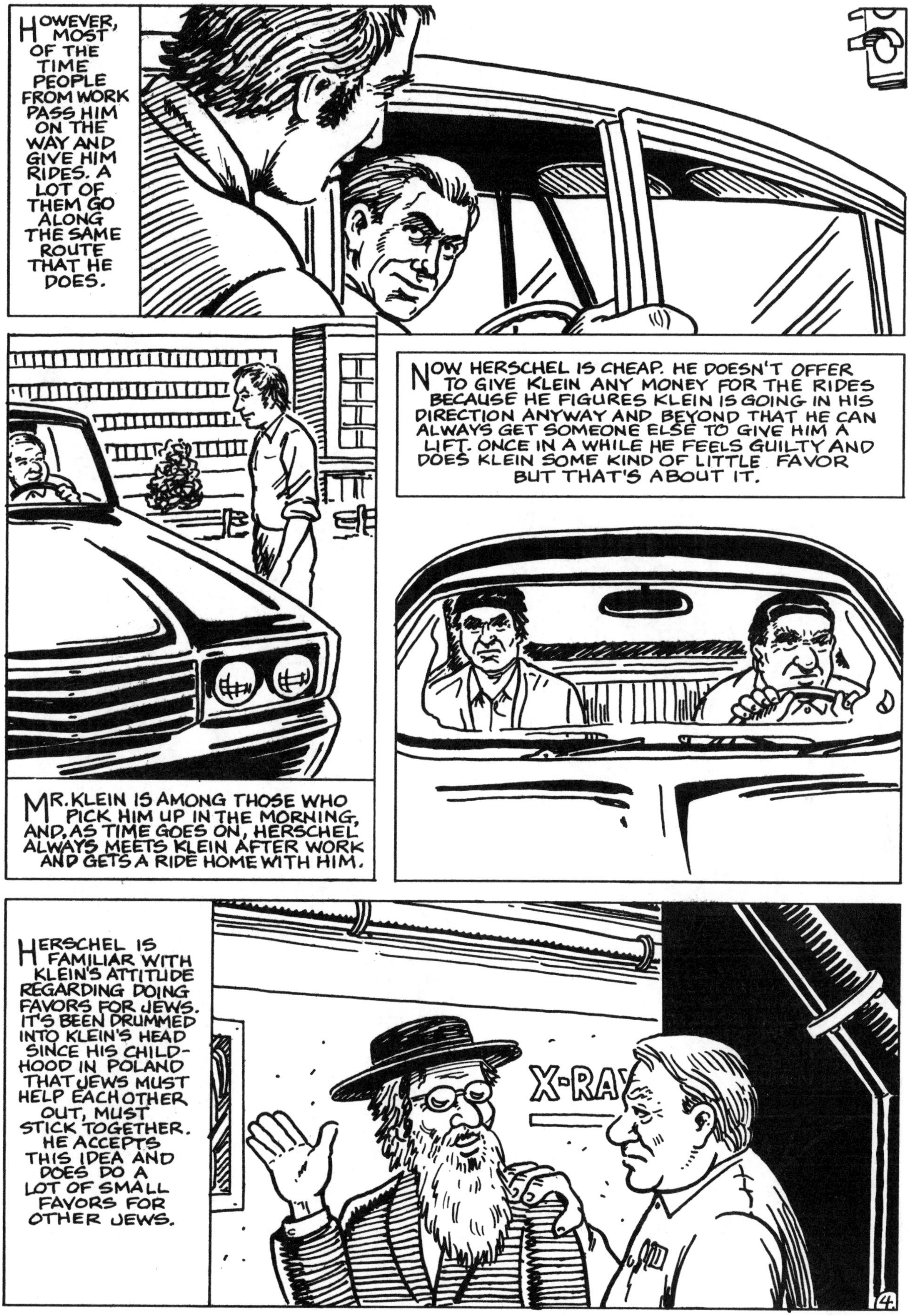
HOWEVER, MOST OF THE TIME PEOPLE FROM WORK PASS HIM ON THE WAY AND GIVE HIM RIDES. A LOT OF THEM GO ALONG THE SAME ROUTE THAT HE DOES.
MR. KLEIN IS AMONG THOSE WHO PICK HIM UP IN THE MORNING, AND, AS TIME GOES ON, HERSCHEL ALWAYS MEETS KLEIN AFTER WORK AND GETS A RIDE HOME WITH HIM.
NOW HERSCHEL IS CHEAP. HE DOESN'T OFFER TO GIVE KLEIN ANY MONEY FOR THE RIDES BECAUSE HE FIGURES KLEIN IS GOING IN HIS DIRECTION ANYWAY AND BEYOND THAT HE CAN ALWAYS GET SOMEONE ELSE TO GIVE HIM A LIFT. ONCE IN A WHILE HE FEELS GUILTY AND DOES KLEIN SOME KIND OF LITTLE FAVOR BUT THAT'S ABOUT IT.
HERSCHEL IS FAMILIAR WITH KLEIN'S ATTITUDE REGARDING DOING FAVORS FOR JEWS. IT'S BEEN DRUMMED INTO KLEIN'S HEAD SINCE HIS CHILDHOOD IN POLAND THAT JEWS MUST HELP EACH OTHER OUT, MUST STICK TOGETHER. HE ACCEPTS THIS IDEA AND DOES DO A LOT OF SMALL FAVORS FOR OTHER JEWS.
4.

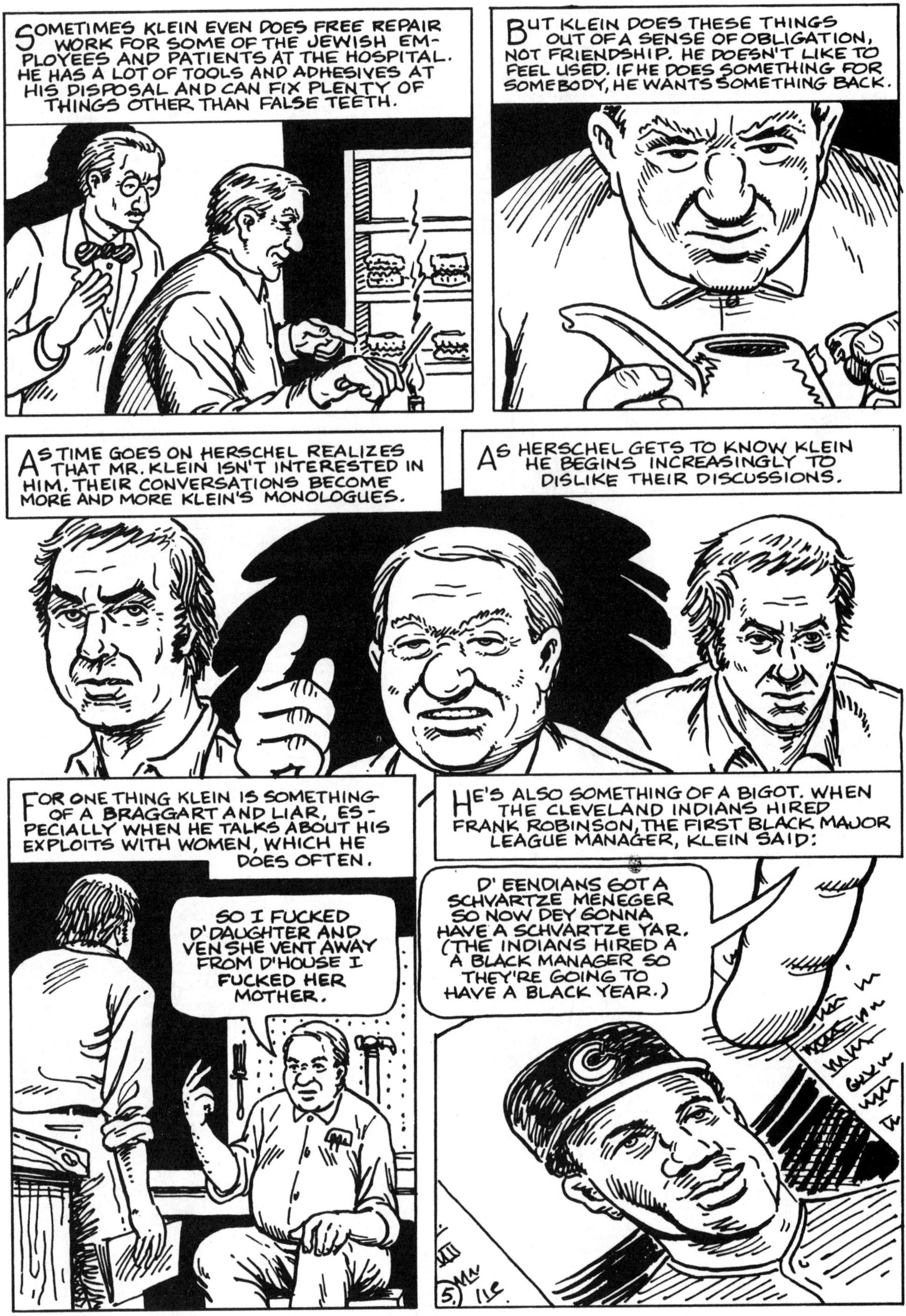
SOMETIMES KLEIN EVEN DOES FREE REPAIR WORK FOR SOME OF THE JEWISH EMPLOYEES AND PATIENTS AT THE HOSPITAL. HE HAS A LOT OF TOOLS AND ADHESIVES AT HIS DISPOSAL AND CAN FIX PLENTY OF THINGS OTHER THAN FALSE TEETH.
BUT KLEIN DOES THESE THINGS OUT OF A SENSE OF OBLIGATION, NOT FRIENDSHIP. HE DOESN'T LIKE TO FEEL USED. IF HE DOES SOMETHING FOR SOMEBODY, HE WANTS SOMETHING BACK.
AS TIME GOES ON HERSCHEL REALIZES THAT MR. KLEIN ISN'T INTERESTED IN HIM. THEIR CONVERSATIONS BECOME MORE AND MORE KLEIN'S MONOLOGUES.
AS HERSCHEL GETS TO KNOW KLEIN HE BEGINS INCREASINGLY TO DISLIKE THEIR DISCUSSIONS.
FOR ONE THING KLEIN IS SOMETHING OF A BRAGGART AND LIAR, ESPECIALLY WHEN HE TALKS ABOUT HIS EXPLOITS WITH WOMEN, WHICH HE DOES OFTEN.
SO I FUCKED D'DAUGHTER AND VEN SHE VENT AWAY FROM D'HOUSE I FUCKED HER MOTHER.
HE'S ALSO SOMETHING OF A BIGOT. WHEN THE CLEVELAND INDIANS HIRED FRANK ROBINSON, THE FIRST BLACK MAJOR LEAGUE MANAGER, KLEIN SAID:
D' EENDIANS GOT A SCHVARTZE MENEGER SO NOW DEY GONNA HAVE A SCHVARTZE YAR. (THE INDIANS HIRED A A BLACK MANAGER SO THEY'RE GOING TO HAVE A BLACK YEAR.)
5.

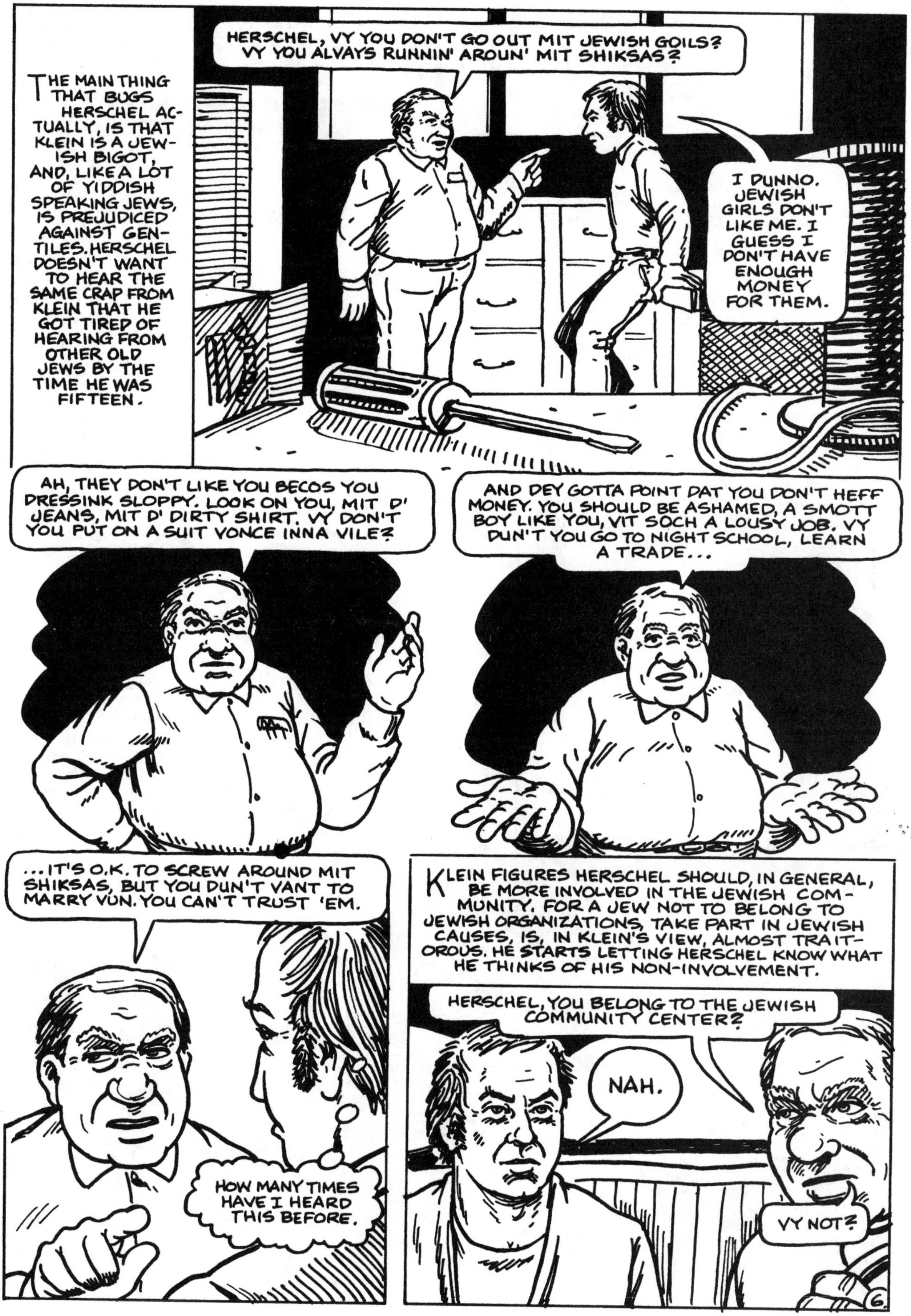
THE MAIN THING THAT BUGS HERSCHEL ACTUALLY, IS THAT KLEIN IS A JEWISH BIGOT, AND, LIKE A LOT OF YIDDISH SPEAKING JEWS, IS PREJUDICED AGAINST GENTILES. HERSCHEL DOESN'T WANT TO HEAR THE SAME CRAP FROM KLEIN THAT HE GOT TIRED OF HEARING FROM OTHER OLD JEWS BY THE TIME HE WAS FIFTEEN.
HERSCHEL, VY YOU DON'T GO OUT MIT JEWISH GOILS? VY YOU ALVAYS RUNNIN' AROUN' MIT SHIKSAS?
I DUNNO. JEWISH GIRLS DON'T LIKE ME. I GUESS I DON'T HAVE ENOUGH MONEY FOR THEM.
AH, THEY DON'T LIKE YOU BECOS YOU DRESSINK SLOPPY. LOOK ON YOU, MIT D' JEANS, MIT D' DIRTY SHIRT. VY DON'T YOU PUT ON A SUIT VONCE INNA VILE?
AND DEY GOTTA POINT DAT YOU DON'T HEFF MONEY. YOU SHOULD BE ASHAMED, A SMOTT BOY LIKE YOU, VIT SOCH A LOUSY JOB. VY DUN'T YOU GO TO NIGHT SCHOOL, LEARN A TRADE...
...IT'S O.K. TO SCREW AROUND MIT SHIKSAS, BUT YOU DUN'T VANT TO MARRY VUN. YOU CAN'T TRUST 'EM.
HOW MANY TIMES HAVE I HEARD THIS BEFORE.
KLEIN FIGURES HERSCHEL SHOULD, IN GENERAL, BE MORE INVOLVED IN THE JEWISH COMMUNITY. FOR A JEW NOT TO BELONG TO JEWISH ORGANIZATIONS, TAKE PART IN JEWISH CAUSES, IS, IN KLEIN'S VIEW, ALMOST TRAITOROUS. HE STARTS LETTING HERSCHEL KNOW WHAT HE THINKS OF HIS NON-INVOLVEMENT.
HERSCHEL, YOU BELONG TO THE JEWISH COMMUNITY CENTER?
NAH.
VY NOT?
6.

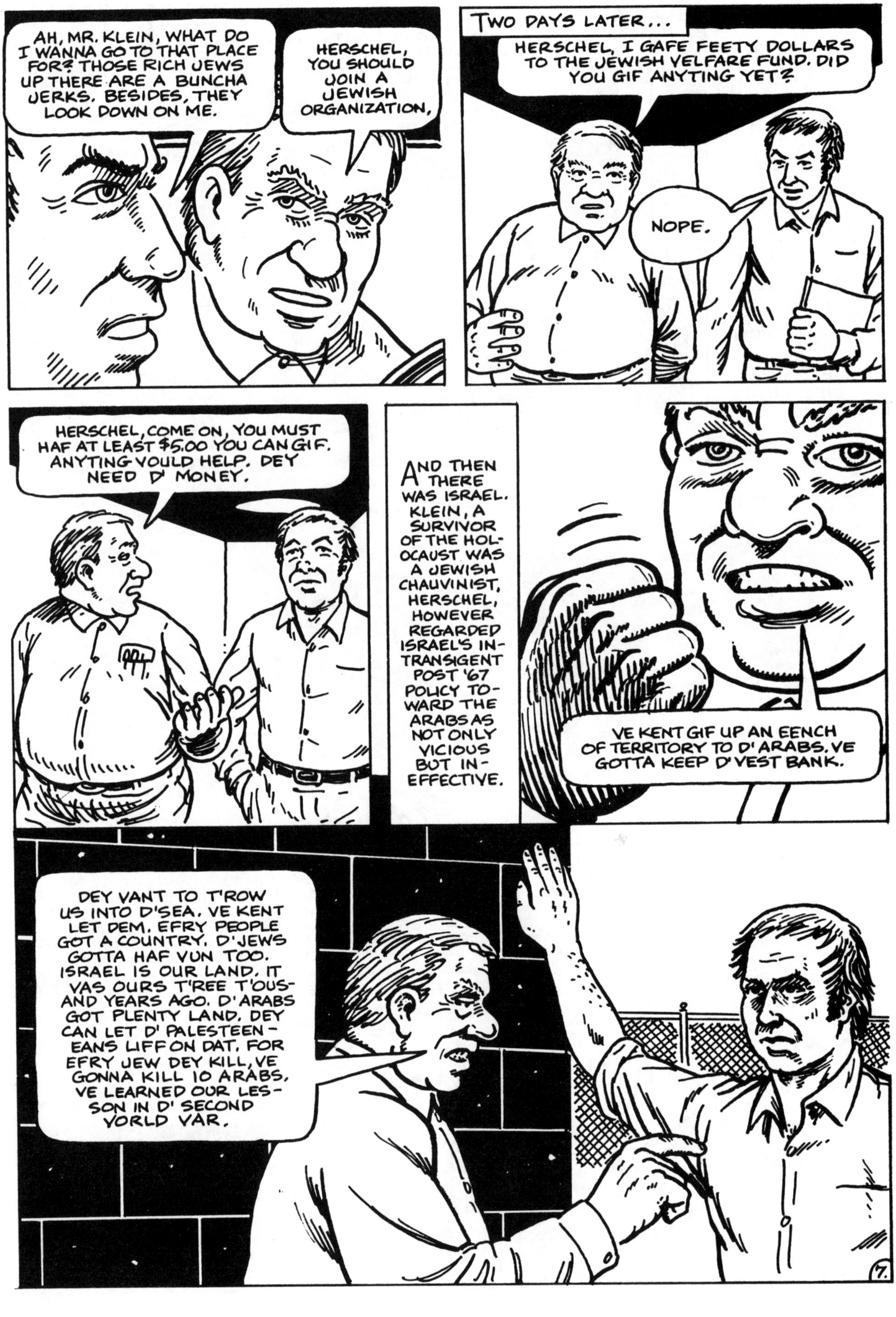
AH, MR. KLEIN, WHAT DO I WANNA GO TO THAT PLACE FOR? THOSE RICH JEWS UP THERE ARE A BUNCHA JERKS. BESIDES, THEY LOOK DOWN ON ME.
HERSCHEL, YOU SHOULD JOIN A JEWISH ORGANIZATION,
TWO DAYS LATER...
HERSCHEL, I GAFE FEETY DOLLARS TO THE JEWISH VELFARE FUND. DID YOU GIF ANYTING YET?
NOPE.
HERSCHEL, COME ON, YOU MUST HAF AT LEAST $5.00 YOU CAN GIF. ANYTING VOULD HELP. DEY NEED D' MONEY.
AND THEN THERE WAS ISRAEL. KLEIN, A SURVIVOR OF THE HOLOCAUST WAS A JEWISH CHAUVINIST, HERSCHEL, HOWEVER REGARDED ISRAEL'S INTRANSIGENT POST '67 POLICY TOWARD THE ARABS AS NOT ONLY VICIOUS BUT INEFFECTIVE.
VE KENT GIF UP AN EENCH OF TERRITORY TO D' ARABS. VE GOTTA KEEP D' VEST BANK.
DEY VANT TO T'ROW US INTO D'SEA. VE KENT LET DEM. EFRY PEOPLE GOT A COUNTRY. D'JEWS GOTTA HAF VUN TOO. ISRAEL IS OUR LAND. IT VAS OURS T'REE T'OUSAND YEARS AGO. D'ARABS GOT PLENTY LAND. DEY CAN LET D' PALESTEENEANS LIFF ON DAT. FOR EFRY JEW DEY KILL, VE GONNA KILL 10 ARABS. VE LEARNED OUR LESSON IN D' SECOND VORLD VAR.
7

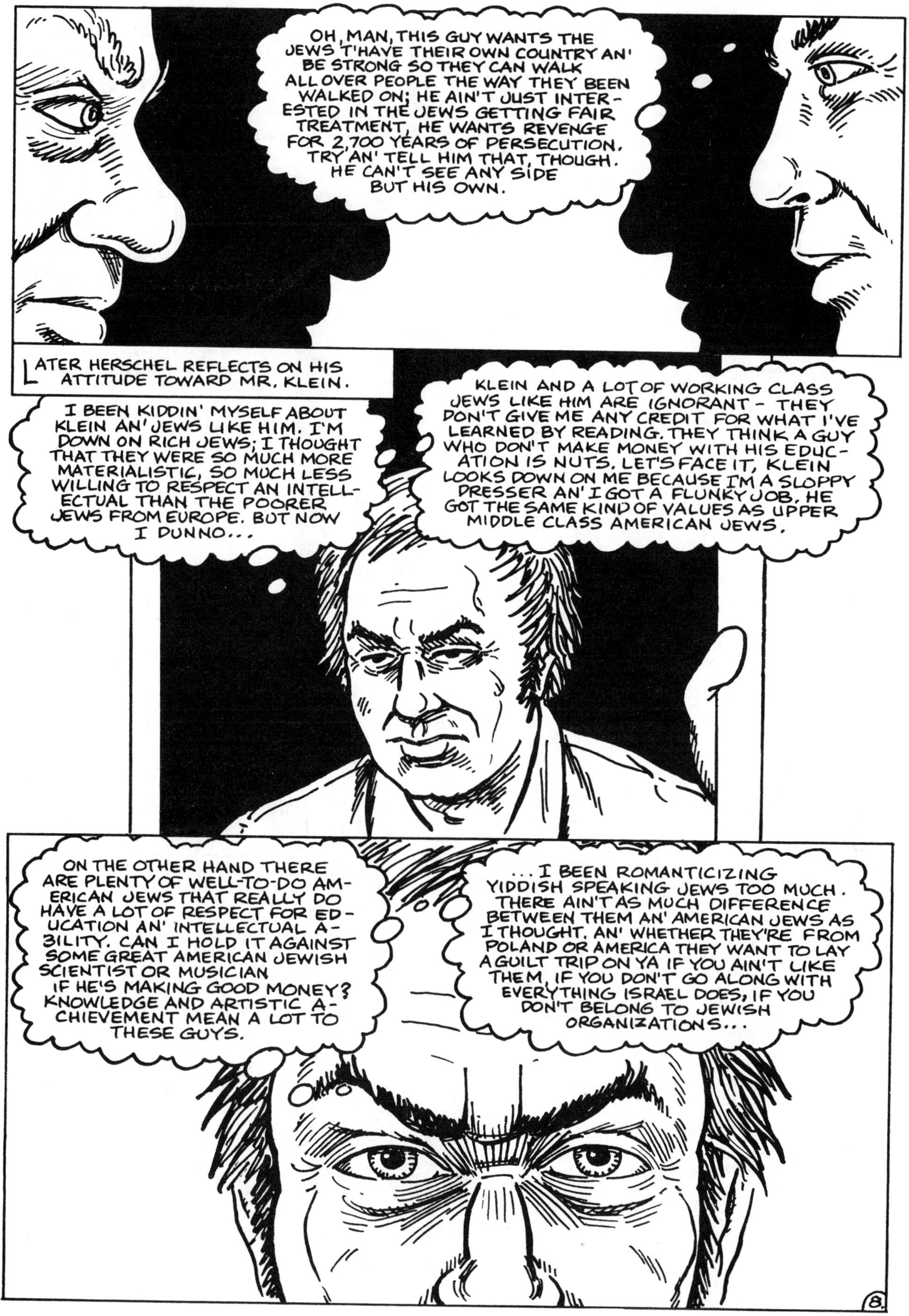
OH, MAN, THIS GUY WANTS THE JEWS T'HAVE THEIR OWN COUNTRY AN' BE STRONG SO THEY CAN WALK ALL OVER PEOPLE THE WAY THEY BEEN WALKED ON; HE AIN'T JUST INTERESTED IN THE JEWS GETTING FAIR TREATMENT, HE WANTS REVENGE FOR 2,700 YEARS OF PERSECUTION. TRY AN' TELL HIM THAT, THOUGH. HE CAN'T SEE ANY SIDE BUT HIS OWN.
LATER HERSCHEL REFLECTS ON HIS ATTITUDE TOWARD MR. KLEIN.
I BEEN KIDDIN' MYSELF ABOUT KLEIN AN' JEWS LIKE HIM. I'M DOWN ON RICH JEWS; I THOUGHT THAT THEY WERE SO MUCH MORE MATERIALISTIC, SO MUCH LESS WILLING TO RESPECT AN INTELLECTUAL THAN THE POORER JEWS FROM EUROPE. BUT NOW I DUNNO...
KLEIN AND A LOT OF WORKING CLASS JEWS LIKE HIM ARE IGNORANT - THEY DON'T GIVE ME ANY CREDIT FOR WHAT I'VE LEARNED BY READING. THEY THINK A GUY WHO DON'T MAKE MONEY WITH HIS EDUCATION IS NUTS. LET'S FACE IT, KLEIN LOOKS DOWN ON ME BECAUSE I'M A SLOPPY DRESSER AN' I GOT A FLUNKY JOB. HE GOT THE SAME KIND OF VALUES AS UPPER MIDDLE CLASS AMERICAN JEWS.
ON THE OTHER HAND THERE ARE PLENTY OF WELL-TO-DO AMERICAN JEWS THAT REALLY DO HAVE A LOT OF RESPECT FOR EDUCATION AN' INTELLECTUAL ABILITY. CAN I HOLD IT AGAINST SOME GREAT AMERICAN JEWISH SCIENTIST OR MUSICIAN IF HE'S MAKING GOOD MONEY? KNOWLEDGE AND ARTISTIC ACHIEVEMENT MEAN A LOT TO THESE GUYS.
...I BEEN ROMANTICIZING YIDDISH SPEAKING JEWS TOO MUCH. THERE AIN'T AS MUCH DIFFERENCE BETWEEN THEM AN' AMERICAN JEWS AS I THOUGHT. AN' WHETHER THEY'RE FROM POLAND OR AMERICA THEY WANT TO LAY A GUILT TRIP ON YA IF YOU AIN'T LIKE THEM, IF YOU DON'T GO ALONG WITH EVERYTHING ISRAEL DOES, IF YOU DON'T BELONG TO JEWISH ORGANIZATIONS...

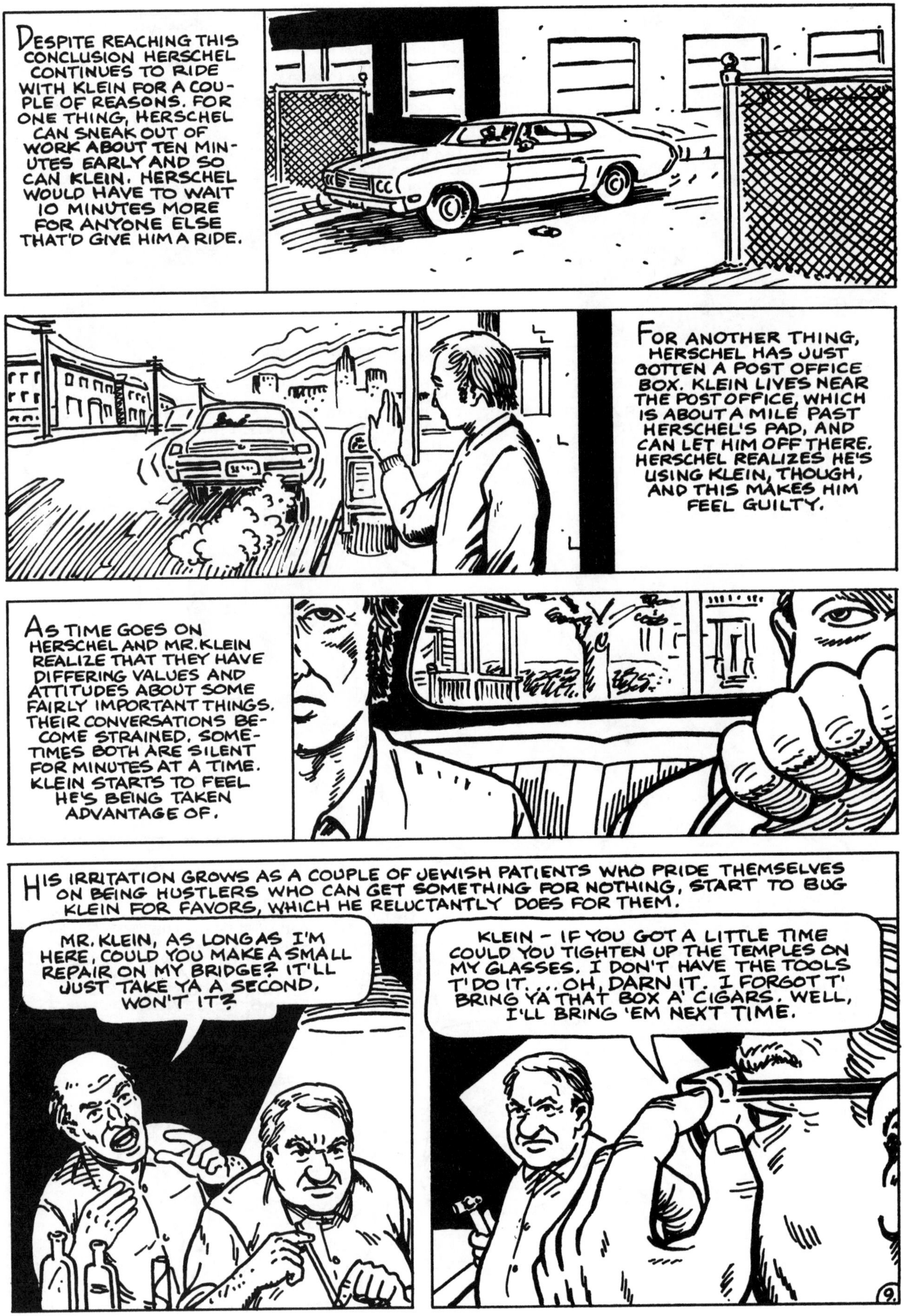
DESPITE REACHING THIS CONCLUSION HERSCHEL CONTINUES TO RIDE WITH KLEIN FOR A COUPLE OF REASONS. FOR ONE THING, HERSCHEL CAN SNEAK OUT OF WORK ABOUT TEN MINUTES EARLY AND SO CAN KLEIN. HERSCHEL WOULD HAVE TO WAIT 10 MINUTES MORE FOR ANYONE ELSE THAT'D GIVE HIM A RIDE.
FOR ANOTHER THING, HERSCHEL HAS JUST GOTTEN A POST OFFICE BOX. KLEIN LIVES NEAR THE POST OFFICE, WHICH IS ABOUT A MILE PAST HERSCHEL'S PAD, AND CAN LET HIM OFF THERE. HERSCHEL REALIZES HE'S USING KLEIN, THOUGH, AND THIS MAKES HIM FEEL GUILTY.
AS TIME GOES ON HERSCHEL AND MR. KLEIN REALIZE THAT THEY HAVE DIFFERING VALUES AND ATTITUDES ABOUT SOME FAIRLY IMPORTANT THINGS. THEIR CONVERSATIONS BECOME STRAINED. SOMETIMES BOTH ARE SILENT FOR MINUTES AT A TIME. KLEIN STARTS TO FEEL HE'S BEING TAKEN ADVANTAGE OF.
HIS IRRITATION GROWS AS A COUPLE OF JEWISH PATIENTS WHO PRIDE THEMSELVES ON BEING HUSTLERS WHO CAN GET SOMETHING FOR NOTHING, START TO BUG KLEIN FOR FAVORS, WHICH HE RELUCTANTLY DOES FOR THEM.
MR. KLEIN, AS LONG AS I'M HERE, COULD YOU MAKE A SMALL REPAIR ON MY BRIDGE? IT'LL JUST TAKE YA A SECOND, WON'T IT?
KLEIN - IF YOU GOT A LITTLE TIME COULD YOU TIGHTEN UP THE TEMPLES ON MY GLASSES. I DON'T HAVE THE TOOLS T'DO IT. . . . OH, DARN IT. I FORGOT T' BRING YA THAT BOX A' CIGARS. WELL, I'LL BRING 'EM NEXT TIME.

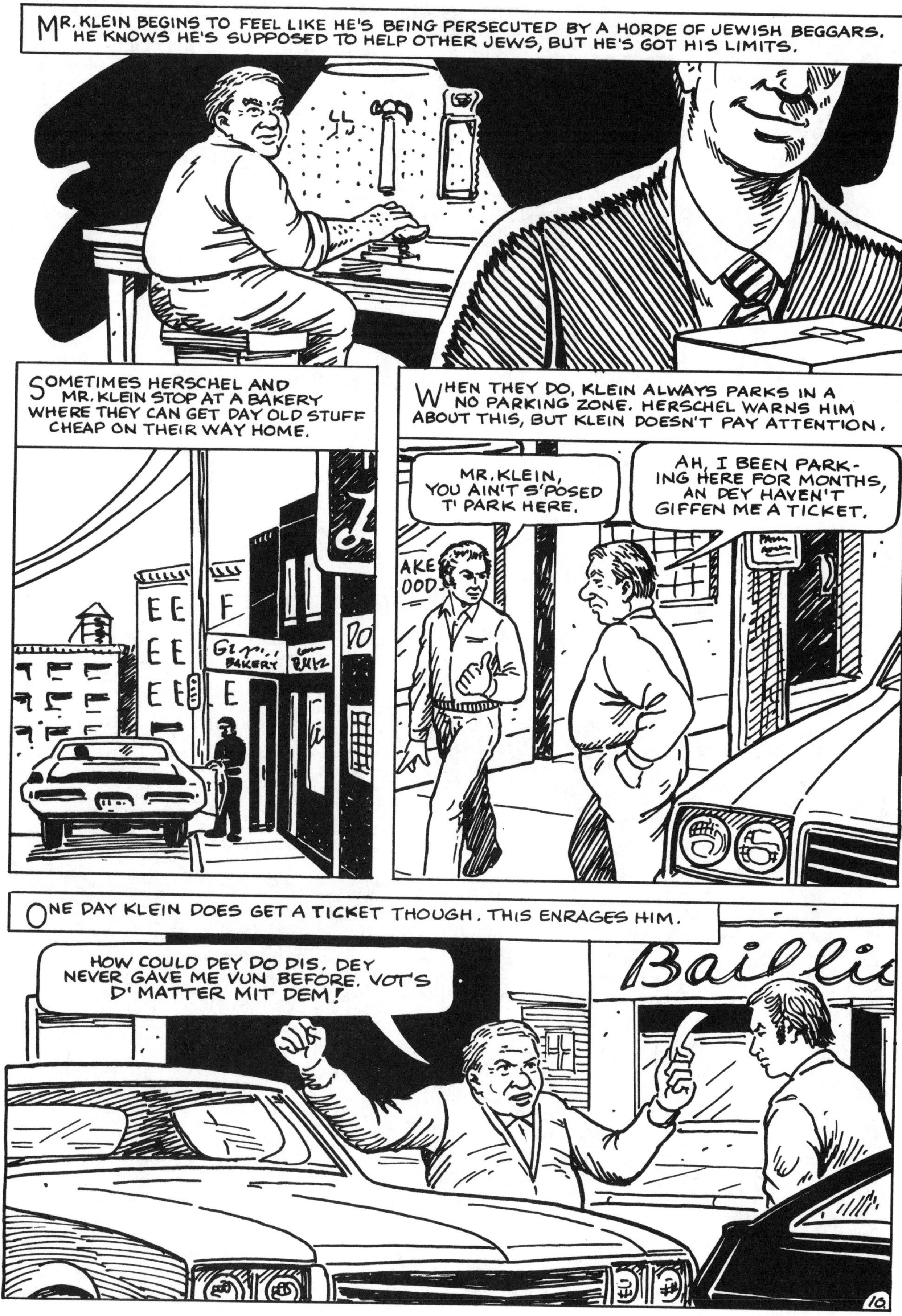
MR. KLEIN BEGINS TO FEEL LIKE HE'S BEING PERSECUTED BY A HORDE OF JEWISH BEGGARS. HE KNOWS HE'S SUPPOSED TO HELP OTHER JEWS, BUT HE'S GOT HIS LIMITS.
SOMETIMES HERSCHEL AND MR. KLEIN STOP AT A BAKERY WHERE THEY CAN GET DAY OLD STUFF CHEAP ON THEIR WAY HOME.
BAKERY
WHEN THEY DO, KLEIN ALWAYS PARKS IN A NO PARKING ZONE. HERSCHEL WARNS HIM ABOUT THIS, BUT KLEIN DOESN'T PAY ATTENTION.
MR. KLEIN, YOU AIN'T S'POSED T' PARK HERE.
AH, I BEEN PARKING HERE FOR MONTHS, AN DEY HAVEN'T GIFFEN ME A TICKET.
ONE DAY KLEIN DOES GET A TICKET THOUGH. THIS ENRAGES HIM.
HOW COULD DEY DO DIS. DEY NEVER GAVE ME VUN BEFORE. VOT'S D' MATTER MIT DEM!
Baili
10

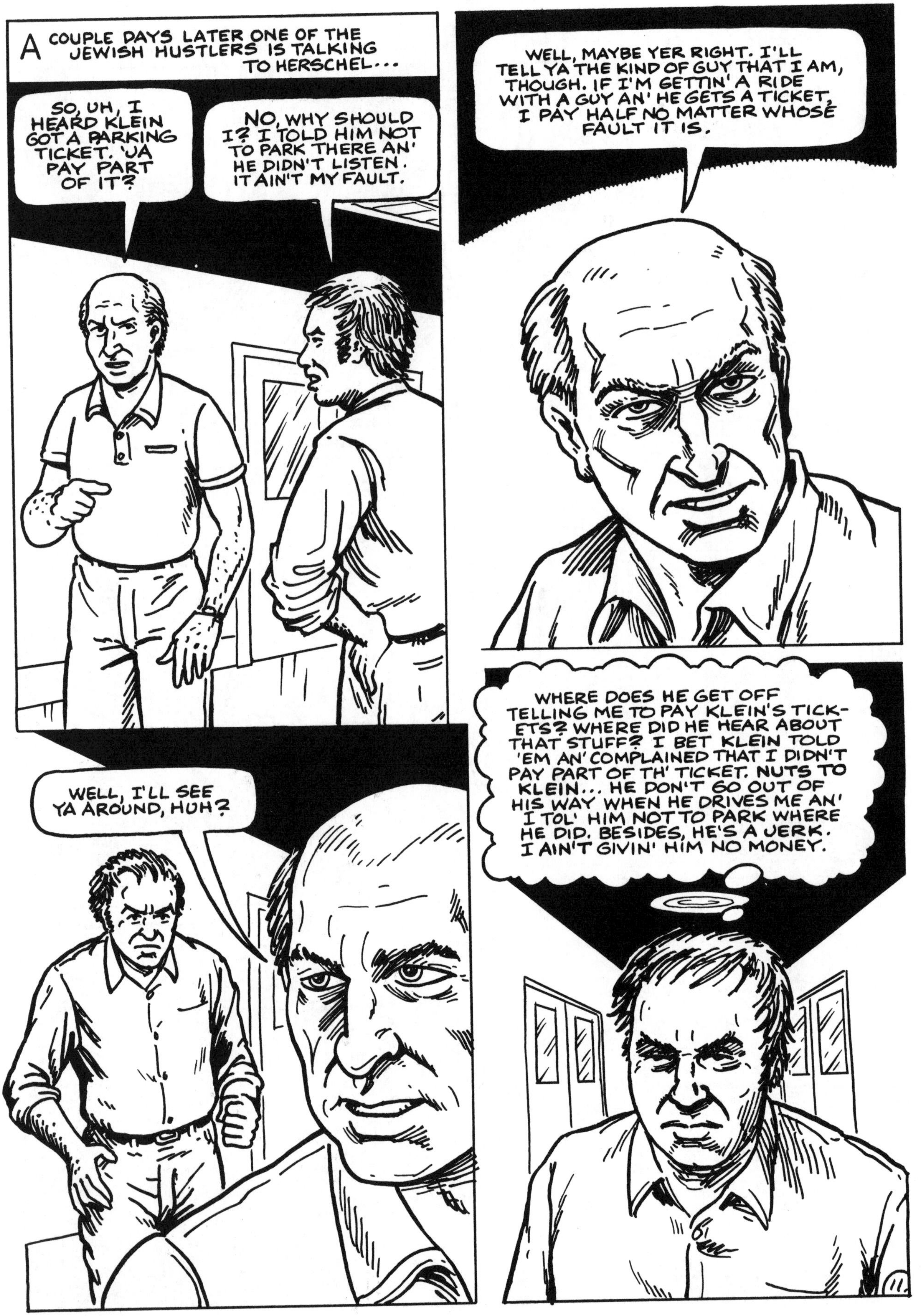
A COUPLE DAYS LATER ONE OF THE JEWISH HUSTLERS IS TALKING TO HERSCHEL...
SO, UH, I HEARD KLEIN GOT A PARKING TICKET. 'JA PAY PART OF IT?
NO, WHY SHOULD I? I TOLD HIM NOT TO PARK THERE AN' HE DIDN'T LISTEN. IT AIN'T MY FAULT.
WELL, MAYBE YER RIGHT. I'LL TELL YA THE KIND OF GUY THAT I AM, THOUGH. IF I'M GETTIN' A RIDE WITH A GUY AN' HE GETS A TICKET, I PAY HALF NO MATTER WHOSE FAULT IT IS.
WELL, I'LL SEE YA AROUND, HUH?
WHERE DOES HE GET OFF TELLING ME TO PAY KLEIN'S TICKETS? WHERE DID HE HEAR ABOUT THAT STUFF? I BET KLEIN TOLD 'EM AN' COMPLAINED THAT I DIDN'T PAY PART OF TH' TICKET. NUTS TO KLEIN... HE DON'T GO OUT OF HIS WAY WHEN HE DRIVES ME AN' I TOL' HIM NOT TO PARK WHERE HE DID. BESIDES, HE'S A JERK. I AIN'T GIVIN' HIM NO MONEY.

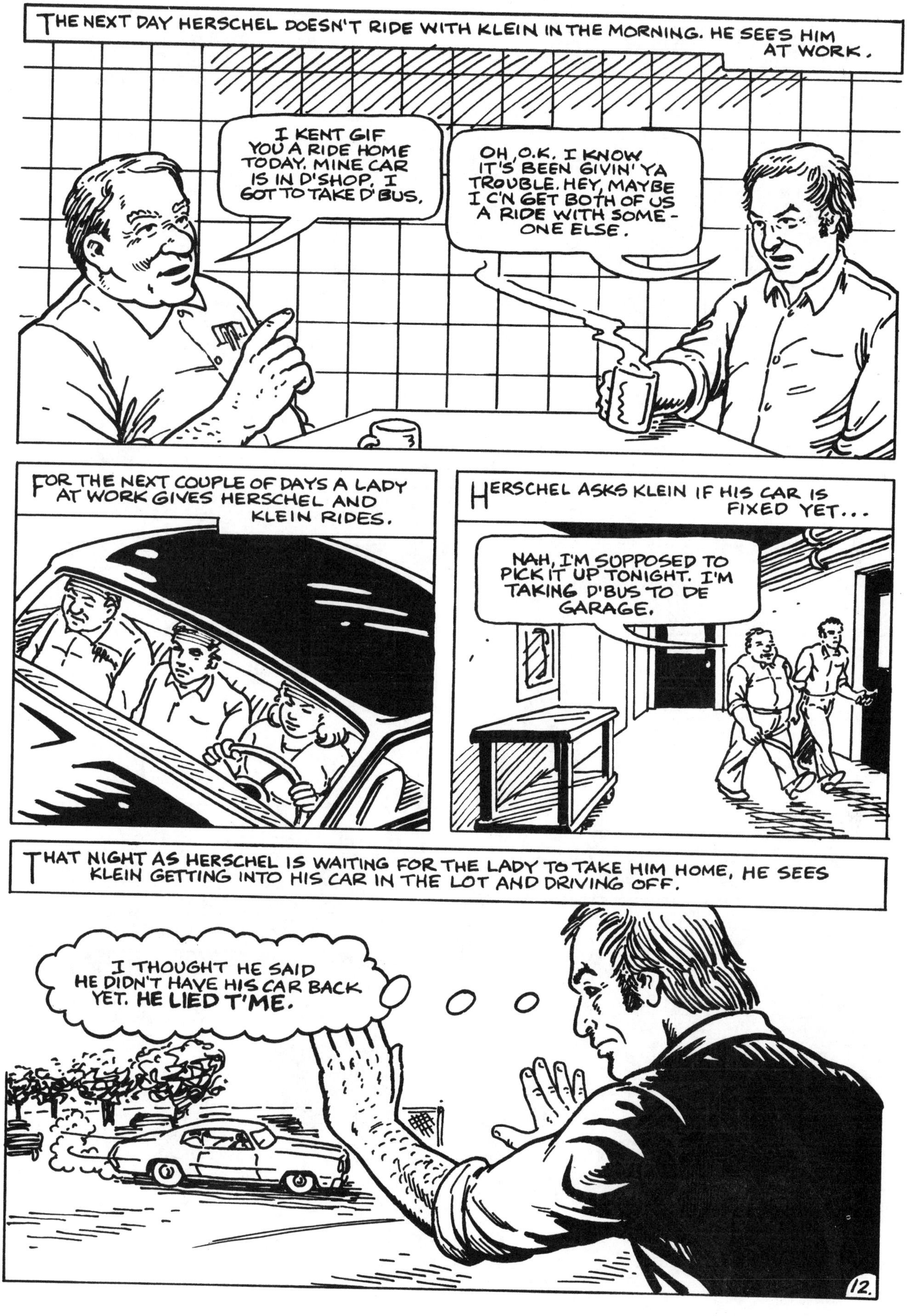
THE NEXT DAY HERSCHEL DOESN'T RIDE WITH KLEIN IN THE MORNING. HE SEES HIM AT WORK.
I KENT GIF YOU A RIDE HOME TODAY. MINE CAR IS IN D'SHOP. I GOT TO TAKE D'BUS.
OH, O.K. I KNOW IT'S BEEN GIVIN' YA TROUBLE. HEY, MAYBE I C'N GET BOTH OF US A RIDE WITH SOME-ONE ELSE.
FOR THE NEXT COUPLE OF DAYS A LADY AT WORK GIVES HERSCHEL AND KLEIN RIDES.
HERSCHEL ASKS KLEIN IF HIS CAR IS FIXED YET...
NAH, I'M SUPPOSED TO PICK IT UP TONIGHT. I'M TAKING D'BUS TO DE GARAGE.
THAT NIGHT AS HERSCHEL IS WAITING FOR THE LADY TO TAKE HIM HOME, HE SEES KLEIN GETTING INTO HIS CAR IN THE LOT AND DRIVING OFF.
I THOUGHT HE SAID HE DIDN'T HAVE HIS CAR BACK YET. HE LIED T'ME.

THE NEXT MORNING AS HE IS WALKING TO WORK KLEIN APPROACHES HERSCHEL IN HIS CAR BUT TURNS OFF A STREET BEFORE HE GETS TO HIM.

I BET HE DELIBER-ATELY AVOIDED ME.

ALL RIGHT, LET IT BE THAT WAY. IF HE LIES T'ME ABOUT HIS CAR, IF HE GOES T'WORK BY A-NOTHER ROUTE T'AVOID ME, WHO NEEDS 'IM. I'LL RIDE WITH OTHER PEOPLE, OR I'LL WALK.

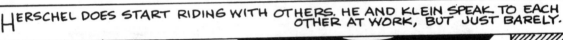

HERSCHEL DOES START RIDING WITH OTHERS. HE AND KLEIN SPEAK TO EACH OTHER AT WORK, BUT JUST BARELY.

GRUNT

HMM.

AS TIME GOES ON THOUGH, HERSCHEL REALIZES THAT WHAT HAPPENED WAS FOR THE BEST.

HE WAS SICKA ME NOT PAYIN' HIM AN' I WAS SICKA HEARIN' HIS BULLSHIT. I SHOULDA STOPPED RIDIN' WITH HIM A LONG TIME AGO.

MR. KLEIN, NOT HAVING TO DRIVE HERSCHEL AROUND, AND FEELING KIND OF BAD BECAUSE HE'S BEEN DE-LIBERATELY AVOIDING HIM ON THE WAY TO WORK, BECOMES FRIEND-LIER; THEIR RELATIONSHIP BE-COMES MORE RELAXED.

HIYA, MR. KLEIN.

HOW ARE YOU, HERSCHEL?

13.

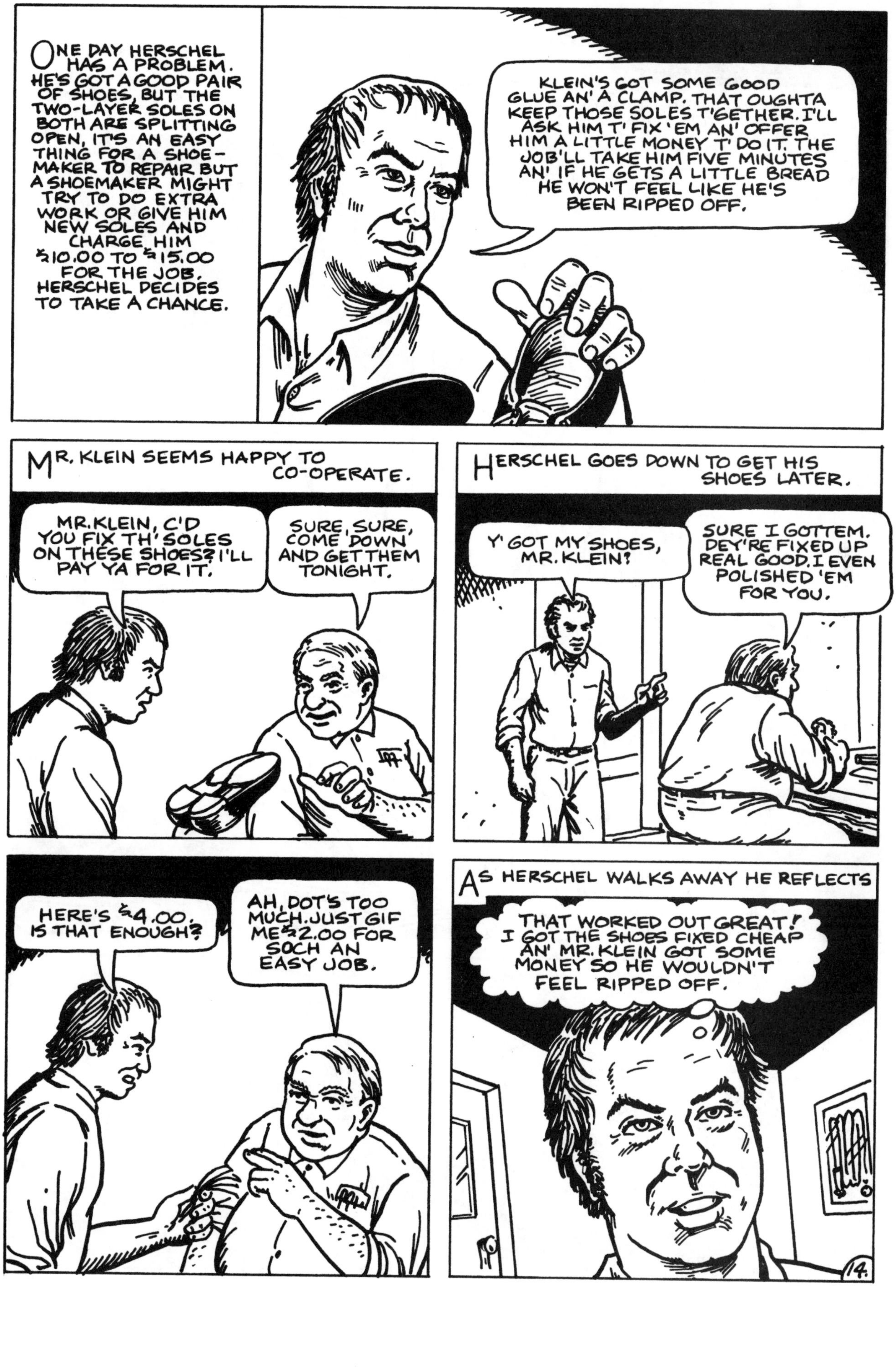

ONE DAY HERSCHEL HAS A PROBLEM. HE'S GOT A GOOD PAIR OF SHOES, BUT THE TWO-LAYER SOLES ON BOTH ARE SPLITTING OPEN. IT'S AN EASY THING FOR A SHOE-MAKER TO REPAIR BUT A SHOEMAKER MIGHT TRY TO DO EXTRA WORK OR GIVE HIM NEW SOLES AND CHARGE HIM $10.00 TO $15.00 FOR THE JOB. HERSCHEL DECIDES TO TAKE A CHANCE.
KLEIN'S GOT SOME GOOD GLUE AN' A CLAMP. THAT OUGHTA KEEP THOSE SOLES T'GETHER. I'LL ASK HIM T' FIX 'EM AN' OFFER HIM A LITTLE MONEY T' DO IT. THE JOB'LL TAKE HIM FIVE MINUTES AN' IF HE GETS A LITTLE BREAD HE WON'T FEEL LIKE HE'S BEEN RIPPED OFF.
MR. KLEIN SEEMS HAPPY TO CO-OPERATE.
MR. KLEIN, C'D YOU FIX TH' SOLES ON THESE SHOES? I'LL PAY YA FOR IT.
SURE, SURE, COME DOWN AND GET THEM TONIGHT.
HERSCHEL GOES DOWN TO GET HIS SHOES LATER.
Y' GOT MY SHOES, MR. KLEIN?
SURE I GOTTEM. DEY'RE FIXED UP REAL GOOD. I EVEN POLISHED 'EM FOR YOU.
HERE'S $4.00. IS THAT ENOUGH?
AH, DOT'S TOO MUCH. JUST GIF ME $2.00 FOR SOCH AN EASY JOB.
AS HERSCHEL WALKS AWAY HE REFLECTS
THAT WORKED OUT GREAT! I GOT THE SHOES FIXED CHEAP AN' MR. KLEIN GOT SOME MONEY SO HE WOULDN'T FEEL RIPPED OFF.

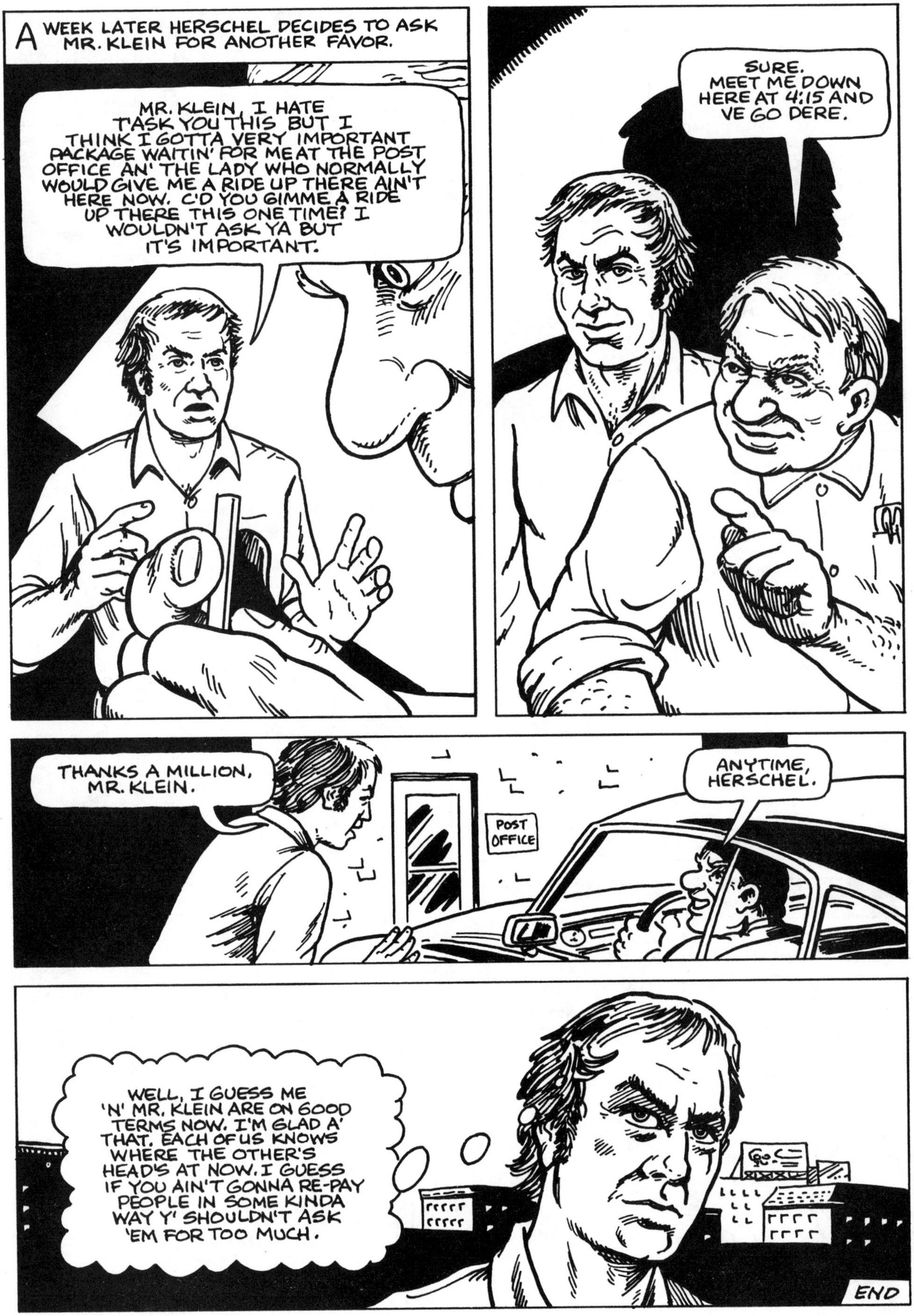
A WEEK LATER HERSCHEL DECIDES TO ASK MR. KLEIN FOR ANOTHER FAVOR.
MR. KLEIN, I HATE T'ASK YOU THIS BUT I THINK I GOTTA VERY IMPORTANT PACKAGE WAITIN' FOR ME AT THE POST OFFICE AN' THE LADY WHO NORMALLY WOULD GIVE ME A RIDE UP THERE AIN'T HERE NOW. C'D YOU GIMME A RIDE UP THERE THIS ONE TIME? I WOULDN'T ASK YA BUT IT'S IMPORTANT.
SURE. MEET ME DOWN HERE AT 4:15 AND VE GO DERE.
THANKS A MILLION, MR. KLEIN.
POST OFFICE
ANYTIME, HERSCHEL.
WELL, I GUESS ME 'N' MR. KLEIN ARE ON GOOD TERMS NOW. I'M GLAD A' THAT. EACH OF US KNOWS WHERE THE OTHER'S HEAD'S AT NOW. I GUESS IF YOU AIN'T GONNA RE-PAY PEOPLE IN SOME KINDA WAY Y' SHOULDN'T ASK 'EM FOR TOO MUCH.
END

OLD CARS

story by
harvey pekar

drawings by
sue cavey

IN 1958 I BOUGHT MY FIRST CAR. IT WAS ALWAYS CONK-ING OUT ON ME. I GOT RID OF IT IN 1960 AND FIGURED I'D NEVER BUY A CAR AGAIN BECAUSE THEY WERE TOO MUCH TROUBLE TO BOTHER WITH.

AND WINTER

WHEN I GOT MARRIED IN 1977 THOUGH, MY WIFE HAD AN OLD STATION WAGON. I GOTTA ADMIT I GOT ADDICTED TO IT. GETTING AROUND IN THE CITY WAS WAY MORE CONVENIENT AND IT WAS NICE TO BE ABLE T'GO AND SEE A MOVIE IN A FAR AWAY SUBURB OR DRIVE AROUND IN THE COUNTRY. I DECIDED THEN THAT OWNING A CAR WAS WELL WORTH THE TROUBLE AND EXPENSE.

IN 1979 I PAID $325.00 TO A GUY FOR A 1970 CHEVELLE WHICH WAS AND IS IN REAL GOOD SHAPE. WUTTA GREAT DEAL. THE CAR WAS IN MY WIFE'S NAME, SO SHE COULD TRANSFER HER INSURANCE FROM OUR OLD CAR TO OUR NEW ONE.

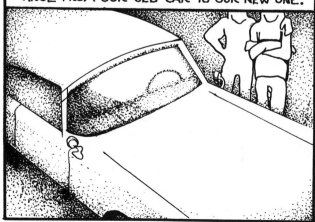

IN FEBRUARY OF '81 I GOT DIVORCED. MY WIFE WAS PLANNING TO LEAVE TOWN AND DIDN'T REALLY WANT THE CAR BECAUSE IT DIDN'T GET GOOD GAS MILEAGE, SO SHE SOLD IT TO ME FOR $500.00. IT WAS A DRAG PAYING FOR THE SAME CAR TWICE, BUT AT LEAST I KNEW WHAT I WAS GETTING. YOU C'N REALLY GET STUCK IF Y' BUY A USED CAR YOU DON'T KNOW ABOUT.

AHHH IT'S ALL MINE

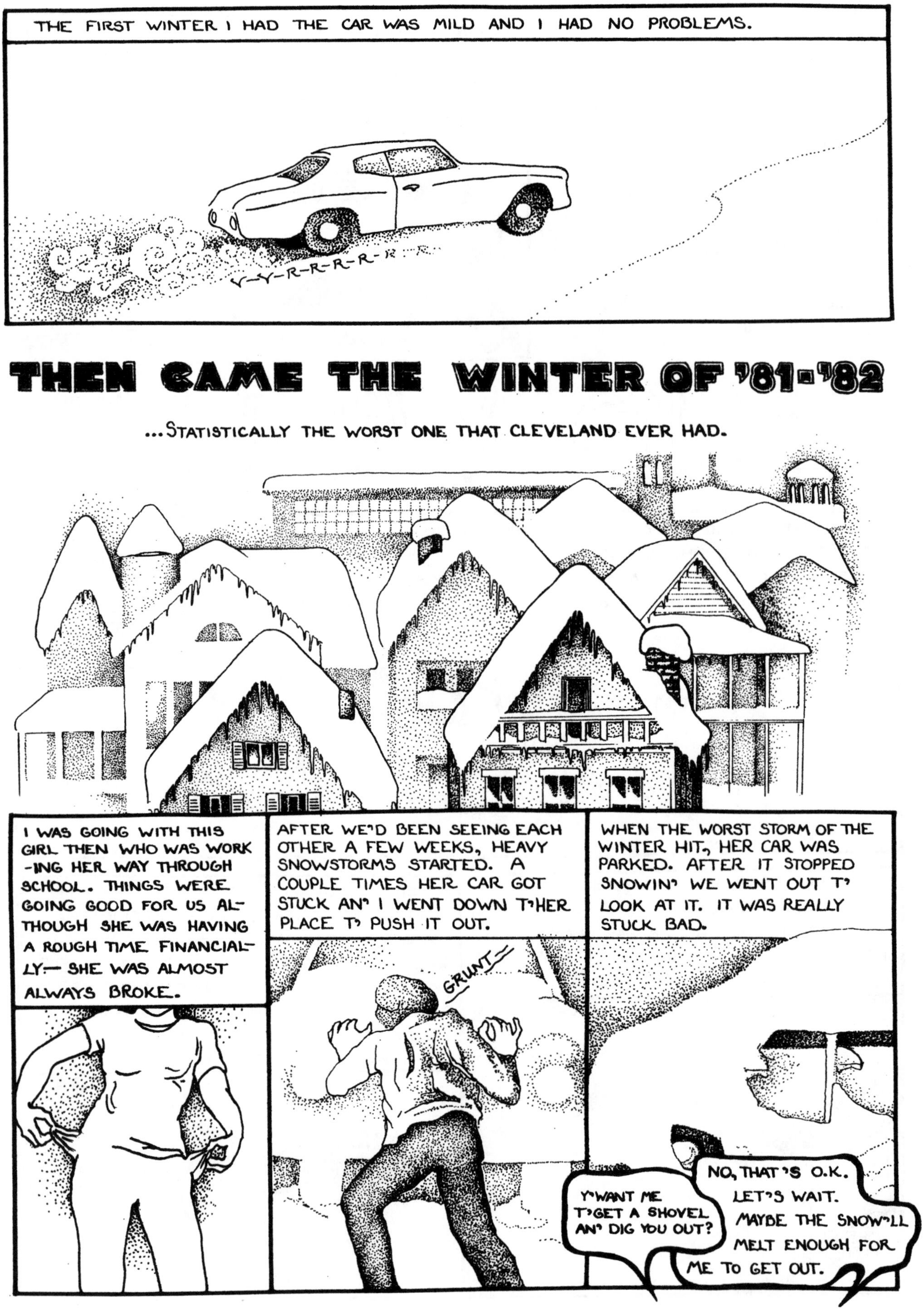
THE FIRST WINTER I HAD THE CAR WAS MILD AND I HAD NO PROBLEMS.
V-Y-R-R-R-R-R
THEN CAME THE WINTER OF '81-'82
...STATISTICALLY THE WORST ONE THAT CLEVELAND EVER HAD.
I WAS GOING WITH THIS GIRL THEN WHO WAS WORK-ING HER WAY THROUGH SCHOOL. THINGS WERE GOING GOOD FOR US AL-THOUGH SHE WAS HAVING A ROUGH TIME FINANCIAL-LY— SHE WAS ALMOST ALWAYS BROKE.
AFTER WE'D BEEN SEEING EACH OTHER A FEW WEEKS, HEAVY SNOWSTORMS STARTED. A COUPLE TIMES HER CAR GOT STUCK AN' I WENT DOWN T'HER PLACE T' PUSH IT OUT.
GRUNT—
WHEN THE WORST STORM OF THE WINTER HIT, HER CAR WAS PARKED. AFTER IT STOPPED SNOWIN' WE WENT OUT T' LOOK AT IT. IT WAS REALLY STUCK BAD.
Y'WANT ME T'GET A SHOVEL AN' DIG YOU OUT?
NO, THAT'S O.K. LET'S WAIT. MAYBE THE SNOW'LL MELT ENOUGH FOR ME TO GET OUT.

SO WE LEFT HER CAR ON THE STREET FOR AWHILE. THEN, TWO DAYS LATER, SHE CALLED ME AT WORK.

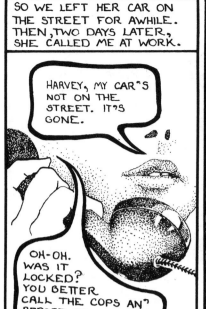

HARVEY, MY CAR'S NOT ON THE STREET. IT'S GONE.

OH-OH. WAS IT LOCKED? YOU BETTER CALL THE COPS AN' REPORT IT.

BUT IT TURNED OUT THAT THE COPS HAD TOWED HER CAR AND IT WAS NOW IMPOUNDED IN A LOT. SHE HADDA PAY A FINE T' GET IT OUT. WE COULDN'T FIGURE OUT WHY THEY'D TOWED THE CAR.

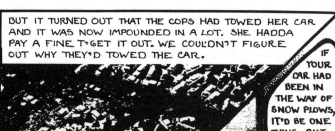

IF YOUR CAR HAD BEEN IN THE WAY OF SNOW PLOWS, IT'D BE ONE THING. BUT ALL THOSE OTHER CARS ONNA STREET HAVE BEEN THERE FOR AS LONG AS YOURS HAS

AN' THEY AIN'T BEEN TOWED.

NOW IT WAS REALLY GONNA GET COMPLICATED T' GET HER CAR BACK BECAUSE SHE DIDN'T OWN IT. HER GIRLFRIEND IN ANOTHER STATE DID! PLUS THE TITLE OF THE CAR WAS IN THE GLOVE COMPARTMENT. SO HER FRIEND HADDA SEND HER A POWER OF ATTORNEY SO SHE HAD LEGAL AUTHORITY T' GET THE CAR OUT.

LUCKILY I HAD A FRIEND WHO HAD CONNECTIONS AT THE POLICE DEPARTMENT. HE WENT DOWN THERE WITH MY GIRLFRIEND BUT STILL IT WAS A HASSLE.

THEY HADDA GO BACK AND FORTH BETWEEN THE JUSTICE CENTER AND THE TOWING LOT T' PAY THE FINE.

FINALLY, WHEN THEY GOT THE FINES PAID, THE CAR WOULDN'T START. THE BATTERY WAS DEAD.

THE CAR WAS ON A LOT OWNED BY A TOWING COMPANY THAT HAD A WORKING ARRANGEMENT WITH THE CITY. THEY WOULDN'T ALLOW ANYONE TO WORK ON THE CAR IN THEIR LOT, BUT THEY WOULD TOW THE CAR OUT OF THE LOT FOR $35.00.

MY GIRLFRIEND WAS ENRAGED BY THE WAY SHE WAS GETTING TREATED. THE WHOLE THING WAS SUCH A RIPOFF. ALTHOUGH SHE GOT A TICKET SHE NEVER DID FIND OUT WHY HER CAR HAD BEEN TOWED.

FINALLY SHE GOT A GAS STATION T' TOW HER CAR FOR A REASONABLE AMOUNT. BUT EVEN THEN SHE HADDA PAY STORAGE CHARGES TO THE TOWING COMPANY BECAUSE HER CAR HAD SAT ON THEIR LOT FOR TWO OR THREE DAYS BEFORE SHE'D BEEN ABLE TO GET IT OUT.

NOW I'VE JUST GIVEN YOU A SUMMARY OF THE STUFF THAT HADDA BE GONE THROUGH T' GET MY GIRLFRIEND'S CAR BACK. ACTUALLY IT WAS A LOT MORE COMPLICATED THAN THAT. SINCE SHE WASN'T FROM CLEVELAND AND DIDN'T KNOW THE ROPES TOO WELL AROUND HERE, I HADDA MAKE A FAIR AMOUNT OF PHONE CALLS FOR HER AND LEND HER SOME MONEY. I GOT IN A COMPLICATED MESS AND BE- LIEVE ME, IT WAS ANNOYING.

THIS INCIDENT STRETCHED OUT OVER ABOUT FIVE DAYS FROM WHEN SHE GOT HER CAR TOWED TO WHEN SHE GOT IT OUT. FOR A COUPLE MONTHS AFTER SHE GOT IT BACK THE WEATHER WAS TERRIBLE; THE CAR KEPT ON BREAKIN' DOWN, AND I KEPT ON LENDIN' HER MONEY TO FIX IT.

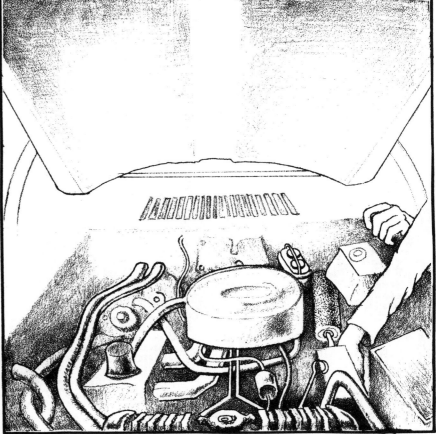

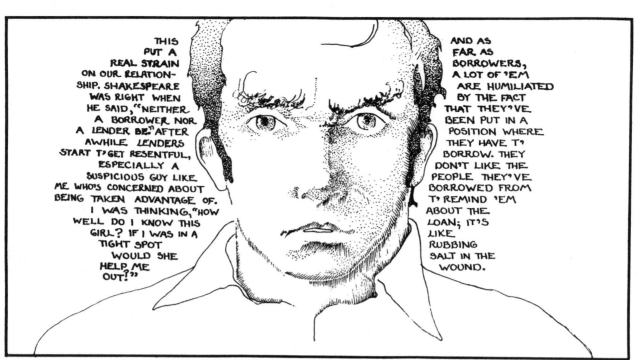

THIS PUT A REAL STRAIN ON OUR RELATIONSHIP. SHAKESPEARE WAS RIGHT WHEN HE SAID, "NEITHER A BORROWER NOR A LENDER BE." AFTER AWHILE LENDERS START T' GET RESENTFUL, ESPECIALLY A SUSPICIOUS GUY LIKE ME WHO'S CONCERNED ABOUT BEING TAKEN ADVANTAGE OF. I WAS THINKING, "HOW WELL DO I KNOW THIS GIRL? IF I WAS IN A TIGHT SPOT WOULD SHE HELP ME OUT?"

AND AS FAR AS BORROWERS, A LOT OF 'EM ARE HUMILIATED BY THE FACT THAT THEY'VE BEEN PUT IN A POSITION WHERE THEY HAVE T' BORROW. THEY DON'T LIKE THE PEOPLE THEY'VE BORROWED FROM T' REMIND 'EM ABOUT THE LOAN; IT'S LIKE RUBBING SALT IN THE WOUND.

ALL THROUGH ALL THIS WE HAD DAY AFTER DAY OF SNOWSTORMS AND SUB-ZERO TEMPERATURES. THERE WAS VIRTUALLY NO BREAK; IT WAS RELENTLESS. MY GIRLFRIEND AND I AND JUST ABOUT EVERYONE ELSE IN CLEVELAND WERE GETTING INCREASINGLY WEARY AND SHORT-TEMPERED.

ONE NIGHT WE WENT T' SEE A FELLINI DOUBLE FEATURE AT CLEVELAND STATE UNIVERSITY. I PUT THE CAR IN A PARKING GARAGE, GOT OUT AND SAW IT WAS STEAMING. A HOSE HAD BROKEN.

WHAT A DRAG. I TAPED UP THE HOSE AND FILLED THE RADIATOR. BY THE TIME I DID, THE MOVIES'D STARTED.

THE CAR STARTED AGAIN AND WE HEADED HOME, BUT PARTWAY THERE IT BROKE DOWN. I COULDN'T GET IT GOING AGAIN.

DAMMIT, IT TURNS OVER BUT IT DON'T CATCH.

FORTUNATELY A COP CAME ALONG AND GAVE ME A LIFT TO A GUY WHO GAVE ME A TOW TO A GAS STATION.

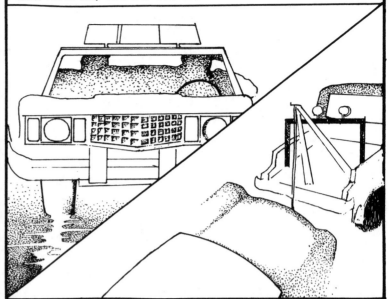

THE GUY DROPS US OFF AT A GAS STATION JUST AS IT'S CLOSING. BUT THE GAS STATION GUY DOESN'T WANT ME TO LEAVE IT THERE. HE CLAIMS HE'S ALREADY GOT TOO MANY CARS PARKED THERE — THAT THE CITY WILL FINE HIM.

CLOSED

LAST YEAR I HAD TO PAY FIVE HUNDRED DOL- LAR. I NOT GOING TO RISK THIS AGAIN.

BUT WHERE'M I GONNA PUT IT! I CAN'T LEAVE IT ON THE STREET AROUND HERE; THEY'LL TICKET ME.

I DON'T CARE. YOU GOTTA GET IT OUT.

ONE OF HIS EMPLOYEES OFFERED TO HELP US......

WELL, IF YOU LIVE NEAR HERE I GOT A ROPE IN MY CAR. I C'D PULL YA HOME.

WOW, WOULDYA? THANKS MAN, I'D BE GLAD T' PAY YA; I'D INSIST ON IT.

BUT FOR SOME REASON THE GAS STATION OWNER CHANGES HIS MIND.

ALRITE, ALRITE, YOU LEAVE IT THERE. I CAN PROBABLY FIX TOMORROW.

SO WE WALKED HOME. IT WAS REAL WINDY AND WE WERE GETTIN' HIT BY A FREEZING RAIN. MY GIRLFRIEND HAD ON A LIGHT COAT. THIS WAS JUST ABOUT THE LAST STRAW.

DAMMIT, WHYN'T YOU CALL A CAB?

WHEN WE GOT BACK WE HAD OUR FIRST ARGUMENT.

YOU COULDA AT LEAST GOTTEN US A CAB!

A CAB?! I ONLY LIVE TWO BLOCKS FROM THE GAS STATION.

YOU LIVE FARTHER AWAY THAN THAT! YOU LIVE EIGHT OR TEN BLOCKS AWAY.

THAT WAS THE WAY IT WAS THAT WINTER.... COLD, A LOTTA SNOW AND PLENTY OF ARGUMENTS. ONCE MY GIRLFRIEND GOT UPSET AND WALKED OUT OF MY APARTMENT.

SHE WENT OVER TO HER SISTER'S HOUSE. A COUPLE OF HOURS LATER SHE CALLED ME AND TOLD ME SHE WANTED A RIDE HOME. I SAID O.K., BUT WHEN I WAS GOING OVER TO GET MY CAR, ON WHICH THE WIPERS DIDN'T WORK, I COULD BARELY SEE.

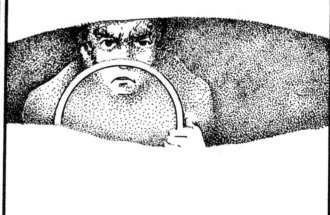

I PICKED UP MY GIRLFRIEND AND WE HEADED BACK TO HER PLACE. WHAT A NIGHTMARE! THE ICY SNOW WAS EXTREMELY HEAVY AND DIFFICULT TO DRIVE THROUGH. I HADDA PUSH MY CAR ABOUT TWENTY FIVE YARDS BEFORE I COULD GET IT ONTO SOME ROAD THAT IT WAS POSSIBLE TO DRIVE ON.

THE ROADS WERE SLICK AS GLASS AND I WAS PRACTICALLY STANDING ON MY HEAD TRYING TO SEE WHERE I WAS GOING.

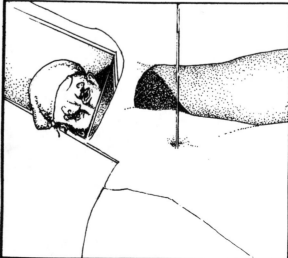

ON TOP OF THAT I'M ARGUING WITH MY GIRL-FRIEND. WE GET TO THE TOP OF A LONG, STEEP HILL AND SHE SAYS SHE WANTS ME TO PARK MY CAR WHEN I GET DOWN TO HER PLACE, COME IN AND TALK SOME MORE.

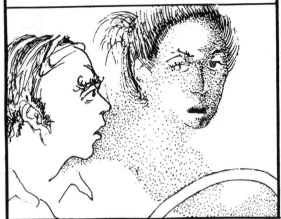

I WANNA RESOLVE OUR HASSLE TOO, BUT IF I CAN GET DOWN THE HILL AND TO HER PLACE IN ONE PIECE, I WANNA KEEP GOING. I'M AFRAID IF I STOP I WON'T BE ABLE T' START AGAIN.

SO I JUST DROP HER OFF AT THE CURB. I'M UPSET BECAUSE I REALLY WANNA KEEP ON TALKIN' TO HER, BUT I'M AFRAID SHE'LL INTERPRET MY NOT WANT-ING T' COME T' HER PAD AS MY SLIGHTING HER.

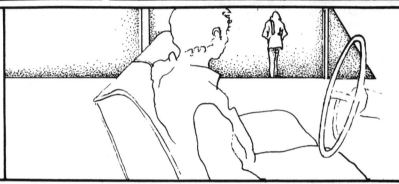

WELL WINTER FINALLY DOES COME TO AN END EVERY YEAR IN CLEVELAND AND IN OTHER CITIES ON OUR "NORTH COAST". I'M WRIT-ING THIS IN MAY. THE HIGH TODAY WAS EIGHTY-ONE. I FELT HOT... BUT SOMEHOW I COULDN'T BELIEVE I WAS. THE COLD AND SNOW OF A COUPLE OF MONTHS BE-FORE IS STILL SO VIVID IN MY MIND THAT NICE WEA-THER SEEMS LIKE A DREAM. I'LL GET USED TO IT THOUGH, EVEN TAKE IT FOR GRANTED BEFORE AUTUMN COMES. I DO EVERY YEAR.

WHAT AM I SAYING IN THIS STORY, WHAT DO I WANT YOU TO COME AWAY WITH? I DUNNO. MAYBE I WANT PEOPLE IN CITIES LIKE BUF-FALO, DETROIT, CHICAGO, AND MINNEAPOLIS TO EMPATHIZE WITH WHAT I'M WRITING HERE... MAYBE WE DESERVE A BADGE OF COURAGE, HUH?

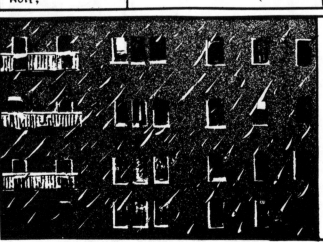

ALSO—IF ANY OF YOU LIVING IN THE SNOW BELT HAVE OLD CARS AND YOU START A ROMANCE WITH SOME-ONE IN DECEMBER OR JANUARY, MAKE UP YOUR MIND TO BE EXTRA PATIENT WITH YOUR OLD MAN OR OLD LADY.

END

A MARRIAGE ALBUM

STORY BY HARVEY PEKAR AND JOYCE BRABNER
ART BY VAL MAYERIK

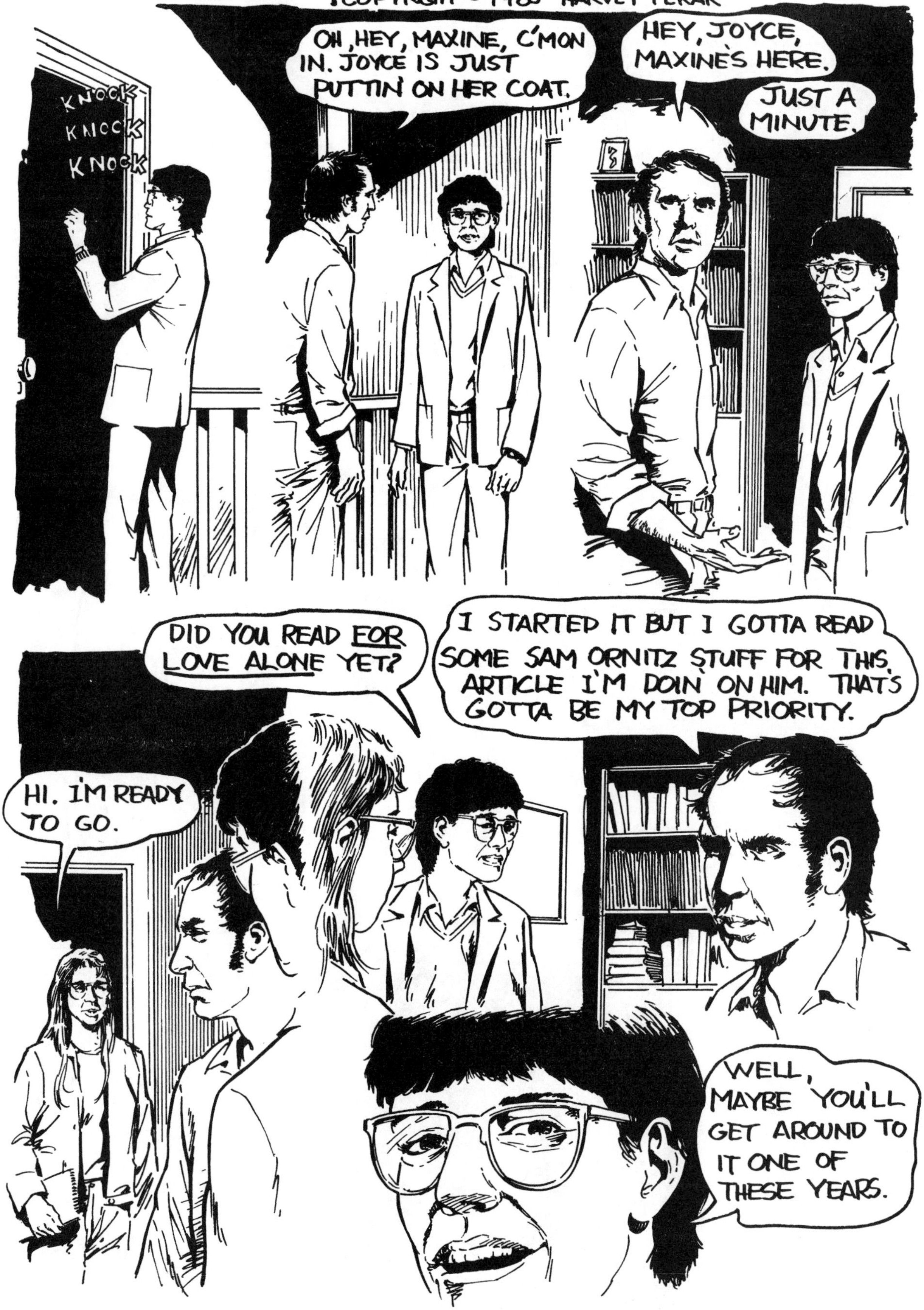
KNOCK
KNOCK
KNOCK
OH, HEY, MAXINE, C'MON IN. JOYCE IS JUST PUTTIN' ON HER COAT.
HEY, JOYCE, MAXINE'S HERE.
JUST A MINUTE.
DID YOU READ FOR LOVE ALONE YET?
I STARTED IT BUT I GOTTA READ SOME SAM ORNITZ STUFF FOR THIS ARTICLE I'M DOIN' ON HIM. THAT'S GOTTA BE MY TOP PRIORITY.
HI. I'M READY TO GO.
WELL, MAYBE YOU'LL GET AROUND TO IT ONE OF THESE YEARS.

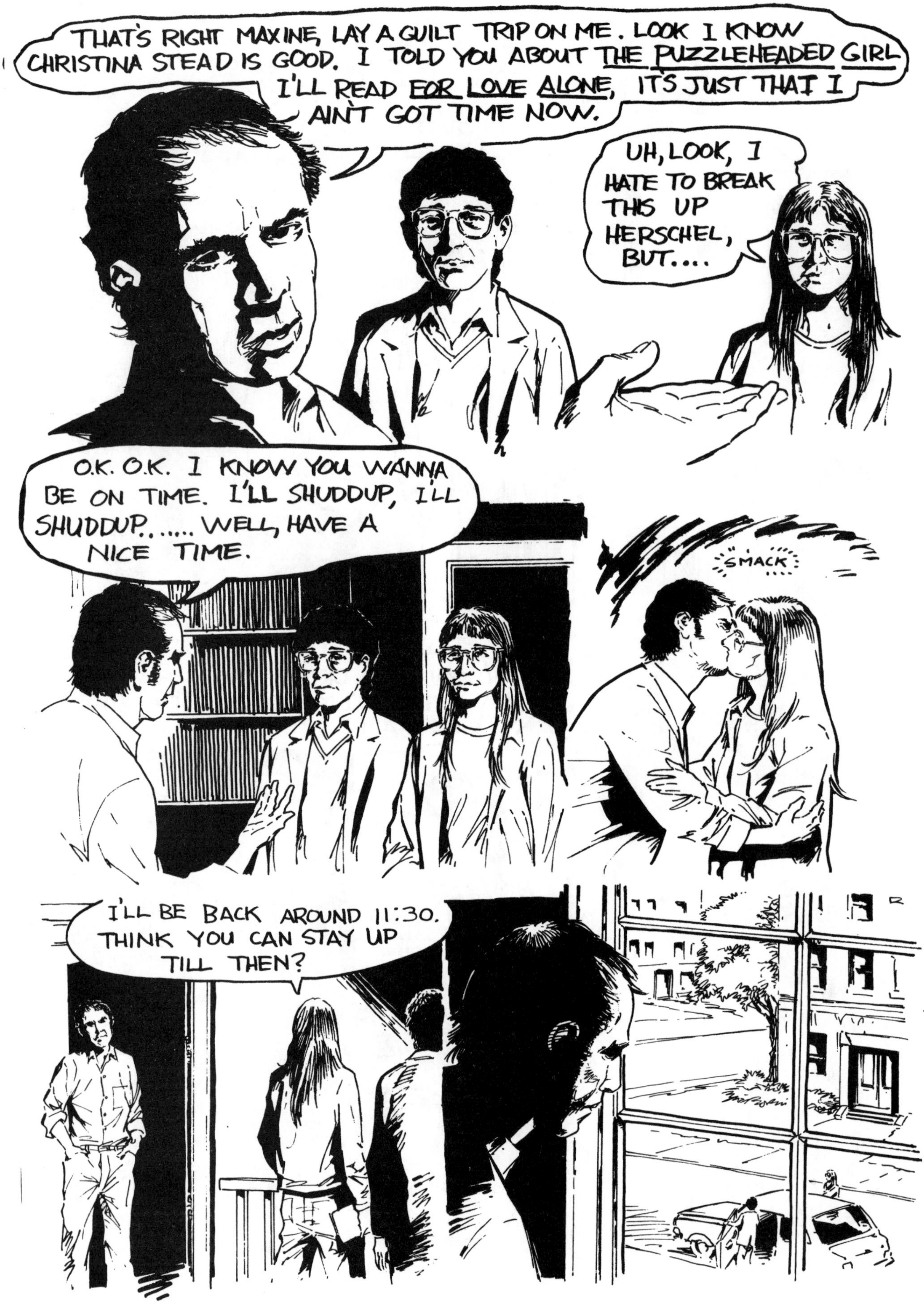
THAT'S RIGHT MAXINE, LAY A GUILT TRIP ON ME. LOOK I KNOW CHRISTINA STEAD IS GOOD. I TOLD YOU ABOUT THE PUZZLEHEADED GIRL I'LL READ FOR LOVE ALONE, IT'S JUST THAT I AIN'T GOT TIME NOW.
UH, LOOK, I HATE TO BREAK THIS UP HERSCHEL, BUT....
O.K. O.K. I KNOW YOU WANNA BE ON TIME. I'LL SHUDDUP, I'LL SHUDDUP....... WELL, HAVE A NICE TIME.
SMACK
I'LL BE BACK AROUND 11:30. THINK YOU CAN STAY UP TILL THEN?

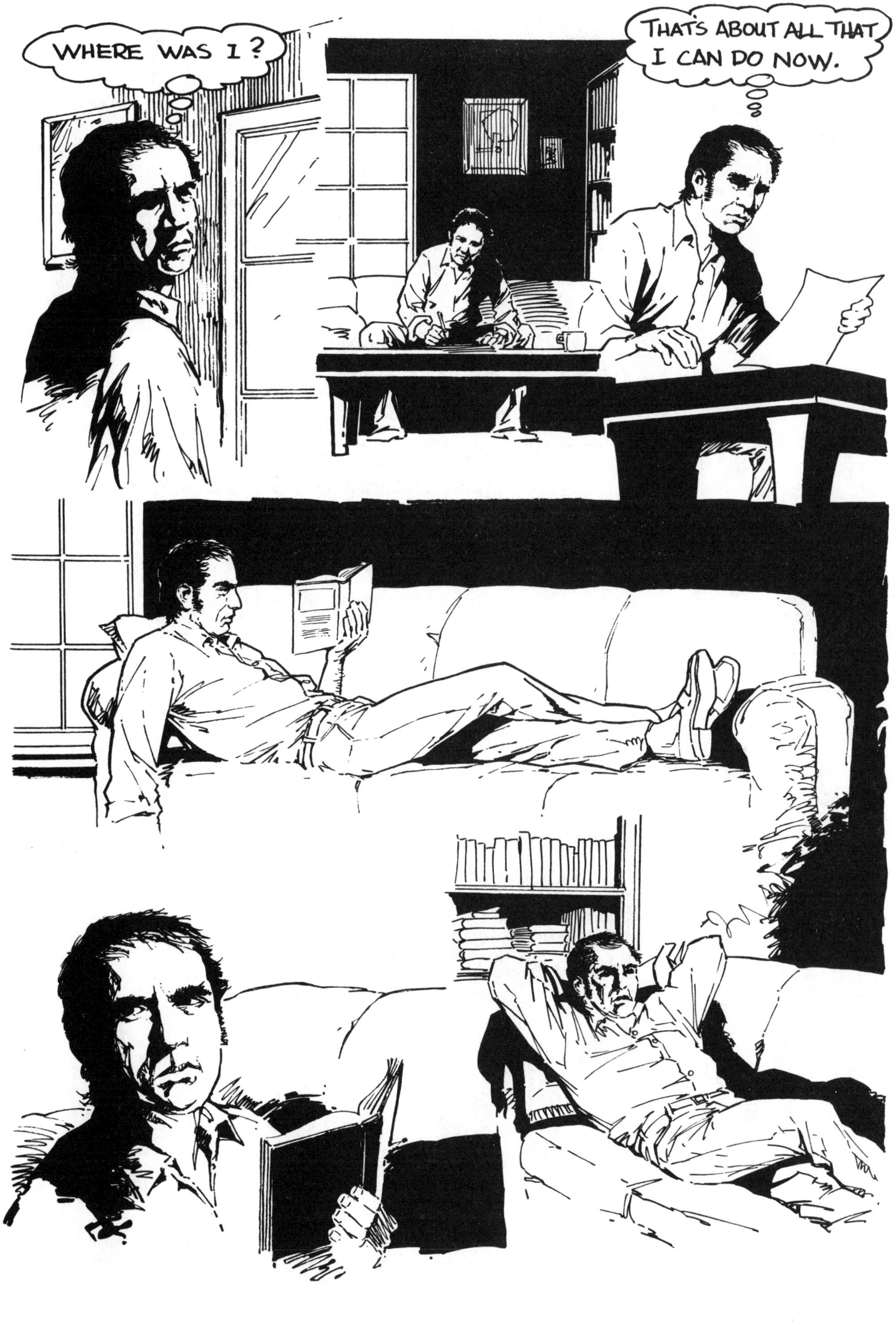
WHERE WAS I?
THAT'S ABOUT ALL THAT I CAN DO NOW.

DEAR MR. PEKAR:

WHAT DO I DO FOR A LIVING?...............COSTUMES, COMICS AND CONVICTS.

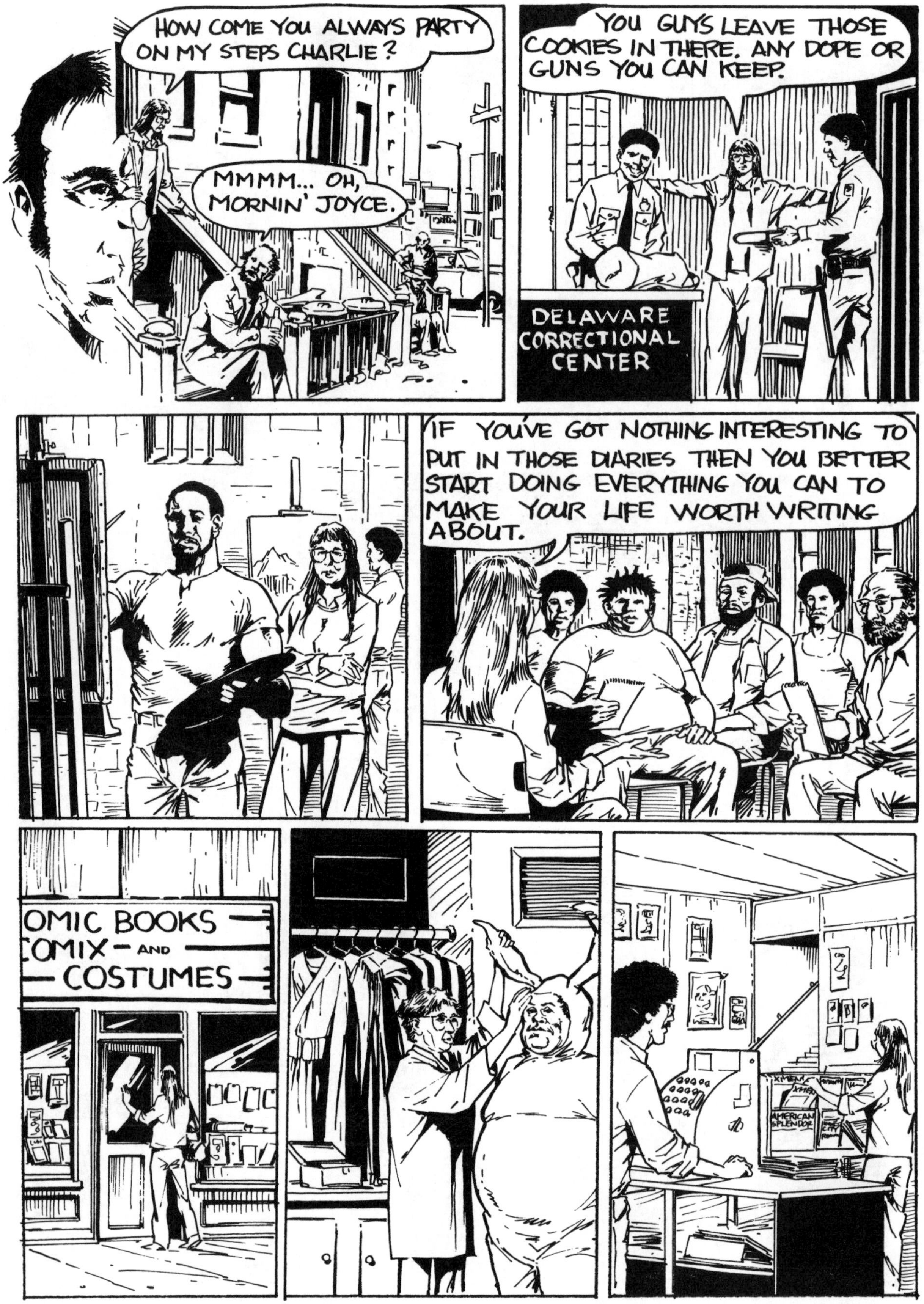
HOW COME YOU ALWAYS PARTY ON MY STEPS CHARLIE?
MMMM... OH, MORNIN' JOYCE.
YOU GUYS LEAVE THOSE COOKIES IN THERE. ANY DOPE OR GUNS YOU CAN KEEP.
DELAWARE CORRECTIONAL CENTER
IF YOU'VE GOT NOTHING INTERESTING TO PUT IN THOSE DIARIES THEN YOU BETTER START DOING EVERYTHING YOU CAN TO MAKE YOUR LIFE WORTH WRITING ABOUT.
OMIC BOOKS
COMIX AND
COSTUMES
AMERICAN SPLENDOR

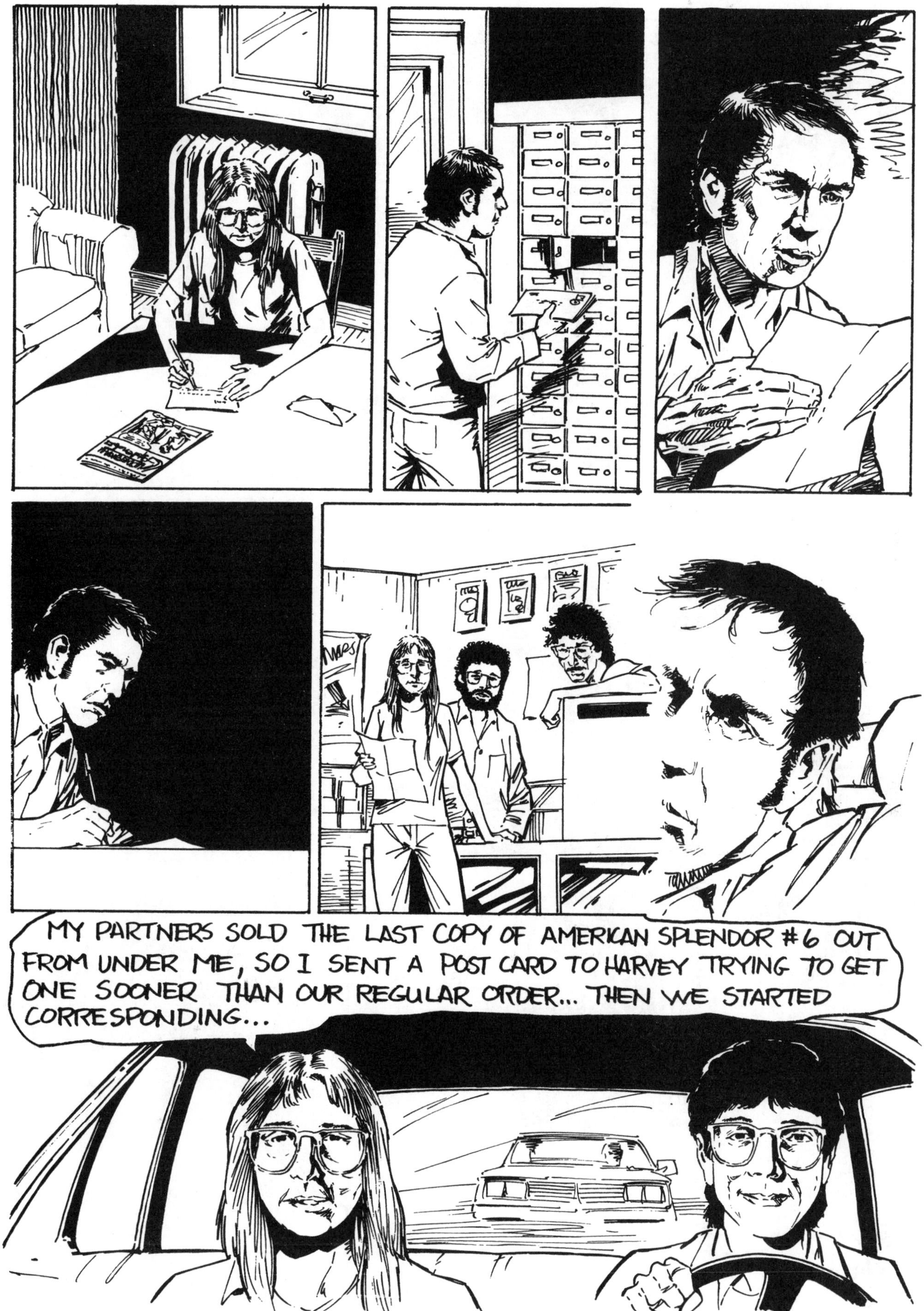
MY PARTNERS SOLD THE LAST COPY OF AMERICAN SPLENDOR #6 OUT FROM UNDER ME, SO I SENT A POST CARD TO HARVEY TRYING TO GET ONE SOONER THAN OUR REGULAR ORDER... THEN WE STARTED CORRESPONDING...

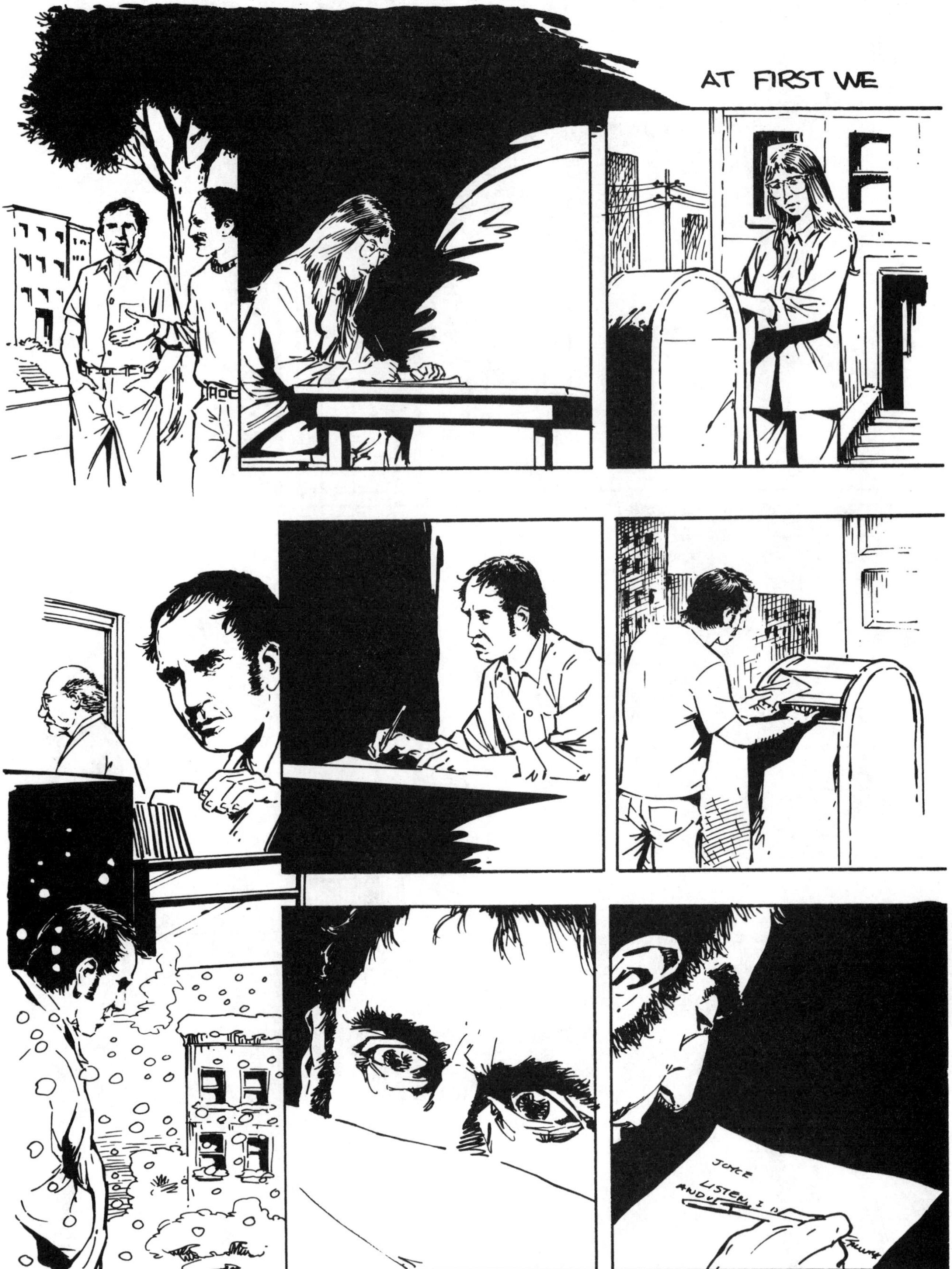
AT FIRST WE
JOYCE
BUT AFTER I CALLED HIM.....

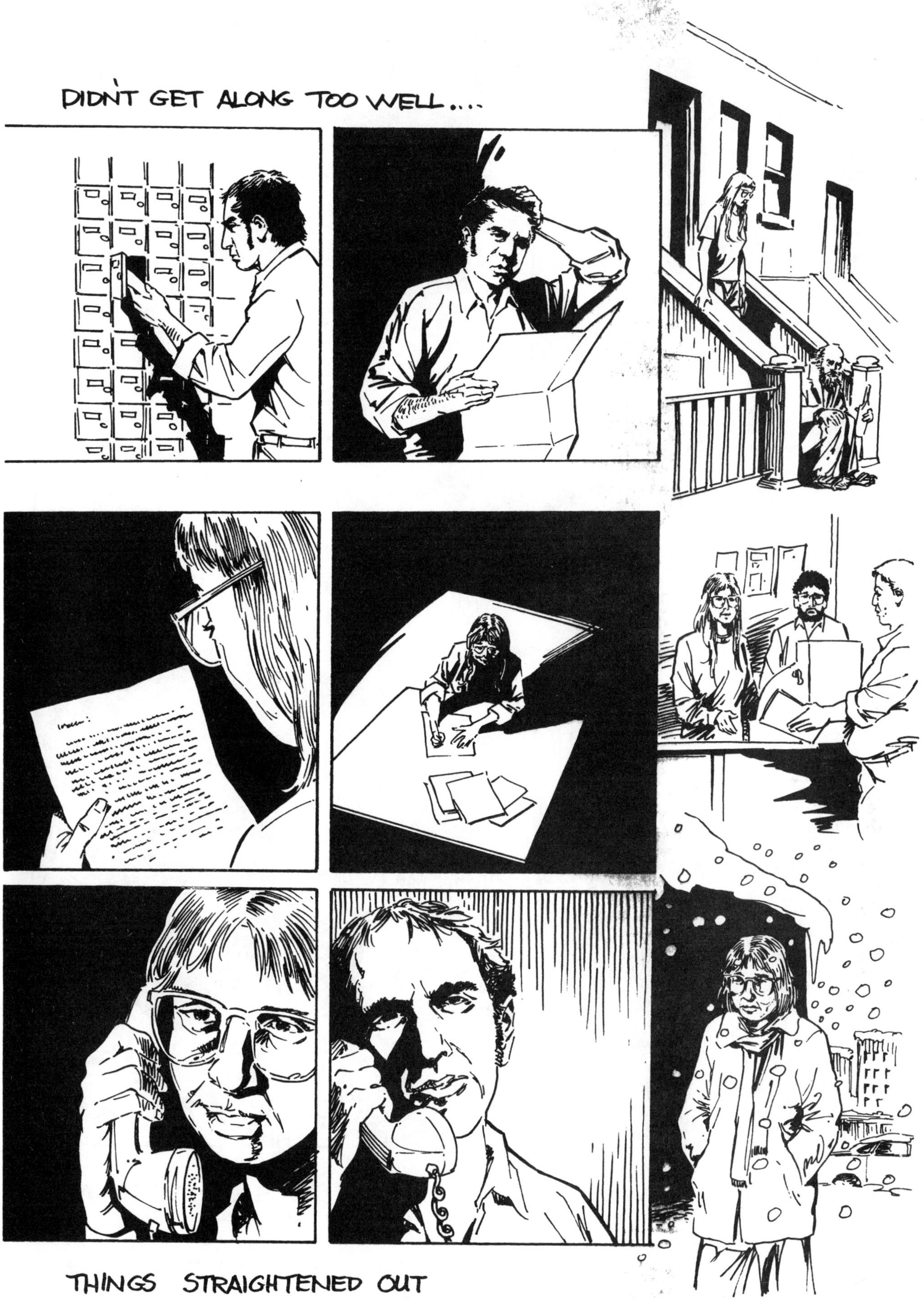
DIDN'T GET ALONG TOO WELL....
THINGS STRAIGHTENED OUT

MEANWHILE..... AS WE WERE CORRESPONDING,

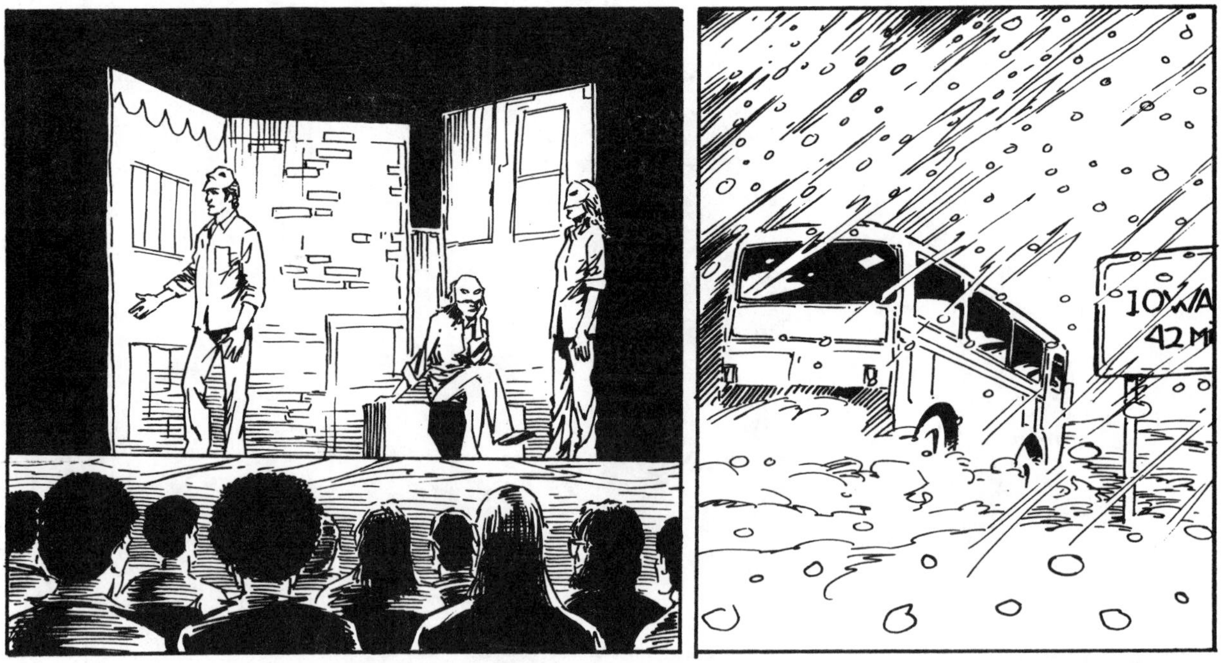

IOWA
42 MI

I WAS INVOLVED WITH A THEATER COMPANY THAT WORKS IN PRISONS. IN JANUARY I SPENT TWO WEEKS IN IOWA WORKING WITH THEM. I WAS SUPPOSED TO RETURN IN FEBRUARY, AFTER I GOT OUT OF THE HOSPITAL.

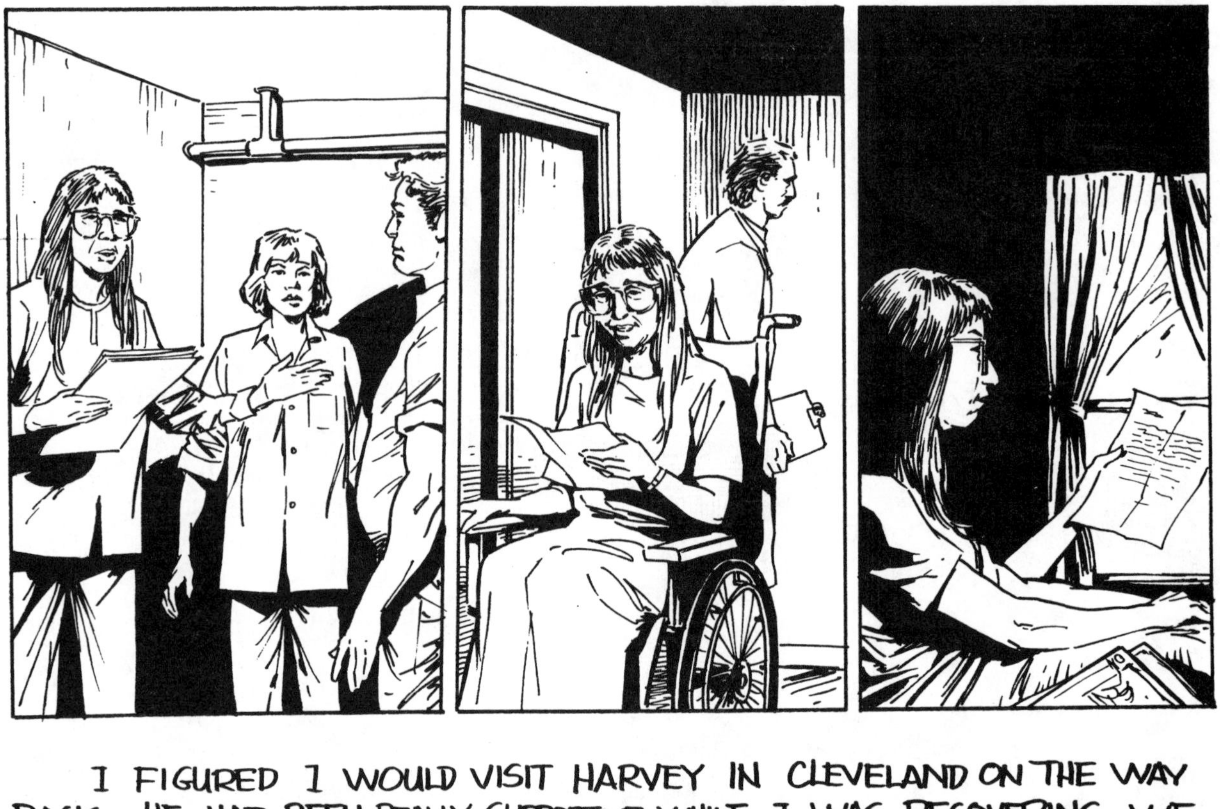

I FIGURED I WOULD VISIT HARVEY IN CLEVELAND ON THE WAY BACK. HE HAD BEEN REALLY SUPPORTIVE WHILE I WAS RECOVERING. WE TALKED ALMOST EVERY DAY AND HE SENT ME A BUNCH OF GREAT OLD RECORDS. THE COMPANY CHANGED PLANS BUT I WAS PSYCHED TO MEET HIM, SO I FLEW OUT TO CLEVELAND.

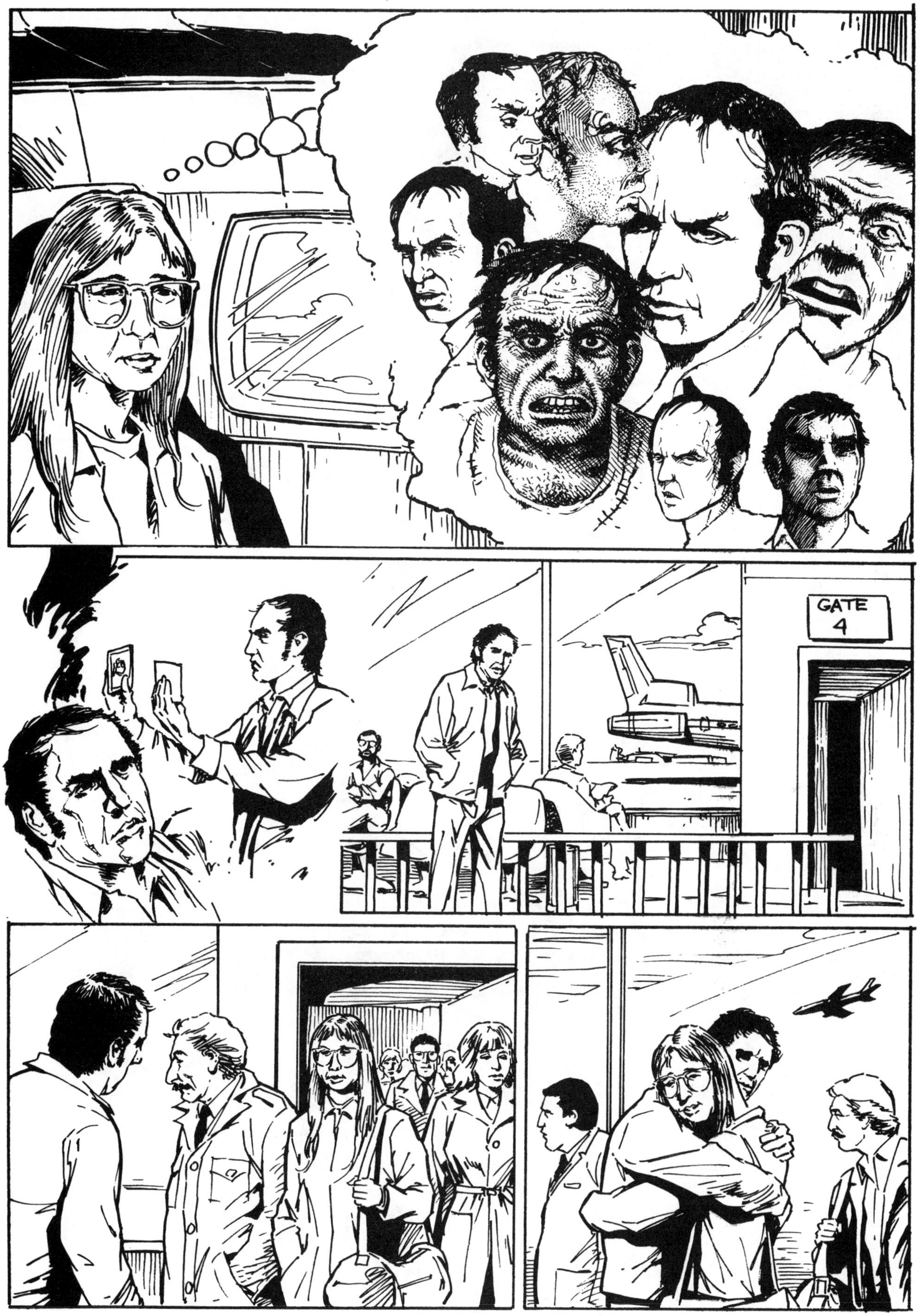
GATE
4

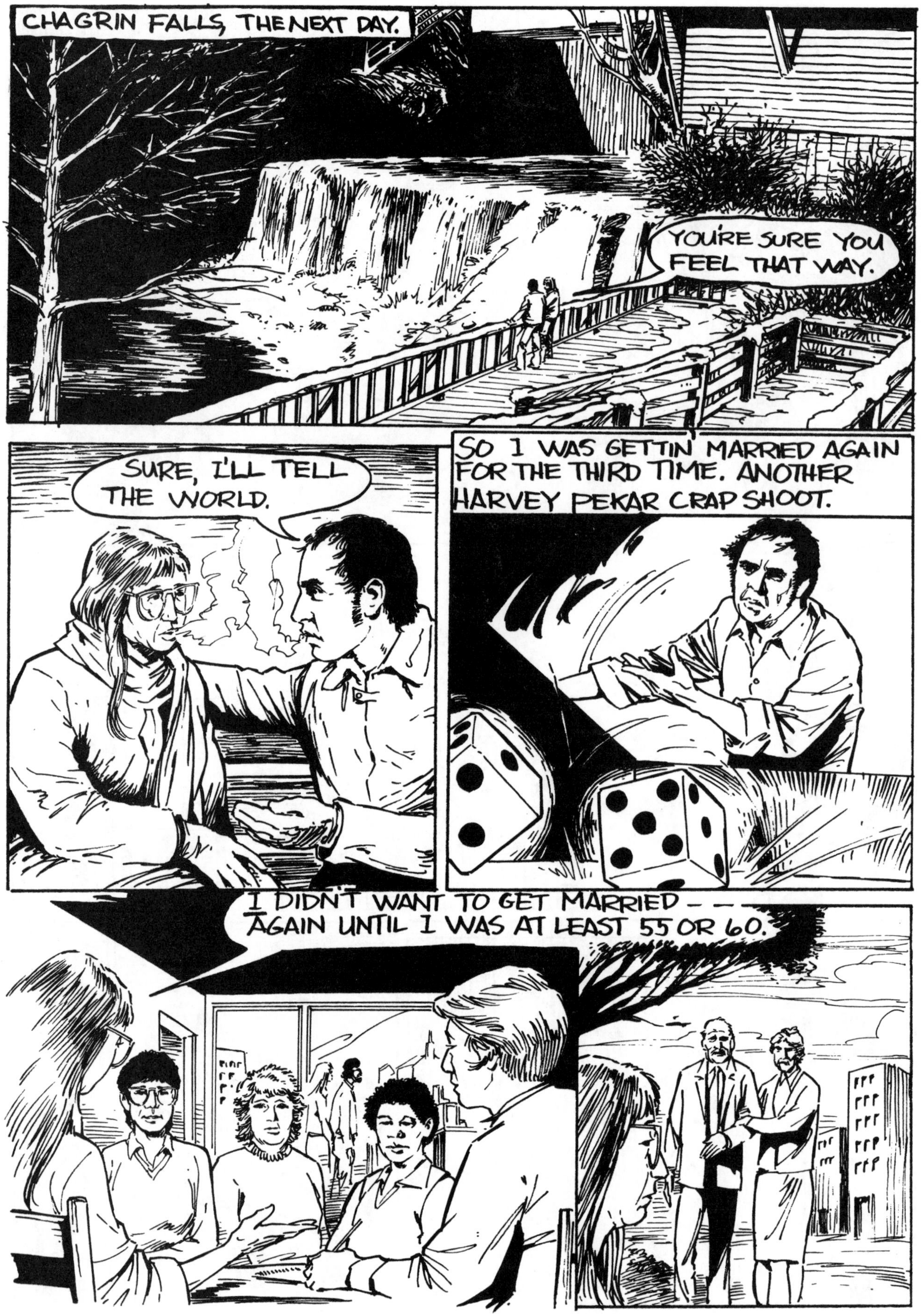
CHAGRIN FALLS, THE NEXT DAY.
YOU'RE SURE YOU FEEL THAT WAY.
SURE, I'LL TELL THE WORLD.
SO I WAS GETTIN MARRIED AGAIN FOR THE THIRD TIME. ANOTHER HARVEY PEKAR CRAP SHOOT.
I DIDN'T WANT TO GET MARRIED--- AGAIN UNTIL I WAS AT LEAST 55 OR 60.

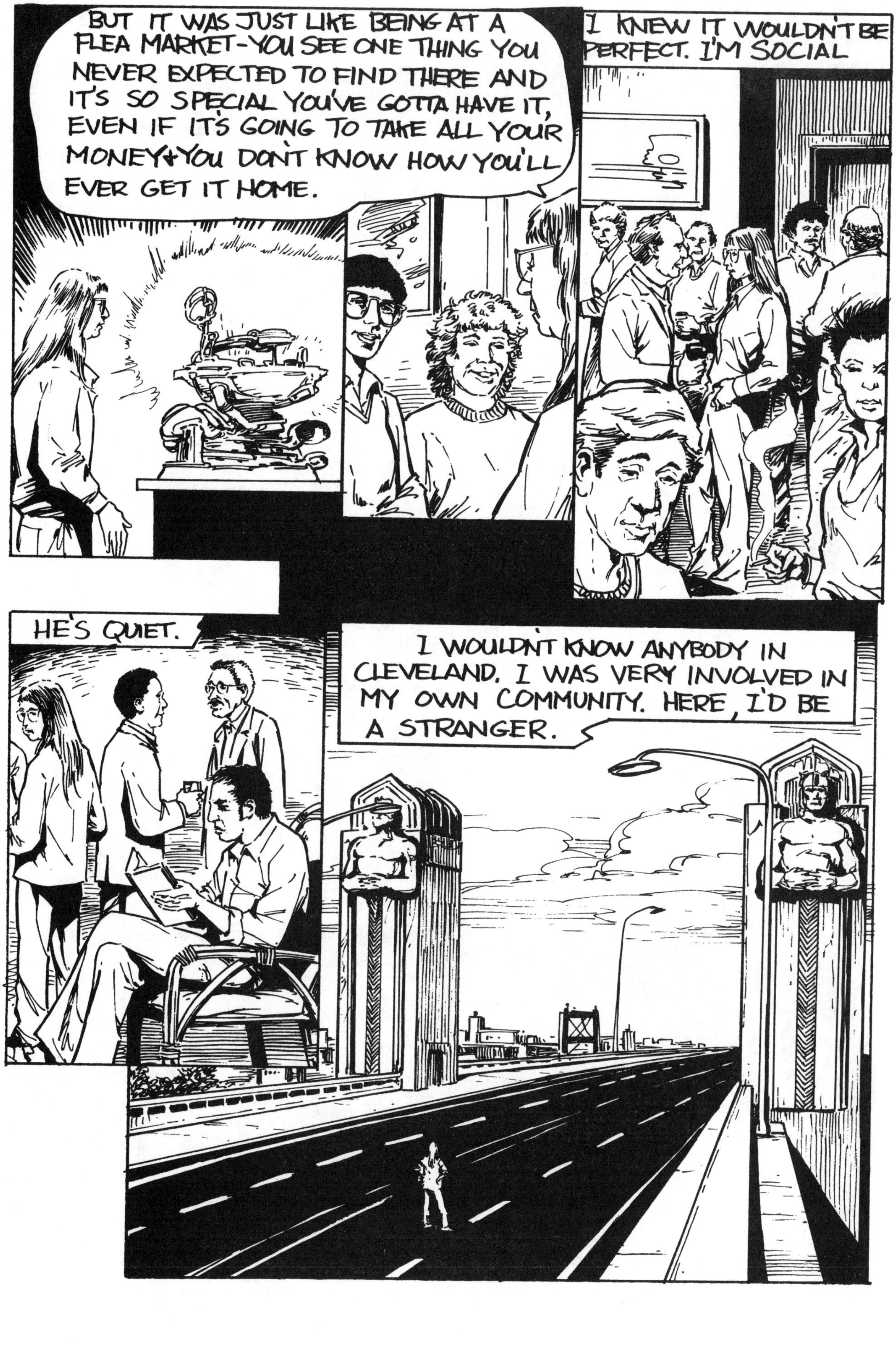
BUT IT WAS JUST LIKE BEING AT A FLEA MARKET-YOU SEE ONE THING YOU NEVER EXPECTED TO FIND THERE AND IT'S SO SPECIAL YOU'VE GOTTA HAVE IT, EVEN IF IT'S GOING TO TAKE ALL YOUR MONEY+YOU DON'T KNOW HOW YOU'LL EVER GET IT HOME.
I KNEW IT WOULDN'T BE PERFECT. I'M SOCIAL
HE'S QUIET.
I WOULDN'T KNOW ANYBODY IN CLEVELAND. I WAS VERY INVOLVED IN MY OWN COMMUNITY. HERE, I'D BE A STRANGER.

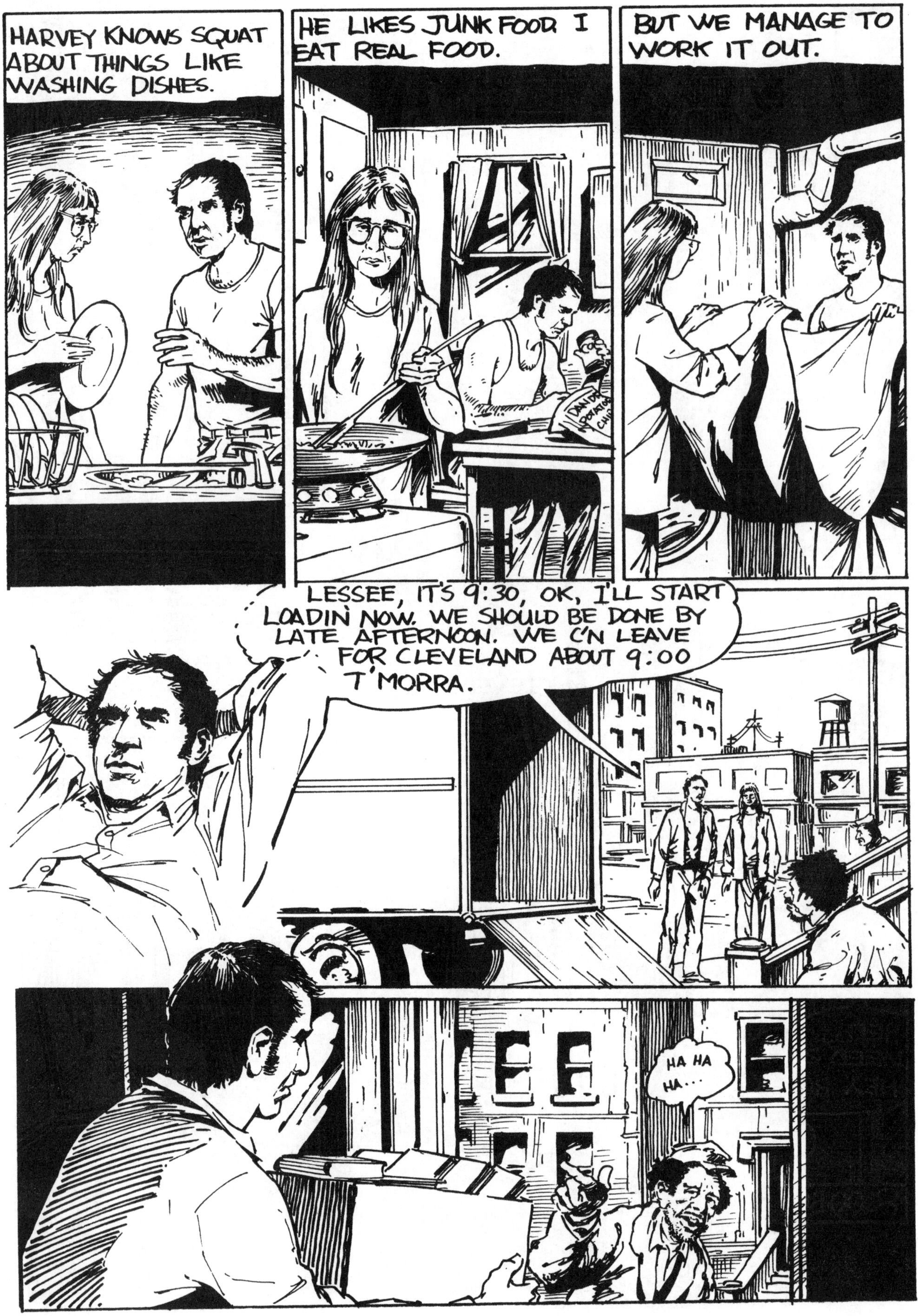
HARVEY KNOWS SQUAT ABOUT THINGS LIKE WASHING DISHES.
HE LIKES JUNK FOOD. I EAT REAL FOOD.
BUT WE MANAGE TO WORK IT OUT.
LESSEE, IT'S 9:30, OK, I'LL START LOADIN' NOW. WE SHOULD BE DONE BY LATE AFTERNOON. WE C'N LEAVE FOR CLEVELAND ABOUT 9:00 T'MORRA.
HA HA HA...

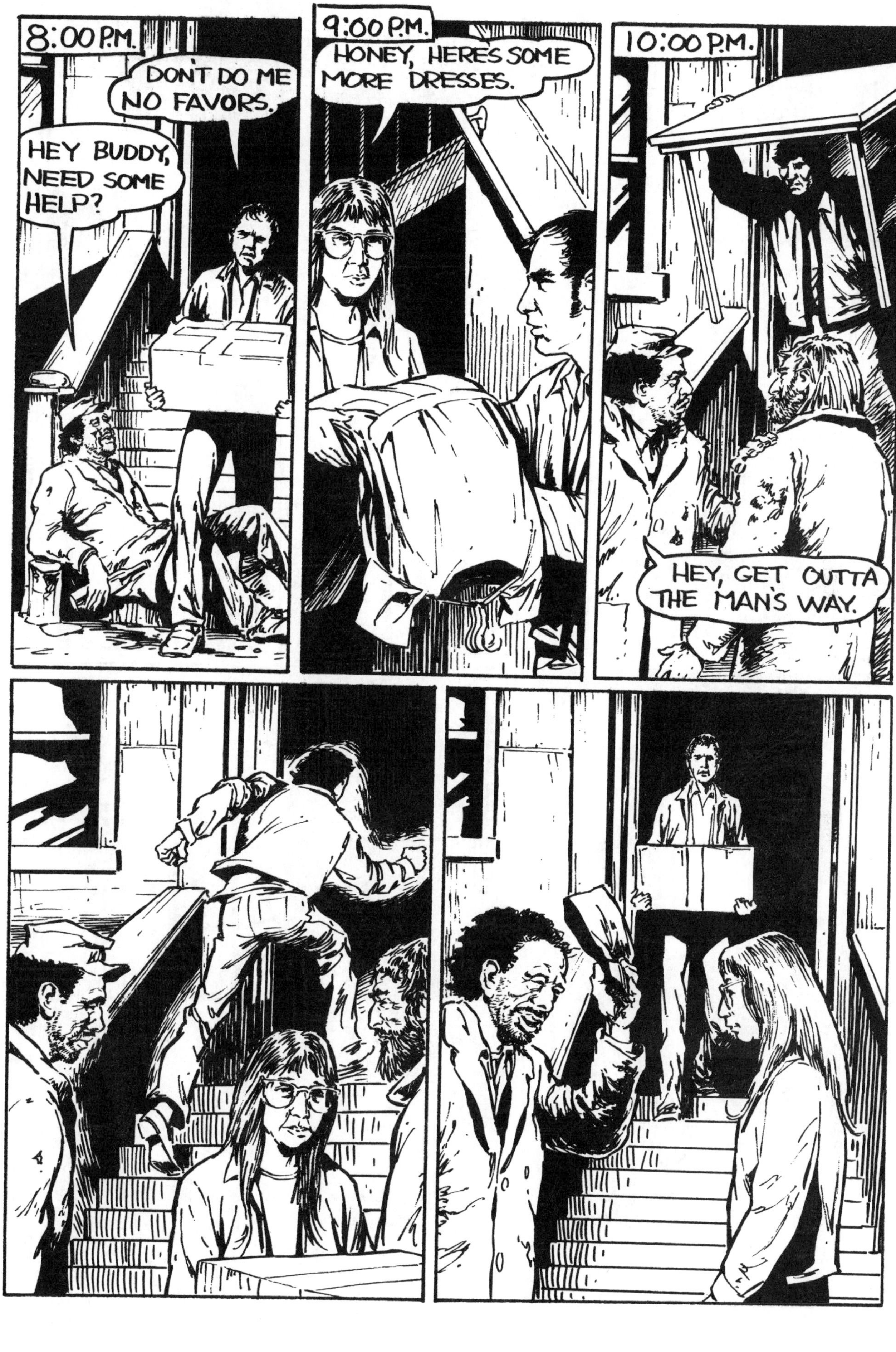
8:00 P.M.
HEY BUDDY, NEED SOME HELP?
DON'T DO ME NO FAVORS.
9:00 P.M.
HONEY, HERES SOME MORE DRESSES.
10:00 P.M.
HEY, GET OUTTA THE MAN'S WAY.

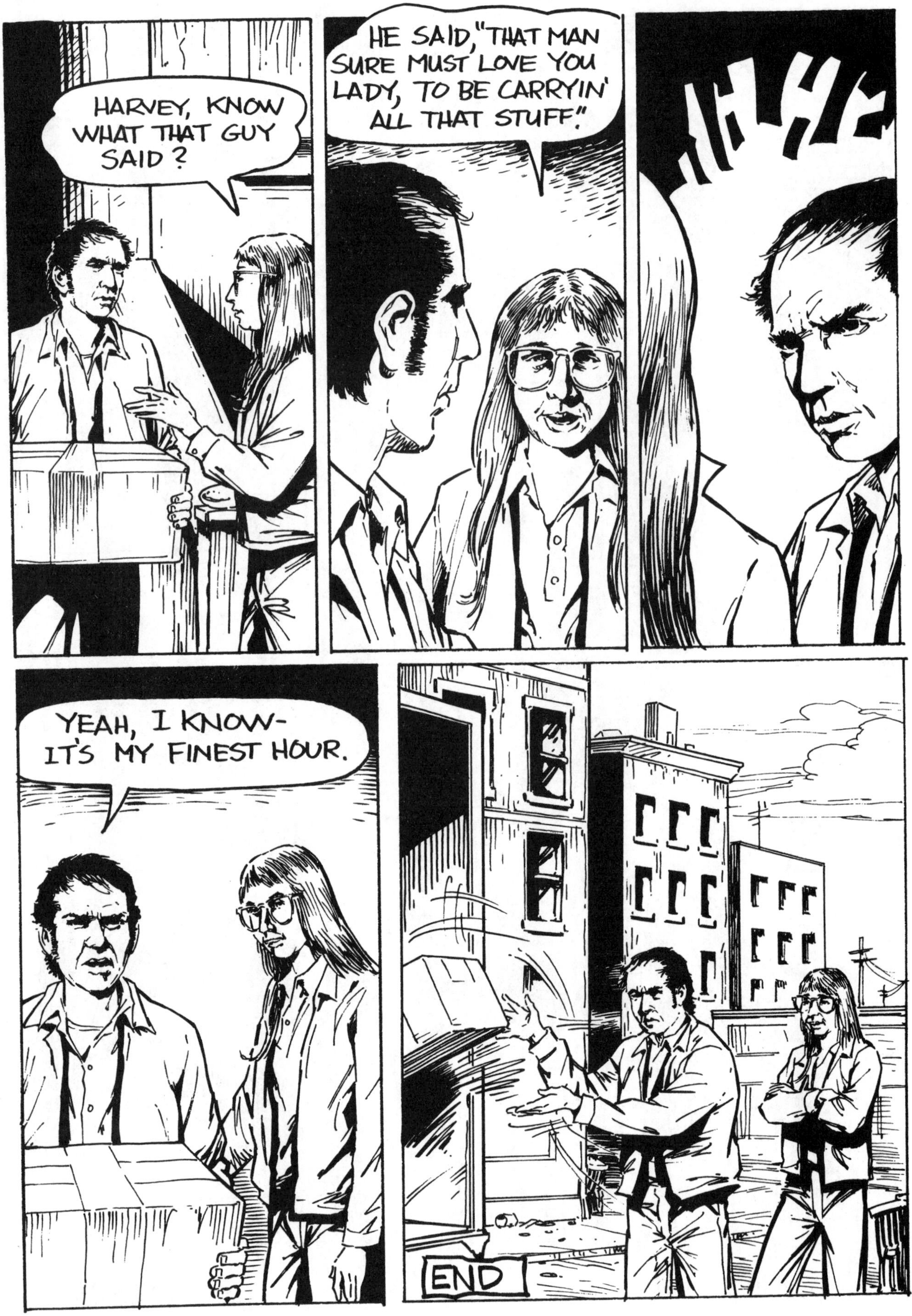
HARVEY, KNOW WHAT THAT GUY SAID?
HE SAID, "THAT MAN SURE MUST LOVE YOU LADY, TO BE CARRYIN' ALL THAT STUFF."
HE HE
YEAH, I KNOW- IT'S MY FINEST HOUR.
END

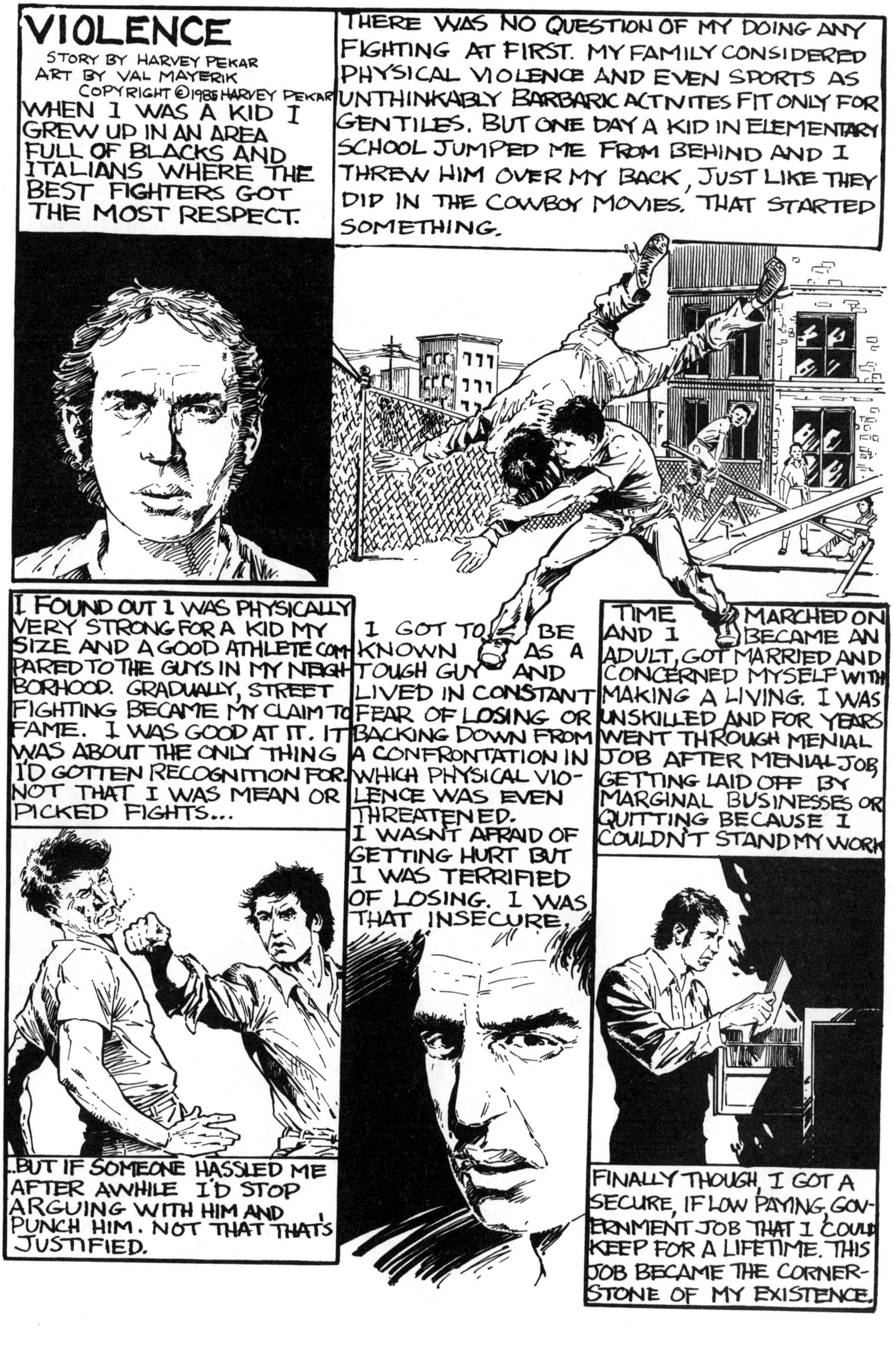
VIOLENCE
STORY BY HARVEY PEKAR
ART BY VAL MAYERIK
COPYRIGHT © 1985 HARVEY PEKAR
WHEN I WAS A KID I GREW UP IN AN AREA FULL OF BLACKS AND ITALIANS WHERE THE BEST FIGHTERS GOT THE MOST RESPECT.
THERE WAS NO QUESTION OF MY DOING ANY FIGHTING AT FIRST. MY FAMILY CONSIDERED PHYSICAL VIOLENCE AND EVEN SPORTS AS UNTHINKABLY BARBARIC ACTIVITES FIT ONLY FOR GENTILES. BUT ONE DAY A KID IN ELEMENTARY SCHOOL JUMPED ME FROM BEHIND AND I THREW HIM OVER MY BACK, JUST LIKE THEY DID IN THE COWBOY MOVIES. THAT STARTED SOMETHING.
I FOUND OUT I WAS PHYSICALLY VERY STRONG FOR A KID MY SIZE AND A GOOD ATHLETE COMPARED TO THE GUYS IN MY NEIGHBORHOOD. GRADUALLY, STREET FIGHTING BECAME MY CLAIM TO FAME. I WAS GOOD AT IT. IT WAS ABOUT THE ONLY THING I'D GOTTEN RECOGNITION FOR. NOT THAT I WAS MEAN OR PICKED FIGHTS...
..BUT IF SOMEONE HASSLED ME AFTER AWHILE I'D STOP ARGUING WITH HIM AND PUNCH HIM. NOT THAT THAT'S JUSTIFIED.
I GOT TO BE KNOWN AS A TOUGH GUY AND LIVED IN CONSTANT FEAR OF LOSING OR BACKING DOWN FROM A CONFRONTATION IN WHICH PHYSICAL VIOLENCE WAS EVEN THREATENED.
I WASN'T AFRAID OF GETTING HURT BUT I WAS TERRIFIED OF LOSING. I WAS THAT INSECURE.
TIME MARCHED ON AND I BECAME AN ADULT, GOT MARRIED AND CONCERNED MYSELF WITH MAKING A LIVING. I WAS UNSKILLED AND FOR YEARS WENT THROUGH MENIAL JOB AFTER MENIAL JOB, GETTING LAID OFF BY MARGINAL BUSINESSES OR QUITTING BECAUSE I COULDN'T STAND MY WORK
FINALLY THOUGH, I GOT A SECURE, IF LOW PAYING, GOVERNMENT JOB THAT I COULD KEEP FOR A LIFETIME. THIS JOB BECAME THE CORNERSTONE OF MY EXISTENCE.

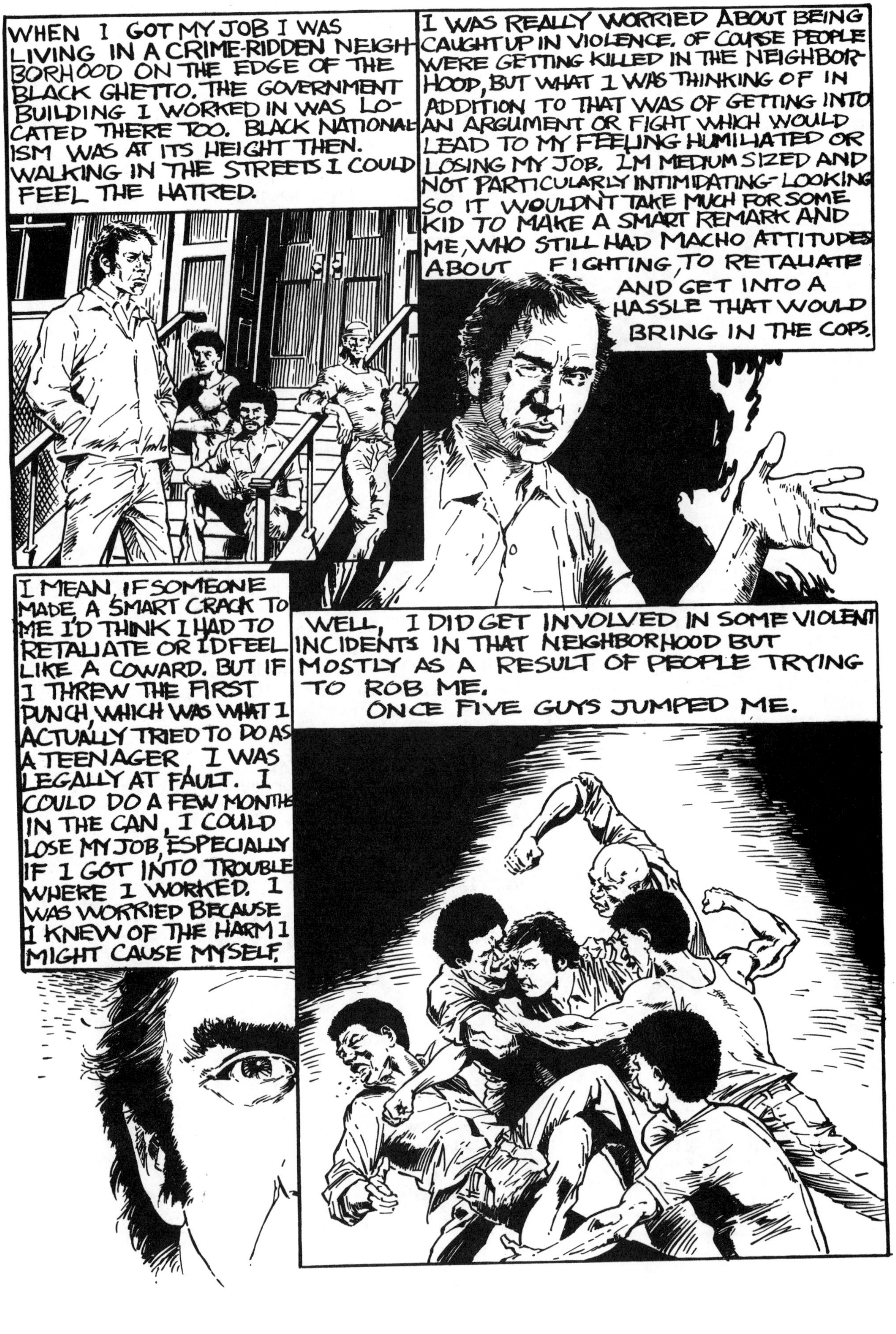
WHEN I GOT MY JOB I WAS LIVING IN A CRIME-RIDDEN NEIGHBORHOOD ON THE EDGE OF THE BLACK GHETTO. THE GOVERNMENT BUILDING I WORKED IN WAS LOCATED THERE TOO. BLACK NATIONALISM WAS AT ITS HEIGHT THEN. WALKING IN THE STREETS I COULD FEEL THE HATRED.
I WAS REALLY WORRIED ABOUT BEING CAUGHT UP IN VIOLENCE. OF COURSE PEOPLE WERE GETTING KILLED IN THE NEIGHBORHOOD, BUT WHAT I WAS THINKING OF IN ADDITION TO THAT WAS OF GETTING INTO AN ARGUMENT OR FIGHT WHICH WOULD LEAD TO MY FEELING HUMILIATED OR LOSING MY JOB. I'M MEDIUM SIZED AND NOT PARTICULARLY INTIMIDATING-LOOKING SO IT WOULDN'T TAKE MUCH FOR SOME KID TO MAKE A SMART REMARK AND ME, WHO STILL HAD MACHO ATTITUDES ABOUT FIGHTING, TO RETALIATE AND GET INTO A HASSLE THAT WOULD BRING IN THE COPS.
I MEAN, IF SOMEONE MADE A SMART CRACK TO ME I'D THINK I HAD TO RETALIATE OR I'D FEEL LIKE A COWARD. BUT IF I THREW THE FIRST PUNCH, WHICH WAS WHAT I ACTUALLY TRIED TO DO AS A TEENAGER, I WAS LEGALLY AT FAULT. I COULD DO A FEW MONTHS IN THE CAN, I COULD LOSE MY JOB, ESPECIALLY IF I GOT INTO TROUBLE WHERE I WORKED. I WAS WORRIED BECAUSE I KNEW OF THE HARM I MIGHT CAUSE MYSELF.
WELL, I DID GET INVOLVED IN SOME VIOLENT INCIDENTS IN THAT NEIGHBORHOOD BUT MOSTLY AS A RESULT OF PEOPLE TRYING TO ROB ME.
ONCE FIVE GUYS JUMPED ME.

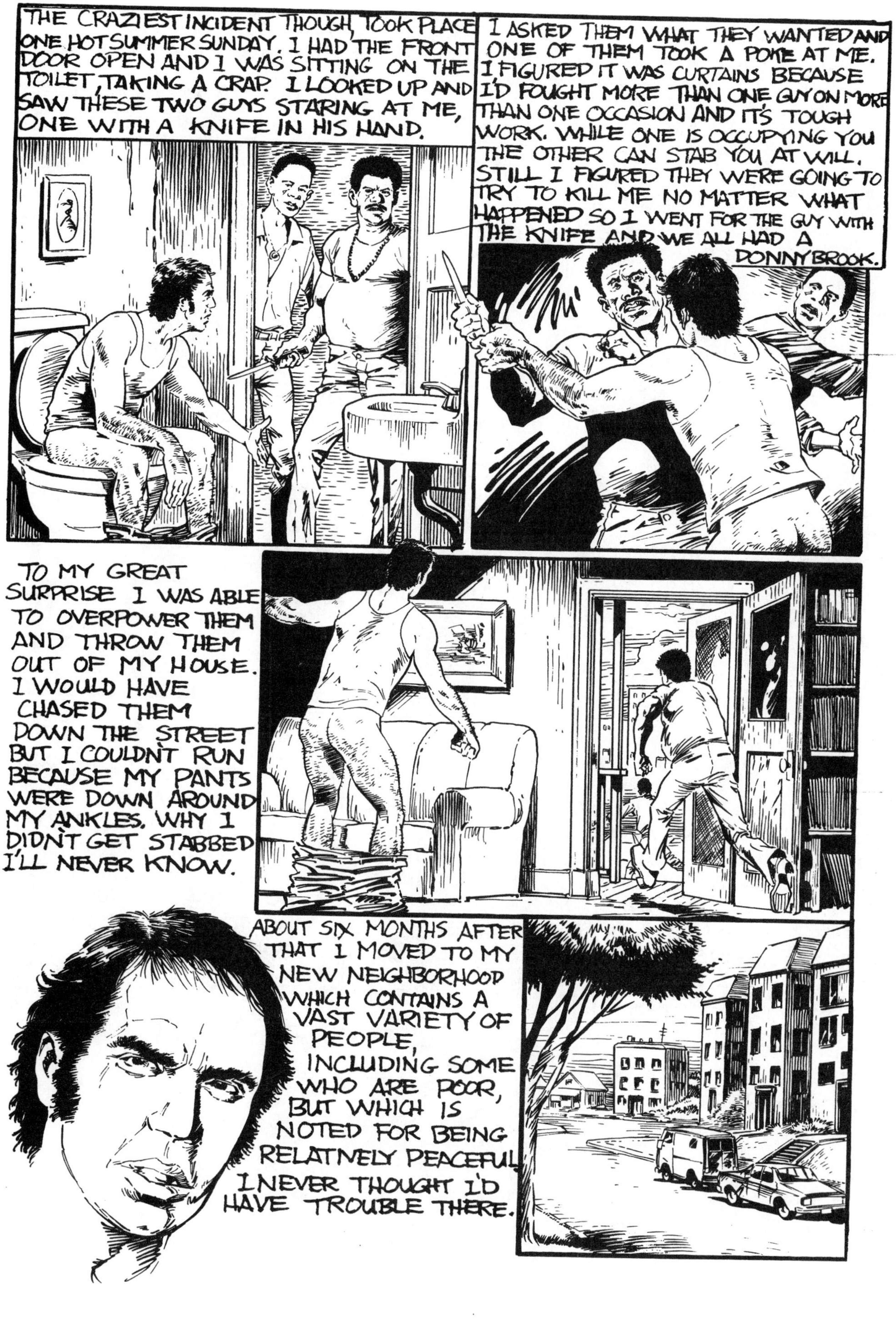
THE CRAZIEST INCIDENT THOUGH, TOOK PLACE ONE HOT SUMMER SUNDAY. I HAD THE FRONT DOOR OPEN AND I WAS SITTING ON THE TOILET, TAKING A CRAP. I LOOKED UP AND SAW THESE TWO GUYS STARING AT ME, ONE WITH A KNIFE IN HIS HAND.
I ASKED THEM WHAT THEY WANTED AND ONE OF THEM TOOK A POKE AT ME. I FIGURED IT WAS CURTAINS BECAUSE I'D FOUGHT MORE THAN ONE GUY ON MORE THAN ONE OCCASION AND IT'S TOUGH WORK. WHILE ONE IS OCCUPYING YOU THE OTHER CAN STAB YOU AT WILL. STILL I FIGURED THEY WERE GOING TO TRY TO KILL ME NO MATTER WHAT HAPPENED SO I WENT FOR THE GUY WITH THE KNIFE AND WE ALL HAD A DONNYBROOK.
TO MY GREAT SURPRISE I WAS ABLE TO OVERPOWER THEM AND THROW THEM OUT OF MY HOUSE. I WOULD HAVE CHASED THEM DOWN THE STREET BUT I COULDN'T RUN BECAUSE MY PANTS WERE DOWN AROUND MY ANKLES. WHY I DIDN'T GET STABBED I'LL NEVER KNOW.
ABOUT SIX MONTHS AFTER THAT I MOVED TO MY NEW NEIGHBORHOOD WHICH CONTAINS A VAST VARIETY OF PEOPLE, INCLUDING SOME WHO ARE POOR, BUT WHICH IS NOTED FOR BEING RELATNELY PEACEFUL.
I NEVER THOUGHT I'D HAVE TROUBLE THERE.

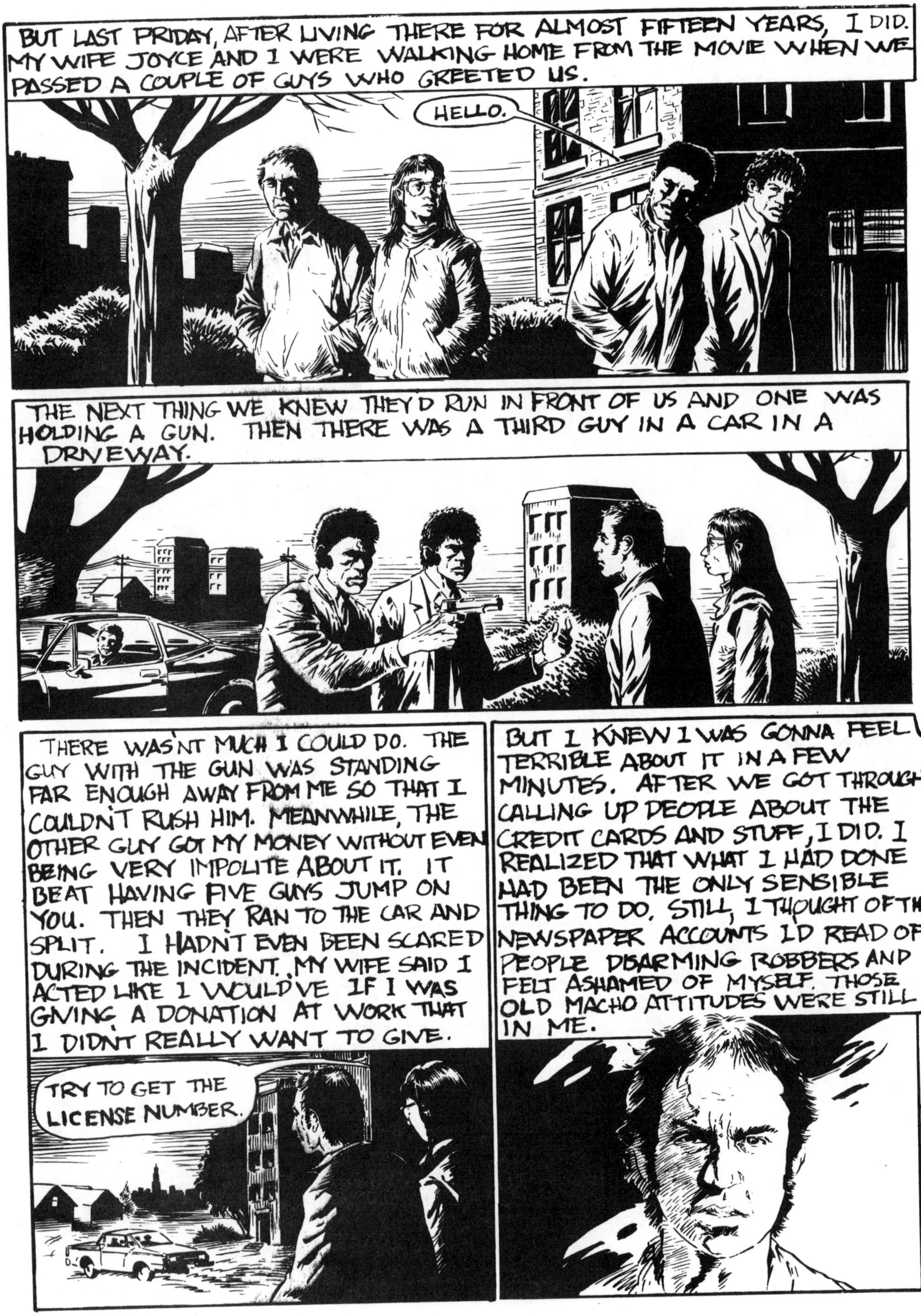
BUT LAST FRIDAY, AFTER LIVING THERE FOR ALMOST FIFTEEN YEARS, I DID. MY WIFE JOYCE AND I WERE WALKING HOME FROM THE MOVIE WHEN WE PASSED A COUPLE OF GUYS WHO GREETED US.
HELLO.
THE NEXT THING WE KNEW THEY'D RUN IN FRONT OF US AND ONE WAS HOLDING A GUN. THEN THERE WAS A THIRD GUY IN A CAR IN A DRIVEWAY.
THERE WAS'NT MUCH I COULD DO. THE GUY WITH THE GUN WAS STANDING FAR ENOUGH AWAY FROM ME SO THAT I COULDN'T RUSH HIM. MEANWHILE, THE OTHER GUY GOT MY MONEY WITHOUT EVEN BEING VERY IMPOLITE ABOUT IT. IT BEAT HAVING FIVE GUYS JUMP ON YOU. THEN THEY RAN TO THE CAR AND SPLIT. I HADN'T EVEN BEEN SCARED DURING THE INCIDENT. MY WIFE SAID I ACTED LIKE I WOULD'VE IF I WAS GIVING A DONATION AT WORK THAT I DIDN'T REALLY WANT TO GIVE.
TRY TO GET THE LICENSE NUMBER.
BUT I KNEW I WAS GONNA FEEL TERRIBLE ABOUT IT IN A FEW MINUTES. AFTER WE GOT THROUGH CALLING UP PEOPLE ABOUT THE CREDIT CARDS AND STUFF, I DID. I REALIZED THAT WHAT I HAD DONE HAD BEEN THE ONLY SENSIBLE THING TO DO. STILL, I THOUGHT OF THE NEWSPAPER ACCOUNTS I'D READ OF PEOPLE DISARMING ROBBERS AND FELT ASHAMED OF MYSELF. THOSE OLD MACHO ATTITUDES WERE STILL IN ME.

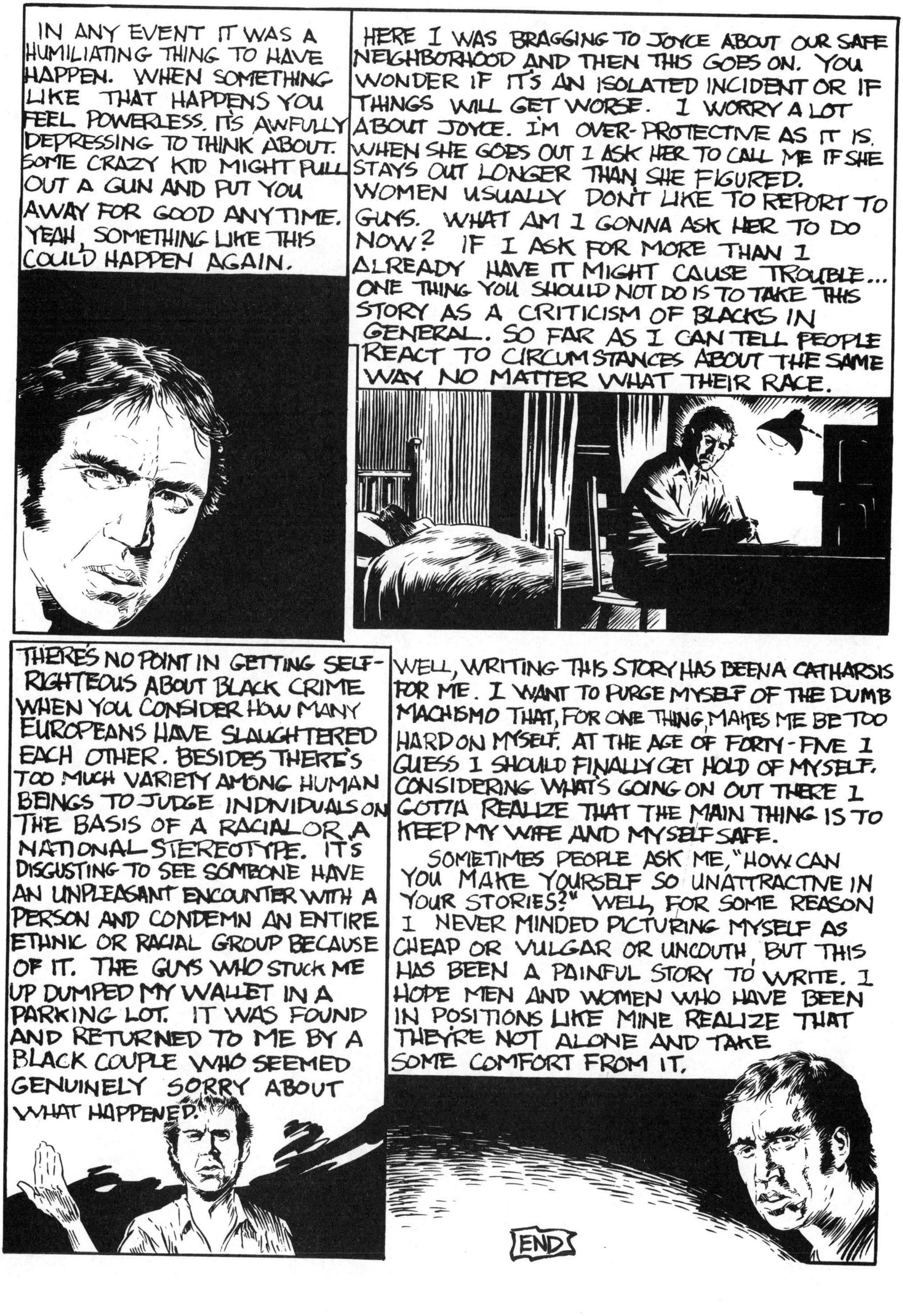
IN ANY EVENT IT WAS A HUMILIATING THING TO HAVE HAPPEN. WHEN SOMETHING LIKE THAT HAPPENS YOU FEEL POWERLESS. IT'S AWFULLY DEPRESSING TO THINK ABOUT. SOME CRAZY KID MIGHT PULL OUT A GUN AND PUT YOU AWAY FOR GOOD ANYTIME. YEAH, SOMETHING LIKE THIS COULD HAPPEN AGAIN.
HERE I WAS BRAGGING TO JOYCE ABOUT OUR SAFE NEIGHBORHOOD AND THEN THIS GOES ON. YOU WONDER IF IT'S AN ISOLATED INCIDENT OR IF THINGS WILL GET WORSE. I WORRY A LOT ABOUT JOYCE. I'M OVER-PROTECTIVE AS IT IS. WHEN SHE GOES OUT I ASK HER TO CALL ME IF SHE STAYS OUT LONGER THAN SHE FIGURED. WOMEN USUALLY DON'T LIKE TO REPORT TO GUYS. WHAT AM I GONNA ASK HER TO DO NOW? IF I ASK FOR MORE THAN I ALREADY HAVE IT MIGHT CAUSE TROUBLE... ONE THING YOU SHOULD NOT DO IS TO TAKE THIS STORY AS A CRITICISM OF BLACKS IN GENERAL. SO FAR AS I CAN TELL PEOPLE REACT TO CIRCUMSTANCES ABOUT THE SAME WAY NO MATTER WHAT THEIR RACE.
THERE'S NO POINT IN GETTING SELF-RIGHTEOUS ABOUT BLACK CRIME WHEN YOU CONSIDER HOW MANY EUROPEANS HAVE SLAUGHTERED EACH OTHER. BESIDES THERE'S TOO MUCH VARIETY AMONG HUMAN BEINGS TO JUDGE INDIVIDUALS ON THE BASIS OF A RACIAL OR A NATIONAL STEREOTYPE. IT'S DISGUSTING TO SEE SOMBONE HAVE AN UNPLEASANT ENCOUNTER WITH A PERSON AND CONDEMN AN ENTIRE ETHNIC OR RACIAL GROUP BECAUSE OF IT. THE GUYS WHO STUCK ME UP DUMPED MY WALLET IN A PARKING LOT. IT WAS FOUND AND RETURNED TO ME BY A BLACK COUPLE WHO SEEMED GENUINELY SORRY ABOUT WHAT HAPPENED.
WELL, WRITING THIS STORY HAS BEEN A CATHARSIS FOR ME. I WANT TO PURGE MYSELF OF THE DUMB MACHISMO THAT, FOR ONE THING, MAKES ME BE TOO HARD ON MYSELF. AT THE AGE OF FORTY-FIVE I GUESS I SHOULD FINALLY GET HOLD OF MYSELF. CONSIDERING WHAT'S GOING ON OUT THERE I GOTTA REALIZE THAT THE MAIN THING IS TO KEEP MY WIFE AND MYSELF SAFE.
SOMETIMES PEOPLE ASK ME, "HOW CAN YOU MAKE YOURSELF SO UNATTRACTIVE IN YOUR STORIES?" WELL, FOR SOME REASON I NEVER MINDED PICTURING MYSELF AS CHEAP OR VULGAR OR UNCOUTH, BUT THIS HAS BEEN A PAINFUL STORY TO WRITE. I HOPE MEN AND WOMEN WHO HAVE BEEN IN POSITIONS LIKE MINE REALIZE THAT THEY'RE NOT ALONE AND TAKE SOME COMFORT FROM IT.
END

HISTORY REPEATS ITSELF

Story By: HARVEY PEKAR
Art By: SEÁN CARROLL

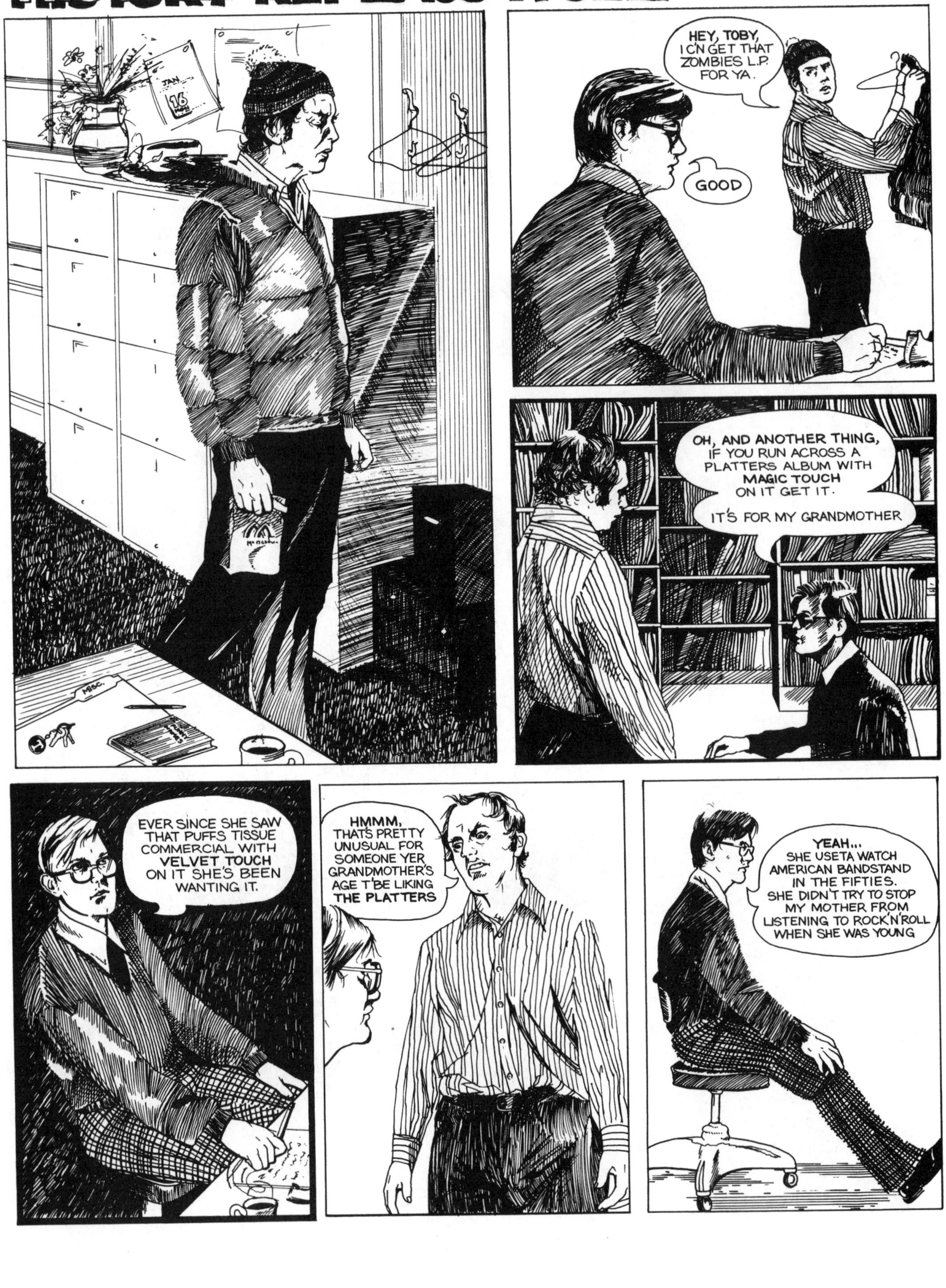
HEY, TOBY, I C'N GET THAT ZOMBIES L.P. FOR YA.
GOOD
OH, AND ANOTHER THING, IF YOU RUN ACROSS A PLATTERS ALBUM WITH MAGIC TOUCH ON IT GET IT.
IT'S FOR MY GRANDMOTHER
EVER SINCE SHE SAW THAT PUFFS TISSUE COMMERCIAL WITH VELVET TOUCH ON IT SHE'S BEEN WANTING IT.
HMMM, THAT'S PRETTY UNUSUAL FOR SOMEONE YER GRANDMOTHER'S AGE T'BE LIKING THE PLATTERS
YEAH... SHE USETA WATCH AMERICAN BANDSTAND IN THE FIFTIES. SHE DIDN'T TRY TO STOP MY MOTHER FROM LISTENING TO ROCK'N'ROLL WHEN SHE WAS YOUNG

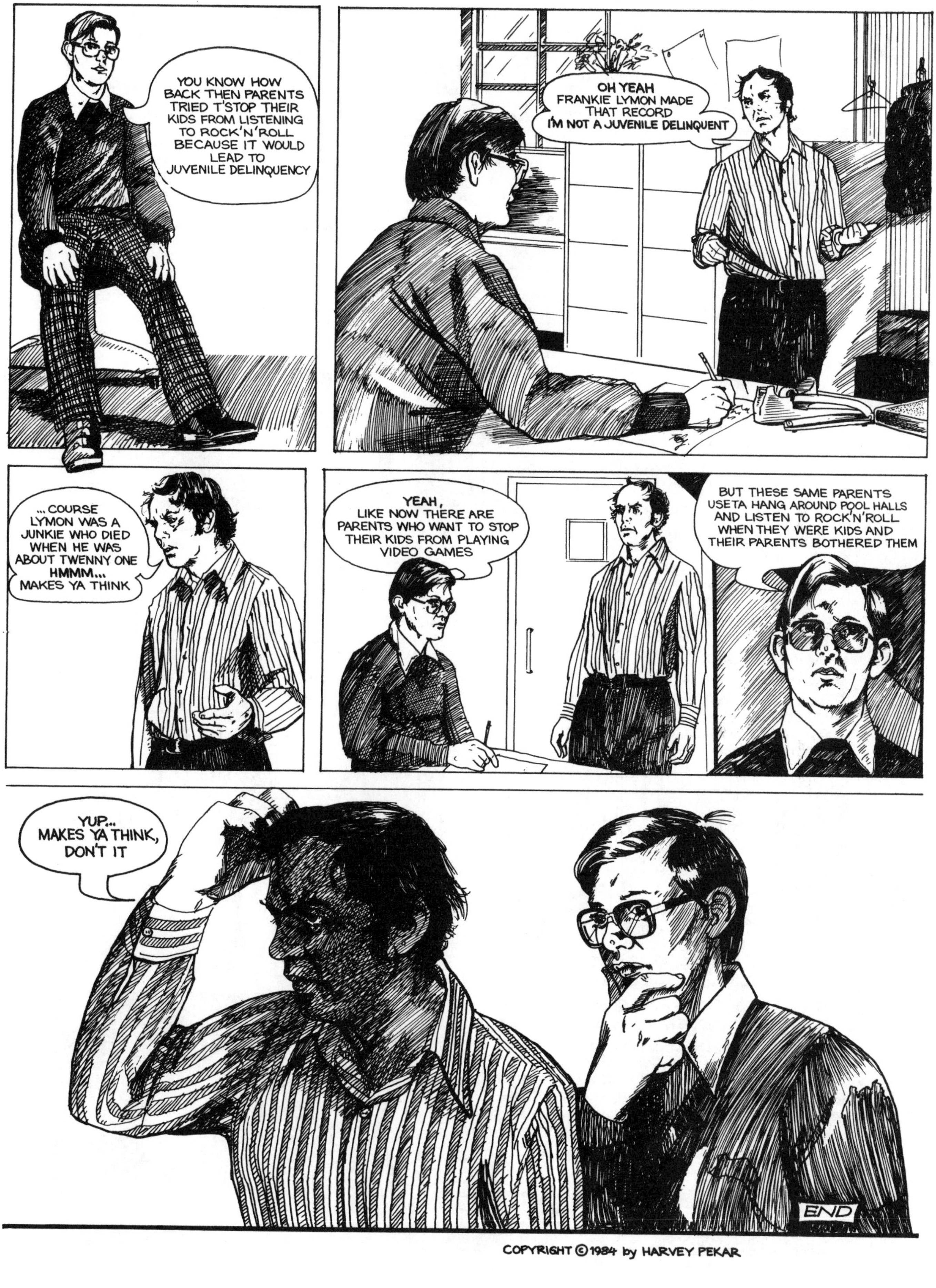

YOU KNOW HOW BACK THEN PARENTS TRIED T'STOP THEIR KIDS FROM LISTENING TO ROCK'N'ROLL BECAUSE IT WOULD LEAD TO JUVENILE DELINQUENCY
OH YEAH FRANKIE LYMON MADE THAT RECORD I'M NOT A JUVENILE DELINQUENT
...COURSE LYMON WAS A JUNKIE WHO DIED WHEN HE WAS ABOUT TWENNY ONE HMMM... MAKES YA THINK
YEAH, LIKE NOW THERE ARE PARENTS WHO WANT TO STOP THEIR KIDS FROM PLAYING VIDEO GAMES
BUT THESE SAME PARENTS USETA HANG AROUND POOL HALLS AND LISTEN TO ROCK'N'ROLL WHEN THEY WERE KIDS AND THEIR PARENTS BOTHERED THEM
YUP... MAKES YA THINK, DON'T IT
END

A MATTER OF LIFE AND...

STORY BY HARVEY PEKAR
ART BY VAL MAYERIK

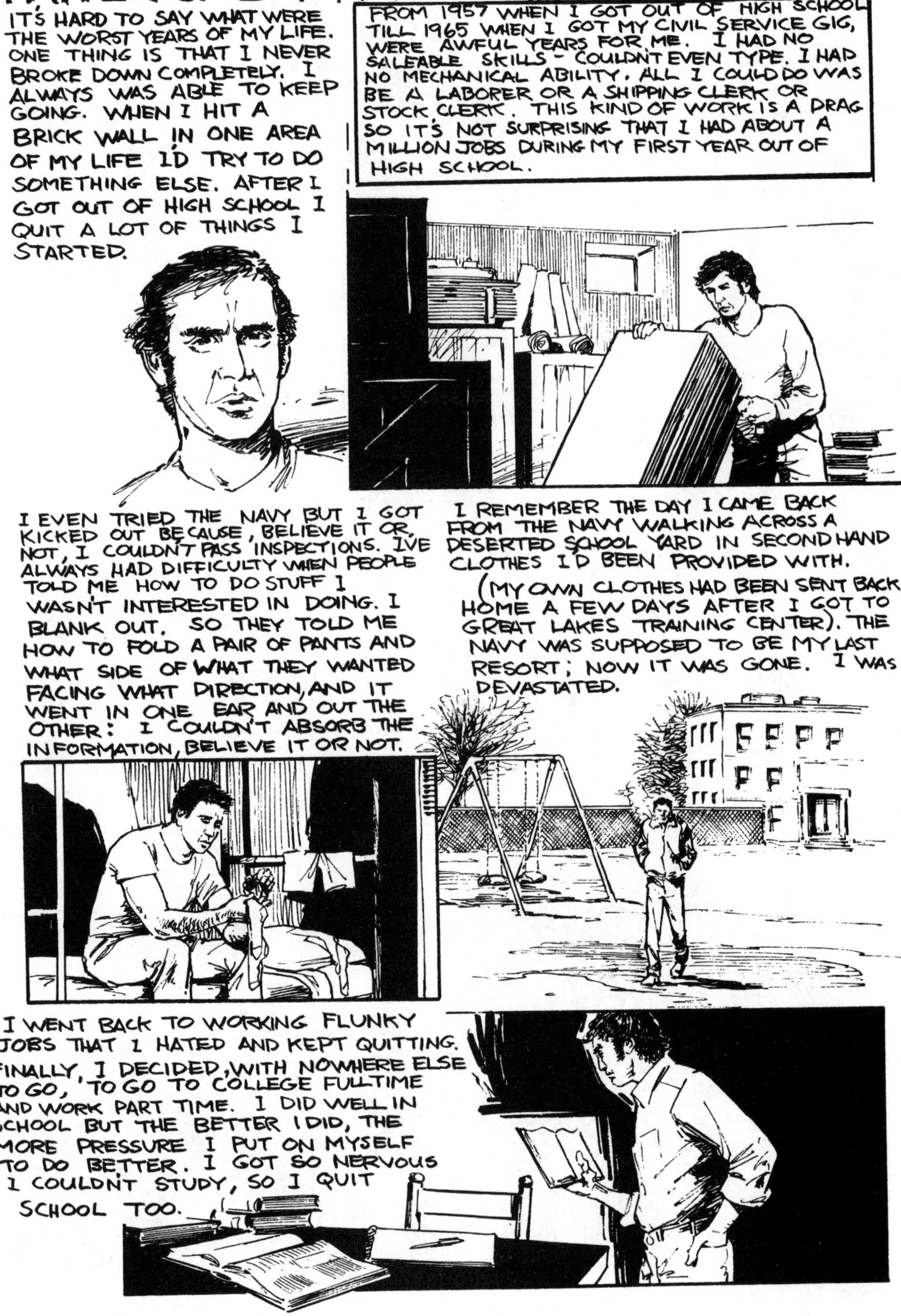
IT'S HARD TO SAY WHAT WERE THE WORST YEARS OF MY LIFE. ONE THING IS THAT I NEVER BROKE DOWN COMPLETELY. I ALWAYS WAS ABLE TO KEEP GOING. WHEN I HIT A BRICK WALL IN ONE AREA OF MY LIFE I'D TRY TO DO SOMETHING ELSE. AFTER I GOT OUT OF HIGH SCHOOL I QUIT A LOT OF THINGS I STARTED.
FROM 1957 WHEN I GOT OUT OF HIGH SCHOOL TILL 1965 WHEN I GOT MY CIVIL SERVICE GIG, WERE AWFUL YEARS FOR ME. I HAD NO SALEABLE SKILLS - COULDN'T EVEN TYPE. I HAD NO MECHANICAL ABILITY. ALL I COULD DO WAS BE A LABORER OR A SHIPPING CLERK OR STOCK CLERK. THIS KIND OF WORK IS A DRAG SO IT'S NOT SURPRISING THAT I HAD ABOUT A MILLION JOBS DURING MY FIRST YEAR OUT OF HIGH SCHOOL.
I EVEN TRIED THE NAVY BUT I GOT KICKED OUT BECAUSE, BELIEVE IT OR NOT, I COULDN'T PASS INSPECTIONS. I'VE ALWAYS HAD DIFFICULTY WHEN PEOPLE TOLD ME HOW TO DO STUFF I WASN'T INTERESTED IN DOING. I BLANK OUT. SO THEY TOLD ME HOW TO FOLD A PAIR OF PANTS AND WHAT SIDE OF WHAT THEY WANTED FACING WHAT DIRECTION, AND IT WENT IN ONE EAR AND OUT THE OTHER: I COULDN'T ABSORB THE INFORMATION, BELIEVE IT OR NOT.
I REMEMBER THE DAY I CAME BACK FROM THE NAVY WALKING ACROSS A DESERTED SCHOOL YARD IN SECOND HAND CLOTHES I'D BEEN PROVIDED WITH.
(MY OWN CLOTHES HAD BEEN SENT BACK HOME A FEW DAYS AFTER I GOT TO GREAT LAKES TRAINING CENTER). THE NAVY WAS SUPPOSED TO BE MY LAST RESORT; NOW IT WAS GONE. I WAS DEVASTATED.
I WENT BACK TO WORKING FLUNKY JOBS THAT I HATED AND KEPT QUITTING. FINALLY, I DECIDED, WITH NOWHERE ELSE TO GO, TO GO TO COLLEGE FULLTIME AND WORK PART TIME. I DID WELL IN SCHOOL BUT THE BETTER I DID, THE MORE PRESSURE I PUT ON MYSELF TO DO BETTER. I GOT SO NERVOUS I COULDN'T STUDY, SO I QUIT SCHOOL TOO.

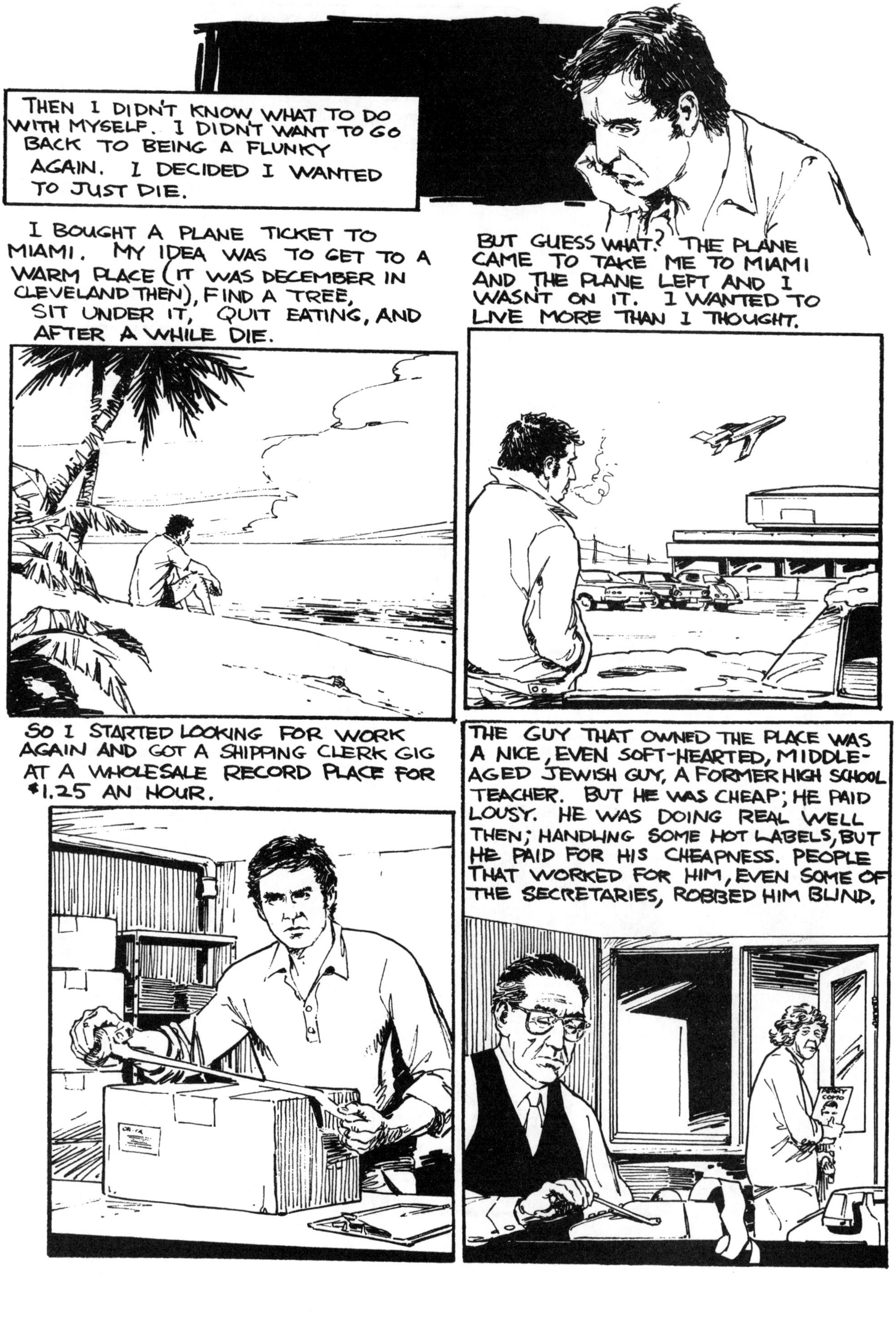
THEN I DIDN'T KNOW WHAT TO DO WITH MYSELF. I DIDN'T WANT TO GO BACK TO BEING A FLUNKY AGAIN. I DECIDED I WANTED TO JUST DIE.
I BOUGHT A PLANE TICKET TO MIAMI. MY IDEA WAS TO GET TO A WARM PLACE (IT WAS DECEMBER IN CLEVELAND THEN), FIND A TREE, SIT UNDER IT, QUIT EATING, AND AFTER A WHILE DIE.
BUT GUESS WHAT? THE PLANE CAME TO TAKE ME TO MIAMI AND THE PLANE LEFT AND I WASN'T ON IT. I WANTED TO LIVE MORE THAN I THOUGHT.
SO I STARTED LOOKING FOR WORK AGAIN AND GOT A SHIPPING CLERK GIG AT A WHOLESALE RECORD PLACE FOR $1.25 AN HOUR.
THE GUY THAT OWNED THE PLACE WAS A NICE, EVEN SOFT-HEARTED, MIDDLE-AGED JEWISH GUY, A FORMER HIGH SCHOOL TEACHER. BUT HE WAS CHEAP; HE PAID LOUSY. HE WAS DOING REAL WELL THEN; HANDLING SOME HOT LABELS, BUT HE PAID FOR HIS CHEAPNESS. PEOPLE THAT WORKED FOR HIM, EVEN SOME OF THE SECRETARIES, ROBBED HIM BLIND.
PERRY COMO

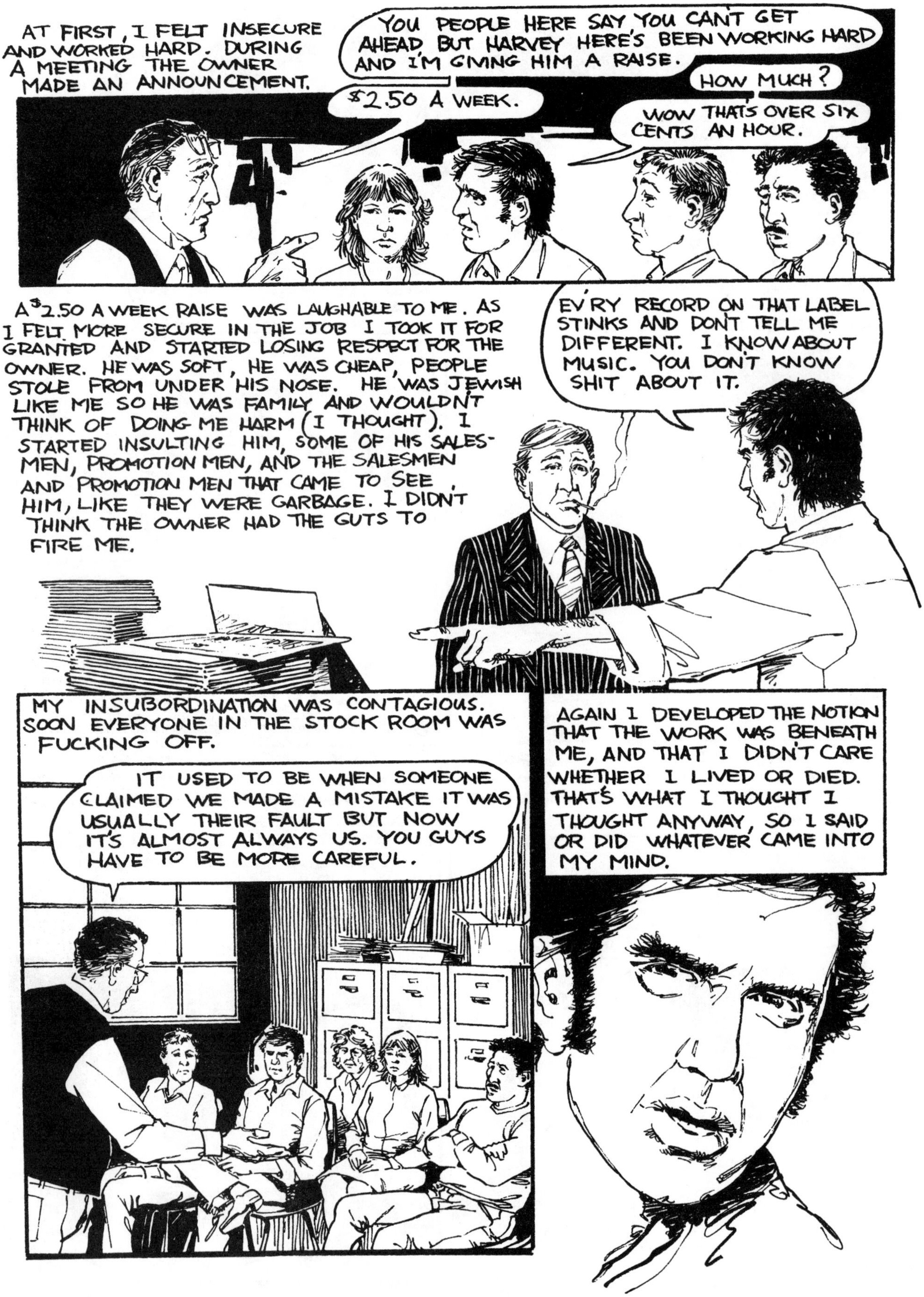
AT FIRST, I FELT INSECURE AND WORKED HARD. DURING A MEETING THE OWNER MADE AN ANNOUNCEMENT.
YOU PEOPLE HERE SAY YOU CAN'T GET AHEAD BUT HARVEY HERE'S BEEN WORKING HARD AND I'M GIVING HIM A RAISE.
HOW MUCH?
$2.50 A WEEK.
WOW THAT'S OVER SIX CENTS AN HOUR.
A $2.50 A WEEK RAISE WAS LAUGHABLE TO ME. AS I FELT MORE SECURE IN THE JOB I TOOK IT FOR GRANTED AND STARTED LOSING RESPECT FOR THE OWNER. HE WAS SOFT, HE WAS CHEAP, PEOPLE STOLE FROM UNDER HIS NOSE. HE WAS JEWISH LIKE ME SO HE WAS FAMILY AND WOULDN'T THINK OF DOING ME HARM (I THOUGHT). I STARTED INSULTING HIM, SOME OF HIS SALESMEN, PROMOTION MEN, AND THE SALESMEN AND PROMOTION MEN THAT CAME TO SEE HIM, LIKE THEY WERE GARBAGE. I DIDN'T THINK THE OWNER HAD THE GUTS TO FIRE ME.
EV'RY RECORD ON THAT LABEL STINKS AND DON'T TELL ME DIFFERENT. I KNOW ABOUT MUSIC. YOU DON'T KNOW SHIT ABOUT IT.
MY INSUBORDINATION WAS CONTAGIOUS. SOON EVERYONE IN THE STOCK ROOM WAS FUCKING OFF.
IT USED TO BE WHEN SOMEONE CLAIMED WE MADE A MISTAKE IT WAS USUALLY THEIR FAULT BUT NOW IT'S ALMOST ALWAYS US. YOU GUYS HAVE TO BE MORE CAREFUL.
AGAIN I DEVELOPED THE NOTION THAT THE WORK WAS BENEATH ME, AND THAT I DIDN'T CARE WHETHER I LIVED OR DIED. THAT'S WHAT I THOUGHT I THOUGHT ANYWAY, SO I SAID OR DID WHATEVER CAME INTO MY MIND.

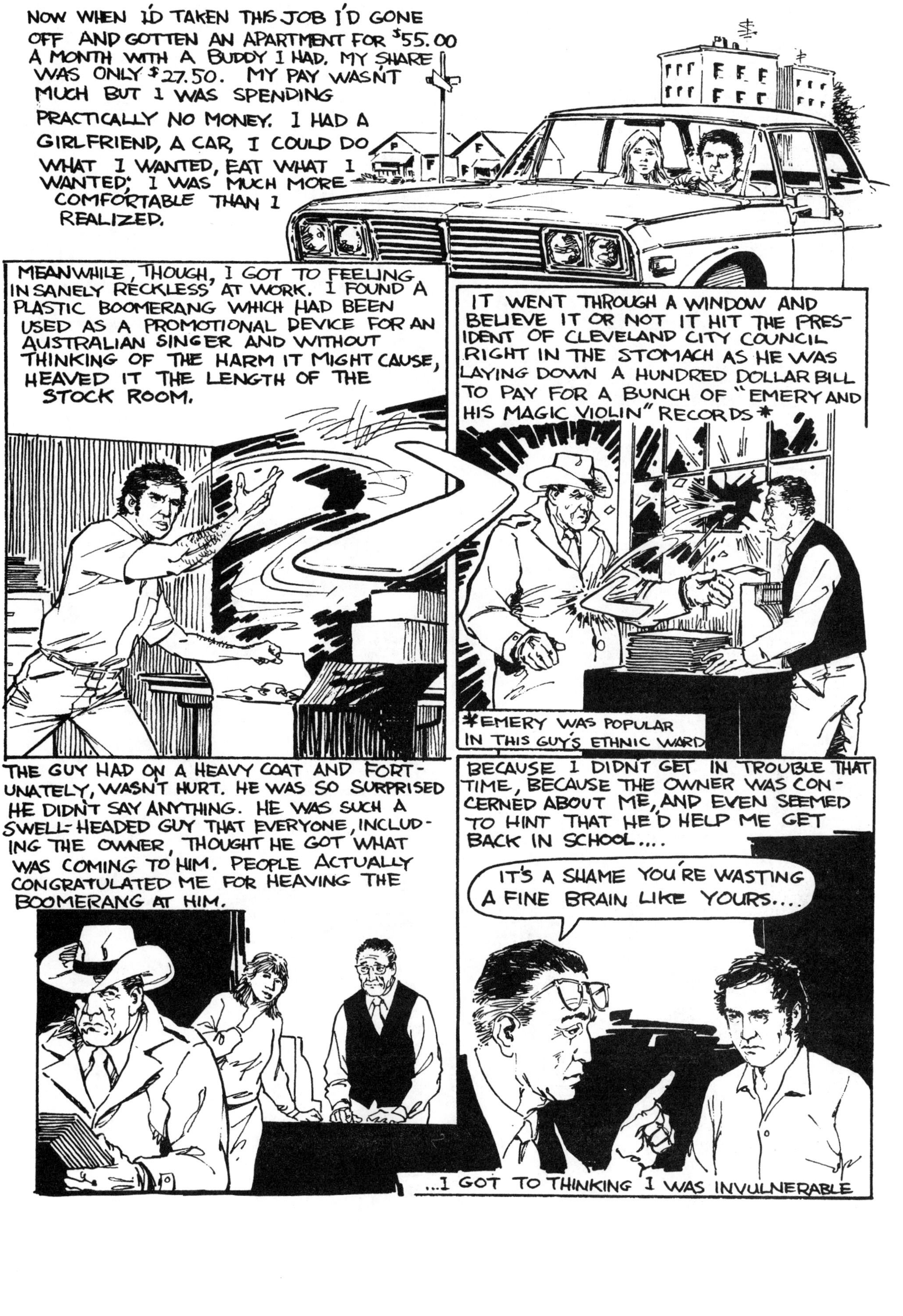
NOW WHEN I'D TAKEN THIS JOB I'D GONE OFF AND GOTTEN AN APARTMENT FOR $55.00 A MONTH WITH A BUDDY I HAD. MY SHARE WAS ONLY $27.50. MY PAY WASN'T MUCH BUT I WAS SPENDING PRACTICALLY NO MONEY. I HAD A GIRLFRIEND, A CAR, I COULD DO WHAT I WANTED, EAT WHAT I WANTED; I WAS MUCH MORE COMFORTABLE THAN I REALIZED.
MEANWHILE, THOUGH, I GOT TO FEELING INSANELY RECKLESS AT WORK. I FOUND A PLASTIC BOOMERANG WHICH HAD BEEN USED AS A PROMOTIONAL DEVICE FOR AN AUSTRALIAN SINGER AND WITHOUT THINKING OF THE HARM IT MIGHT CAUSE, HEAVED IT THE LENGTH OF THE STOCK ROOM.
IT WENT THROUGH A WINDOW AND BELIEVE IT OR NOT IT HIT THE PRESIDENT OF CLEVELAND CITY COUNCIL RIGHT IN THE STOMACH AS HE WAS LAYING DOWN A HUNDRED DOLLAR BILL TO PAY FOR A BUNCH OF "EMERY AND HIS MAGIC VIOLIN" RECORDS*
*EMERY WAS POPULAR IN THIS GUY'S ETHNIC WARD
THE GUY HAD ON A HEAVY COAT AND FORTUNATELY, WASN'T HURT. HE WAS SO SURPRISED HE DIDN'T SAY ANYTHING. HE WAS SUCH A SWELL-HEADED GUY THAT EVERYONE, INCLUDING THE OWNER, THOUGHT HE GOT WHAT WAS COMING TO HIM. PEOPLE ACTUALLY CONGRATULATED ME FOR HEAVING THE BOOMERANG AT HIM.
BECAUSE I DIDNT GET IN TROUBLE THAT TIME, BECAUSE THE OWNER WAS CONCERNED ABOUT ME, AND EVEN SEEMED TO HINT THAT HE'D HELP ME GET BACK IN SCHOOL....
IT'S A SHAME YOU'RE WASTING A FINE BRAIN LIKE YOURS...
...I GOT TO THINKING I WAS INVULNERABLE

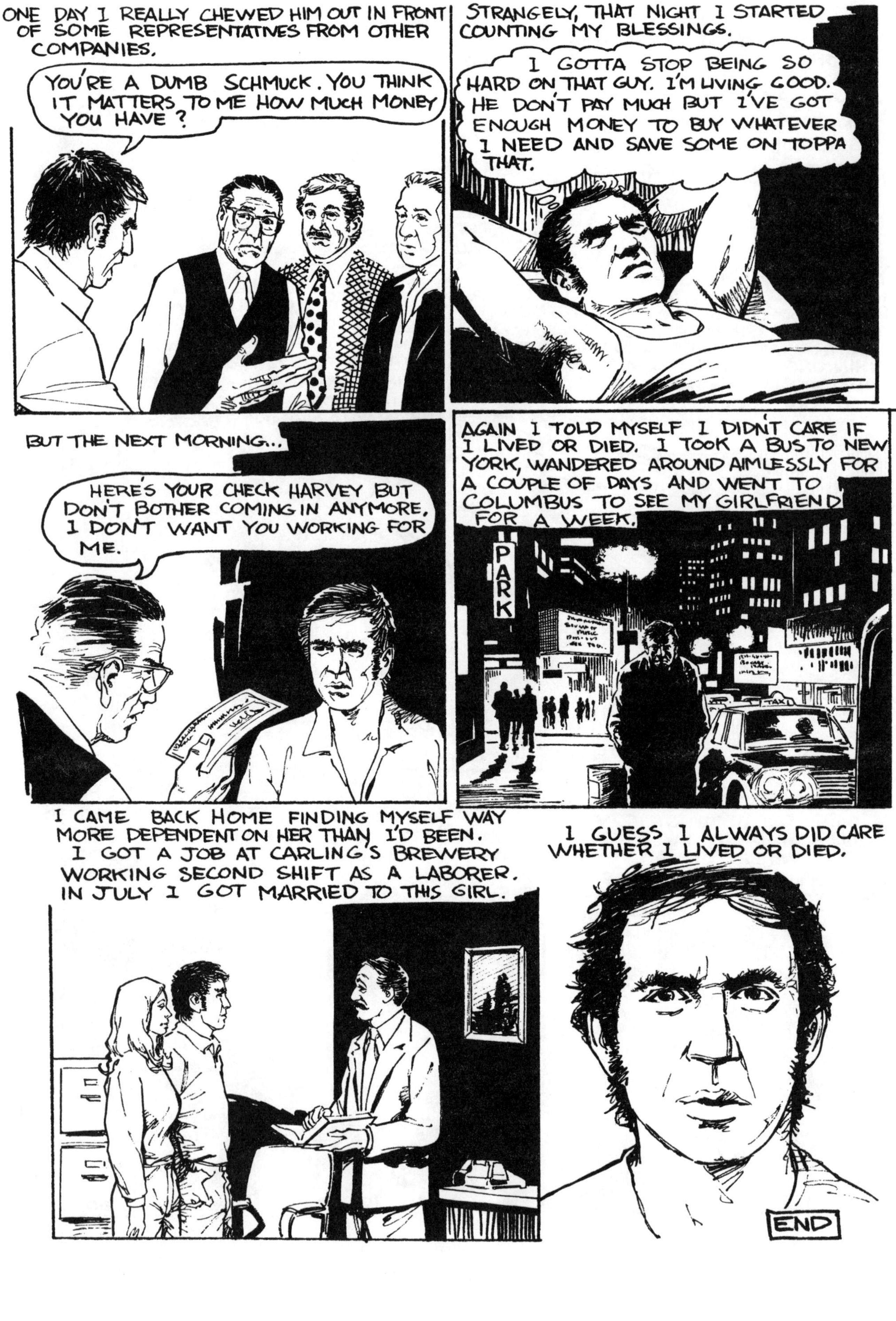
ONE DAY I REALLY CHEWED HIM OUT IN FRONT OF SOME REPRESENTATIVES FROM OTHER COMPANIES.
YOU'RE A DUMB SCHMUCK. YOU THINK IT MATTERS TO ME HOW MUCH MONEY YOU HAVE?
STRANGELY, THAT NIGHT I STARTED COUNTING MY BLESSINGS.
I GOTTA STOP BEING SO HARD ON THAT GUY. I'M LIVING GOOD. HE DON'T PAY MUCH BUT I'VE GOT ENOUGH MONEY TO BUY WHATEVER I NEED AND SAVE SOME ON TOPPA THAT.
BUT THE NEXT MORNING...
HERE'S YOUR CHECK HARVEY BUT DON'T BOTHER COMING IN ANYMORE, I DON'T WANT YOU WORKING FOR ME.
AGAIN I TOLD MYSELF I DIDN'T CARE IF I LIVED OR DIED. I TOOK A BUS TO NEW YORK, WANDERED AROUND AIMLESSLY FOR A COUPLE OF DAYS AND WENT TO COLUMBUS TO SEE MY GIRLFRIEND FOR A WEEK.
PARK
TAXI
I CAME BACK HOME FINDING MYSELF WAY MORE DEPENDENT ON HER THAN I'D BEEN. I GOT A JOB AT CARLING'S BREWERY WORKING SECOND SHIFT AS A LABORER. IN JULY I GOT MARRIED TO THIS GIRL.
I GUESS I ALWAYS DID CARE WHETHER I LIVED OR DIED.
END

COMMON SENSE

STORY BY HARVEY PEKAR
ART BY VAL MAYERIK

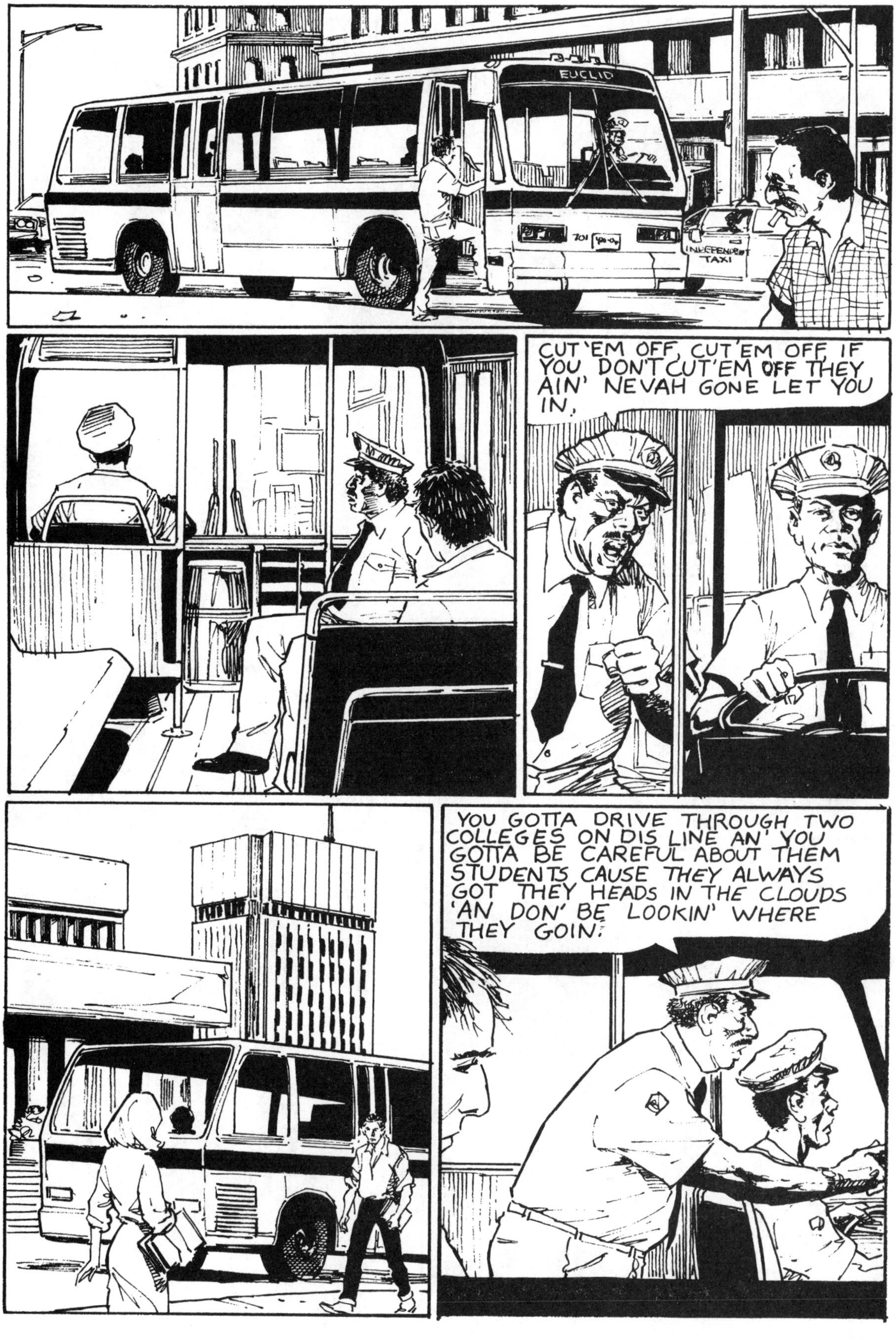
EUCLID
INDEPENDENT TAXI
CUT'EM OFF, CUT'EM OFF IF YOU DON'T CUT'EM OFF THEY AIN' NEVAH GONE LET YOU IN.
YOU GOTTA DRIVE THROUGH TWO COLLEGES ON DIS LINE AN' YOU GOTTA BE CAREFUL ABOUT THEM STUDENTS CAUSE THEY ALWAYS GOT THEY HEADS IN THE CLOUDS 'AN DON' BE LOOKIN' WHERE THEY GOIN.

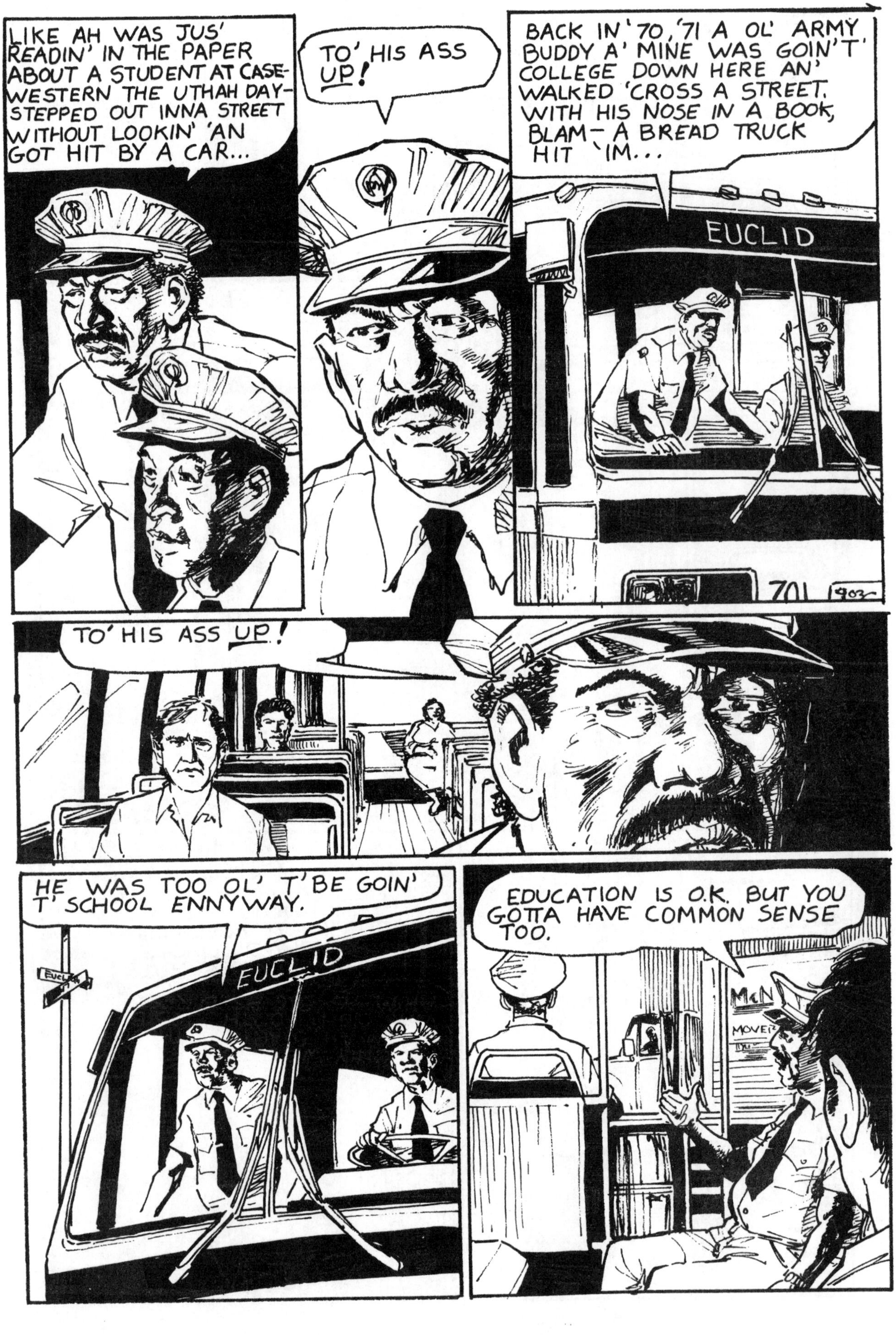
LIKE AH WAS JUS' READIN' IN THE PAPER ABOUT A STUDENT AT CASE-WESTERN THE UTHAH DAY-STEPPED OUT INNA STREET WITHOUT LOOKIN' 'AN GOT HIT BY A CAR...
TO' HIS ASS UP!
BACK IN '70, '71 A OL' ARMY BUDDY A' MINE WAS GOIN' T' COLLEGE DOWN HERE AN' WALKED 'CROSS A STREET, WITH HIS NOSE IN A BOOK, BLAM— A BREAD TRUCK HIT 'IM...
EUCLID
701
TO' HIS ASS UP!
HE WAS TOO OL' T' BE GOIN' T' SCHOOL ENNYWAY.
EUCLID
EDUCATION IS O.K. BUT YOU GOTTA HAVE COMMON SENSE TOO.

M' FRIENDS DON' B'LIEVE ME, BUT, B'LIEVE IT 'UH NOT AH GOT TAHD A' THEM HOES COMIN' ON THE BUS AN' MESSIN' WITH ME. YOU GET SICK O' THEM AFTUH WHAHLE.
AH ONLY WEIGHED ONE SIXTY-TWO WHEN AH STARTED. THOUGHT AH WAS LIGHT FO' TH' JOB BUT NOW AH'M AS BIG AS D'REST OF 'EM
ARMY
CLINIC
DRUG REHABILITATIO
Y'GOTTA WATCH F'DEM PEOPLE TOO. THEY GET FULLA METHADONE, THEY GET BLIND... LIABLE T'WALK INTUH TH' SIDE A' THE BUS

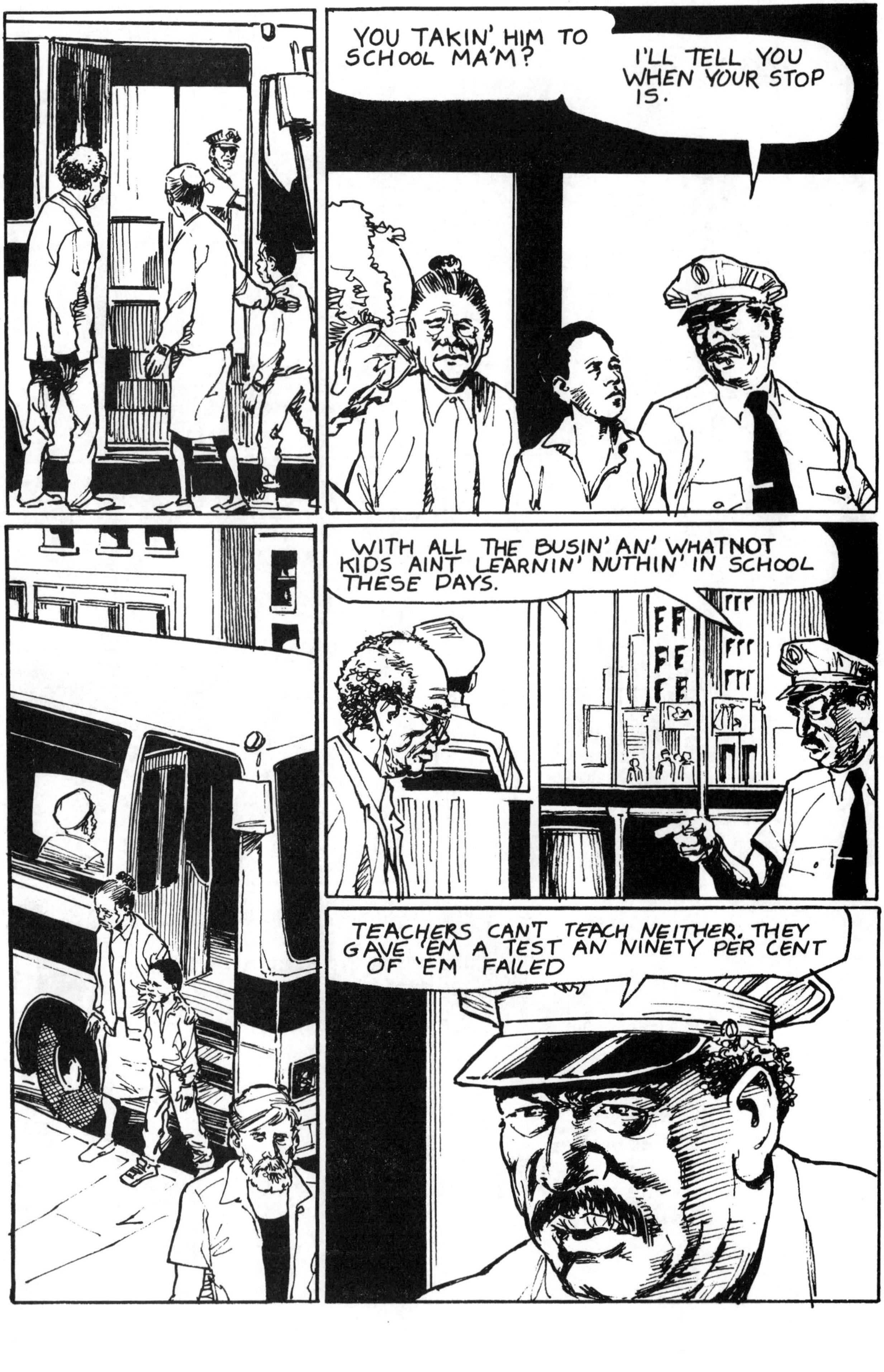
YOU TAKIN' HIM TO SCHOOL MA'M?
I'LL TELL YOU WHEN YOUR STOP IS.
WITH ALL THE BUSIN' AN' WHATNOT KIDS AINT LEARNIN' NUTHIN' IN SCHOOL THESE DAYS.
TEACHERS CAN'T TEACH NEITHER. THEY GAVE 'EM A TEST AN NINETY PER CENT OF 'EM FAILED

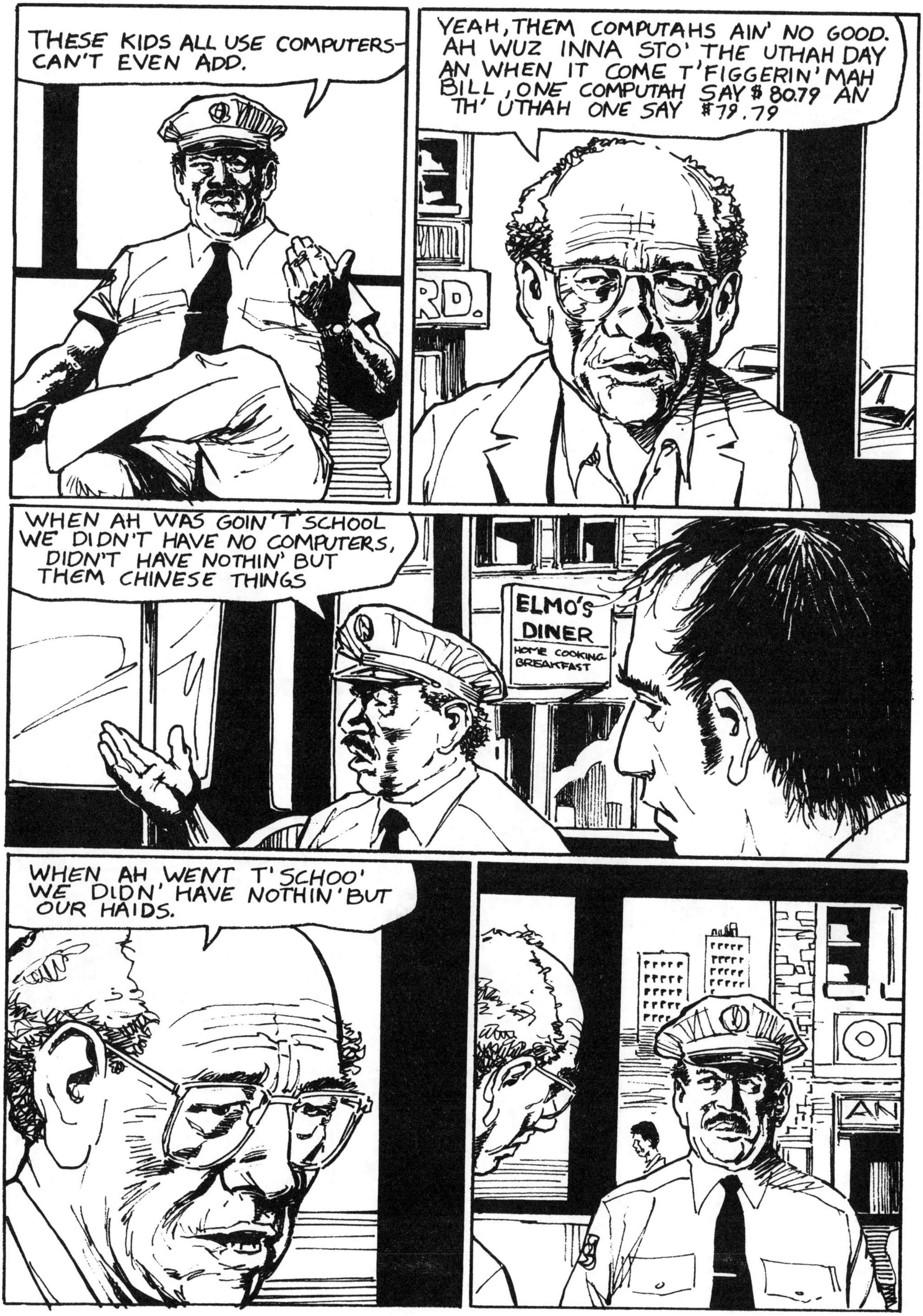
THESE KIDS ALL USE COMPUTERS- CAN'T EVEN ADD.
YEAH, THEM COMPUTAHS AIN' NO GOOD. AH WUZ INNA STO' THE UTHAH DAY AN WHEN IT COME T'FIGGERIN' MAH BILL, ONE COMPUTAH SAY $80.79 AN TH' UTHAH ONE SAY $79.79
WHEN AH WAS GOIN' T'SCHOOL WE DIDN'T HAVE NO COMPUTERS, DIDN'T HAVE NOTHIN' BUT THEM CHINESE THINGS
ELMO'S DINER
HOME COOKING
BREAKFAST
WHEN AH WENT T'SCHOO' WE DIDN' HAVE NOTHIN' BUT OUR HAIDS.

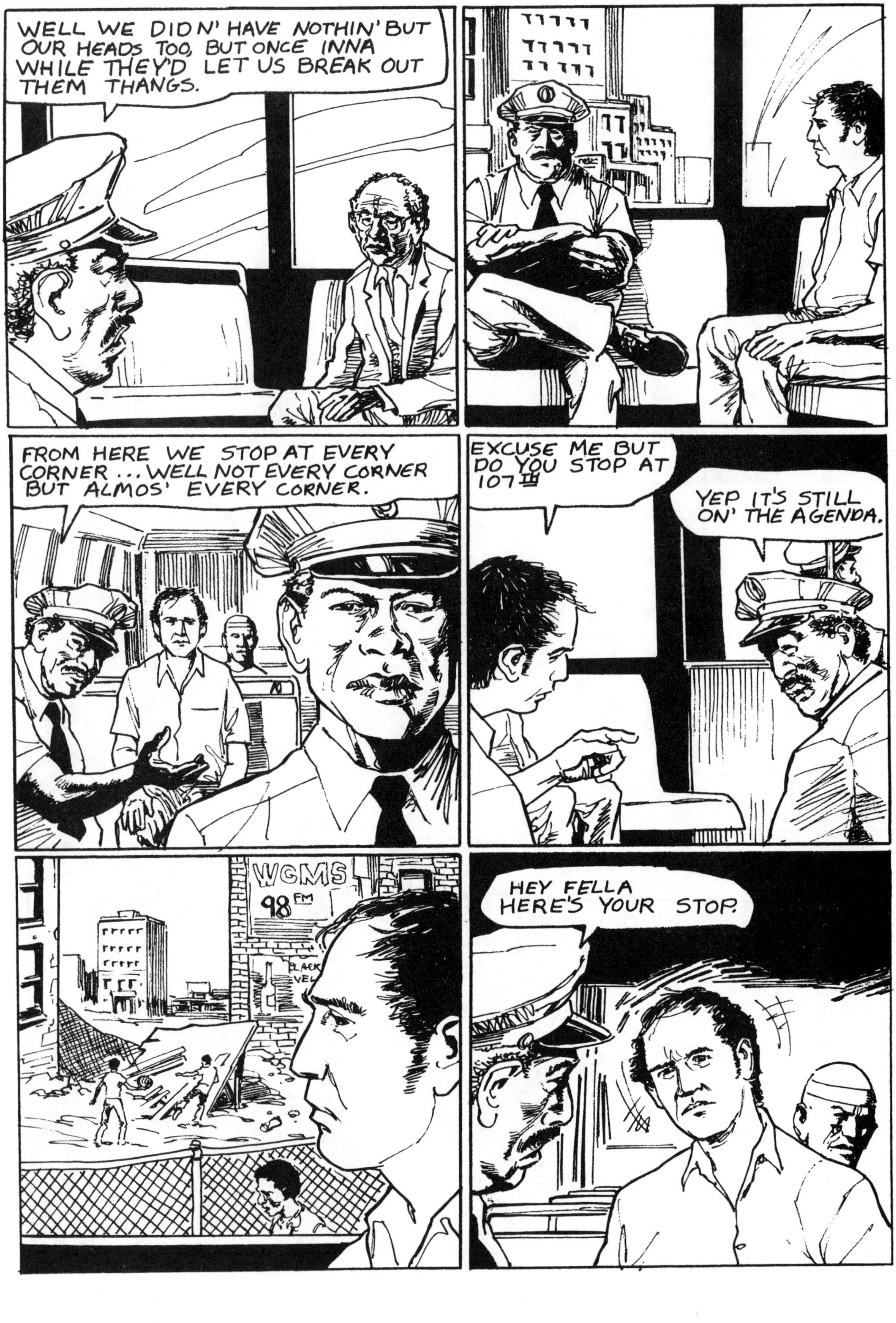
WELL WE DIDN' HAVE NOTHIN' BUT OUR HEADS TOO, BUT ONCE INNA WHILE THEY'D LET US BREAK OUT THEM THANGS.
FROM HERE WE STOP AT EVERY CORNER ... WELL NOT EVERY CORNER BUT ALMOS' EVERY CORNER.
EXCUSE ME BUT DO YOU STOP AT 107TH
YEP IT'S STILL ON' THE AGENDA.
WGMS
98 FM
HEY FELLA HERE'S YOUR STOP.

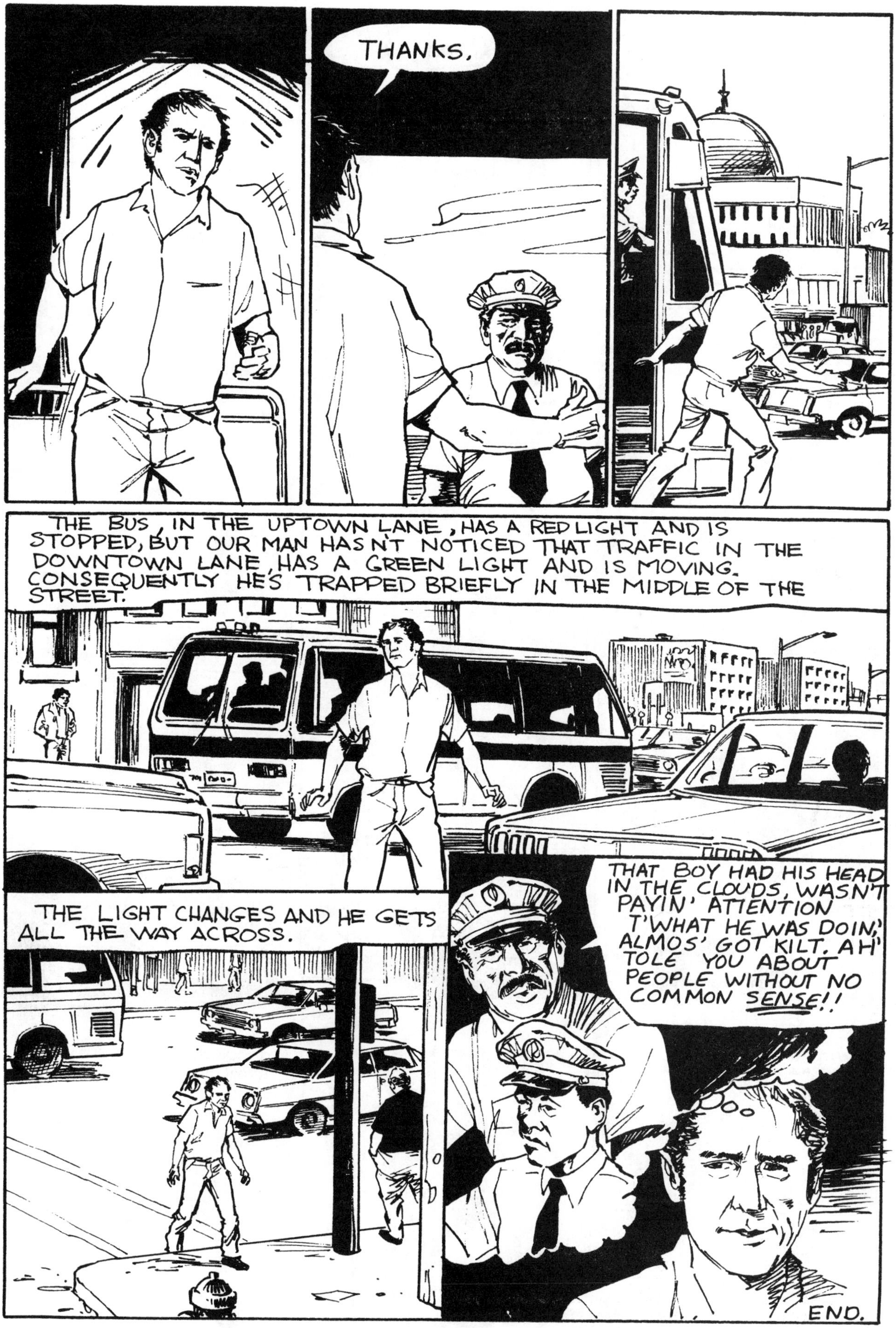
THANKS.
THE BUS, IN THE UPTOWN LANE, HAS A RED LIGHT AND IS STOPPED, BUT OUR MAN HASN'T NOTICED THAT TRAFFIC IN THE DOWNTOWN LANE, HAS A GREEN LIGHT AND IS MOVING. CONSEQUENTLY HE'S TRAPPED BRIEFLY IN THE MIDDLE OF THE STREET.
THE LIGHT CHANGES AND HE GETS ALL THE WAY ACROSS.
THAT BOY HAD HIS HEAD IN THE CLOUDS, WASN'T PAYIN' ATTENTION T'WHAT HE WAS DOIN', ALMOS' GOT KILT. AH' TOLE YOU ABOUT PEOPLE WITHOUT NO COMMON SENSE!!
END.

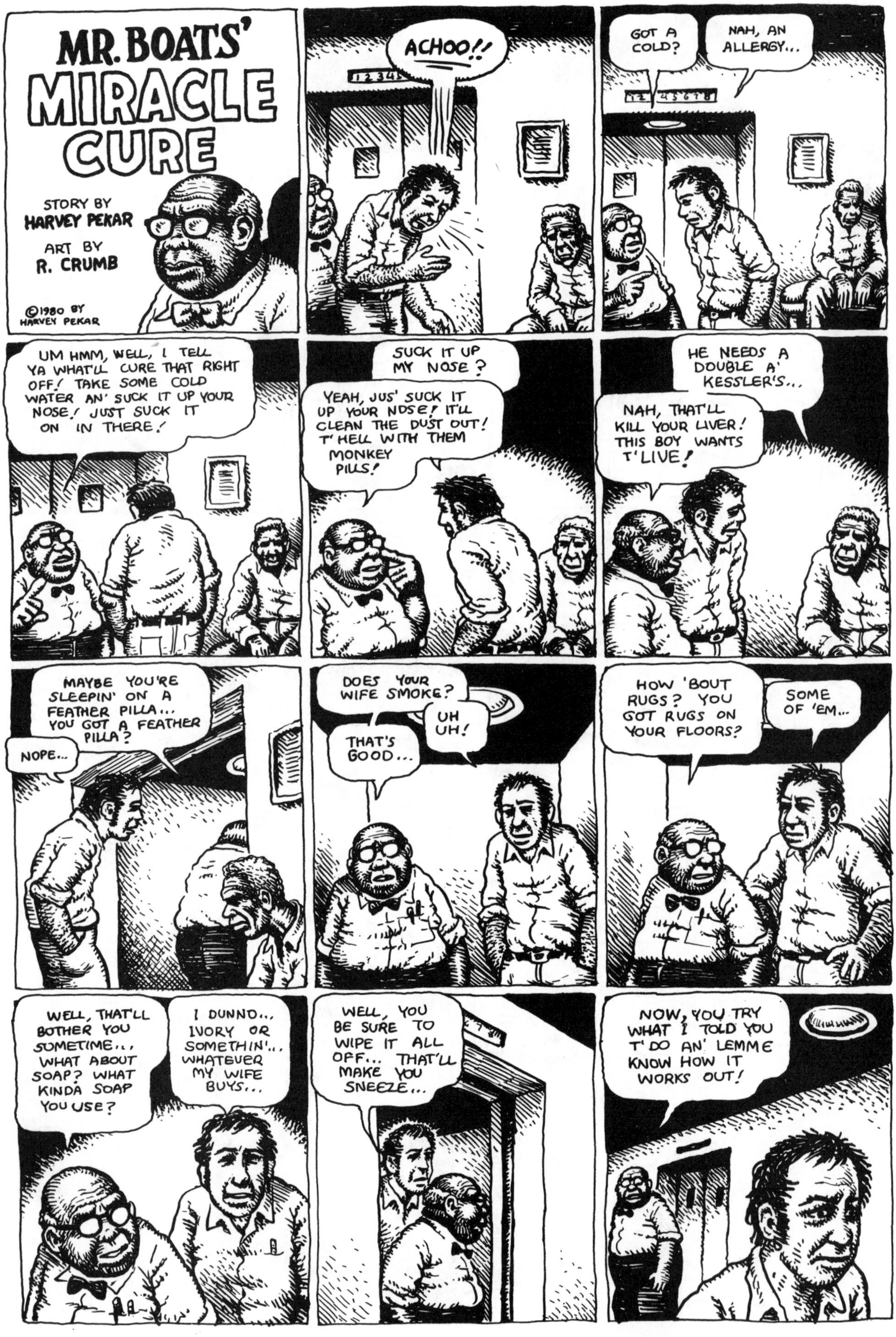
MR. BOATS' MIRACLE CURE
STORY BY HARVEY PEKAR
ART BY R. CRUMB
©1980 BY HARVEY PEKAR
ACHOO!!
GOT A COLD?
NAH, AN ALLERGY...
UM HMM, WELL, I TELL YA WHAT'LL CURE THAT RIGHT OFF! TAKE SOME COLD WATER AN' SUCK IT UP YOUR NOSE! JUST SUCK IT ON IN THERE!
SUCK IT UP MY NOSE?
YEAH, JUS' SUCK IT UP YOUR NOSE! IT'LL CLEAN THE DUST OUT! T'HELL WITH THEM MONKEY PILLS!
HE NEEDS A DOUBLE A' KESSLER'S...
NAH, THAT'LL KILL YOUR LIVER! THIS BOY WANTS T'LIVE!
MAYBE YOU'RE SLEEPIN' ON A FEATHER PILLA... YOU GOT A FEATHER PILLA?
NOPE...
DOES YOUR WIFE SMOKE?
UH UH!
THAT'S GOOD...
HOW 'BOUT RUGS? YOU GOT RUGS ON YOUR FLOORS?
SOME OF 'EM...
WELL, THAT'LL BOTHER YOU SOMETIME... WHAT ABOUT SOAP? WHAT KINDA SOAP YOU USE?
I DUNNO... IVORY OR SOMETHIN'... WHATEVER MY WIFE BUYS...
WELL, YOU BE SURE TO WIPE IT ALL OFF... THAT'LL MAKE YOU SNEEZE...
NOW, YOU TRY WHAT I TOLD YOU T'DO AN' LEMME KNOW HOW IT WORKS OUT!